WARRIORS

RAVENPAW'S PATH

#1: SHATTERED PEACE

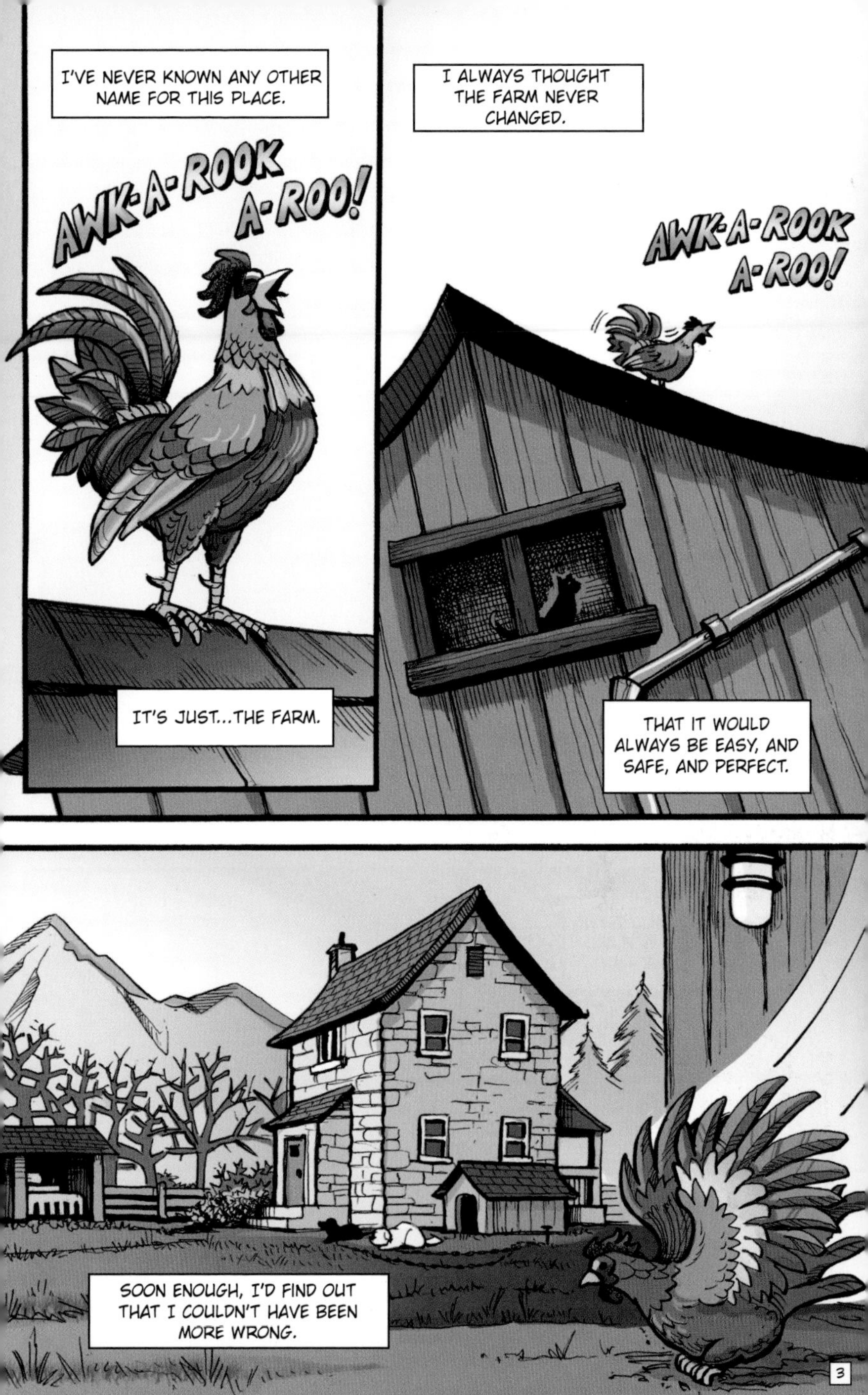
I'VE NEVER KNOWN ANY OTHER NAME FOR THIS PLACE.
AWK-A-ROOK A-ROO!
IT'S JUST...THE FARM.
I ALWAYS THOUGHT THE FARM NEVER CHANGED.
AWK-A-ROOK A-ROO!
THAT IT WOULD ALWAYS BE EASY, AND SAFE, AND PERFECT.
SOON ENOUGH, I'D FIND OUT THAT I COULDN'T HAVE BEEN MORE WRONG.

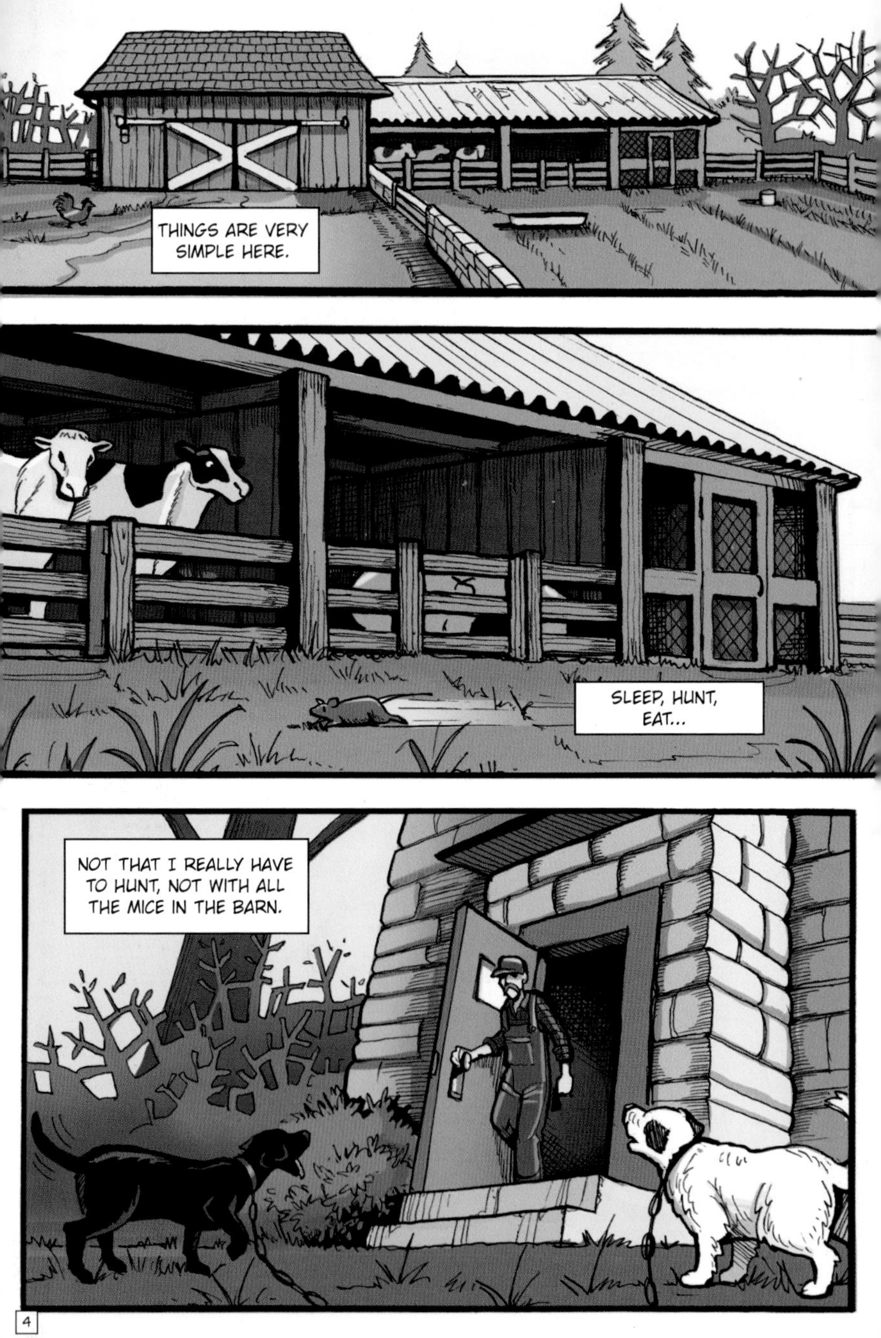
THINGS ARE VERY SIMPLE HERE.
SLEEP, HUNT, EAT...
NOT THAT I REALLY HAVE TO HUNT, NOT WITH ALL THE MICE IN THE BARN.

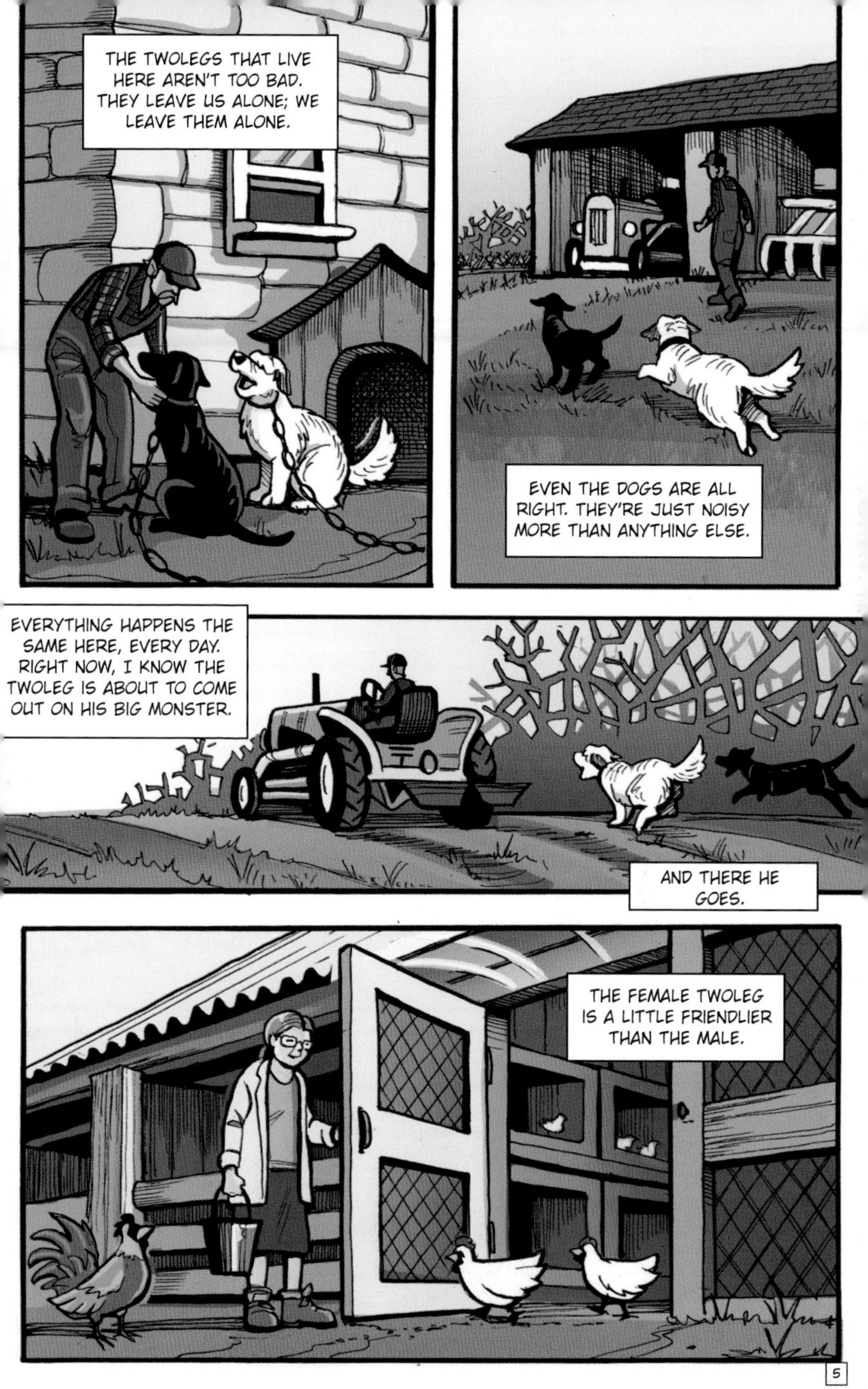
THE TWOLEGS THAT LIVE HERE AREN'T TOO BAD. THEY LEAVE US ALONE; WE LEAVE THEM ALONE.
EVEN THE DOGS ARE ALL RIGHT. THEY'RE JUST NOISY MORE THAN ANYTHING ELSE.
EVERYTHING HAPPENS THE SAME HERE, EVERY DAY. RIGHT NOW, I KNOW THE TWOLEG IS ABOUT TO COME OUT ON HIS BIG MONSTER.
AND THERE HE GOES.
THE FEMALE TWOLEG IS A LITTLE FRIENDLIER THAN THE MALE.

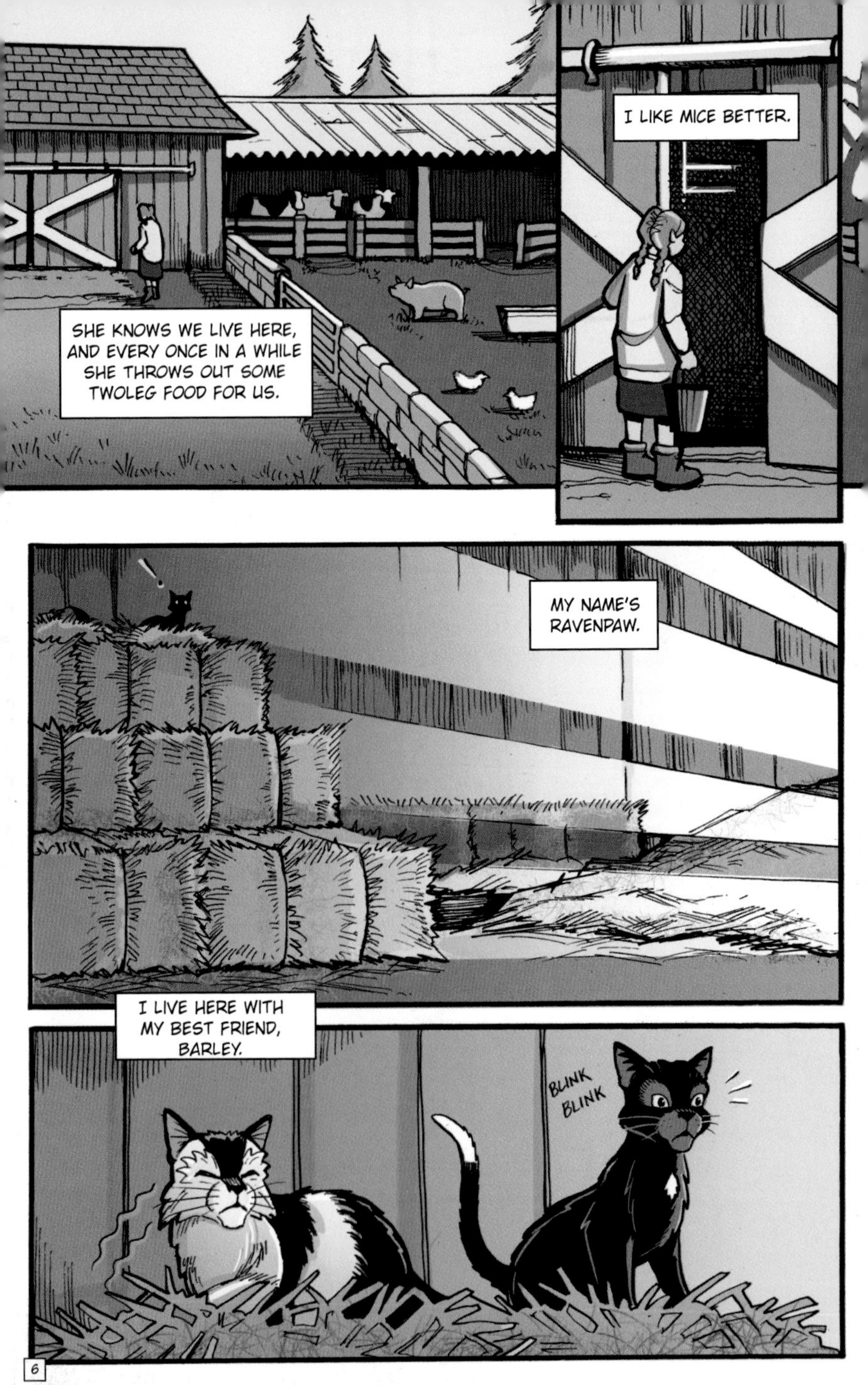
SHE KNOWS WE LIVE HERE, AND EVERY ONCE IN A WHILE SHE THROWS OUT SOME TWOLEG FOOD FOR US.
I LIKE MICE BETTER.
MY NAME'S RAVENPAW.
I LIVE HERE WITH MY BEST FRIEND, BARLEY.
BLINK BLINK

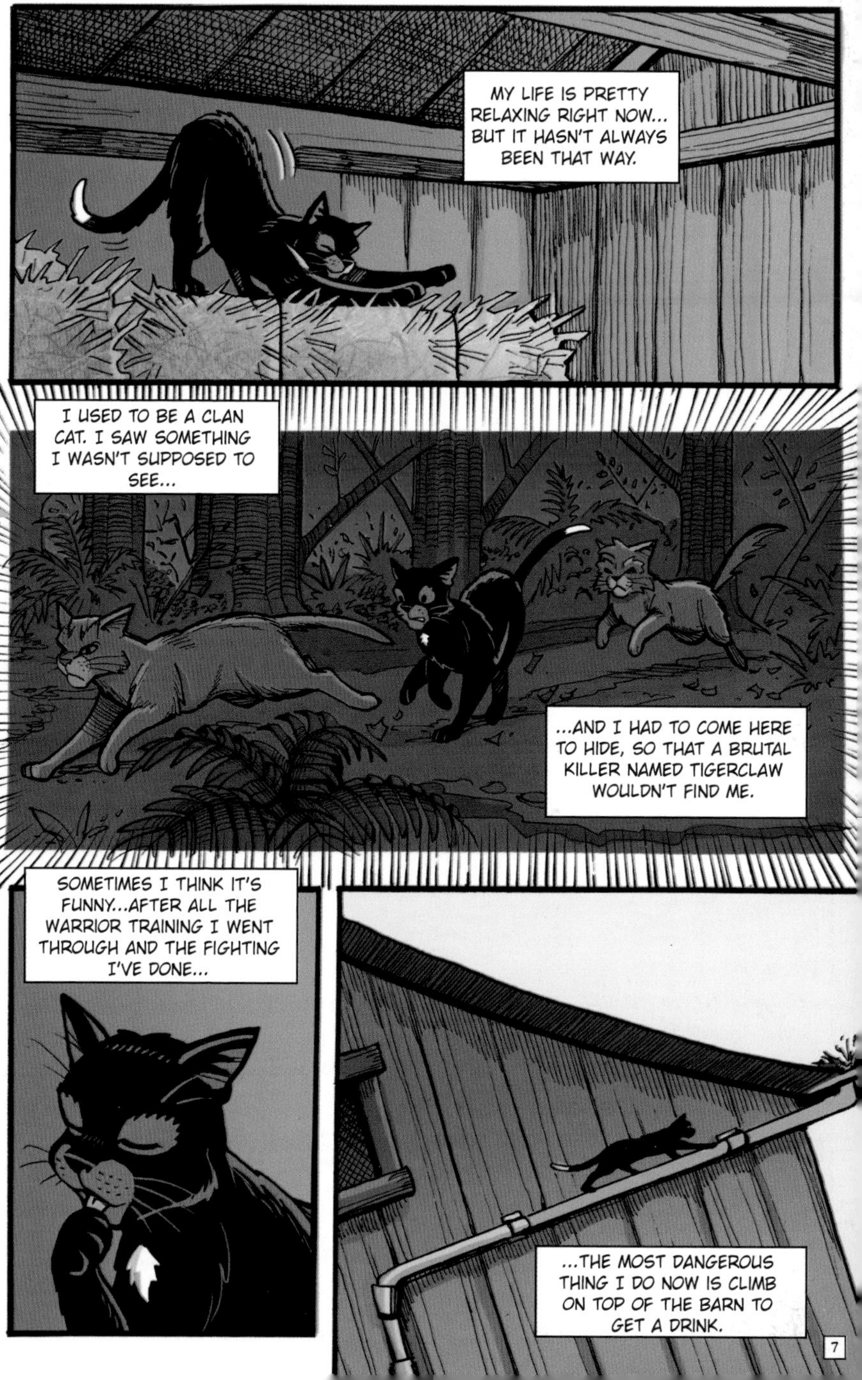

MY LIFE IS PRETTY RELAXING RIGHT NOW... BUT IT HASN'T ALWAYS BEEN THAT WAY.
I USED TO BE A CLAN CAT. I SAW SOMETHING I WASN'T SUPPOSED TO SEE...
...AND I HAD TO COME HERE TO HIDE, SO THAT A BRUTAL KILLER NAMED TIGERCLAW WOULDN'T FIND ME.
SOMETIMES I THINK IT'S FUNNY...AFTER ALL THE WARRIOR TRAINING I WENT THROUGH AND THE FIGHTING I'VE DONE...
...THE MOST DANGEROUS THING I DO NOW IS CLIMB ON TOP OF THE BARN TO GET A DRINK.

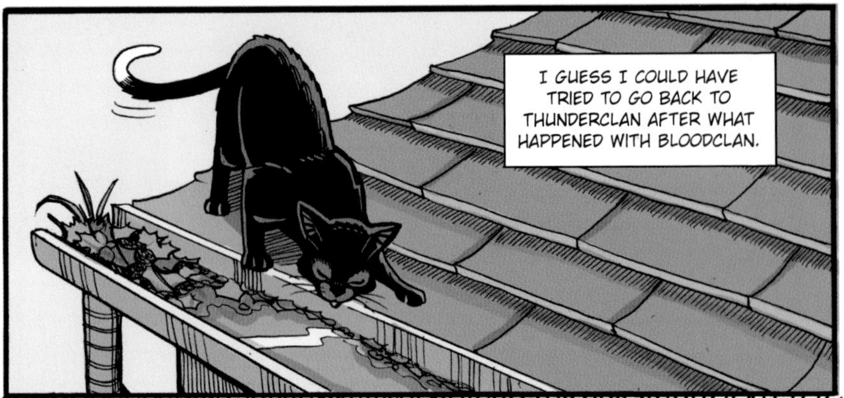
I GUESS I COULD HAVE TRIED TO GO BACK TO THUNDERCLAN AFTER WHAT HAPPENED WITH BLOODCLAN.

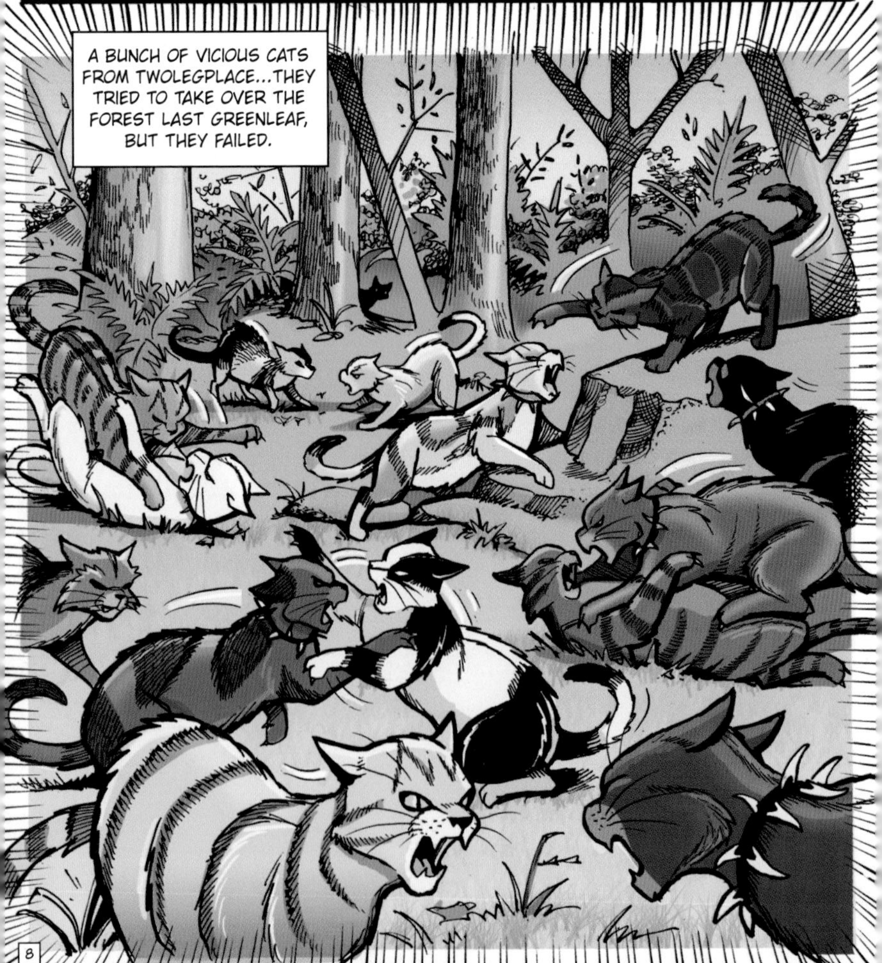
A BUNCH OF VICIOUS CATS FROM TWOLEGPLACE...THEY TRIED TO TAKE OVER THE FOREST LAST GREENLEAF, BUT THEY FAILED.

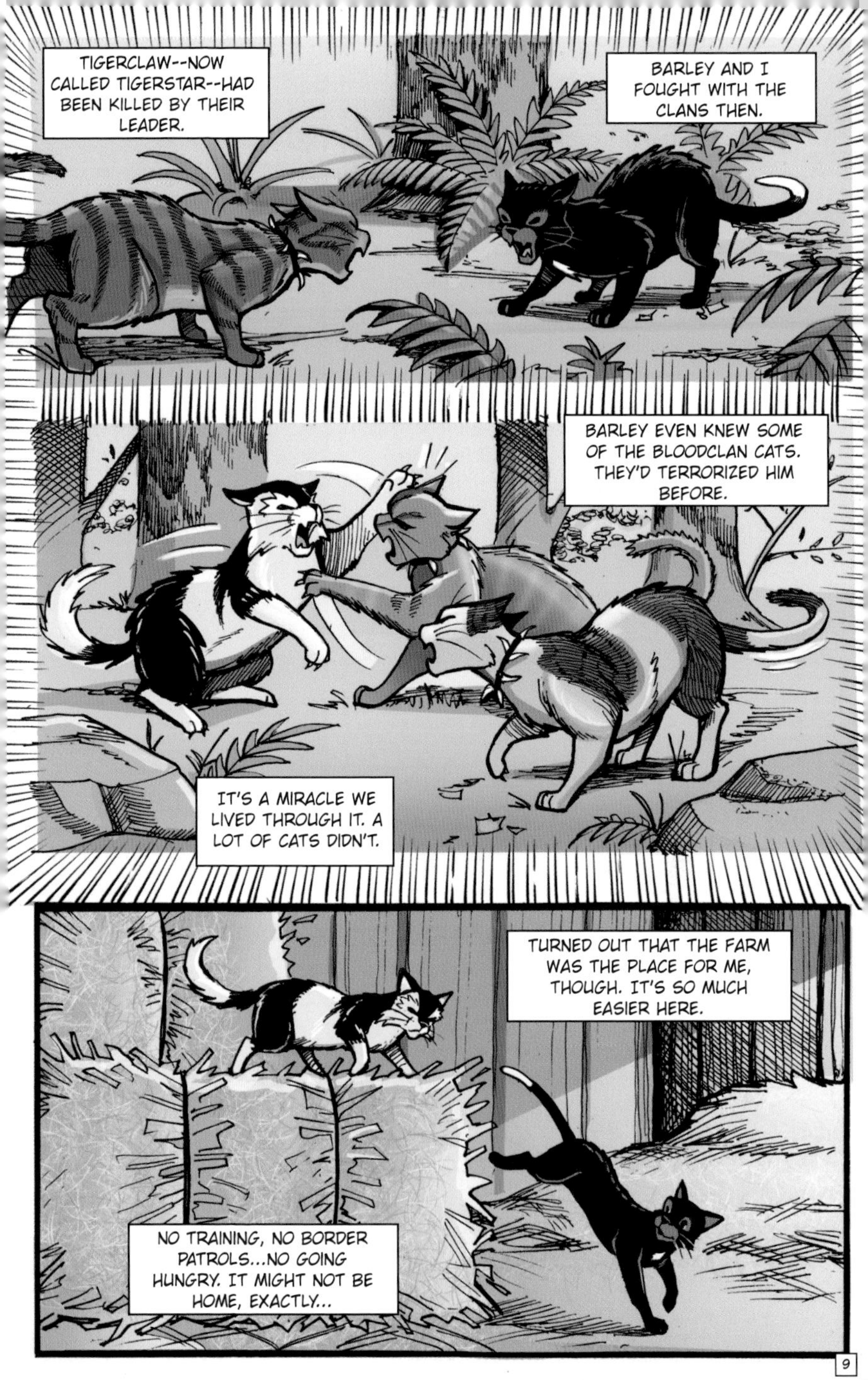
TIGERCLAW--NOW CALLED TIGERSTAR--HAD BEEN KILLED BY THEIR LEADER.
BARLEY AND I FOUGHT WITH THE CLANS THEN.
BARLEY EVEN KNEW SOME OF THE BLOODCLAN CATS. THEY'D TERRORIZED HIM BEFORE.
IT'S A MIRACLE WE LIVED THROUGH IT. A LOT OF CATS DIDN'T.
TURNED OUT THAT THE FARM WAS THE PLACE FOR ME, THOUGH. IT'S SO MUCH EASIER HERE.
NO TRAINING, NO BORDER PATROLS...NO GOING HUNGRY. IT MIGHT NOT BE HOME, EXACTLY...

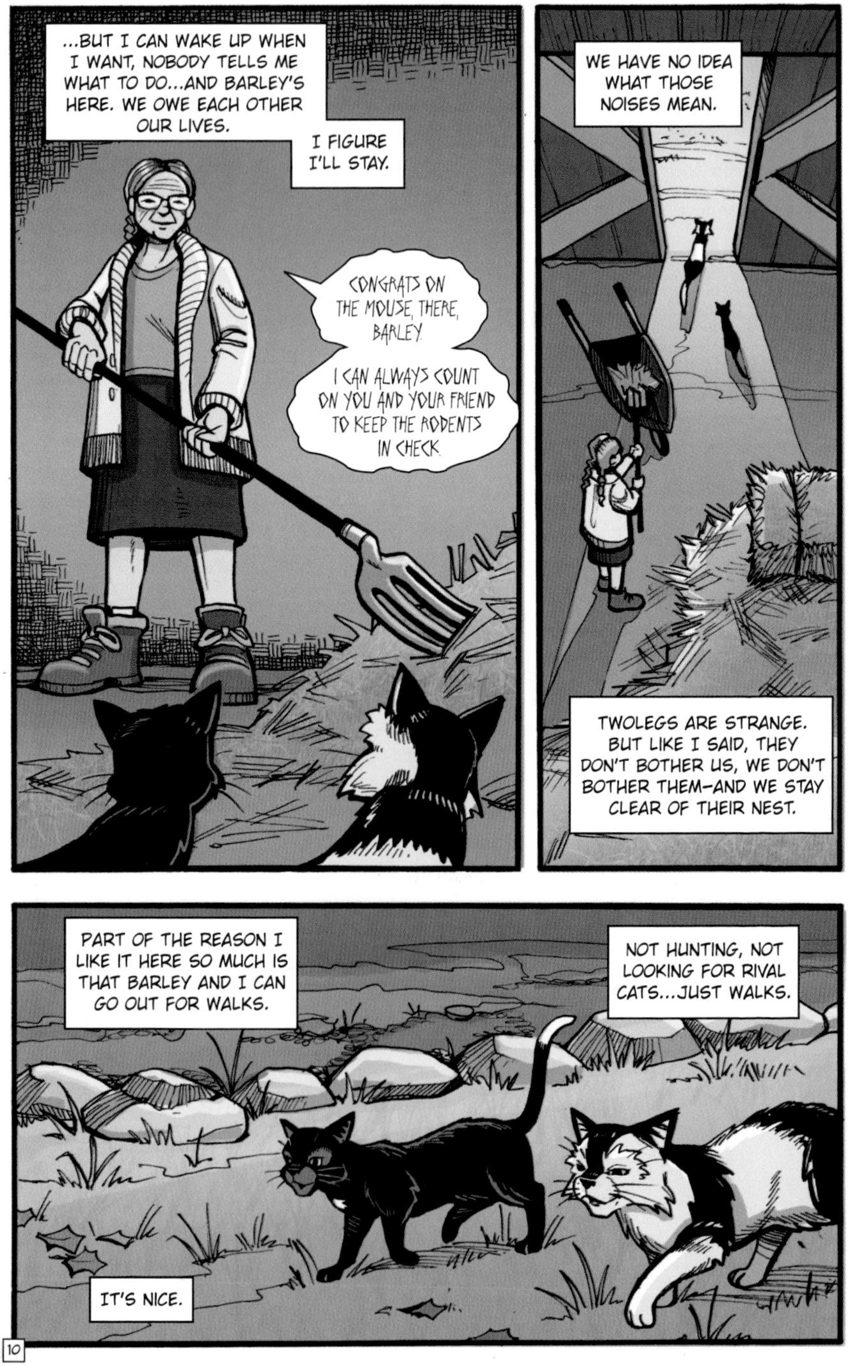
...BUT I CAN WAKE UP WHEN I WANT, NOBODY TELLS ME WHAT TO DO...AND BARLEY'S HERE. WE OWE EACH OTHER OUR LIVES.
I FIGURE I'LL STAY.
CONGRATS ON THE MOUSE, THERE, BARLEY.
I CAN ALWAYS COUNT ON YOU AND YOUR FRIEND TO KEEP THE RODENTS IN CHECK.
WE HAVE NO IDEA WHAT THOSE NOISES MEAN.
TWOLEGS ARE STRANGE. BUT LIKE I SAID, THEY DON'T BOTHER US, WE DON'T BOTHER THEM—AND WE STAY CLEAR OF THEIR NEST.
PART OF THE REASON I LIKE IT HERE SO MUCH IS THAT BARLEY AND I CAN GO OUT FOR WALKS.
NOT HUNTING, NOT LOOKING FOR RIVAL CATS...JUST WALKS.
IT'S NICE.

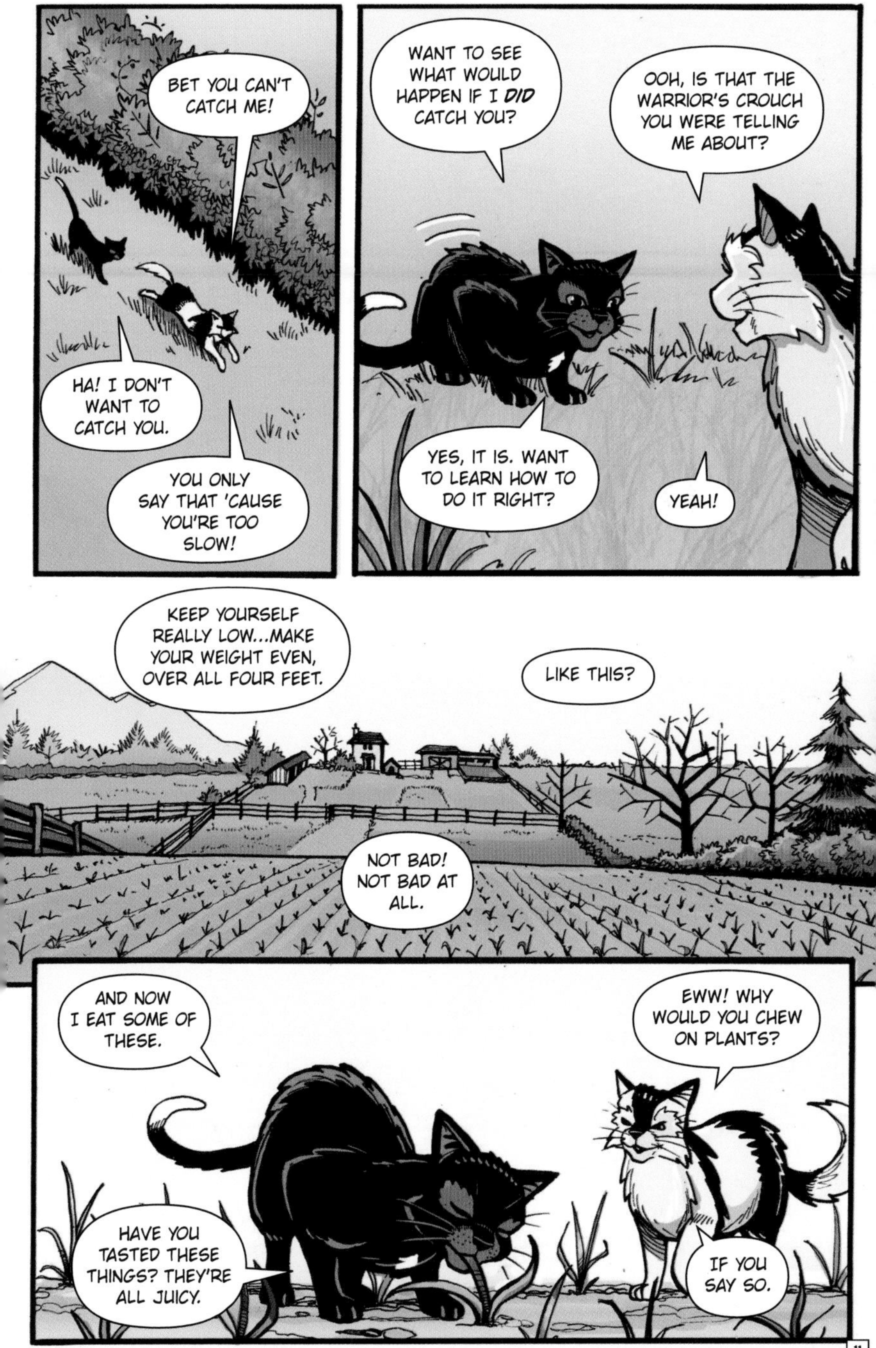
BET YOU CAN'T CATCH ME!
HA! I DON'T WANT TO CATCH YOU.
YOU ONLY SAY THAT 'CAUSE YOU'RE TOO SLOW!
WANT TO SEE WHAT WOULD HAPPEN IF I *DID* CATCH YOU?
OOH, IS THAT THE WARRIOR'S CROUCH YOU WERE TELLING ME ABOUT?
YES, IT IS. WANT TO LEARN HOW TO DO IT RIGHT?
YEAH!
KEEP YOURSELF REALLY LOW...MAKE YOUR WEIGHT EVEN, OVER ALL FOUR FEET.
LIKE THIS?
NOT BAD! NOT BAD AT ALL.
AND NOW I EAT SOME OF THESE.
EWW! WHY WOULD YOU CHEW ON PLANTS?
HAVE YOU TASTED THESE THINGS? THEY'RE ALL JUICY.
IF YOU SAY SO.

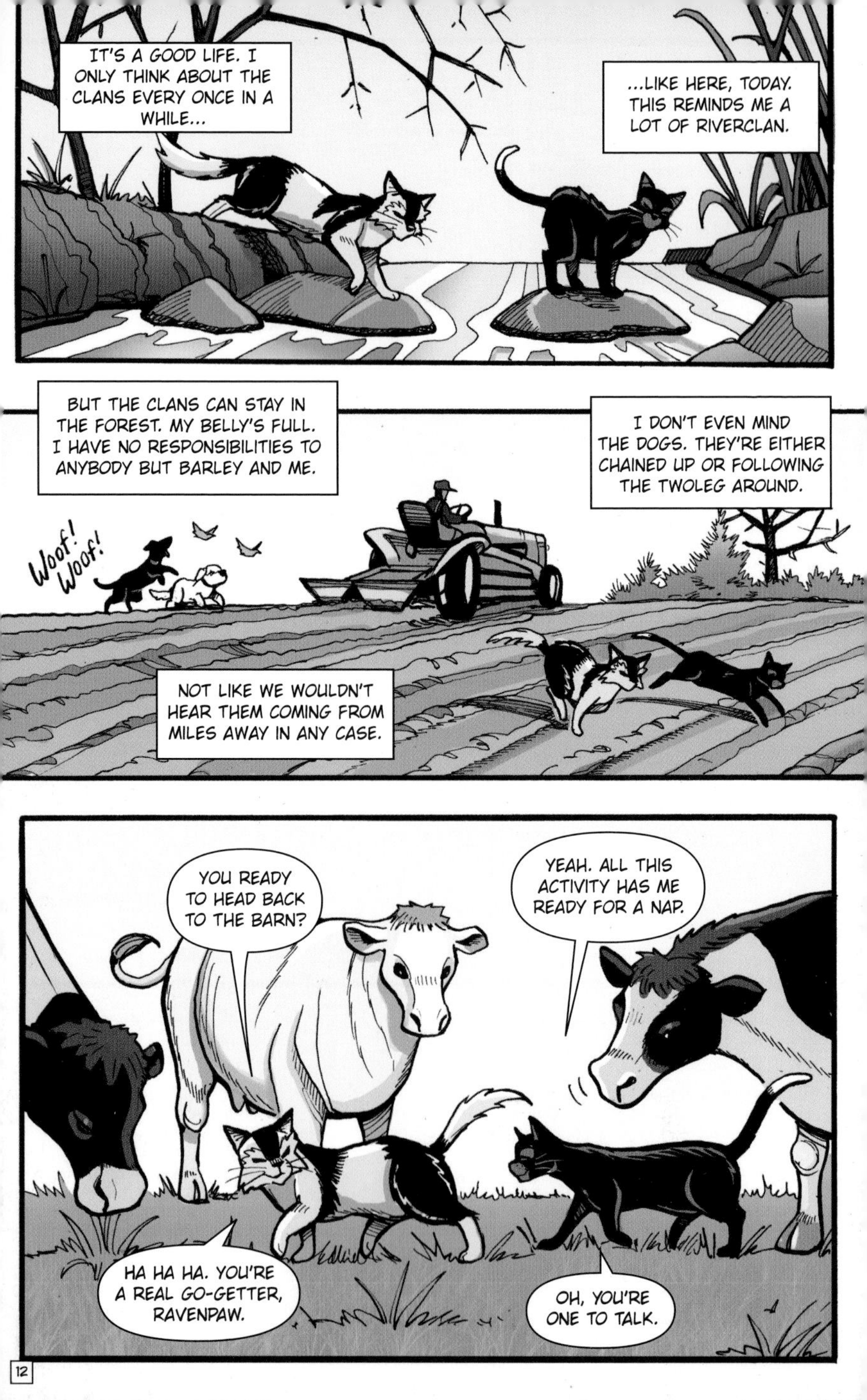
IT'S A GOOD LIFE. I ONLY THINK ABOUT THE CLANS EVERY ONCE IN A WHILE...
...LIKE HERE, TODAY. THIS REMINDS ME A LOT OF RIVERCLAN.
BUT THE CLANS CAN STAY IN THE FOREST. MY BELLY'S FULL. I HAVE NO RESPONSIBILITIES TO ANYBODY BUT BARLEY AND ME.
I DON'T EVEN MIND THE DOGS. THEY'RE EITHER CHAINED UP OR FOLLOWING THE TWOLEG AROUND.
Woof! Woof!
NOT LIKE WE WOULDN'T HEAR THEM COMING FROM MILES AWAY IN ANY CASE.
YOU READY TO HEAD BACK TO THE BARN?
YEAH. ALL THIS ACTIVITY HAS ME READY FOR A NAP.
HA HA HA. YOU'RE A REAL GO-GETTER, RAVENPAW.
OH, YOU'RE ONE TO TALK.

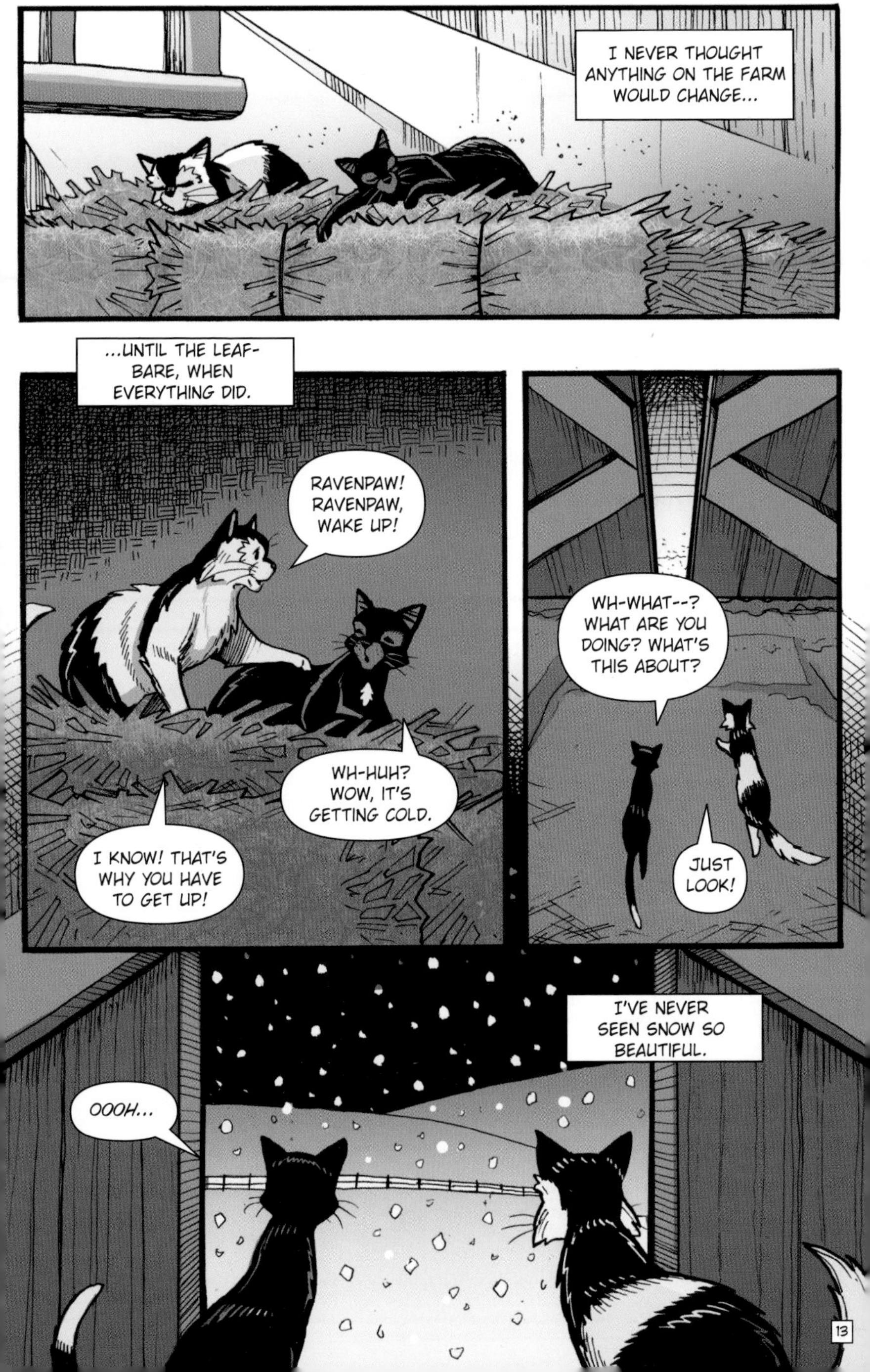
I NEVER THOUGHT ANYTHING ON THE FARM WOULD CHANGE...
...UNTIL THE LEAF-BARE, WHEN EVERYTHING DID.
RAVENPAW! RAVENPAW, WAKE UP!
WH-HUH? WOW, IT'S GETTING COLD.
I KNOW! THAT'S WHY YOU HAVE TO GET UP!
WH-WHAT--? WHAT ARE YOU DOING? WHAT'S THIS ABOUT?
JUST LOOK!
I'VE NEVER SEEN SNOW SO BEAUTIFUL.
OOOH...

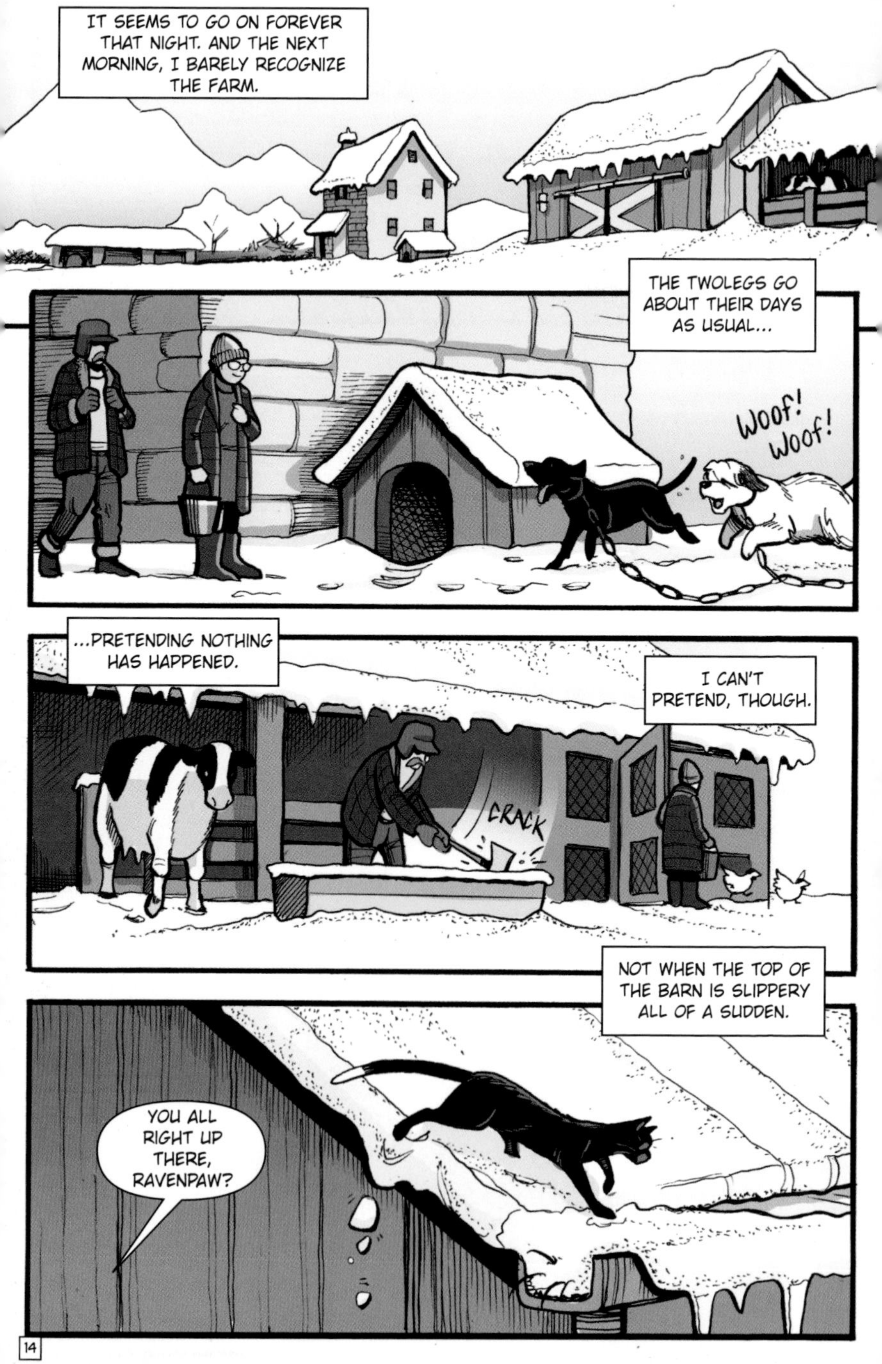
IT SEEMS TO GO ON FOREVER THAT NIGHT. AND THE NEXT MORNING, I BARELY RECOGNIZE THE FARM.
THE TWOLEGS GO ABOUT THEIR DAYS AS USUAL...
Woof! Woof!
...PRETENDING NOTHING HAS HAPPENED.
I CAN'T PRETEND, THOUGH.
CRACK
NOT WHEN THE TOP OF THE BARN IS SLIPPERY ALL OF A SUDDEN.
YOU ALL RIGHT UP THERE, RAVENPAW?

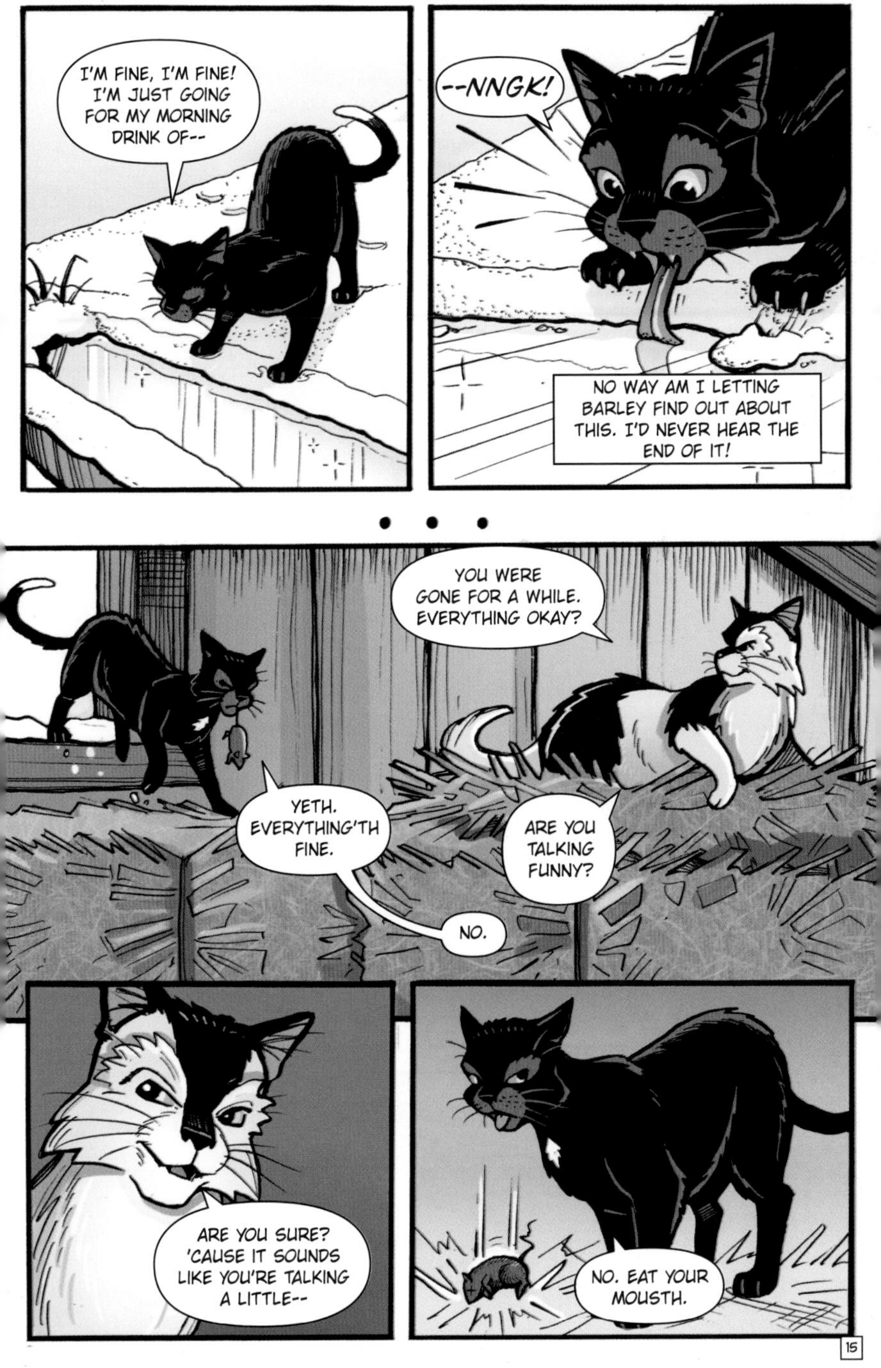
I'M FINE, I'M FINE! I'M JUST GOING FOR MY MORNING DRINK OF--
--NNGK!
NO WAY AM I LETTING BARLEY FIND OUT ABOUT THIS. I'D NEVER HEAR THE END OF IT!
YOU WERE GONE FOR A WHILE. EVERYTHING OKAY?
YETH. EVERYTHING'TH FINE.
ARE YOU TALKING FUNNY?
NO.
ARE YOU SURE? 'CAUSE IT SOUNDS LIKE YOU'RE TALKING A LITTLE--
NO. EAT YOUR MOUSTH.

BARLEY IS NICE ENOUGH TO DROP THE SUBJECT.

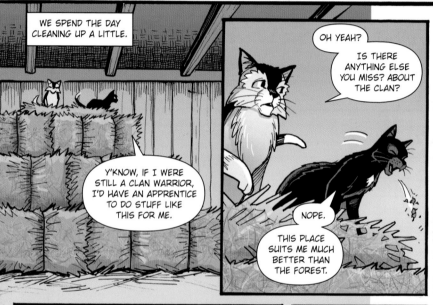

WE SPEND THE DAY CLEANING UP A LITTLE.

Y'KNOW, IF I WERE STILL A CLAN WARRIOR, I'D HAVE AN APPRENTICE TO DO STUFF LIKE THIS FOR ME.

OH YEAH?

IS THERE ANYTHING ELSE YOU MISS? ABOUT THE CLAN?

NOPE.

THIS PLACE SUITS ME MUCH BETTER THAN THE FOREST.

PLUS, YOU KNOW, **YOU** ARE MY BEST FRIEND.

ALL RIGHT.

RELAX, BARLEY. I'M NOT GOING ANYWHERE.

ME? HEY, I'M TOTALLY RELAXED. YOU'RE THE ONE GETTING ALL SENTIMENTAL. MAYBE **YOU** SHOULD RELAX.

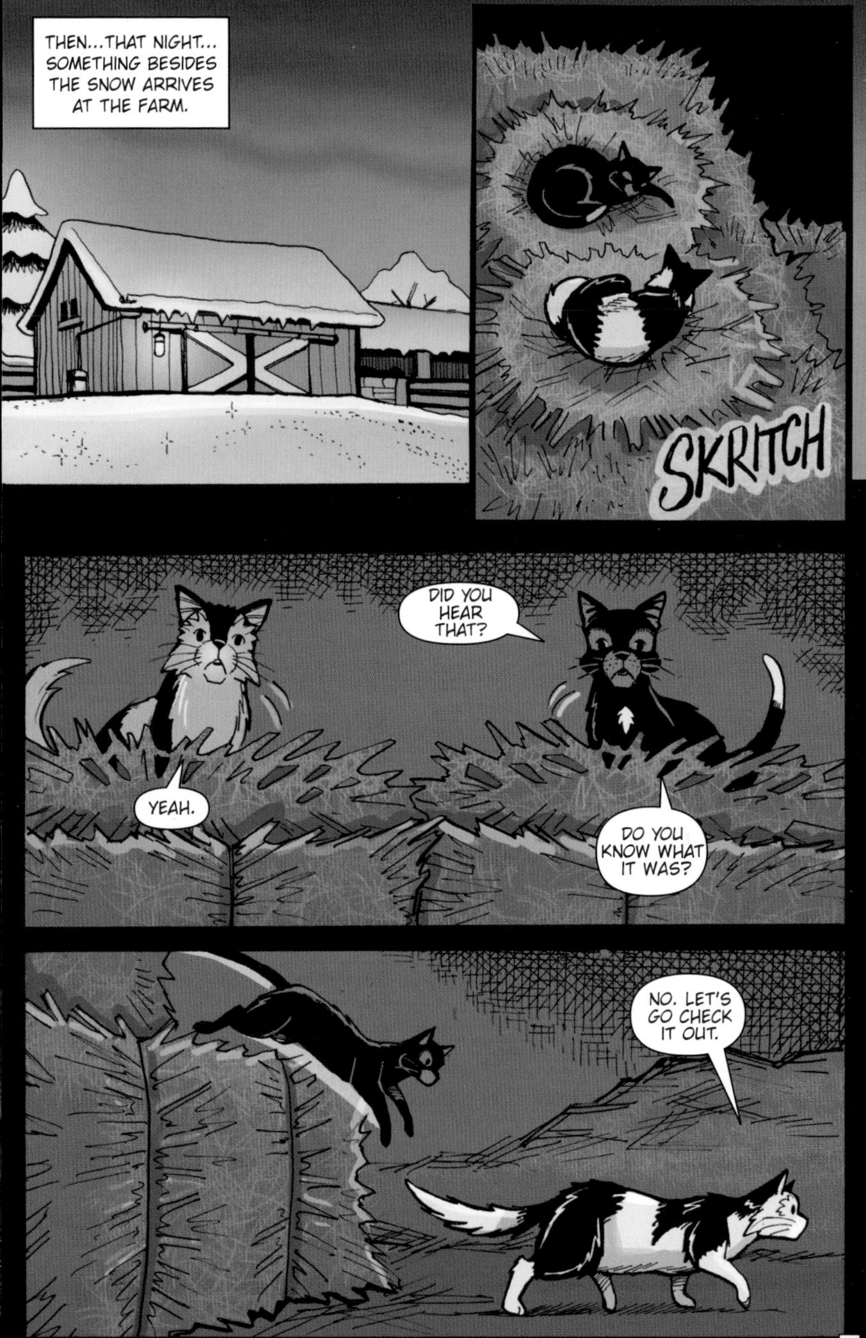
THEN...THAT NIGHT... SOMETHING BESIDES THE SNOW ARRIVES AT THE FARM.
SKRITCH
DID YOU HEAR THAT?
YEAH.
DO YOU KNOW WHAT IT WAS?
NO. LET'S GO CHECK IT OUT.

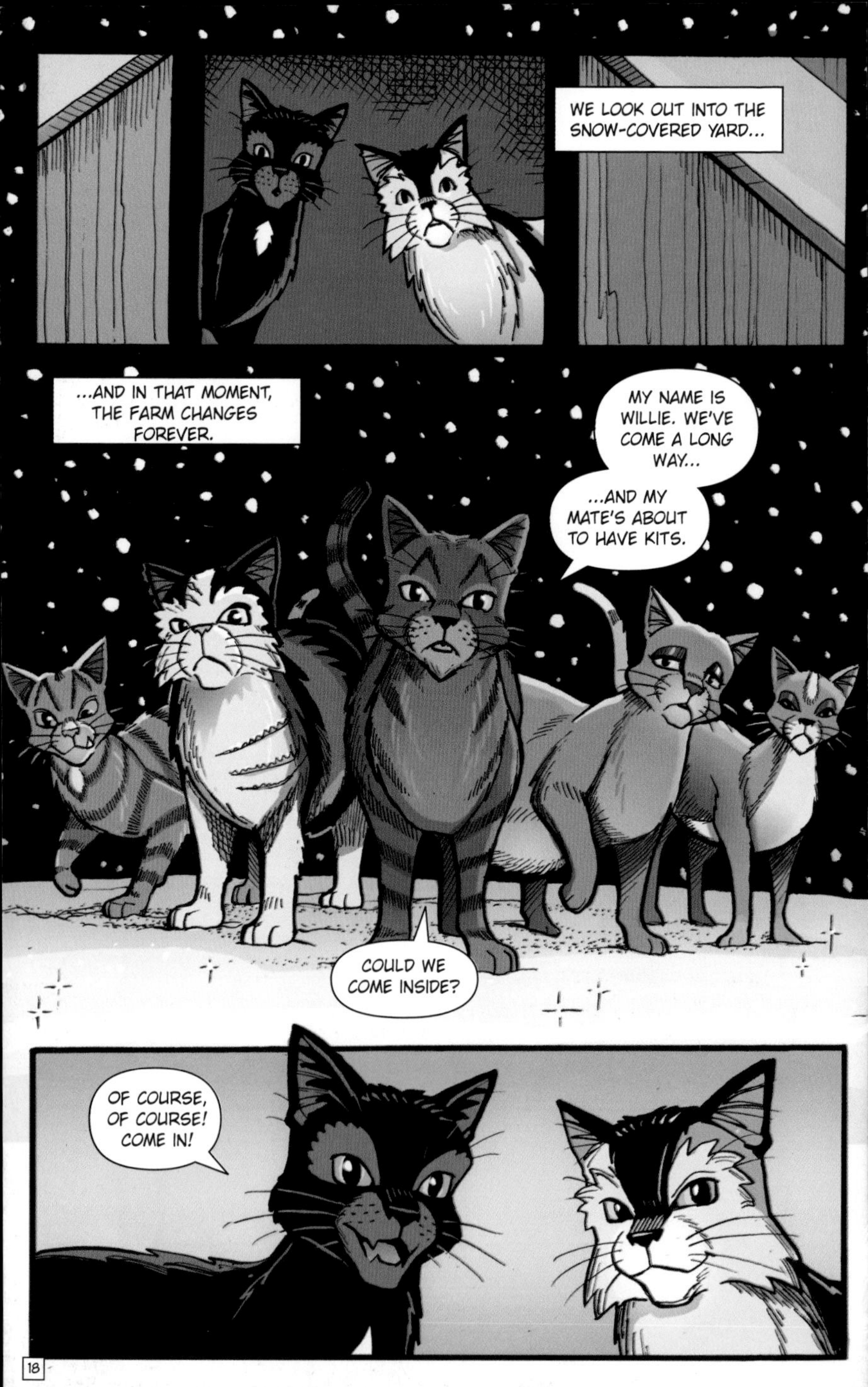
WE LOOK OUT INTO THE SNOW-COVERED YARD...
...AND IN THAT MOMENT, THE FARM CHANGES FOREVER.
MY NAME IS WILLIE. WE'VE COME A LONG WAY...
...AND MY MATE'S ABOUT TO HAVE KITS.
COULD WE COME INSIDE?
OF COURSE, OF COURSE! COME IN!

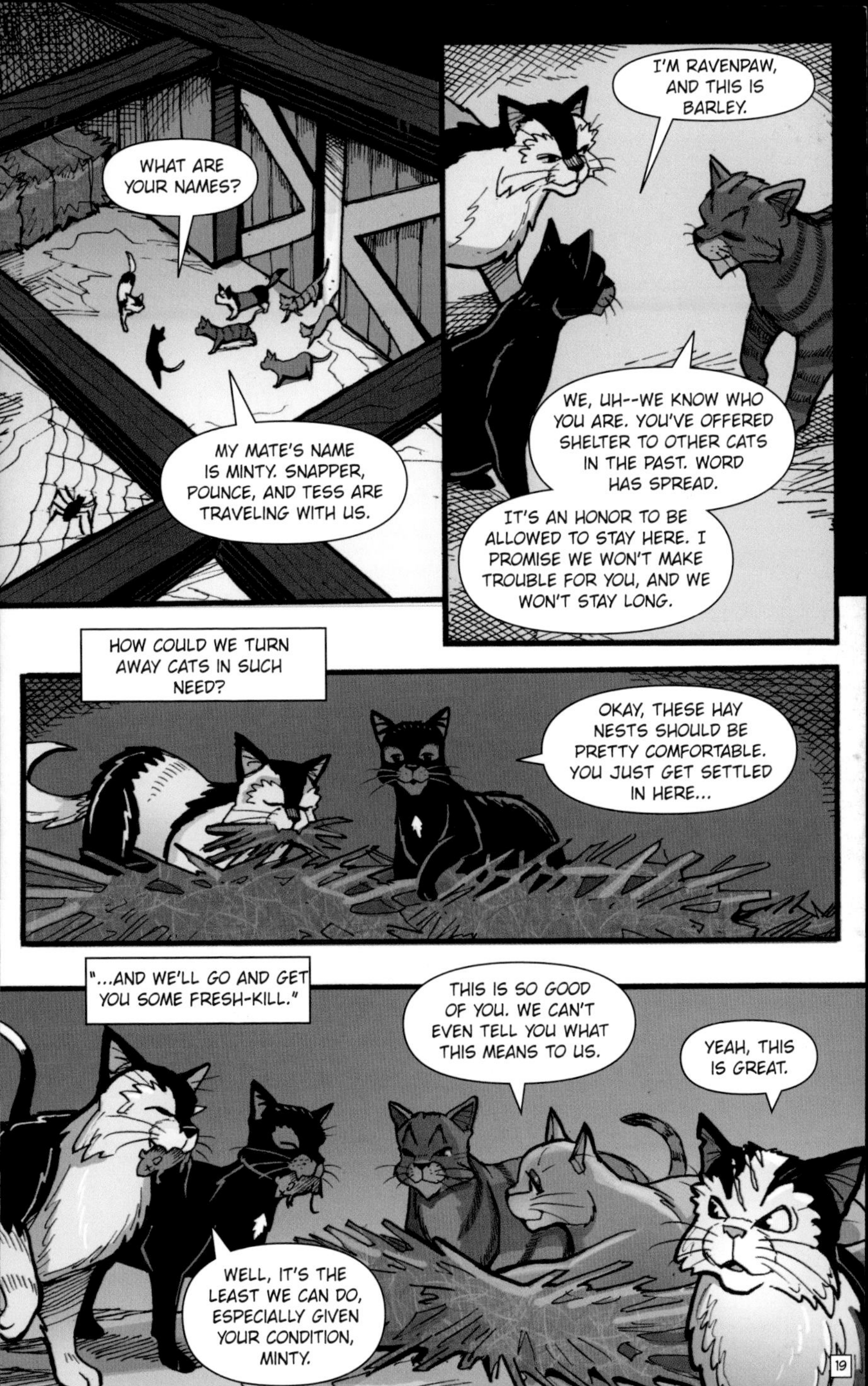
WHAT ARE YOUR NAMES?
MY MATE'S NAME IS MINTY. SNAPPER, POUNCE, AND TESS ARE TRAVELING WITH US.
I'M RAVENPAW, AND THIS IS BARLEY.
WE, UH--WE KNOW WHO YOU ARE. YOU'VE OFFERED SHELTER TO OTHER CATS IN THE PAST. WORD HAS SPREAD.
IT'S AN HONOR TO BE ALLOWED TO STAY HERE. I PROMISE WE WON'T MAKE TROUBLE FOR YOU, AND WE WON'T STAY LONG.
HOW COULD WE TURN AWAY CATS IN SUCH NEED?
OKAY, THESE HAY NESTS SHOULD BE PRETTY COMFORTABLE. YOU JUST GET SETTLED IN HERE...
"...AND WE'LL GO AND GET YOU SOME FRESH-KILL."
THIS IS SO GOOD OF YOU. WE CAN'T EVEN TELL YOU WHAT THIS MEANS TO US.
YEAH, THIS IS GREAT.
WELL, IT'S THE LEAST WE CAN DO, ESPECIALLY GIVEN YOUR CONDITION, MINTY.

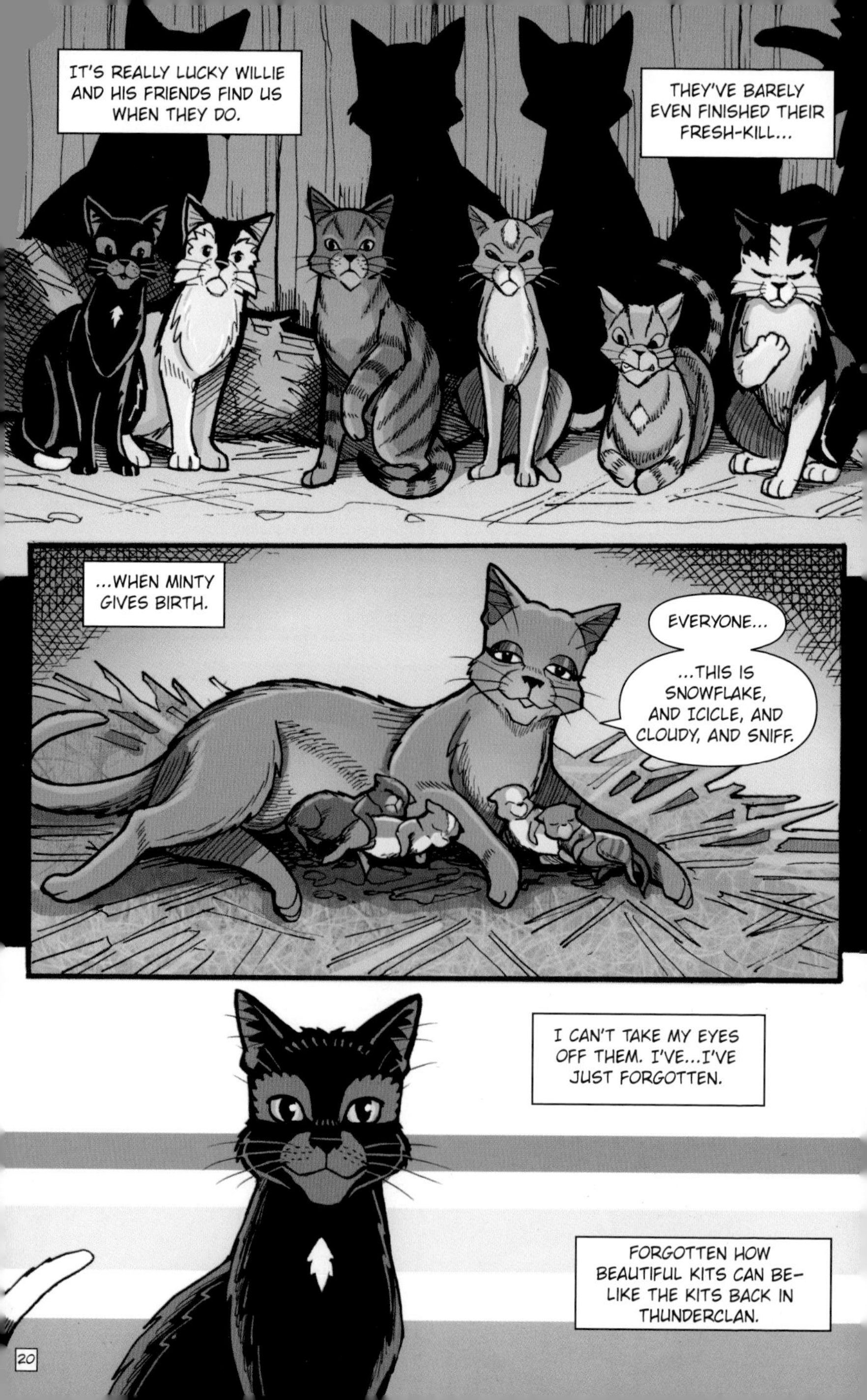
IT'S REALLY LUCKY WILLIE AND HIS FRIENDS FIND US WHEN THEY DO.
THEY'VE BARELY EVEN FINISHED THEIR FRESH-KILL...
...WHEN MINTY GIVES BIRTH.
EVERYONE...
...THIS IS SNOWFLAKE, AND ICICLE, AND CLOUDY, AND SNIFF.
I CAN'T TAKE MY EYES OFF THEM. I'VE...I'VE JUST FORGOTTEN.
FORGOTTEN HOW BEAUTIFUL KITS CAN BE-LIKE THE KITS BACK IN THUNDERCLAN.

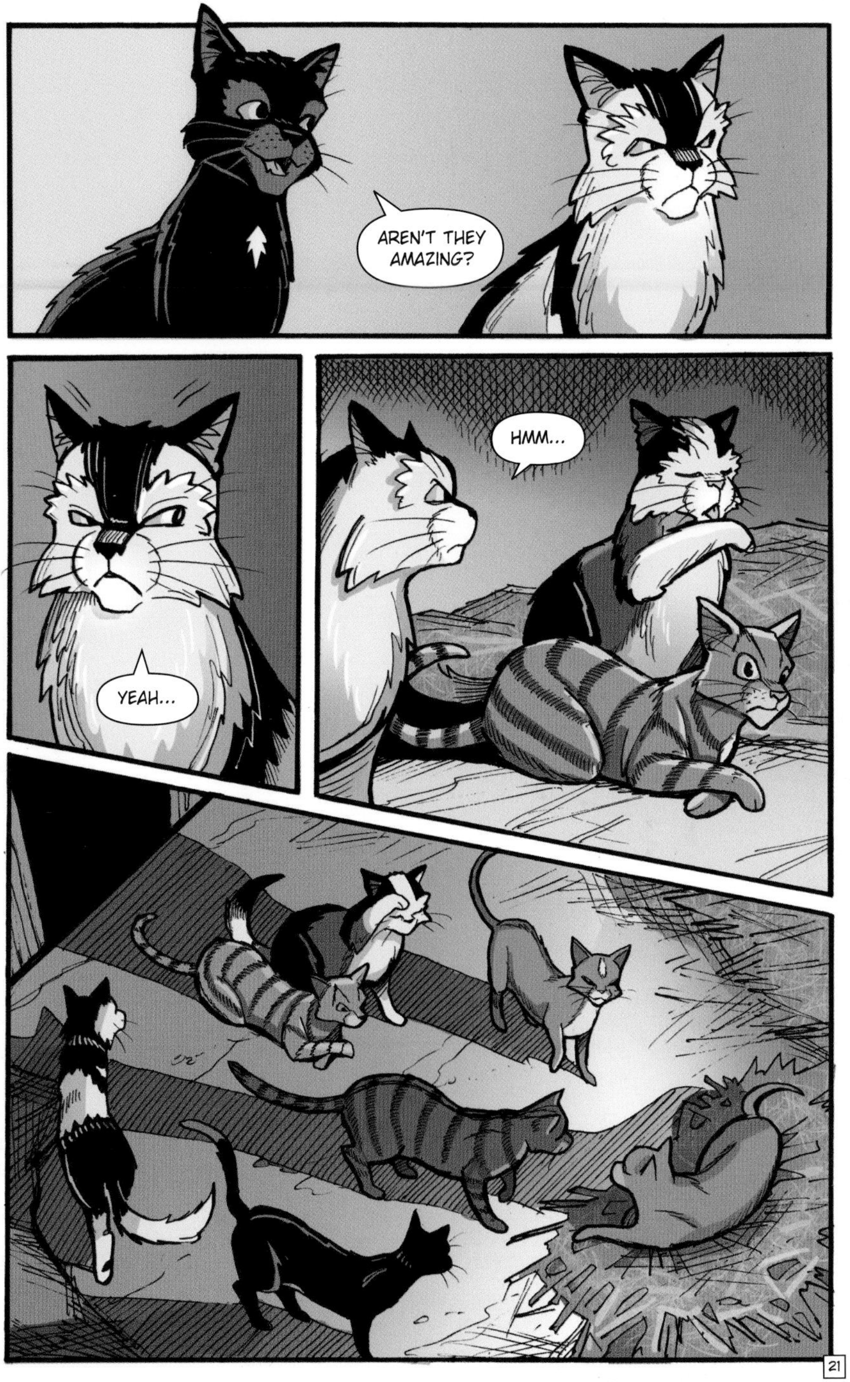
AREN'T THEY AMAZING?
YEAH...
HMM...

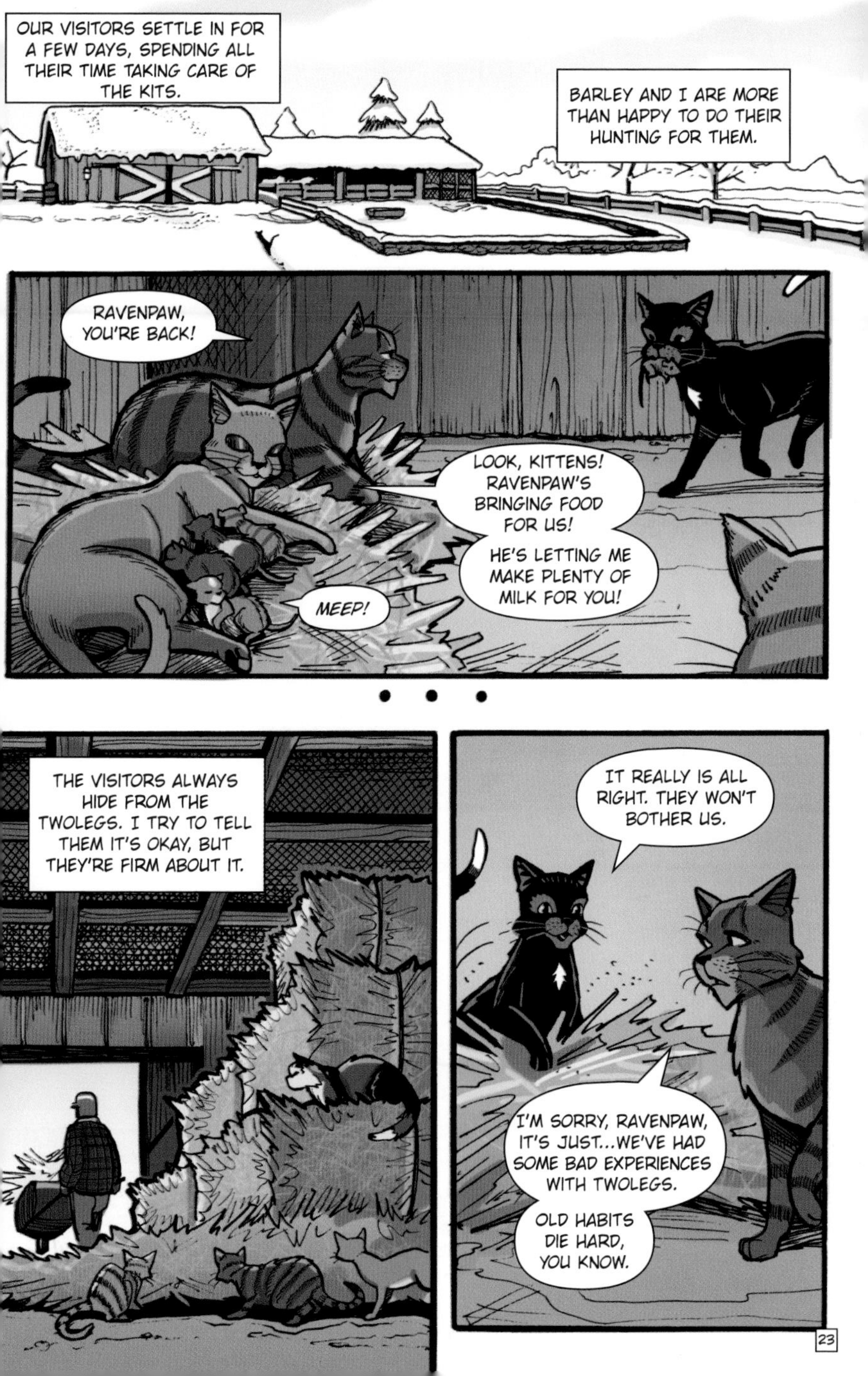
OUR VISITORS SETTLE IN FOR A FEW DAYS, SPENDING ALL THEIR TIME TAKING CARE OF THE KITS.
BARLEY AND I ARE MORE THAN HAPPY TO DO THEIR HUNTING FOR THEM.
RAVENPAW, YOU'RE BACK!
LOOK, KITTENS! RAVENPAW'S BRINGING FOOD FOR US!
HE'S LETTING ME MAKE PLENTY OF MILK FOR YOU!
MEEP!
THE VISITORS ALWAYS HIDE FROM THE TWOLEGS. I TRY TO TELL THEM IT'S OKAY, BUT THEY'RE FIRM ABOUT IT.
IT REALLY IS ALL RIGHT. THEY WON'T BOTHER US.
I'M SORRY, RAVENPAW, IT'S JUST...WE'VE HAD SOME BAD EXPERIENCES WITH TWOLEGS.
OLD HABITS DIE HARD, YOU KNOW.

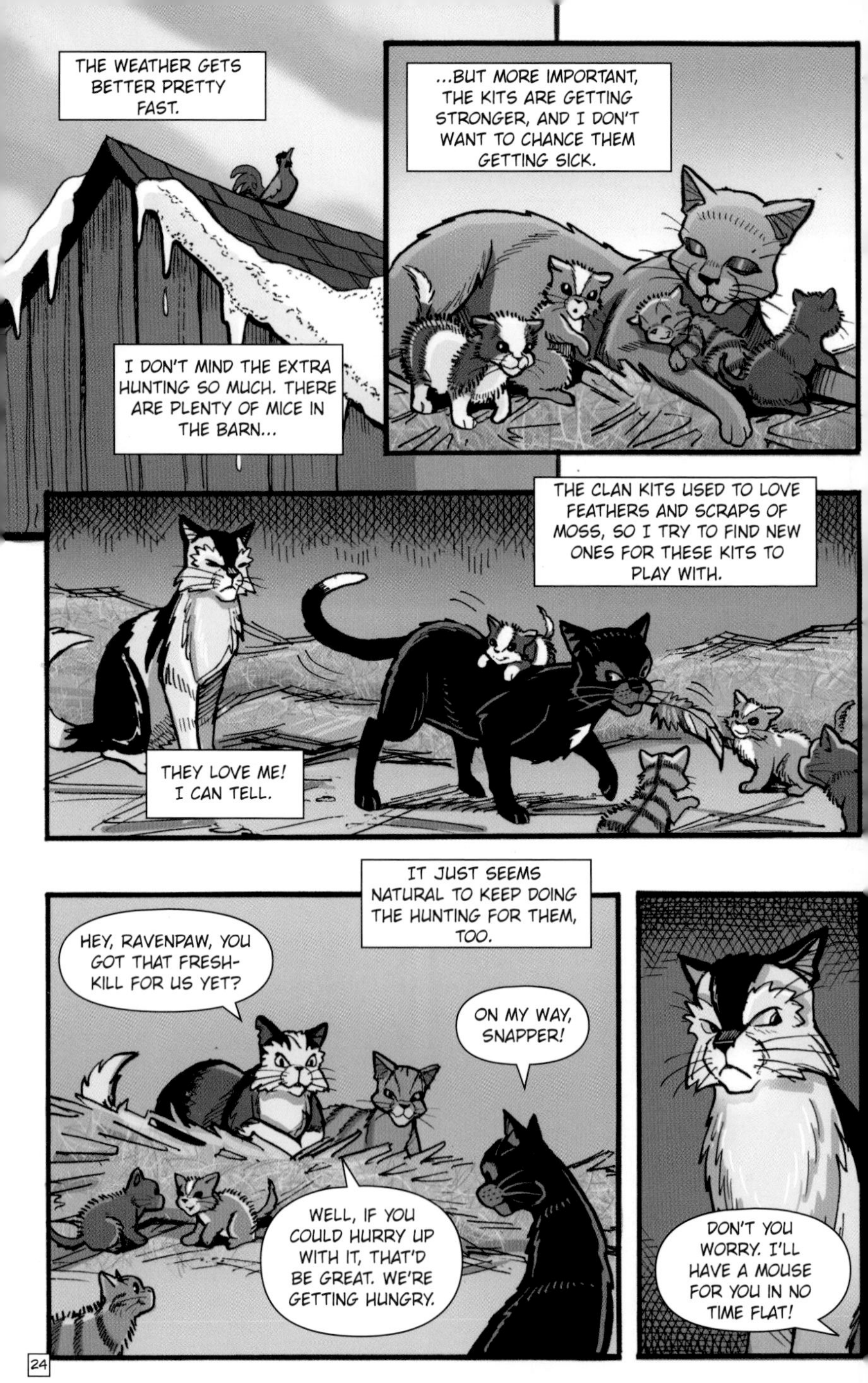
THE WEATHER GETS BETTER PRETTY FAST.
I DON'T MIND THE EXTRA HUNTING SO MUCH. THERE ARE PLENTY OF MICE IN THE BARN...
...BUT MORE IMPORTANT, THE KITS ARE GETTING STRONGER, AND I DON'T WANT TO CHANCE THEM GETTING SICK.
THE CLAN KITS USED TO LOVE FEATHERS AND SCRAPS OF MOSS, SO I TRY TO FIND NEW ONES FOR THESE KITS TO PLAY WITH.
THEY LOVE ME! I CAN TELL.
IT JUST SEEMS NATURAL TO KEEP DOING THE HUNTING FOR THEM, TOO.
HEY, RAVENPAW, YOU GOT THAT FRESH-KILL FOR US YET?
ON MY WAY, SNAPPER!
WELL, IF YOU COULD HURRY UP WITH IT, THAT'D BE GREAT. WE'RE GETTING HUNGRY.
DON'T YOU WORRY. I'LL HAVE A MOUSE FOR YOU IN NO TIME FLAT!

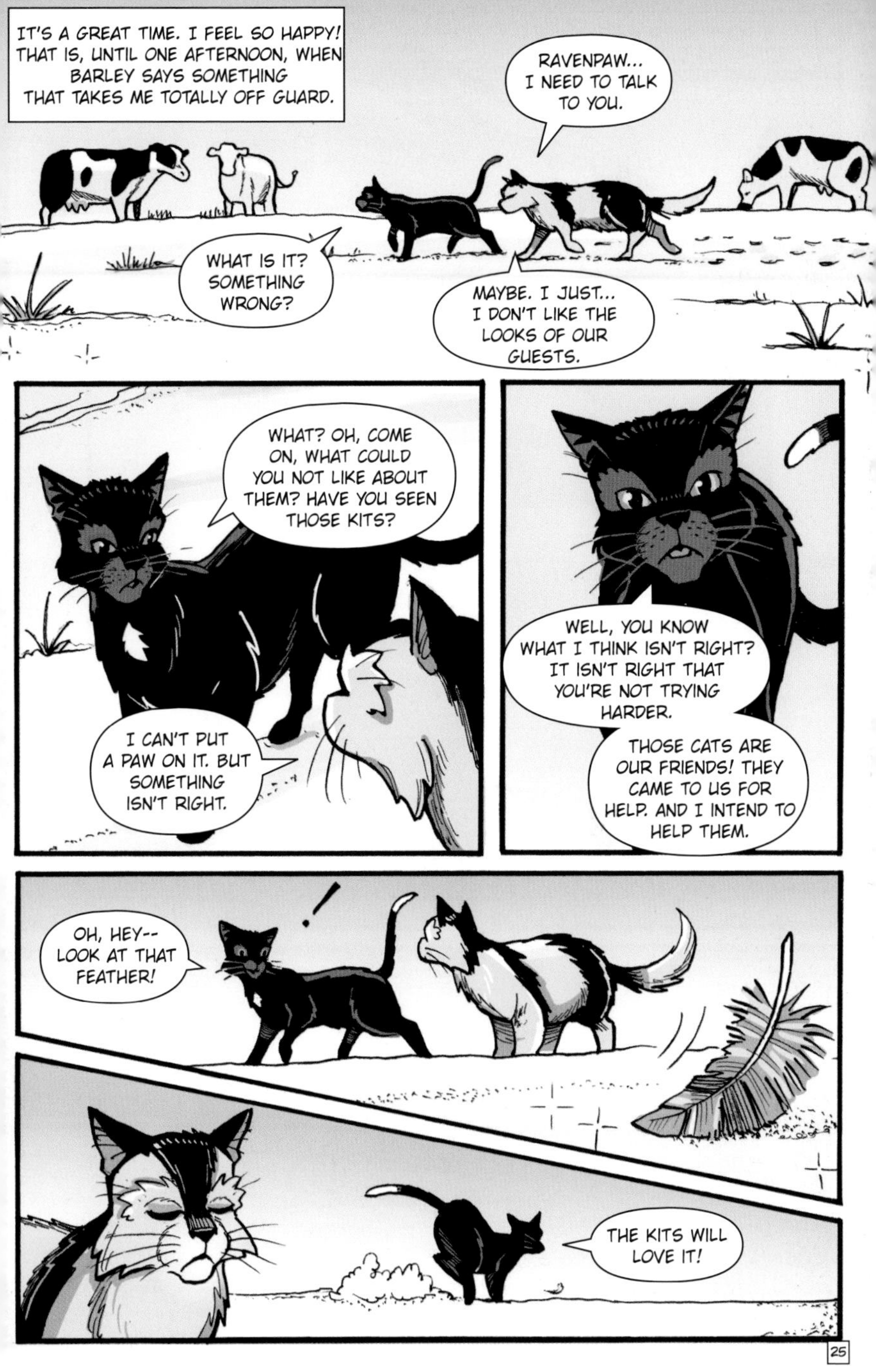

IT'S A GREAT TIME. I FEEL SO HAPPY! THAT IS, UNTIL ONE AFTERNOON, WHEN BARLEY SAYS SOMETHING THAT TAKES ME TOTALLY OFF GUARD.
RAVENPAW... I NEED TO TALK TO YOU.
WHAT IS IT? SOMETHING WRONG?
MAYBE. I JUST... I DON'T LIKE THE LOOKS OF OUR GUESTS.
WHAT? OH, COME ON, WHAT COULD YOU NOT LIKE ABOUT THEM? HAVE YOU SEEN THOSE KITS?
I CAN'T PUT A PAW ON IT. BUT SOMETHING ISN'T RIGHT.
WELL, YOU KNOW WHAT I THINK ISN'T RIGHT? IT ISN'T RIGHT THAT YOU'RE NOT TRYING HARDER.
THOSE CATS ARE OUR FRIENDS! THEY CAME TO US FOR HELP. AND I INTEND TO HELP THEM.
OH, HEY-- LOOK AT THAT FEATHER!
!
THE KITS WILL LOVE IT!

I DON'T KNOW WHAT'S BOTHERING BARLEY ABOUT WILLIE AND THE OTHER VISITORS.

I THINK THEY'RE GREAT. WILLIE ESPECIALLY--HE'S ALWAYS SO INTERESTED IN HOW THE FARM WORKS...

...EVEN IF HE DOESN'T UNDERSTAND EVERYTHING TO BEGIN WITH.

WILLIE! HEY, WILLIE!

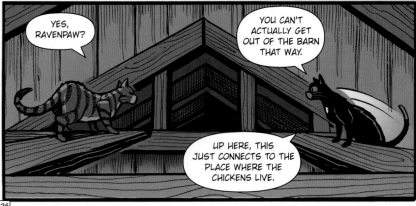

YES, RAVENPAW?

YOU CAN'T ACTUALLY GET OUT OF THE BARN THAT WAY.

UP HERE, THIS JUST CONNECTS TO THE PLACE WHERE THE CHICKENS LIVE.

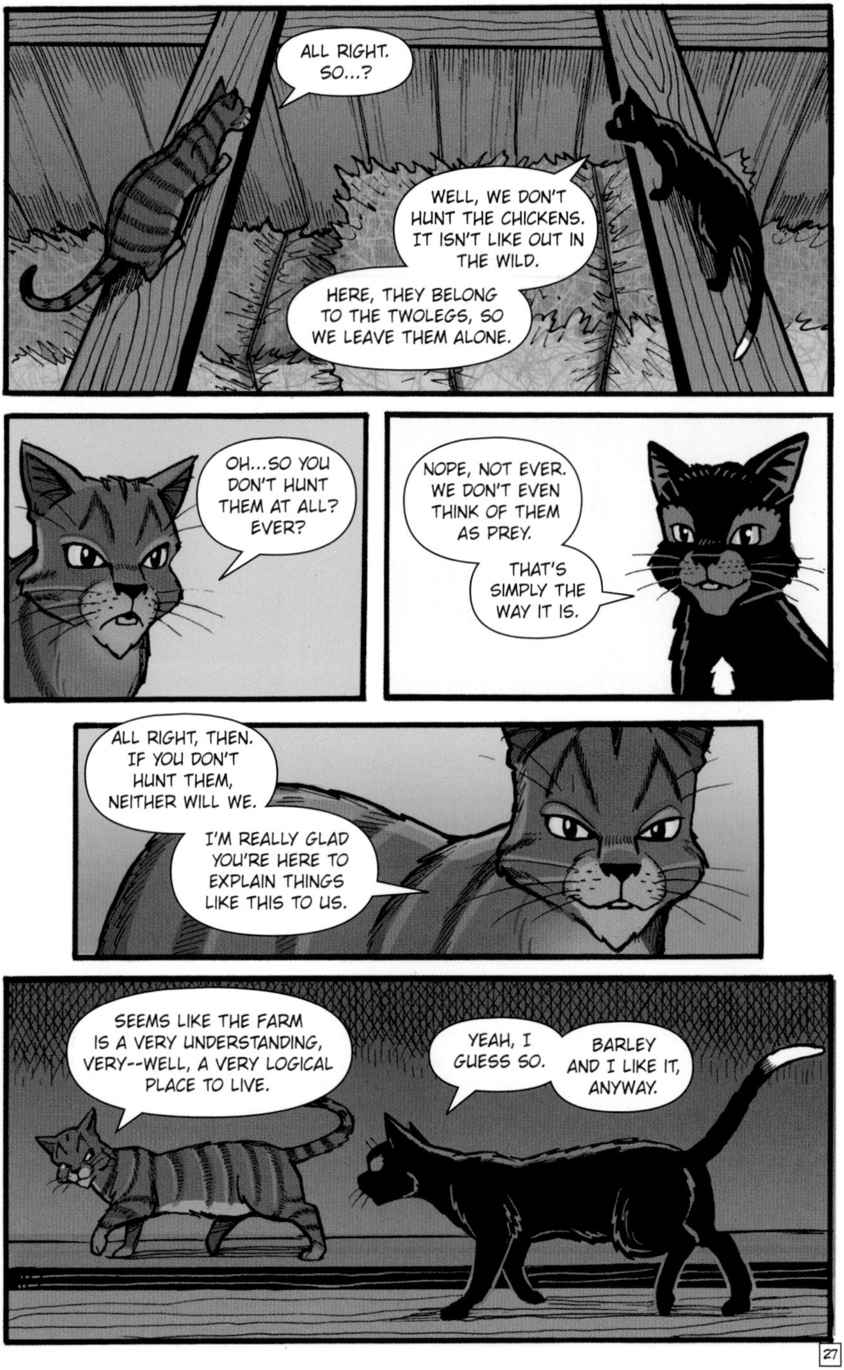
ALL RIGHT. SO...?
WELL, WE DON'T HUNT THE CHICKENS. IT ISN'T LIKE OUT IN THE WILD.
HERE, THEY BELONG TO THE TWOLEGS, SO WE LEAVE THEM ALONE.
OH...SO YOU DON'T HUNT THEM AT ALL? EVER?
NOPE, NOT EVER. WE DON'T EVEN THINK OF THEM AS PREY.
THAT'S SIMPLY THE WAY IT IS.
ALL RIGHT, THEN. IF YOU DON'T HUNT THEM, NEITHER WILL WE.
I'M REALLY GLAD YOU'RE HERE TO EXPLAIN THINGS LIKE THIS TO US.
SEEMS LIKE THE FARM IS A VERY UNDERSTANDING, VERY--WELL, A VERY LOGICAL PLACE TO LIVE.
YEAH, I GUESS SO.
BARLEY AND I LIKE IT, ANYWAY.

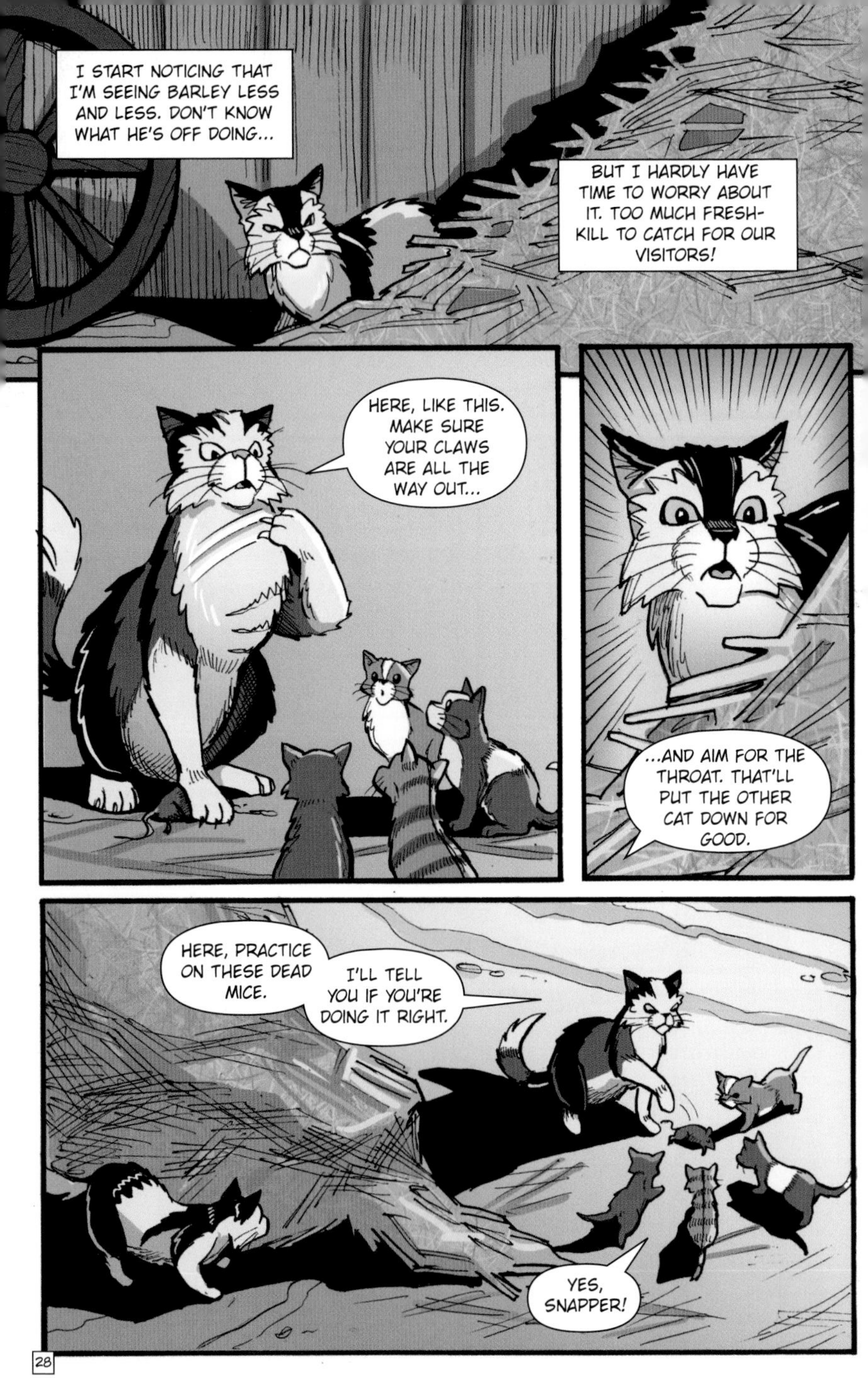
I START NOTICING THAT I'M SEEING BARLEY LESS AND LESS. DON'T KNOW WHAT HE'S OFF DOING...
BUT I HARDLY HAVE TIME TO WORRY ABOUT IT. TOO MUCH FRESH-KILL TO CATCH FOR OUR VISITORS!
HERE, LIKE THIS. MAKE SURE YOUR CLAWS ARE ALL THE WAY OUT...
...AND AIM FOR THE THROAT. THAT'LL PUT THE OTHER CAT DOWN FOR GOOD.
HERE, PRACTICE ON THESE DEAD MICE.
I'LL TELL YOU IF YOU'RE DOING IT RIGHT.
YES, SNAPPER!

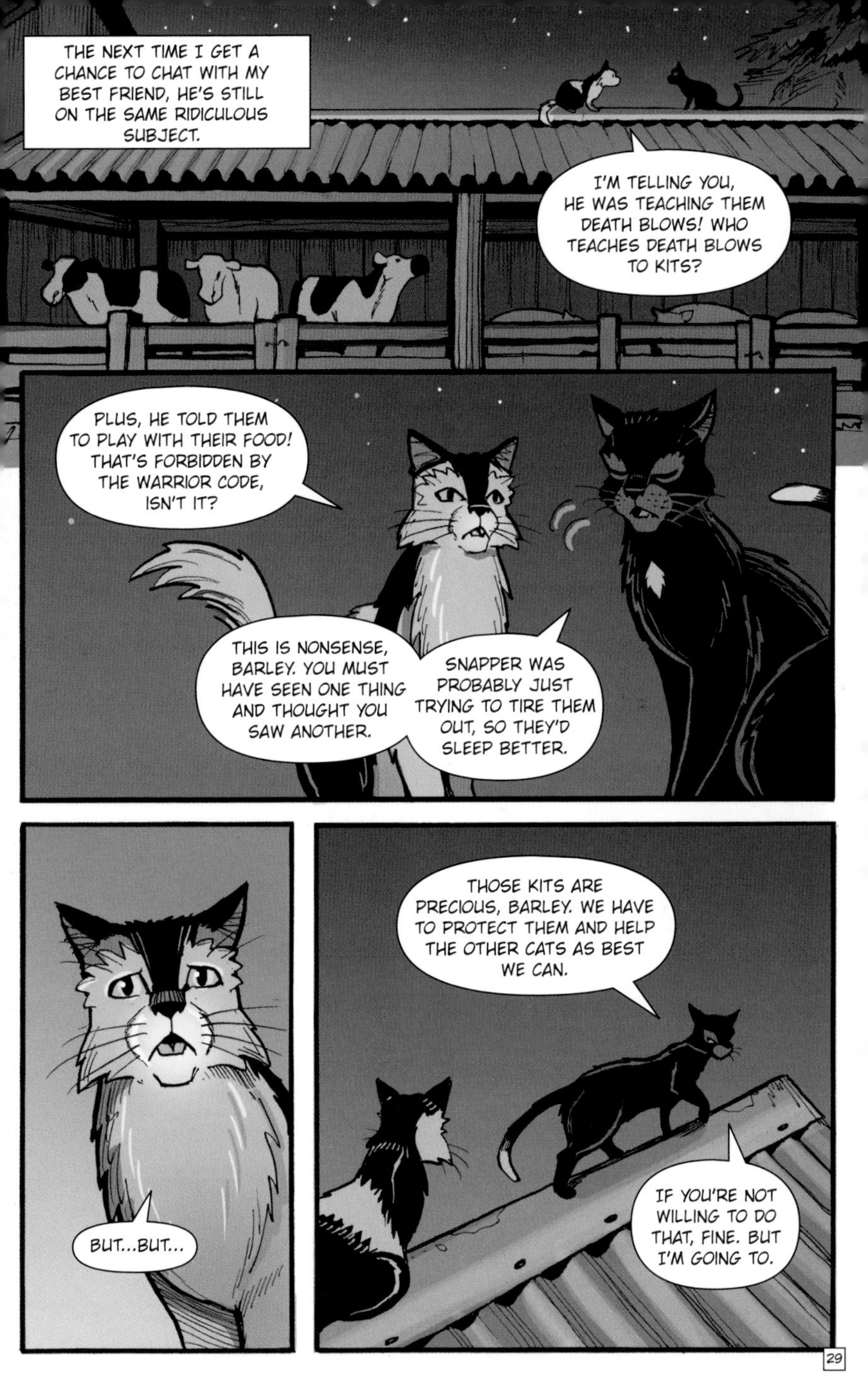
THE NEXT TIME I GET A CHANCE TO CHAT WITH MY BEST FRIEND, HE'S STILL ON THE SAME RIDICULOUS SUBJECT.
I'M TELLING YOU, HE WAS TEACHING THEM DEATH BLOWS! WHO TEACHES DEATH BLOWS TO KITS?
PLUS, HE TOLD THEM TO PLAY WITH THEIR FOOD! THAT'S FORBIDDEN BY THE WARRIOR CODE, ISN'T IT?
THIS IS NONSENSE, BARLEY. YOU MUST HAVE SEEN ONE THING AND THOUGHT YOU SAW ANOTHER.
SNAPPER WAS PROBABLY JUST TRYING TO TIRE THEM OUT, SO THEY'D SLEEP BETTER.
BUT...BUT...
THOSE KITS ARE PRECIOUS, BARLEY. WE HAVE TO PROTECT THEM AND HELP THE OTHER CATS AS BEST WE CAN.
IF YOU'RE NOT WILLING TO DO THAT, FINE. BUT I'M GOING TO.

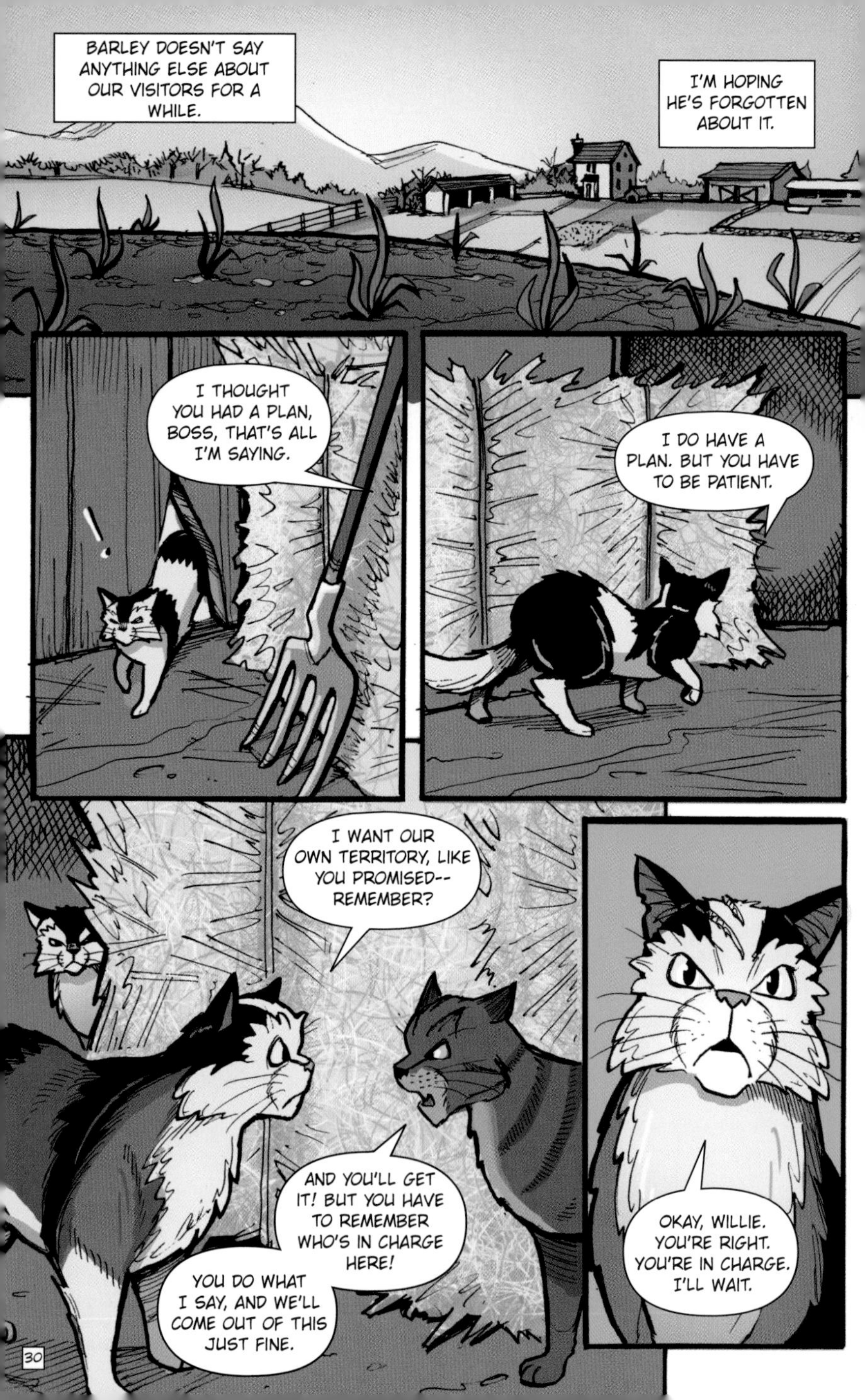
BARLEY DOESN'T SAY ANYTHING ELSE ABOUT OUR VISITORS FOR A WHILE.
I'M HOPING HE'S FORGOTTEN ABOUT IT.
I THOUGHT YOU HAD A PLAN, BOSS, THAT'S ALL I'M SAYING.
!
I DO HAVE A PLAN. BUT YOU HAVE TO BE PATIENT.
I WANT OUR OWN TERRITORY, LIKE YOU PROMISED-- REMEMBER?
AND YOU'LL GET IT! BUT YOU HAVE TO REMEMBER WHO'S IN CHARGE HERE!
YOU DO WHAT I SAY, AND WE'LL COME OUT OF THIS JUST FINE.
OKAY, WILLIE. YOU'RE RIGHT. YOU'RE IN CHARGE. I'LL WAIT.

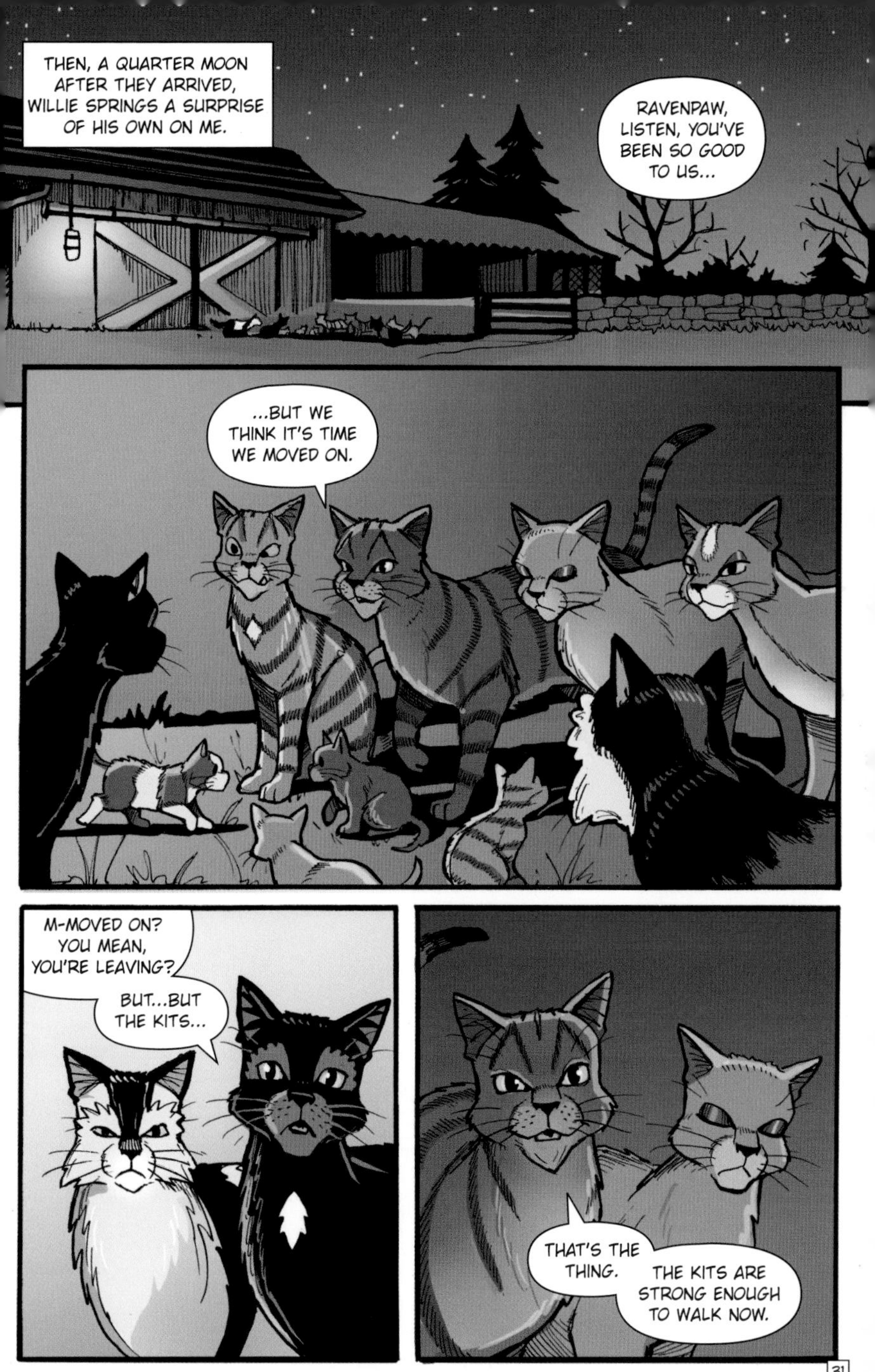
THEN, A QUARTER MOON AFTER THEY ARRIVED, WILLIE SPRINGS A SURPRISE OF HIS OWN ON ME.
RAVENPAW, LISTEN, YOU'VE BEEN SO GOOD TO US...
...BUT WE THINK IT'S TIME WE MOVED ON.
M-MOVED ON? YOU MEAN, YOU'RE LEAVING?
BUT...BUT THE KITS...
THAT'S THE THING.
THE KITS ARE STRONG ENOUGH TO WALK NOW.

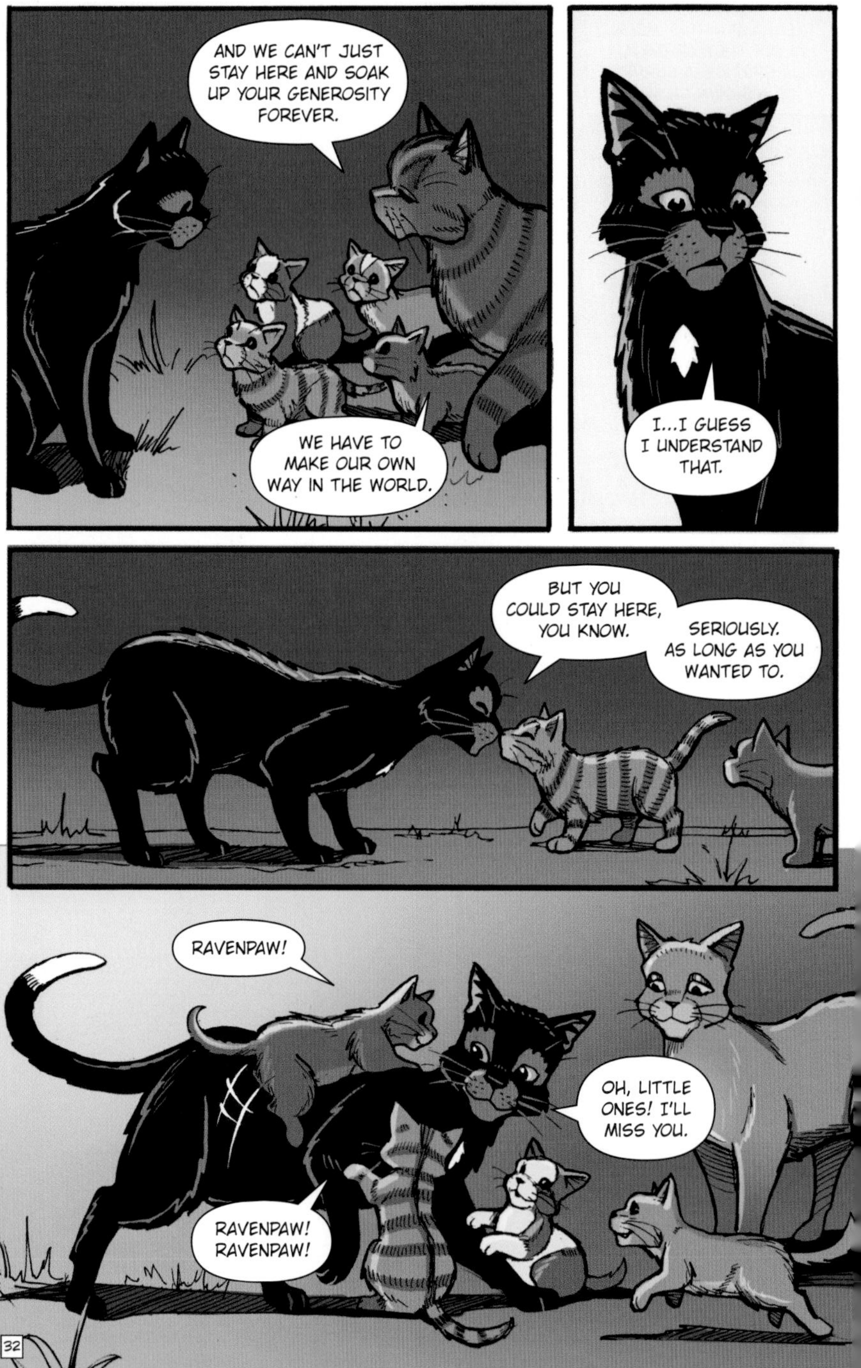
AND WE CAN'T JUST STAY HERE AND SOAK UP YOUR GENEROSITY FOREVER.
WE HAVE TO MAKE OUR OWN WAY IN THE WORLD.
I...I GUESS I UNDERSTAND THAT.
BUT YOU COULD STAY HERE, YOU KNOW.
SERIOUSLY. AS LONG AS YOU WANTED TO.
RAVENPAW!
OH, LITTLE ONES! I'LL MISS YOU.
RAVENPAW! RAVENPAW!

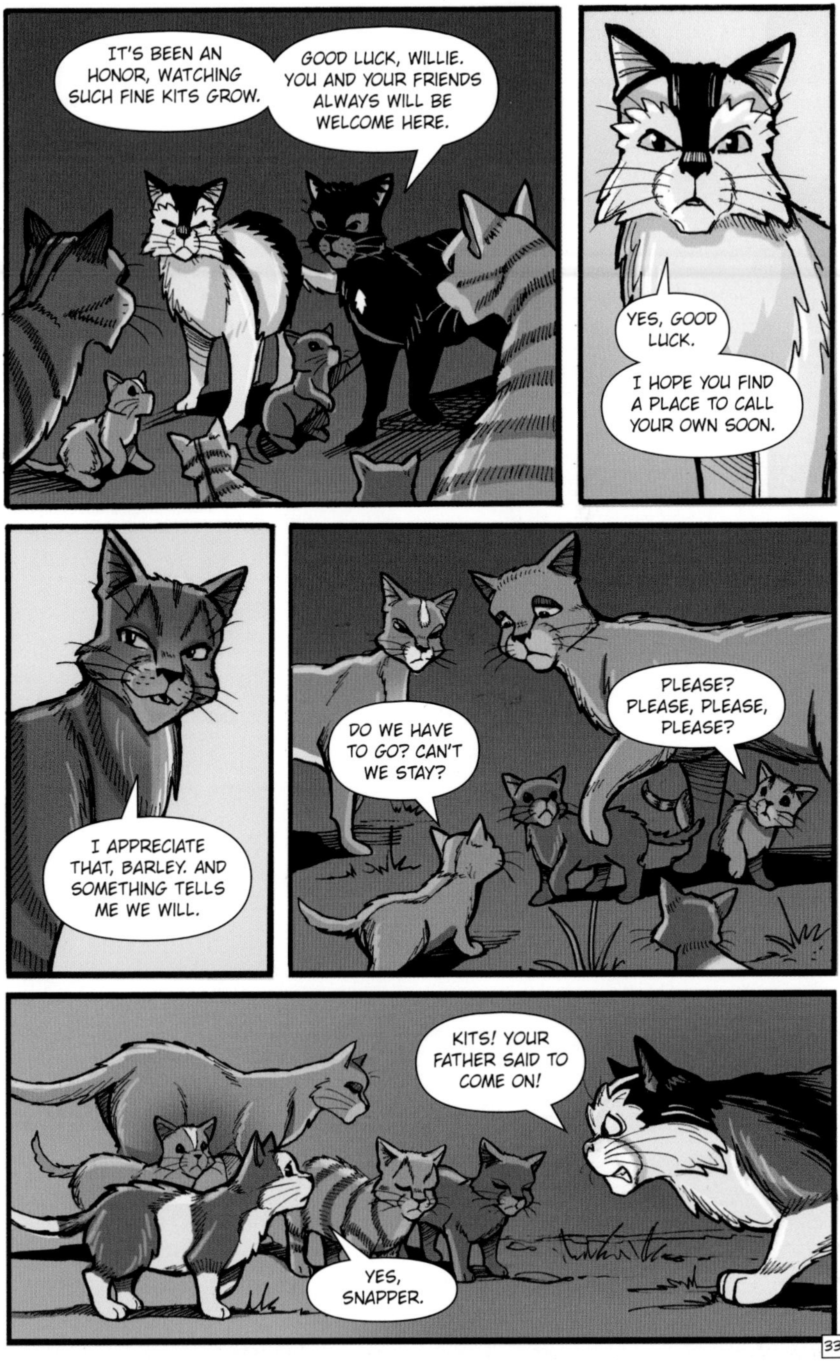
IT'S BEEN AN HONOR, WATCHING SUCH FINE KITS GROW.
GOOD LUCK, WILLIE. YOU AND YOUR FRIENDS ALWAYS WILL BE WELCOME HERE.
YES, GOOD LUCK.
I HOPE YOU FIND A PLACE TO CALL YOUR OWN SOON.
I APPRECIATE THAT, BARLEY. AND SOMETHING TELLS ME WE WILL.
DO WE HAVE TO GO? CAN'T WE STAY?
PLEASE? PLEASE, PLEASE, PLEASE?
KITS! YOUR FATHER SAID TO COME ON!
YES, SNAPPER.

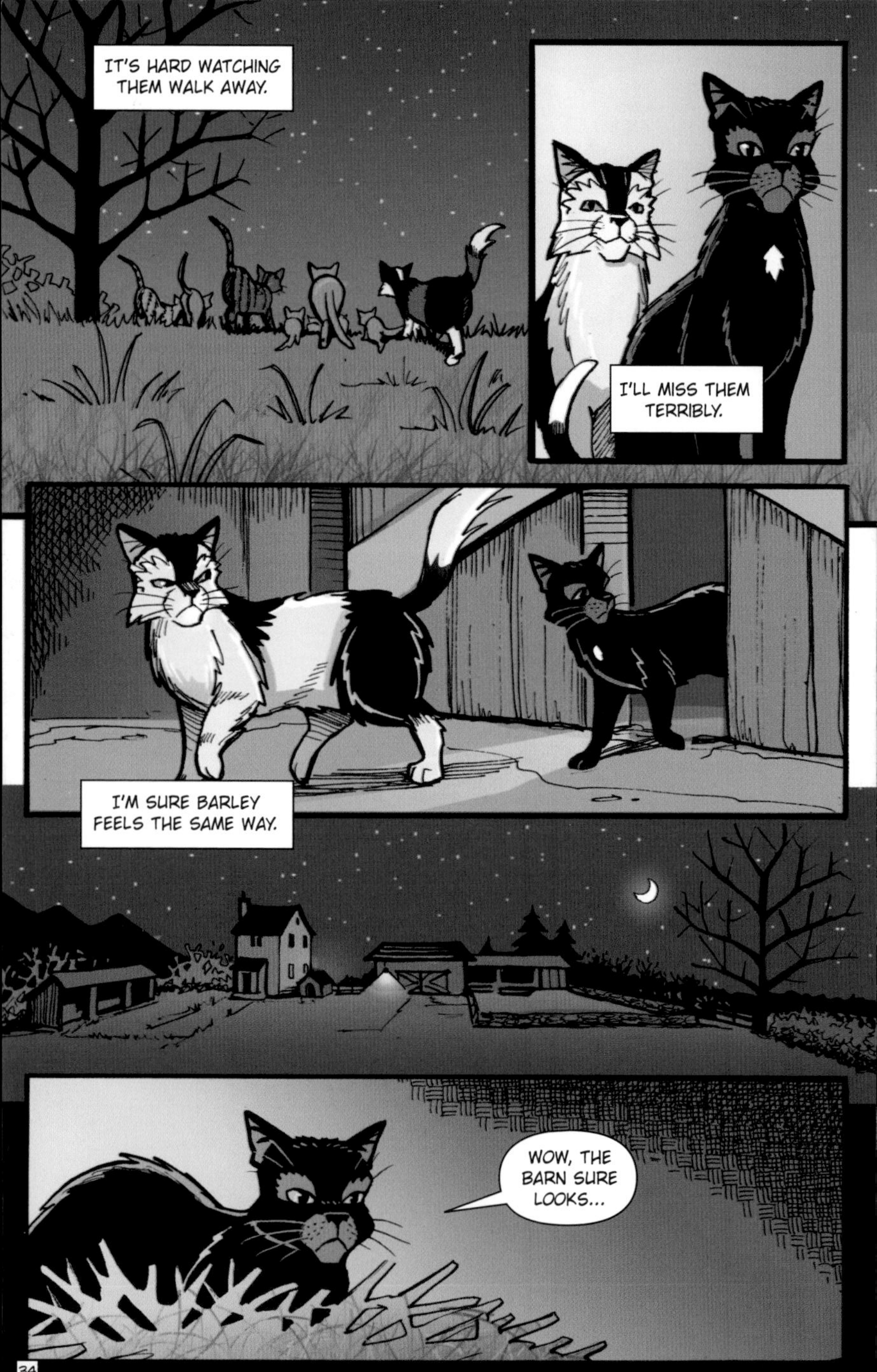
IT'S HARD WATCHING THEM WALK AWAY.
I'LL MISS THEM TERRIBLY.
I'M SURE BARLEY FEELS THE SAME WAY.
WOW, THE BARN SURE LOOKS...

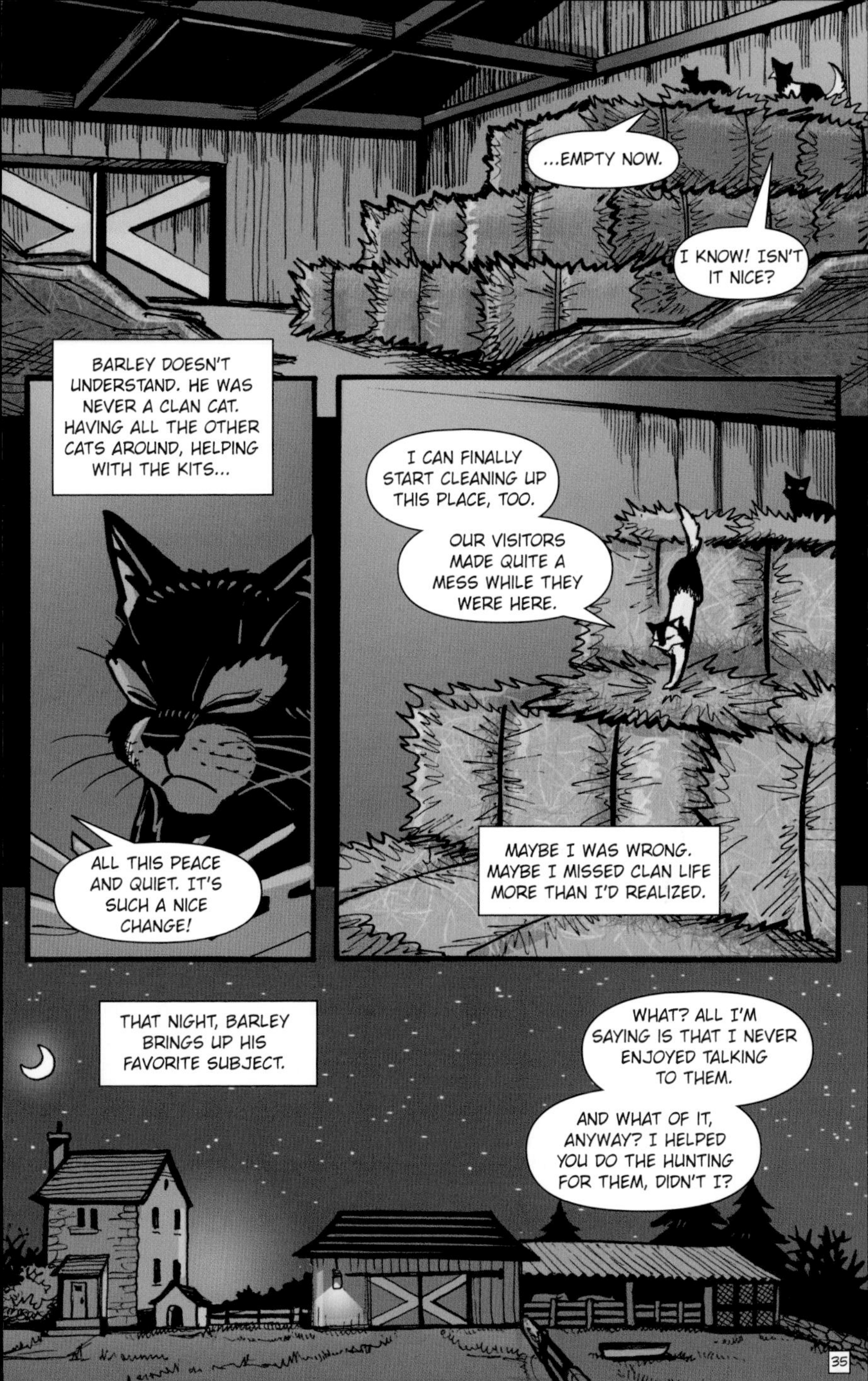
...EMPTY NOW.
I KNOW! ISN'T IT NICE?
BARLEY DOESN'T UNDERSTAND. HE WAS NEVER A CLAN CAT. HAVING ALL THE OTHER CATS AROUND, HELPING WITH THE KITS...
ALL THIS PEACE AND QUIET. IT'S SUCH A NICE CHANGE!
I CAN FINALLY START CLEANING UP THIS PLACE, TOO.
OUR VISITORS MADE QUITE A MESS WHILE THEY WERE HERE.
MAYBE I WAS WRONG. MAYBE I MISSED CLAN LIFE MORE THAN I'D REALIZED.
THAT NIGHT, BARLEY BRINGS UP HIS FAVORITE SUBJECT.
WHAT? ALL I'M SAYING IS THAT I NEVER ENJOYED TALKING TO THEM.
AND WHAT OF IT, ANYWAY? I HELPED YOU DO THE HUNTING FOR THEM, DIDN'T I?

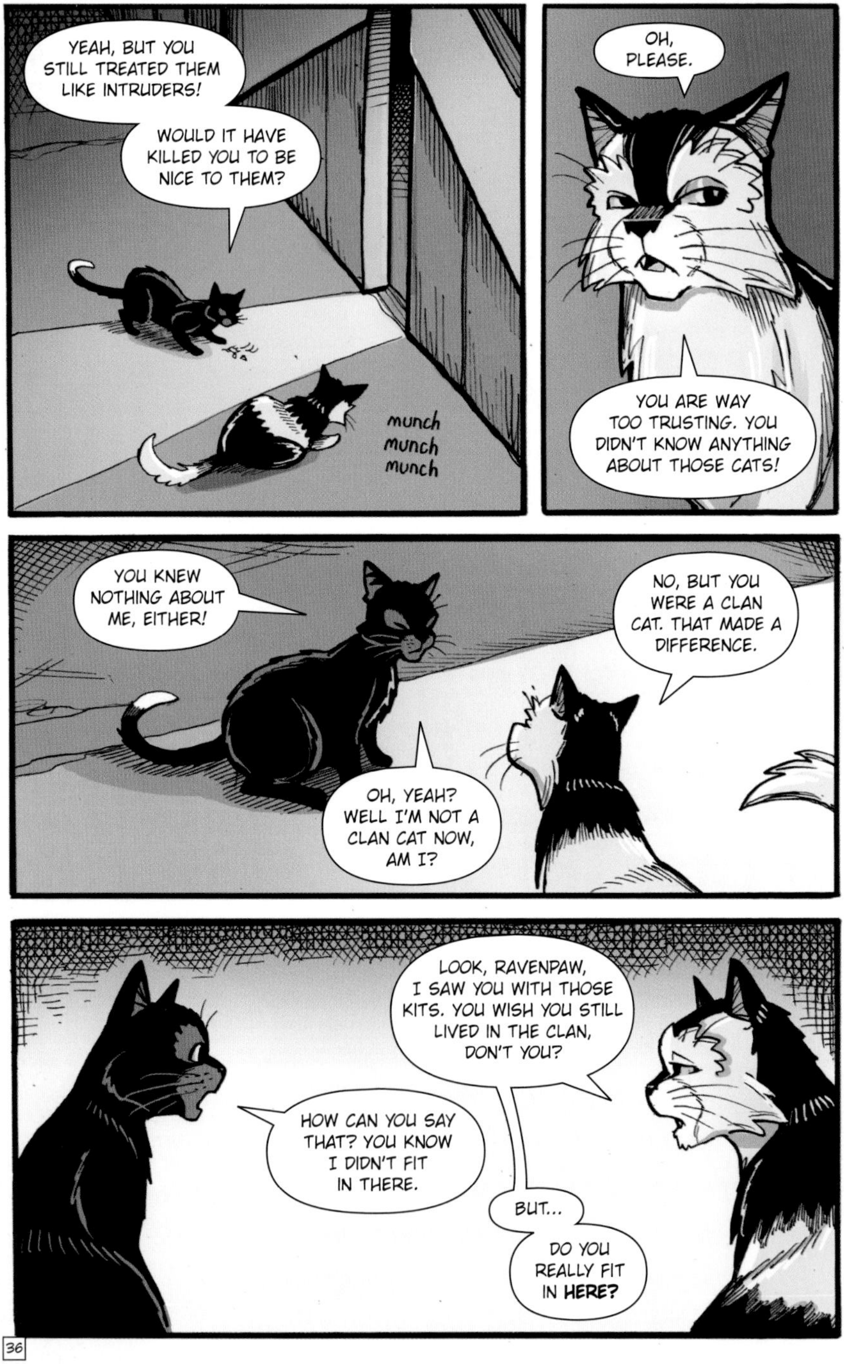
YEAH, BUT YOU STILL TREATED THEM LIKE INTRUDERS!
WOULD IT HAVE KILLED YOU TO BE NICE TO THEM?
munch munch munch
OH, PLEASE.
YOU ARE WAY TOO TRUSTING. YOU DIDN'T KNOW ANYTHING ABOUT THOSE CATS!
YOU KNEW NOTHING ABOUT ME, EITHER!
NO, BUT YOU WERE A CLAN CAT. THAT MADE A DIFFERENCE.
OH, YEAH? WELL I'M NOT A CLAN CAT NOW, AM I?
LOOK, RAVENPAW, I SAW YOU WITH THOSE KITS. YOU WISH YOU STILL LIVED IN THE CLAN, DON'T YOU?
HOW CAN YOU SAY THAT? YOU KNOW I DIDN'T FIT IN THERE.
BUT...
DO YOU REALLY FIT IN **HERE?**

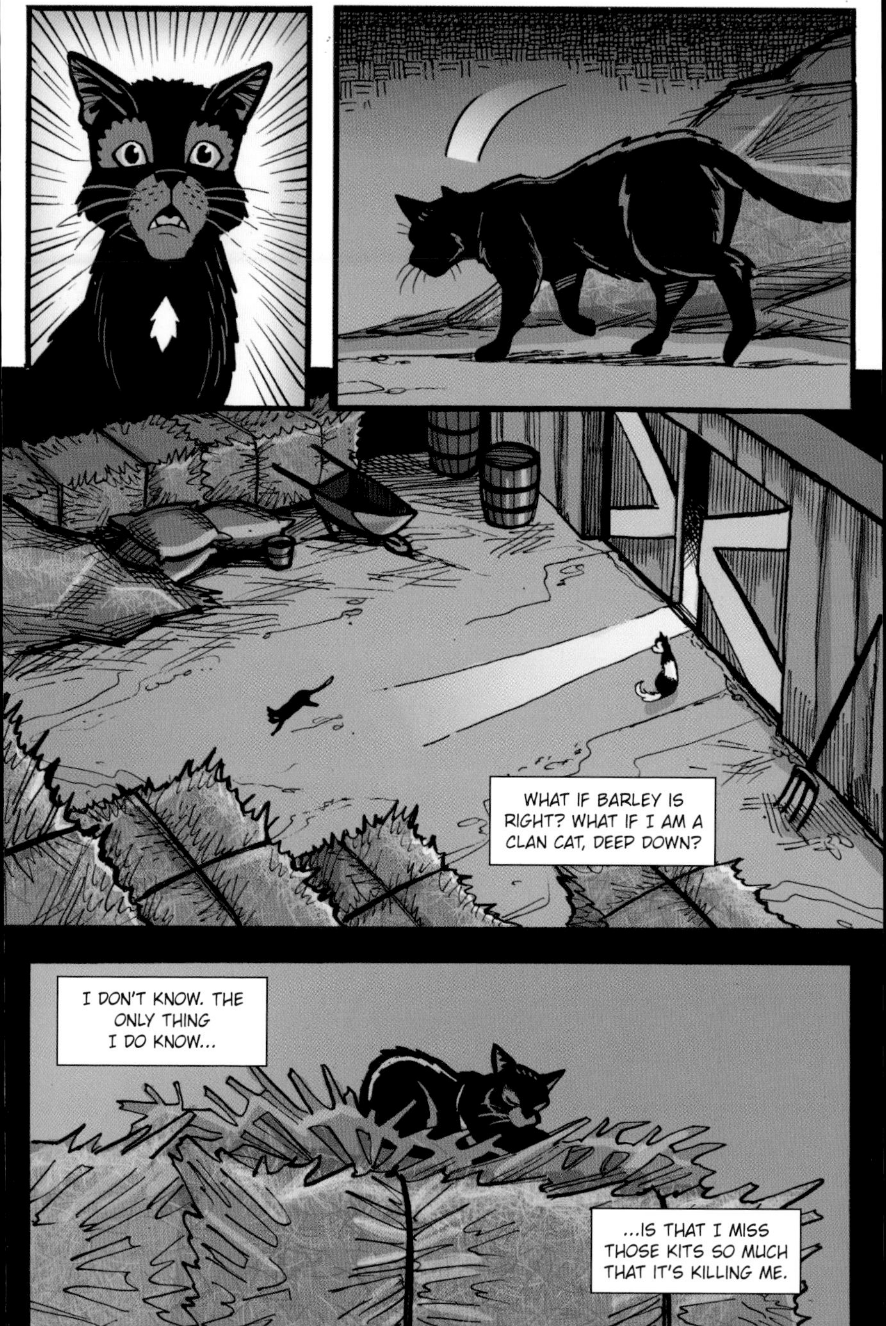
WHAT IF BARLEY IS RIGHT? WHAT IF I AM A CLAN CAT, DEEP DOWN?
I DON'T KNOW. THE ONLY THING I DO KNOW...
...IS THAT I MISS THOSE KITS SO MUCH THAT IT'S KILLING ME.

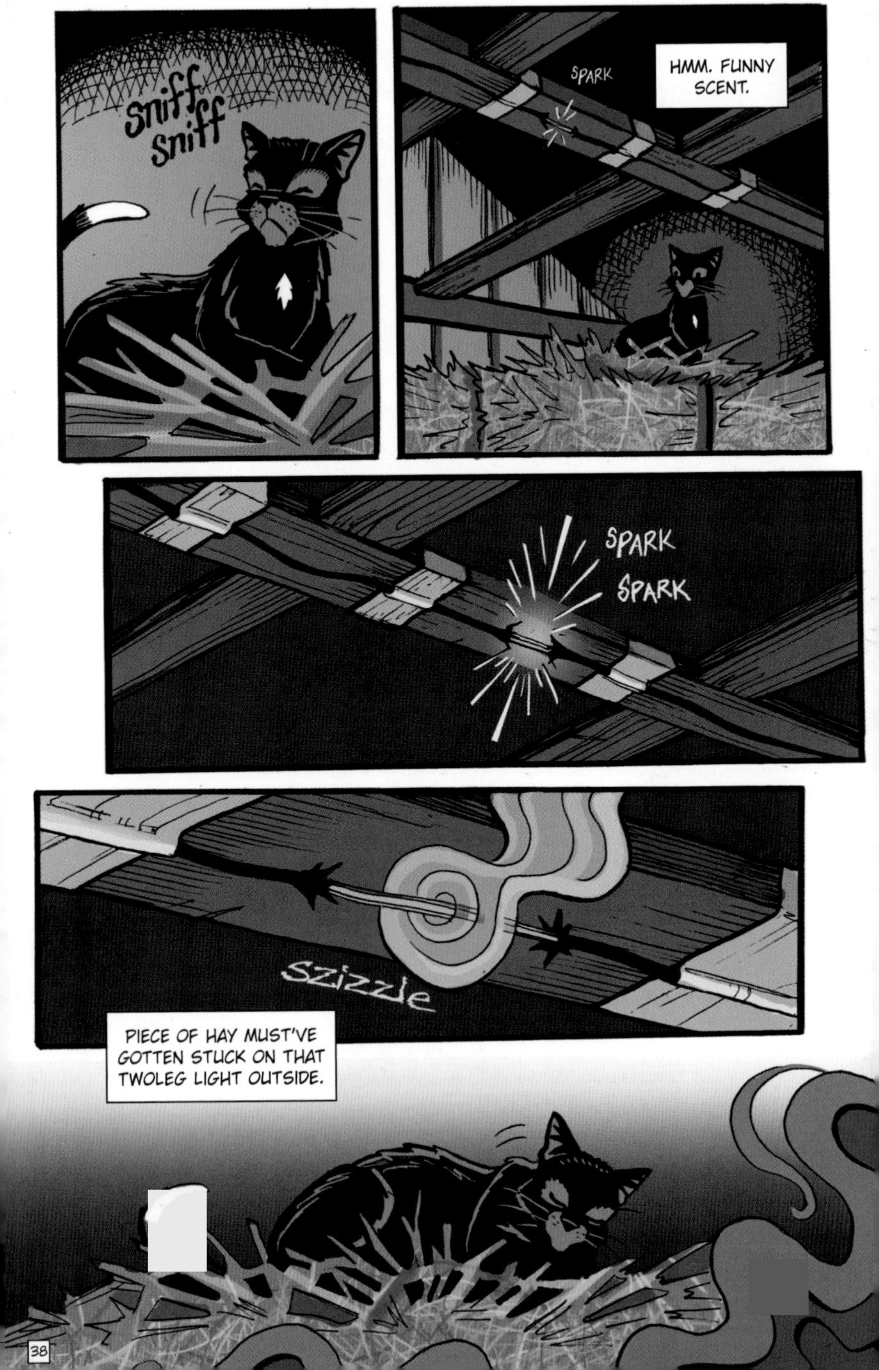
sniff sniff
SPARK
HMM. FUNNY SCENT.
SPARK
SPARK
szizzle
PIECE OF HAY MUST'VE GOTTEN STUCK ON THAT TWOLEG LIGHT OUTSIDE.

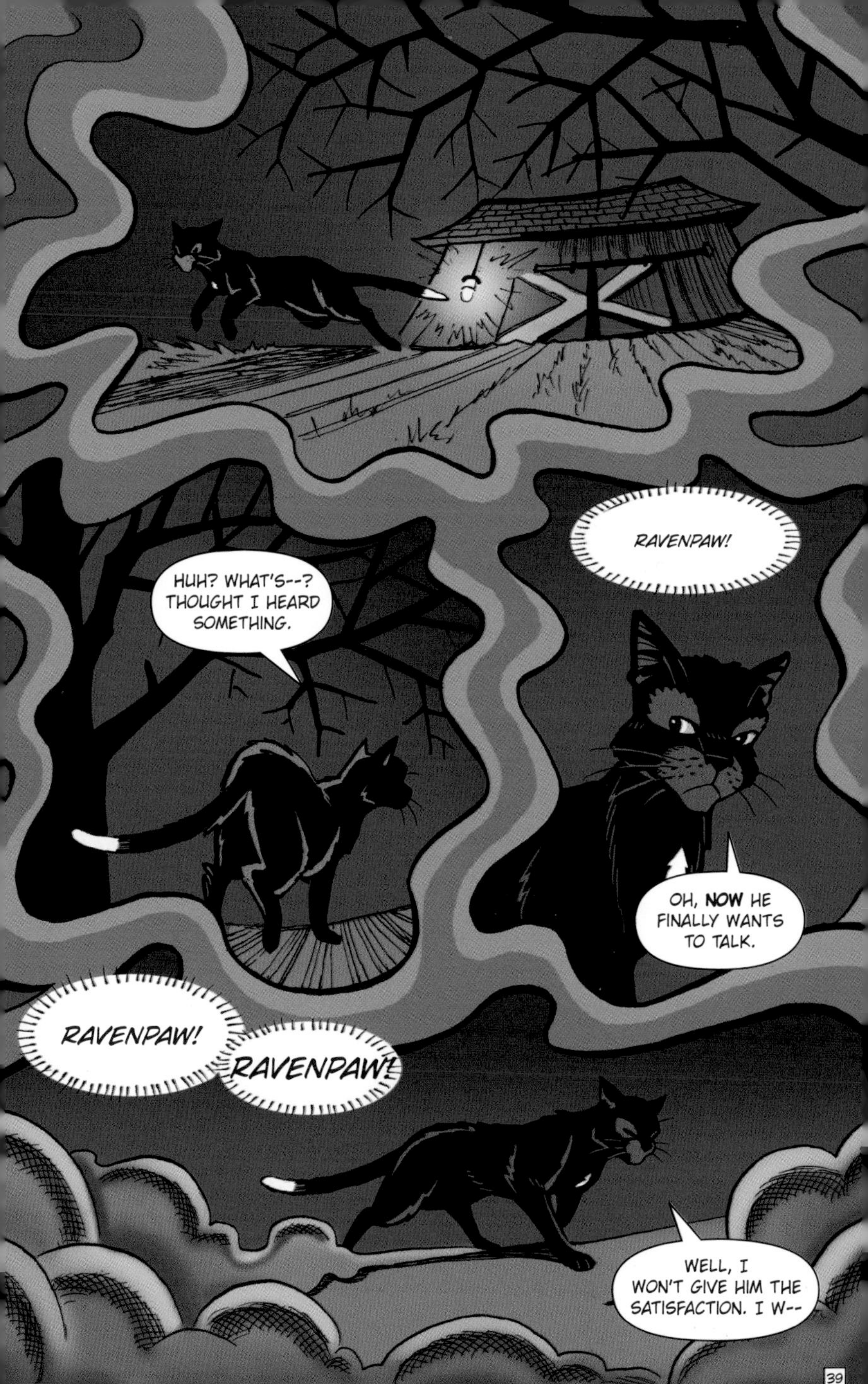
RAVENPAW!
HUH? WHAT'S--? THOUGHT I HEARD SOMETHING.
OH, NOW HE FINALLY WANTS TO TALK.
RAVENPAW!
RAVENPAW!
WELL, I WON'T GIVE HIM THE SATISFACTION. I W--

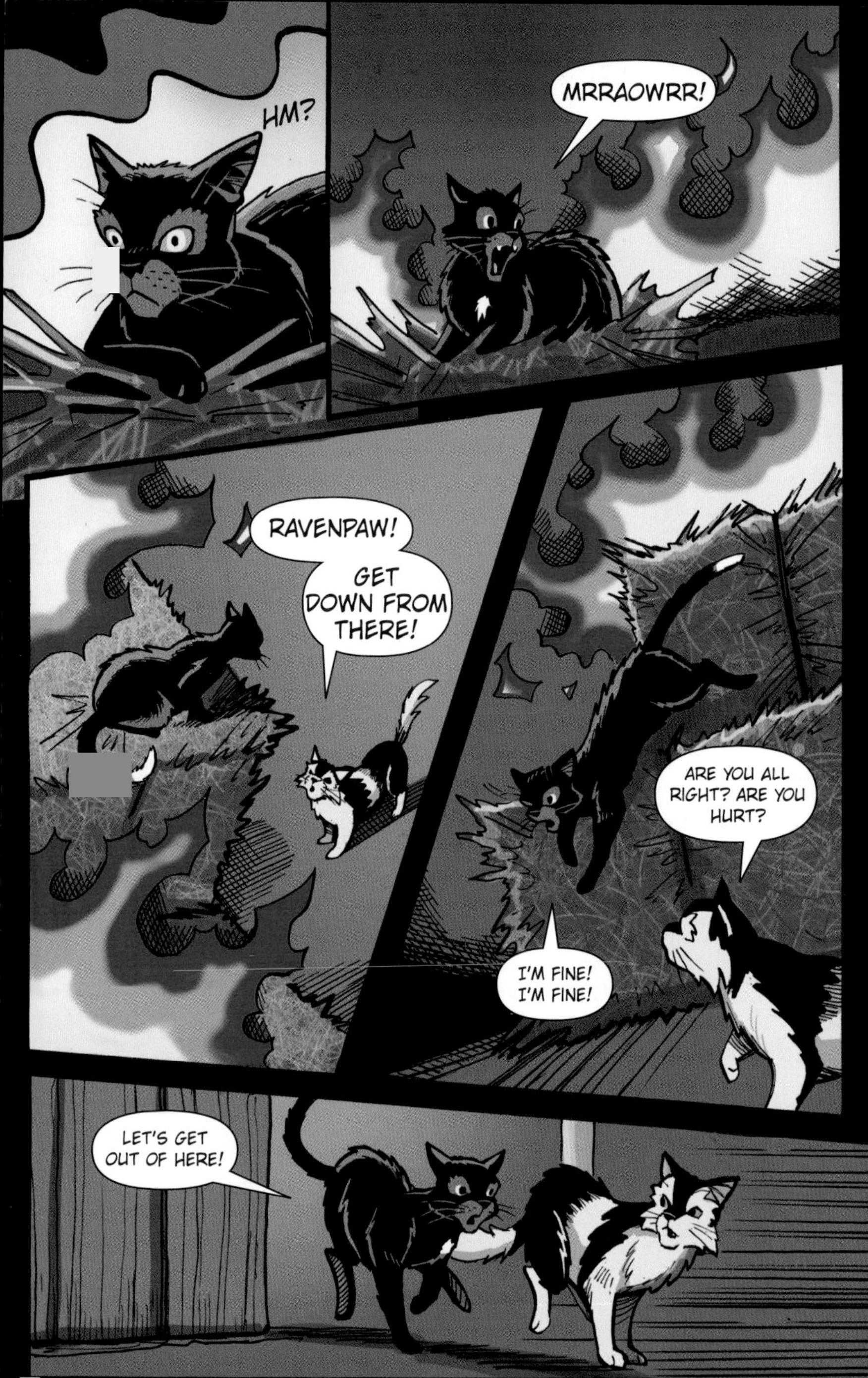
HM?
MRRAOWRR!
RAVENPAW!
GET DOWN FROM THERE!
ARE YOU ALL RIGHT? ARE YOU HURT?
I'M FINE! I'M FINE!
LET'S GET OUT OF HERE!

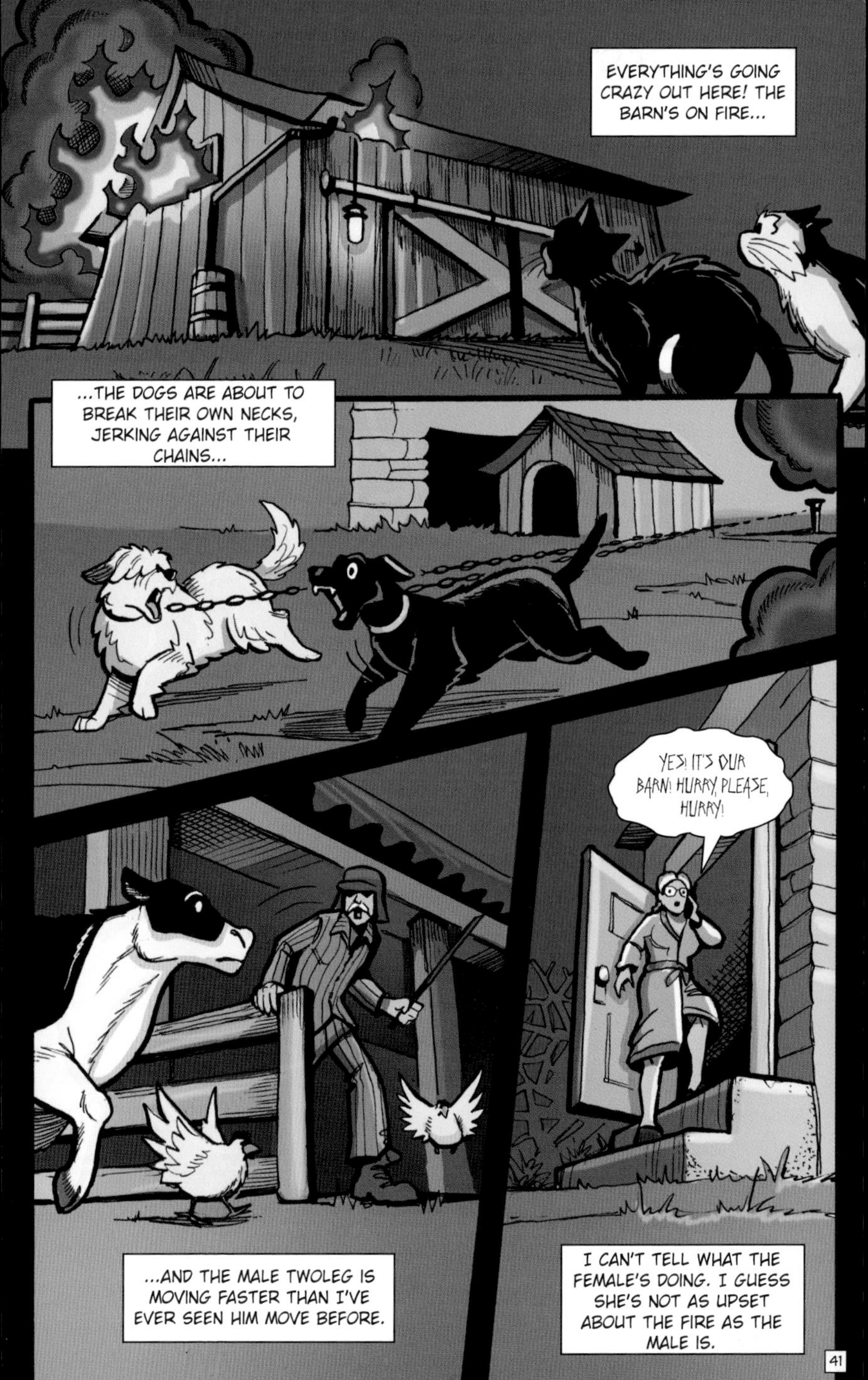
EVERYTHING'S GOING CRAZY OUT HERE! THE BARN'S ON FIRE...
...THE DOGS ARE ABOUT TO BREAK THEIR OWN NECKS, JERKING AGAINST THEIR CHAINS...
...AND THE MALE TWOLEG IS MOVING FASTER THAN I'VE EVER SEEN HIM MOVE BEFORE.
YES! IT'S OUR BARN! HURRY, PLEASE, HURRY!
I CAN'T TELL WHAT THE FEMALE'S DOING. I GUESS SHE'S NOT AS UPSET ABOUT THE FIRE AS THE MALE IS.

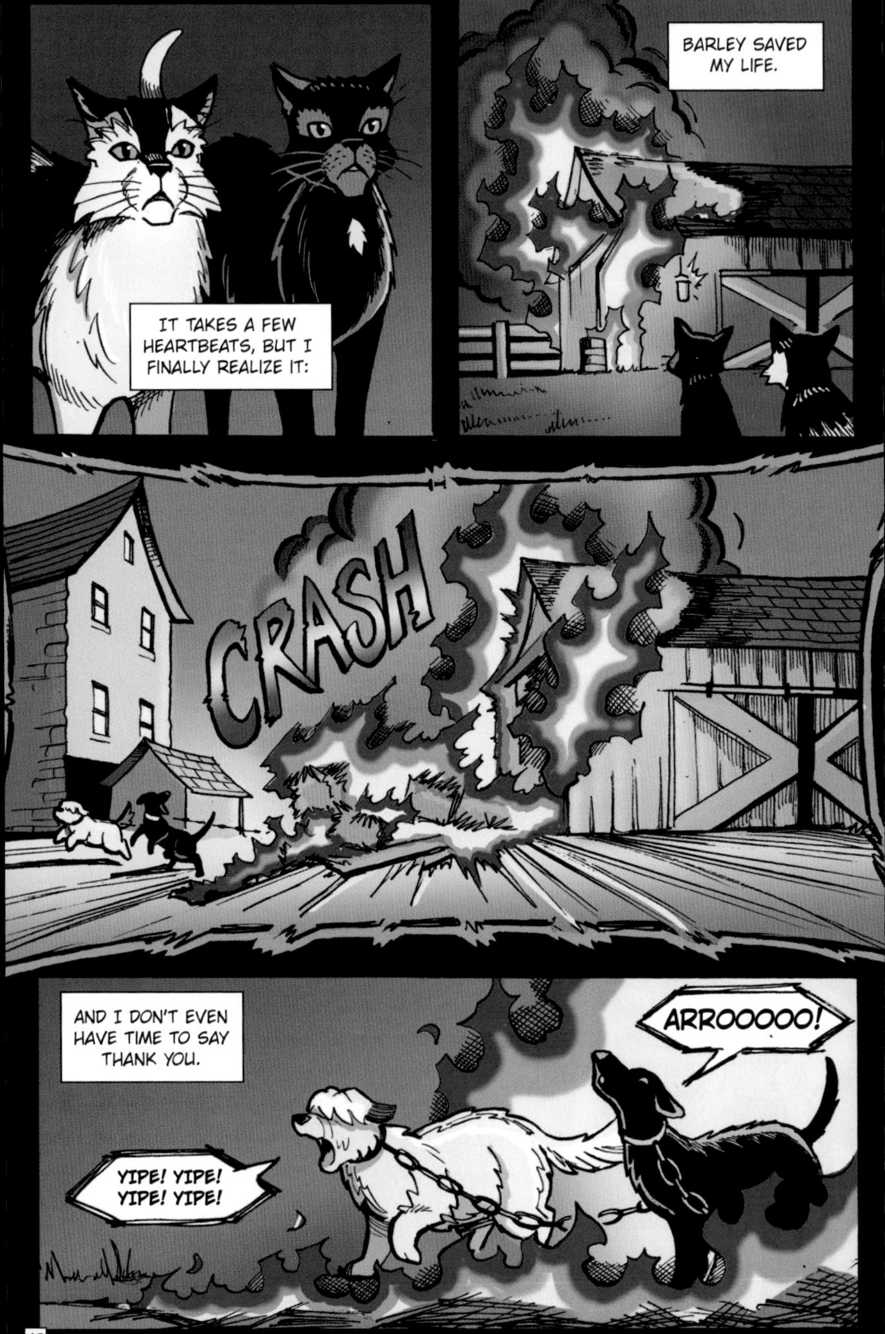
IT TAKES A FEW HEARTBEATS, BUT I FINALLY REALIZE IT:
BARLEY SAVED MY LIFE.
CRASH
AND I DON'T EVEN HAVE TIME TO SAY THANK YOU.
ARROOOOO!
YIPE! YIPE! YIPE! YIPE!

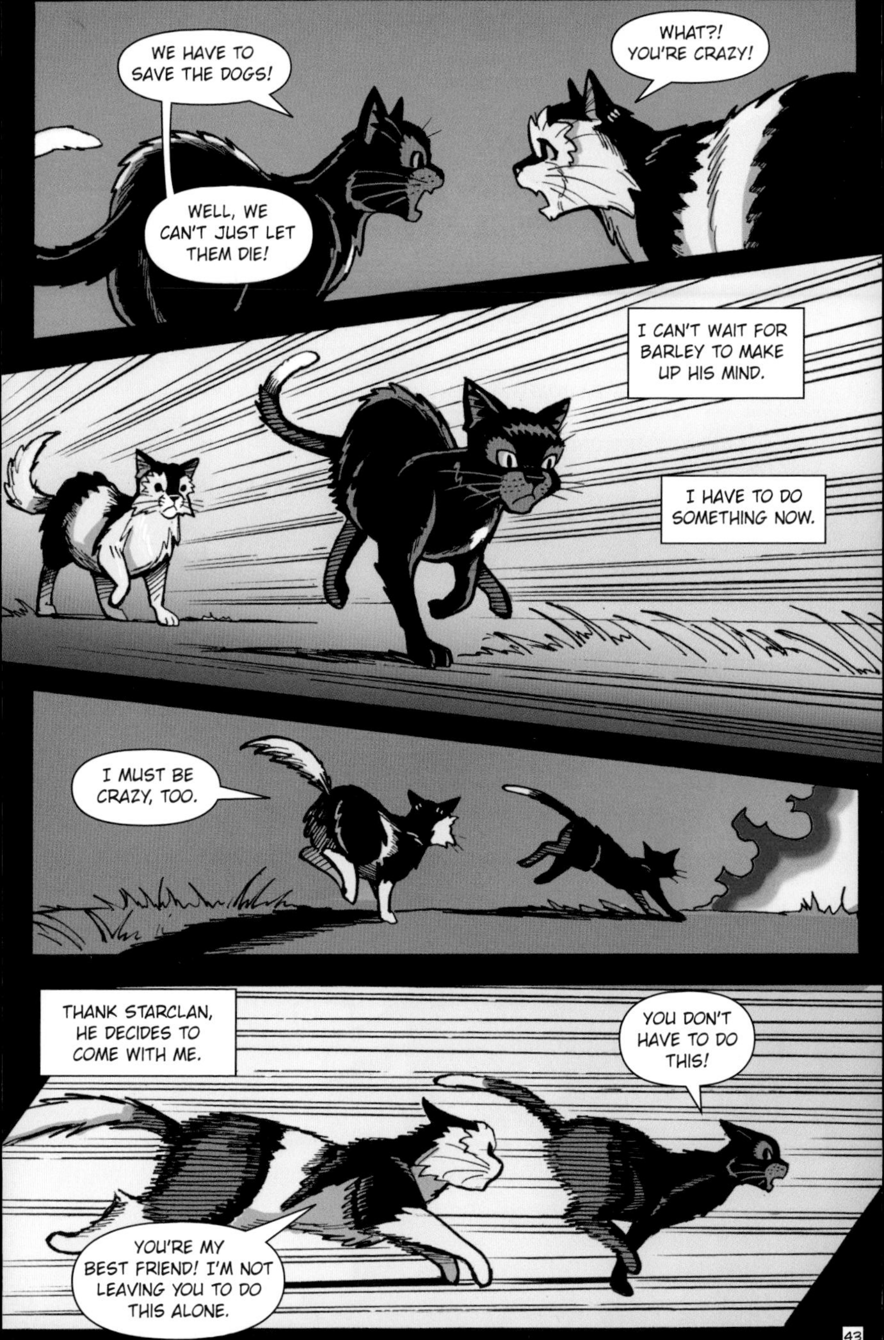
WE HAVE TO SAVE THE DOGS!
WHAT?! YOU'RE CRAZY!
WELL, WE CAN'T JUST LET THEM DIE!
I CAN'T WAIT FOR BARLEY TO MAKE UP HIS MIND.
I HAVE TO DO SOMETHING NOW.
I MUST BE CRAZY, TOO.
THANK STARCLAN, HE DECIDES TO COME WITH ME.
YOU DON'T HAVE TO DO THIS!
YOU'RE MY BEST FRIEND! I'M NOT LEAVING YOU TO DO THIS ALONE.

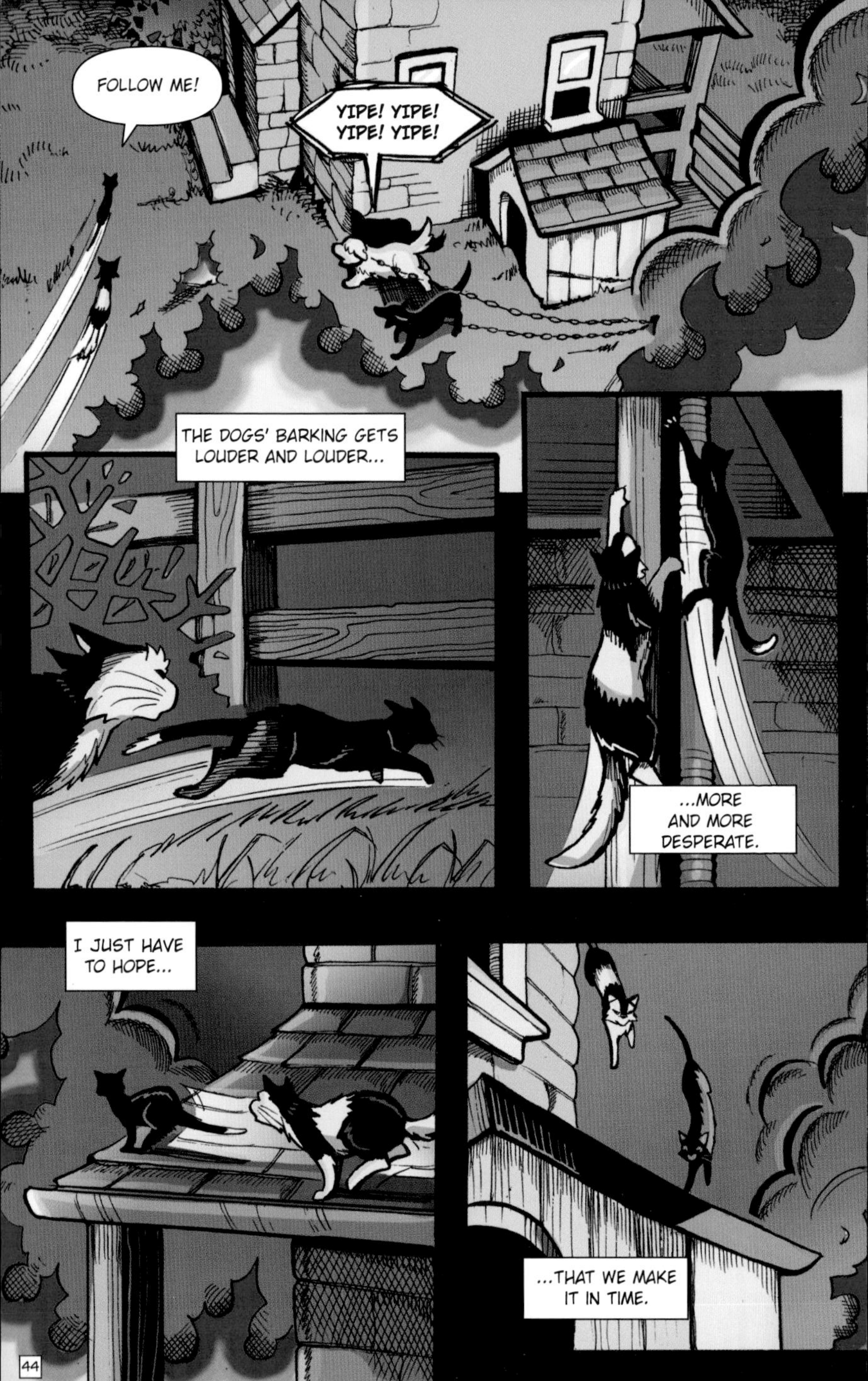
FOLLOW ME!
YIPE! YIPE! YIPE! YIPE!
THE DOGS' BARKING GETS LOUDER AND LOUDER...
...MORE AND MORE DESPERATE.
I JUST HAVE TO HOPE...
...THAT WE MAKE IT IN TIME.

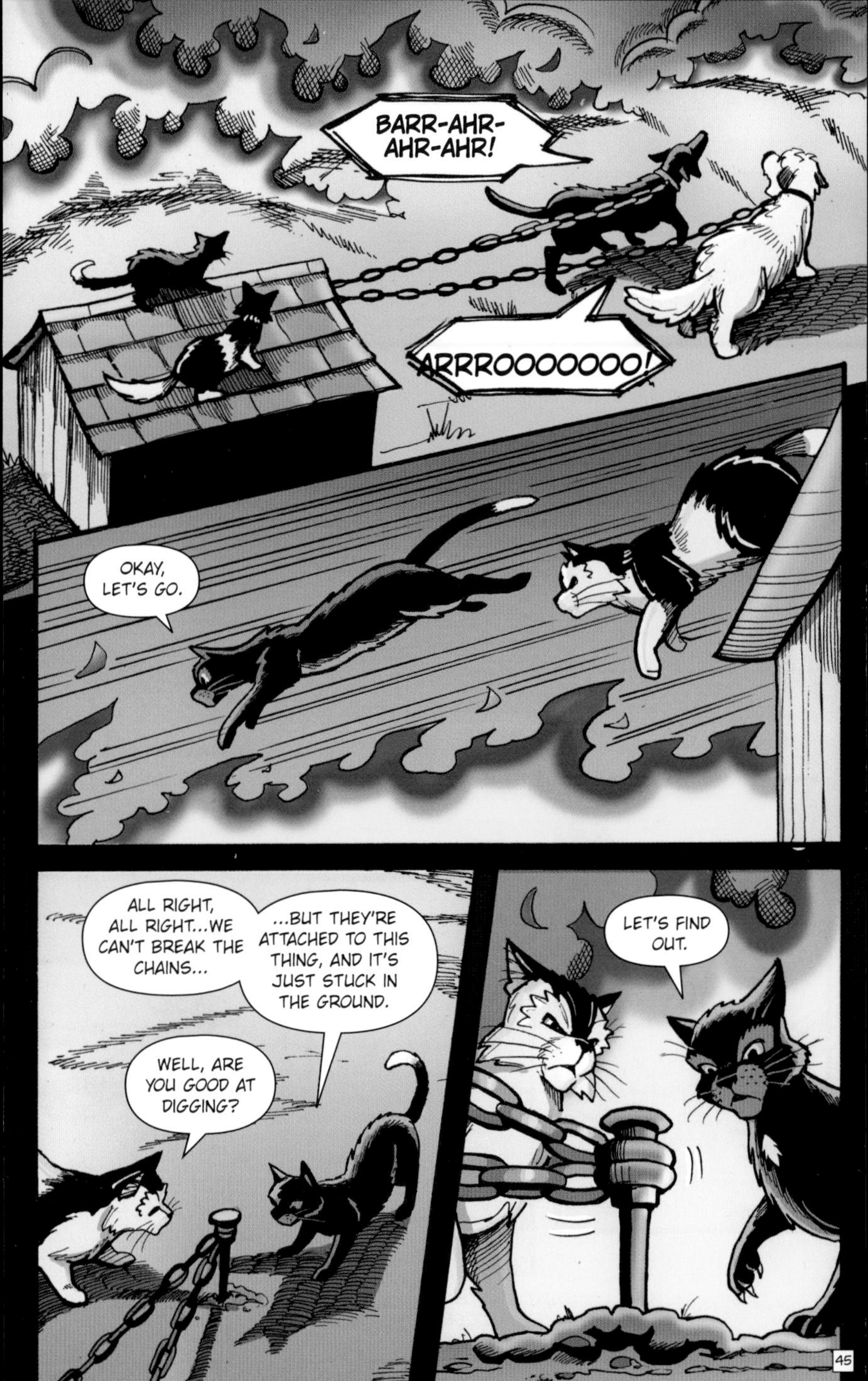
BARR-AHR-AHR-AHR!
ARRROOOOOOO!
OKAY, LET'S GO.
ALL RIGHT, ALL RIGHT...WE CAN'T BREAK THE CHAINS...
...BUT THEY'RE ATTACHED TO THIS THING, AND IT'S JUST STUCK IN THE GROUND.
WELL, ARE YOU GOOD AT DIGGING?
LET'S FIND OUT.

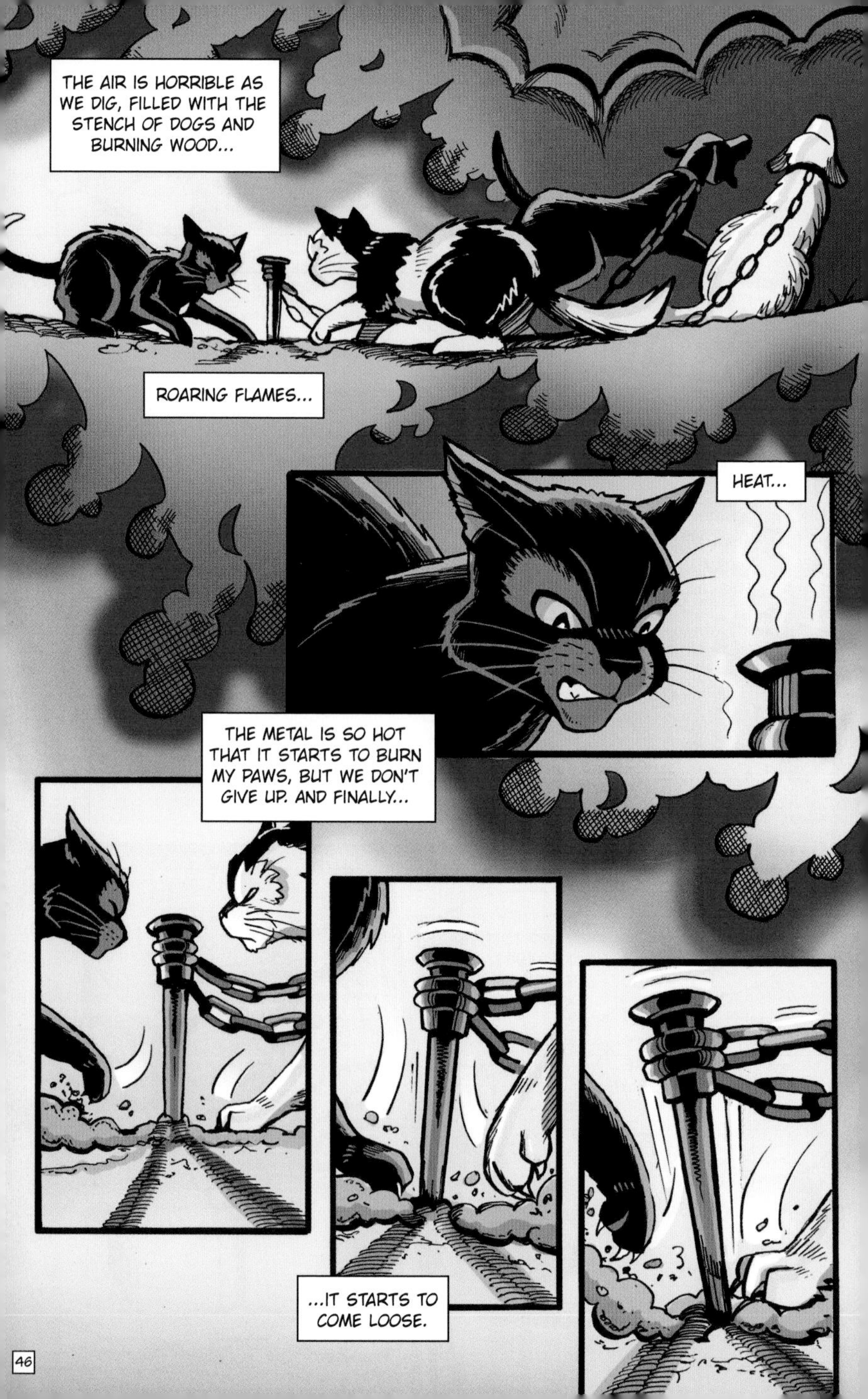
THE AIR IS HORRIBLE AS WE DIG, FILLED WITH THE STENCH OF DOGS AND BURNING WOOD...
ROARING FLAMES...
HEAT...
THE METAL IS SO HOT THAT IT STARTS TO BURN MY PAWS, BUT WE DON'T GIVE UP. AND FINALLY...
...IT STARTS TO COME LOOSE.

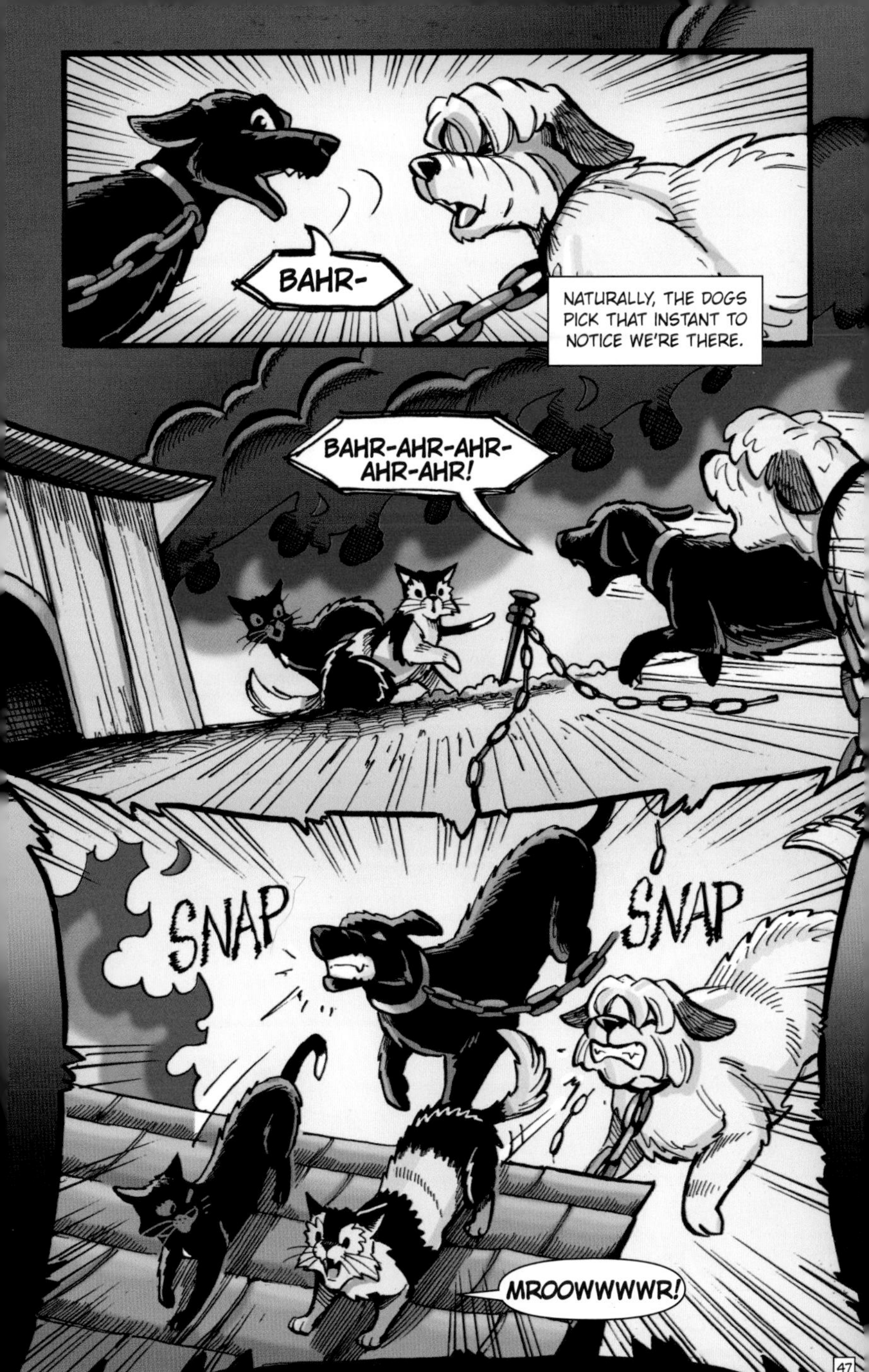
BAHR-
NATURALLY, THE DOGS PICK THAT INSTANT TO NOTICE WE'RE THERE.
BAHR-AHR-AHR-AHR-AHR!
SNAP
SNAP
MROOWWWWR!

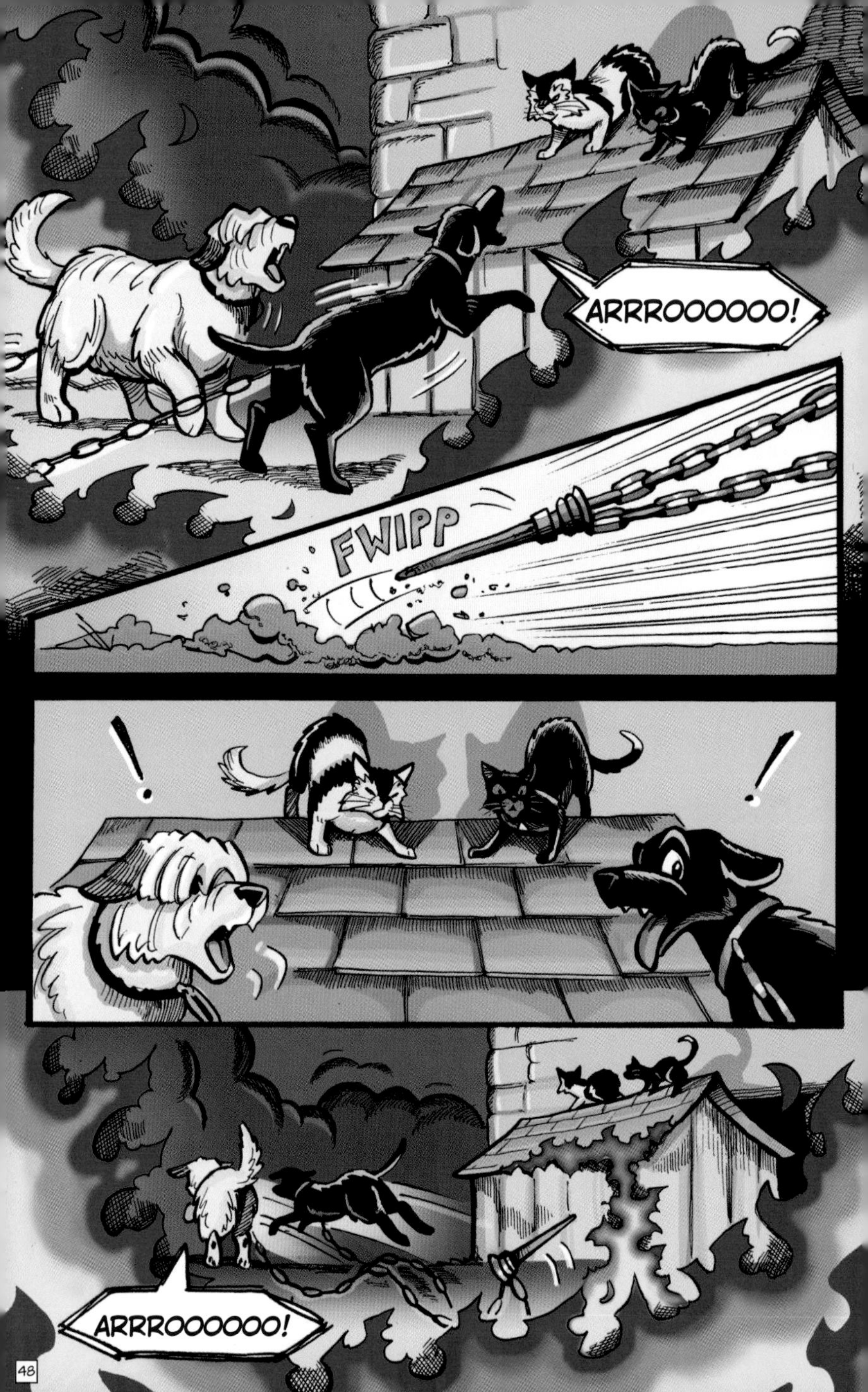
ARRROOOOOO!
FWIPP
!
!
ARRROOOOOO!

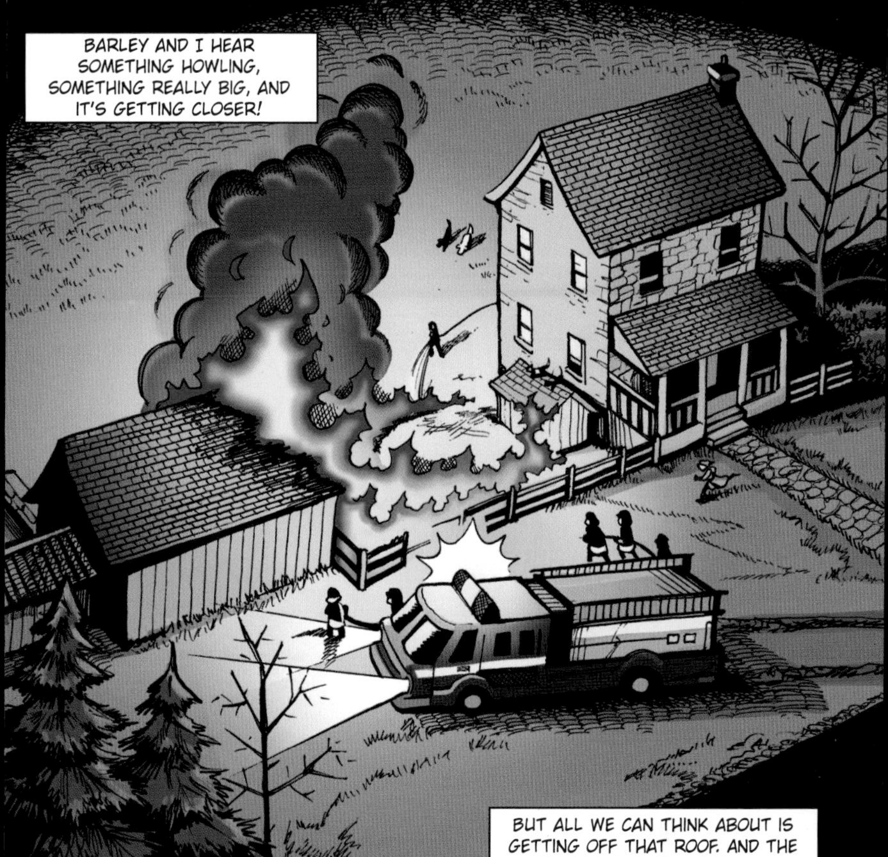
BARLEY AND I HEAR SOMETHING HOWLING, SOMETHING REALLY BIG, AND IT'S GETTING CLOSER!

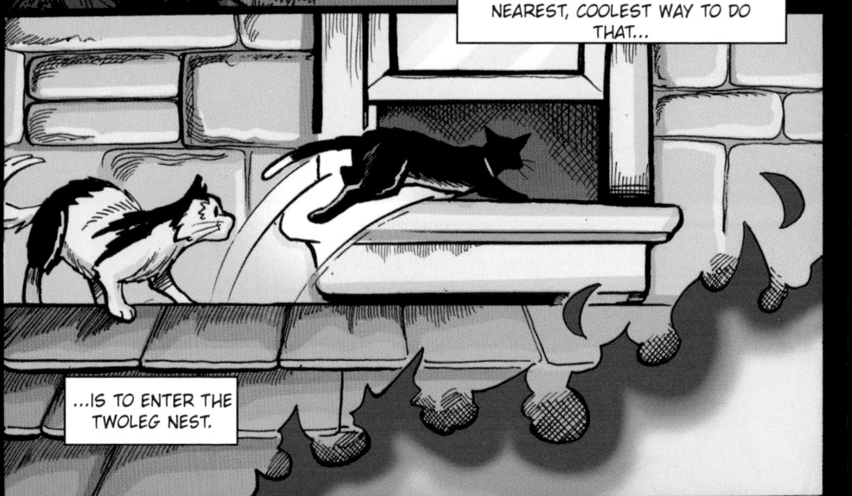
BUT ALL WE CAN THINK ABOUT IS GETTING OFF THAT ROOF. AND THE NEAREST, COOLEST WAY TO DO THAT...
...IS TO ENTER THE TWOLEG NEST.

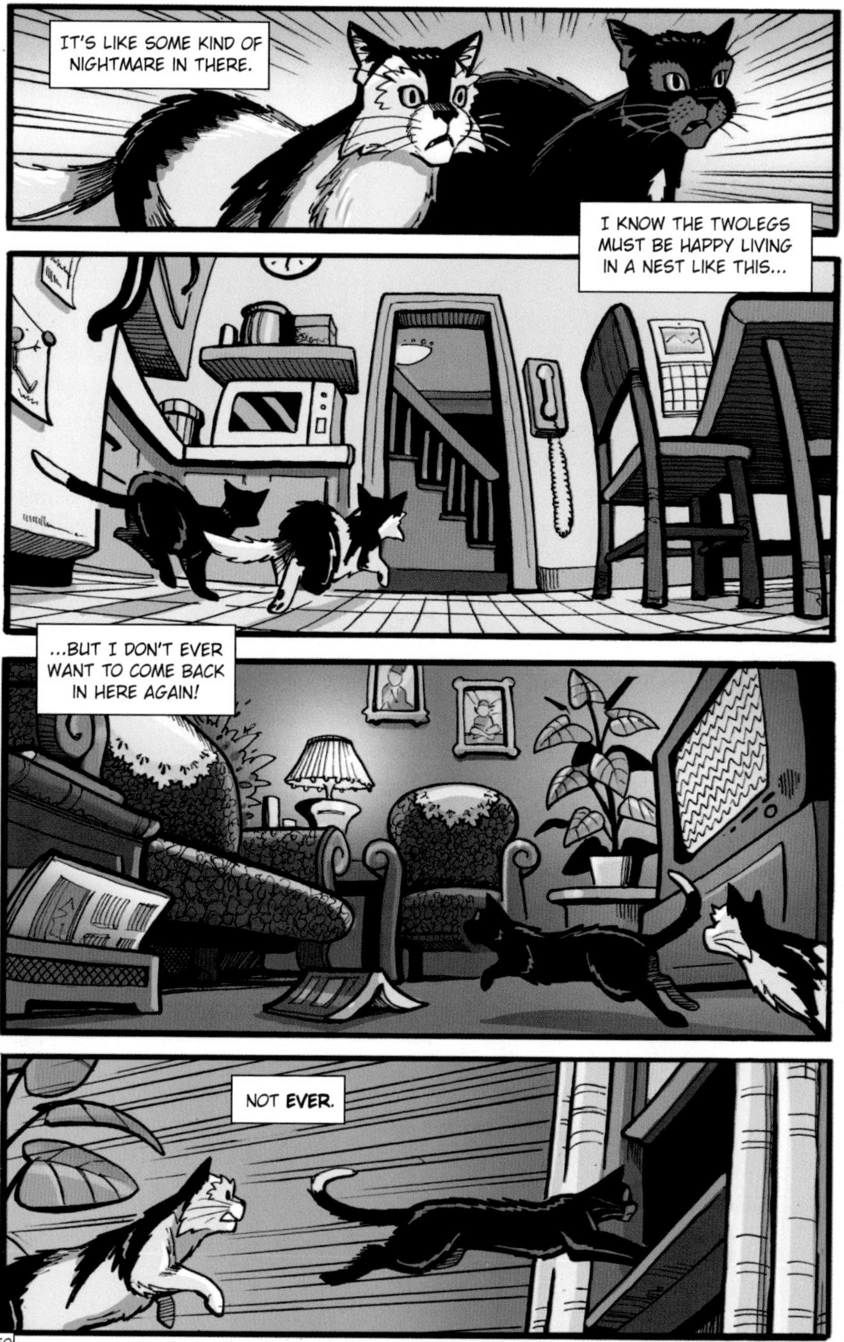
IT'S LIKE SOME KIND OF NIGHTMARE IN THERE.
I KNOW THE TWOLEGS MUST BE HAPPY LIVING IN A NEST LIKE THIS...
...BUT I DON'T EVER WANT TO COME BACK IN HERE AGAIN!
NOT **EVER**.

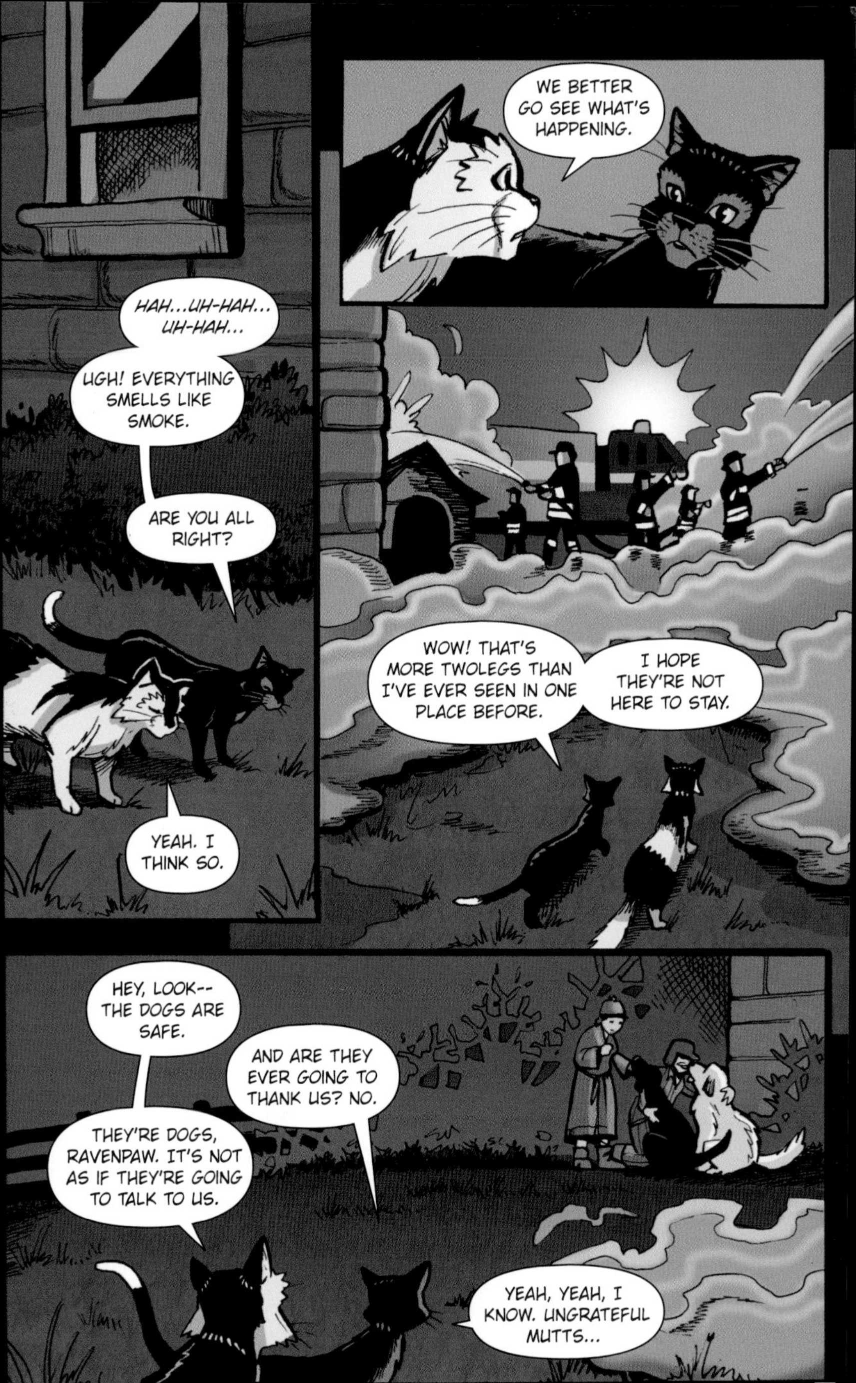
WE BETTER GO SEE WHAT'S HAPPENING.
HAH...UH-HAH... UH-HAH...
UGH! EVERYTHING SMELLS LIKE SMOKE.
ARE YOU ALL RIGHT?
YEAH. I THINK SO.
WOW! THAT'S MORE TWOLEGS THAN I'VE EVER SEEN IN ONE PLACE BEFORE.
I HOPE THEY'RE NOT HERE TO STAY.
HEY, LOOK-- THE DOGS ARE SAFE.
AND ARE THEY EVER GOING TO THANK US? NO.
THEY'RE DOGS, RAVENPAW. IT'S NOT AS IF THEY'RE GOING TO TALK TO US.
YEAH, YEAH, I KNOW. UNGRATEFUL MUTTS...

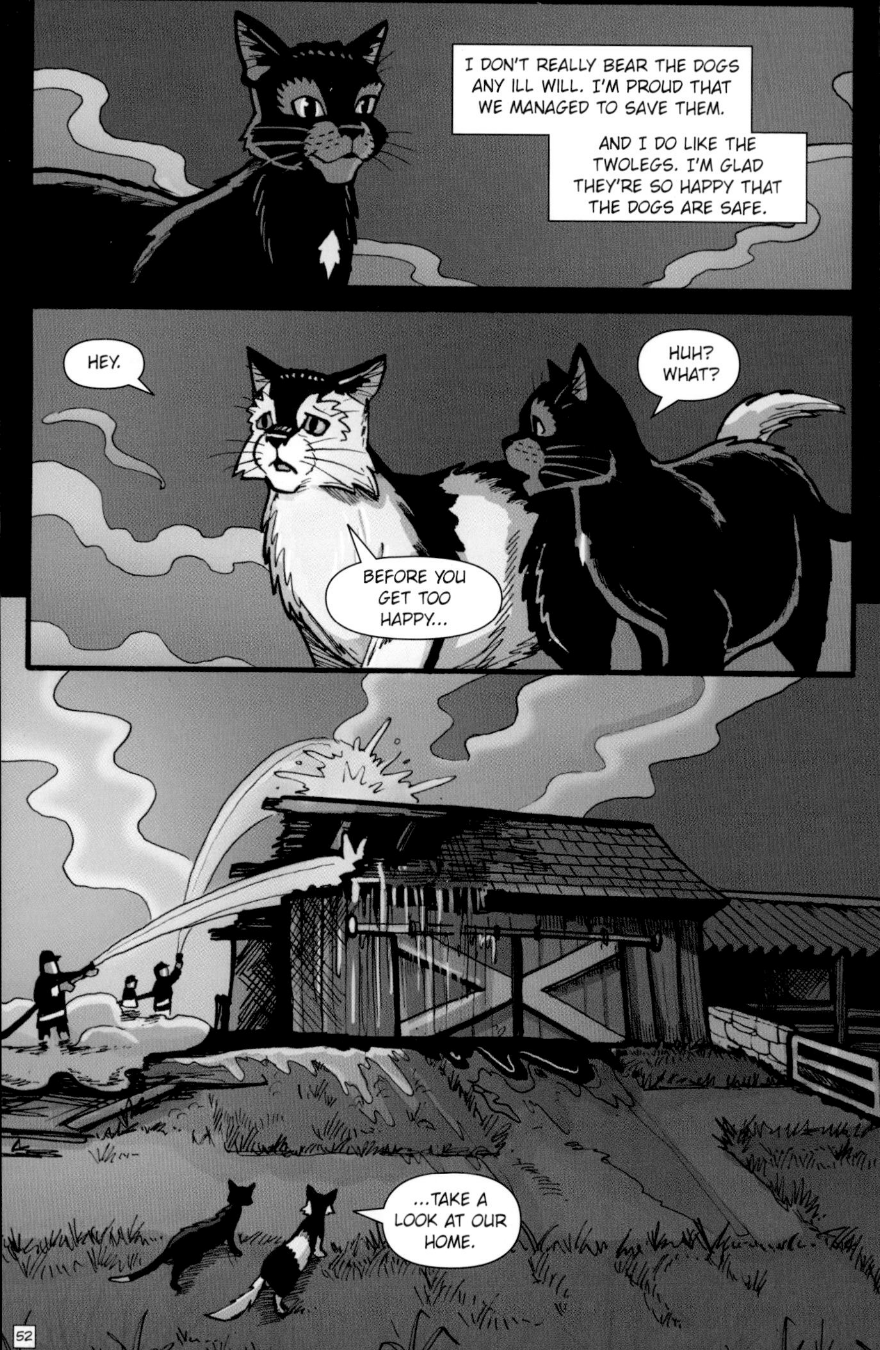
I DON'T REALLY BEAR THE DOGS ANY ILL WILL. I'M PROUD THAT WE MANAGED TO SAVE THEM.
AND I DO LIKE THE TWOLEGS. I'M GLAD THEY'RE SO HAPPY THAT THE DOGS ARE SAFE.
HEY.
HUH? WHAT?
BEFORE YOU GET TOO HAPPY...
...TAKE A LOOK AT OUR HOME.

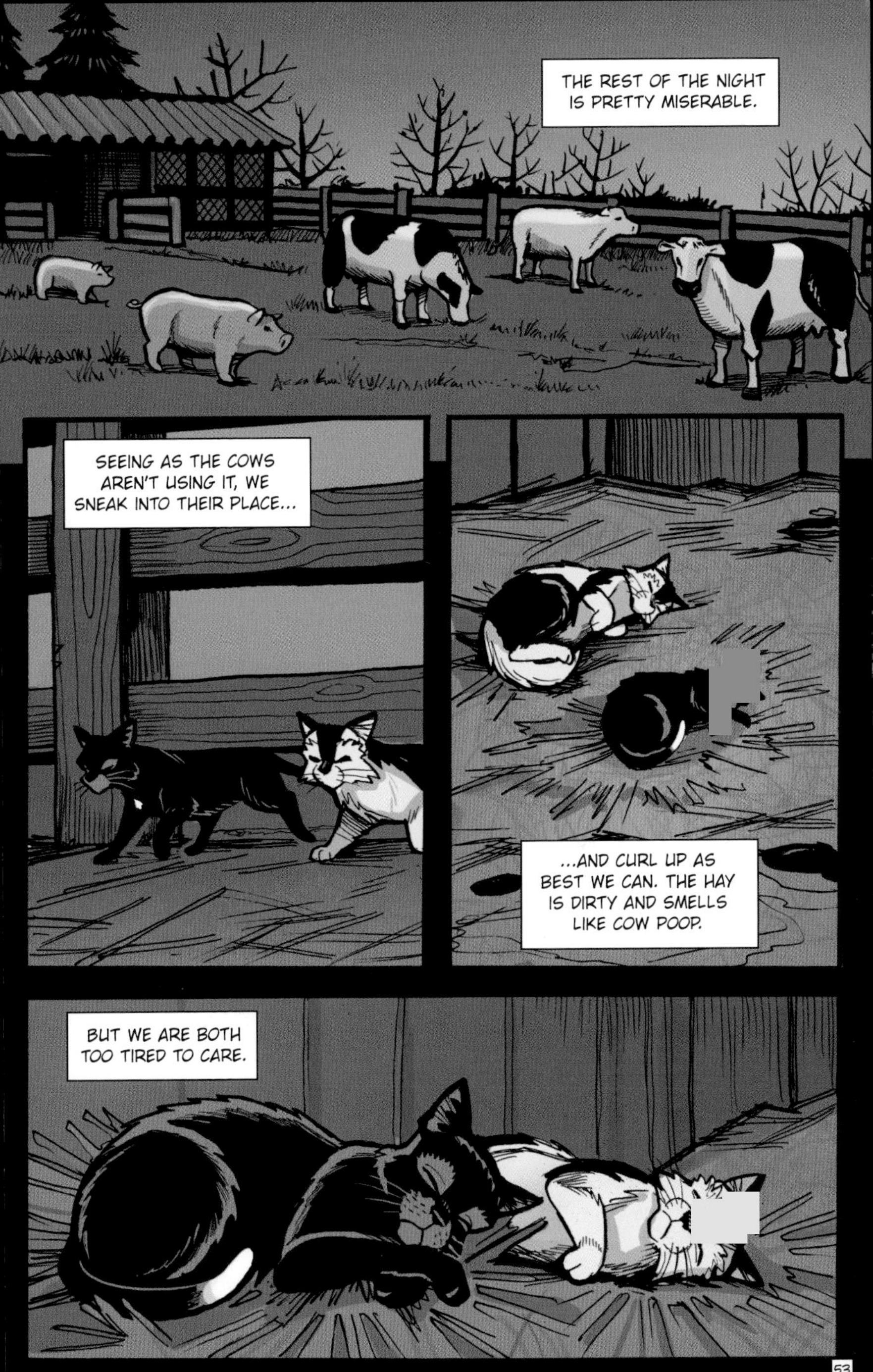
THE REST OF THE NIGHT IS PRETTY MISERABLE.
SEEING AS THE COWS AREN'T USING IT, WE SNEAK INTO THEIR PLACE...
...AND CURL UP AS BEST WE CAN. THE HAY IS DIRTY AND SMELLS LIKE COW POOP.
BUT WE ARE BOTH TOO TIRED TO CARE.

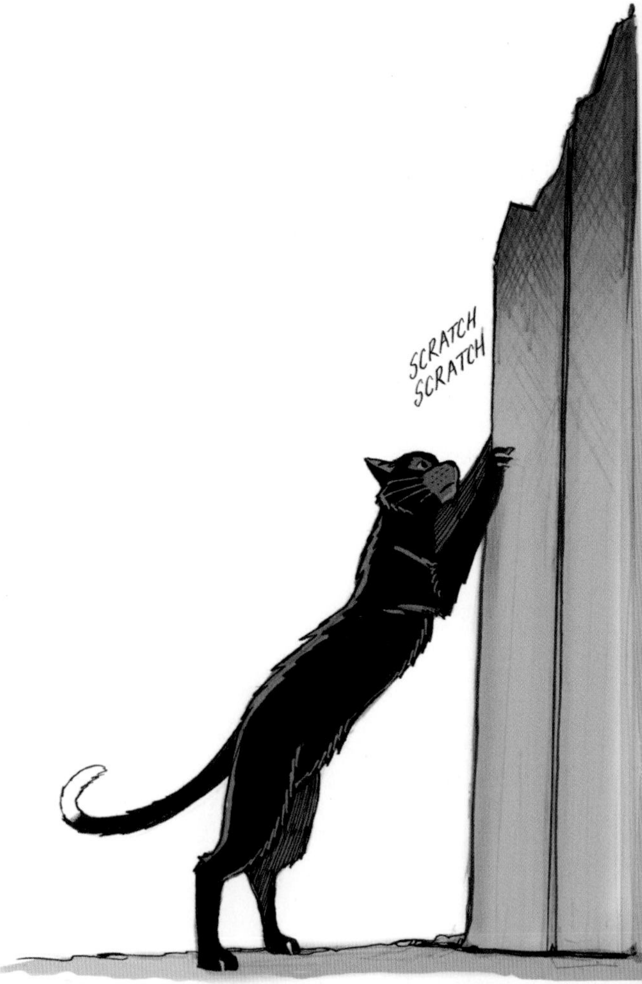
SCRATCH
SCRATCH

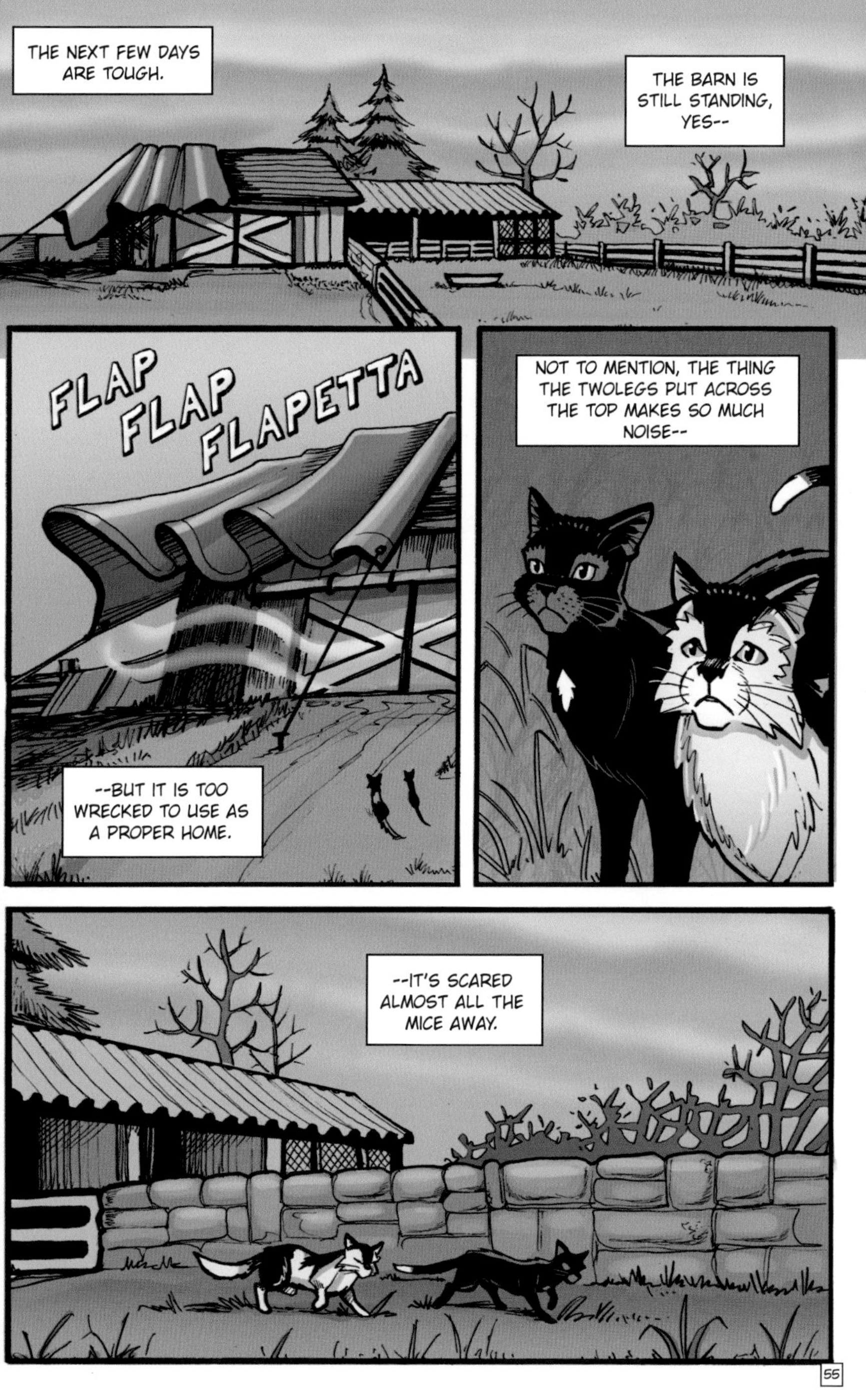

THE NEXT FEW DAYS ARE TOUGH.
THE BARN IS STILL STANDING, YES--
FLAP FLAP FLAPETTA
--BUT IT IS TOO WRECKED TO USE AS A PROPER HOME.
NOT TO MENTION, THE THING THE TWOLEGS PUT ACROSS THE TOP MAKES SO MUCH NOISE--
--IT'S SCARED ALMOST ALL THE MICE AWAY.

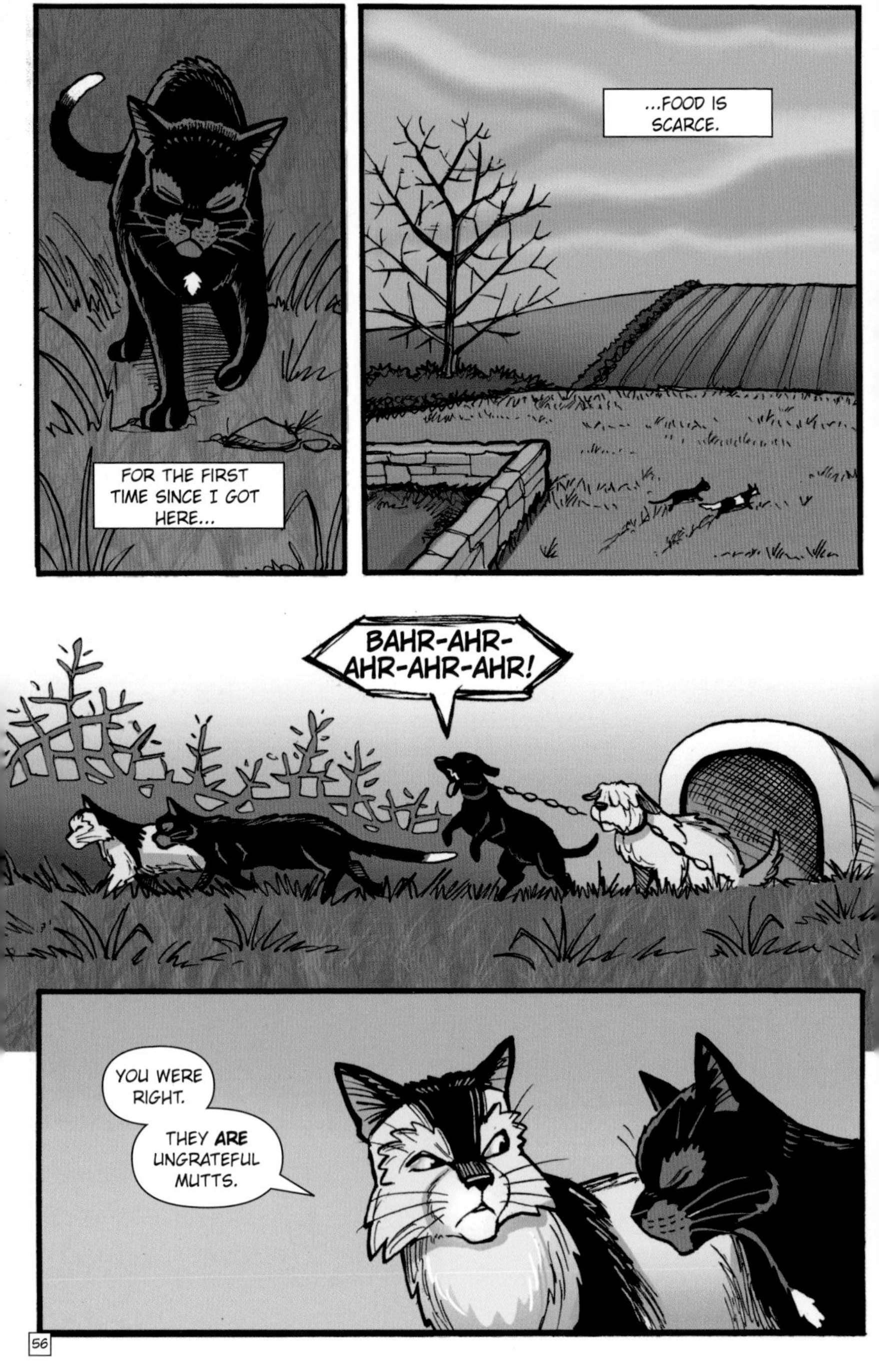
FOR THE FIRST TIME SINCE I GOT HERE...
...FOOD IS SCARCE.
BAHR-AHR-AHR-AHR-AHR!
YOU WERE RIGHT.
THEY ARE UNGRATEFUL MUTTS.

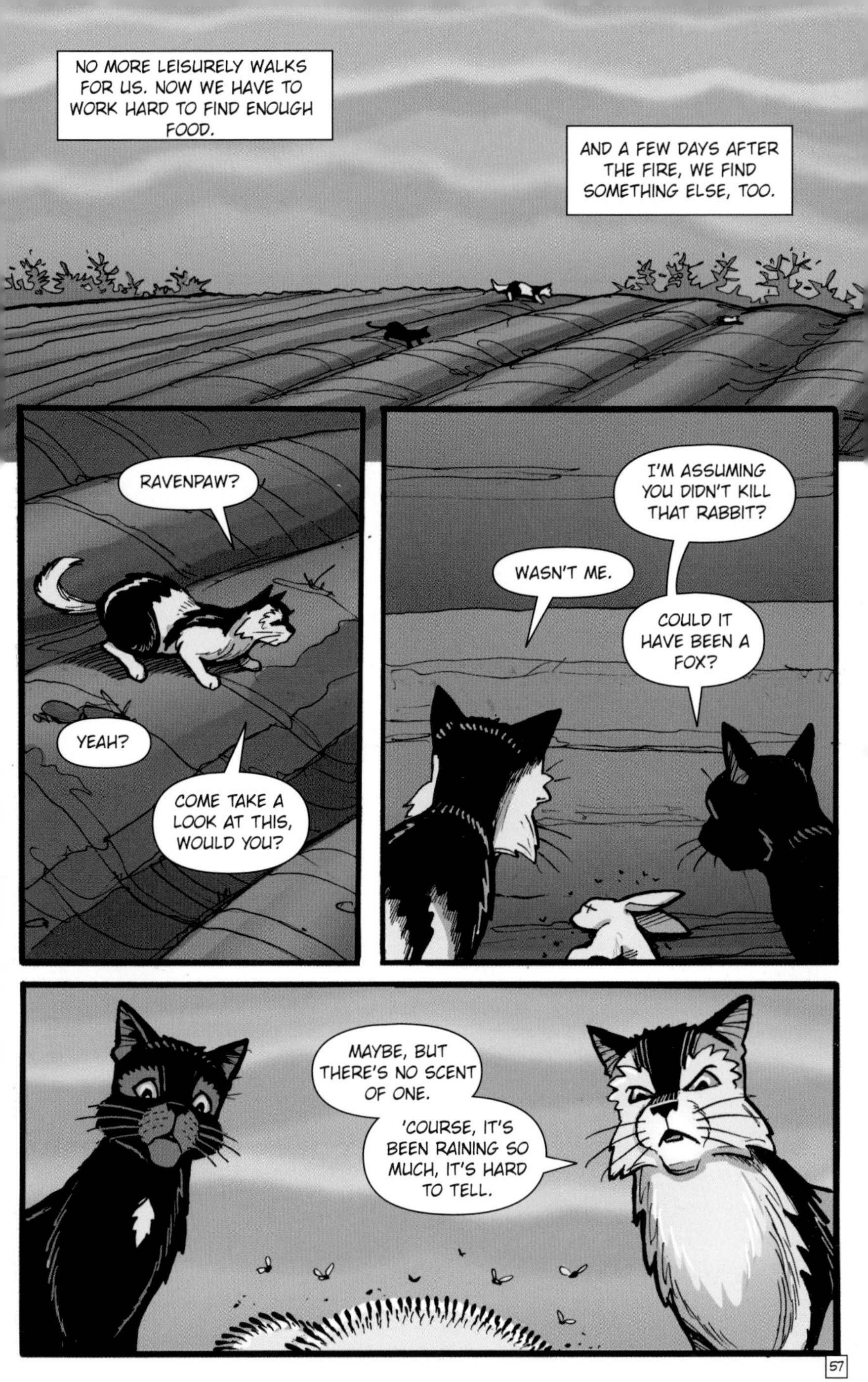
NO MORE LEISURELY WALKS FOR US. NOW WE HAVE TO WORK HARD TO FIND ENOUGH FOOD.
AND A FEW DAYS AFTER THE FIRE, WE FIND SOMETHING ELSE, TOO.
RAVENPAW?
YEAH?
COME TAKE A LOOK AT THIS, WOULD YOU?
I'M ASSUMING YOU DIDN'T KILL THAT RABBIT?
WASN'T ME.
COULD IT HAVE BEEN A FOX?
MAYBE, BUT THERE'S NO SCENT OF ONE.
'COURSE, IT'S BEEN RAINING SO MUCH, IT'S HARD TO TELL.

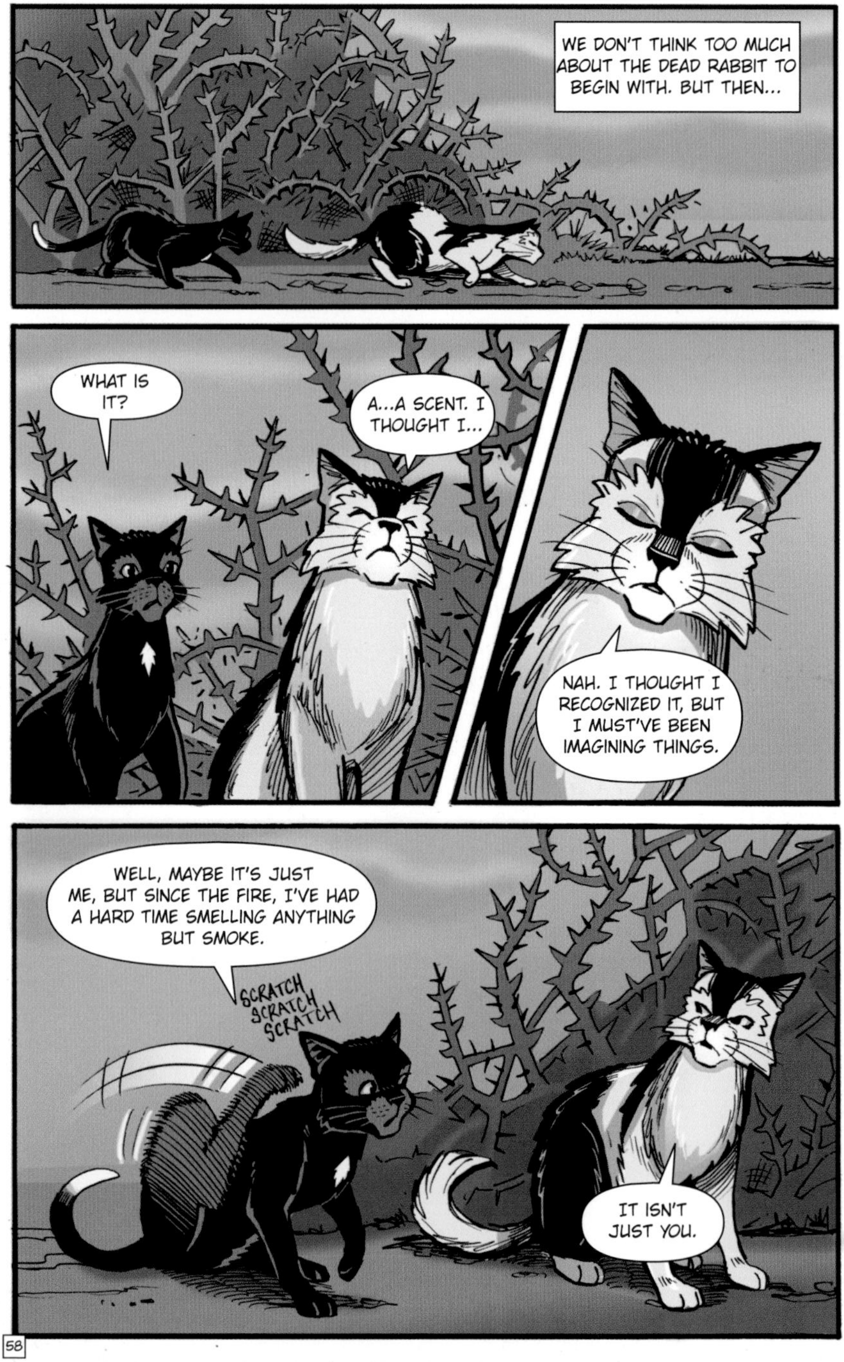
WE DON'T THINK TOO MUCH ABOUT THE DEAD RABBIT TO BEGIN WITH. BUT THEN...
WHAT IS IT?
A...A SCENT. I THOUGHT I...
NAH. I THOUGHT I RECOGNIZED IT, BUT I MUST'VE BEEN IMAGINING THINGS.
WELL, MAYBE IT'S JUST ME, BUT SINCE THE FIRE, I'VE HAD A HARD TIME SMELLING ANYTHING BUT SMOKE.
SCRATCH SCRATCH SCRATCH
IT ISN'T JUST YOU.

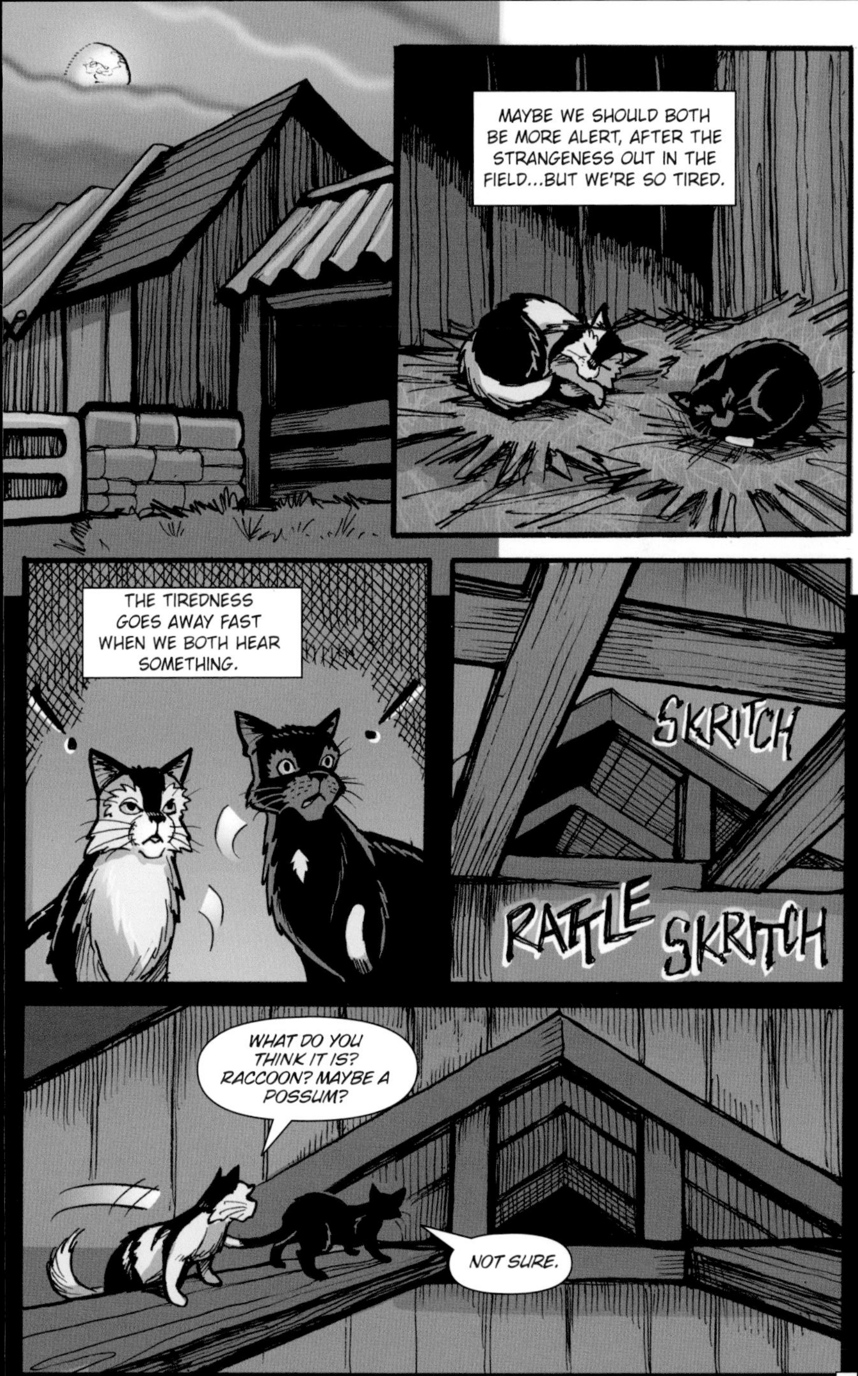
MAYBE WE SHOULD BOTH BE MORE ALERT, AFTER THE STRANGENESS OUT IN THE FIELD...BUT WE'RE SO TIRED.
THE TIREDNESS GOES AWAY FAST WHEN WE BOTH HEAR SOMETHING.
SKRITCH
RATTLE
SKRITCH
WHAT DO YOU THINK IT IS? RACCOON? MAYBE A POSSUM?
NOT SURE.

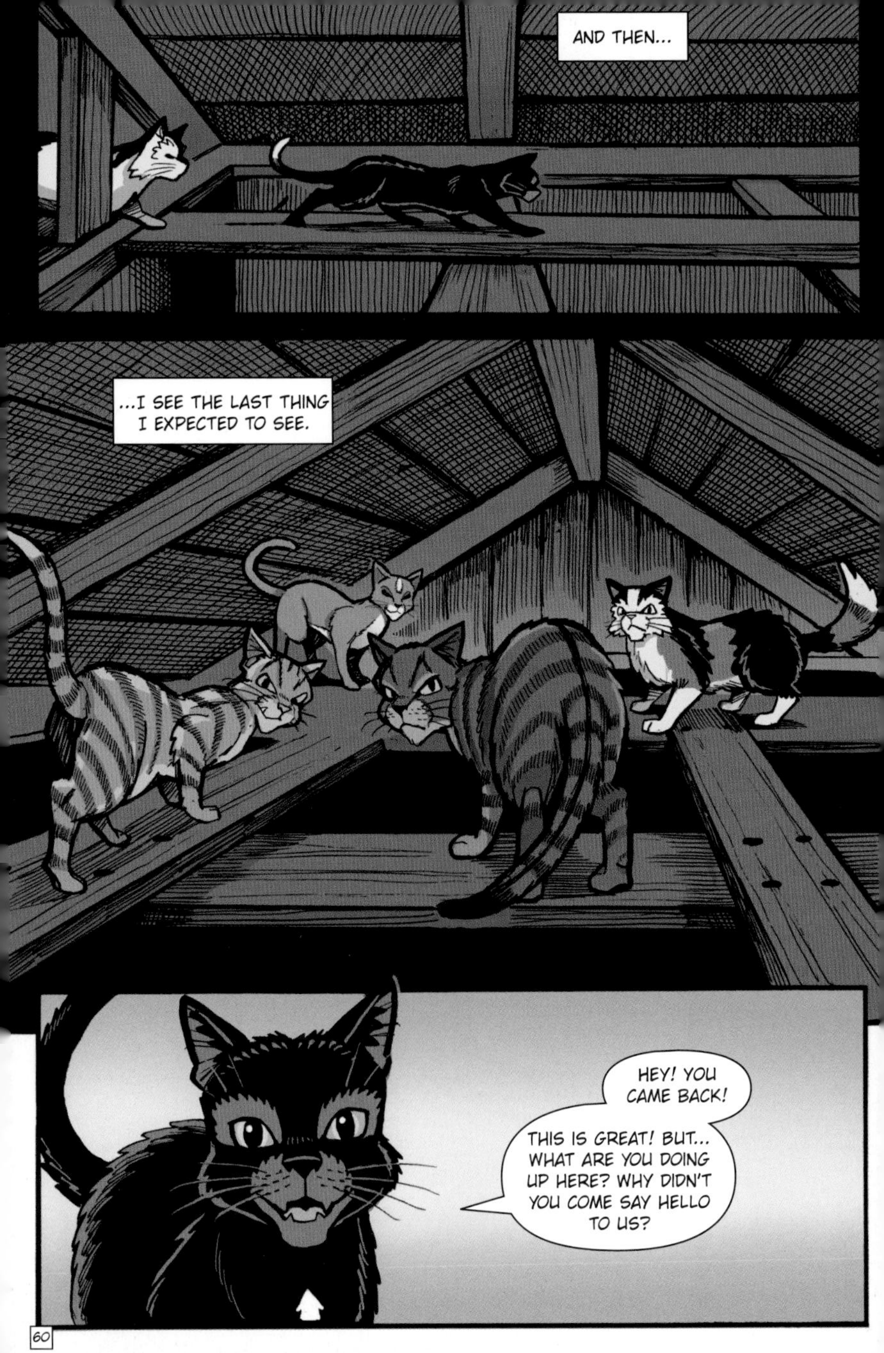
AND THEN...
...I SEE THE LAST THING I EXPECTED TO SEE.
HEY! YOU CAME BACK!
THIS IS GREAT! BUT... WHAT ARE YOU DOING UP HERE? WHY DIDN'T YOU COME SAY HELLO TO US?

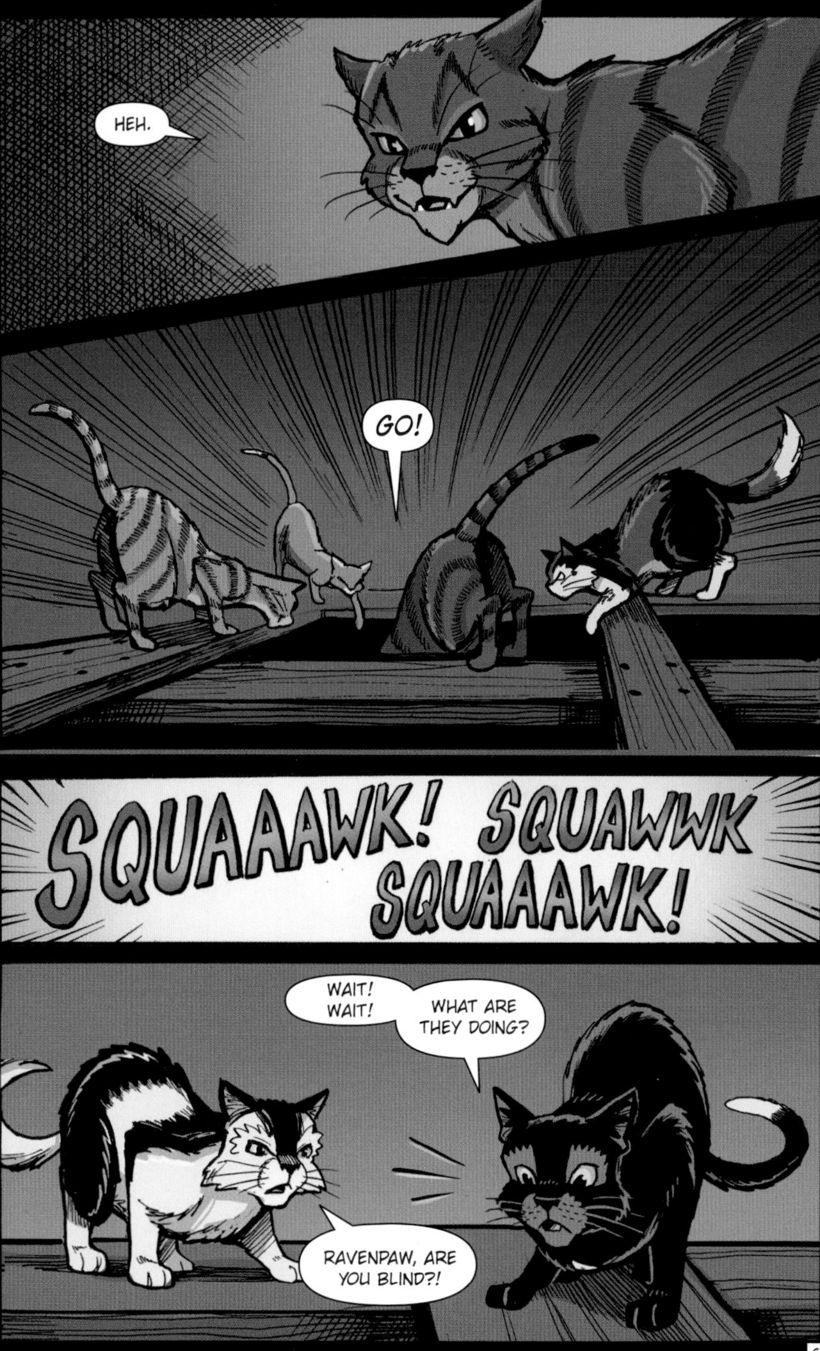
HEH.
GO!
SQUAAAWK! SQUAWWK
SQUAAAWK!
WAIT! WAIT!
WHAT ARE THEY DOING?
RAVENPAW, ARE YOU BLIND?!

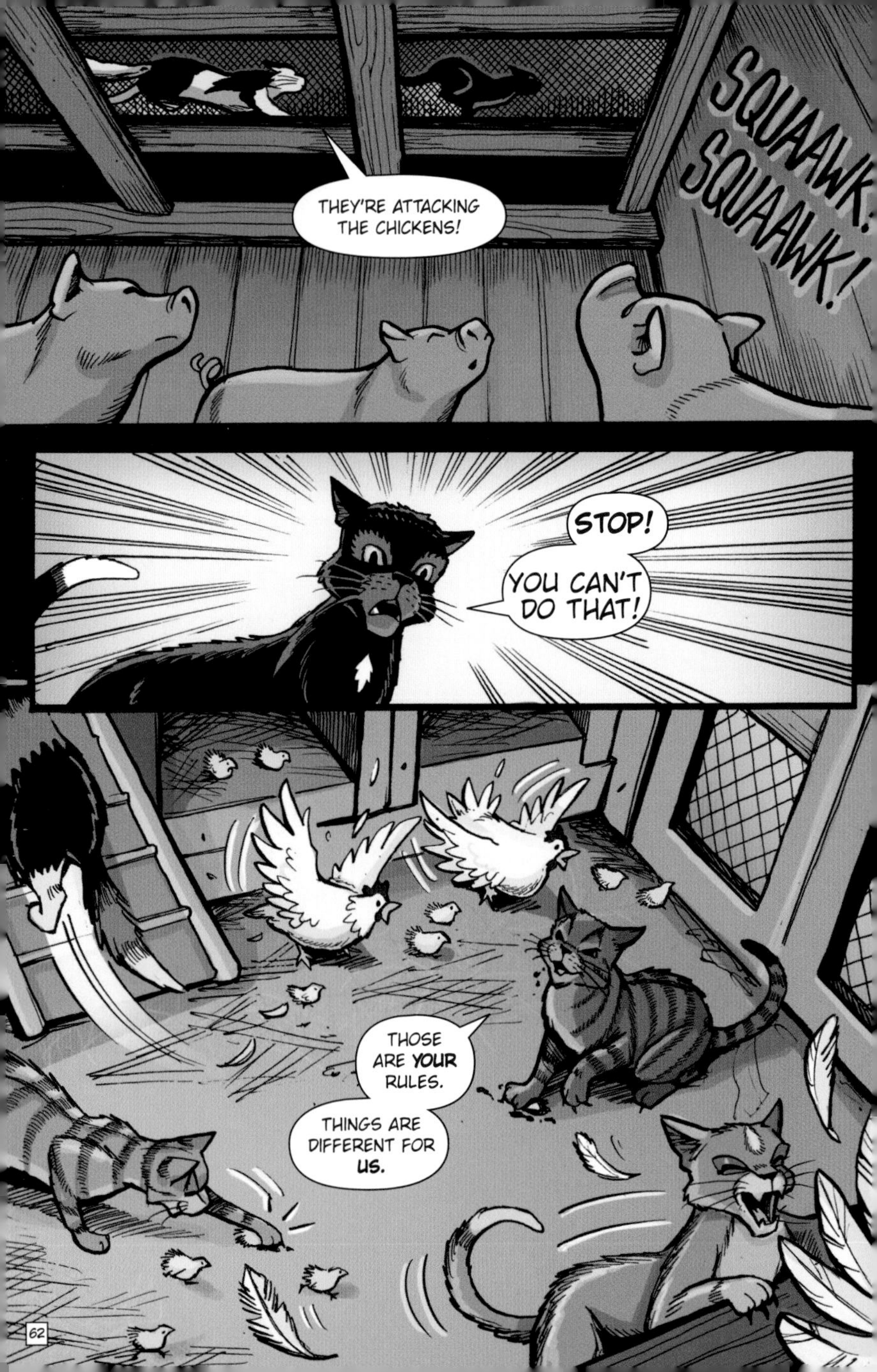

THEY'RE ATTACKING THE CHICKENS!
SQUAAAWK! SQUAAAWK!
STOP!
YOU CAN'T DO THAT!
THOSE ARE **YOUR** RULES.
THINGS ARE DIFFERENT FOR **US.**

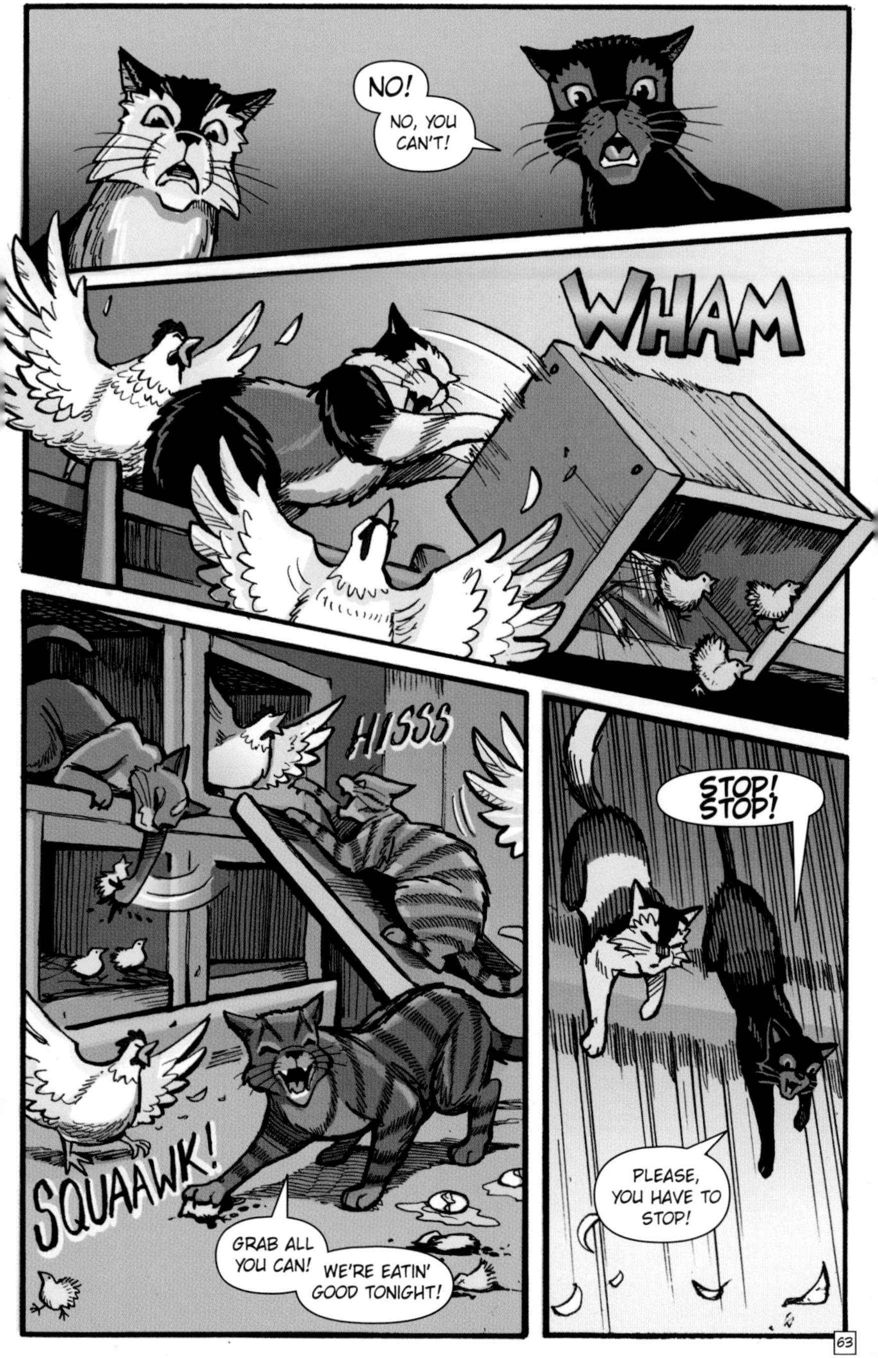
NO!
NO, YOU CAN'T!
WHAM
HISSS
SQUAAWK!
GRAB ALL YOU CAN!
WE'RE EATIN' GOOD TONIGHT!
STOP! STOP!
PLEASE, YOU HAVE TO STOP!

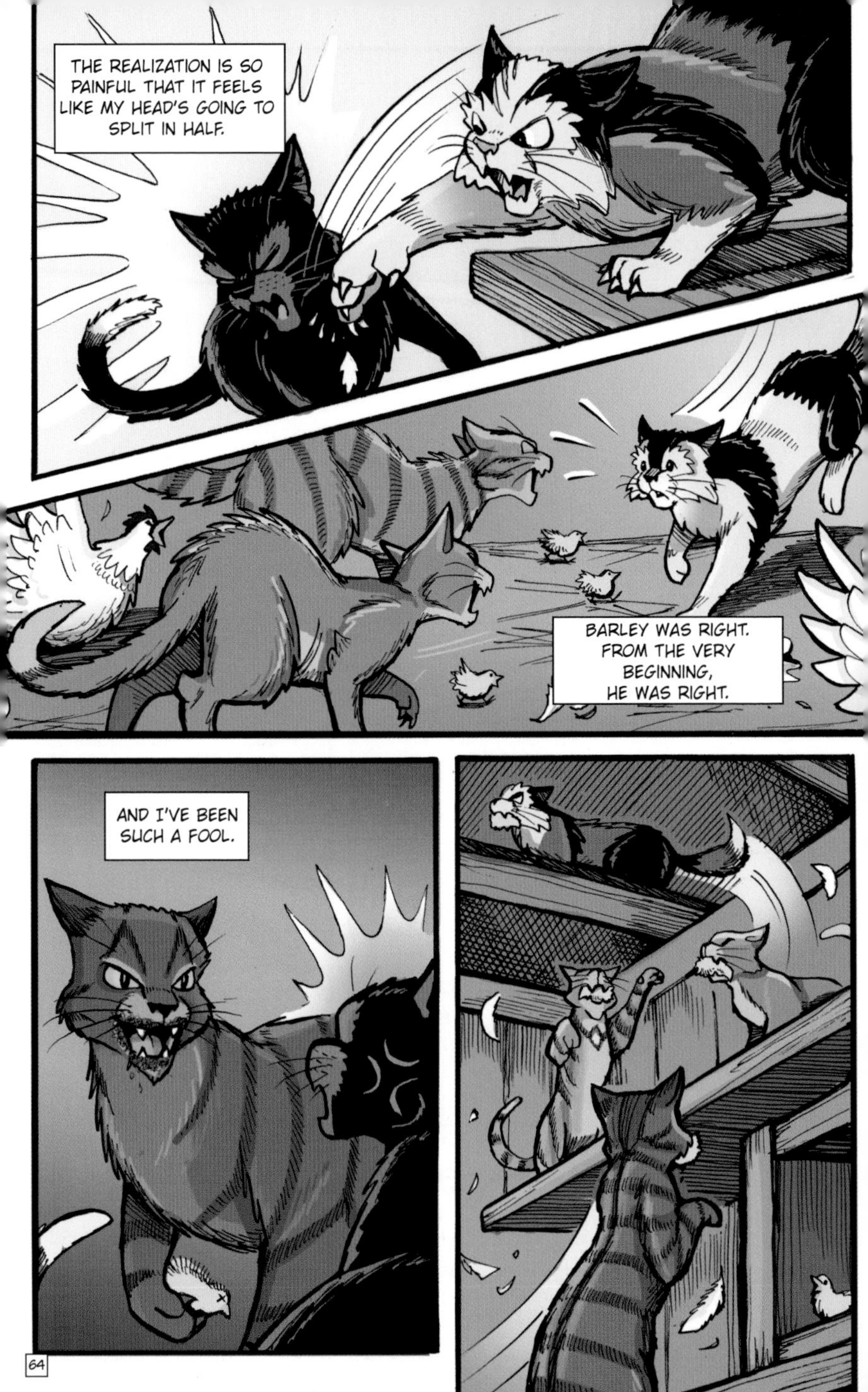
THE REALIZATION IS SO PAINFUL THAT IT FEELS LIKE MY HEAD'S GOING TO SPLIT IN HALF.
BARLEY WAS RIGHT. FROM THE VERY BEGINNING, HE WAS RIGHT.
AND I'VE BEEN SUCH A FOOL.

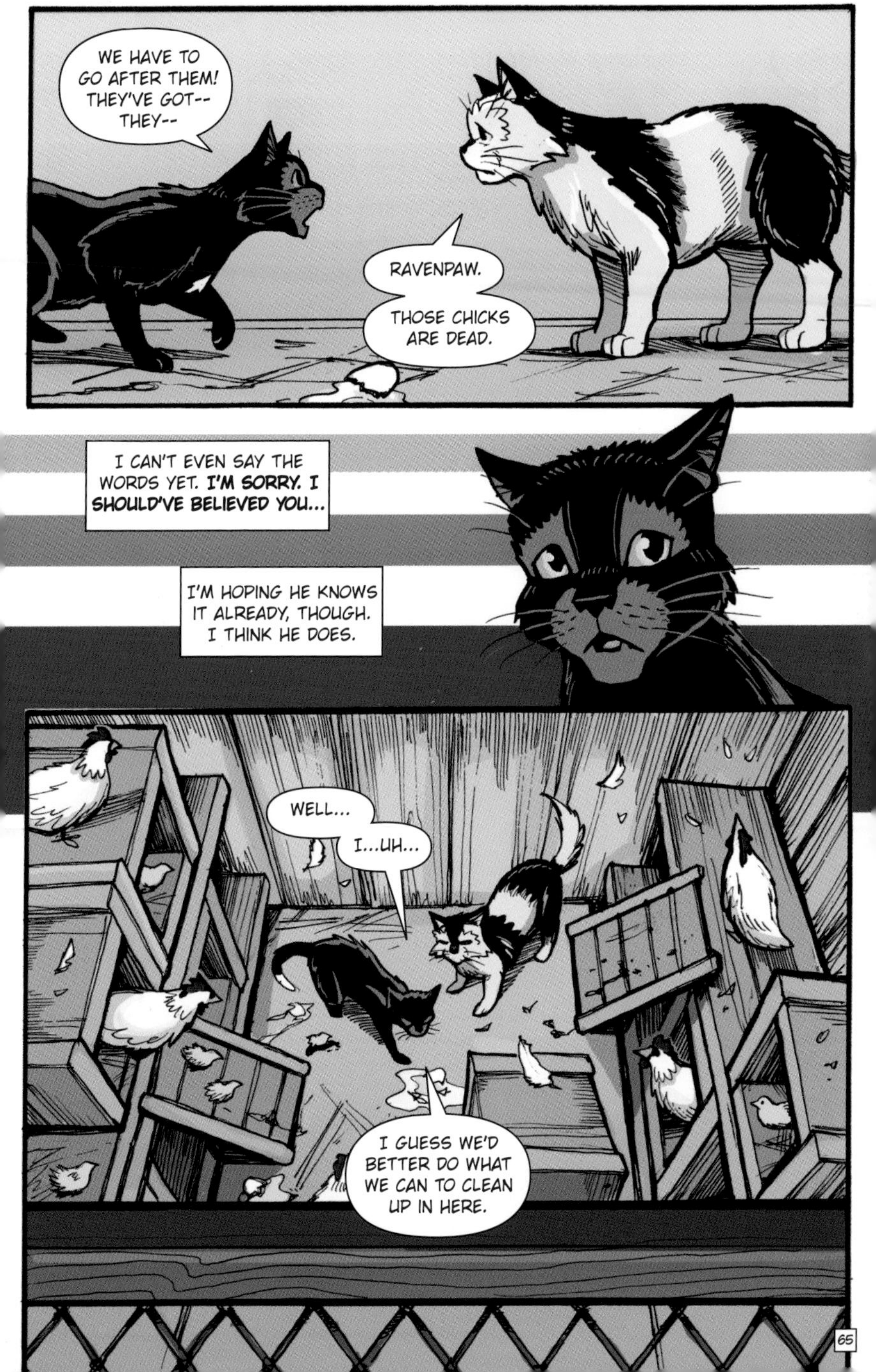
WE HAVE TO GO AFTER THEM! THEY'VE GOT-- THEY--
RAVENPAW.
THOSE CHICKS ARE DEAD.
I CAN'T EVEN SAY THE WORDS YET. **I'M SORRY. I SHOULD'VE BELIEVED YOU...**
I'M HOPING HE KNOWS IT ALREADY, THOUGH. I THINK HE DOES.
WELL...
I...UH...
I GUESS WE'D BETTER DO WHAT WE CAN TO CLEAN UP IN HERE.

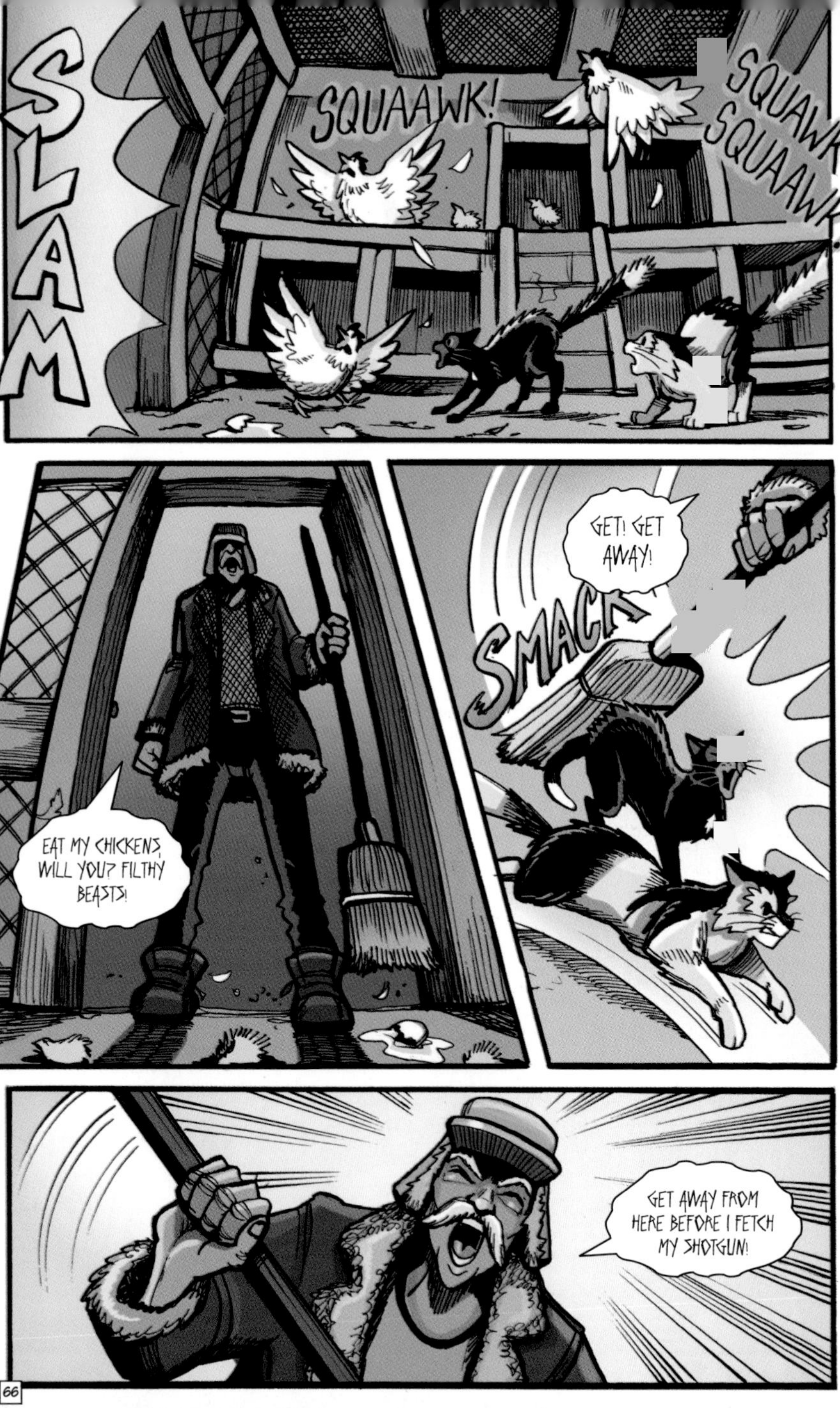
SLAM
SQUAAWK!
SQUAWK
SQUAAAWK!
EAT MY CHICKENS, WILL YOU? FILTHY BEASTS!
GET! GET AWAY!
SMACK
GET AWAY FROM HERE BEFORE I FETCH MY SHOTGUN!

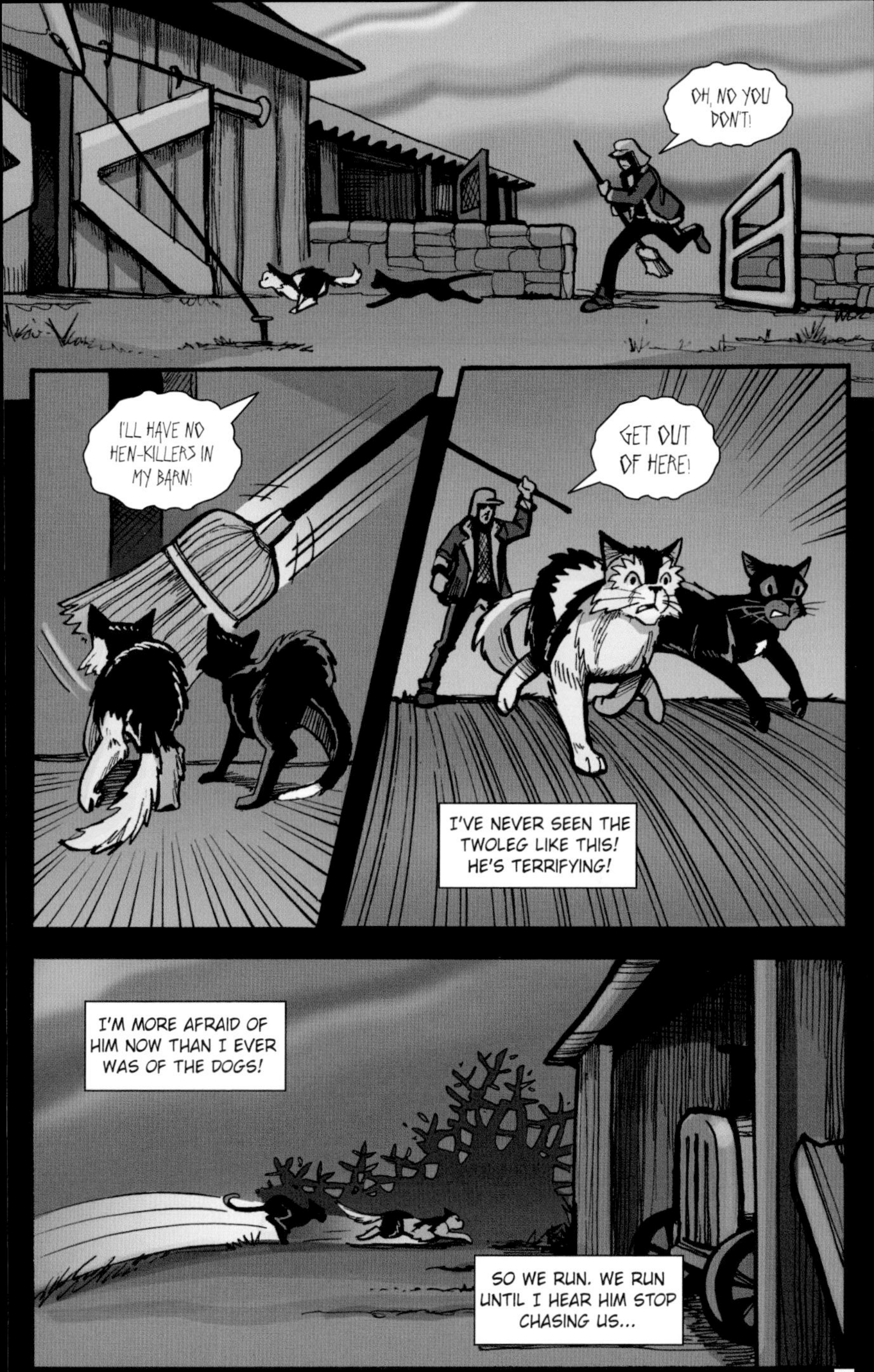
OH, NO YOU DON'T!
I'LL HAVE NO HEN-KILLERS IN MY BARN!
GET OUT OF HERE!
I'VE NEVER SEEN THE TWOLEG LIKE THIS! HE'S TERRIFYING!
I'M MORE AFRAID OF HIM NOW THAN I EVER WAS OF THE DOGS!
SO WE RUN. WE RUN UNTIL I HEAR HIM STOP CHASING US...

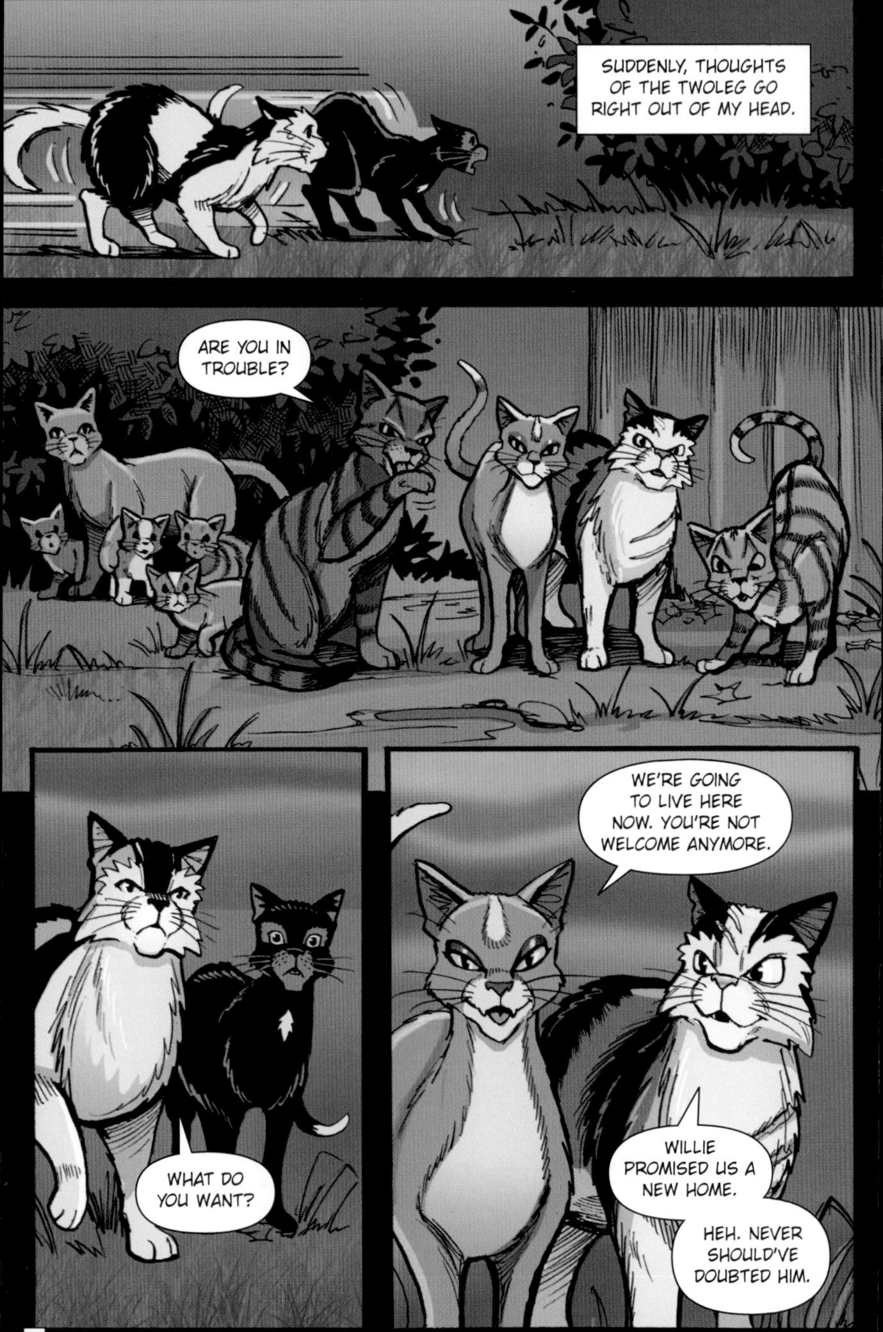
SUDDENLY, THOUGHTS OF THE TWOLEG GO RIGHT OUT OF MY HEAD.
ARE YOU IN TROUBLE?
WHAT DO YOU WANT?
WE'RE GOING TO LIVE HERE NOW. YOU'RE NOT WELCOME ANYMORE.
WILLIE PROMISED US A NEW HOME.
HEH. NEVER SHOULD'VE DOUBTED HIM.

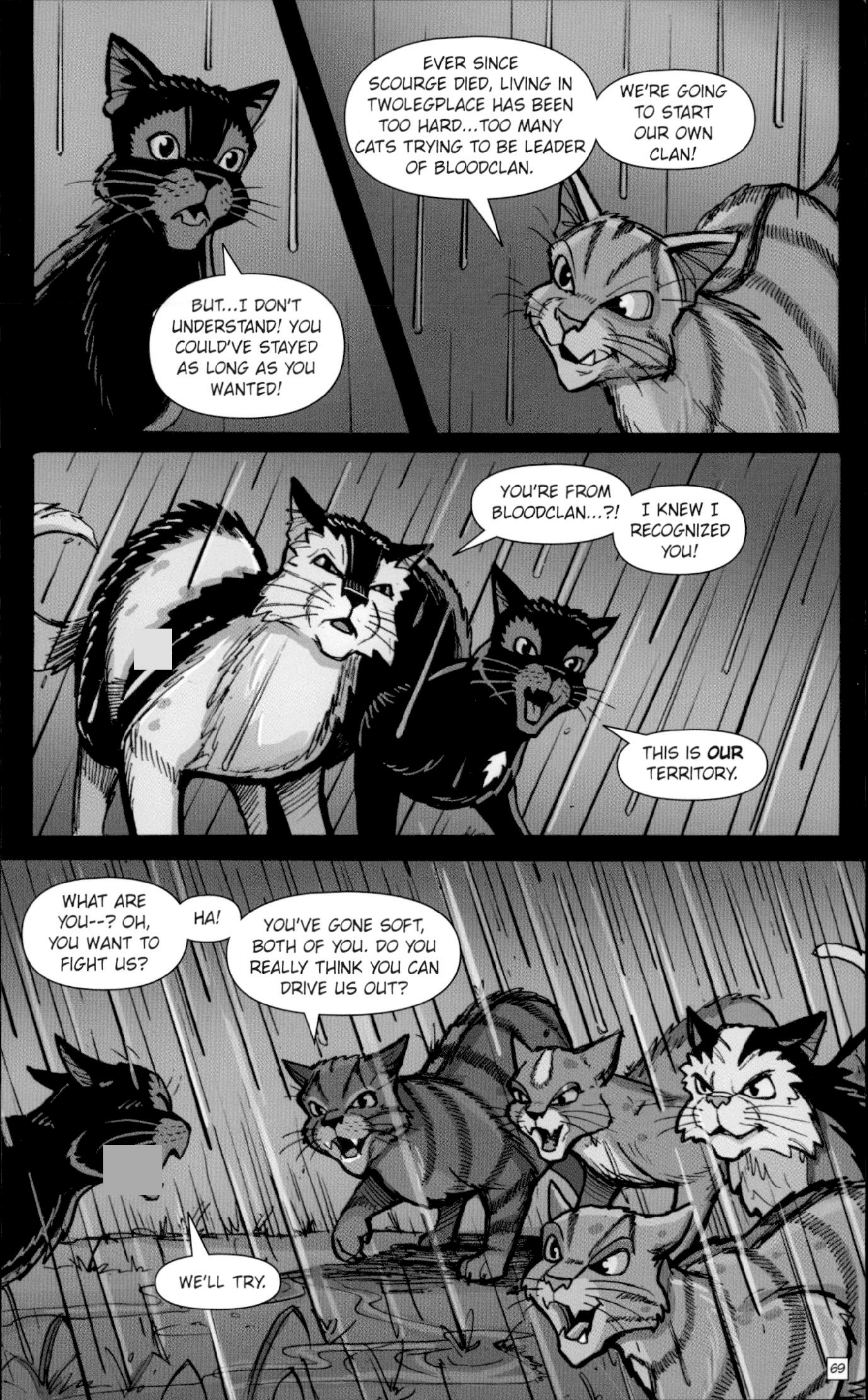
EVER SINCE SCOURGE DIED, LIVING IN TWOLEGPLACE HAS BEEN TOO HARD...TOO MANY CATS TRYING TO BE LEADER OF BLOODCLAN.
WE'RE GOING TO START OUR OWN CLAN!
BUT...I DON'T UNDERSTAND! YOU COULD'VE STAYED AS LONG AS YOU WANTED!
YOU'RE FROM BLOODCLAN...?!
I KNEW I RECOGNIZED YOU!
THIS IS **OUR** TERRITORY.
WHAT ARE YOU--? OH, YOU WANT TO FIGHT US?
HA!
YOU'VE GONE SOFT, BOTH OF YOU. DO YOU REALLY THINK YOU CAN DRIVE US OUT?
WE'LL TRY.

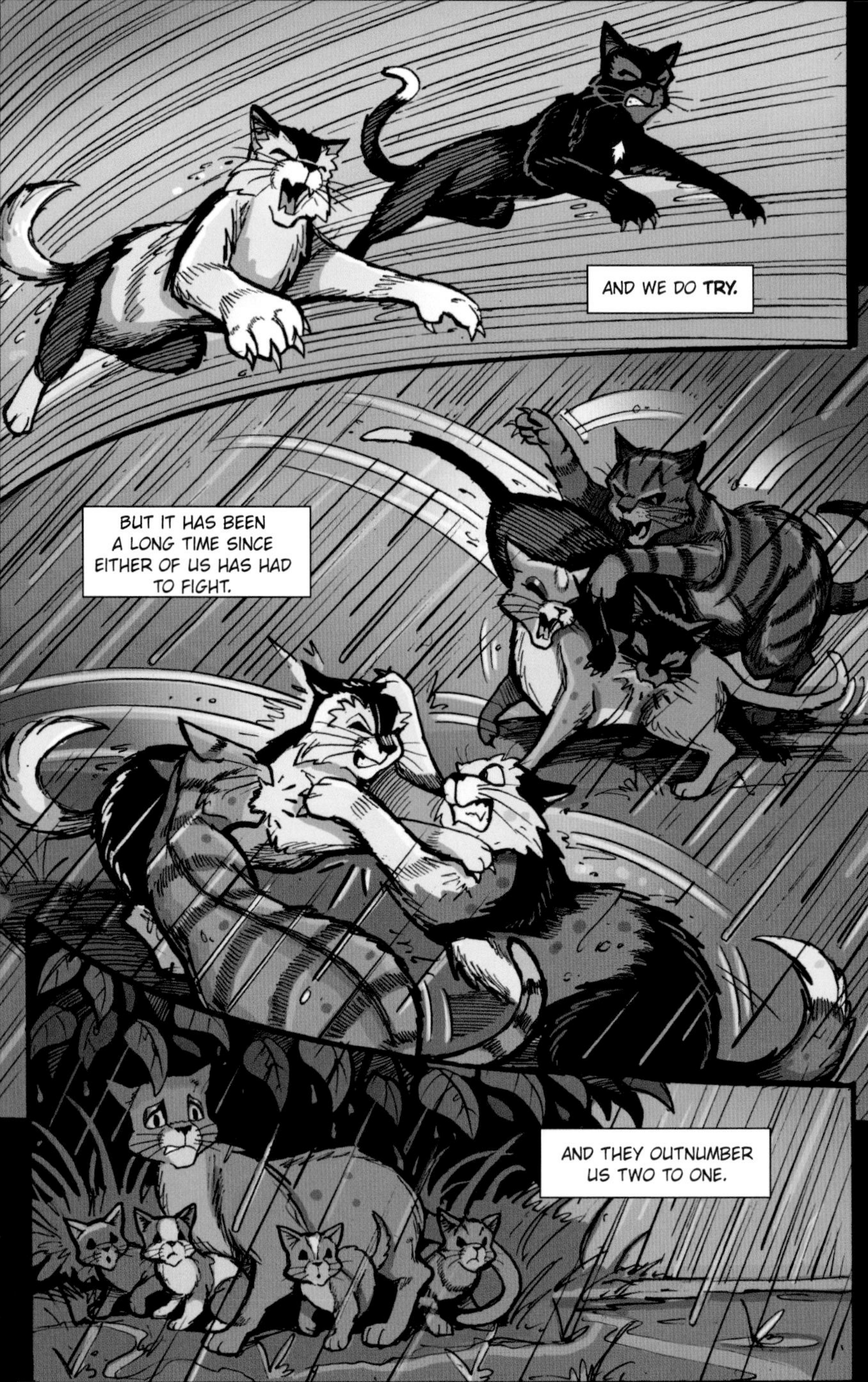
AND WE DO TRY.
BUT IT HAS BEEN A LONG TIME SINCE EITHER OF US HAS HAD TO FIGHT.
AND THEY OUTNUMBER US TWO TO ONE.

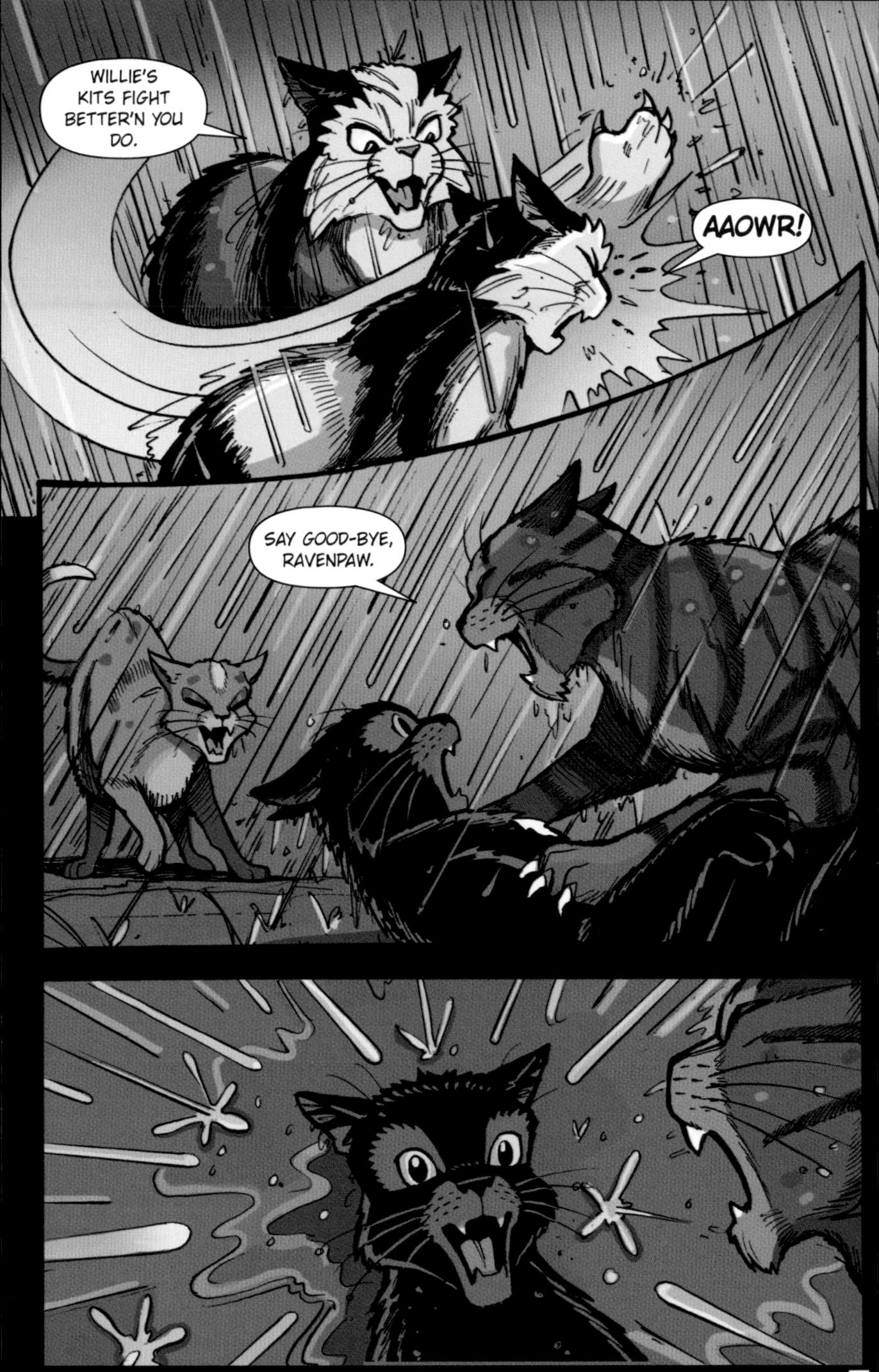
WILLIE'S KITS FIGHT BETTER'N YOU DO.
AAOWR!
SAY GOOD-BYE, RAVENPAW.

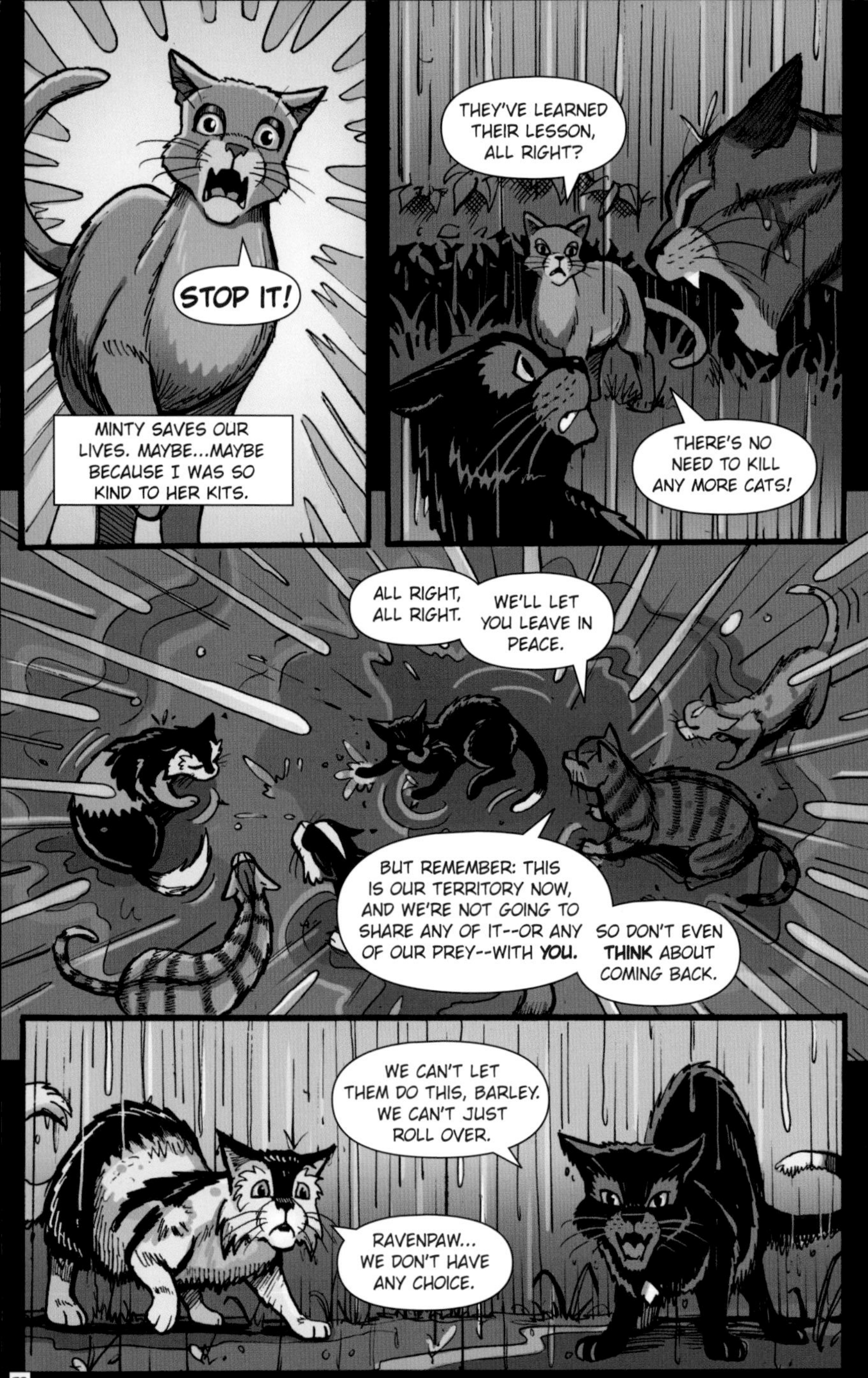
STOP IT!
MINTY SAVES OUR LIVES. MAYBE...MAYBE BECAUSE I WAS SO KIND TO HER KITS.
THEY'VE LEARNED THEIR LESSON, ALL RIGHT?
THERE'S NO NEED TO KILL ANY MORE CATS!
ALL RIGHT, ALL RIGHT.
WE'LL LET YOU LEAVE IN PEACE.
BUT REMEMBER: THIS IS OUR TERRITORY NOW, AND WE'RE NOT GOING TO SHARE ANY OF IT--OR ANY OF OUR PREY--WITH YOU.
SO DON'T EVEN THINK ABOUT COMING BACK.
WE CAN'T LET THEM DO THIS, BARLEY. WE CAN'T JUST ROLL OVER.
RAVENPAW... WE DON'T HAVE ANY CHOICE.

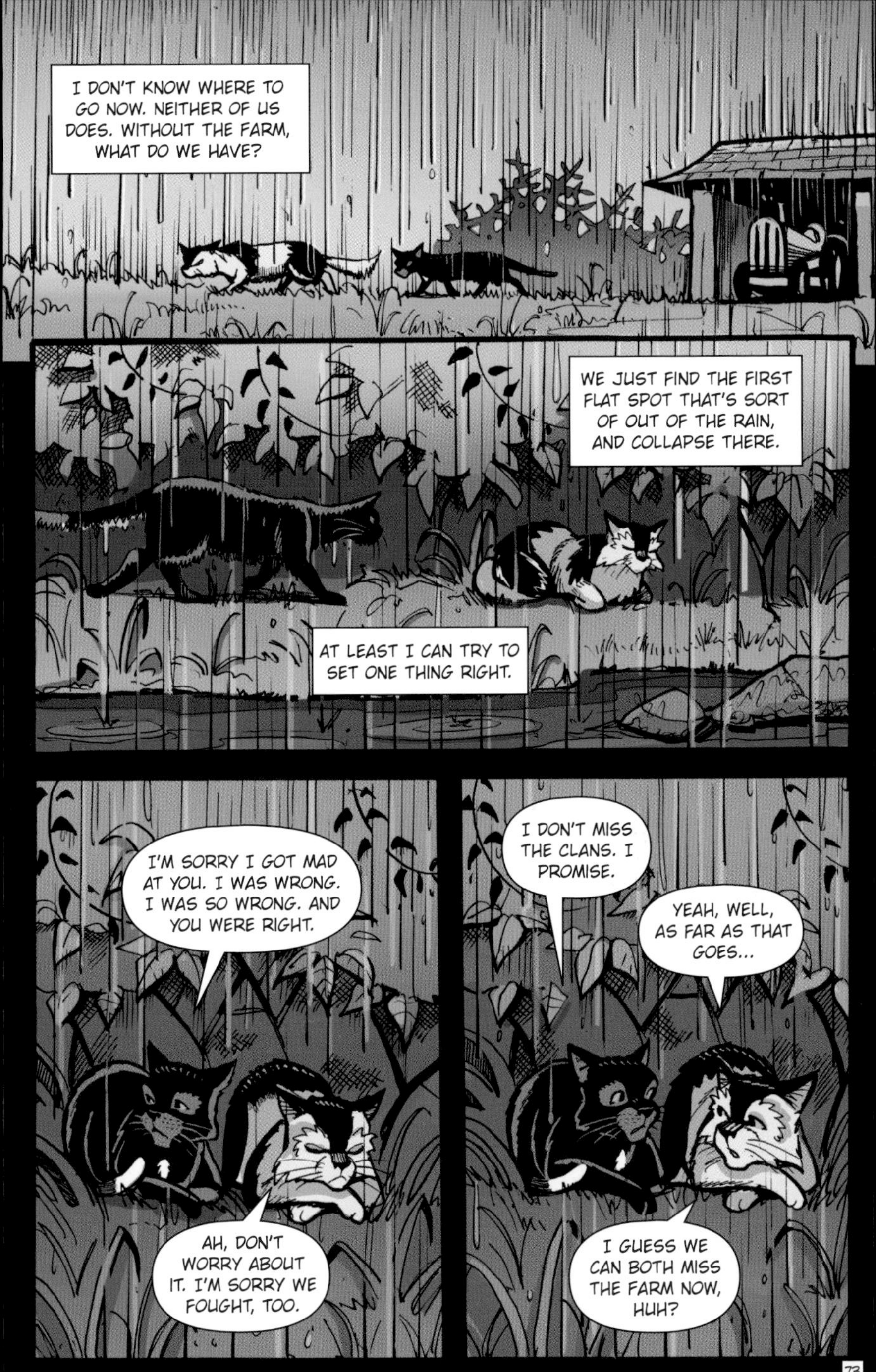

I DON'T KNOW WHERE TO GO NOW. NEITHER OF US DOES. WITHOUT THE FARM, WHAT DO WE HAVE?
WE JUST FIND THE FIRST FLAT SPOT THAT'S SORT OF OUT OF THE RAIN, AND COLLAPSE THERE.
AT LEAST I CAN TRY TO SET ONE THING RIGHT.
I'M SORRY I GOT MAD AT YOU. I WAS WRONG. I WAS SO WRONG. AND YOU WERE RIGHT.
AH, DON'T WORRY ABOUT IT. I'M SORRY WE FOUGHT, TOO.
I DON'T MISS THE CLANS. I PROMISE.
YEAH, WELL, AS FAR AS THAT GOES...
I GUESS WE CAN BOTH MISS THE FARM NOW, HUH?

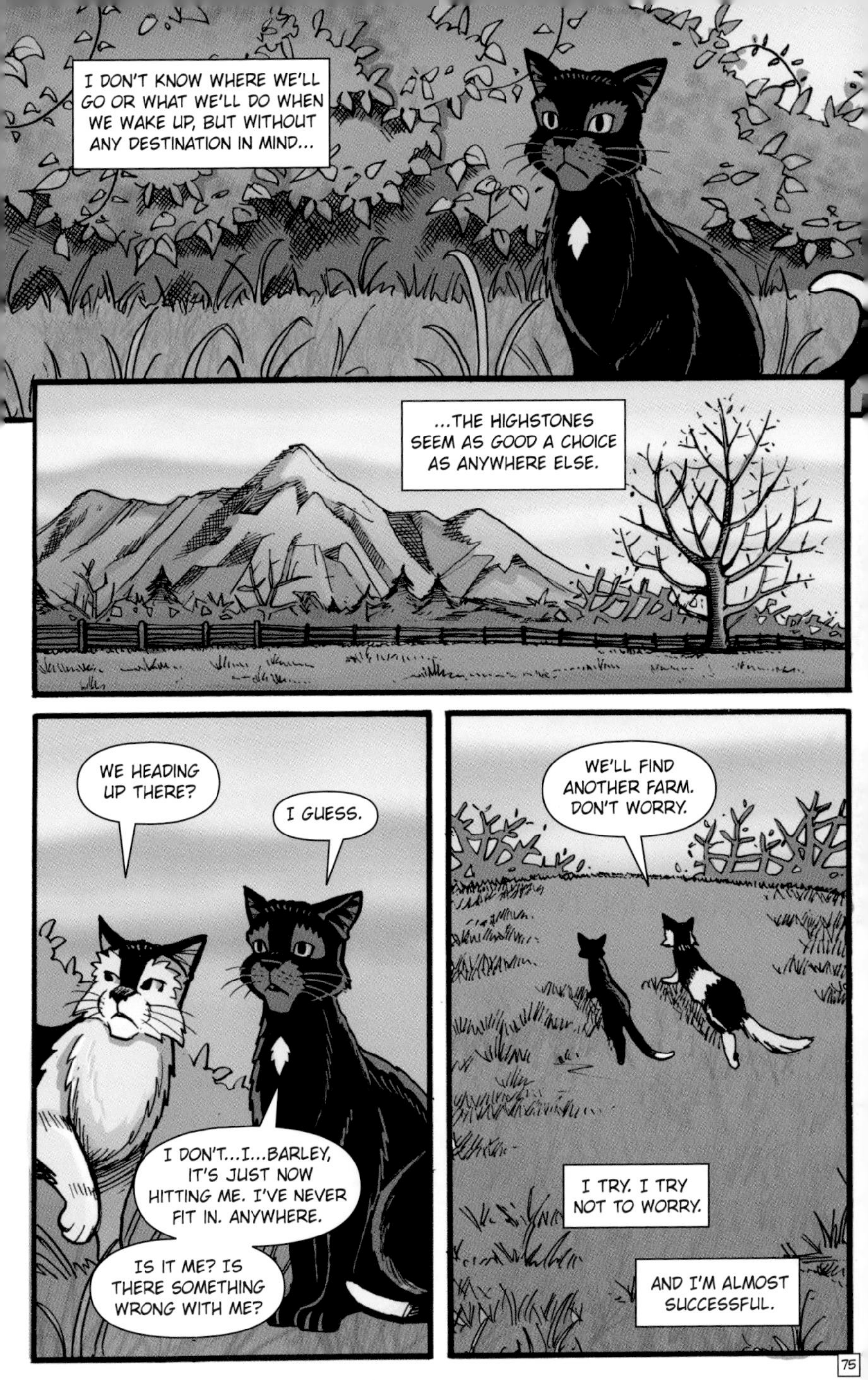
I DON'T KNOW WHERE WE'LL GO OR WHAT WE'LL DO WHEN WE WAKE UP, BUT WITHOUT ANY DESTINATION IN MIND...
...THE HIGHSTONES SEEM AS GOOD A CHOICE AS ANYWHERE ELSE.
WE HEADING UP THERE?
I GUESS.
I DON'T...I...BARLEY, IT'S JUST NOW HITTING ME. I'VE NEVER FIT IN. ANYWHERE.
IS IT ME? IS THERE SOMETHING WRONG WITH ME?
WE'LL FIND ANOTHER FARM. DON'T WORRY.
I TRY. I TRY NOT TO WORRY.
AND I'M ALMOST SUCCESSFUL.

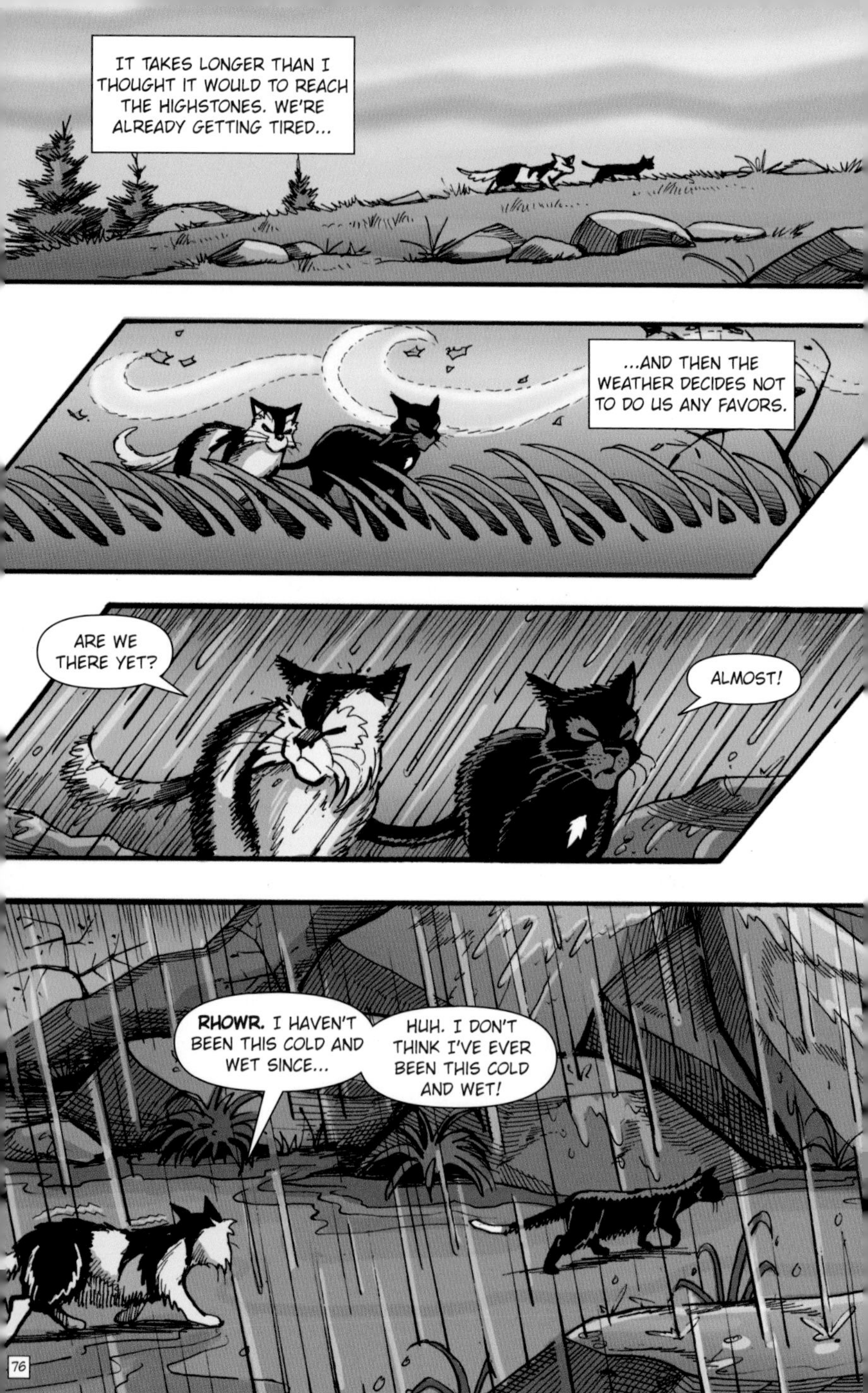
IT TAKES LONGER THAN I THOUGHT IT WOULD TO REACH THE HIGHSTONES. WE'RE ALREADY GETTING TIRED...
...AND THEN THE WEATHER DECIDES NOT TO DO US ANY FAVORS.
ARE WE THERE YET?
ALMOST!
RHOWR. I HAVEN'T BEEN THIS COLD AND WET SINCE...
HUH. I DON'T THINK I'VE EVER BEEN THIS COLD AND WET!

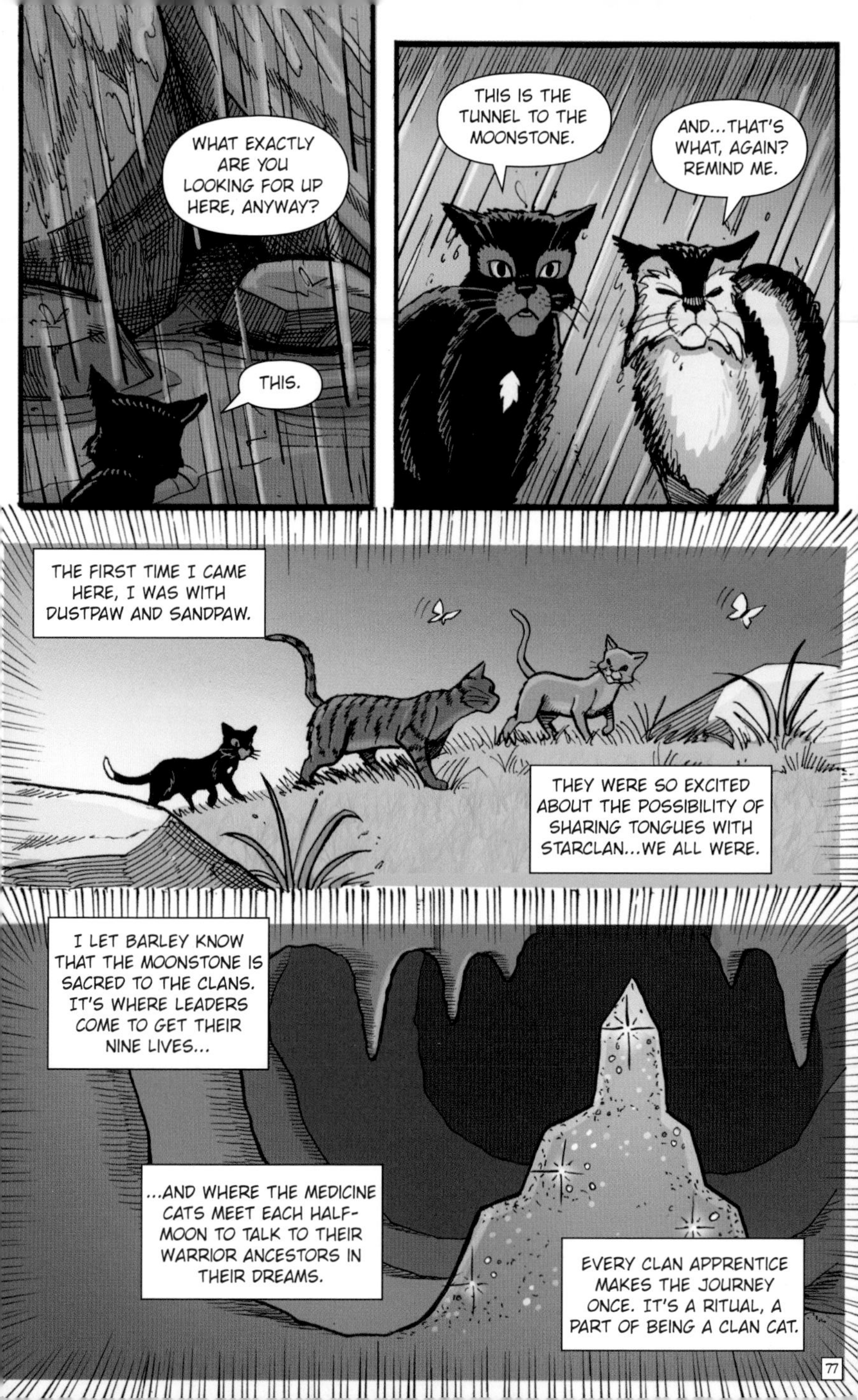
WHAT EXACTLY ARE YOU LOOKING FOR UP HERE, ANYWAY?
THIS.
THIS IS THE TUNNEL TO THE MOONSTONE.
AND...THAT'S WHAT, AGAIN? REMIND ME.
THE FIRST TIME I CAME HERE, I WAS WITH DUSTPAW AND SANDPAW.
THEY WERE SO EXCITED ABOUT THE POSSIBILITY OF SHARING TONGUES WITH STARCLAN...WE ALL WERE.
I LET BARLEY KNOW THAT THE MOONSTONE IS SACRED TO THE CLANS. IT'S WHERE LEADERS COME TO GET THEIR NINE LIVES...
...AND WHERE THE MEDICINE CATS MEET EACH HALF-MOON TO TALK TO THEIR WARRIOR ANCESTORS IN THEIR DREAMS.
EVERY CLAN APPRENTICE MAKES THE JOURNEY ONCE. IT'S A RITUAL, A PART OF BEING A CLAN CAT.

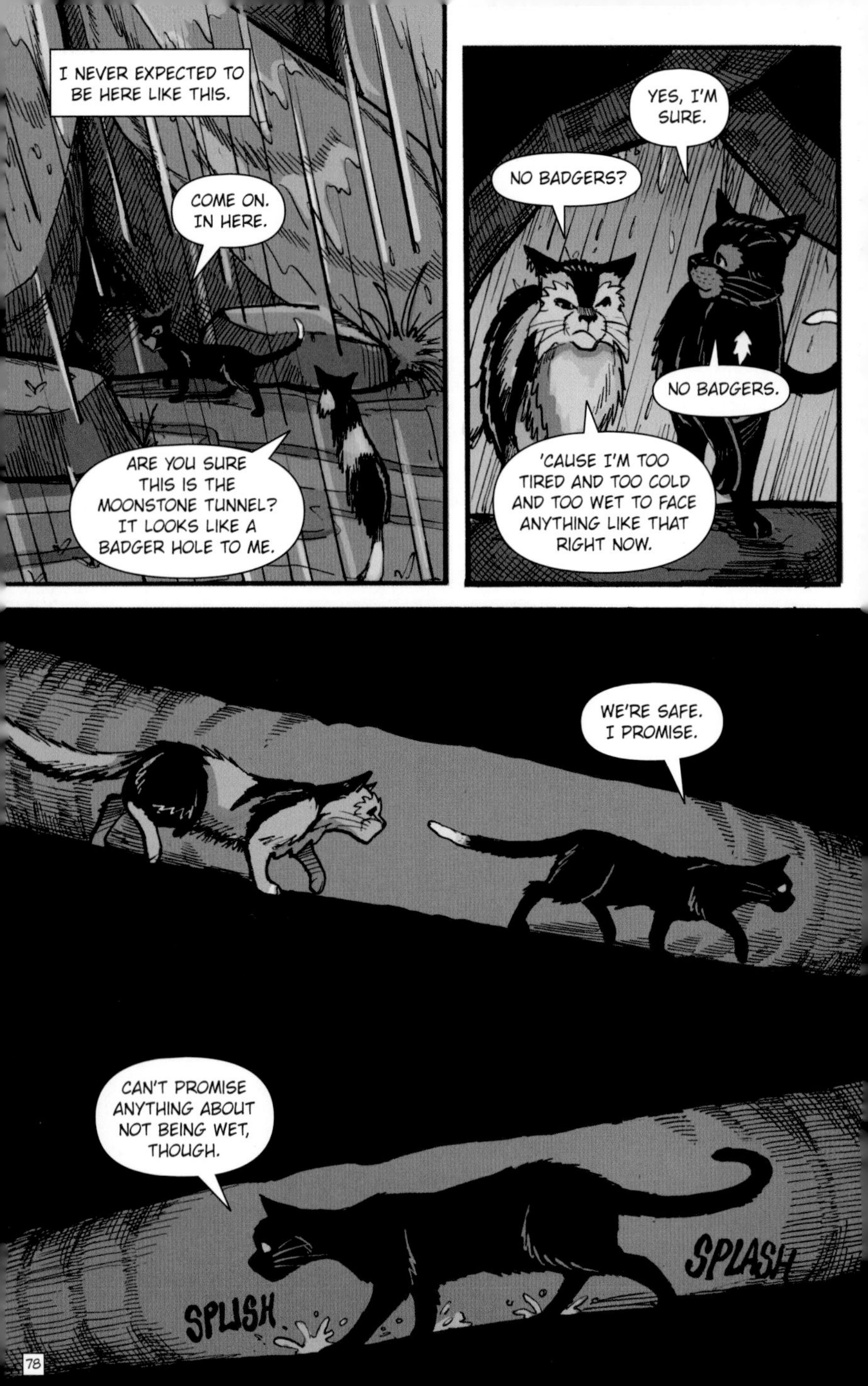
I NEVER EXPECTED TO BE HERE LIKE THIS.
COME ON. IN HERE.
ARE YOU SURE THIS IS THE MOONSTONE TUNNEL? IT LOOKS LIKE A BADGER HOLE TO ME.
YES, I'M SURE.
NO BADGERS?
NO BADGERS.
'CAUSE I'M TOO TIRED AND TOO COLD AND TOO WET TO FACE ANYTHING LIKE THAT RIGHT NOW.
WE'RE SAFE. I PROMISE.
CAN'T PROMISE ANYTHING ABOUT NOT BEING WET, THOUGH.
SPLISH
SPLASH

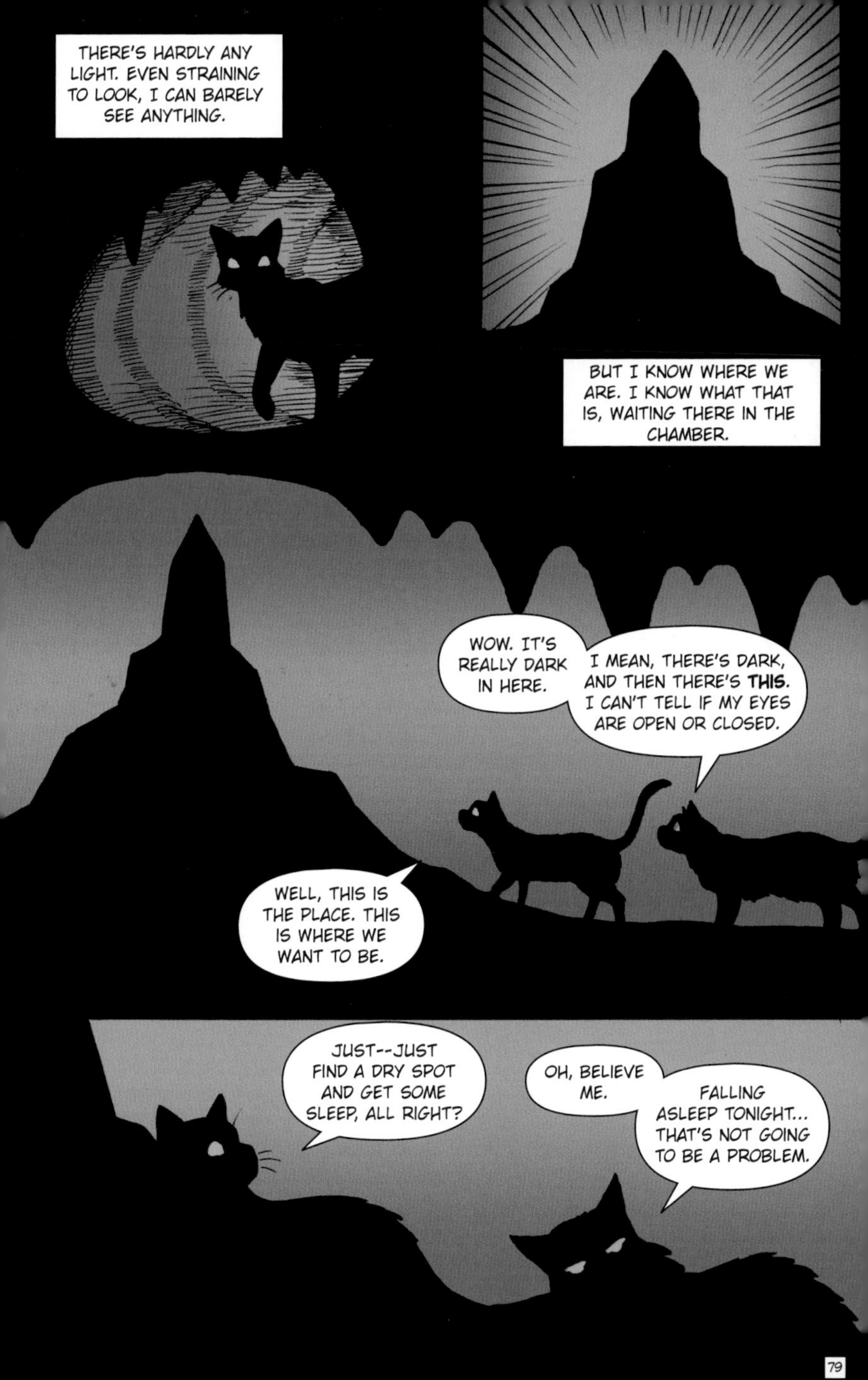
THERE'S HARDLY ANY LIGHT. EVEN STRAINING TO LOOK, I CAN BARELY SEE ANYTHING.
BUT I KNOW WHERE WE ARE. I KNOW WHAT THAT IS, WAITING THERE IN THE CHAMBER.
WOW. IT'S REALLY DARK IN HERE.
I MEAN, THERE'S DARK, AND THEN THERE'S **THIS**. I CAN'T TELL IF MY EYES ARE OPEN OR CLOSED.
WELL, THIS IS THE PLACE. THIS IS WHERE WE WANT TO BE.
JUST--JUST FIND A DRY SPOT AND GET SOME SLEEP, ALL RIGHT?
OH, BELIEVE ME.
FALLING ASLEEP TONIGHT... THAT'S NOT GOING TO BE A PROBLEM.

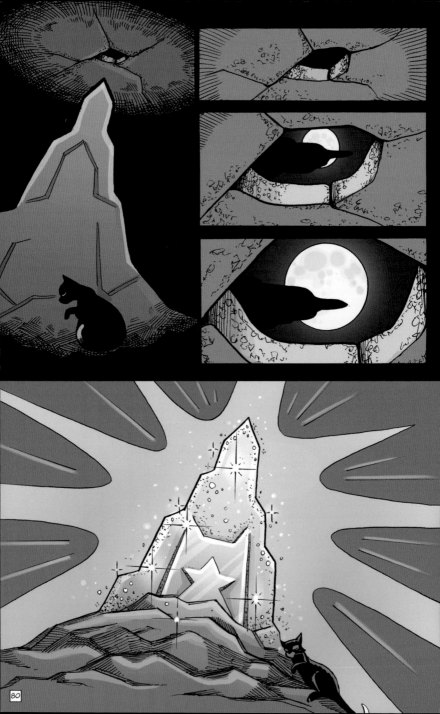

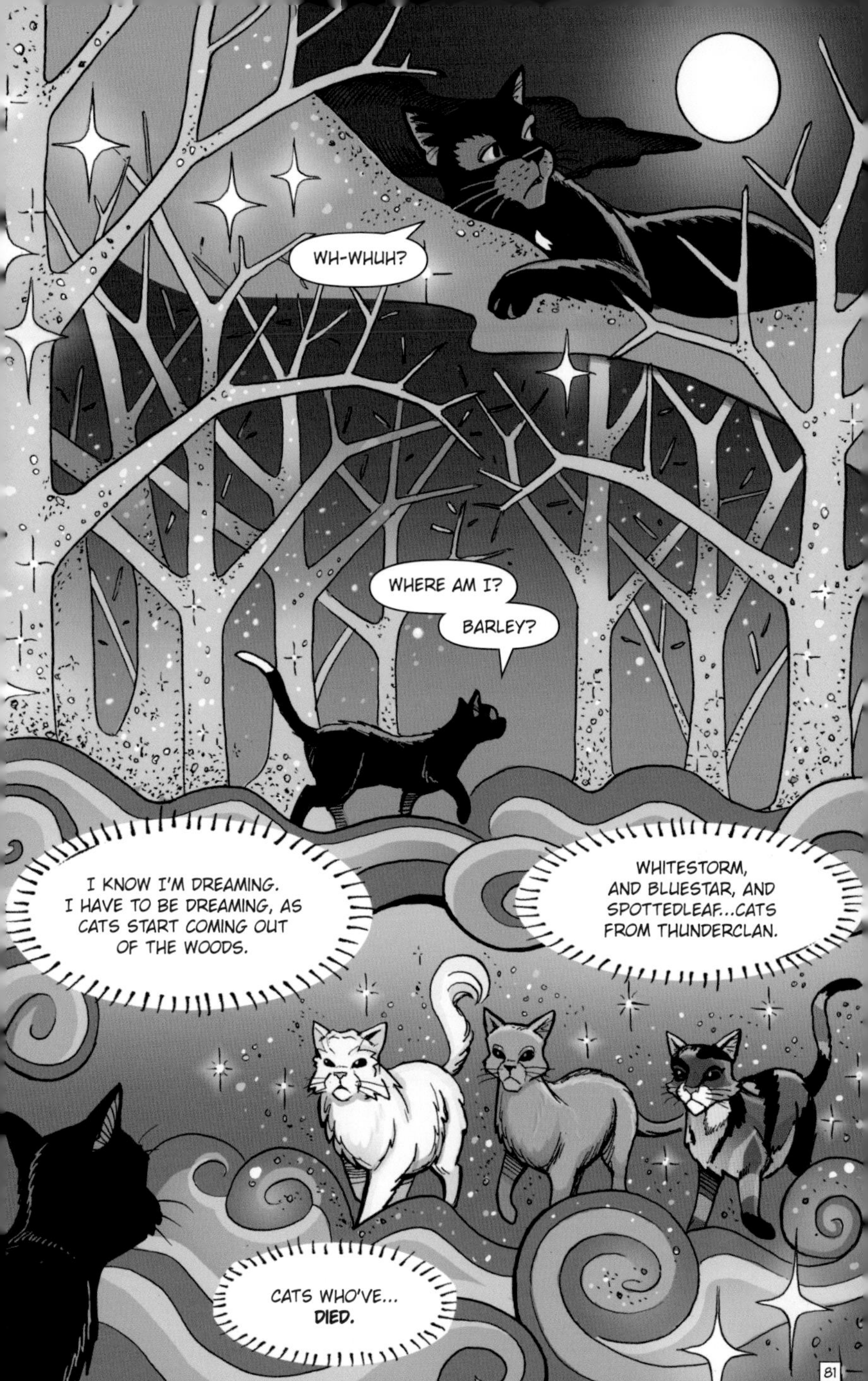
WH-WHUH?
WHERE AM I?
BARLEY?
I KNOW I'M DREAMING. I HAVE TO BE DREAMING, AS CATS START COMING OUT OF THE WOODS.
WHITESTORM, AND BLUESTAR, AND SPOTTEDLEAF...CATS FROM THUNDERCLAN.
CATS WHO'VE... **DIED.**

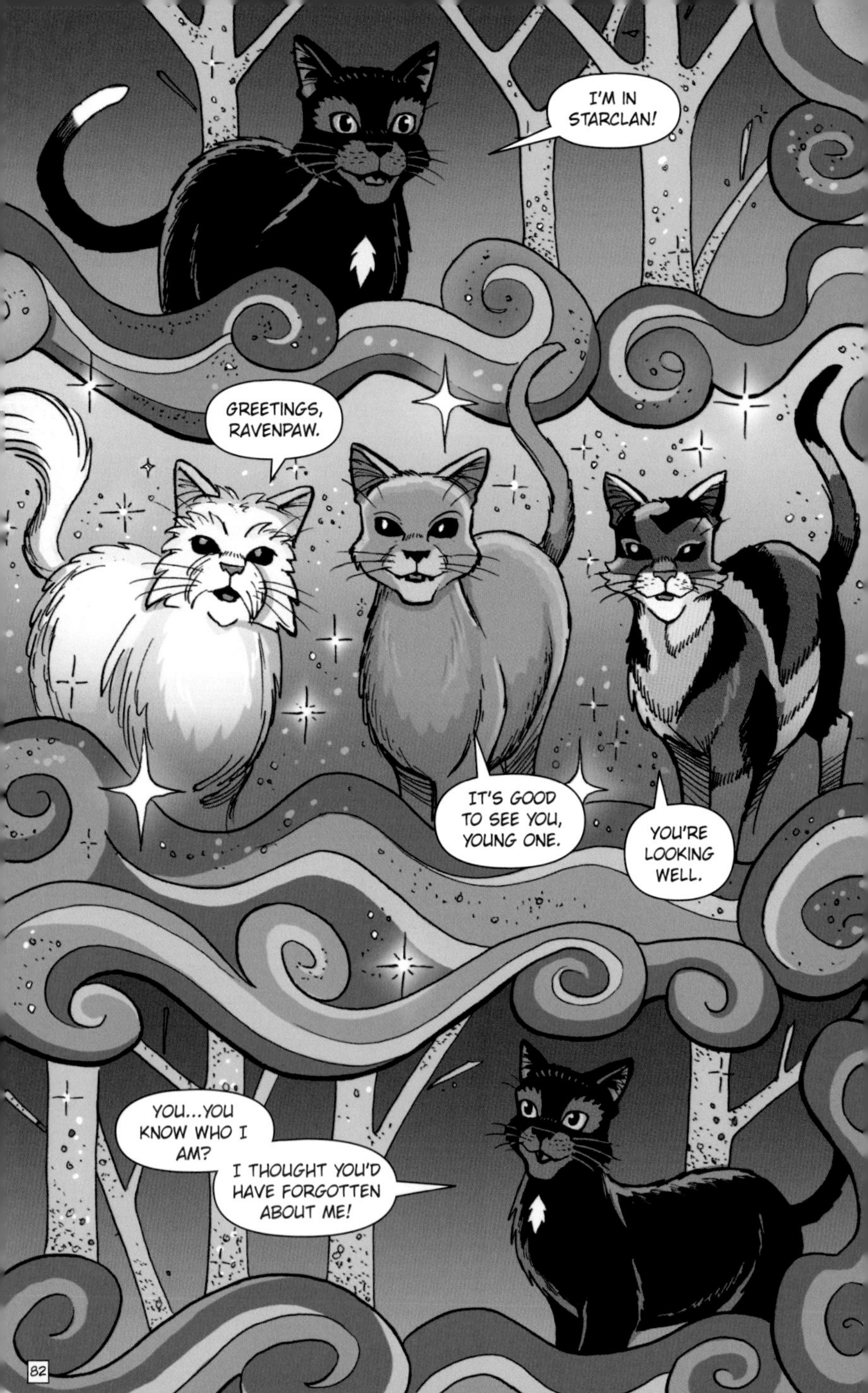
I'M IN STARCLAN!
GREETINGS, RAVENPAW.
IT'S GOOD TO SEE YOU, YOUNG ONE.
YOU'RE LOOKING WELL.
YOU...YOU KNOW WHO I AM?
I THOUGHT YOU'D HAVE FORGOTTEN ABOUT ME!

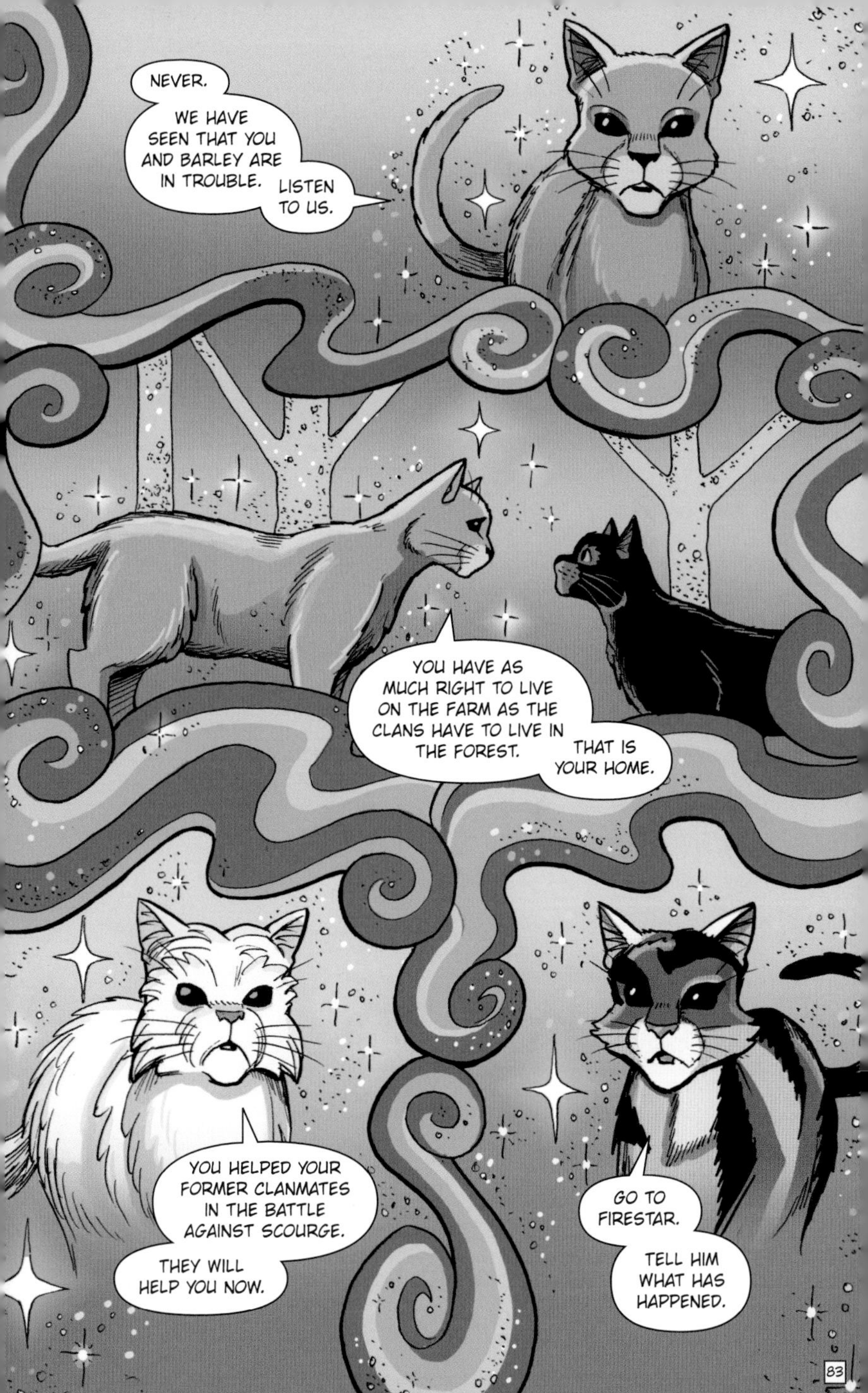
NEVER.
WE HAVE SEEN THAT YOU AND BARLEY ARE IN TROUBLE.
LISTEN TO US.
YOU HAVE AS MUCH RIGHT TO LIVE ON THE FARM AS THE CLANS HAVE TO LIVE IN THE FOREST.
THAT IS YOUR HOME.
YOU HELPED YOUR FORMER CLANMATES IN THE BATTLE AGAINST SCOURGE.
THEY WILL HELP YOU NOW.
GO TO FIRESTAR.
TELL HIM WHAT HAS HAPPENED.

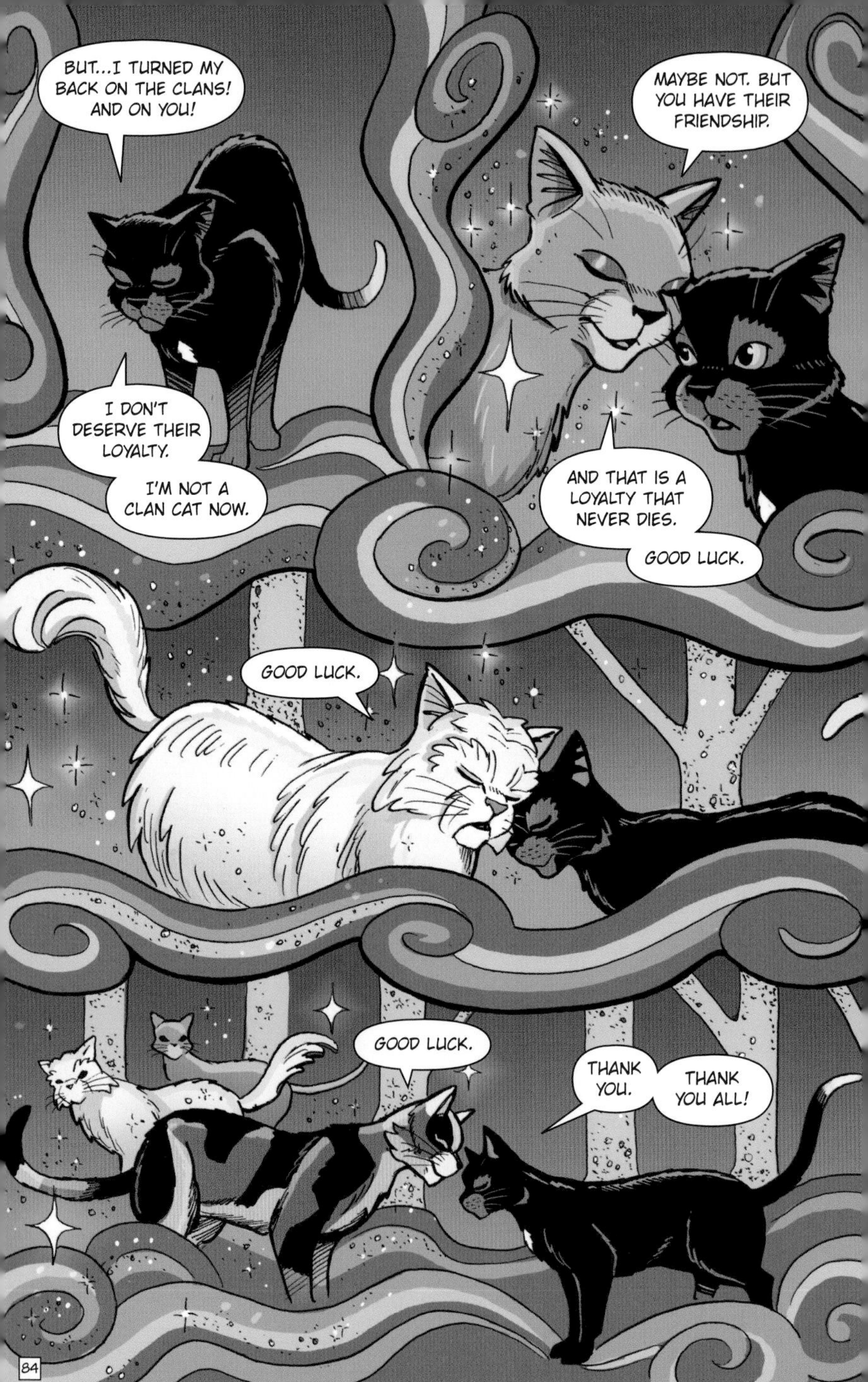
BUT...I TURNED MY BACK ON THE CLANS! AND ON YOU!
MAYBE NOT. BUT YOU HAVE THEIR FRIENDSHIP.
I DON'T DESERVE THEIR LOYALTY.
I'M NOT A CLAN CAT NOW.
AND THAT IS A LOYALTY THAT NEVER DIES.
GOOD LUCK.
GOOD LUCK.
GOOD LUCK.
THANK YOU.
THANK YOU ALL!

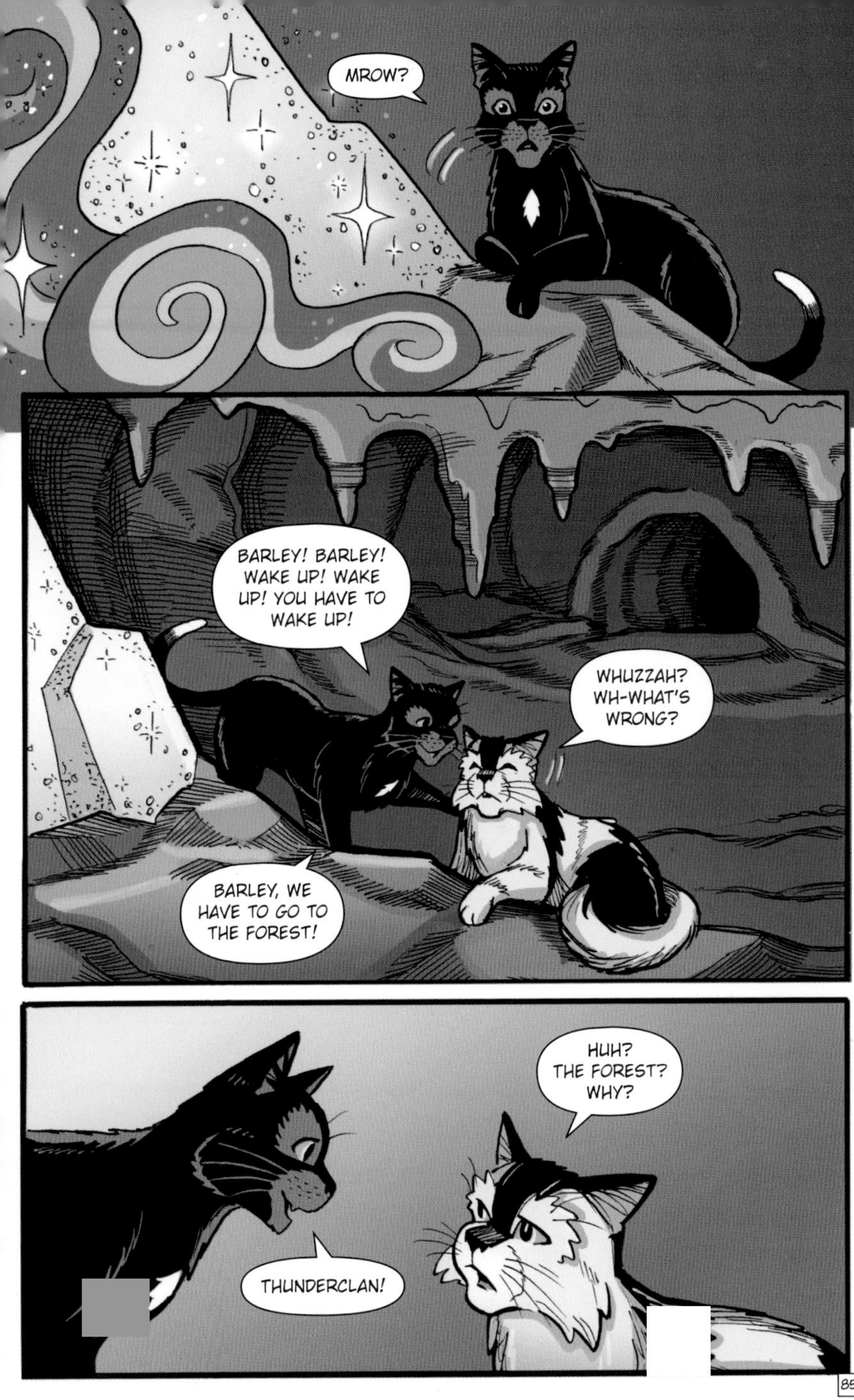
MROW?
BARLEY! BARLEY! WAKE UP! WAKE UP! YOU HAVE TO WAKE UP!
WHUZZAH? WH-WHAT'S WRONG?
BARLEY, WE HAVE TO GO TO THE FOREST!
HUH? THE FOREST? WHY?
THUNDERCLAN!

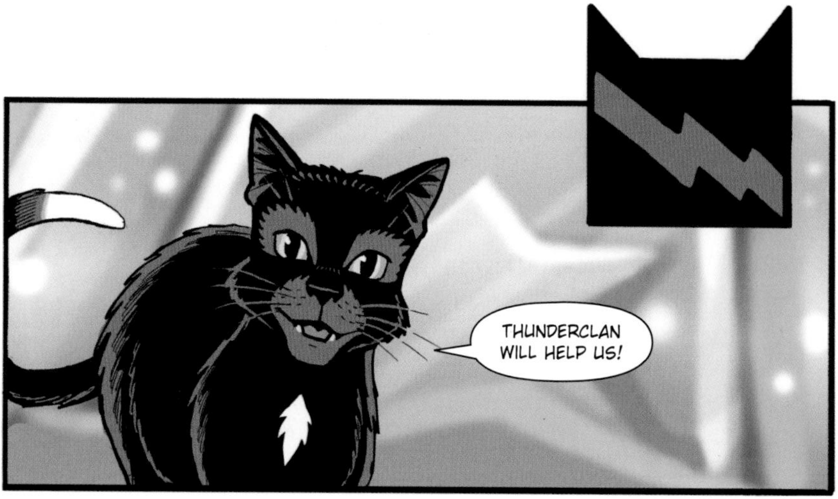
THUNDERCLAN WILL HELP US!

WARRIORS

RAVENPAW'S PATH

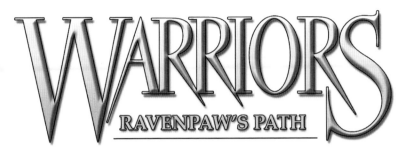

#2: A CLAN IN NEED

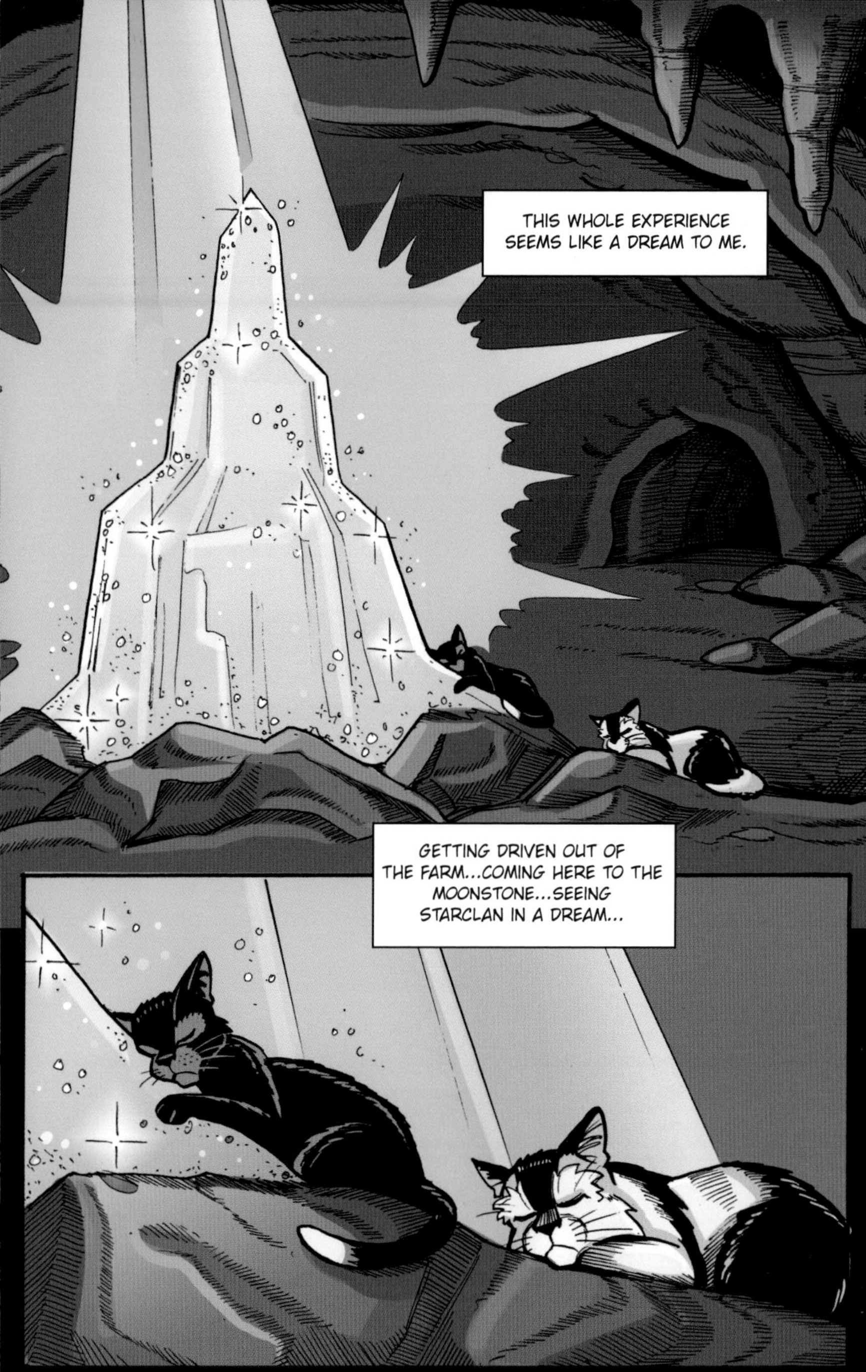
THIS WHOLE EXPERIENCE SEEMS LIKE A DREAM TO ME.
GETTING DRIVEN OUT OF THE FARM...COMING HERE TO THE MOONSTONE...SEEING STARCLAN IN A DREAM...

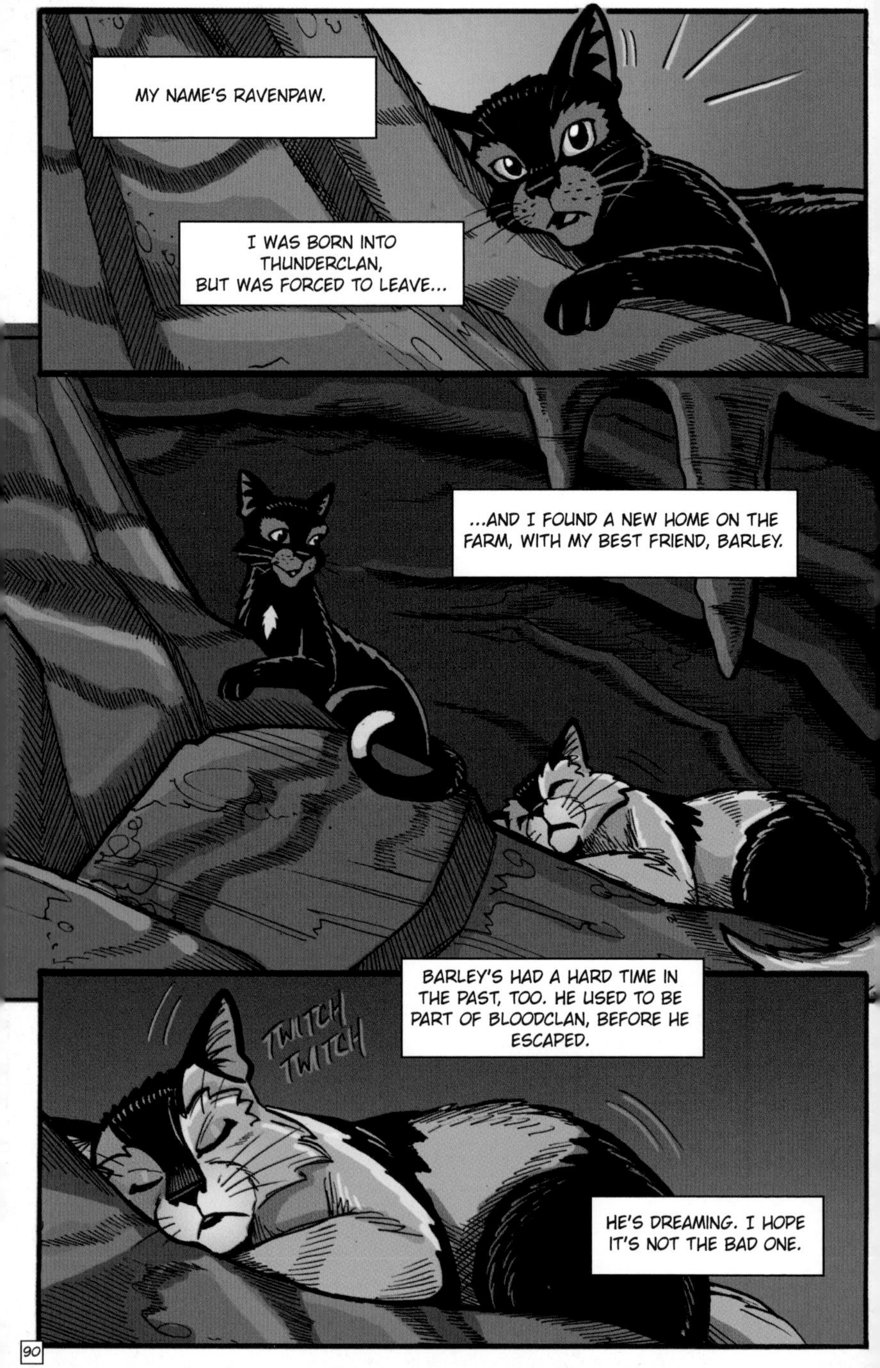
MY NAME'S RAVENPAW.
I WAS BORN INTO THUNDERCLAN, BUT WAS FORCED TO LEAVE...
...AND I FOUND A NEW HOME ON THE FARM, WITH MY BEST FRIEND, BARLEY.
BARLEY'S HAD A HARD TIME IN THE PAST, TOO. HE USED TO BE PART OF BLOODCLAN, BEFORE HE ESCAPED.
TWITCH
TWITCH
HE'S DREAMING. I HOPE IT'S NOT THE BAD ONE.

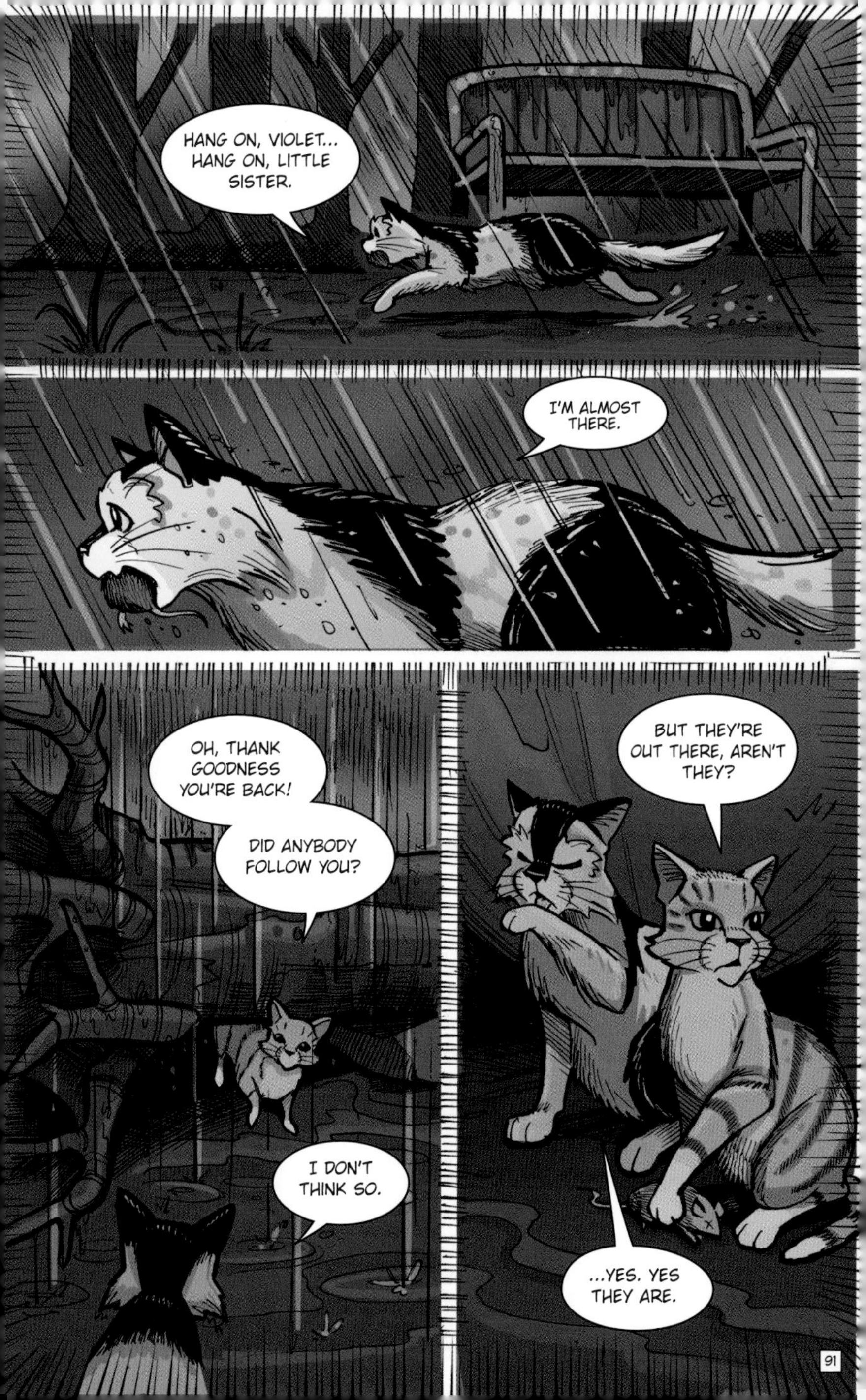
HANG ON, VIOLET...
HANG ON, LITTLE SISTER.
I'M ALMOST THERE.
OH, THANK GOODNESS YOU'RE BACK!
DID ANYBODY FOLLOW YOU?
I DON'T THINK SO.
BUT THEY'RE OUT THERE, AREN'T THEY?
...YES. YES THEY ARE.

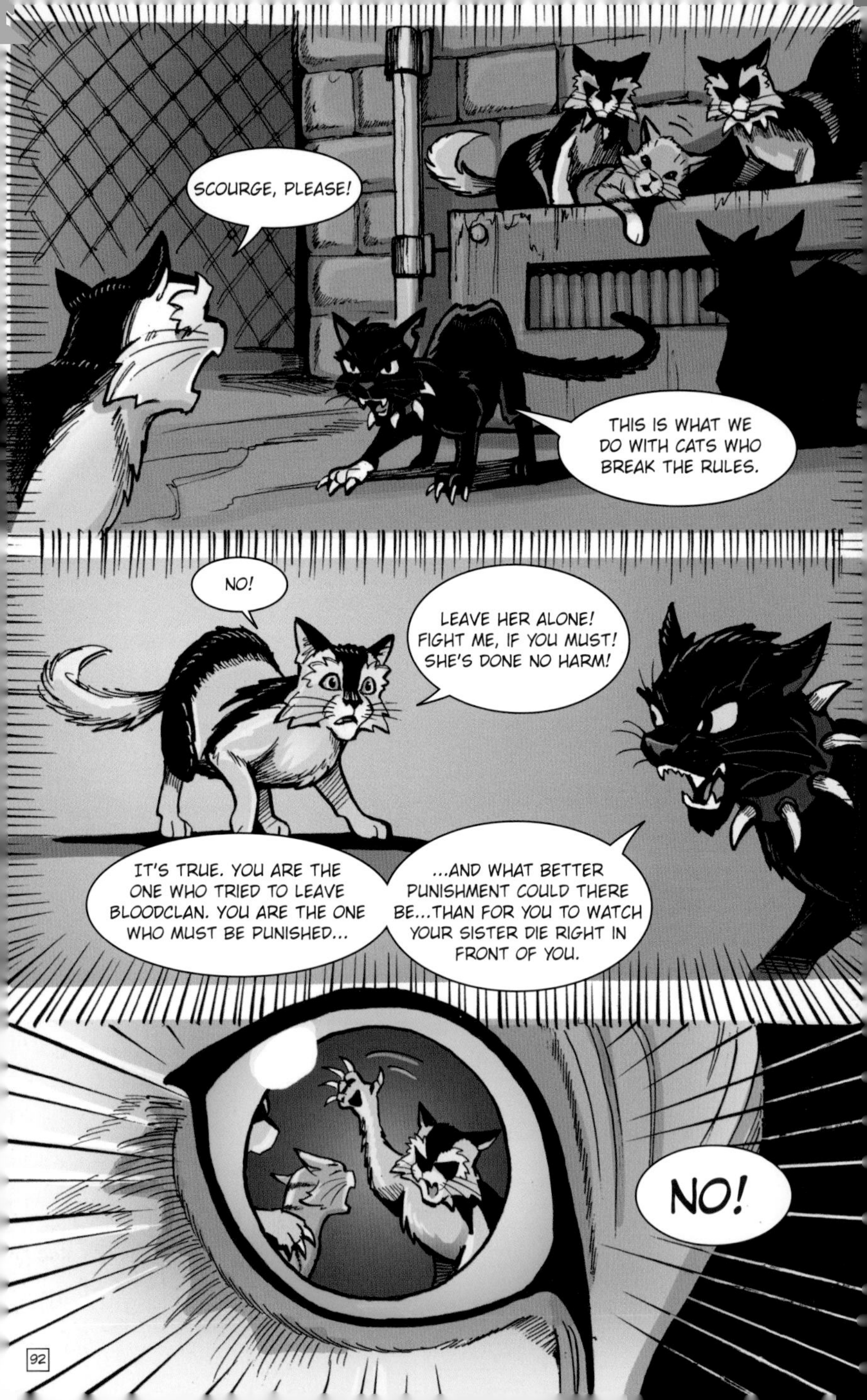
SCOURGE, PLEASE!
THIS IS WHAT WE DO WITH CATS WHO BREAK THE RULES.
NO!
LEAVE HER ALONE! FIGHT ME, IF YOU MUST! SHE'S DONE NO HARM!
IT'S TRUE. YOU ARE THE ONE WHO TRIED TO LEAVE BLOODCLAN. YOU ARE THE ONE WHO MUST BE PUNISHED...
...AND WHAT BETTER PUNISHMENT COULD THERE BE...THAN FOR YOU TO WATCH YOUR SISTER DIE RIGHT IN FRONT OF YOU.
NO!

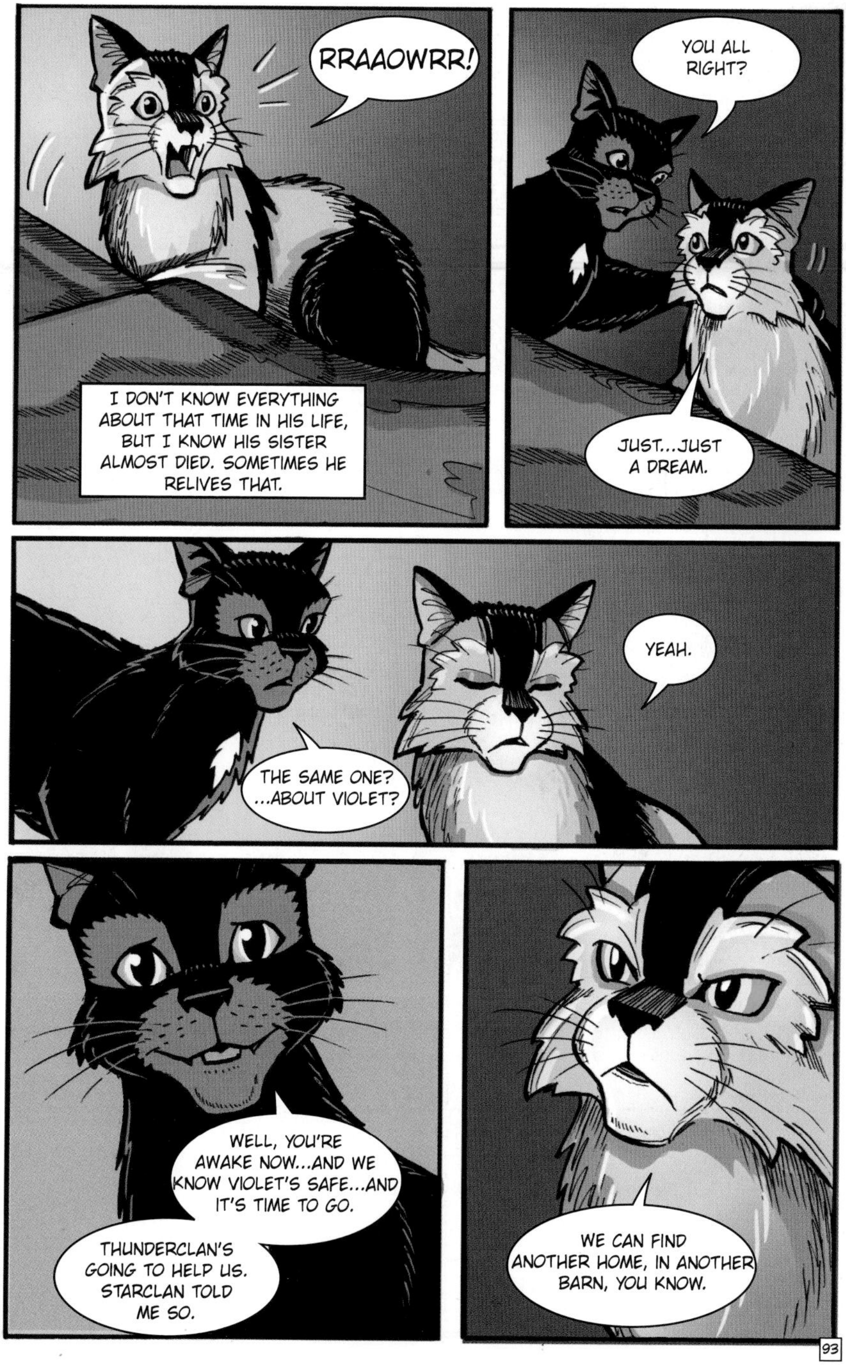
RRAAOWRR!
I DON'T KNOW EVERYTHING ABOUT THAT TIME IN HIS LIFE, BUT I KNOW HIS SISTER ALMOST DIED. SOMETIMES HE RELIVES THAT.
YOU ALL RIGHT?
JUST...JUST A DREAM.
THE SAME ONE? ...ABOUT VIOLET?
YEAH.
WELL, YOU'RE AWAKE NOW...AND WE KNOW VIOLET'S SAFE...AND IT'S TIME TO GO.
THUNDERCLAN'S GOING TO HELP US. STARCLAN TOLD ME SO.
WE CAN FIND ANOTHER HOME, IN ANOTHER BARN, YOU KNOW.

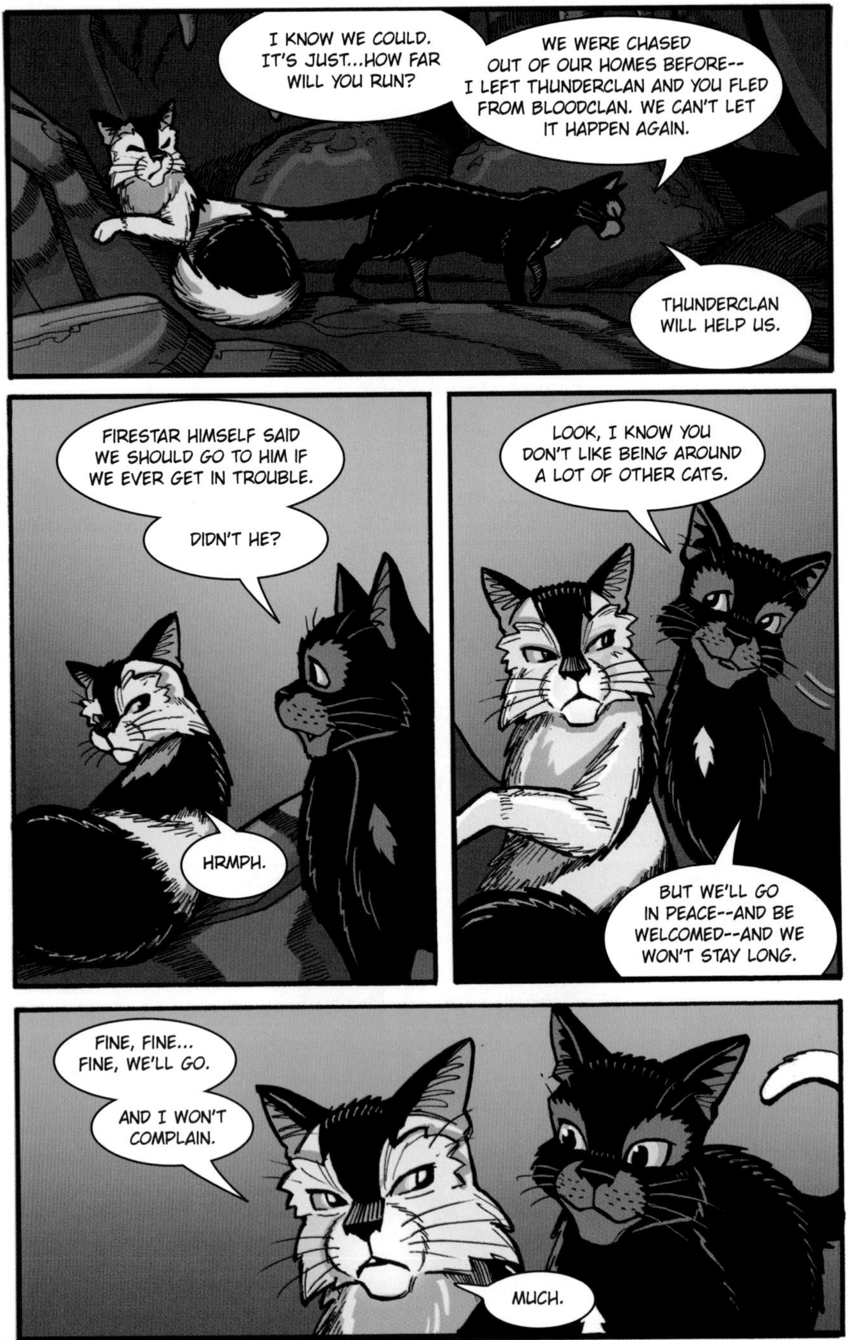
I KNOW WE COULD. IT'S JUST...HOW FAR WILL YOU RUN?
WE WERE CHASED OUT OF OUR HOMES BEFORE-- I LEFT THUNDERCLAN AND YOU FLED FROM BLOODCLAN. WE CAN'T LET IT HAPPEN AGAIN.
THUNDERCLAN WILL HELP US.
FIRESTAR HIMSELF SAID WE SHOULD GO TO HIM IF WE EVER GET IN TROUBLE.
DIDN'T HE?
HRMPH.
LOOK, I KNOW YOU DON'T LIKE BEING AROUND A LOT OF OTHER CATS.
BUT WE'LL GO IN PEACE--AND BE WELCOMED--AND WE WON'T STAY LONG.
FINE, FINE... FINE, WE'LL GO.
AND I WON'T COMPLAIN.
MUCH.

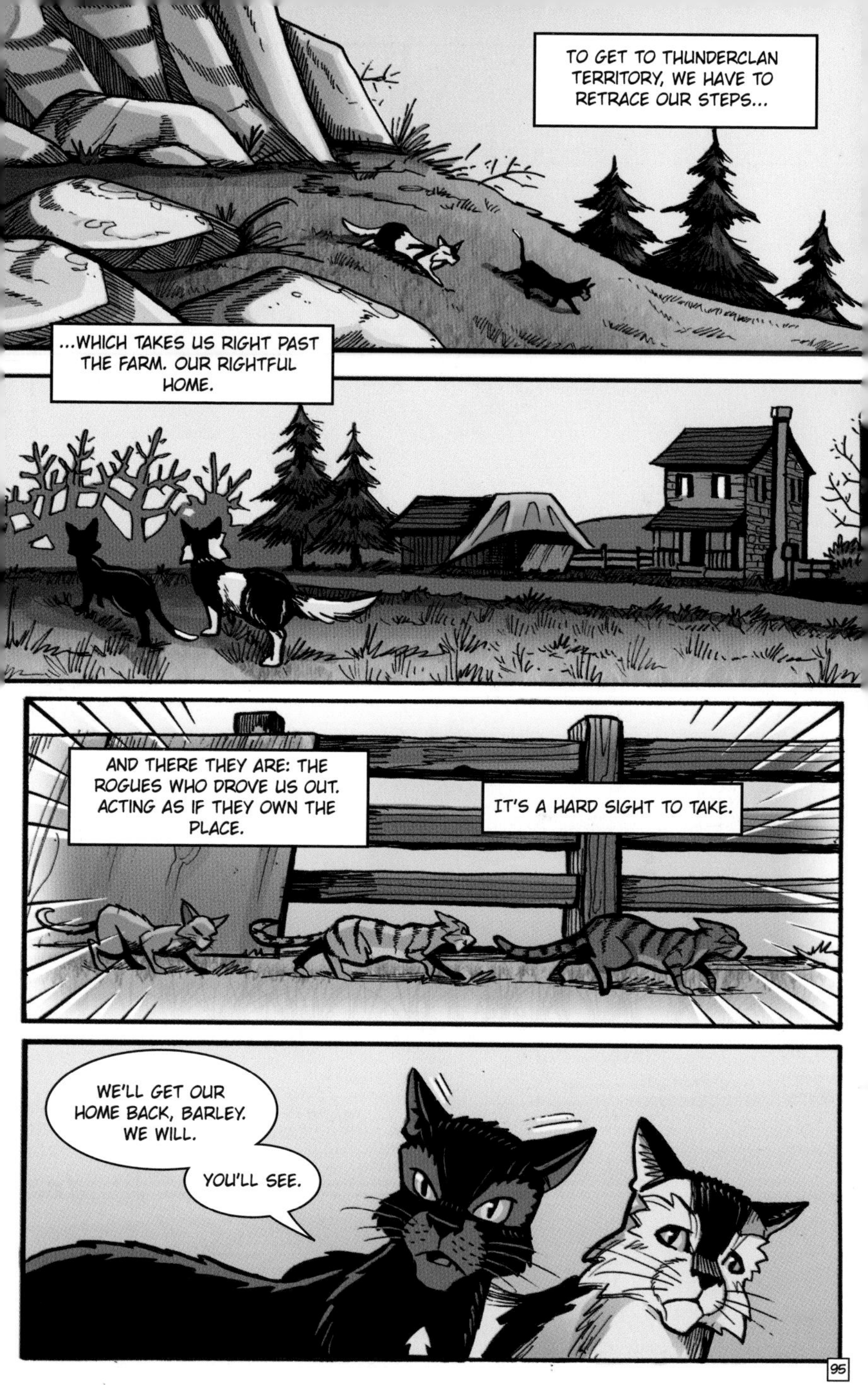
TO GET TO THUNDERCLAN TERRITORY, WE HAVE TO RETRACE OUR STEPS...
...WHICH TAKES US RIGHT PAST THE FARM. OUR RIGHTFUL HOME.
AND THERE THEY ARE: THE ROGUES WHO DROVE US OUT. ACTING AS IF THEY OWN THE PLACE.
IT'S A HARD SIGHT TO TAKE.
WE'LL GET OUR HOME BACK, BARLEY. WE WILL.
YOU'LL SEE.

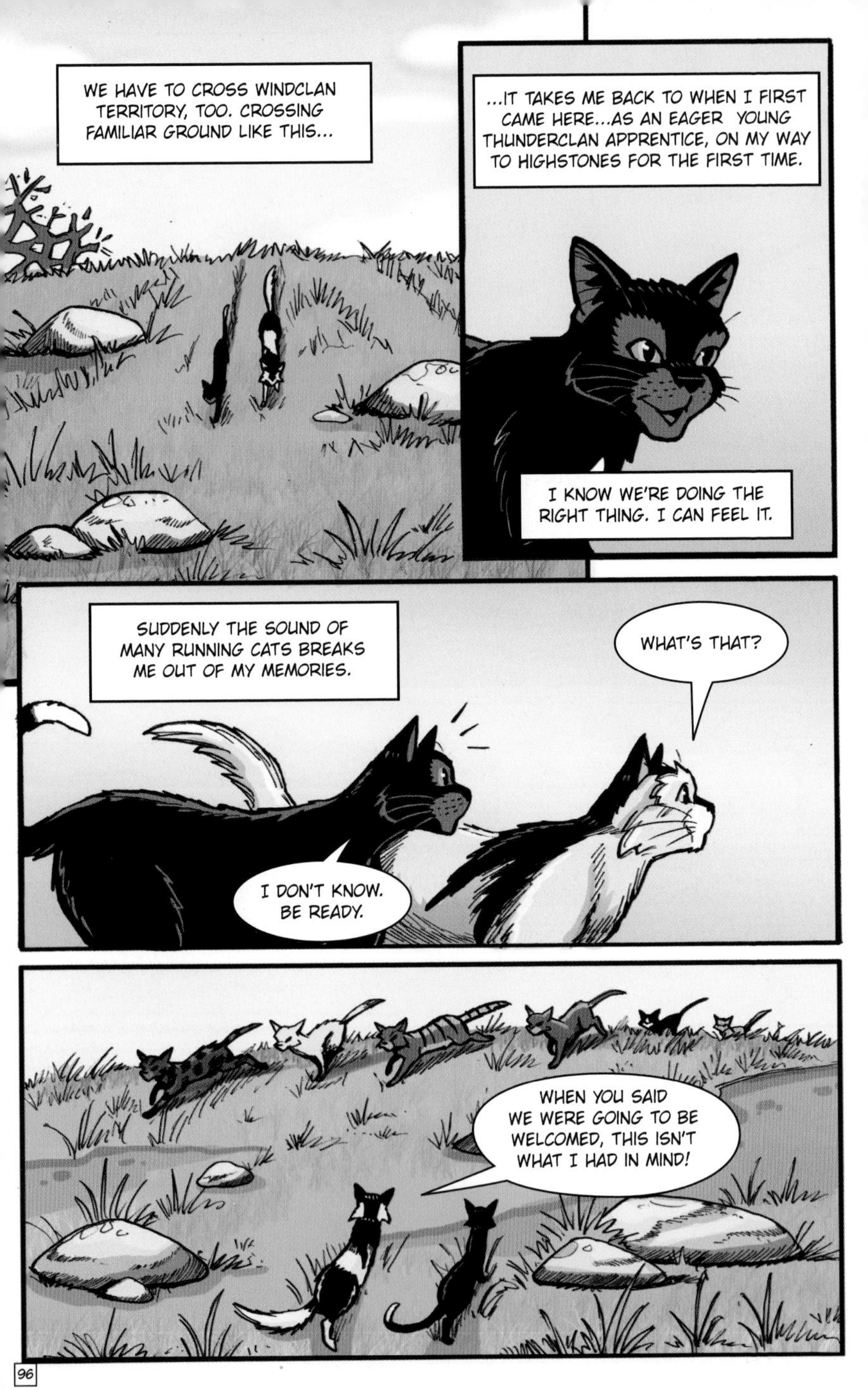

WE HAVE TO CROSS WINDCLAN TERRITORY, TOO. CROSSING FAMILIAR GROUND LIKE THIS...
...IT TAKES ME BACK TO WHEN I FIRST CAME HERE...AS AN EAGER YOUNG THUNDERCLAN APPRENTICE, ON MY WAY TO HIGHSTONES FOR THE FIRST TIME.
I KNOW WE'RE DOING THE RIGHT THING. I CAN FEEL IT.
SUDDENLY THE SOUND OF MANY RUNNING CATS BREAKS ME OUT OF MY MEMORIES.
WHAT'S THAT?
I DON'T KNOW. BE READY.
WHEN YOU SAID WE WERE GOING TO BE WELCOMED, THIS ISN'T WHAT I HAD IN MIND!

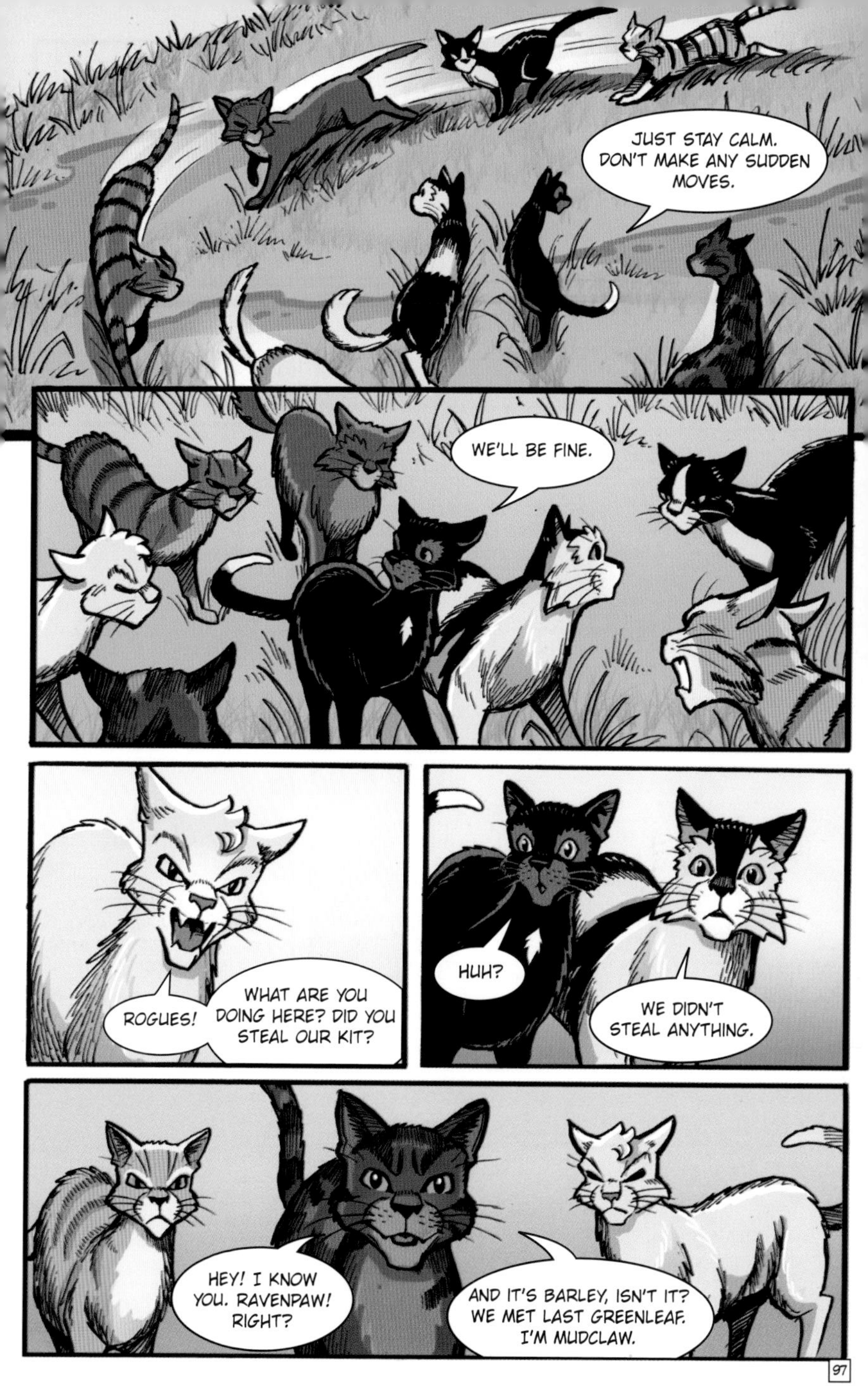
JUST STAY CALM. DON'T MAKE ANY SUDDEN MOVES.
WE'LL BE FINE.
ROGUES!
WHAT ARE YOU DOING HERE? DID YOU STEAL OUR KIT?
HUH?
WE DIDN'T STEAL ANYTHING.
HEY! I KNOW YOU. RAVENPAW! RIGHT?
AND IT'S BARLEY, ISN'T IT? WE MET LAST GREENLEAF. I'M MUDCLAW.

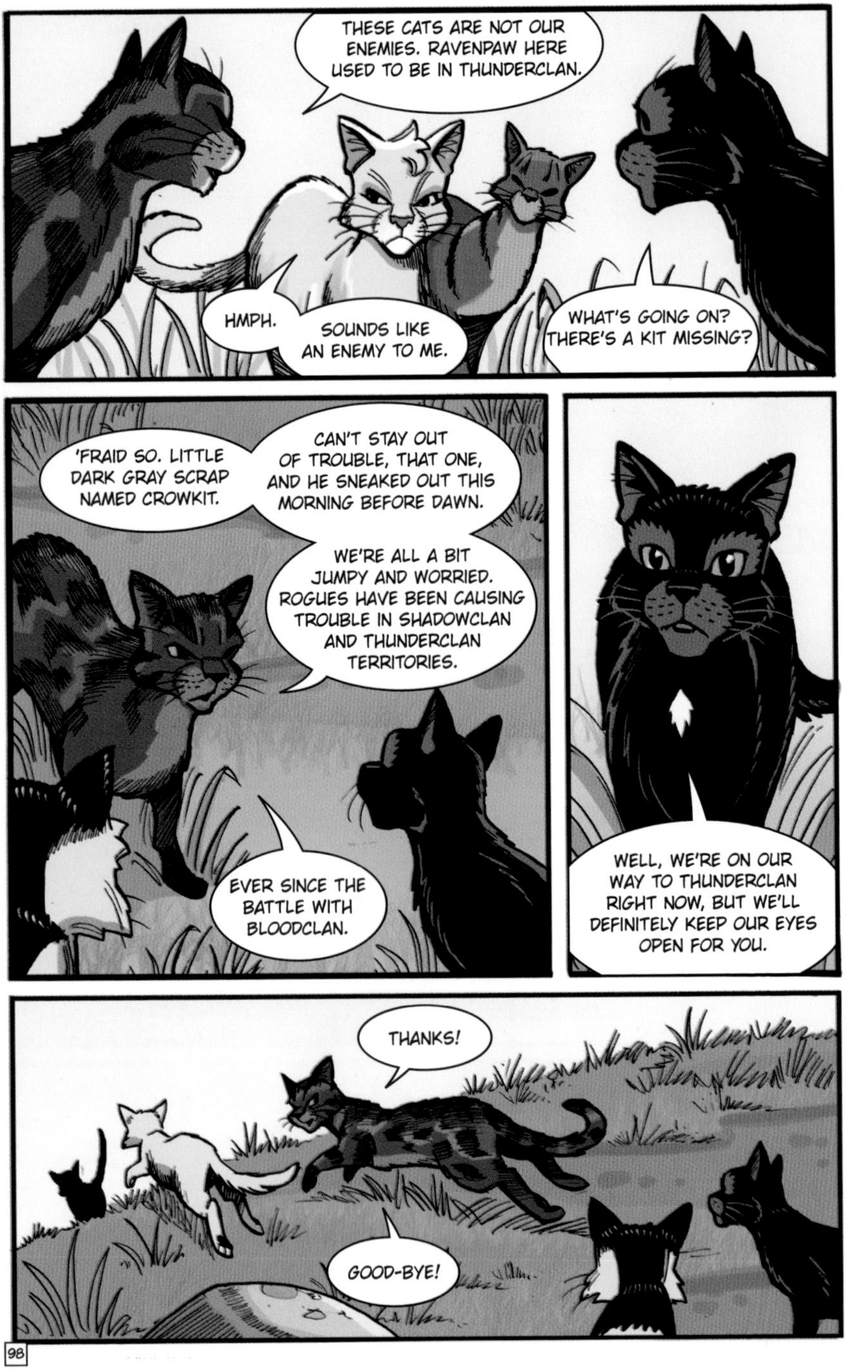
THESE CATS ARE NOT OUR ENEMIES. RAVENPAW HERE USED TO BE IN THUNDERCLAN.
HMPH.
SOUNDS LIKE AN ENEMY TO ME.
WHAT'S GOING ON? THERE'S A KIT MISSING?
'FRAID SO. LITTLE DARK GRAY SCRAP NAMED CROWKIT.
CAN'T STAY OUT OF TROUBLE, THAT ONE, AND HE SNEAKED OUT THIS MORNING BEFORE DAWN.
WE'RE ALL A BIT JUMPY AND WORRIED. ROGUES HAVE BEEN CAUSING TROUBLE IN SHADOWCLAN AND THUNDERCLAN TERRITORIES.
EVER SINCE THE BATTLE WITH BLOODCLAN.
WELL, WE'RE ON OUR WAY TO THUNDERCLAN RIGHT NOW, BUT WE'LL DEFINITELY KEEP OUR EYES OPEN FOR YOU.
THANKS!
GOOD-BYE!

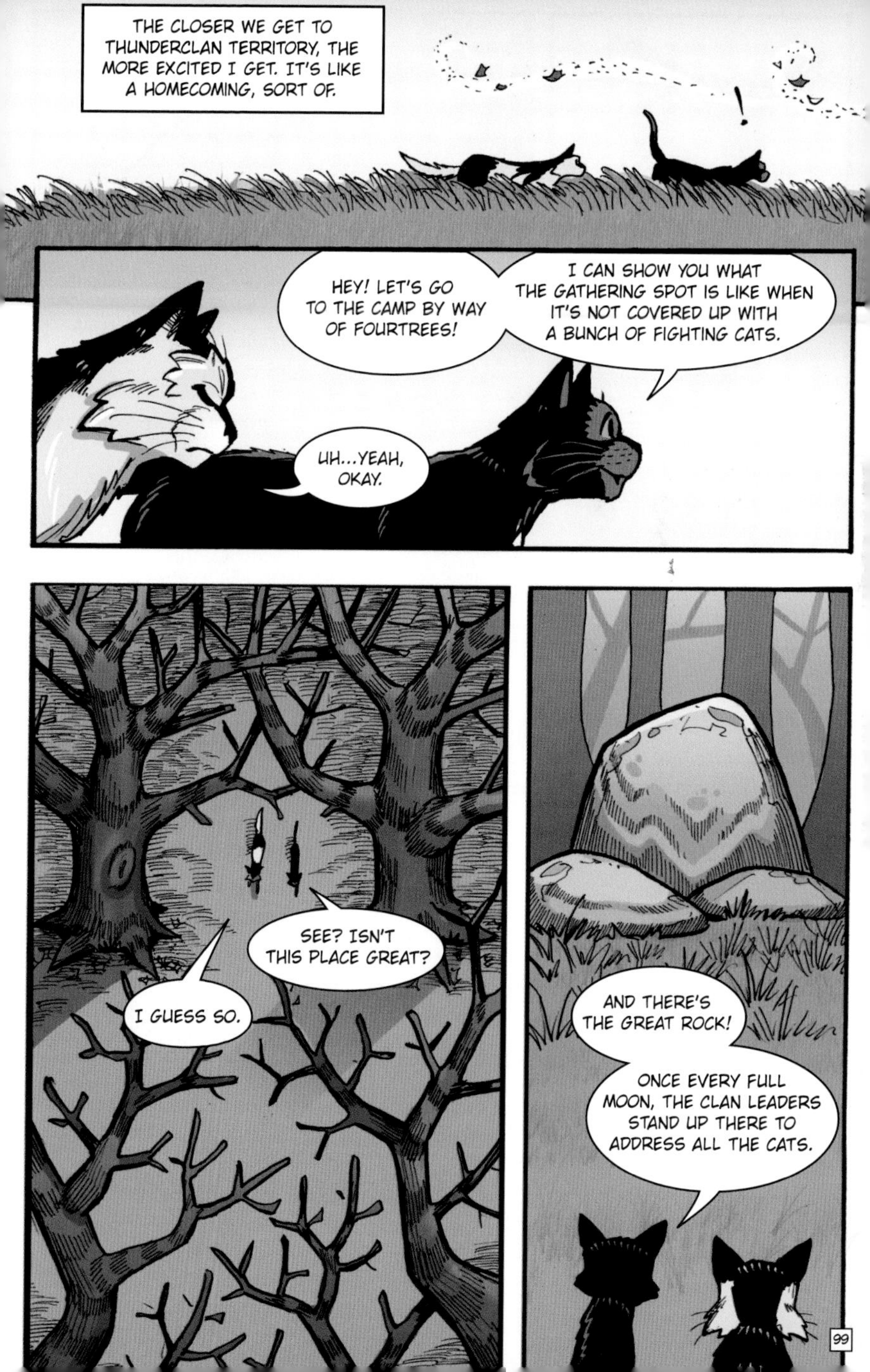
THE CLOSER WE GET TO THUNDERCLAN TERRITORY, THE MORE EXCITED I GET. IT'S LIKE A HOMECOMING, SORT OF.
!
HEY! LET'S GO TO THE CAMP BY WAY OF FOURTREES!
I CAN SHOW YOU WHAT THE GATHERING SPOT IS LIKE WHEN IT'S NOT COVERED UP WITH A BUNCH OF FIGHTING CATS.
UH...YEAH, OKAY.
SEE? ISN'T THIS PLACE GREAT?
I GUESS SO.
AND THERE'S THE GREAT ROCK!
ONCE EVERY FULL MOON, THE CLAN LEADERS STAND UP THERE TO ADDRESS ALL THE CATS.

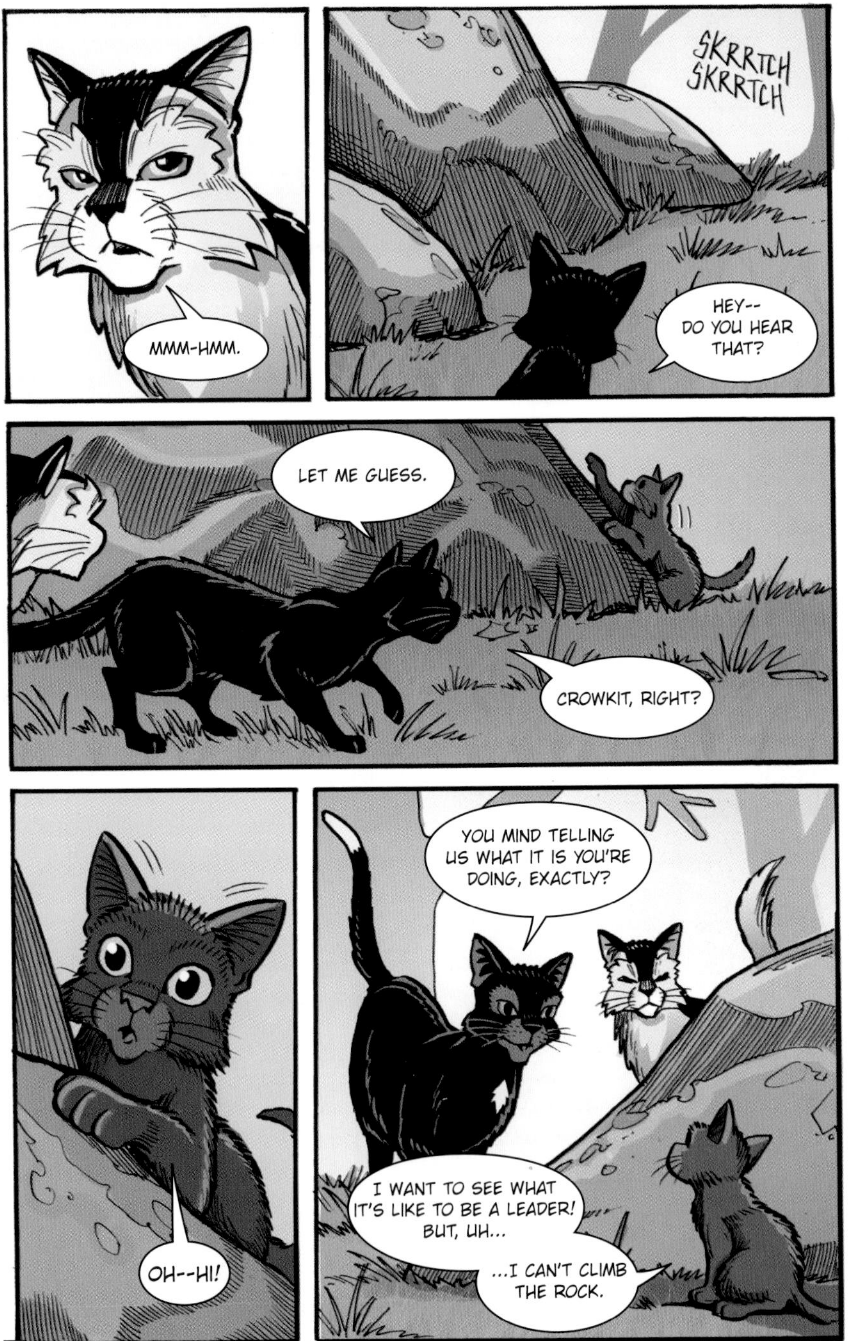
MMM-HMM.
SKRRTCH
SKRRTCH
HEY--
DO YOU HEAR
THAT?
LET ME GUESS.
CROWKIT, RIGHT?
OH--HI!
YOU MIND TELLING
US WHAT IT IS YOU'RE
DOING, EXACTLY?
I WANT TO SEE WHAT
IT'S LIKE TO BE A LEADER!
BUT, UH...
...I CAN'T CLIMB
THE ROCK.

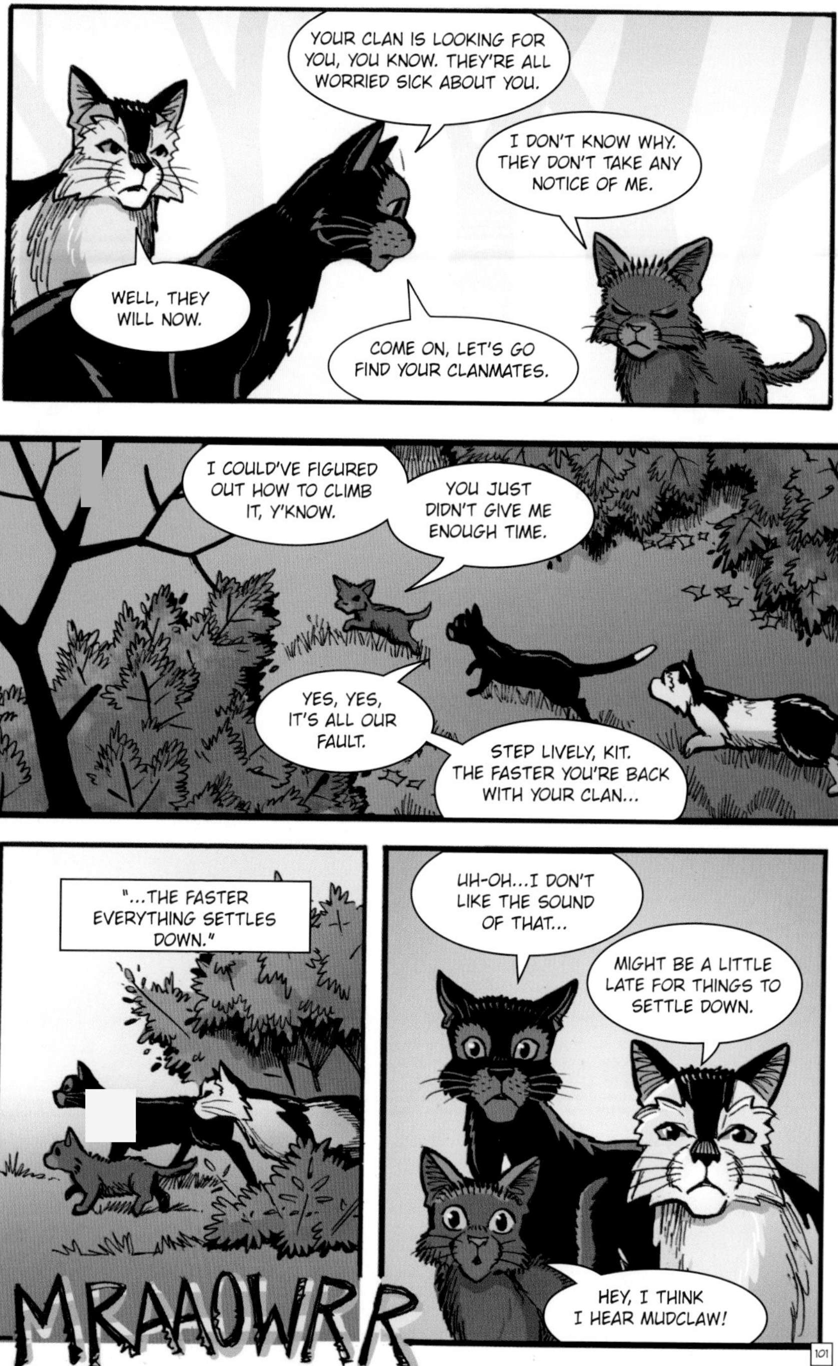
YOUR CLAN IS LOOKING FOR YOU, YOU KNOW. THEY'RE ALL WORRIED SICK ABOUT YOU.
I DON'T KNOW WHY. THEY DON'T TAKE ANY NOTICE OF ME.
WELL, THEY WILL NOW.
COME ON, LET'S GO FIND YOUR CLANMATES.
I COULD'VE FIGURED OUT HOW TO CLIMB IT, Y'KNOW.
YOU JUST DIDN'T GIVE ME ENOUGH TIME.
YES, YES, IT'S ALL OUR FAULT.
STEP LIVELY, KIT. THE FASTER YOU'RE BACK WITH YOUR CLAN...
"...THE FASTER EVERYTHING SETTLES DOWN."
MRAAOWRR
UH-OH...I DON'T LIKE THE SOUND OF THAT...
MIGHT BE A LITTLE LATE FOR THINGS TO SETTLE DOWN.
HEY, I THINK I HEAR MUDCLAW!

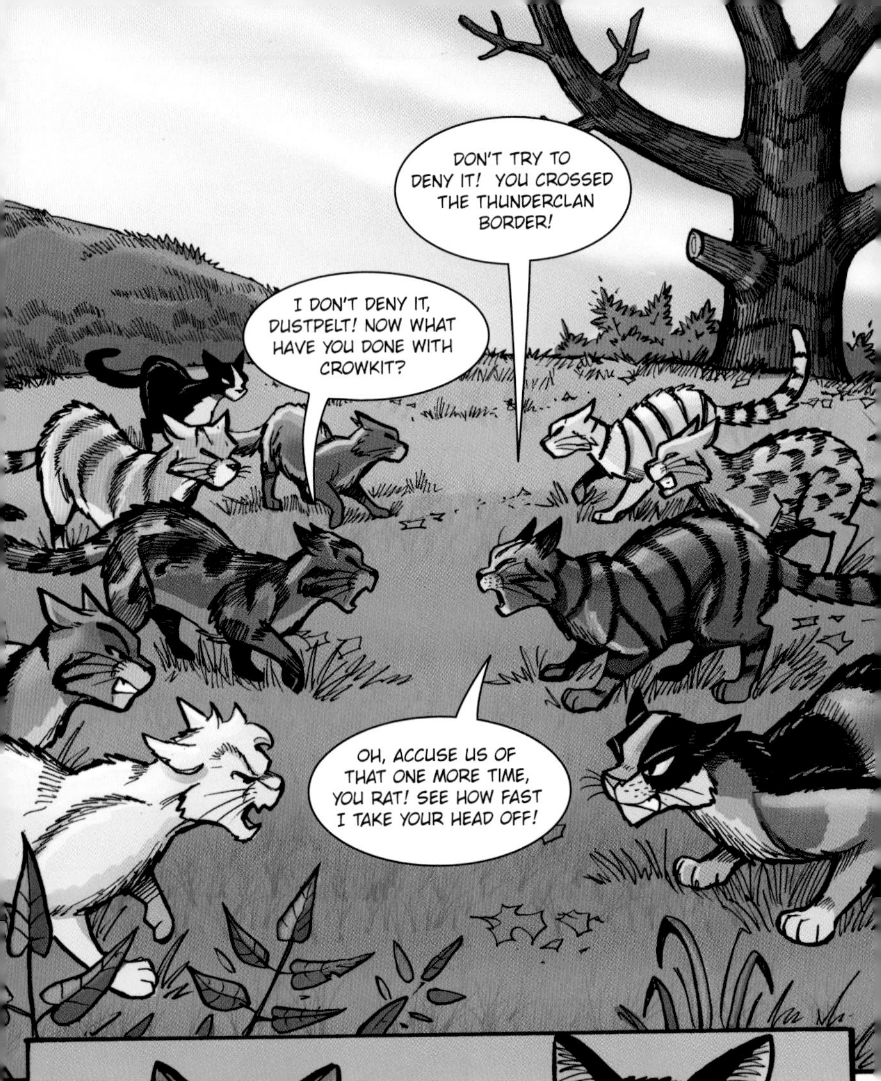
DON'T TRY TO DENY IT! YOU CROSSED THE THUNDERCLAN BORDER!
I DON'T DENY IT, DUSTPELT! NOW WHAT HAVE YOU DONE WITH CROWKIT?
OH, ACCUSE US OF THAT ONE MORE TIME, YOU RAT! SEE HOW FAST I TAKE YOUR HEAD OFF!

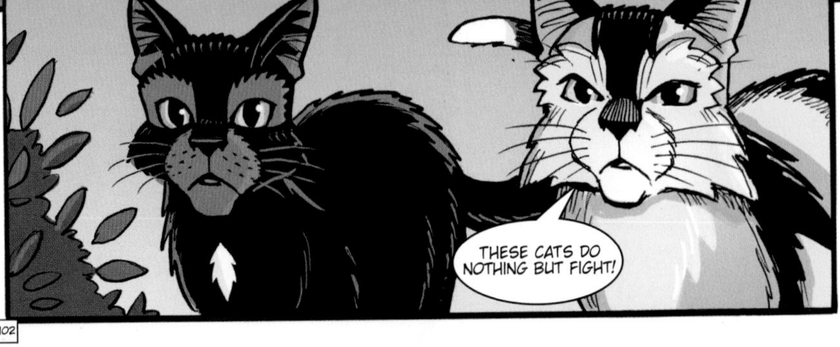
THESE CATS DO NOTHING BUT FIGHT!

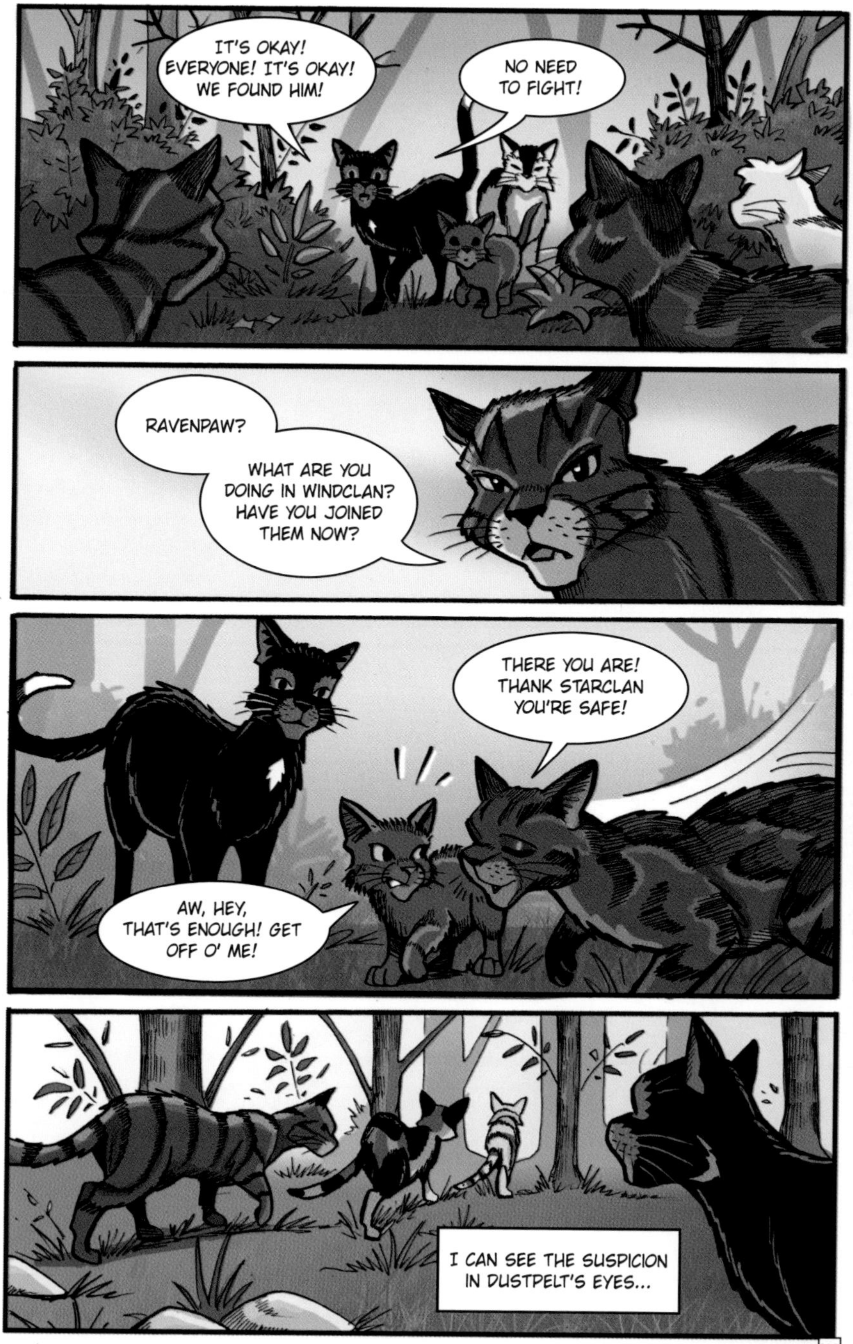
IT'S OKAY! EVERYONE! IT'S OKAY! WE FOUND HIM!
NO NEED TO FIGHT!
RAVENPAW?
WHAT ARE YOU DOING IN WINDCLAN? HAVE YOU JOINED THEM NOW?
THERE YOU ARE! THANK STARCLAN YOU'RE SAFE!
AW, HEY, THAT'S ENOUGH! GET OFF O' ME!
I CAN SEE THE SUSPICION IN DUSTPELT'S EYES...

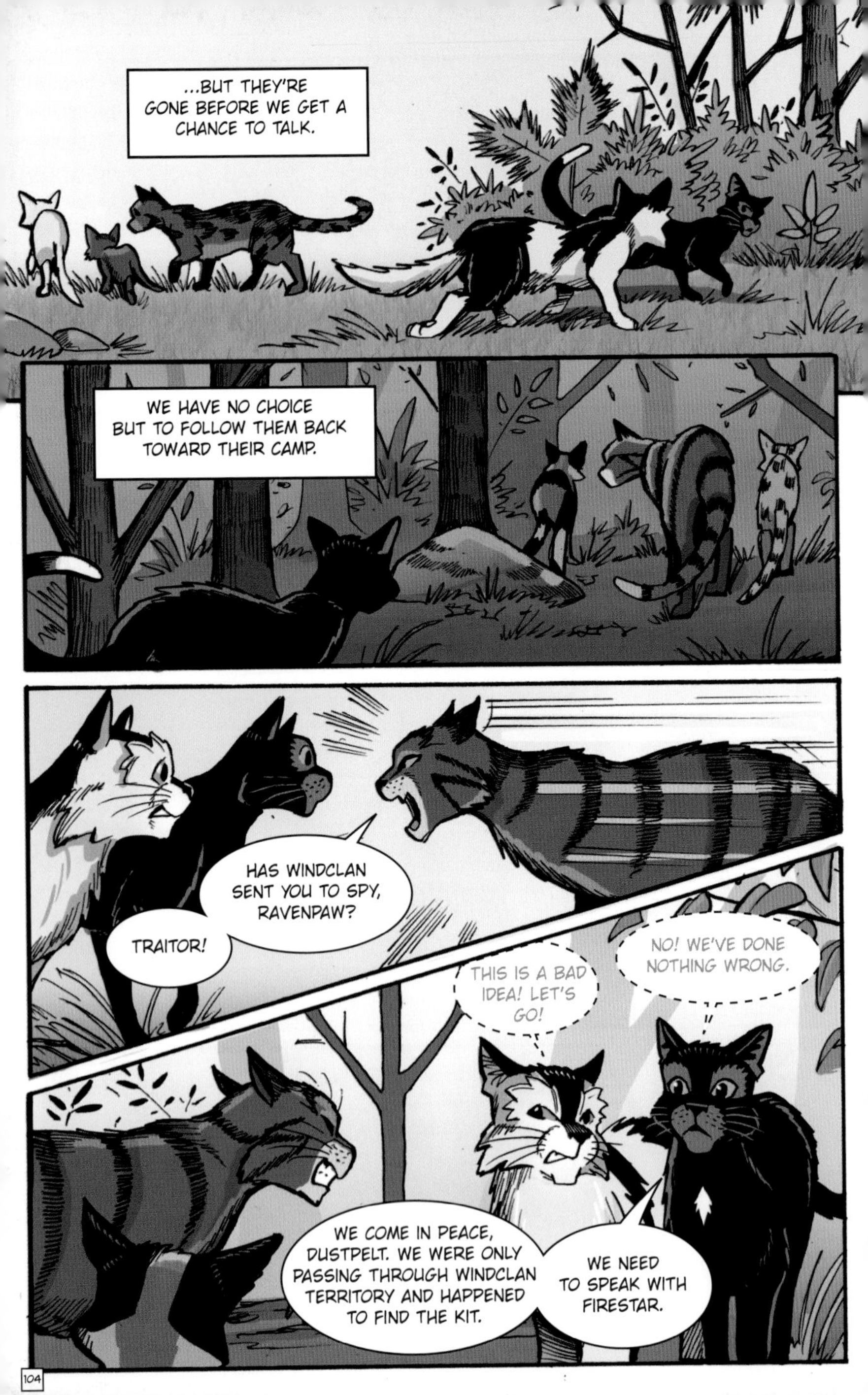

...BUT THEY'RE GONE BEFORE WE GET A CHANCE TO TALK.
WE HAVE NO CHOICE BUT TO FOLLOW THEM BACK TOWARD THEIR CAMP.
HAS WINDCLAN SENT YOU TO SPY, RAVENPAW?
TRAITOR!
THIS IS A BAD IDEA! LET'S GO!
NO! WE'VE DONE NOTHING WRONG.
WE COME IN PEACE, DUSTPELT. WE WERE ONLY PASSING THROUGH WINDCLAN TERRITORY AND HAPPENED TO FIND THE KIT.
WE NEED TO SPEAK WITH FIRESTAR.

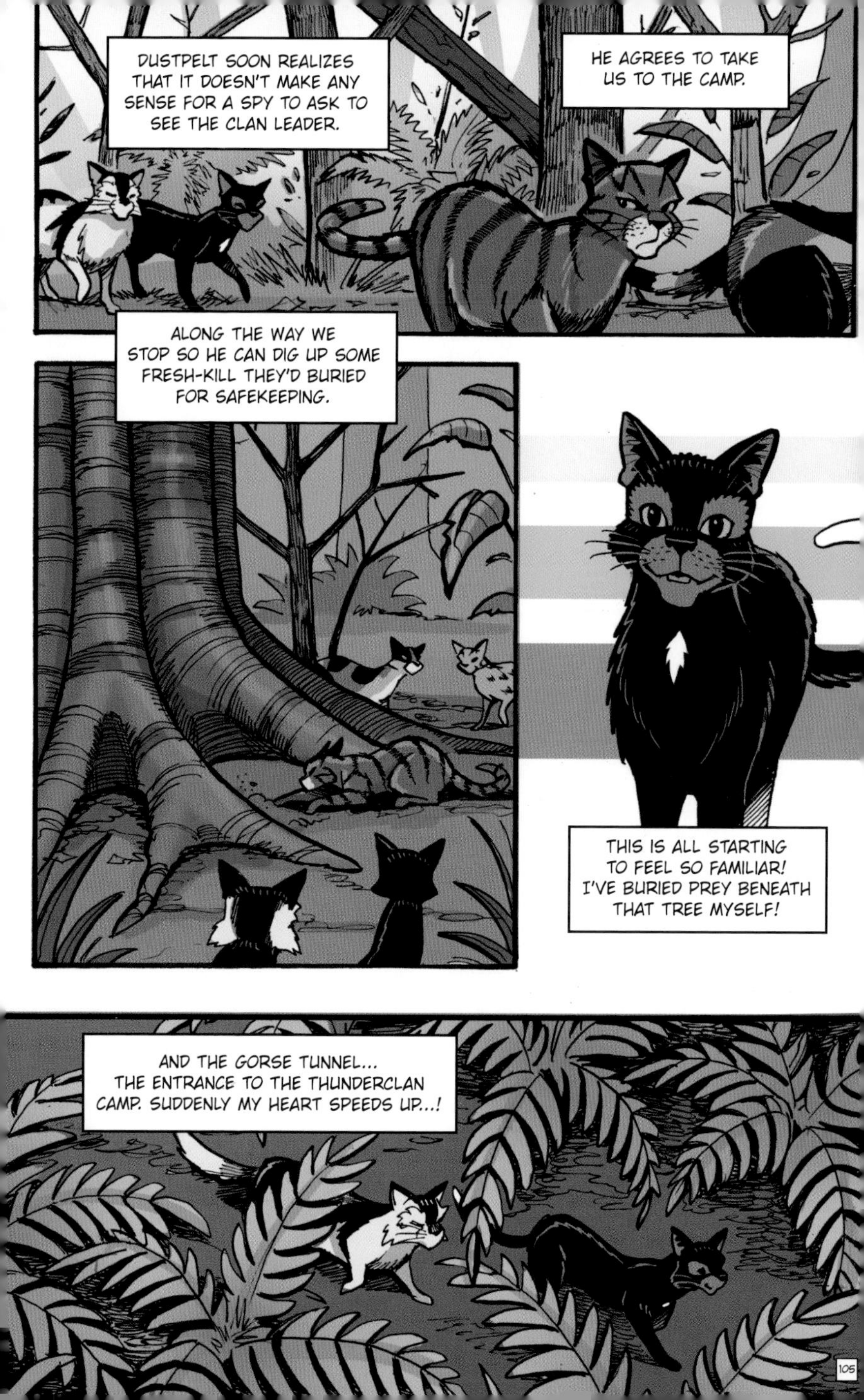
DUSTPELT SOON REALIZES THAT IT DOESN'T MAKE ANY SENSE FOR A SPY TO ASK TO SEE THE CLAN LEADER.
HE AGREES TO TAKE US TO THE CAMP.
ALONG THE WAY WE STOP SO HE CAN DIG UP SOME FRESH-KILL THEY'D BURIED FOR SAFEKEEPING.
THIS IS ALL STARTING TO FEEL SO FAMILIAR! I'VE BURIED PREY BENEATH THAT TREE MYSELF!
AND THE GORSE TUNNEL... THE ENTRANCE TO THE THUNDERCLAN CAMP. SUDDENLY MY HEART SPEEDS UP...!

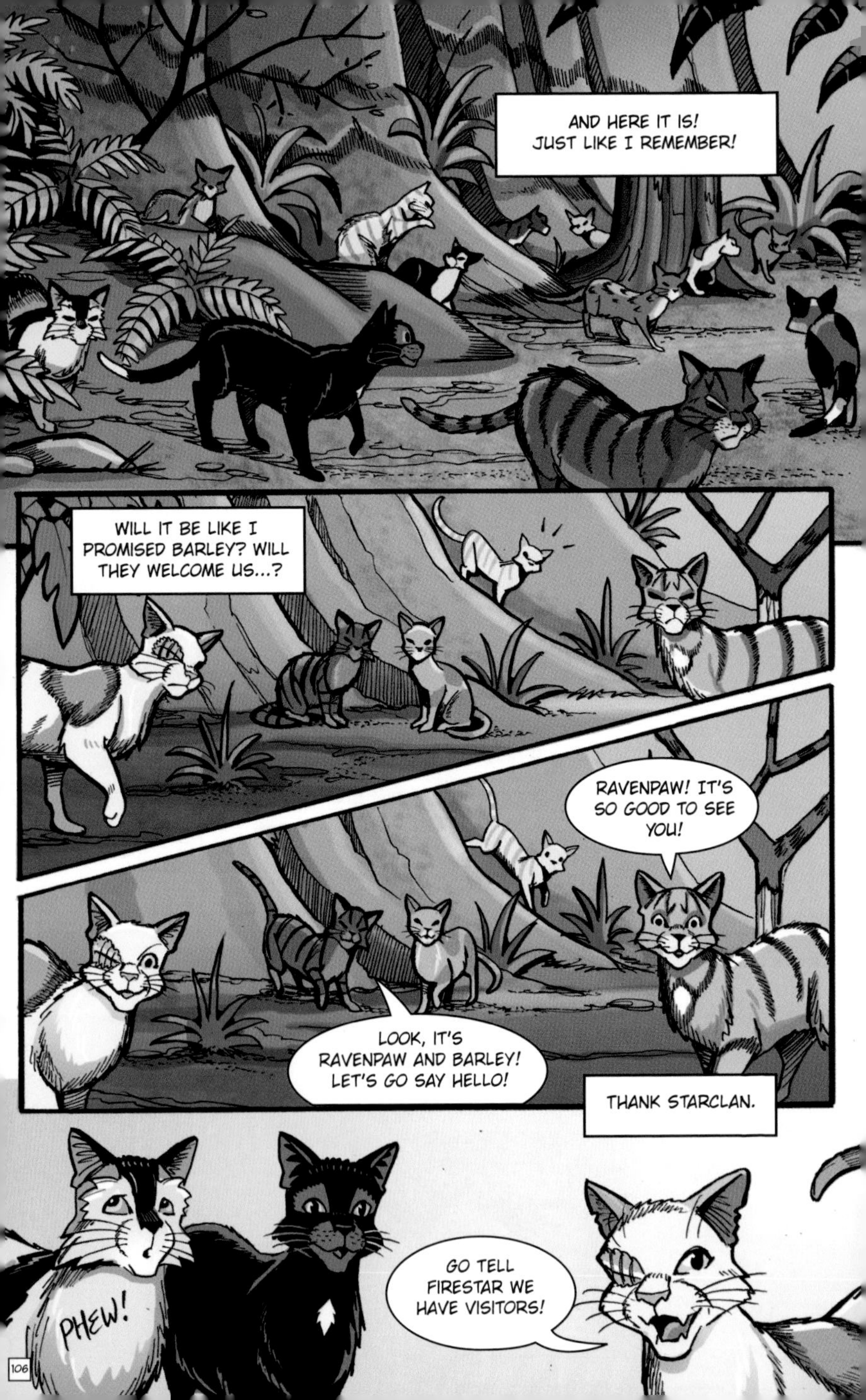
AND HERE IT IS! JUST LIKE I REMEMBER!
WILL IT BE LIKE I PROMISED BARLEY? WILL THEY WELCOME US...?
RAVENPAW! IT'S SO GOOD TO SEE YOU!
LOOK, IT'S RAVENPAW AND BARLEY! LET'S GO SAY HELLO!
THANK STARCLAN.
PHEW!
GO TELL FIRESTAR WE HAVE VISITORS!

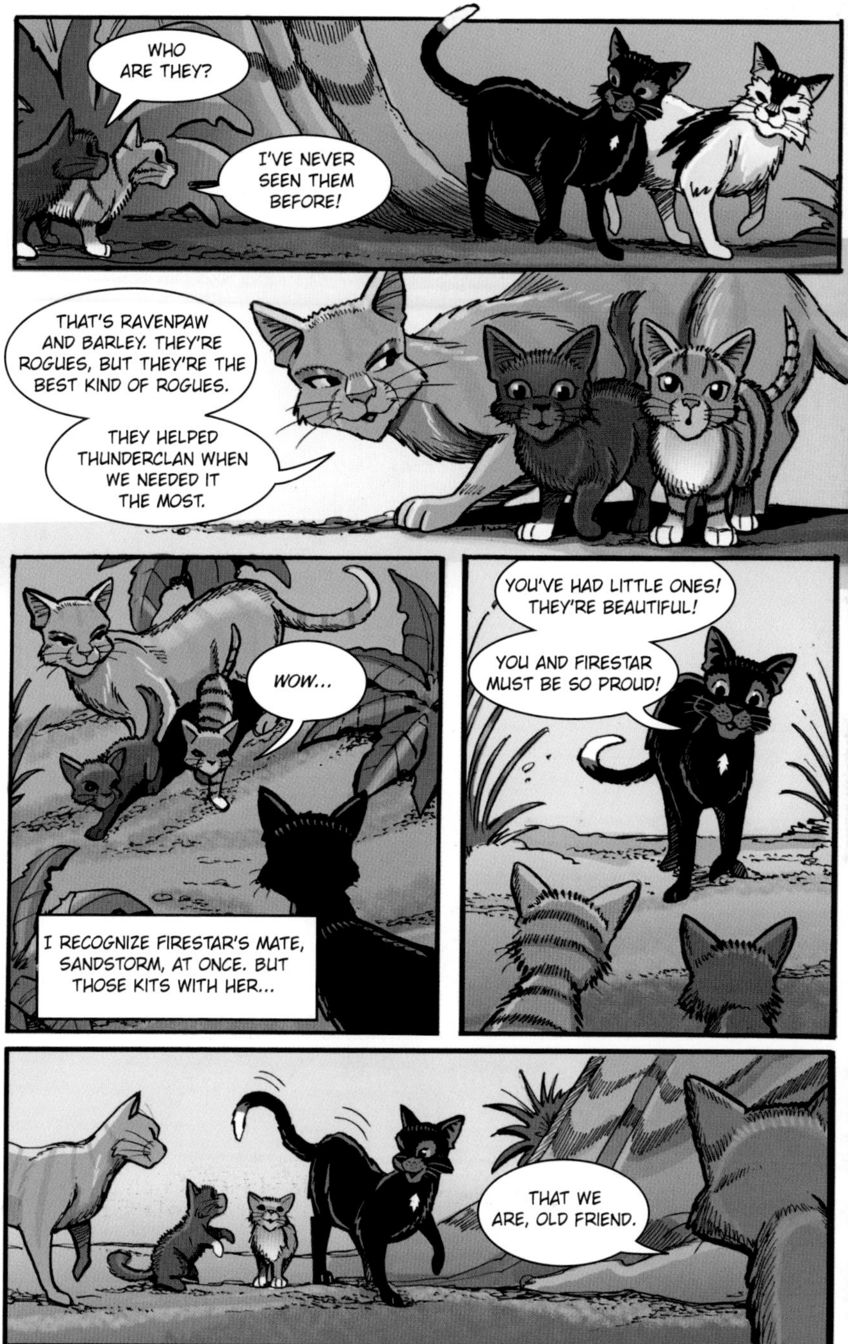
WHO ARE THEY?
I'VE NEVER SEEN THEM BEFORE!
THAT'S RAVENPAW AND BARLEY. THEY'RE ROGUES, BUT THEY'RE THE BEST KIND OF ROGUES.
THEY HELPED THUNDERCLAN WHEN WE NEEDED IT THE MOST.
WOW...
I RECOGNIZE FIRESTAR'S MATE, SANDSTORM, AT ONCE. BUT THOSE KITS WITH HER...
YOU'VE HAD LITTLE ONES! THEY'RE BEAUTIFUL!
YOU AND FIRESTAR MUST BE SO PROUD!
THAT WE ARE, OLD FRIEND.

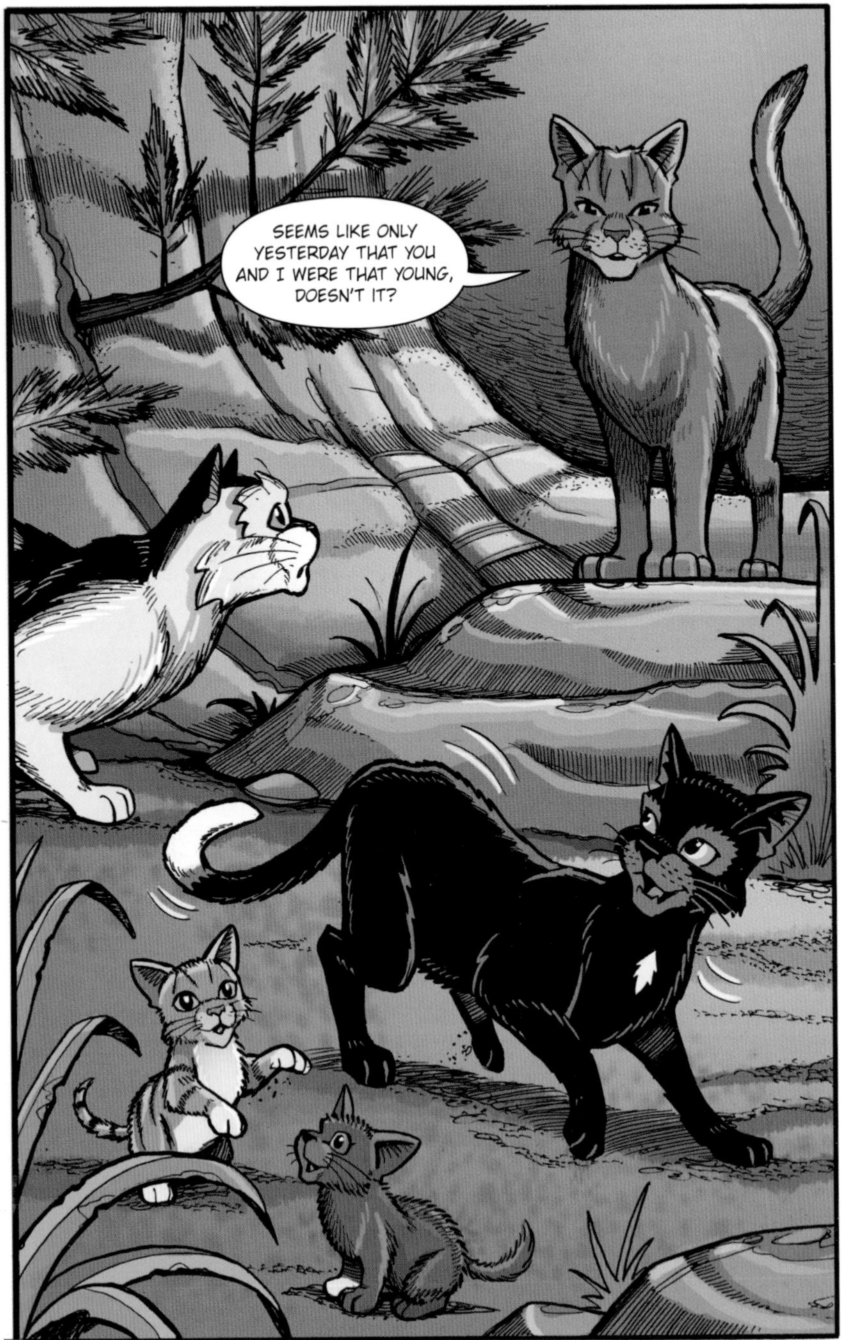
SEEMS LIKE ONLY YESTERDAY THAT YOU AND I WERE THAT YOUNG, DOESN'T IT?

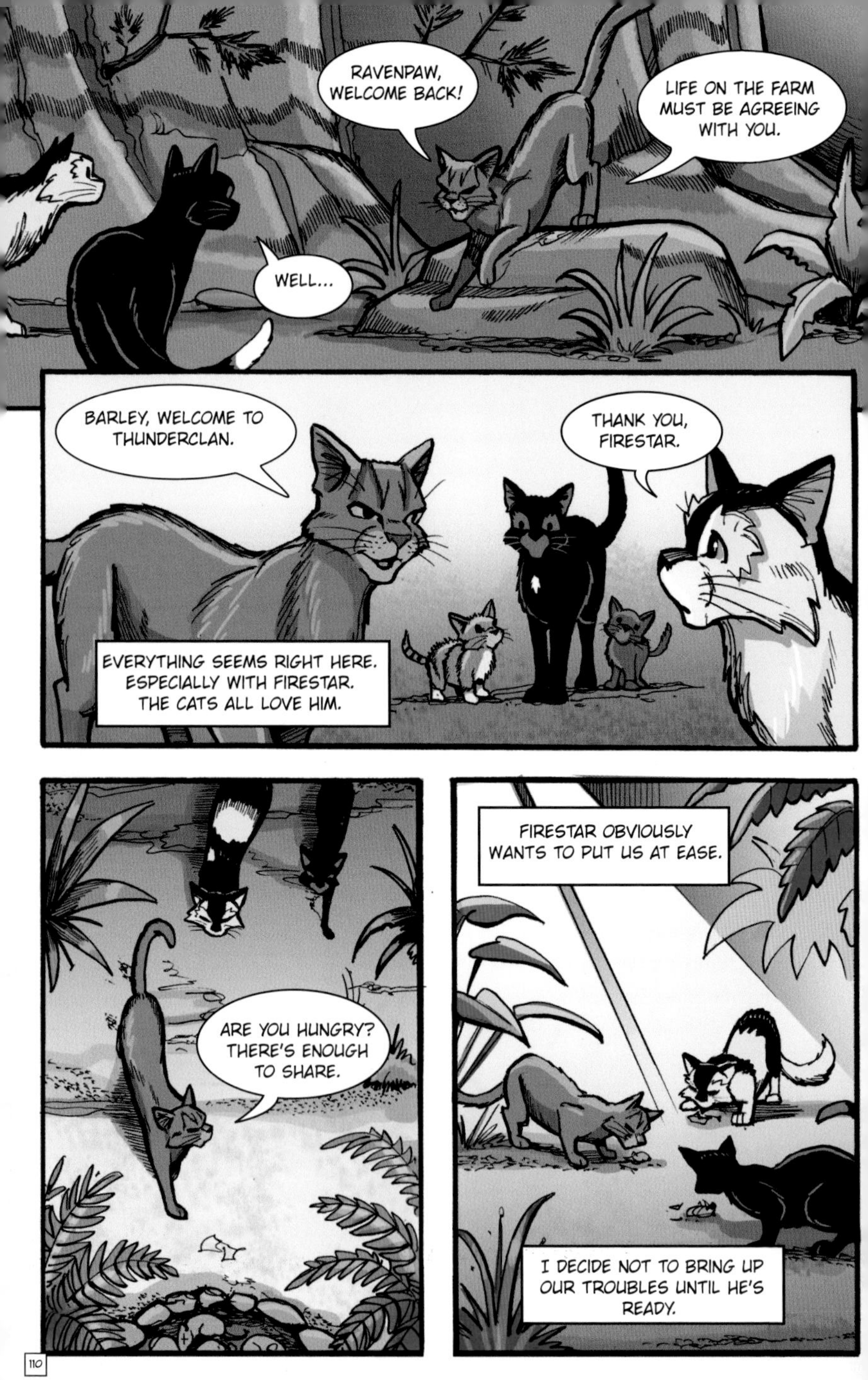
RAVENPAW, WELCOME BACK!
LIFE ON THE FARM MUST BE AGREEING WITH YOU.
WELL...
BARLEY, WELCOME TO THUNDERCLAN.
THANK YOU, FIRESTAR.
EVERYTHING SEEMS RIGHT HERE. ESPECIALLY WITH FIRESTAR. THE CATS ALL LOVE HIM.
ARE YOU HUNGRY? THERE'S ENOUGH TO SHARE.
FIRESTAR OBVIOUSLY WANTS TO PUT US AT EASE.
I DECIDE NOT TO BRING UP OUR TROUBLES UNTIL HE'S READY.

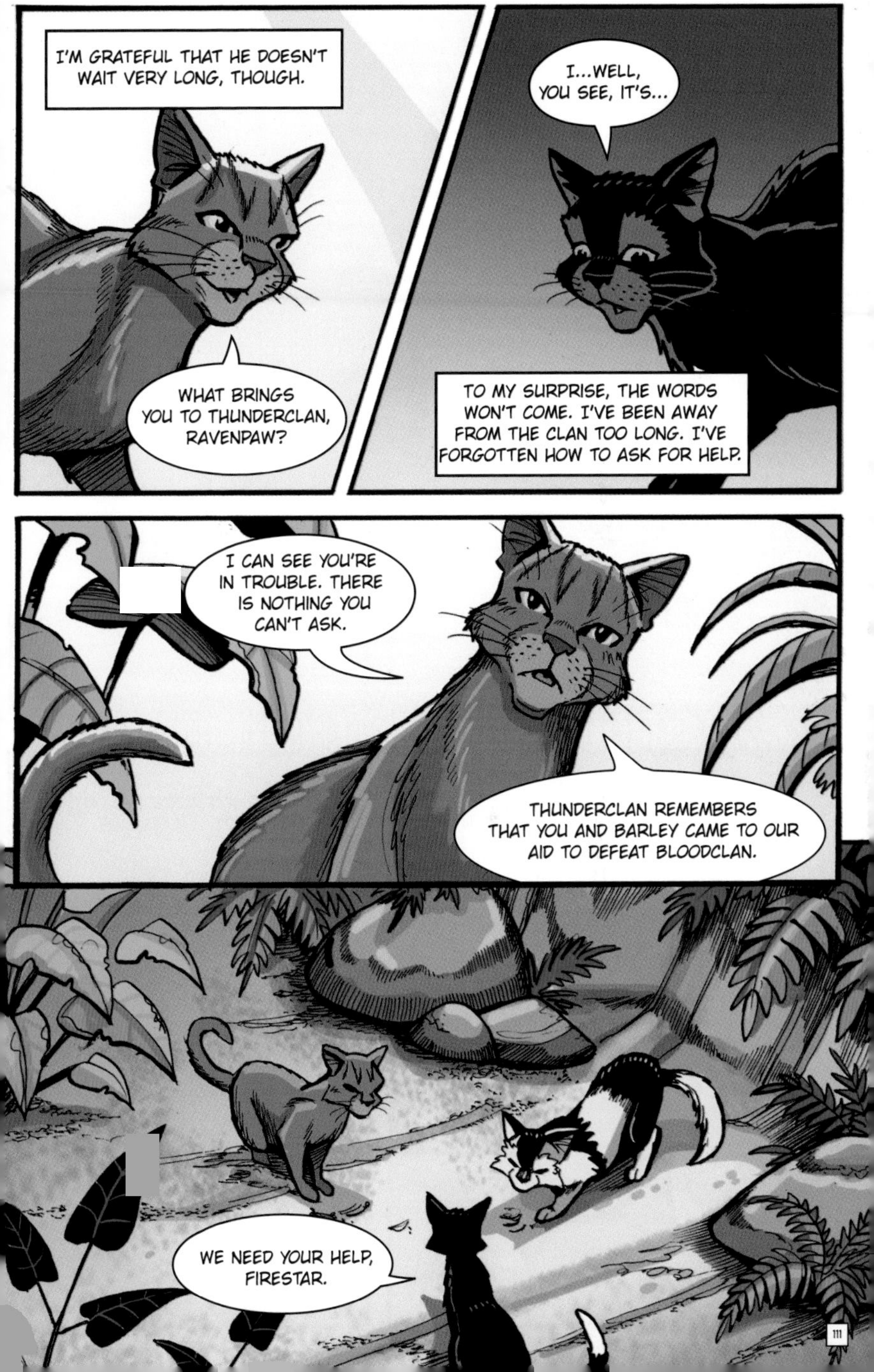
I'M GRATEFUL THAT HE DOESN'T WAIT VERY LONG, THOUGH.
WHAT BRINGS YOU TO THUNDERCLAN, RAVENPAW?
I...WELL, YOU SEE, IT'S...
TO MY SURPRISE, THE WORDS WON'T COME. I'VE BEEN AWAY FROM THE CLAN TOO LONG. I'VE FORGOTTEN HOW TO ASK FOR HELP.
I CAN SEE YOU'RE IN TROUBLE. THERE IS NOTHING YOU CAN'T ASK.
THUNDERCLAN REMEMBERS THAT YOU AND BARLEY CAME TO OUR AID TO DEFEAT BLOODCLAN.
WE NEED YOUR HELP, FIRESTAR.

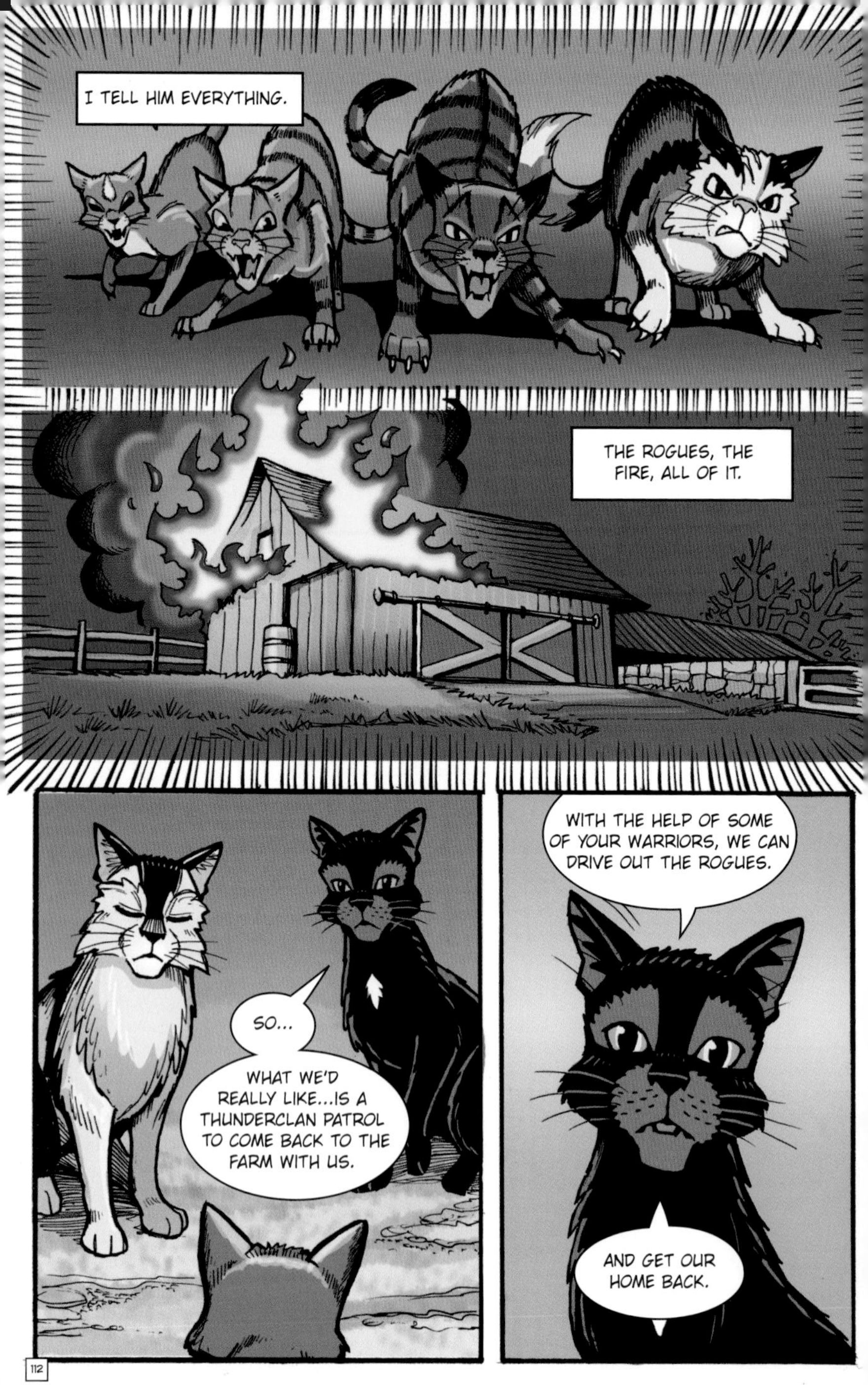
I TELL HIM EVERYTHING.
THE ROGUES, THE FIRE, ALL OF IT.
SO...
WHAT WE'D REALLY LIKE...IS A THUNDERCLAN PATROL TO COME BACK TO THE FARM WITH US.
WITH THE HELP OF SOME OF YOUR WARRIORS, WE CAN DRIVE OUT THE ROGUES.
AND GET OUR HOME BACK.

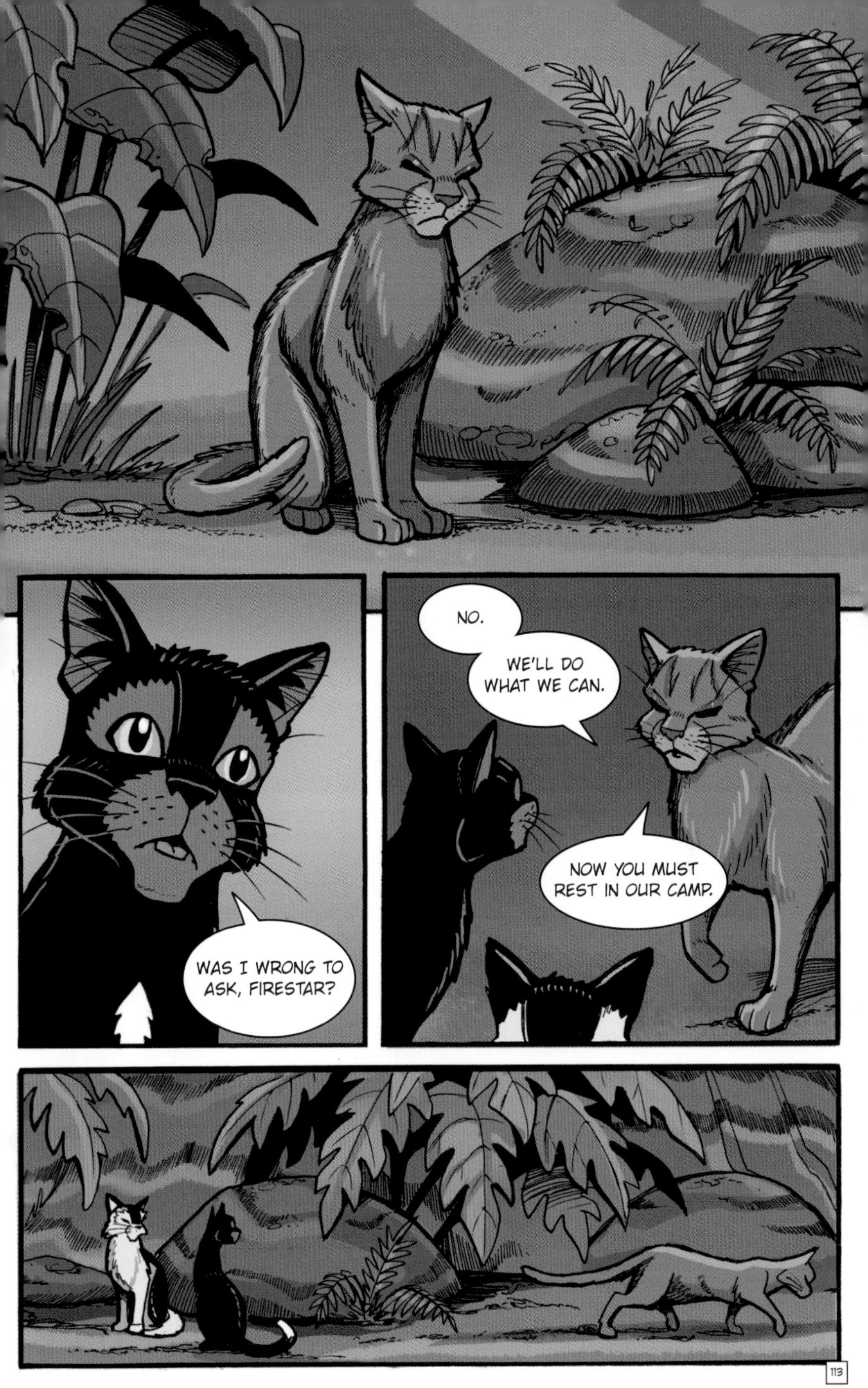
WAS I WRONG TO ASK, FIRESTAR?
NO.
WE'LL DO WHAT WE CAN.
NOW YOU MUST REST IN OUR CAMP.

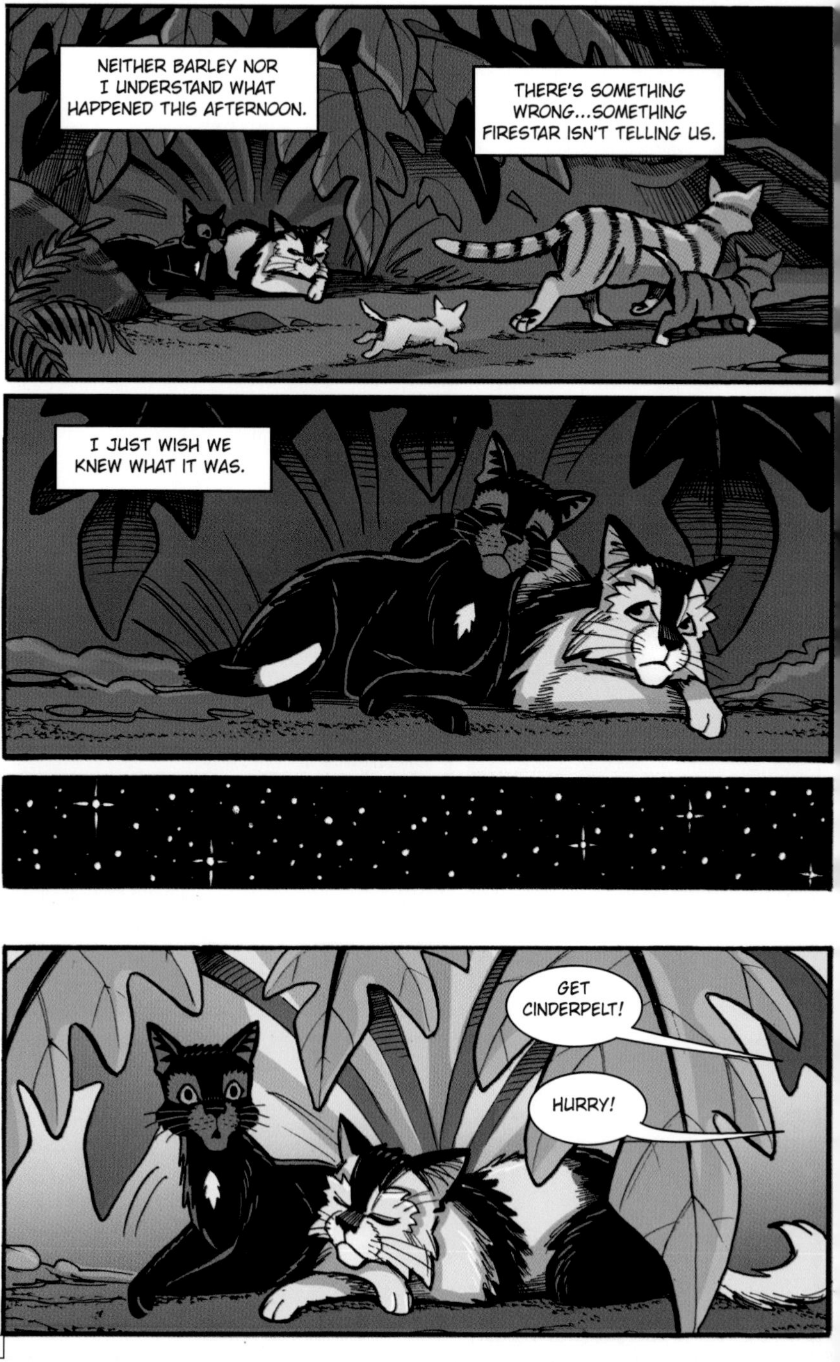
NEITHER BARLEY NOR I UNDERSTAND WHAT HAPPENED THIS AFTERNOON.
THERE'S SOMETHING WRONG...SOMETHING FIRESTAR ISN'T TELLING US.
I JUST WISH WE KNEW WHAT IT WAS.
GET CINDERPELT!
HURRY!

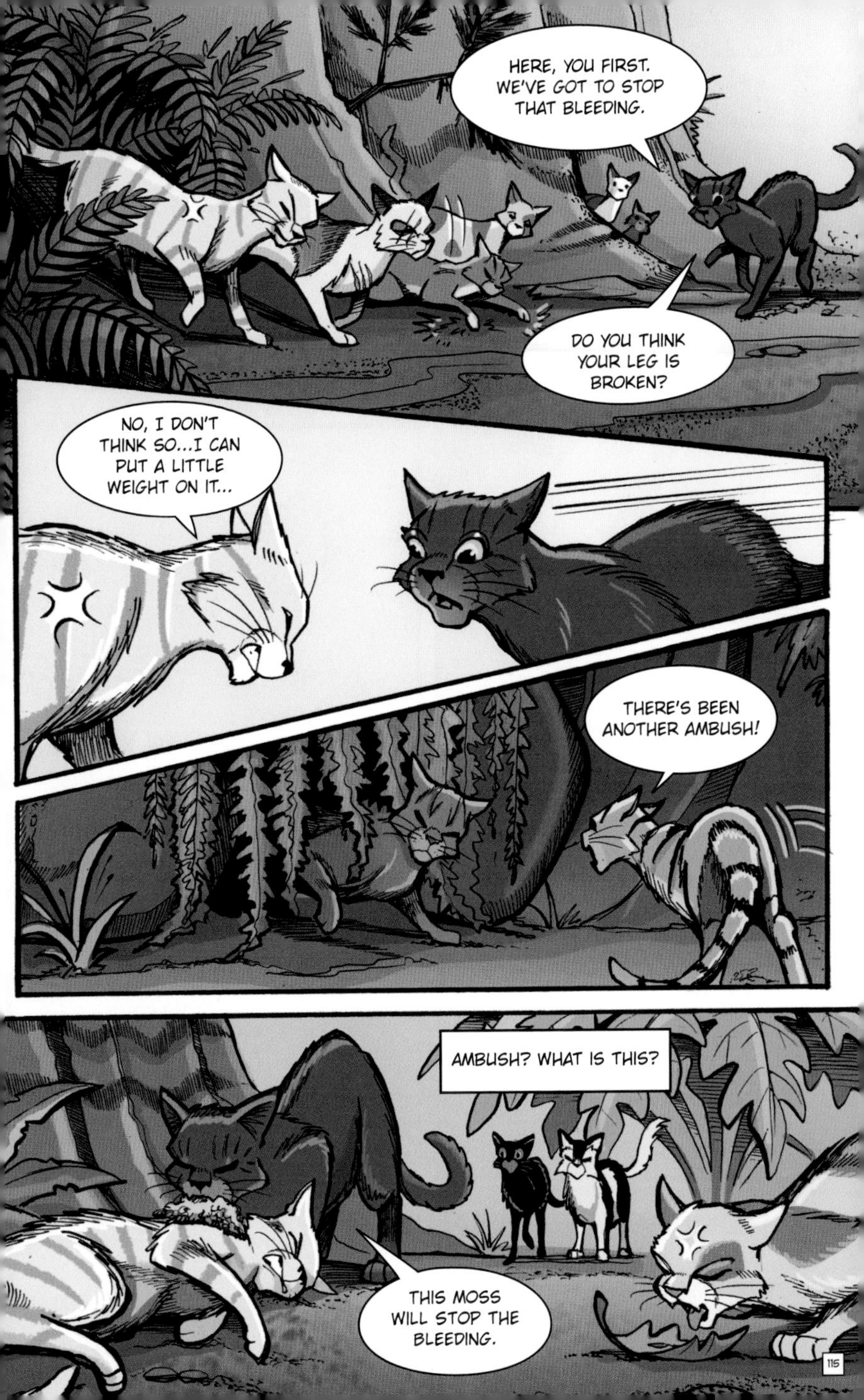
HERE, YOU FIRST. WE'VE GOT TO STOP THAT BLEEDING.
DO YOU THINK YOUR LEG IS BROKEN?
NO, I DON'T THINK SO...I CAN PUT A LITTLE WEIGHT ON IT...
THERE'S BEEN ANOTHER AMBUSH!
AMBUSH? WHAT IS THIS?
THIS MOSS WILL STOP THE BLEEDING.

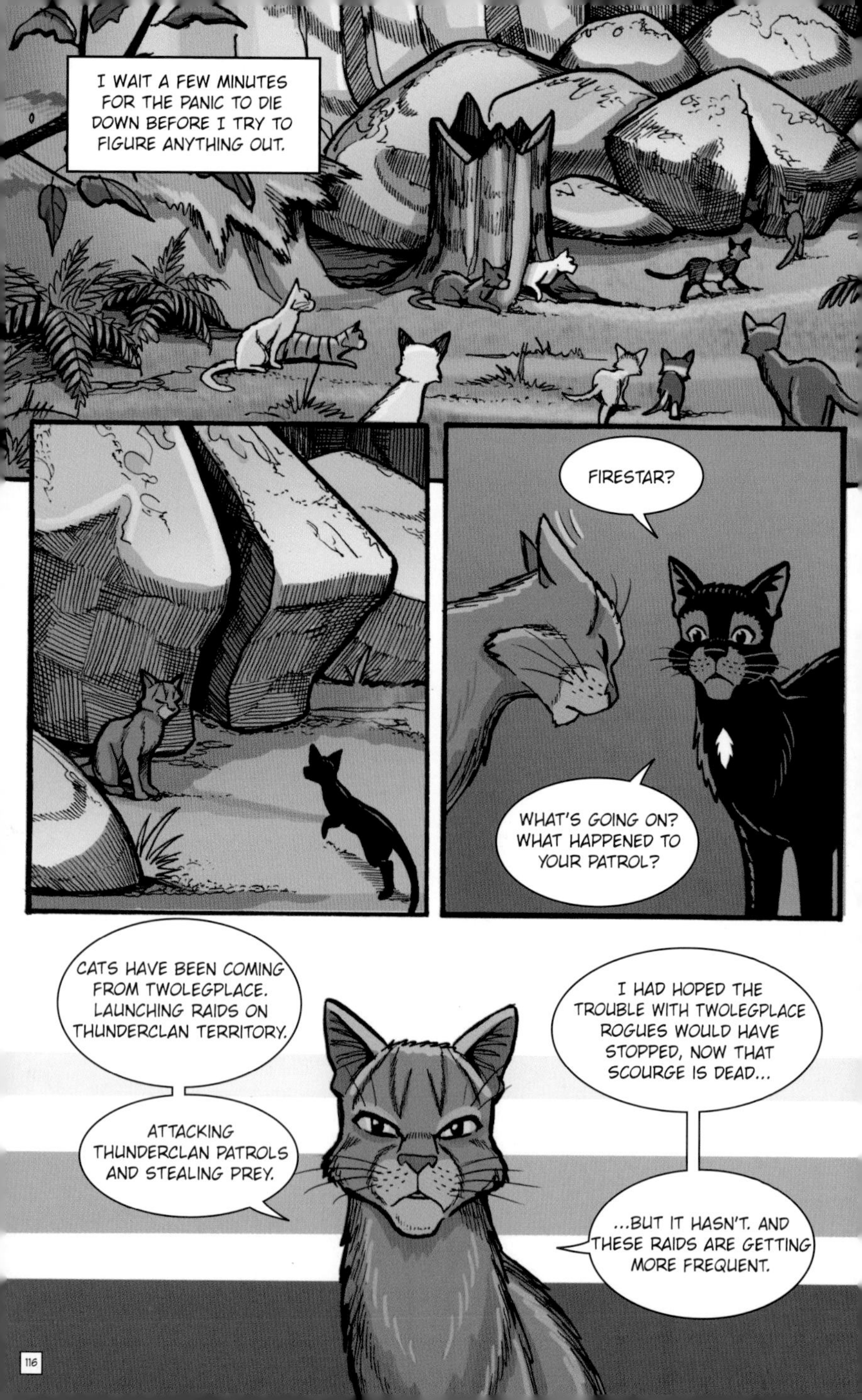

I WAIT A FEW MINUTES FOR THE PANIC TO DIE DOWN BEFORE I TRY TO FIGURE ANYTHING OUT.
FIRESTAR?
WHAT'S GOING ON? WHAT HAPPENED TO YOUR PATROL?
CATS HAVE BEEN COMING FROM TWOLEGPLACE. LAUNCHING RAIDS ON THUNDERCLAN TERRITORY.
ATTACKING THUNDERCLAN PATROLS AND STEALING PREY.
I HAD HOPED THE TROUBLE WITH TWOLEGPLACE ROGUES WOULD HAVE STOPPED, NOW THAT SCOURGE IS DEAD...
...BUT IT HASN'T. AND THESE RAIDS ARE GETTING MORE FREQUENT.

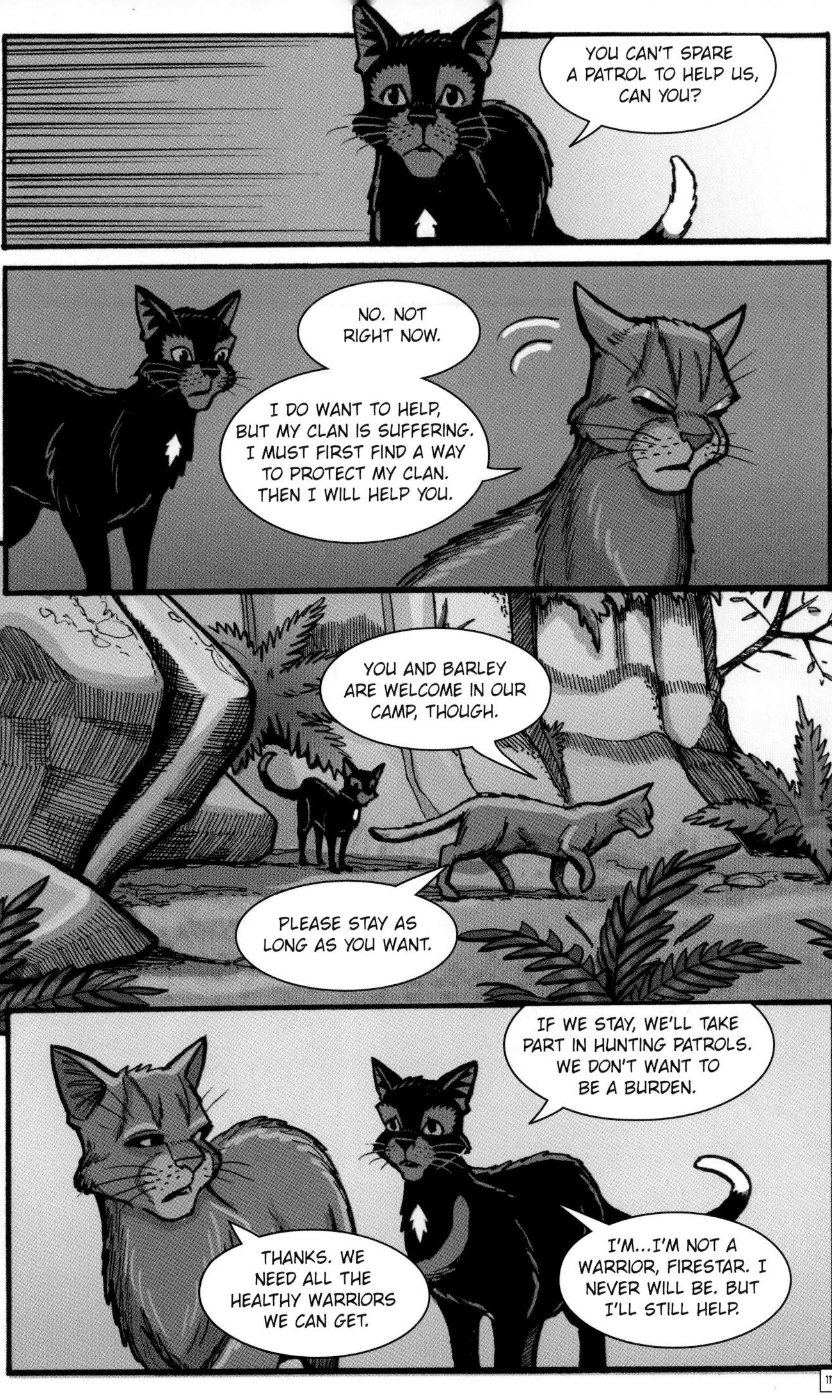
YOU CAN'T SPARE A PATROL TO HELP US, CAN YOU?
NO. NOT RIGHT NOW.
I DO WANT TO HELP, BUT MY CLAN IS SUFFERING. I MUST FIRST FIND A WAY TO PROTECT MY CLAN. THEN I WILL HELP YOU.
YOU AND BARLEY ARE WELCOME IN OUR CAMP, THOUGH.
PLEASE STAY AS LONG AS YOU WANT.
IF WE STAY, WE'LL TAKE PART IN HUNTING PATROLS. WE DON'T WANT TO BE A BURDEN.
THANKS. WE NEED ALL THE HEALTHY WARRIORS WE CAN GET.
I'M...I'M NOT A WARRIOR, FIRESTAR. I NEVER WILL BE. BUT I'LL STILL HELP.

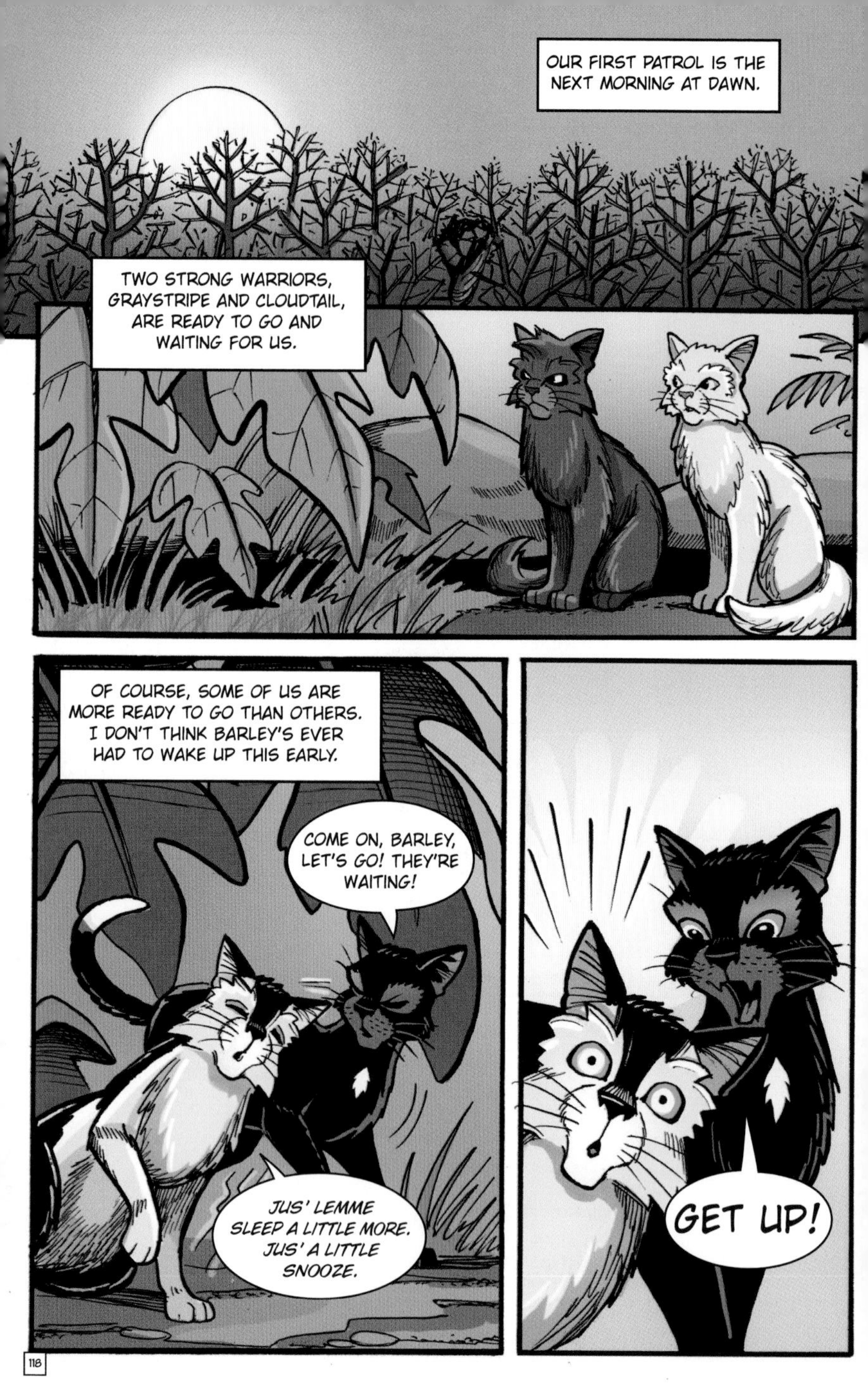
OUR FIRST PATROL IS THE NEXT MORNING AT DAWN.
TWO STRONG WARRIORS, GRAYSTRIPE AND CLOUDTAIL, ARE READY TO GO AND WAITING FOR US.
OF COURSE, SOME OF US ARE MORE READY TO GO THAN OTHERS. I DON'T THINK BARLEY'S EVER HAD TO WAKE UP THIS EARLY.
COME ON, BARLEY, LET'S GO! THEY'RE WAITING!
JUS' LEMME SLEEP A LITTLE MORE. JUS' A LITTLE SNOOZE.
GET UP!

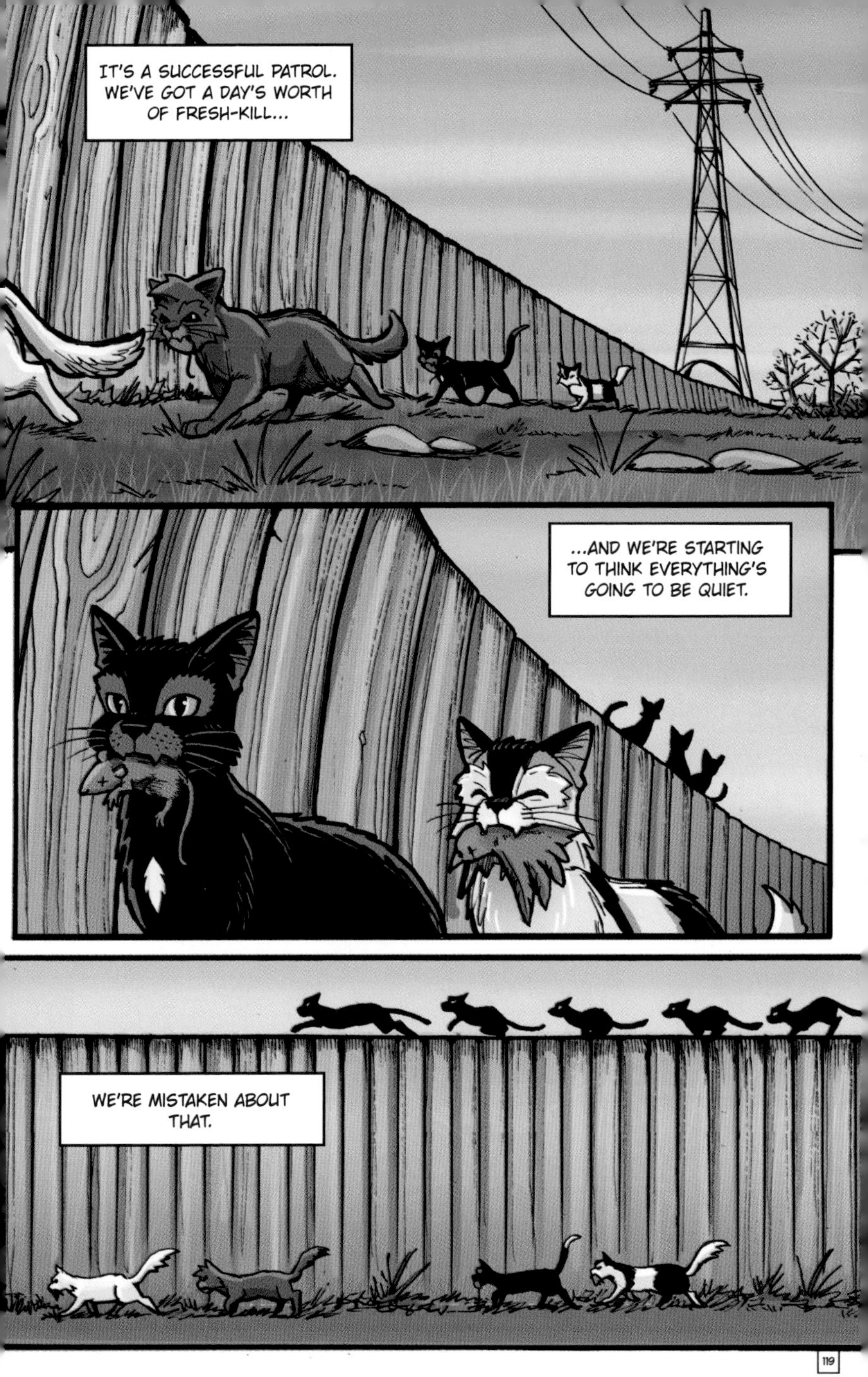
IT'S A SUCCESSFUL PATROL. WE'VE GOT A DAY'S WORTH OF FRESH-KILL...
...AND WE'RE STARTING TO THINK EVERYTHING'S GOING TO BE QUIET.
WE'RE MISTAKEN ABOUT THAT.

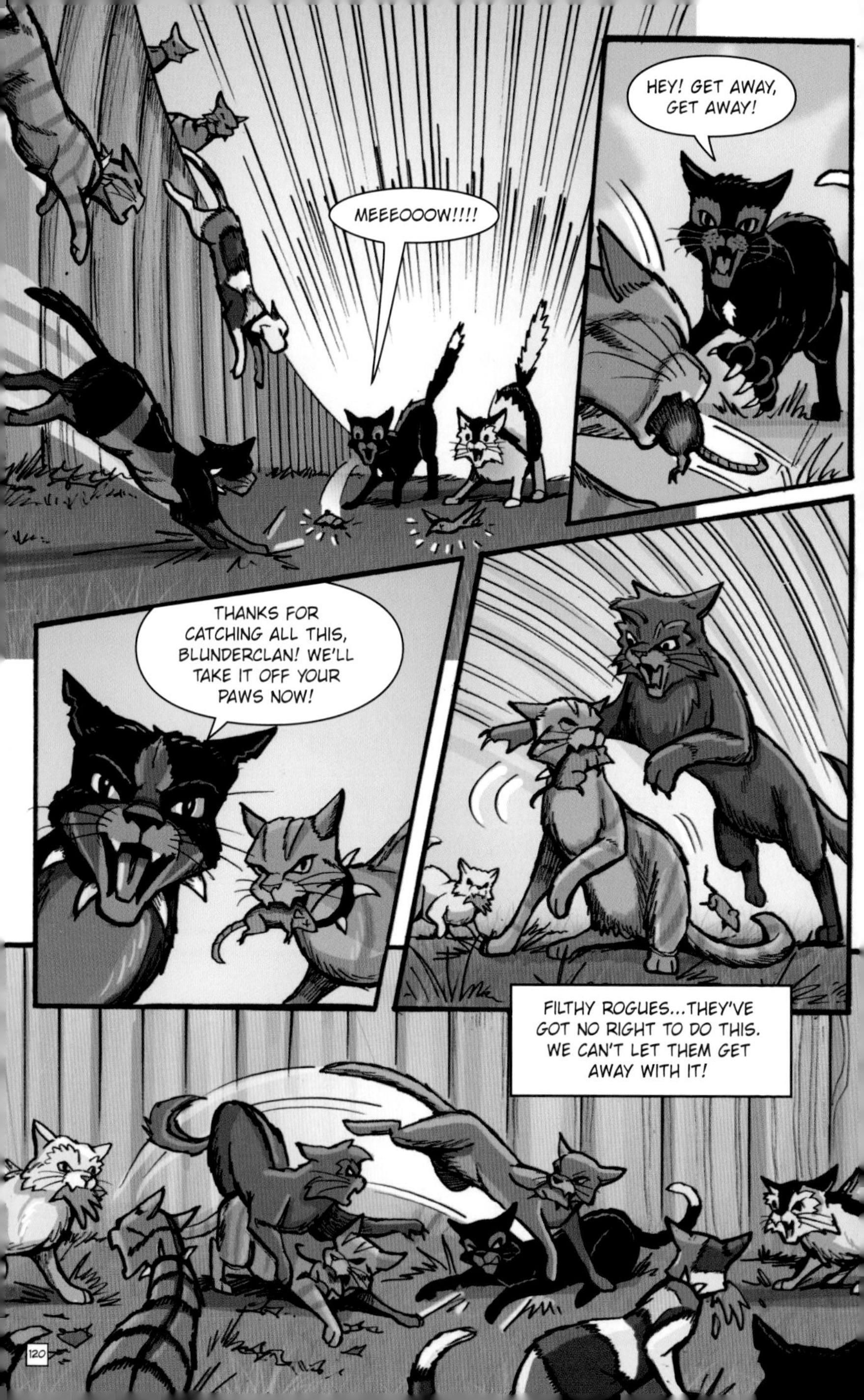
MEEEOOOW!!!!
HEY! GET AWAY, GET AWAY!
THANKS FOR CATCHING ALL THIS, BLUNDERCLAN! WE'LL TAKE IT OFF YOUR PAWS NOW!
FILTHY ROGUES...THEY'VE GOT NO RIGHT TO DO THIS. WE CAN'T LET THEM GET AWAY WITH IT!

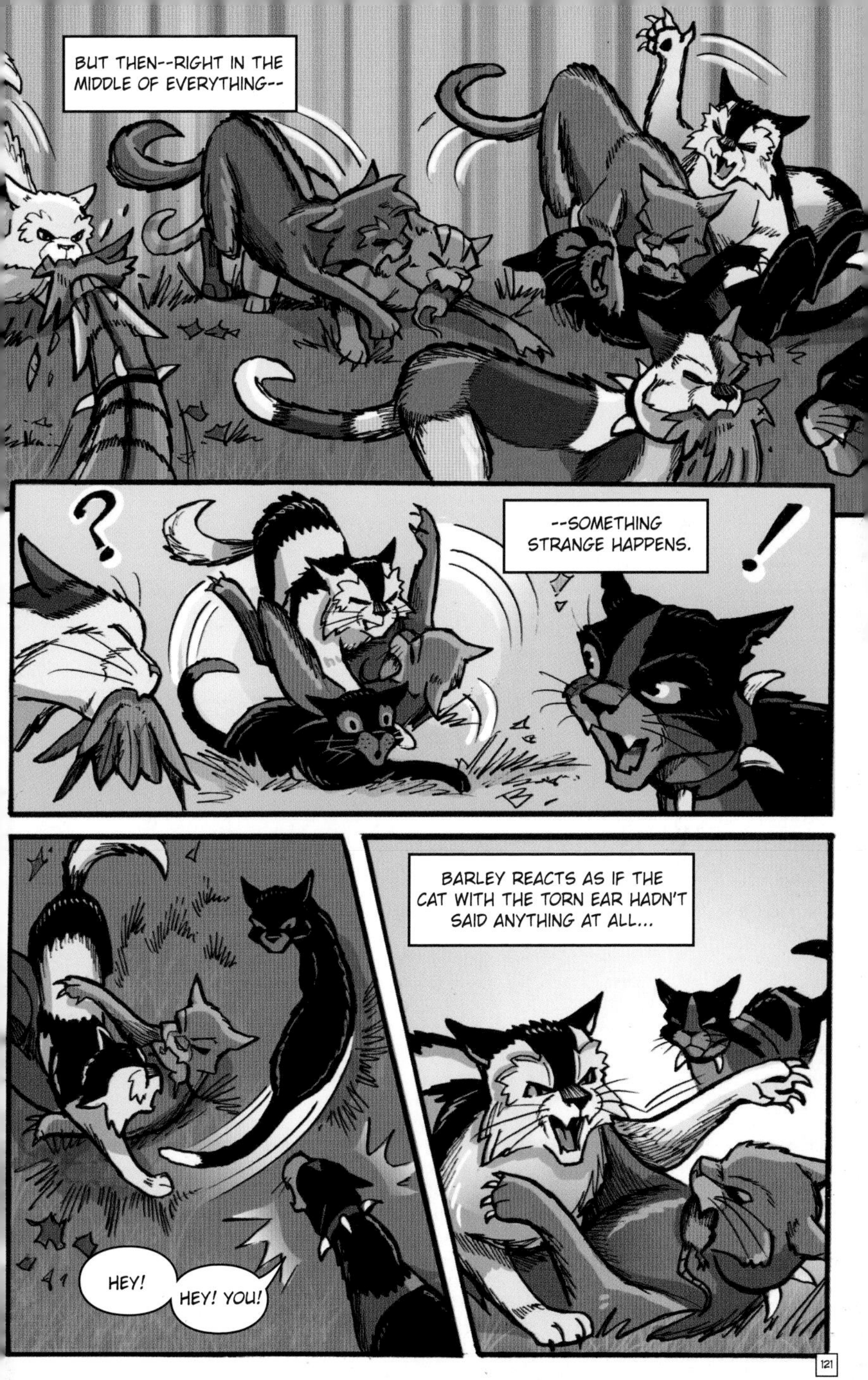
BUT THEN--RIGHT IN THE MIDDLE OF EVERYTHING--
--SOMETHING STRANGE HAPPENS.
?
!
HEY!
HEY! YOU!
BARLEY REACTS AS IF THE CAT WITH THE TORN EAR HADN'T SAID ANYTHING AT ALL...

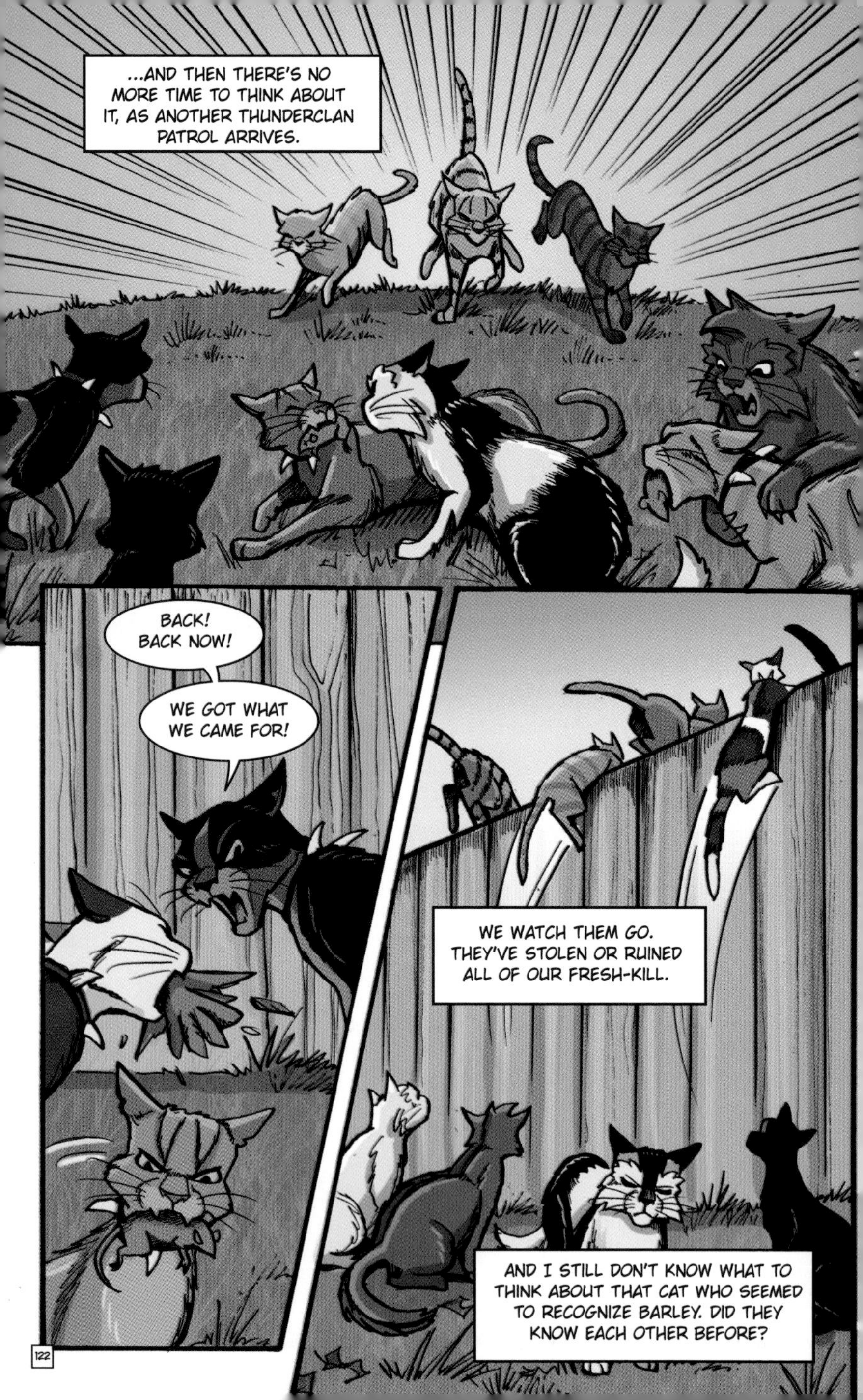

...AND THEN THERE'S NO MORE TIME TO THINK ABOUT IT, AS ANOTHER THUNDERCLAN PATROL ARRIVES.
BACK! BACK NOW!
WE GOT WHAT WE CAME FOR!
WE WATCH THEM GO. THEY'VE STOLEN OR RUINED ALL OF OUR FRESH-KILL.
AND I STILL DON'T KNOW WHAT TO THINK ABOUT THAT CAT WHO SEEMED TO RECOGNIZE BARLEY. DID THEY KNOW EACH OTHER BEFORE?

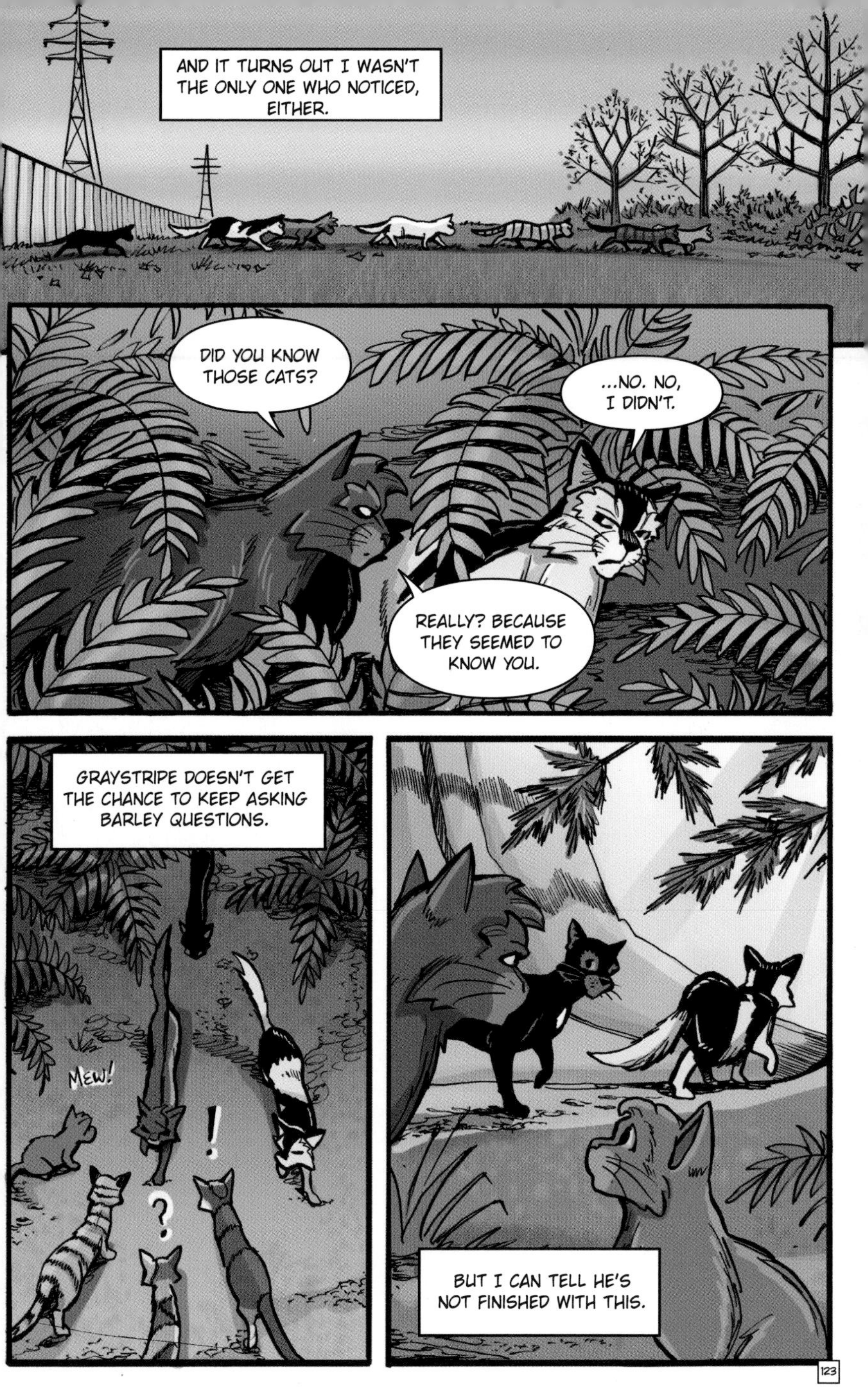
AND IT TURNS OUT I WASN'T THE ONLY ONE WHO NOTICED, EITHER.
DID YOU KNOW THOSE CATS?
...NO. NO, I DIDN'T.
REALLY? BECAUSE THEY SEEMED TO KNOW YOU.
GRAYSTRIPE DOESN'T GET THE CHANCE TO KEEP ASKING BARLEY QUESTIONS.
MEW!
BUT I CAN TELL HE'S NOT FINISHED WITH THIS.

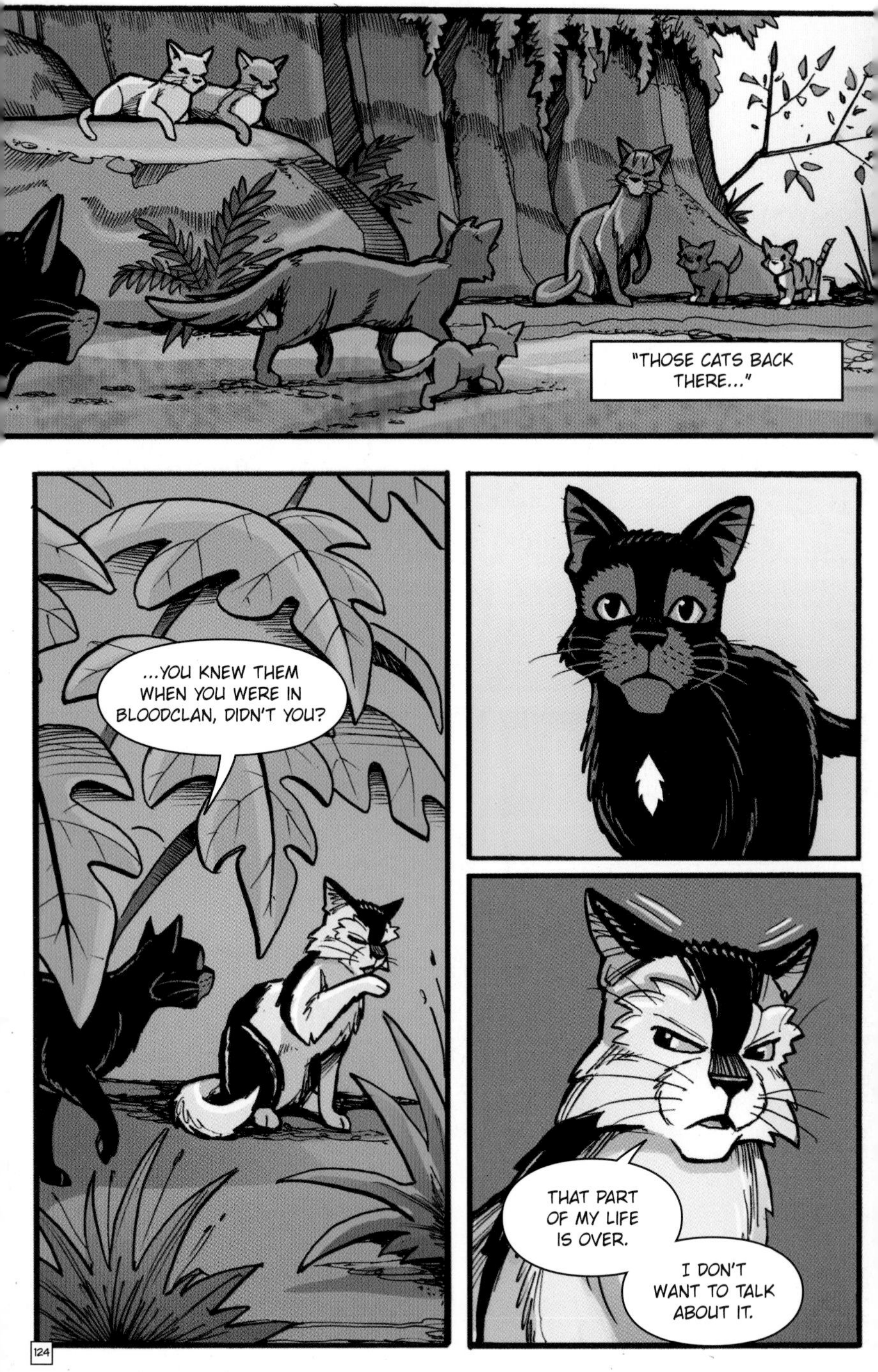
"THOSE CATS BACK THERE..."
...YOU KNEW THEM WHEN YOU WERE IN BLOODCLAN, DIDN'T YOU?
THAT PART OF MY LIFE IS OVER.
I DON'T WANT TO TALK ABOUT IT.

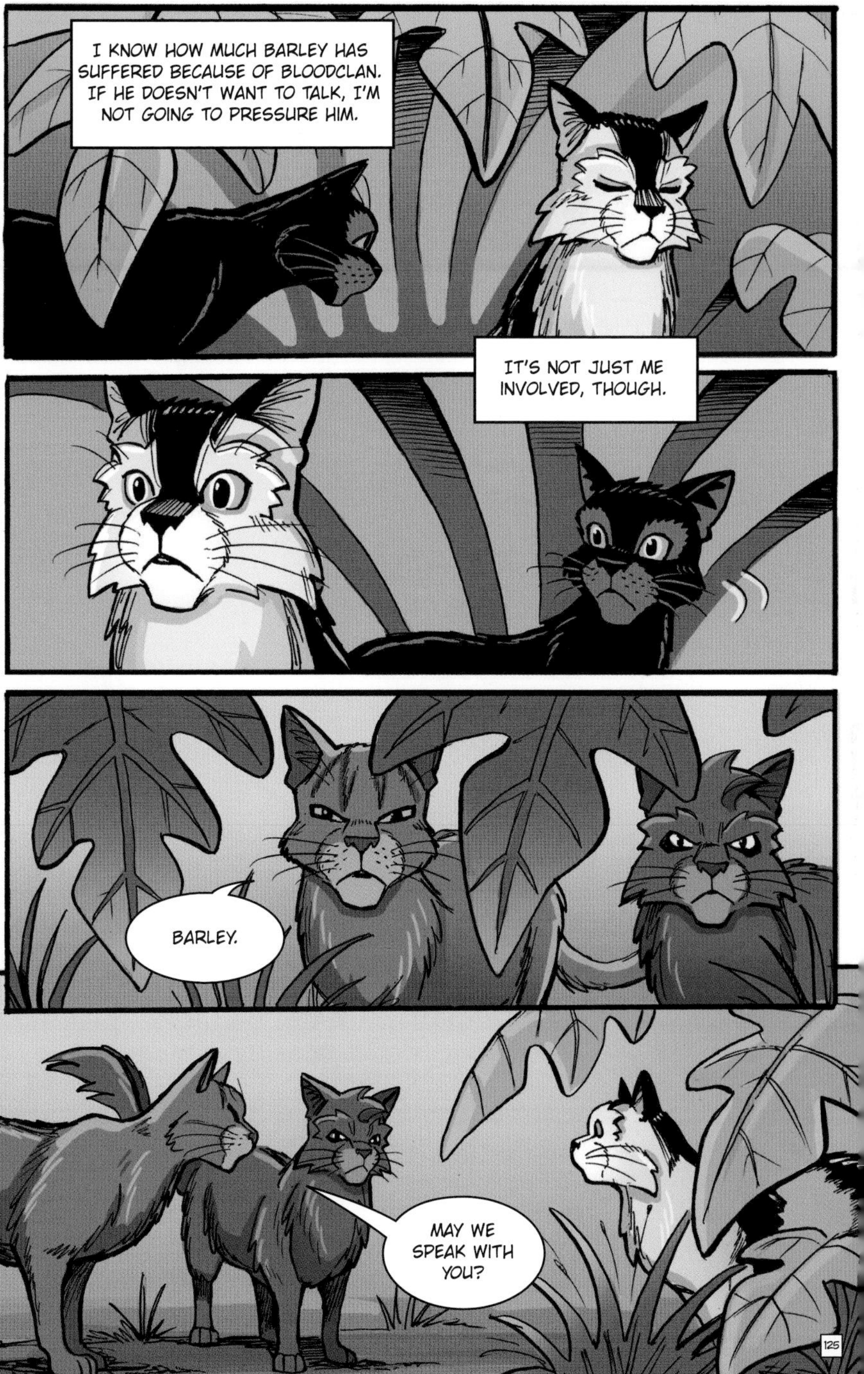
I KNOW HOW MUCH BARLEY HAS SUFFERED BECAUSE OF BLOODCLAN. IF HE DOESN'T WANT TO TALK, I'M NOT GOING TO PRESSURE HIM.
IT'S NOT JUST ME INVOLVED, THOUGH.
BARLEY.
MAY WE SPEAK WITH YOU?

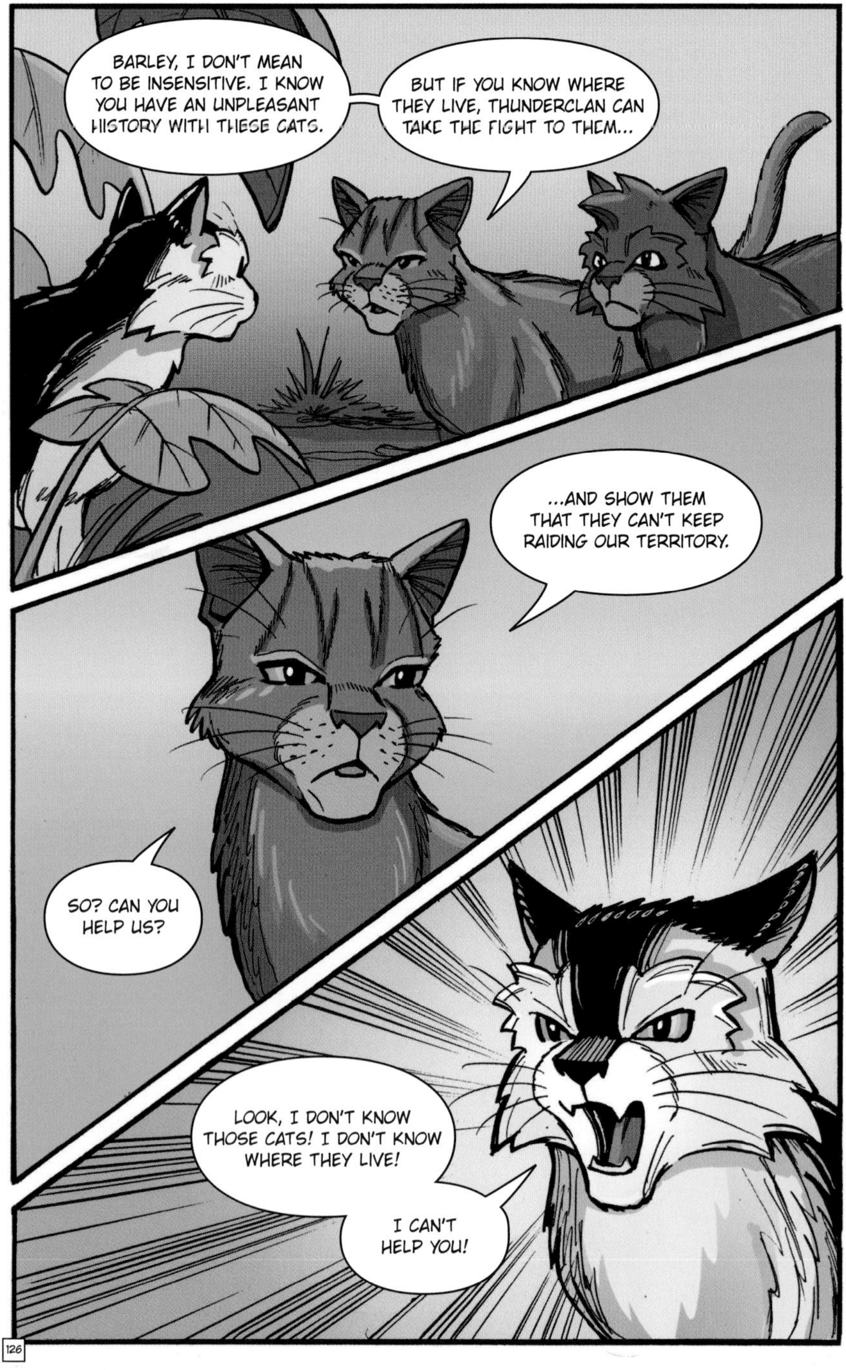
BARLEY, I DON'T MEAN TO BE INSENSITIVE. I KNOW YOU HAVE AN UNPLEASANT HISTORY WITH THESE CATS.
BUT IF YOU KNOW WHERE THEY LIVE, THUNDERCLAN CAN TAKE THE FIGHT TO THEM...
...AND SHOW THEM THAT THEY CAN'T KEEP RAIDING OUR TERRITORY.
SO? CAN YOU HELP US?
LOOK, I DON'T KNOW THOSE CATS! I DON'T KNOW WHERE THEY LIVE!
I CAN'T HELP YOU!

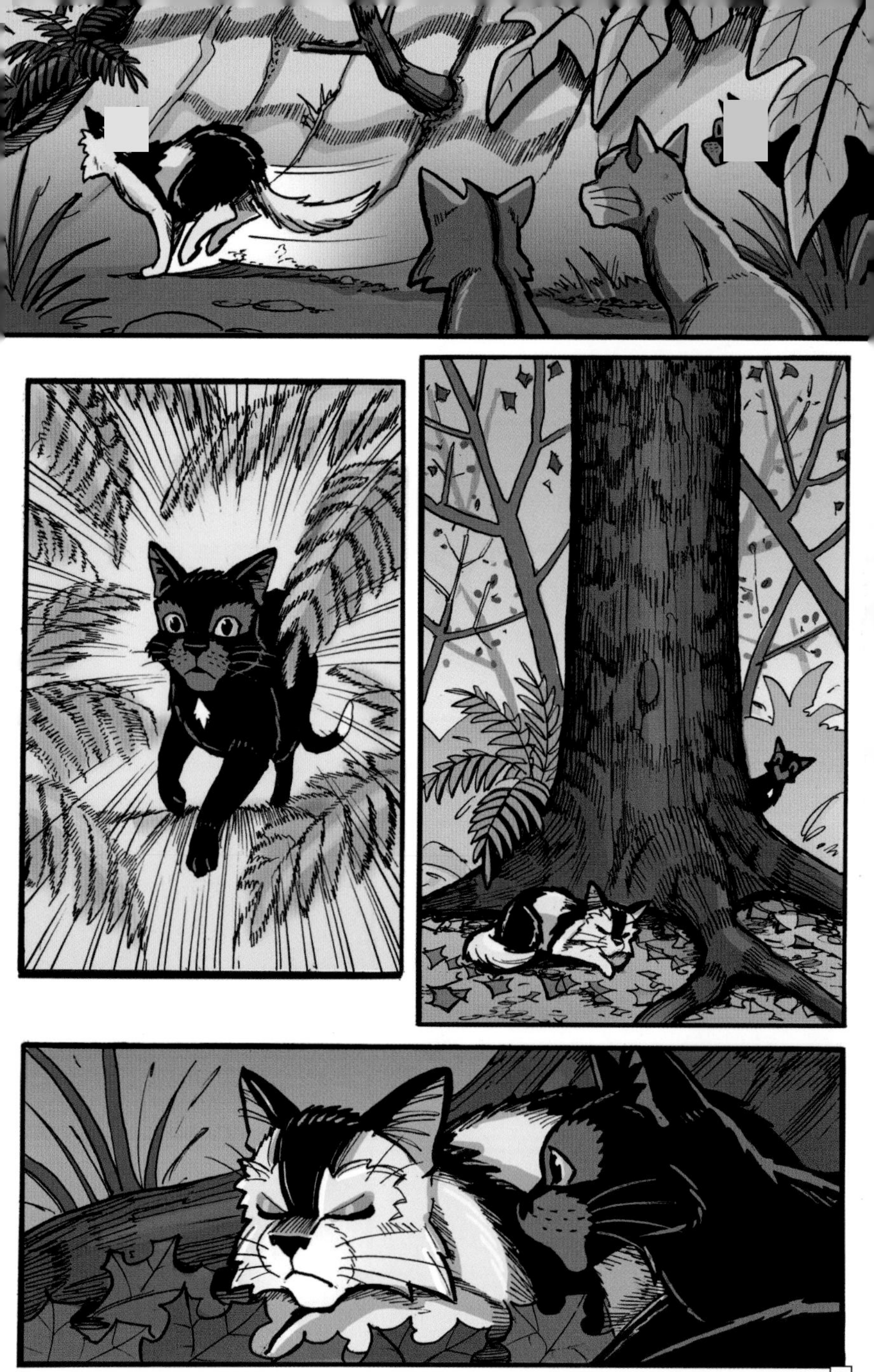

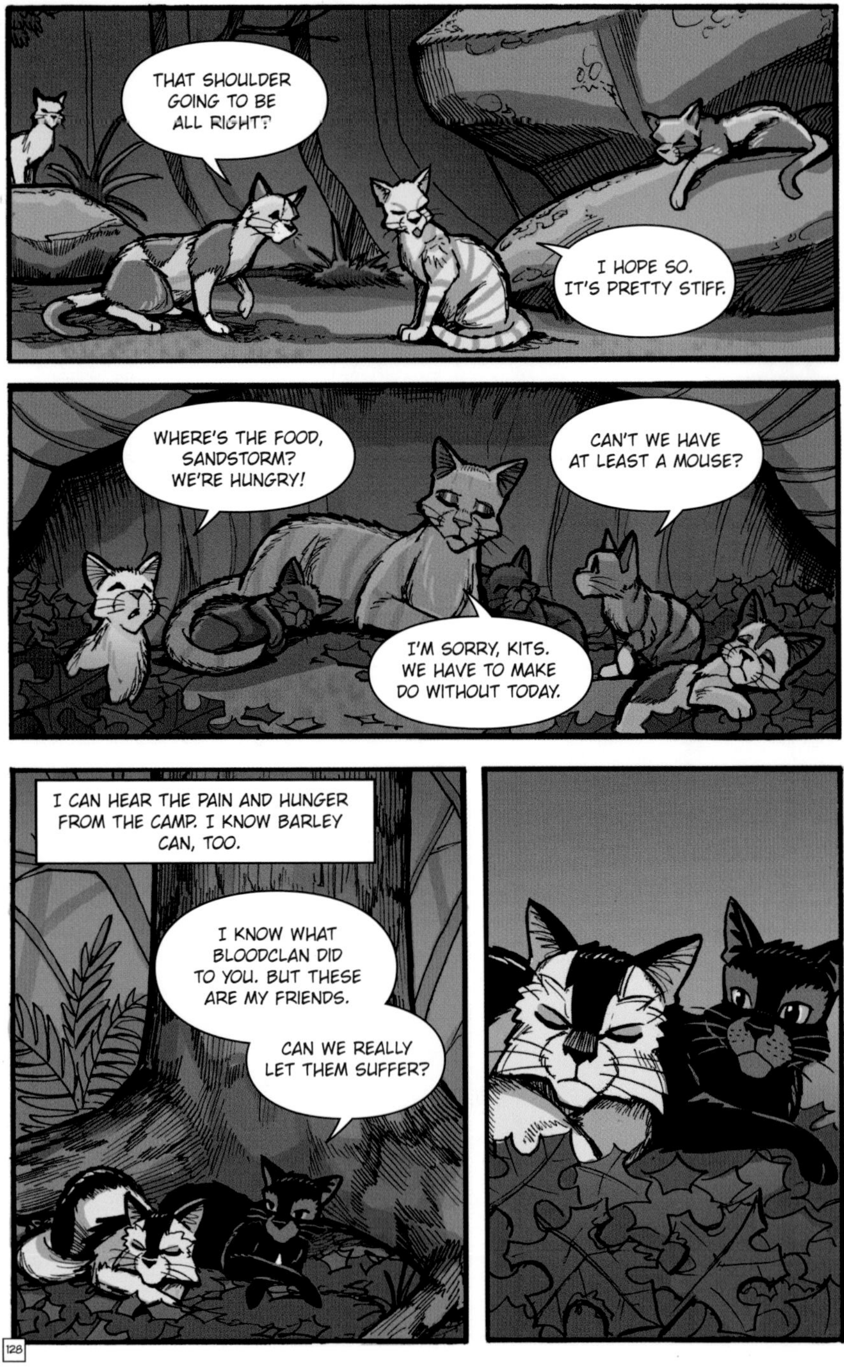
THAT SHOULDER GOING TO BE ALL RIGHT?
I HOPE SO. IT'S PRETTY STIFF.
WHERE'S THE FOOD, SANDSTORM? WE'RE HUNGRY!
CAN'T WE HAVE AT LEAST A MOUSE?
I'M SORRY, KITS. WE HAVE TO MAKE DO WITHOUT TODAY.
I CAN HEAR THE PAIN AND HUNGER FROM THE CAMP. I KNOW BARLEY CAN, TOO.
I KNOW WHAT BLOODCLAN DID TO YOU. BUT THESE ARE MY FRIENDS.
CAN WE REALLY LET THEM SUFFER?

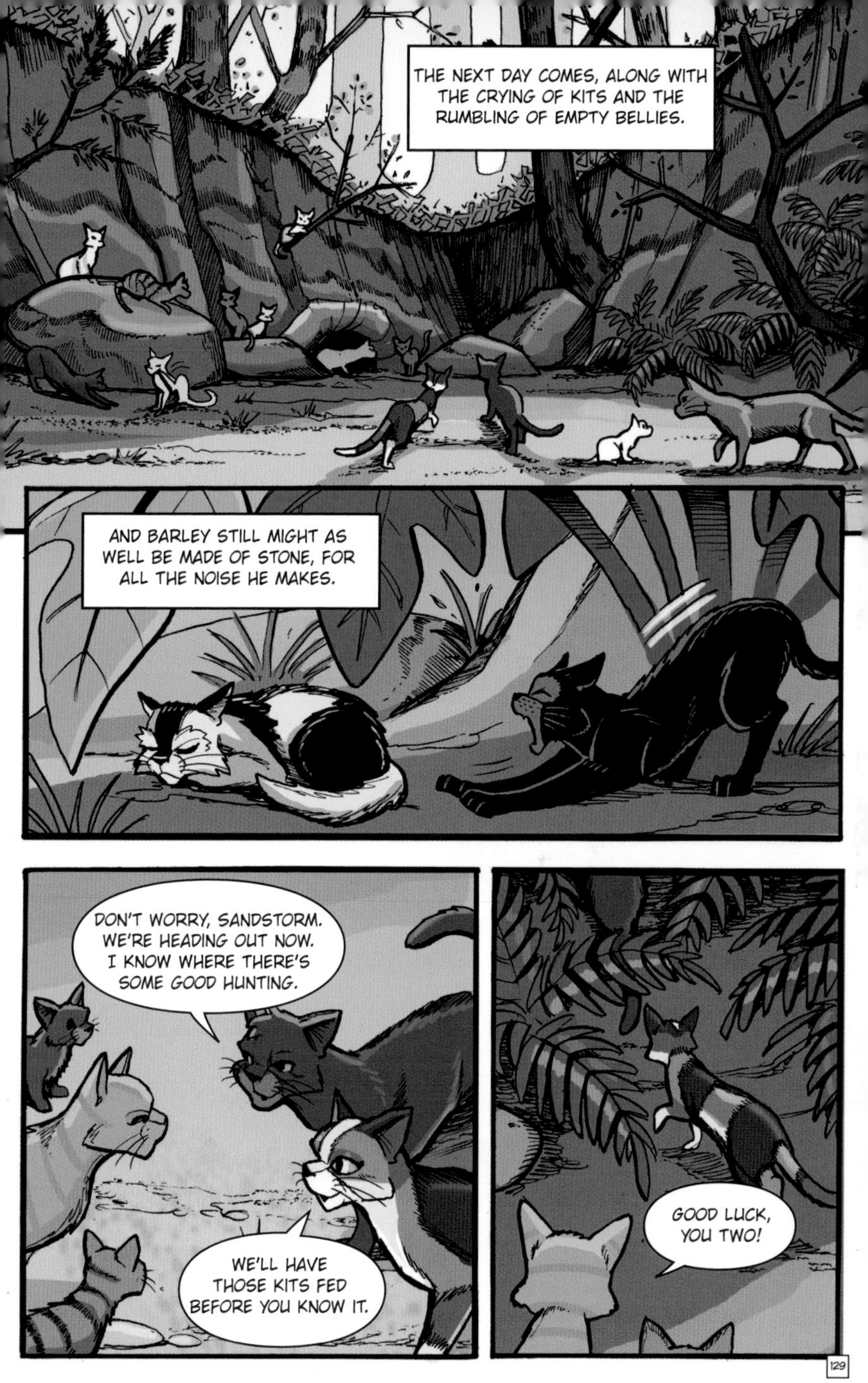
THE NEXT DAY COMES, ALONG WITH THE CRYING OF KITS AND THE RUMBLING OF EMPTY BELLIES.
AND BARLEY STILL MIGHT AS WELL BE MADE OF STONE, FOR ALL THE NOISE HE MAKES.
DON'T WORRY, SANDSTORM. WE'RE HEADING OUT NOW. I KNOW WHERE THERE'S SOME GOOD HUNTING.
WE'LL HAVE THOSE KITS FED BEFORE YOU KNOW IT.
GOOD LUCK, YOU TWO!

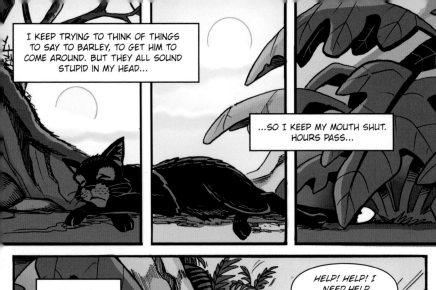

I KEEP TRYING TO THINK OF THINGS TO SAY TO BARLEY, TO GET HIM TO COME AROUND. BUT THEY ALL SOUND STUPID IN MY HEAD...

...SO I KEEP MY MOUTH SHUT. HOURS PASS...

...AND THEN...

HELP! HELP! I NEED HELP, PLEASE!

RAINPAW! WHAT'S WRONG? WHERE'S YOUR SISTER?

SORRELPAW--IT WAS ROGUES! THEY HURT HER BAD!

PLEASE, FIRESTAR--

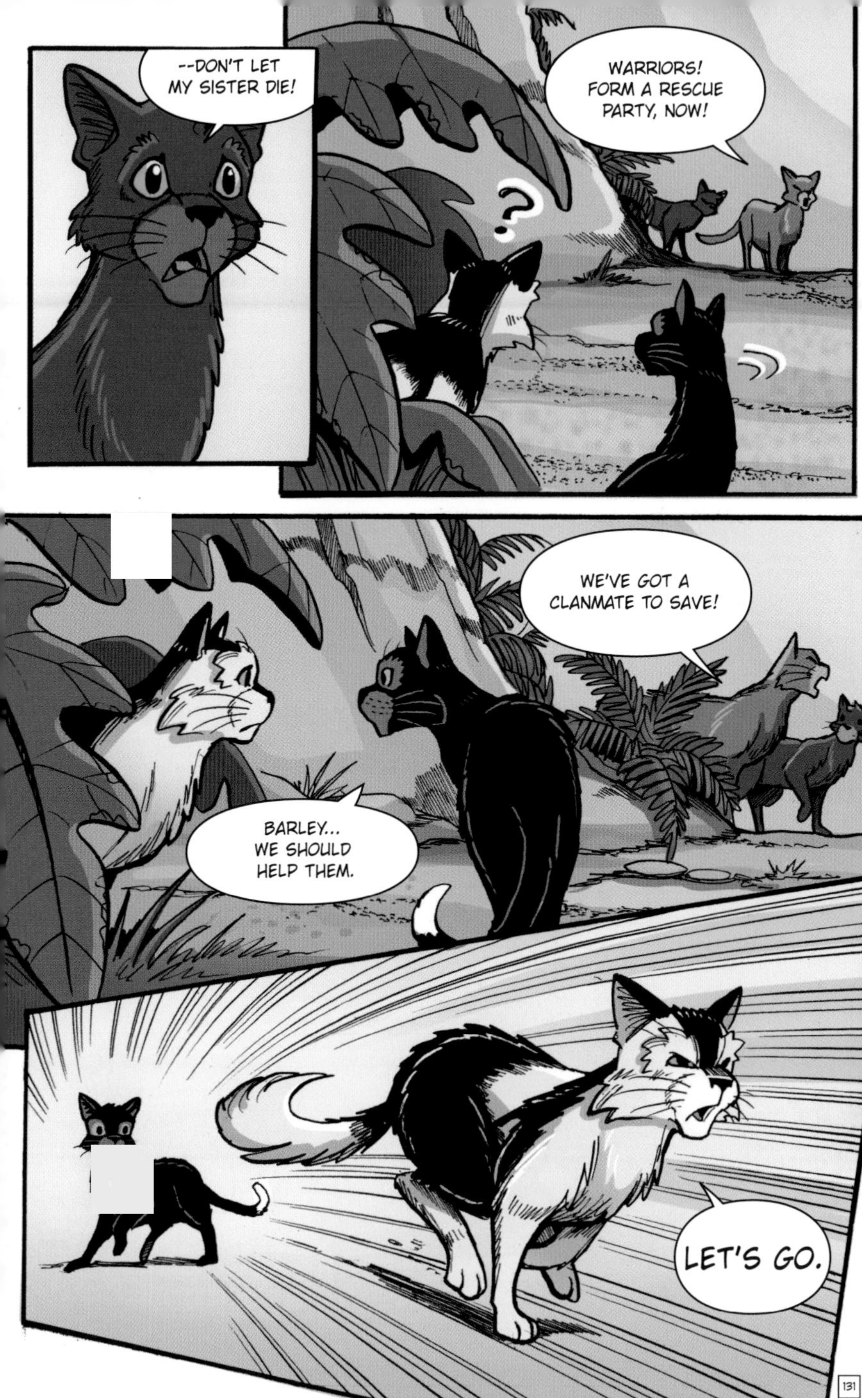
--DON'T LET MY SISTER DIE!
WARRIORS! FORM A RESCUE PARTY, NOW!
?
WE'VE GOT A CLANMATE TO SAVE!
BARLEY... WE SHOULD HELP THEM.
LET'S GO.

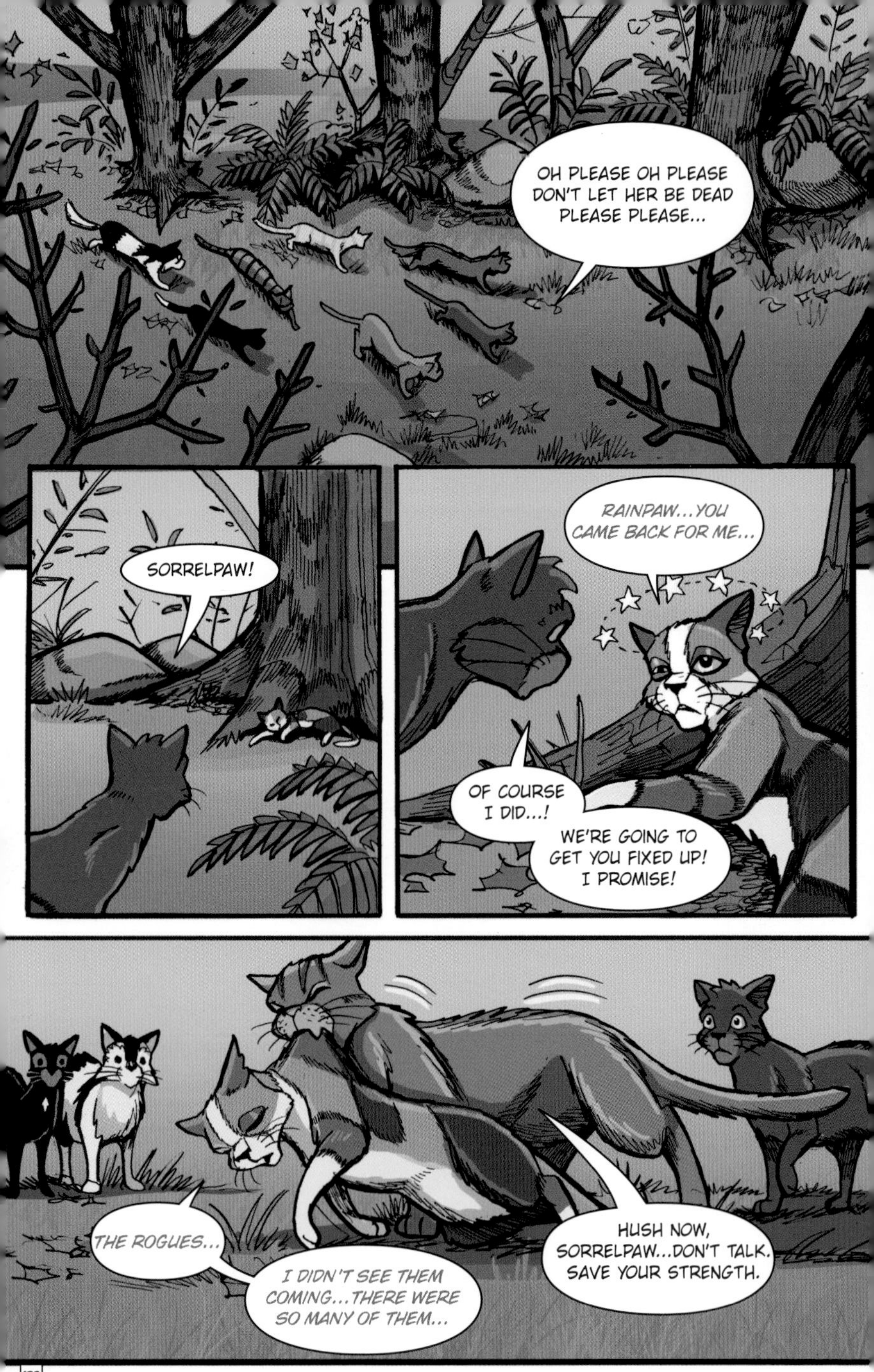
OH PLEASE OH PLEASE DON'T LET HER BE DEAD PLEASE PLEASE...
SORRELPAW!
RAINPAW...YOU CAME BACK FOR ME...
OF COURSE I DID...!
WE'RE GOING TO GET YOU FIXED UP! I PROMISE!
THE ROGUES...
I DIDN'T SEE THEM COMING...THERE WERE SO MANY OF THEM...
HUSH NOW, SORRELPAW...DON'T TALK. SAVE YOUR STRENGTH.

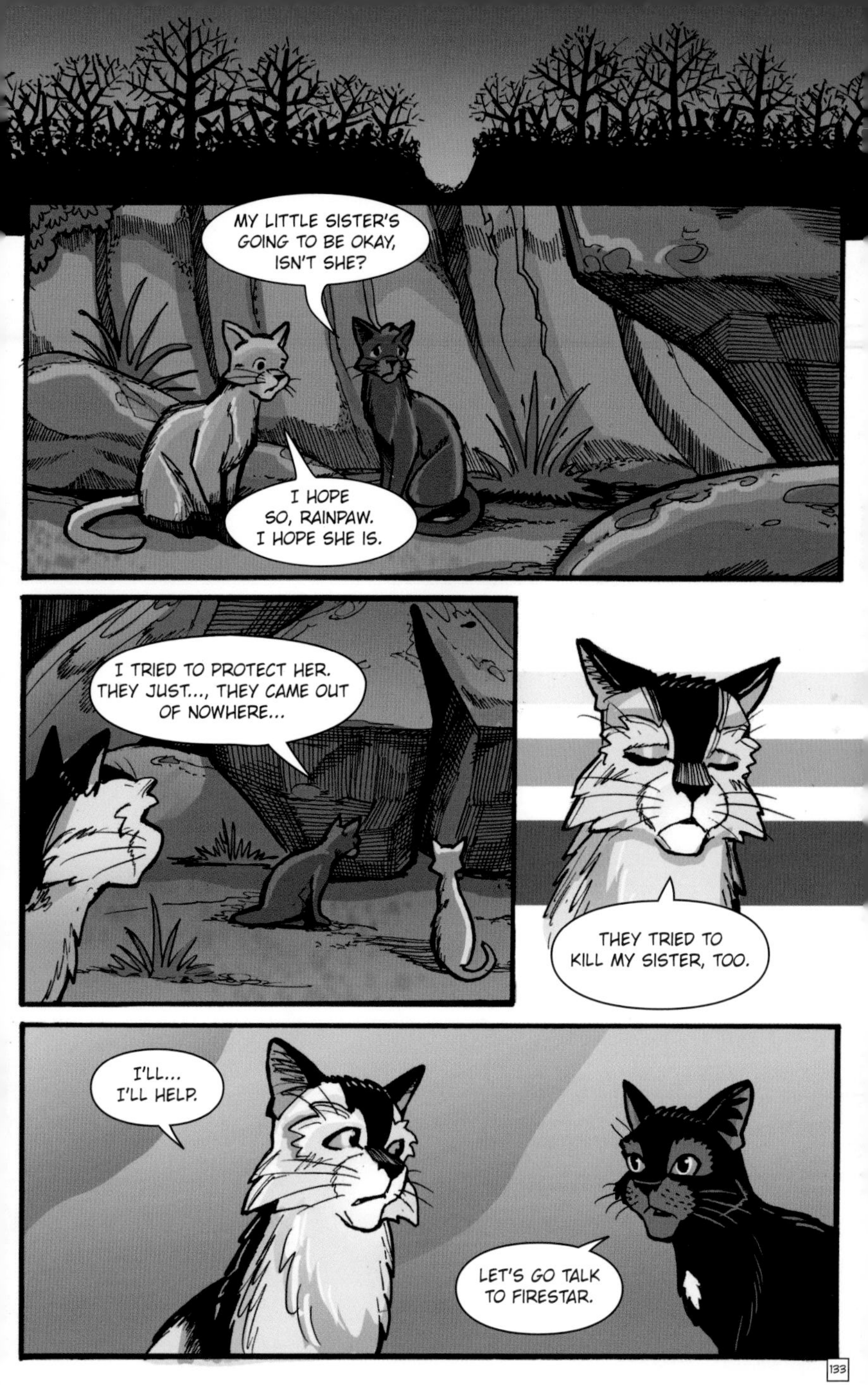
MY LITTLE SISTER'S GOING TO BE OKAY, ISN'T SHE?
I HOPE SO, RAINPAW. I HOPE SHE IS.
I TRIED TO PROTECT HER. THEY JUST..., THEY CAME OUT OF NOWHERE...
THEY TRIED TO KILL MY SISTER, TOO.
I'LL... I'LL HELP.
LET'S GO TALK TO FIRESTAR.

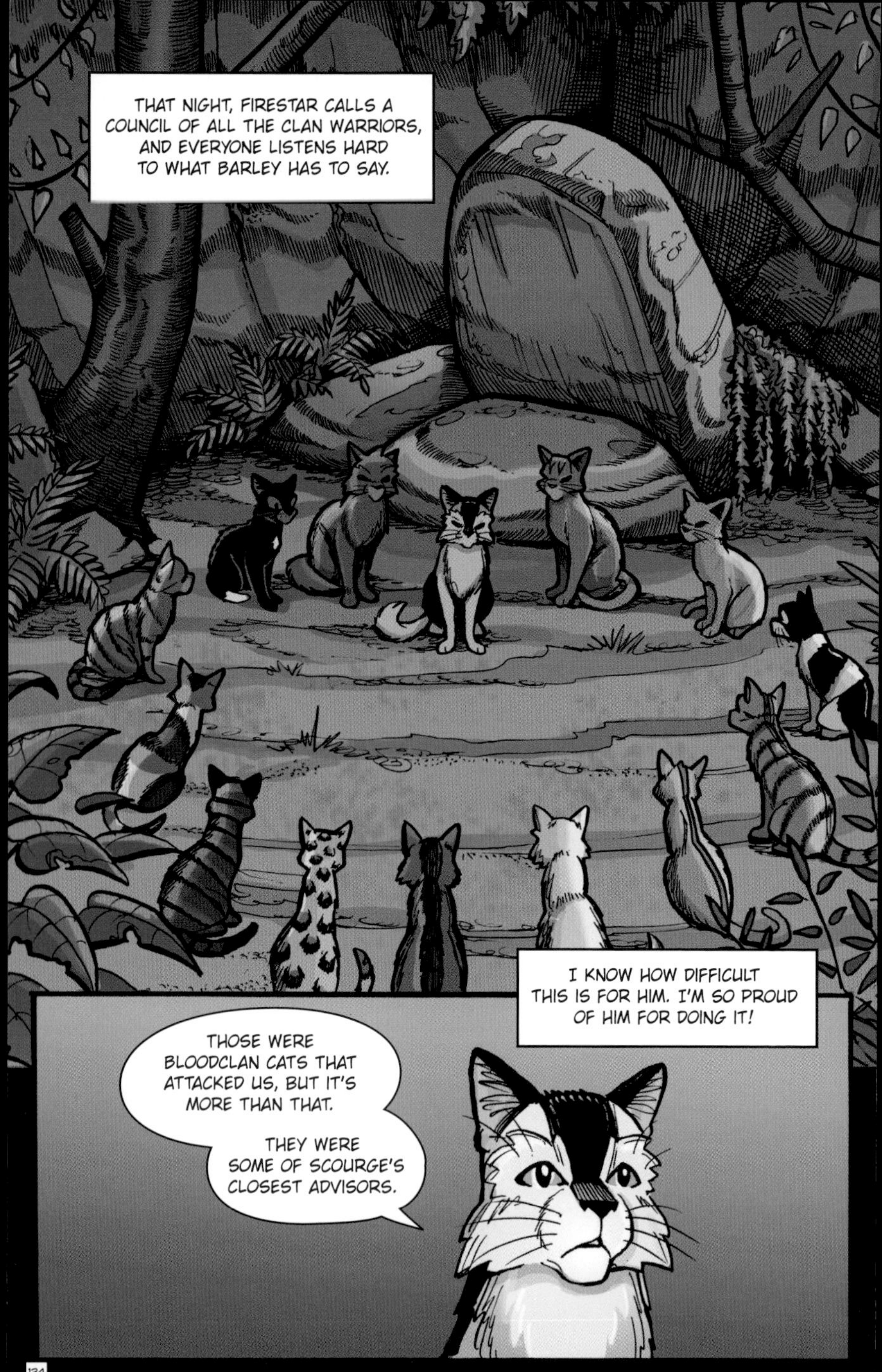
THAT NIGHT, FIRESTAR CALLS A COUNCIL OF ALL THE CLAN WARRIORS, AND EVERYONE LISTENS HARD TO WHAT BARLEY HAS TO SAY.
I KNOW HOW DIFFICULT THIS IS FOR HIM. I'M SO PROUD OF HIM FOR DOING IT!
THOSE WERE BLOODCLAN CATS THAT ATTACKED US, BUT IT'S MORE THAN THAT.
THEY WERE SOME OF SCOURGE'S CLOSEST ADVISORS.

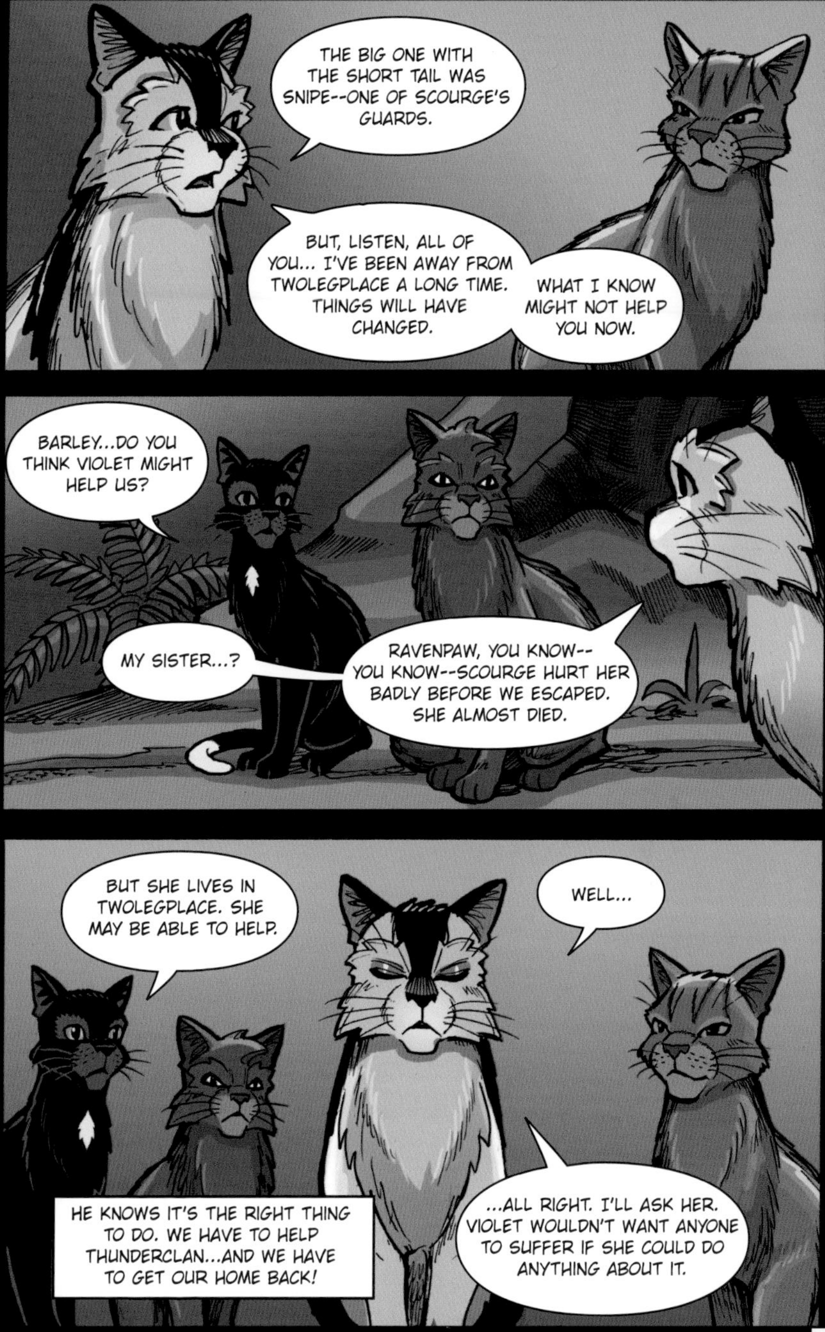
THE BIG ONE WITH THE SHORT TAIL WAS SNIPE--ONE OF SCOURGE'S GUARDS.
BUT, LISTEN, ALL OF YOU... I'VE BEEN AWAY FROM TWOLEGPLACE A LONG TIME. THINGS WILL HAVE CHANGED.
WHAT I KNOW MIGHT NOT HELP YOU NOW.
BARLEY...DO YOU THINK VIOLET MIGHT HELP US?
MY SISTER...?
RAVENPAW, YOU KNOW-- YOU KNOW--SCOURGE HURT HER BADLY BEFORE WE ESCAPED. SHE ALMOST DIED.
BUT SHE LIVES IN TWOLEGPLACE. SHE MAY BE ABLE TO HELP.
WELL...
HE KNOWS IT'S THE RIGHT THING TO DO. WE HAVE TO HELP THUNDERCLAN...AND WE HAVE TO GET OUR HOME BACK!
...ALL RIGHT. I'LL ASK HER. VIOLET WOULDN'T WANT ANYONE TO SUFFER IF SHE COULD DO ANYTHING ABOUT IT.

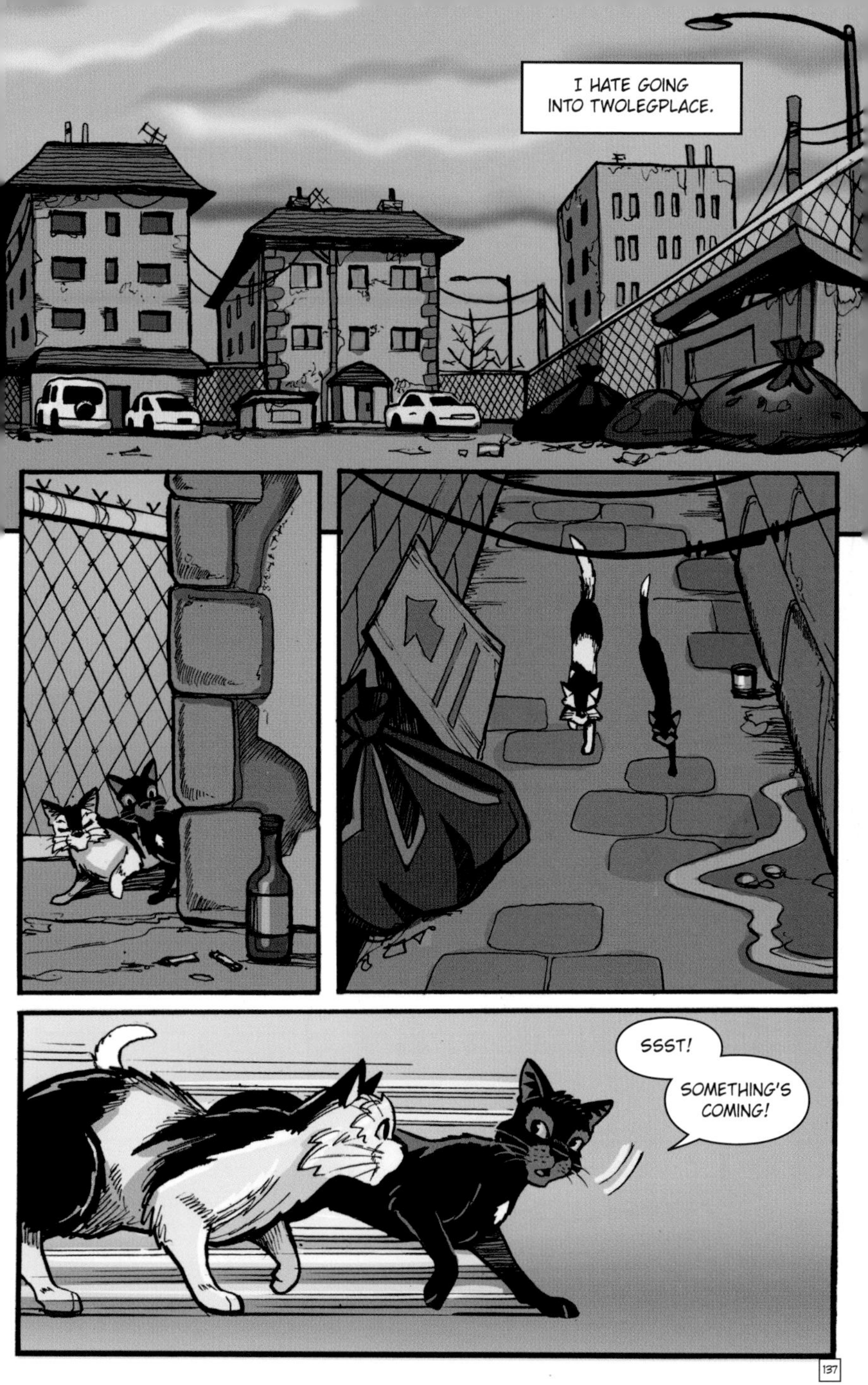
I HATE GOING INTO TWOLEGPLACE.
SSST!
SOMETHING'S COMING!

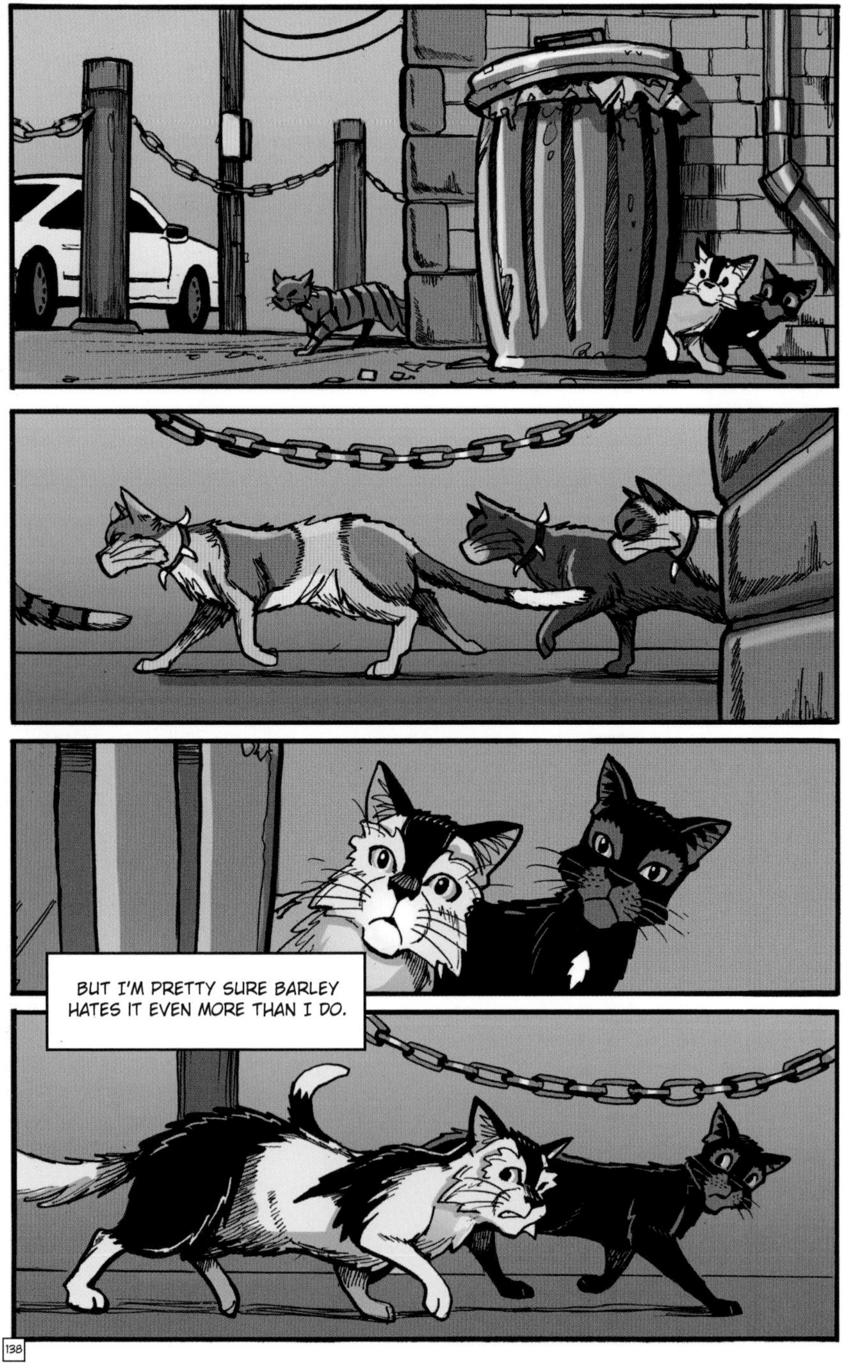
BUT I'M PRETTY SURE BARLEY HATES IT EVEN MORE THAN I DO.

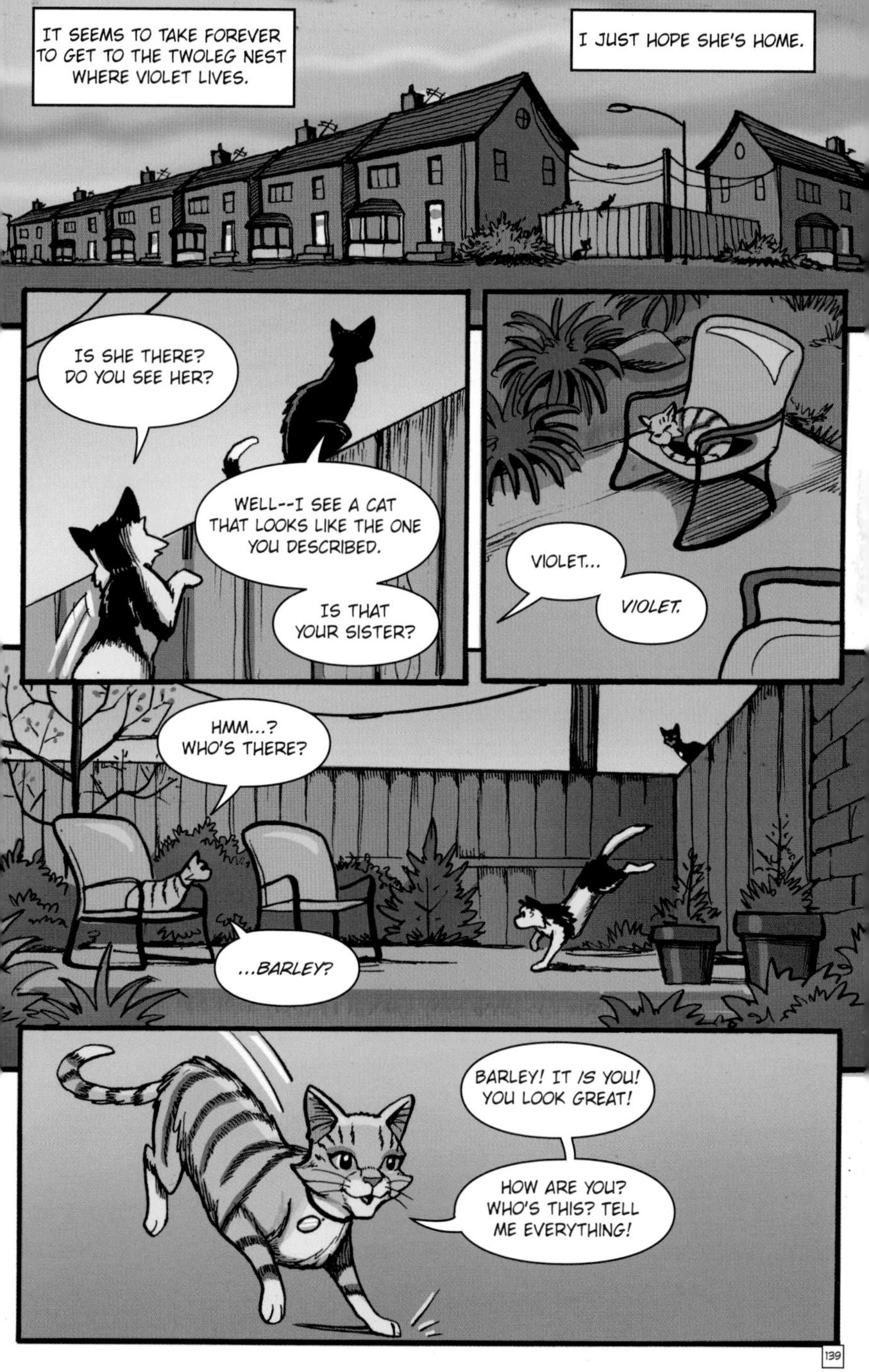
IT SEEMS TO TAKE FOREVER TO GET TO THE TWOLEG NEST WHERE VIOLET LIVES.
I JUST HOPE SHE'S HOME.
IS SHE THERE? DO YOU SEE HER?
WELL--I SEE A CAT THAT LOOKS LIKE THE ONE YOU DESCRIBED.
IS THAT YOUR SISTER?
VIOLET...
VIOLET.
HMM...? WHO'S THERE?
...BARLEY?
BARLEY! IT IS YOU! YOU LOOK GREAT!
HOW ARE YOU? WHO'S THIS? TELL ME EVERYTHING!

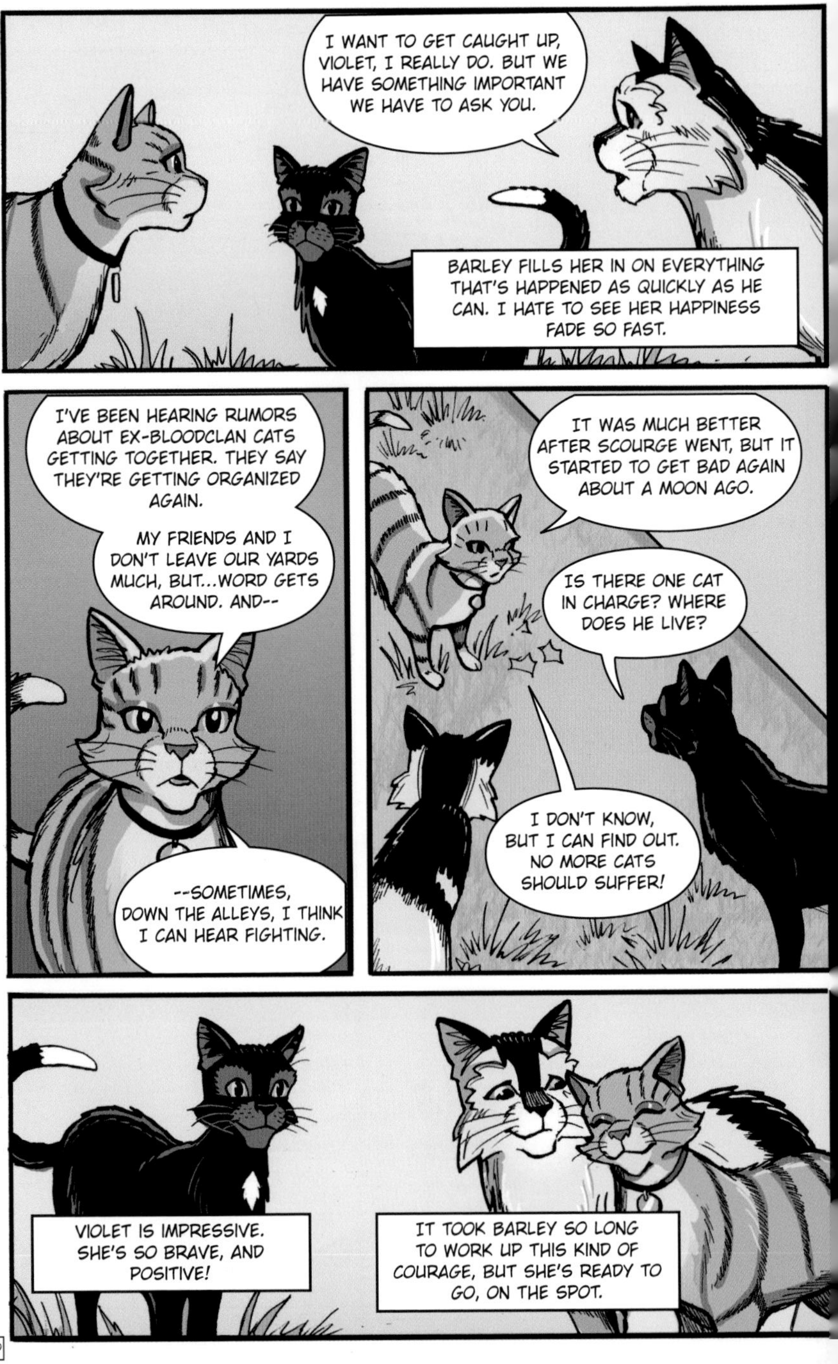
I WANT TO GET CAUGHT UP, VIOLET, I REALLY DO. BUT WE HAVE SOMETHING IMPORTANT WE HAVE TO ASK YOU.
BARLEY FILLS HER IN ON EVERYTHING THAT'S HAPPENED AS QUICKLY AS HE CAN. I HATE TO SEE HER HAPPINESS FADE SO FAST.
I'VE BEEN HEARING RUMORS ABOUT EX-BLOODCLAN CATS GETTING TOGETHER. THEY SAY THEY'RE GETTING ORGANIZED AGAIN.
MY FRIENDS AND I DON'T LEAVE OUR YARDS MUCH, BUT...WORD GETS AROUND. AND--
--SOMETIMES, DOWN THE ALLEYS, I THINK I CAN HEAR FIGHTING.
IT WAS MUCH BETTER AFTER SCOURGE WENT, BUT IT STARTED TO GET BAD AGAIN ABOUT A MOON AGO.
IS THERE ONE CAT IN CHARGE? WHERE DOES HE LIVE?
I DON'T KNOW, BUT I CAN FIND OUT. NO MORE CATS SHOULD SUFFER!
VIOLET IS IMPRESSIVE. SHE'S SO BRAVE, AND POSITIVE!
IT TOOK BARLEY SO LONG TO WORK UP THIS KIND OF COURAGE, BUT SHE'S READY TO GO, ON THE SPOT.

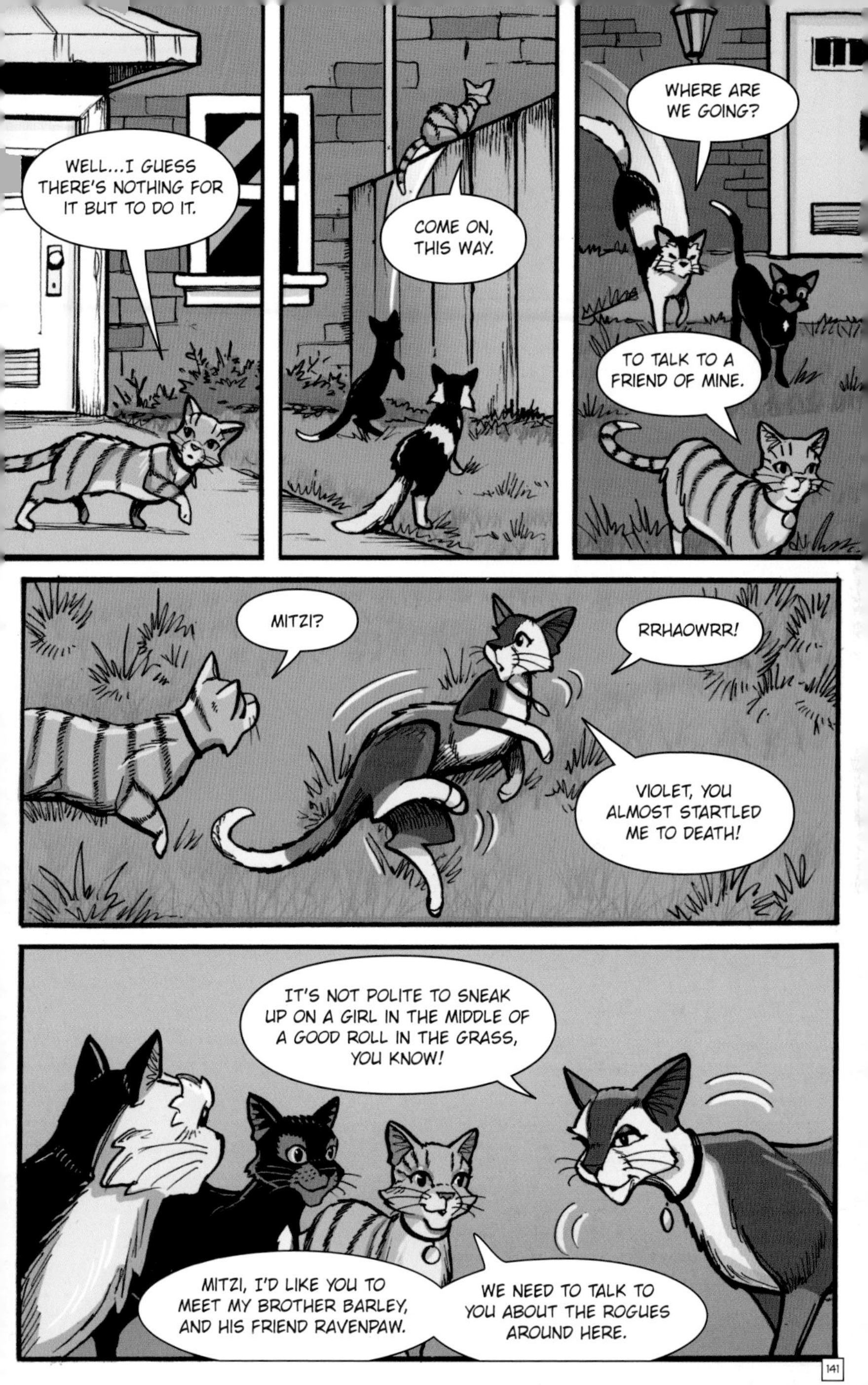
WELL...I GUESS THERE'S NOTHING FOR IT BUT TO DO IT.
COME ON, THIS WAY.
WHERE ARE WE GOING?
TO TALK TO A FRIEND OF MINE.
MITZI?
RRHAOWRR!
VIOLET, YOU ALMOST STARTLED ME TO DEATH!
IT'S NOT POLITE TO SNEAK UP ON A GIRL IN THE MIDDLE OF A GOOD ROLL IN THE GRASS, YOU KNOW!
MITZI, I'D LIKE YOU TO MEET MY BROTHER BARLEY, AND HIS FRIEND RAVENPAW.
WE NEED TO TALK TO YOU ABOUT THE ROGUES AROUND HERE.

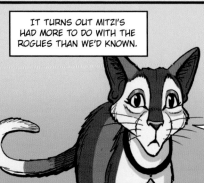

IT TURNS OUT MITZI'S HAD MORE TO DO WITH THE ROGUES THAN WE'D KNOWN.

THEY...THEY TOOK MY SON. THOSE MONSTERS FROM BLOODCLAN. THEY JUST TOOK HIM ONE NIGHT, AND I HAVEN'T SEEN HIM SINCE.

I FOLLOWED THEM, FOLLOWED HIS SCENT, BUT I DIDN'T DARE GET CLOSE. THEY'RE RECRUITING A NEW BLOODCLAN NOW, WITH NEW LEADERSHIP.

TAKE US THERE, MITZI. PLEASE.

MAYBE WE CAN FIND YOUR SON.

I-I DON'T KNOW, VIOLET. WHAT CAN YOU THREE DO?

IT WON'T BE JUST US. IF WE CAN FIND OUT WHERE THESE CATS LIVE, THERE ARE MORE WHO WOULD FIGHT THEM, TOO.

A LOT MORE.

WITH MITZI CONVINCED, WE SET OUT... AND THE CLOSER WE GOT TO THIS PLACE, EVEN THOUGH I HADN'T SEEN IT YET, THE TENSER I GOT.

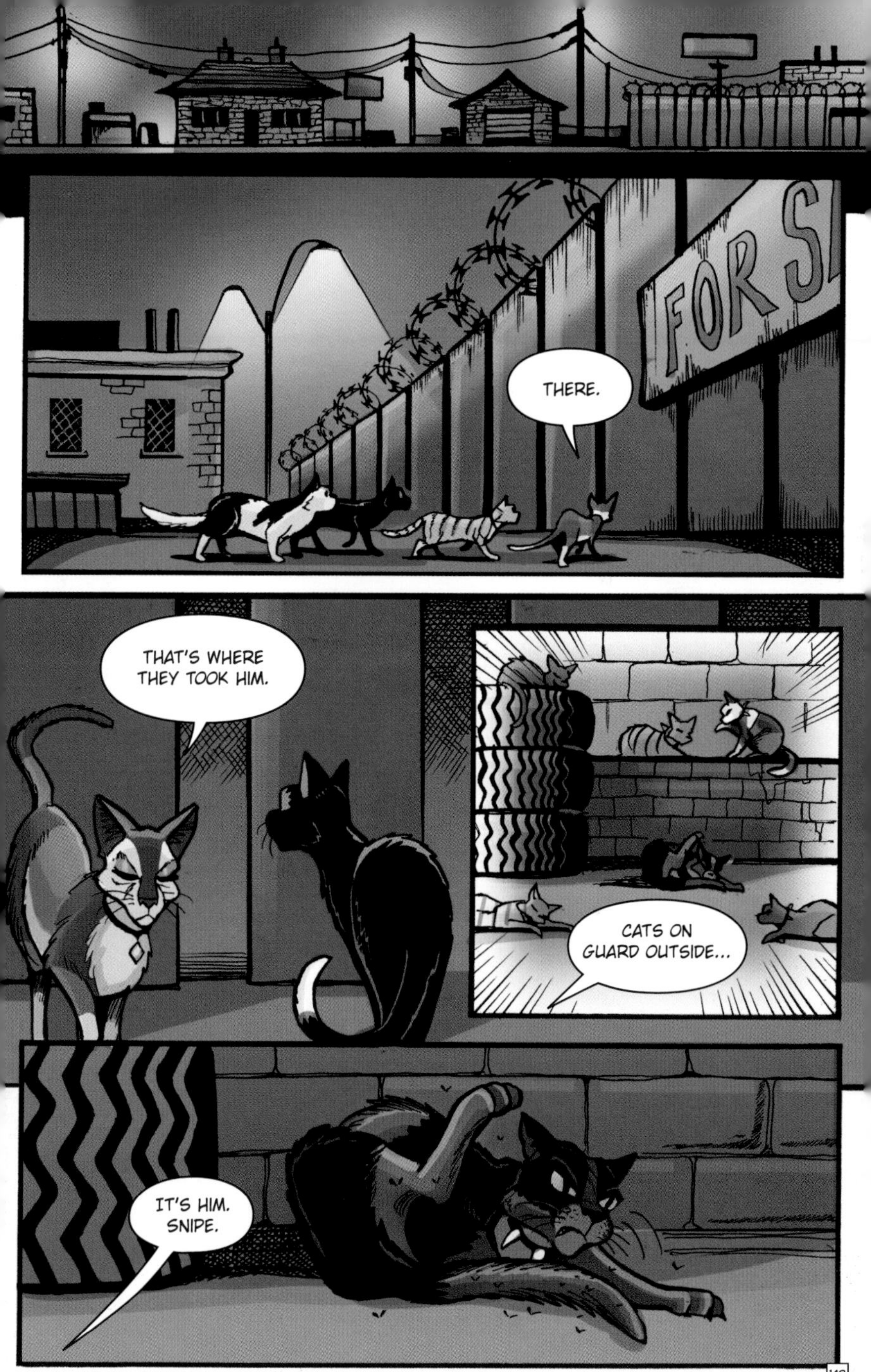
FOR S
THERE.
THAT'S WHERE THEY TOOK HIM.
CATS ON GUARD OUTSIDE...
IT'S HIM. SNIPE.

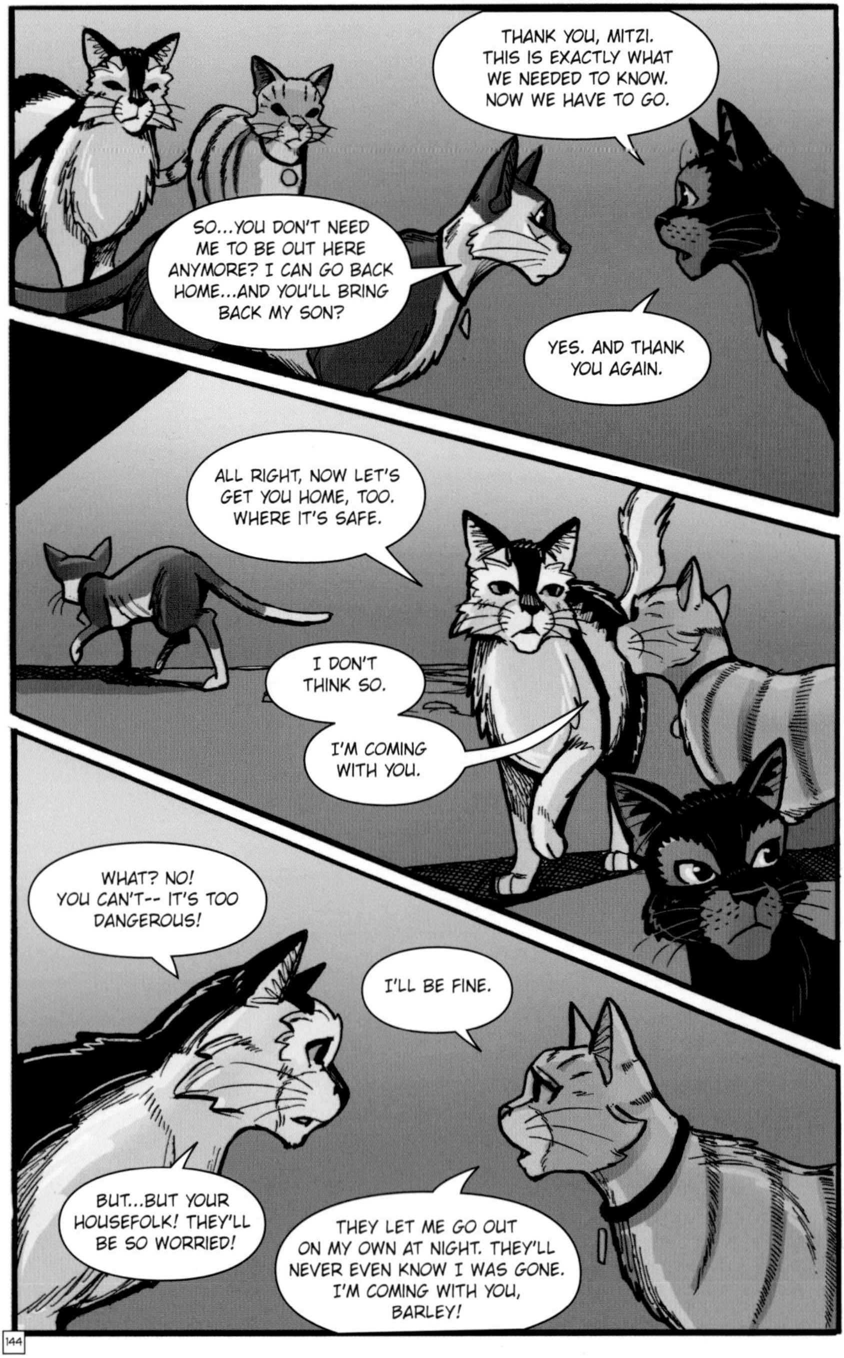
THANK YOU, MITZI. THIS IS EXACTLY WHAT WE NEEDED TO KNOW. NOW WE HAVE TO GO.
SO...YOU DON'T NEED ME TO BE OUT HERE ANYMORE? I CAN GO BACK HOME...AND YOU'LL BRING BACK MY SON?
YES. AND THANK YOU AGAIN.
ALL RIGHT, NOW LET'S GET YOU HOME, TOO. WHERE IT'S SAFE.
I DON'T THINK SO.
I'M COMING WITH YOU.
WHAT? NO! YOU CAN'T-- IT'S TOO DANGEROUS!
I'LL BE FINE.
BUT...BUT YOUR HOUSEFOLK! THEY'LL BE SO WORRIED!
THEY LET ME GO OUT ON MY OWN AT NIGHT. THEY'LL NEVER EVEN KNOW I WAS GONE. I'M COMING WITH YOU, BARLEY!

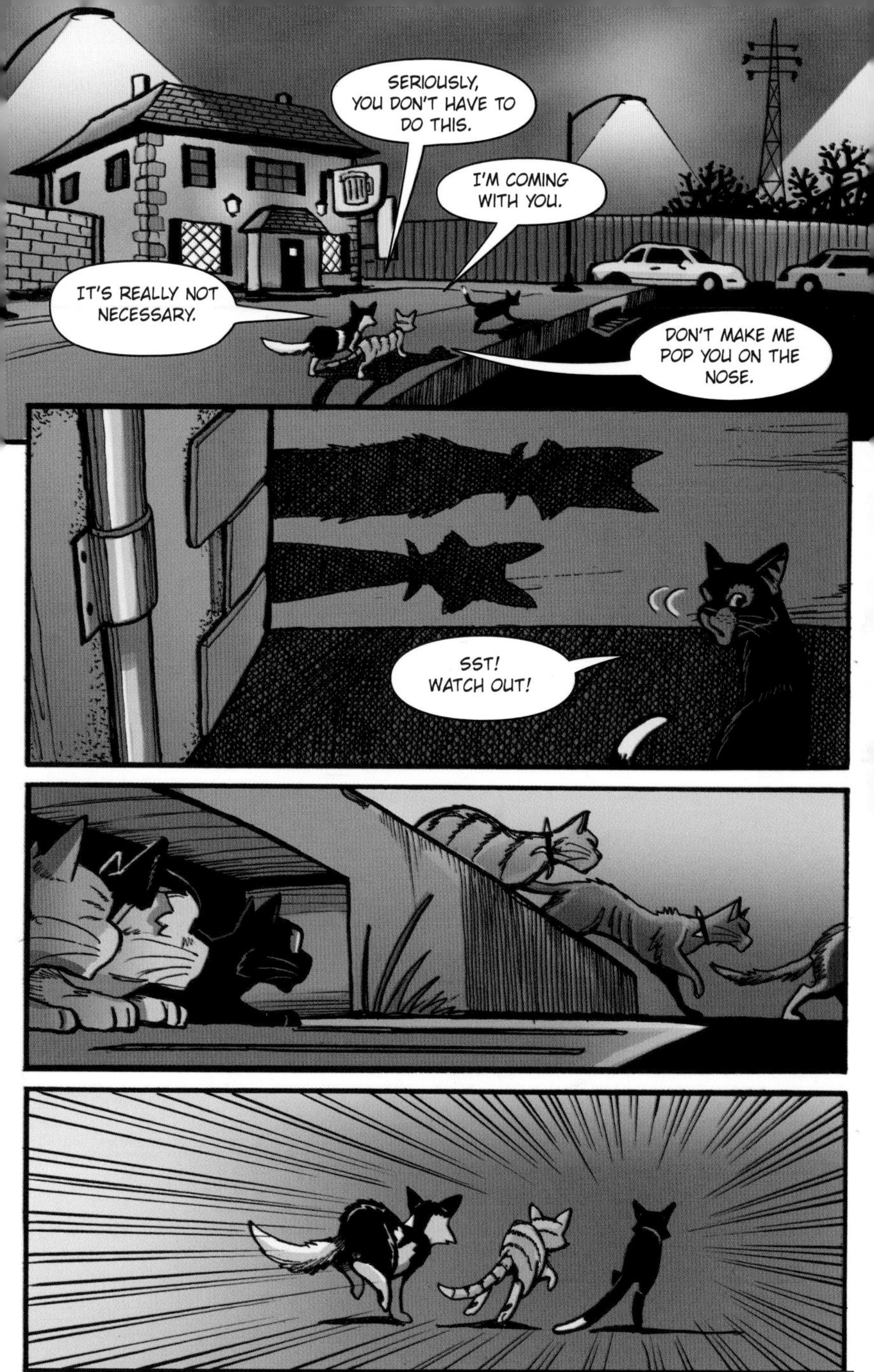
SERIOUSLY, YOU DON'T HAVE TO DO THIS.
I'M COMING WITH YOU.
IT'S REALLY NOT NECESSARY.
DON'T MAKE ME POP YOU ON THE NOSE.
SST! WATCH OUT!

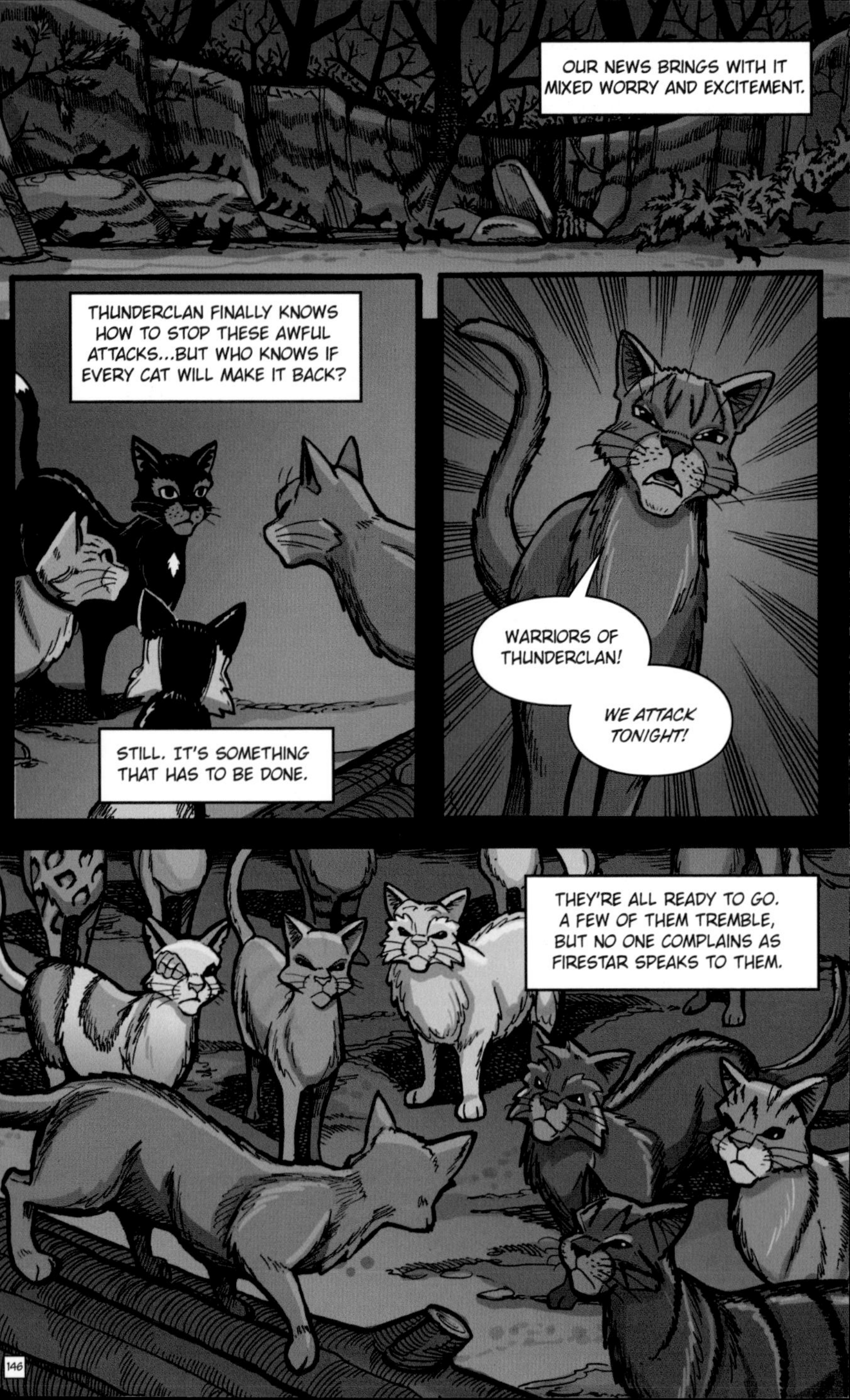
OUR NEWS BRINGS WITH IT MIXED WORRY AND EXCITEMENT.
THUNDERCLAN FINALLY KNOWS HOW TO STOP THESE AWFUL ATTACKS...BUT WHO KNOWS IF EVERY CAT WILL MAKE IT BACK?
STILL, IT'S SOMETHING THAT HAS TO BE DONE.
WARRIORS OF THUNDERCLAN!
WE ATTACK TONIGHT!
THEY'RE ALL READY TO GO. A FEW OF THEM TREMBLE, BUT NO ONE COMPLAINS AS FIRESTAR SPEAKS TO THEM.

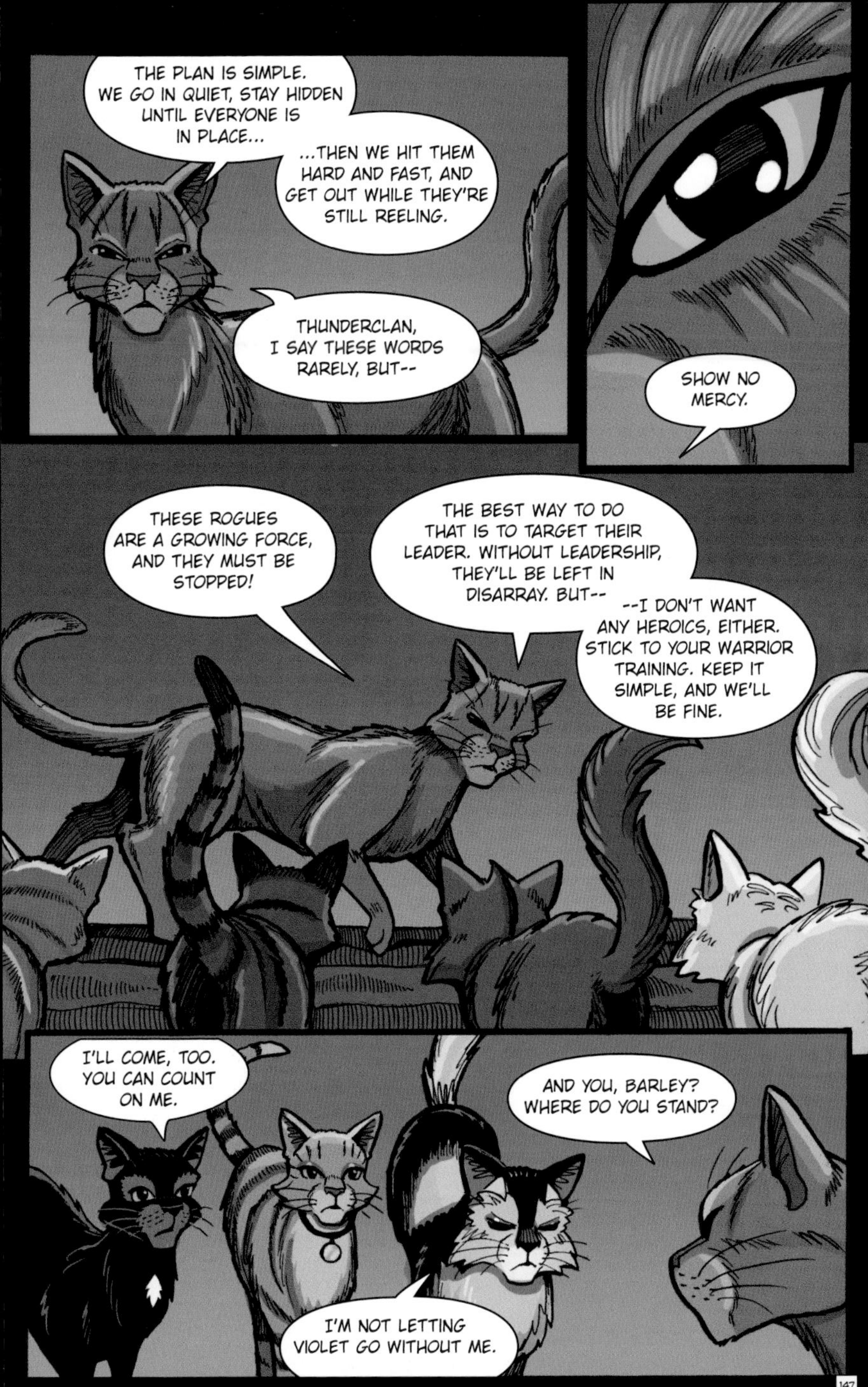
THE PLAN IS SIMPLE. WE GO IN QUIET, STAY HIDDEN UNTIL EVERYONE IS IN PLACE...
...THEN WE HIT THEM HARD AND FAST, AND GET OUT WHILE THEY'RE STILL REELING.
THUNDERCLAN, I SAY THESE WORDS RARELY, BUT--
SHOW NO MERCY.
THESE ROGUES ARE A GROWING FORCE, AND THEY MUST BE STOPPED!
THE BEST WAY TO DO THAT IS TO TARGET THEIR LEADER. WITHOUT LEADERSHIP, THEY'LL BE LEFT IN DISARRAY. BUT--
--I DON'T WANT ANY HEROICS, EITHER. STICK TO YOUR WARRIOR TRAINING. KEEP IT SIMPLE, AND WE'LL BE FINE.
I'LL COME, TOO. YOU CAN COUNT ON ME.
AND YOU, BARLEY? WHERE DO YOU STAND?
I'M NOT LETTING VIOLET GO WITHOUT ME.

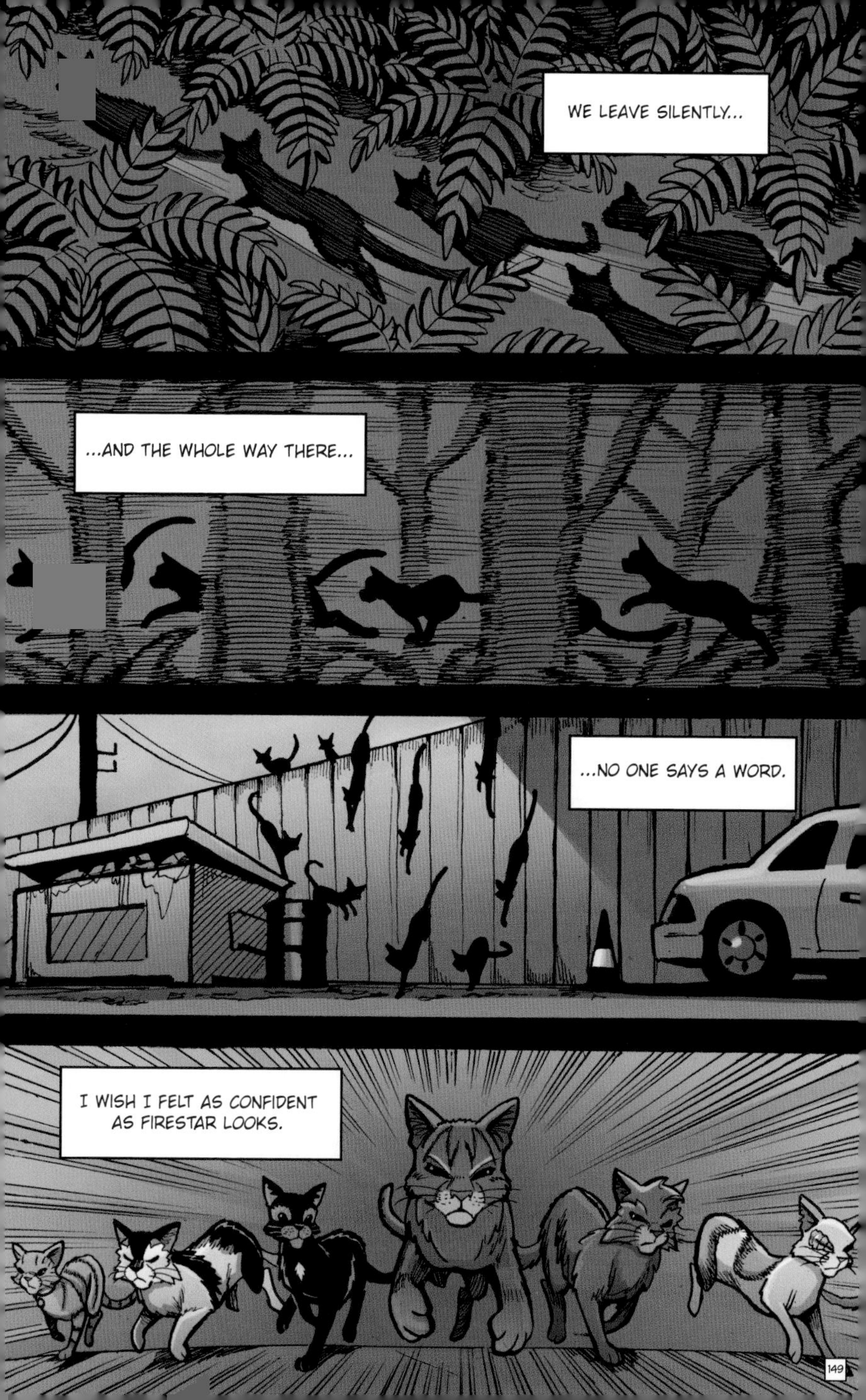
WE LEAVE SILENTLY...
...AND THE WHOLE WAY THERE...
...NO ONE SAYS A WORD.
I WISH I FELT AS CONFIDENT AS FIRESTAR LOOKS.

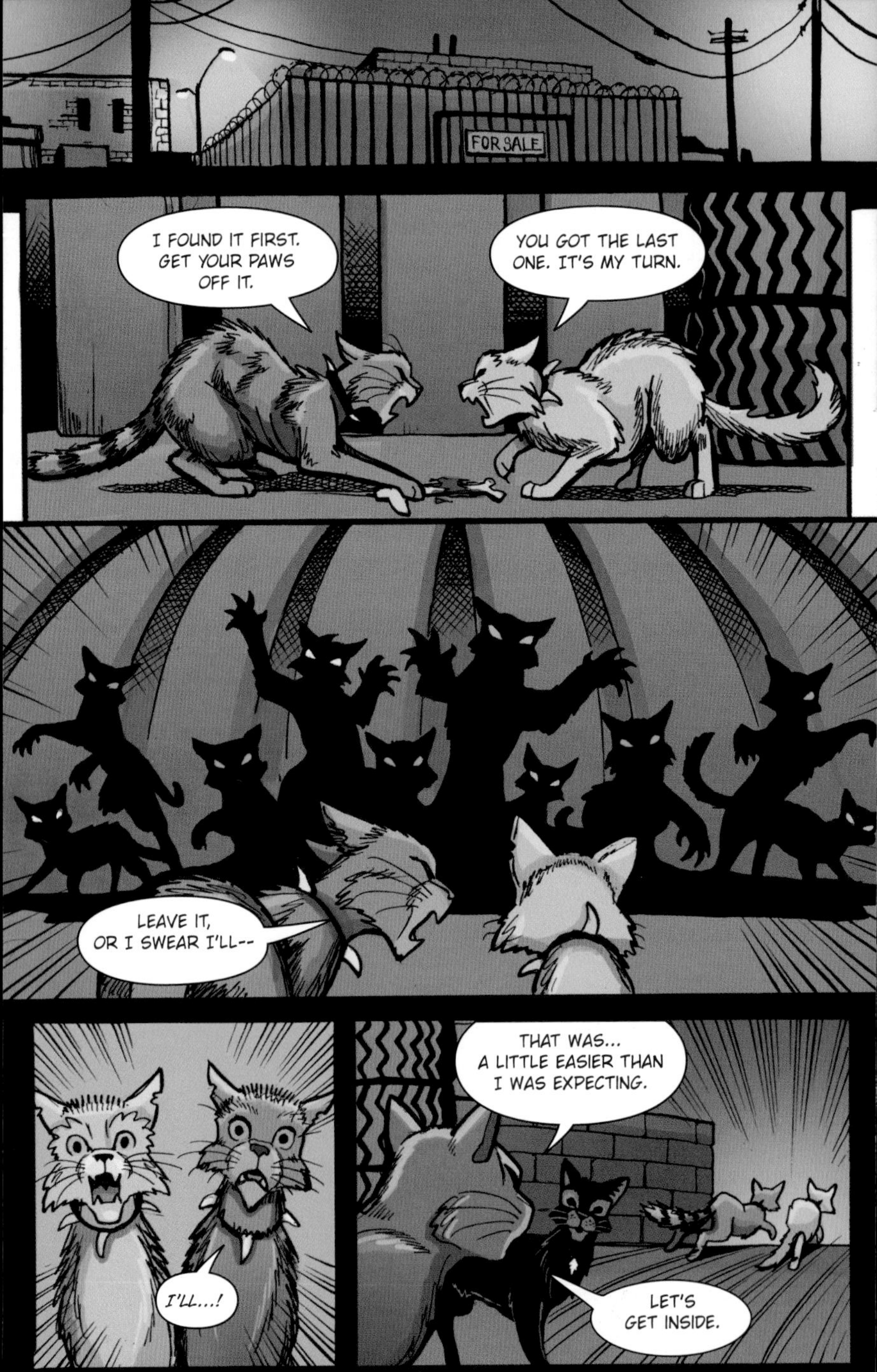
FOR SALE
I FOUND IT FIRST. GET YOUR PAWS OFF IT.
YOU GOT THE LAST ONE. IT'S MY TURN.
LEAVE IT, OR I SWEAR I'LL--
I'LL...!
THAT WAS... A LITTLE EASIER THAN I WAS EXPECTING.
LET'S GET INSIDE.

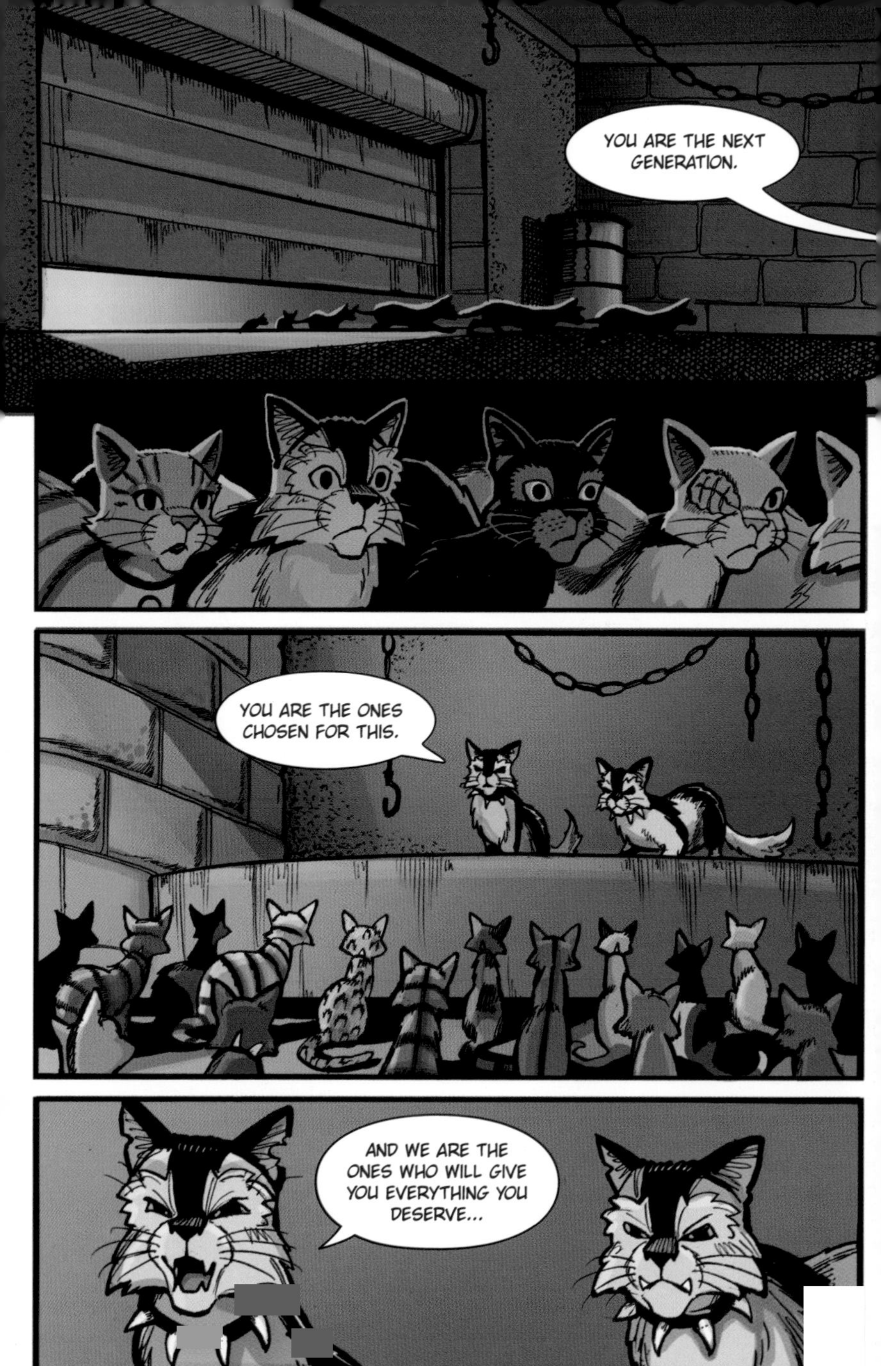
YOU ARE THE NEXT GENERATION.
YOU ARE THE ONES CHOSEN FOR THIS.
AND WE ARE THE ONES WHO WILL GIVE YOU EVERYTHING YOU DESERVE...

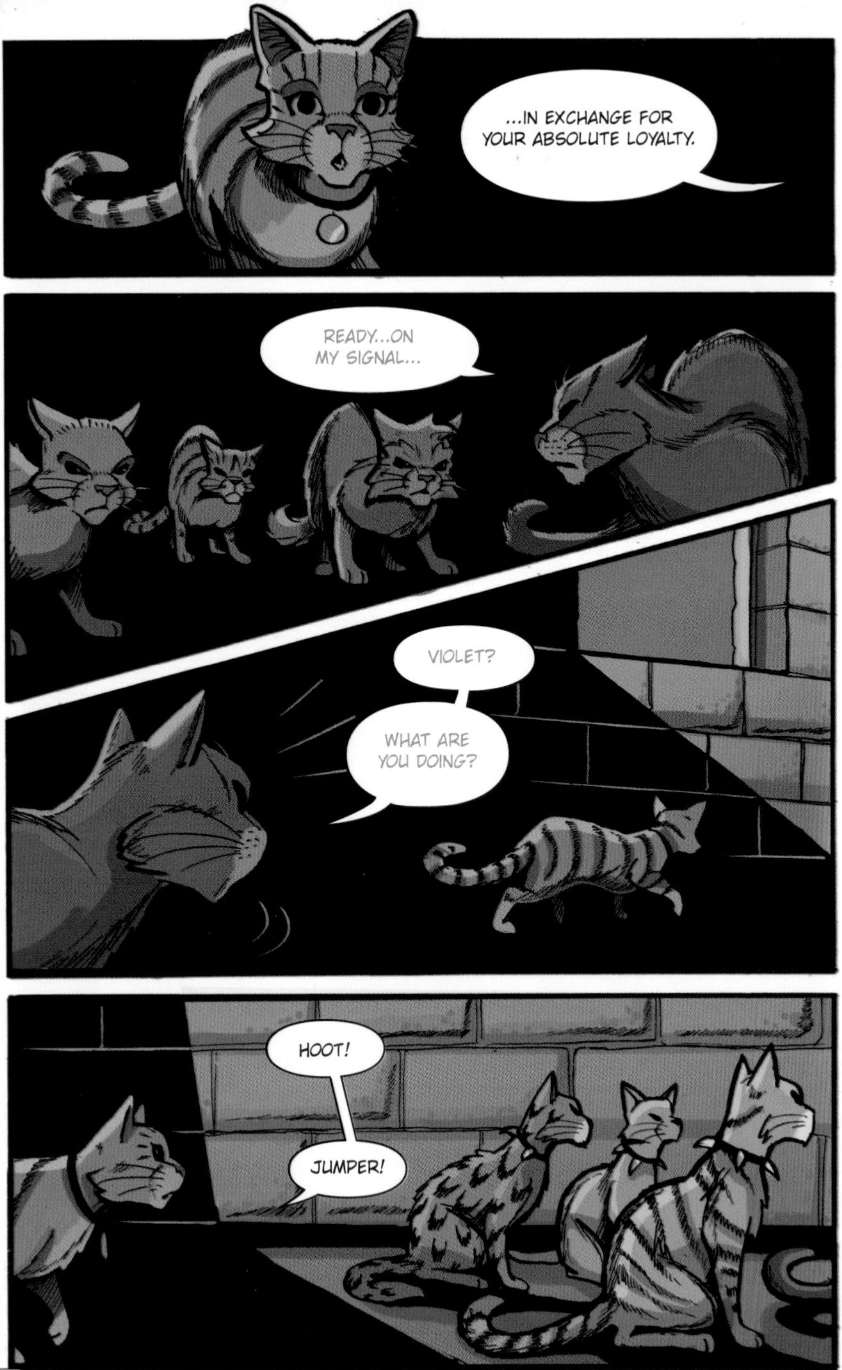
...IN EXCHANGE FOR YOUR ABSOLUTE LOYALTY.
READY...ON MY SIGNAL...
VIOLET?
WHAT ARE YOU DOING?
HOOT!
JUMPER!

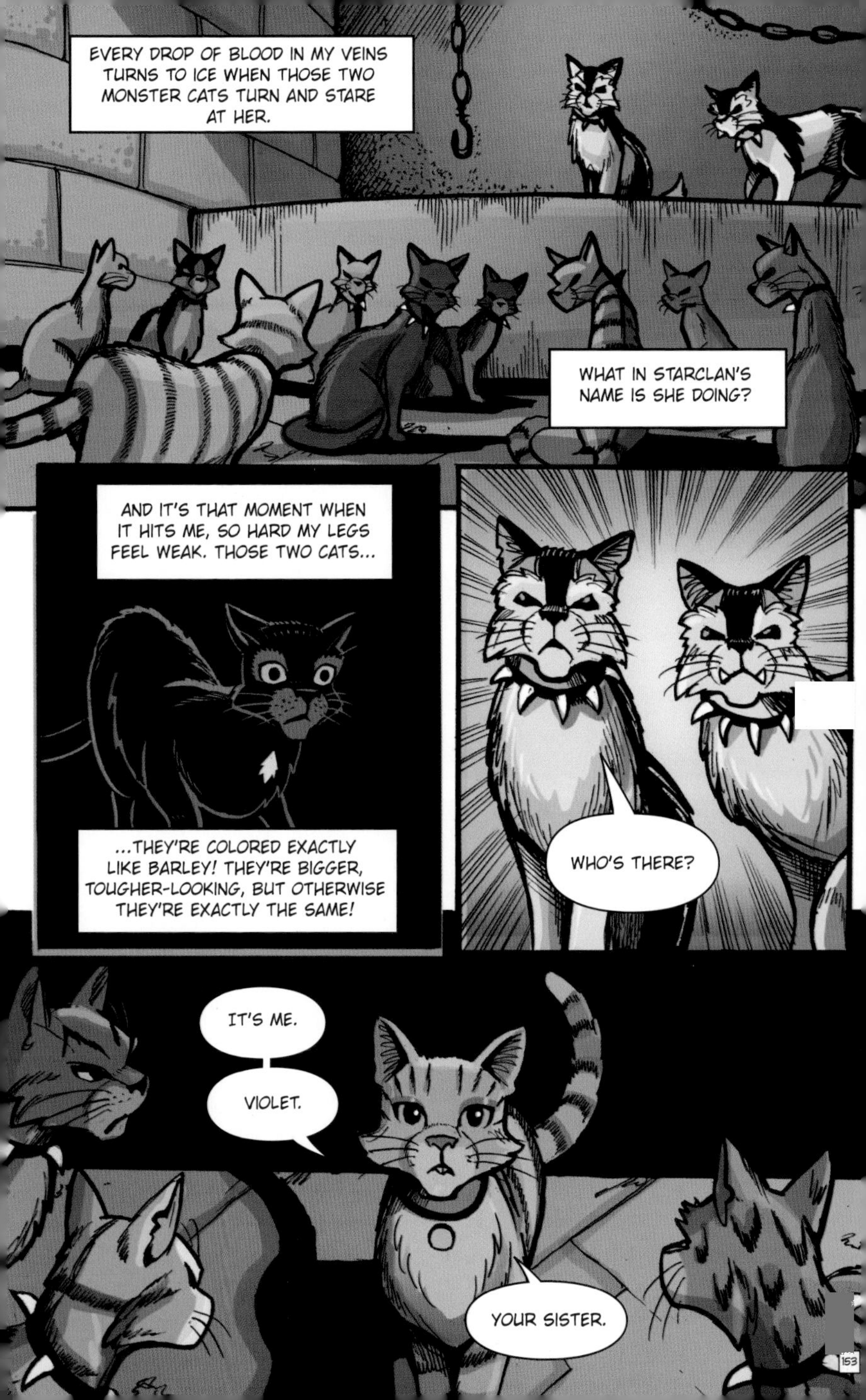
EVERY DROP OF BLOOD IN MY VEINS TURNS TO ICE WHEN THOSE TWO MONSTER CATS TURN AND STARE AT HER.
WHAT IN STARCLAN'S NAME IS SHE DOING?
AND IT'S THAT MOMENT WHEN IT HITS ME, SO HARD MY LEGS FEEL WEAK. THOSE TWO CATS...
...THEY'RE COLORED EXACTLY LIKE BARLEY! THEY'RE BIGGER, TOUGHER-LOOKING, BUT OTHERWISE THEY'RE EXACTLY THE SAME!
WHO'S THERE?
IT'S ME.
VIOLET.
YOUR SISTER.

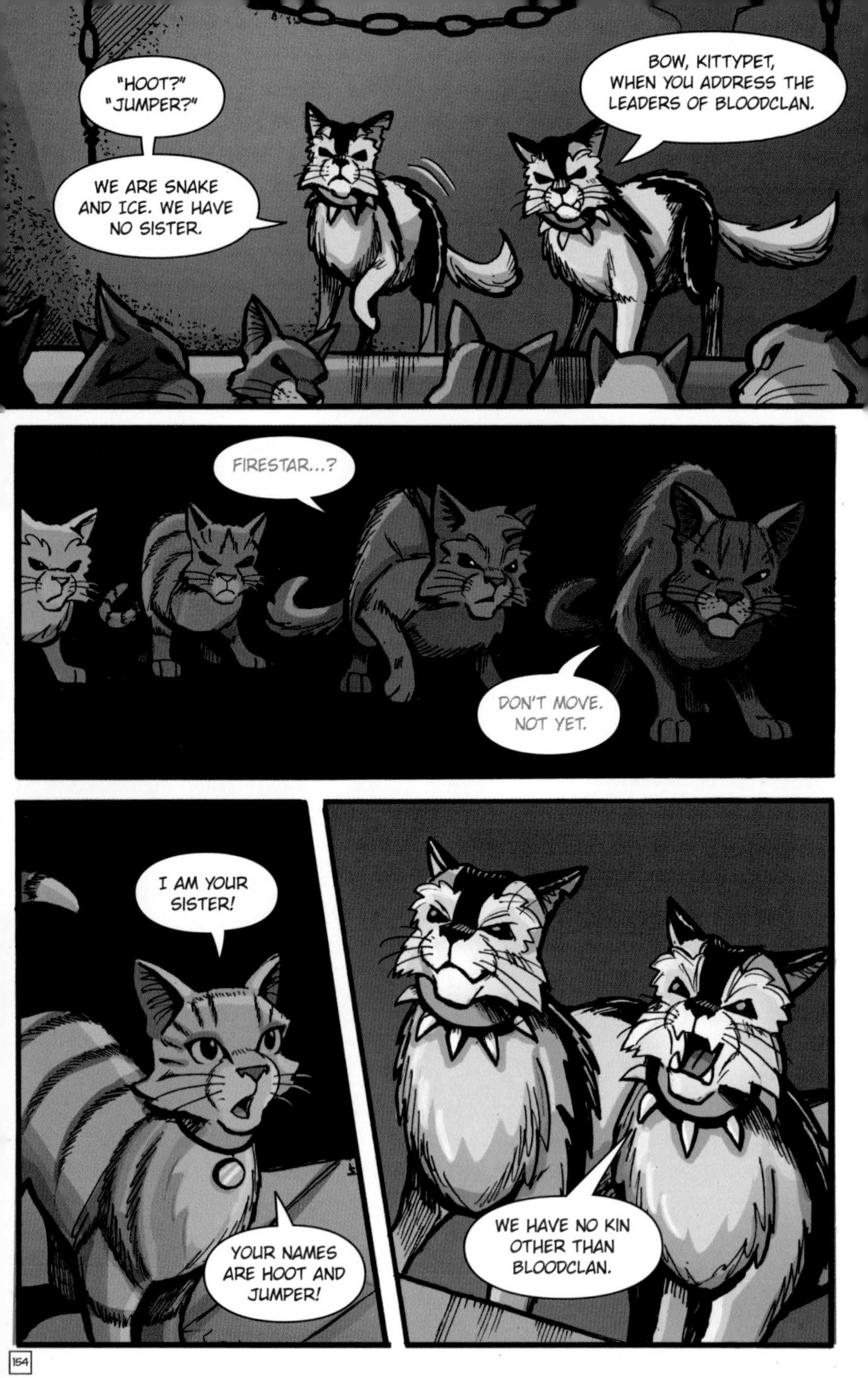
"HOOT?" "JUMPER?"
WE ARE SNAKE AND ICE. WE HAVE NO SISTER.
BOW, KITTYPET, WHEN YOU ADDRESS THE LEADERS OF BLOODCLAN.
FIRESTAR...?
DON'T MOVE. NOT YET.
I AM YOUR SISTER!
YOUR NAMES ARE HOOT AND JUMPER!
WE HAVE NO KIN OTHER THAN BLOODCLAN.

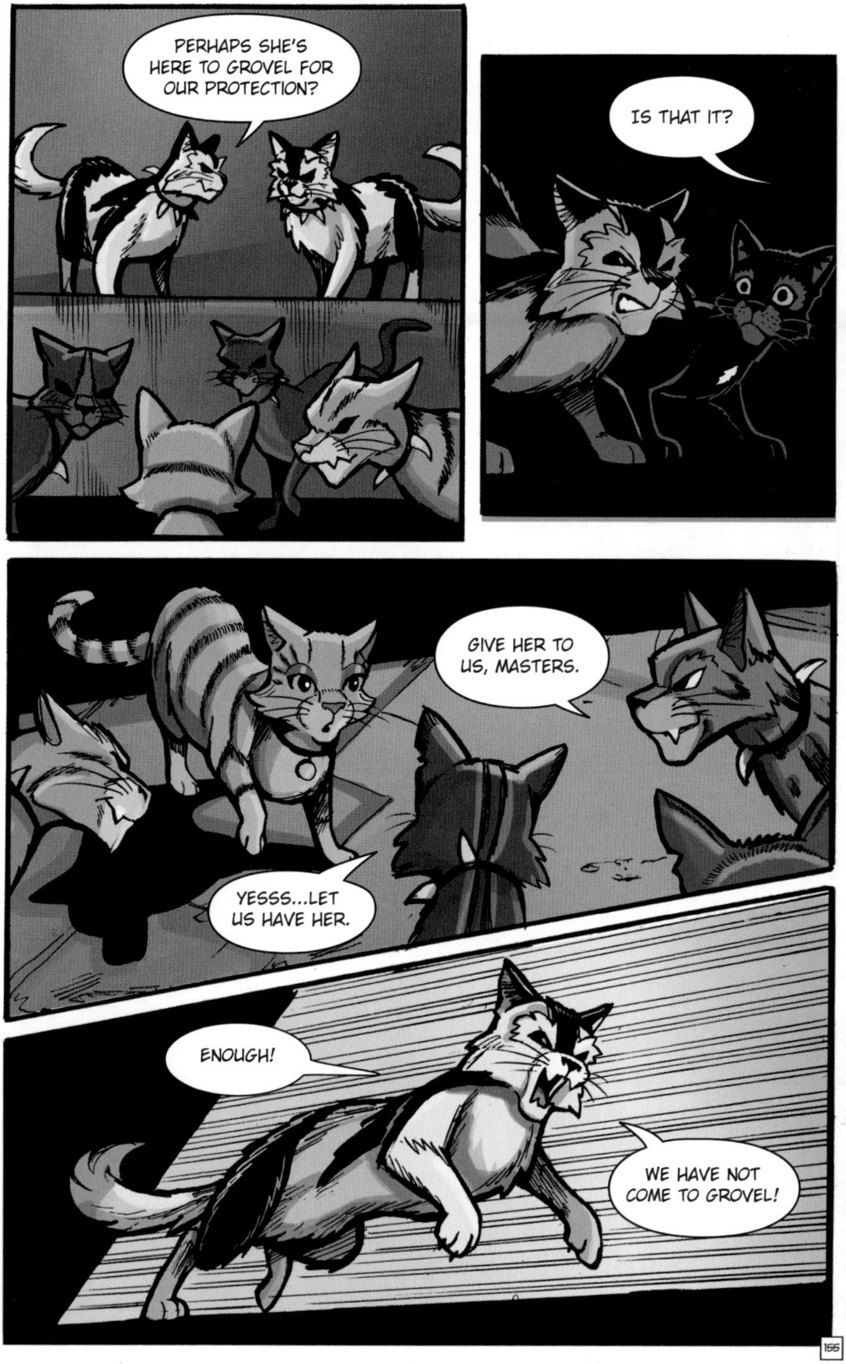
PERHAPS SHE'S HERE TO GROVEL FOR OUR PROTECTION?
IS THAT IT?
GIVE HER TO US, MASTERS.
YESSS...LET US HAVE HER.
ENOUGH!
WE HAVE NOT COME TO GROVEL!

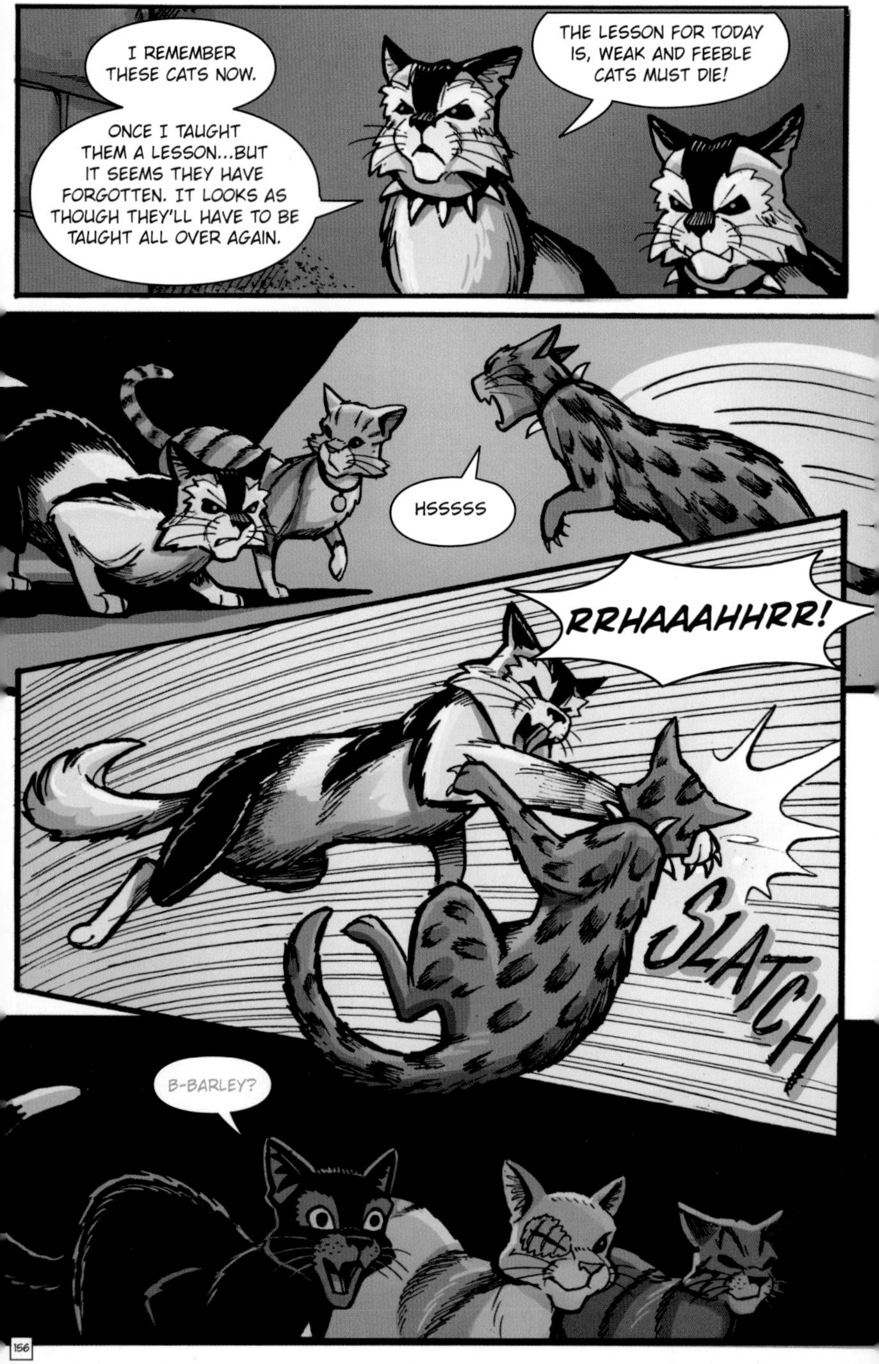
I REMEMBER THESE CATS NOW.
ONCE I TAUGHT THEM A LESSON...BUT IT SEEMS THEY HAVE FORGOTTEN. IT LOOKS AS THOUGH THEY'LL HAVE TO BE TAUGHT ALL OVER AGAIN.
THE LESSON FOR TODAY IS, WEAK AND FEEBLE CATS MUST DIE!
HSSSSS
RRHAAAHHRR!
SLATCH!
B-BARLEY?

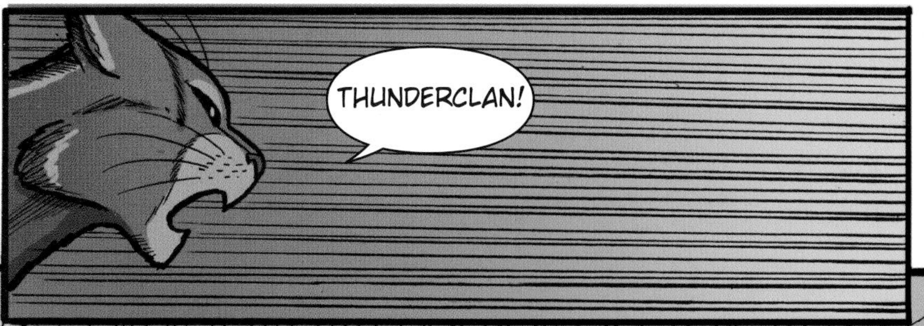
THUNDERCLAN!

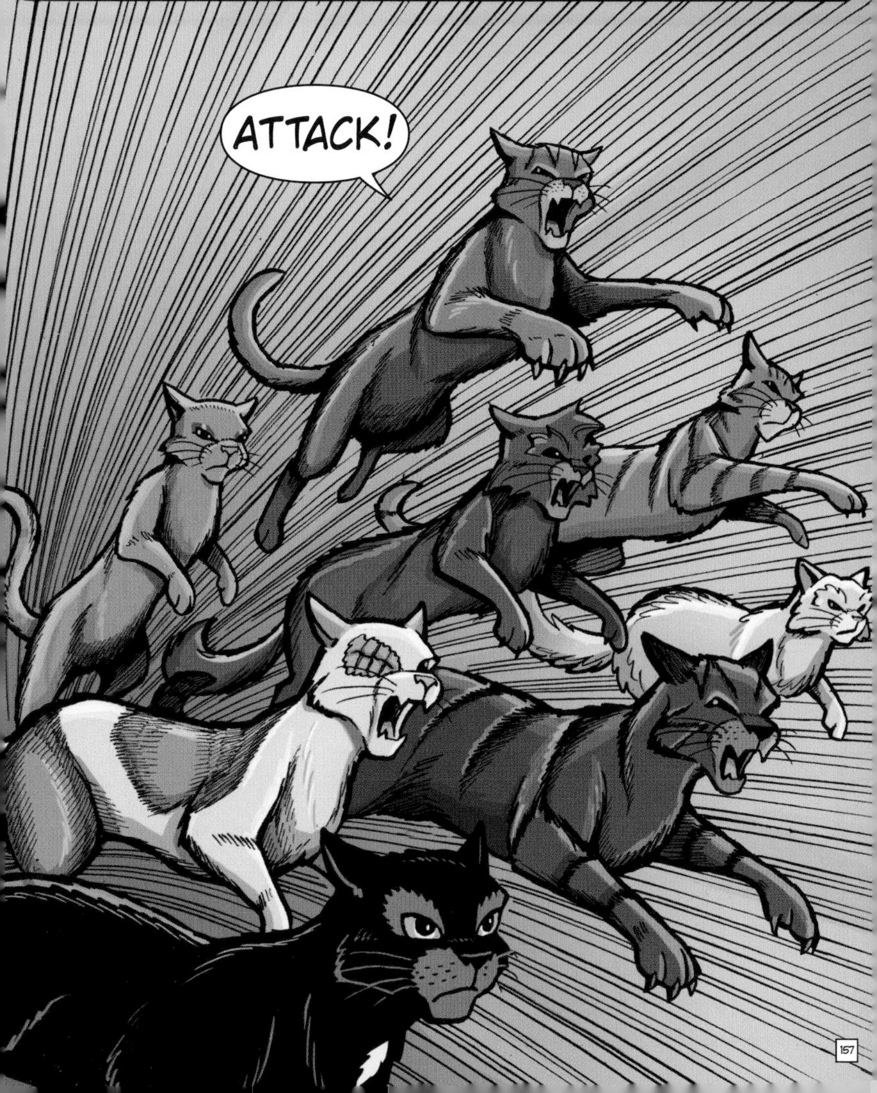
ATTACK!

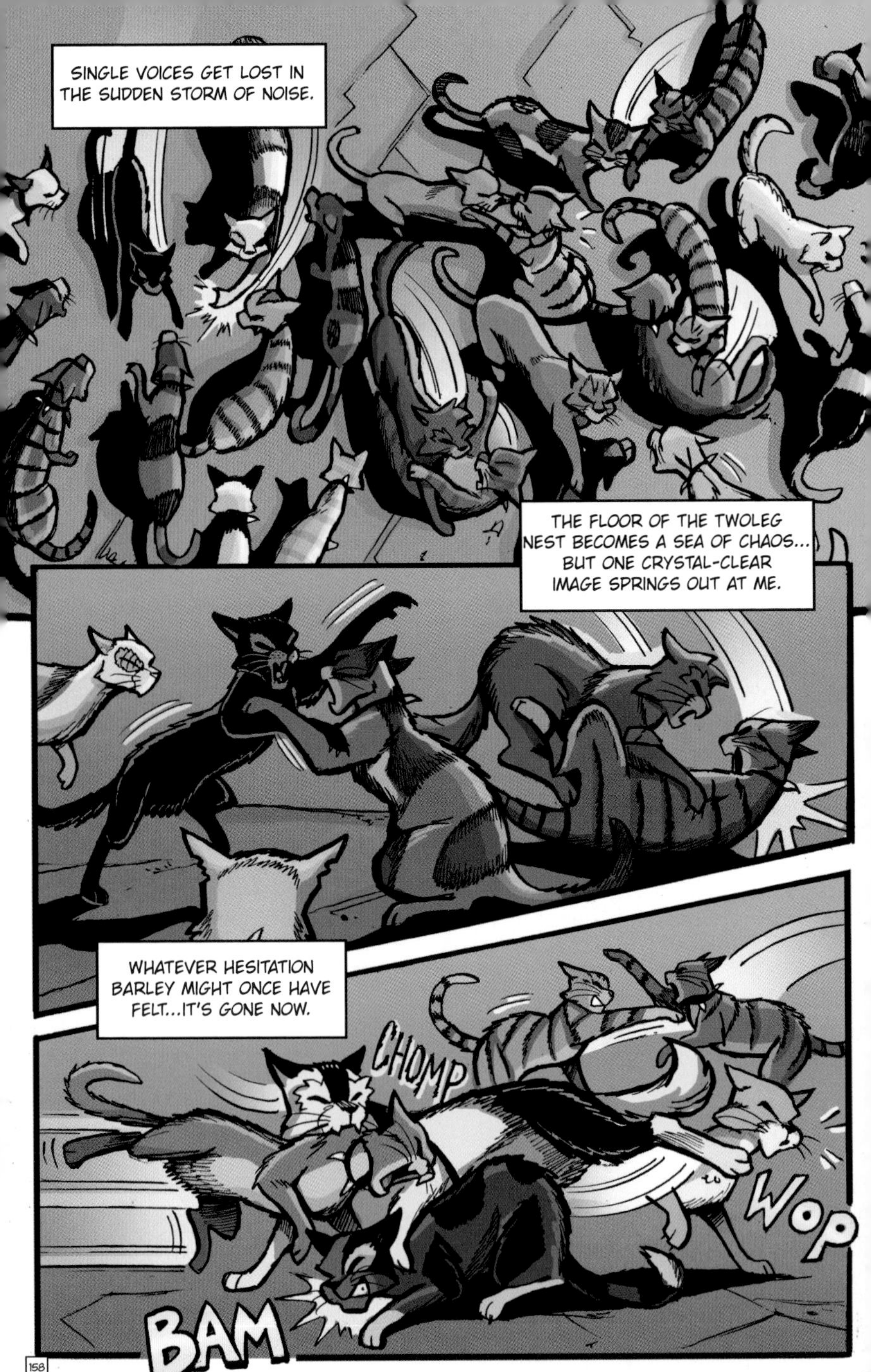
SINGLE VOICES GET LOST IN THE SUDDEN STORM OF NOISE.
THE FLOOR OF THE TWOLEG NEST BECOMES A SEA OF CHAOS... BUT ONE CRYSTAL-CLEAR IMAGE SPRINGS OUT AT ME.
WHATEVER HESITATION BARLEY MIGHT ONCE HAVE FELT...IT'S GONE NOW.
CHOMP
WOP
BAM

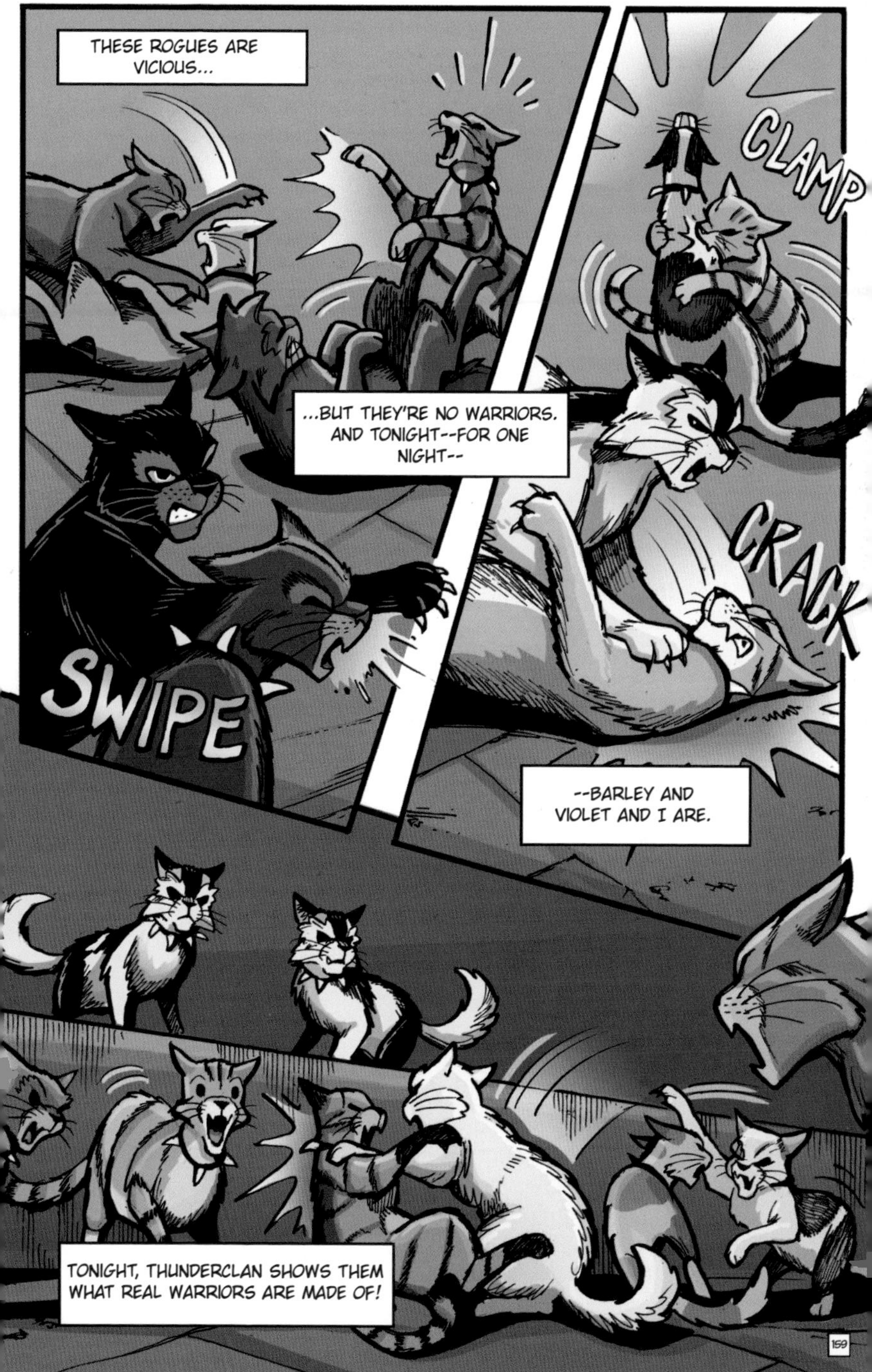
THESE ROGUES ARE VICIOUS...
SWIPE
...BUT THEY'RE NO WARRIORS. AND TONIGHT--FOR ONE NIGHT--
CLAMP
CRACK
--BARLEY AND VIOLET AND I ARE.
TONIGHT, THUNDERCLAN SHOWS THEM WHAT REAL WARRIORS ARE MADE OF!

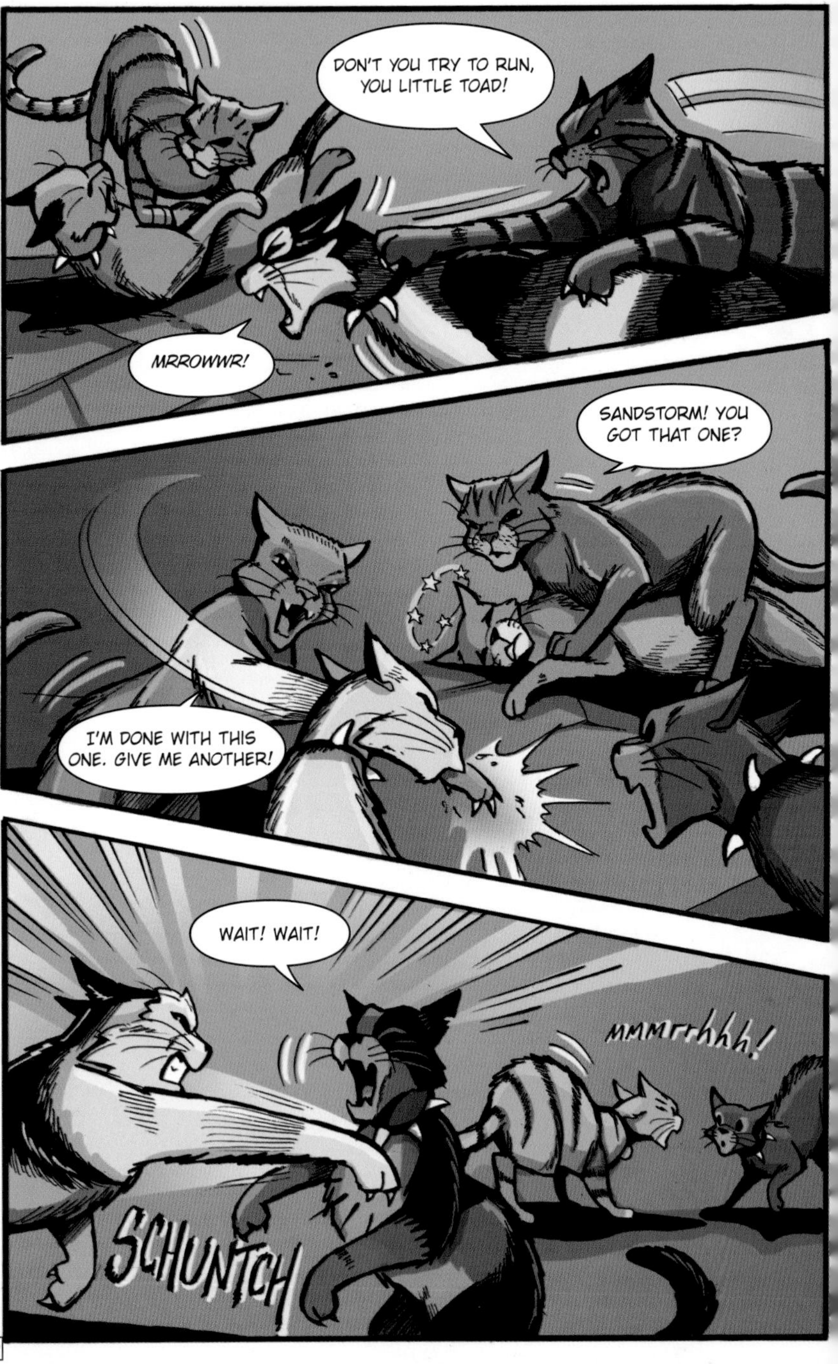
DON'T YOU TRY TO RUN, YOU LITTLE TOAD!
MRROWWR!
SANDSTORM! YOU GOT THAT ONE?
I'M DONE WITH THIS ONE. GIVE ME ANOTHER!
WAIT! WAIT!
MMMrrhhh!
SCHUNTCH

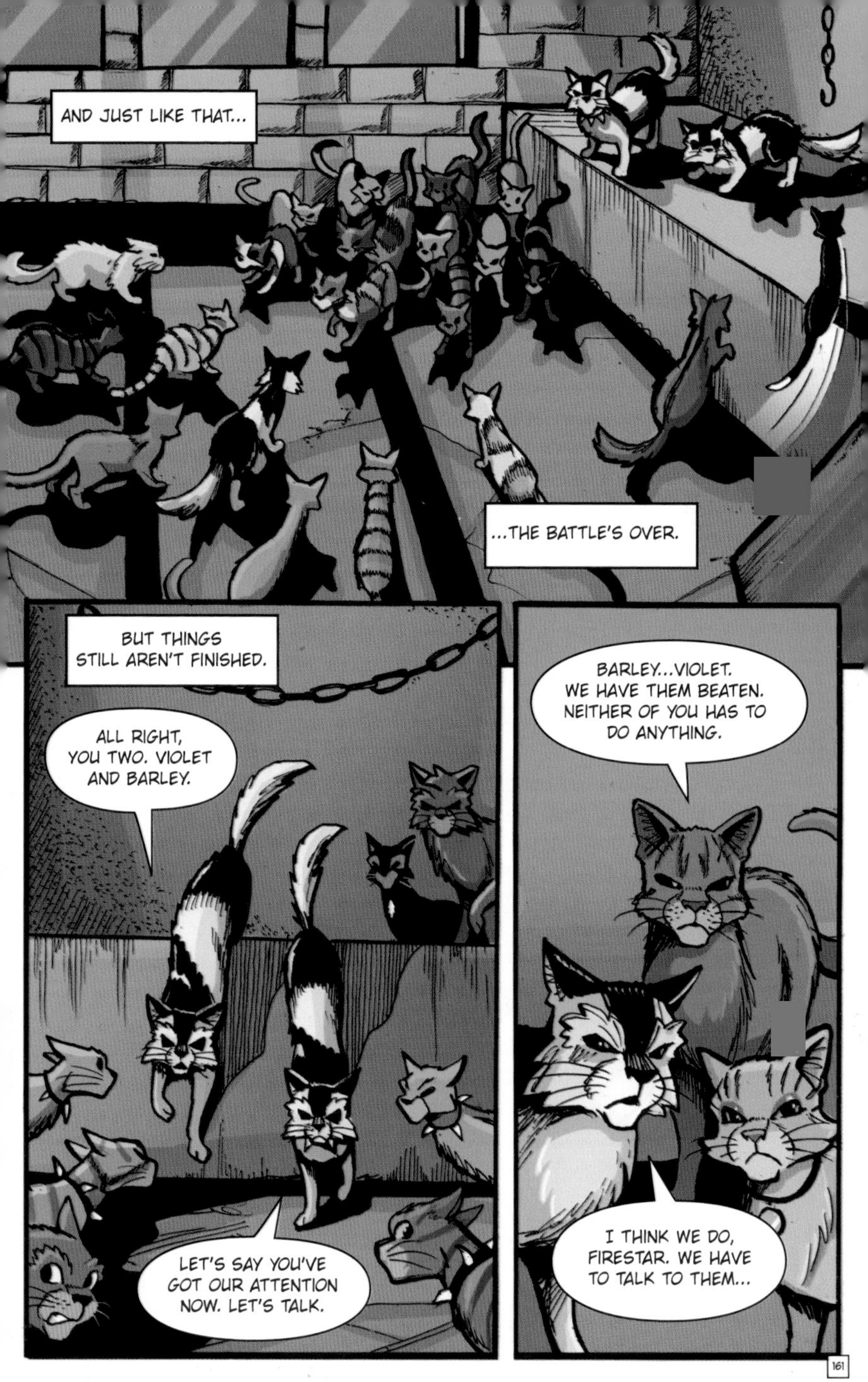
AND JUST LIKE THAT...
...THE BATTLE'S OVER.
BUT THINGS STILL AREN'T FINISHED.
ALL RIGHT, YOU TWO. VIOLET AND BARLEY.
LET'S SAY YOU'VE GOT OUR ATTENTION NOW. LET'S TALK.
BARLEY...VIOLET. WE HAVE THEM BEATEN. NEITHER OF YOU HAS TO DO ANYTHING.
I THINK WE DO, FIRESTAR. WE HAVE TO TALK TO THEM...

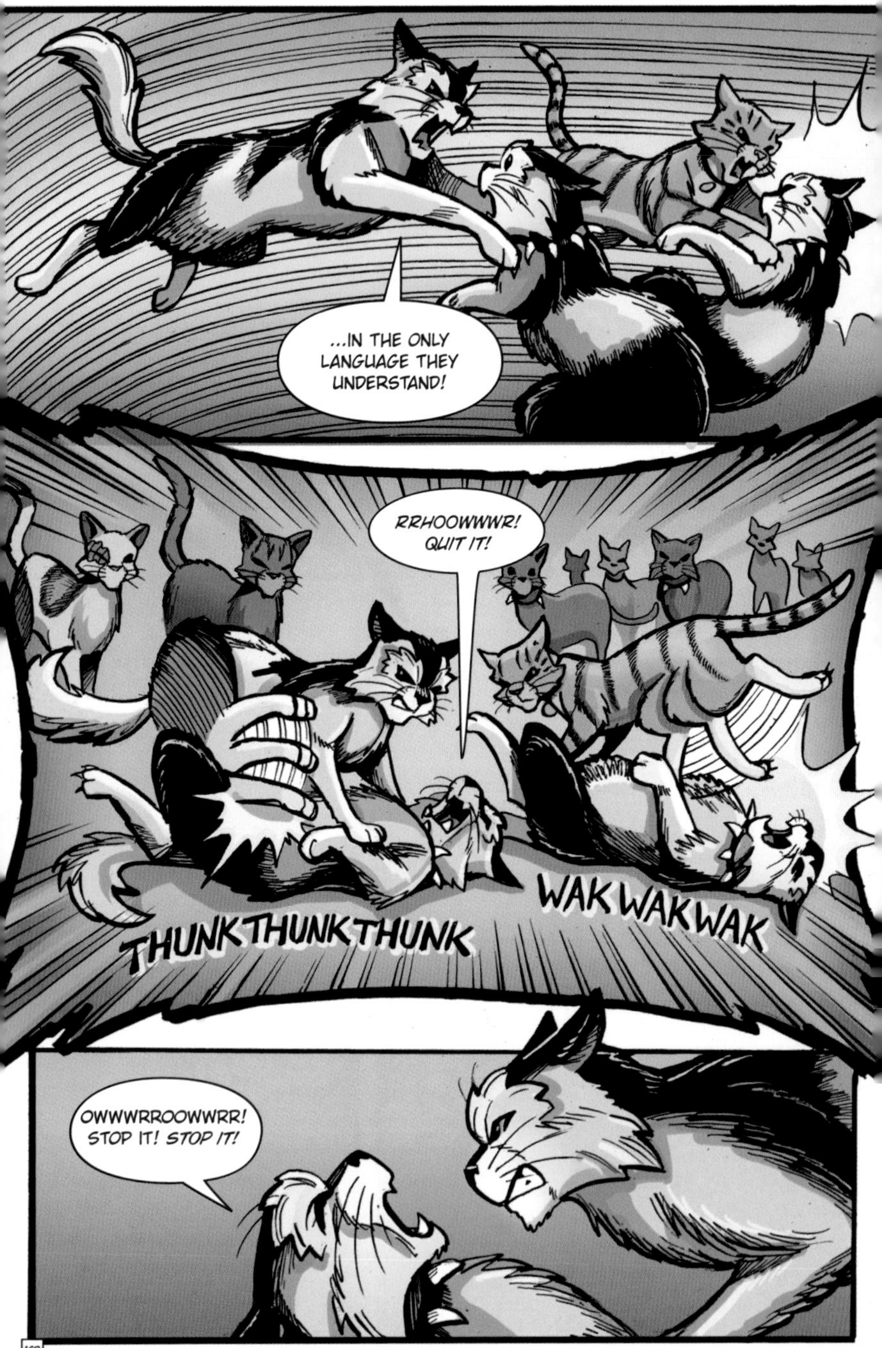
...IN THE ONLY LANGUAGE THEY UNDERSTAND!
RRHOOWWWR! QUIT IT!
THUNK THUNK THUNK
WAK WAK WAK
OWWWRROOWWRR! STOP IT! STOP IT!

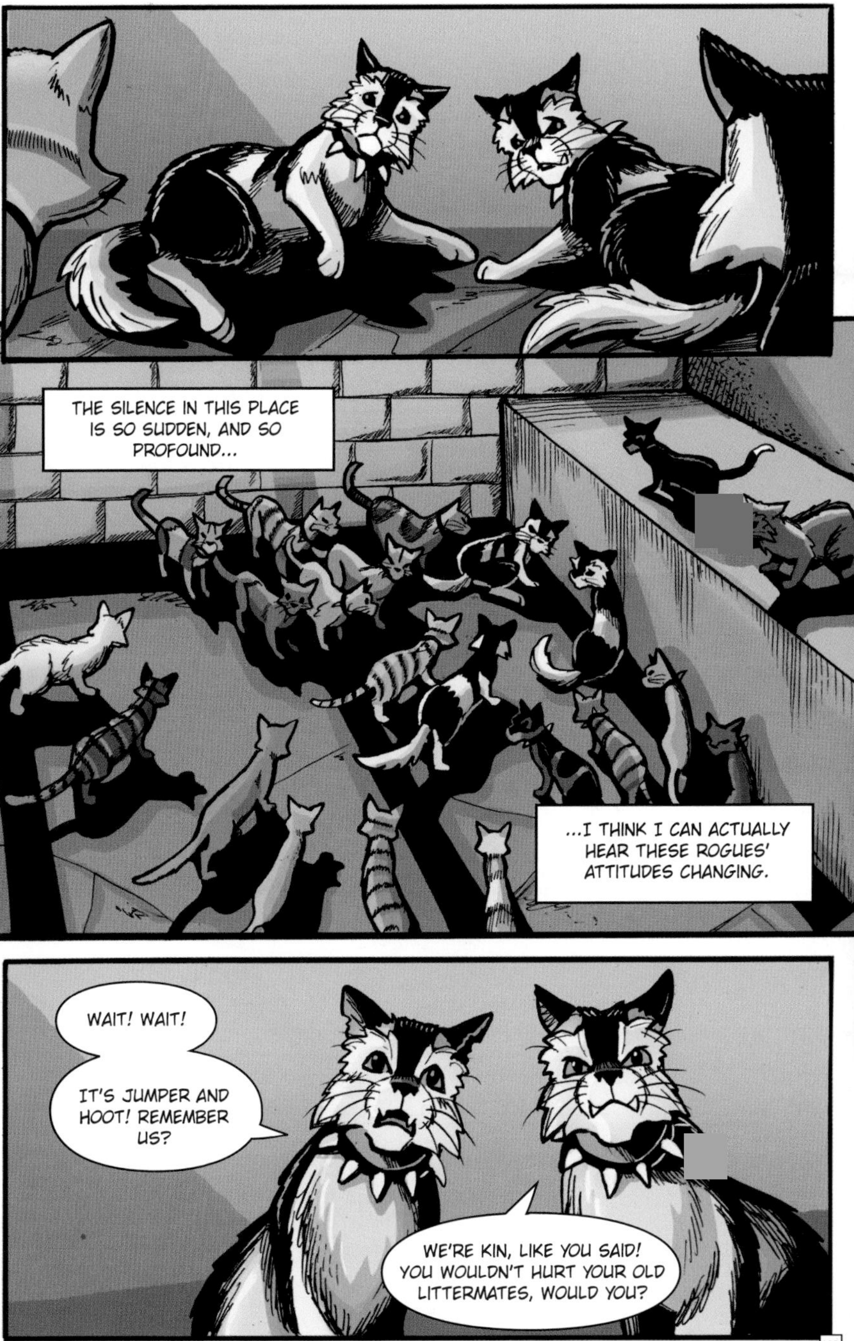
THE SILENCE IN THIS PLACE IS SO SUDDEN, AND SO PROFOUND...
...I THINK I CAN ACTUALLY HEAR THESE ROGUES' ATTITUDES CHANGING.
WAIT! WAIT!
IT'S JUMPER AND HOOT! REMEMBER US?
WE'RE KIN, LIKE YOU SAID! YOU WOULDN'T HURT YOUR OLD LITTERMATES, WOULD YOU?

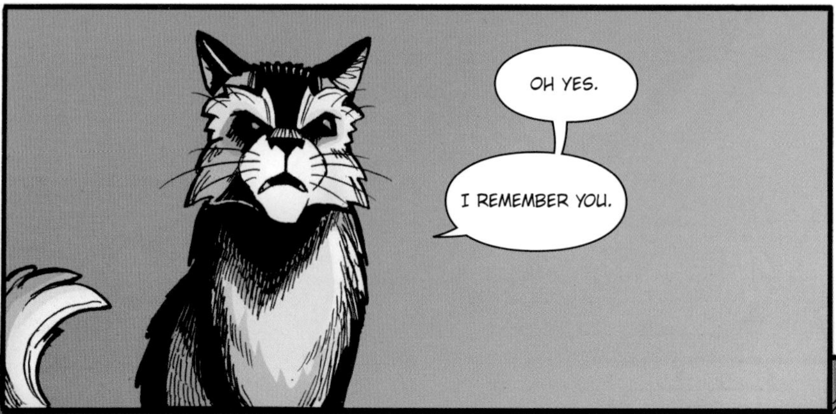
OH YES.
I REMEMBER YOU.

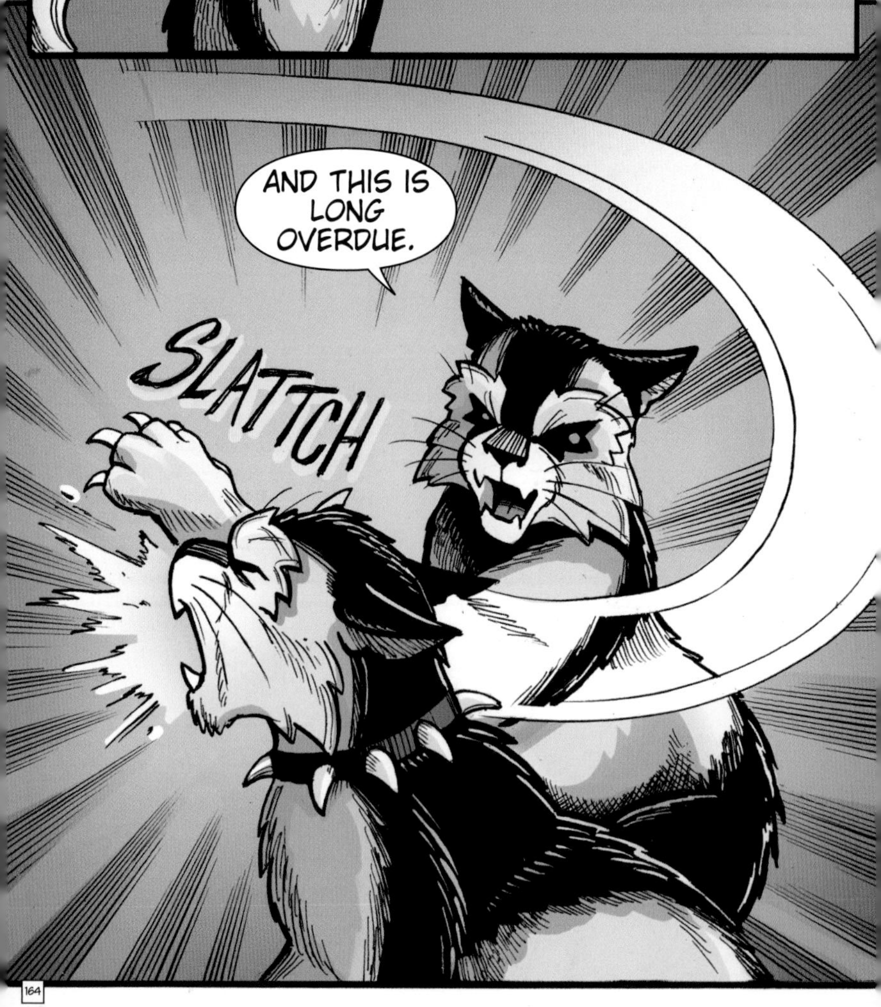
AND THIS IS LONG OVERDUE.
SLATTCH

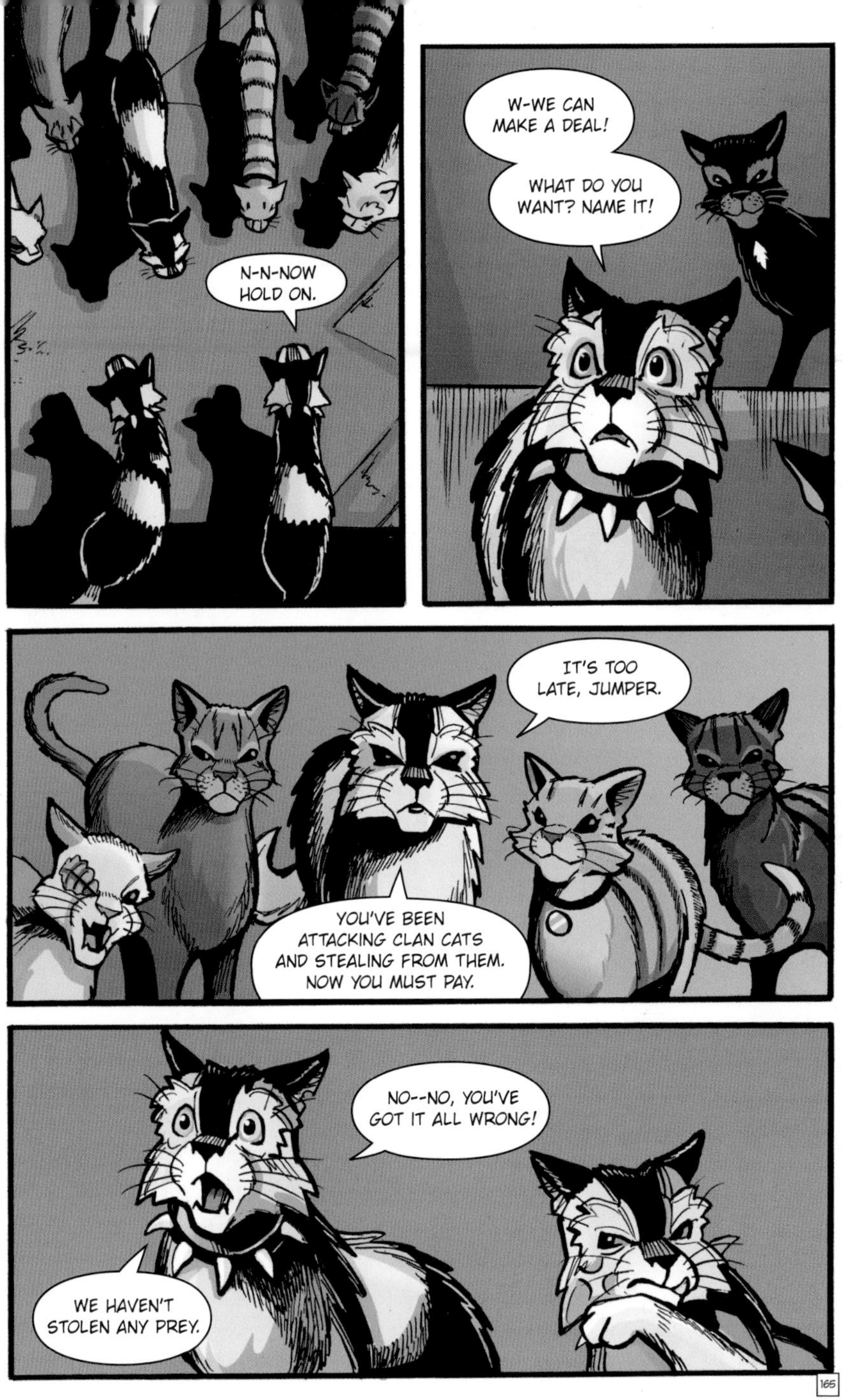
N-N-NOW HOLD ON.
W-WE CAN MAKE A DEAL!
WHAT DO YOU WANT? NAME IT!
IT'S TOO LATE, JUMPER.
YOU'VE BEEN ATTACKING CLAN CATS AND STEALING FROM THEM. NOW YOU MUST PAY.
NO--NO, YOU'VE GOT IT ALL WRONG!
WE HAVEN'T STOLEN ANY PREY.

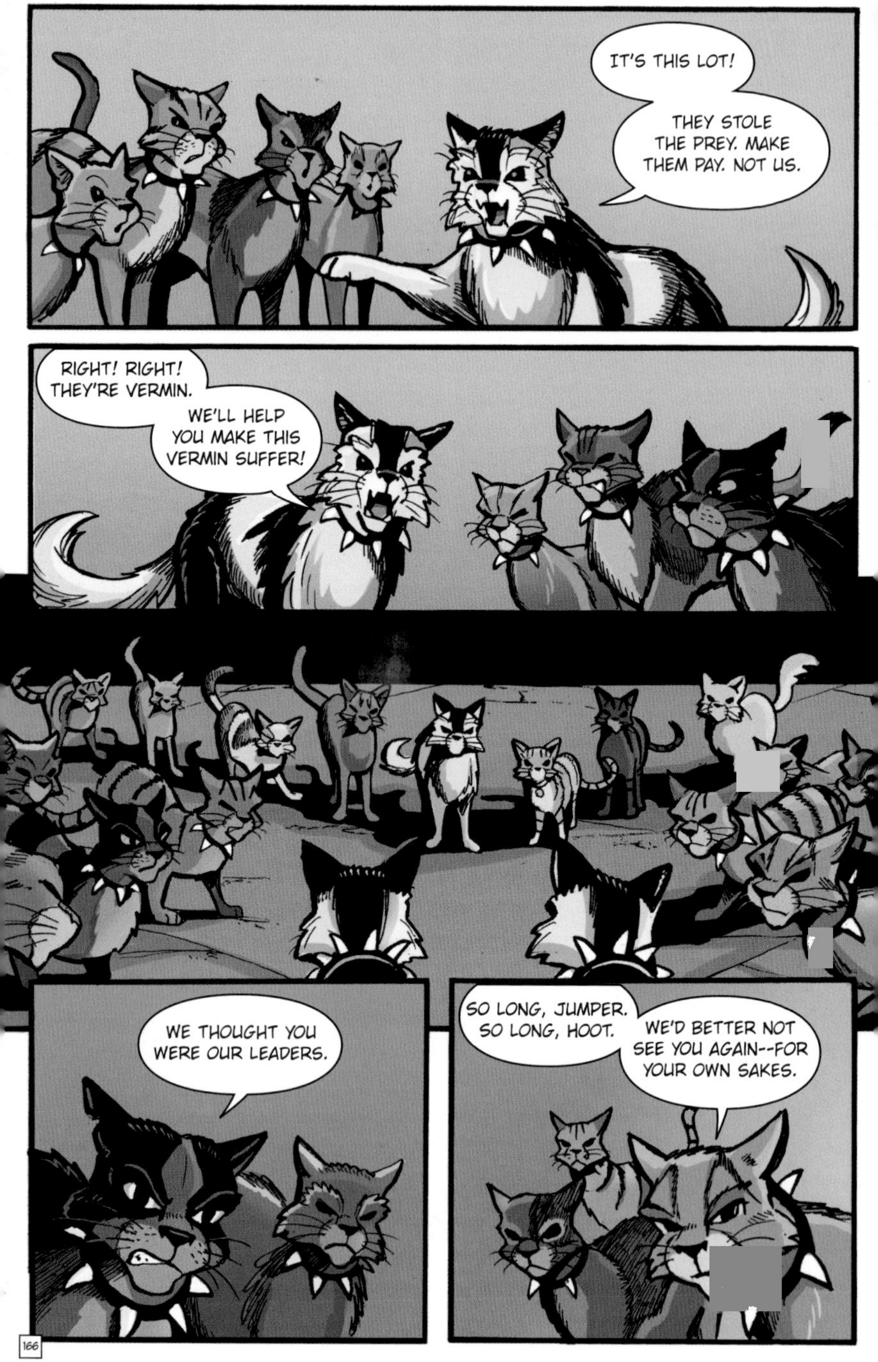
IT'S THIS LOT!
THEY STOLE THE PREY. MAKE THEM PAY. NOT US.
RIGHT! RIGHT! THEY'RE VERMIN.
WE'LL HELP YOU MAKE THIS VERMIN SUFFER!
WE THOUGHT YOU WERE OUR LEADERS.
SO LONG, JUMPER. SO LONG, HOOT.
WE'D BETTER NOT SEE YOU AGAIN--FOR YOUR OWN SAKES.

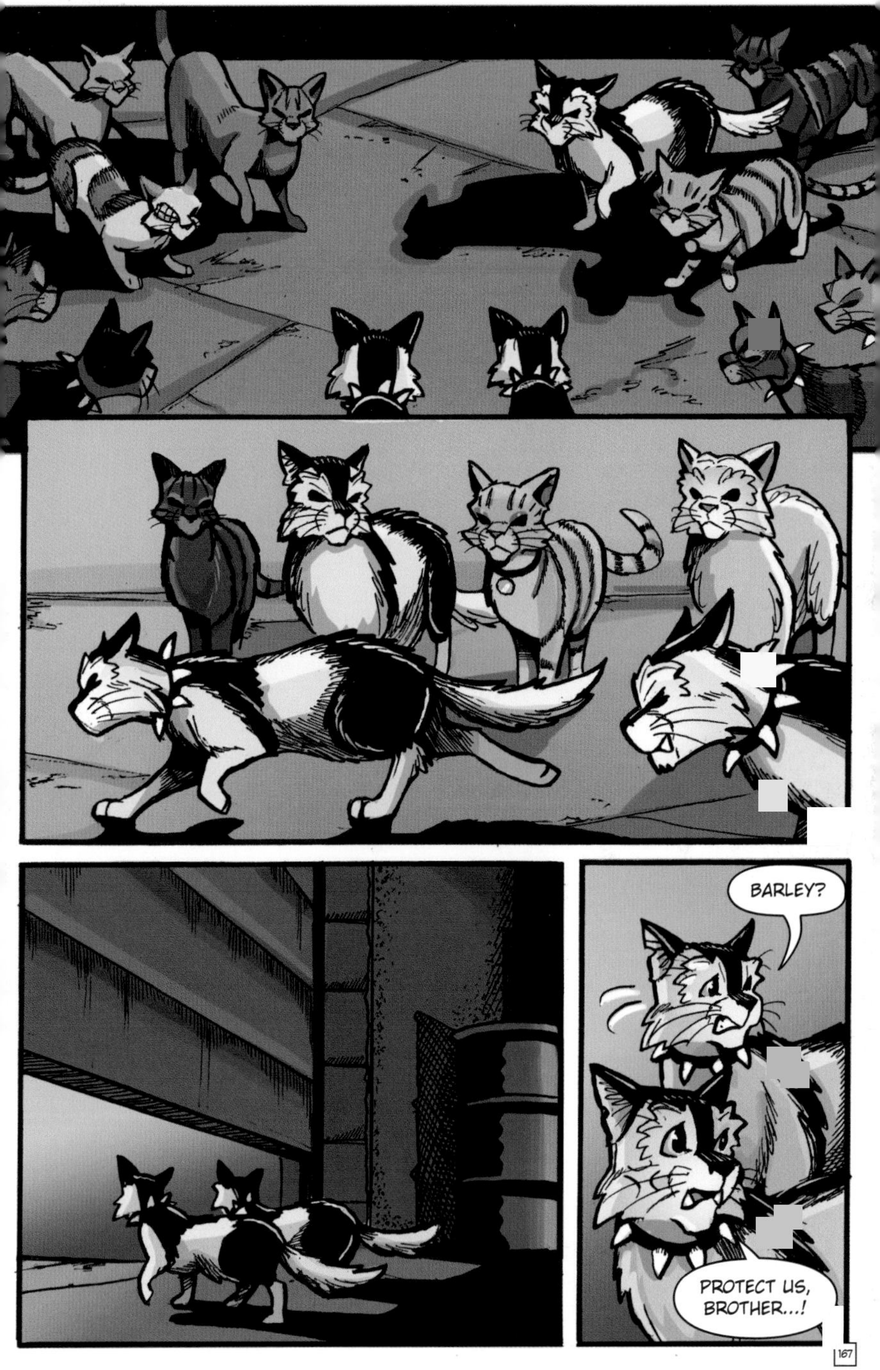
BARLEY?
PROTECT US, BROTHER...!

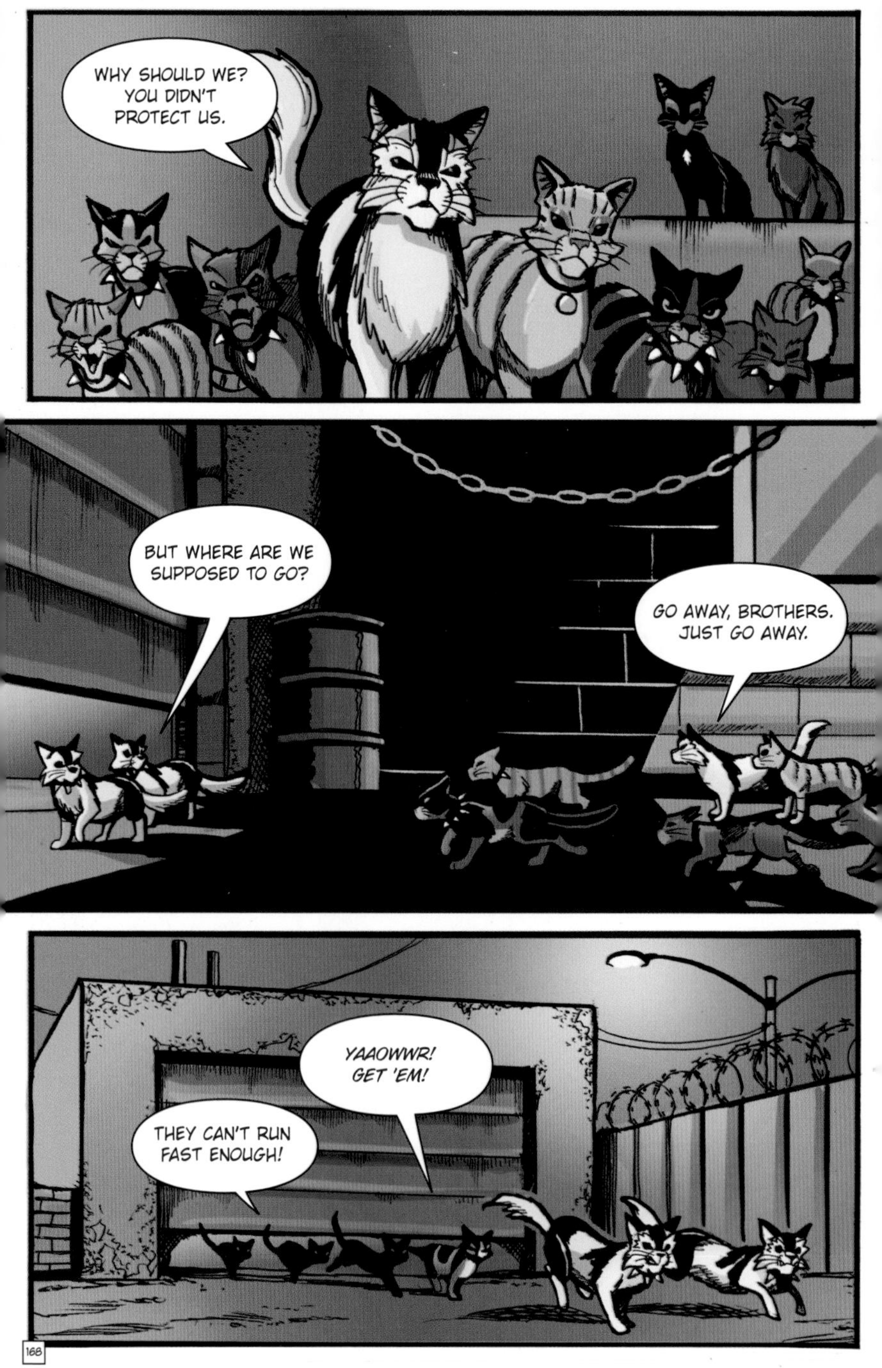
WHY SHOULD WE? YOU DIDN'T PROTECT US.
BUT WHERE ARE WE SUPPOSED TO GO?
GO AWAY, BROTHERS. JUST GO AWAY.
YAAOWWR! GET 'EM!
THEY CAN'T RUN FAST ENOUGH!

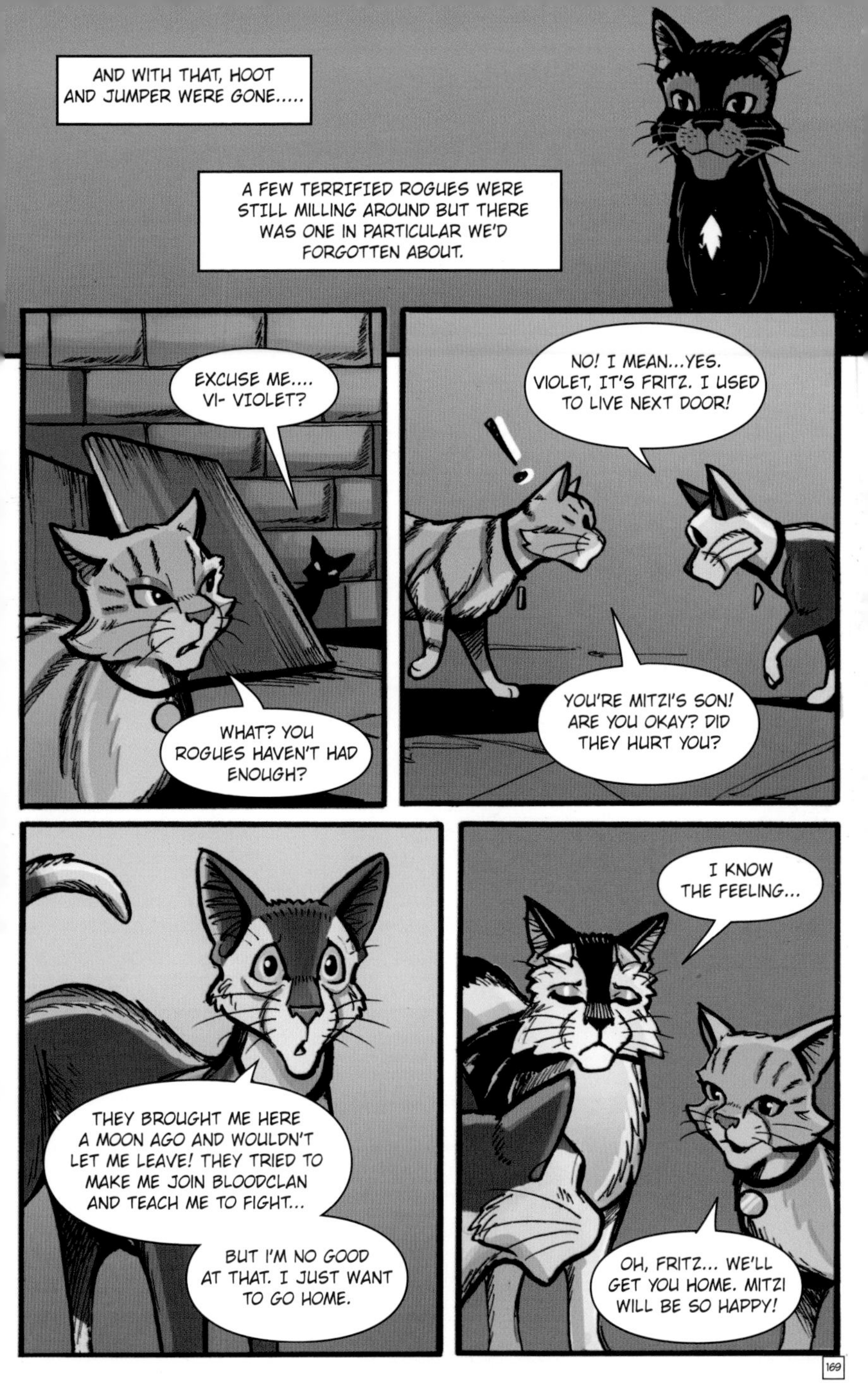
AND WITH THAT, HOOT AND JUMPER WERE GONE.....
A FEW TERRIFIED ROGUES WERE STILL MILLING AROUND BUT THERE WAS ONE IN PARTICULAR WE'D FORGOTTEN ABOUT.
EXCUSE ME.... VI- VIOLET?
WHAT? YOU ROGUES HAVEN'T HAD ENOUGH?
NO! I MEAN...YES. VIOLET, IT'S FRITZ. I USED TO LIVE NEXT DOOR!
!
YOU'RE MITZI'S SON! ARE YOU OKAY? DID THEY HURT YOU?
THEY BROUGHT ME HERE A MOON AGO AND WOULDN'T LET ME LEAVE! THEY TRIED TO MAKE ME JOIN BLOODCLAN AND TEACH ME TO FIGHT...
BUT I'M NO GOOD AT THAT. I JUST WANT TO GO HOME.
I KNOW THE FEELING...
OH, FRITZ... WE'LL GET YOU HOME. MITZI WILL BE SO HAPPY!

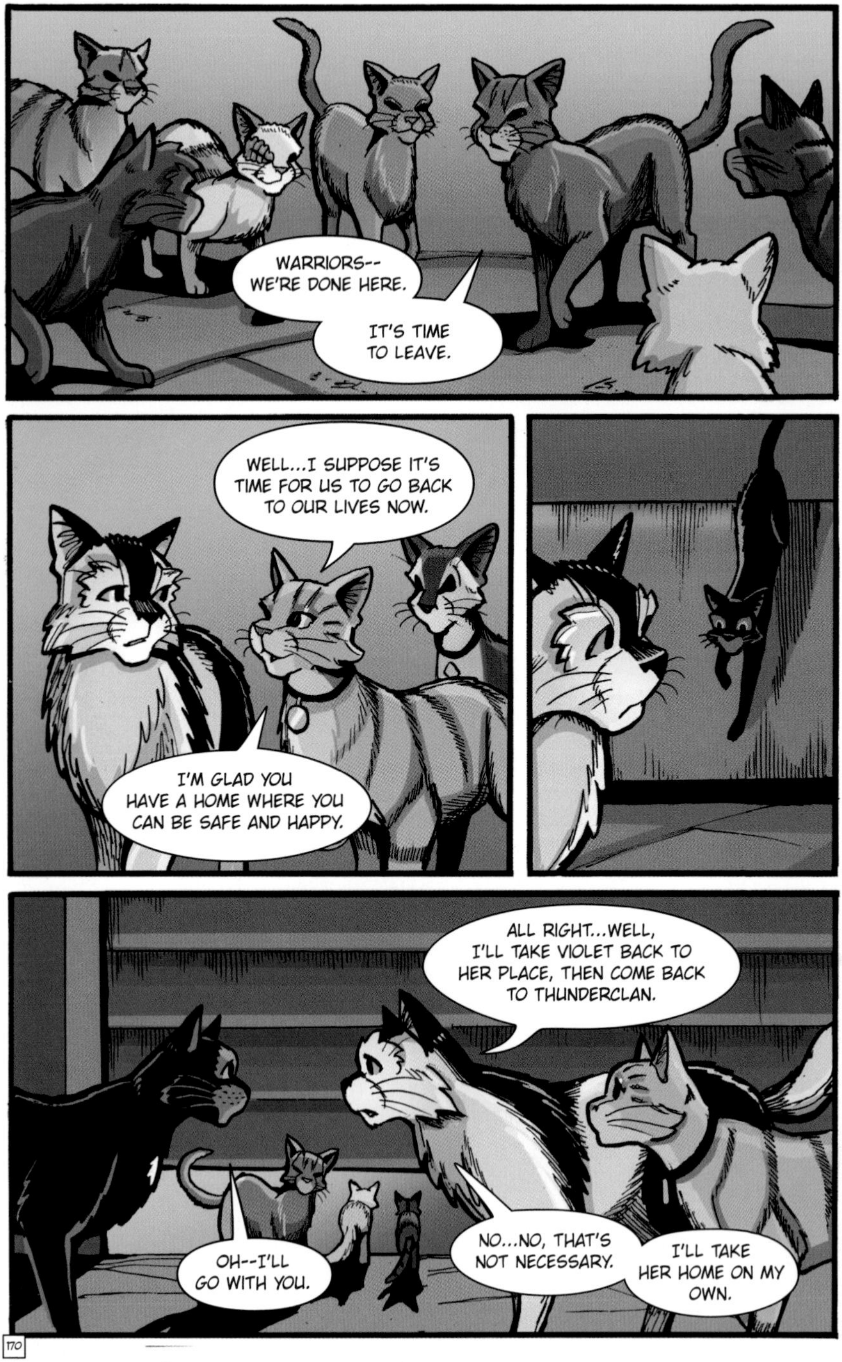
WARRIORS--
WE'RE DONE HERE.
IT'S TIME
TO LEAVE.
WELL...I SUPPOSE IT'S
TIME FOR US TO GO BACK
TO OUR LIVES NOW.
I'M GLAD YOU
HAVE A HOME WHERE YOU
CAN BE SAFE AND HAPPY.
ALL RIGHT...WELL,
I'LL TAKE VIOLET BACK TO
HER PLACE, THEN COME BACK
TO THUNDERCLAN.
OH--I'LL
GO WITH YOU.
NO...NO, THAT'S
NOT NECESSARY.
I'LL TAKE
HER HOME ON MY
OWN.

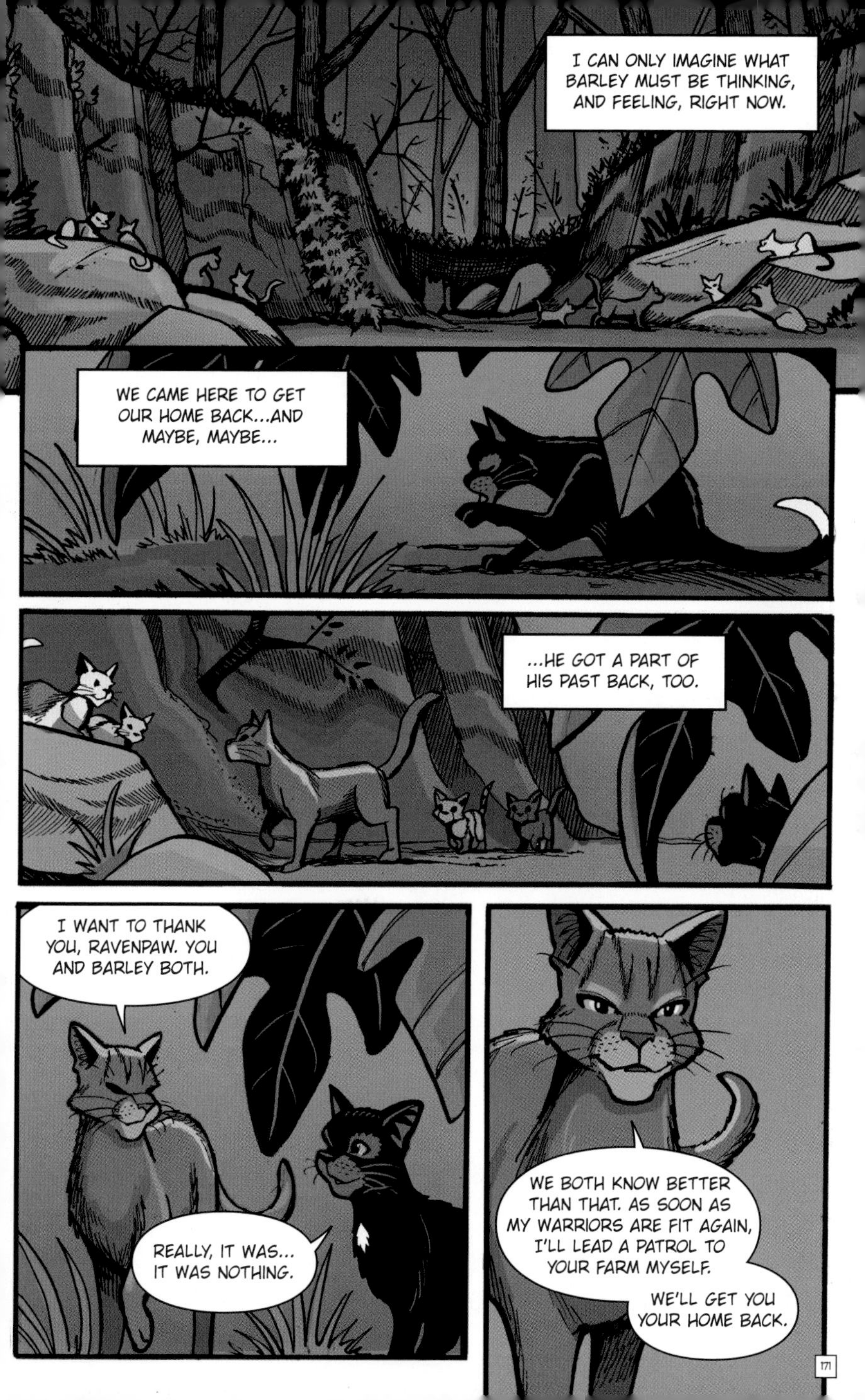

I CAN ONLY IMAGINE WHAT BARLEY MUST BE THINKING, AND FEELING, RIGHT NOW.
WE CAME HERE TO GET OUR HOME BACK...AND MAYBE, MAYBE...
...HE GOT A PART OF HIS PAST BACK, TOO.
I WANT TO THANK YOU, RAVENPAW. YOU AND BARLEY BOTH.
REALLY, IT WAS... IT WAS NOTHING.
WE BOTH KNOW BETTER THAN THAT. AS SOON AS MY WARRIORS ARE FIT AGAIN, I'LL LEAD A PATROL TO YOUR FARM MYSELF.
WE'LL GET YOU YOUR HOME BACK.

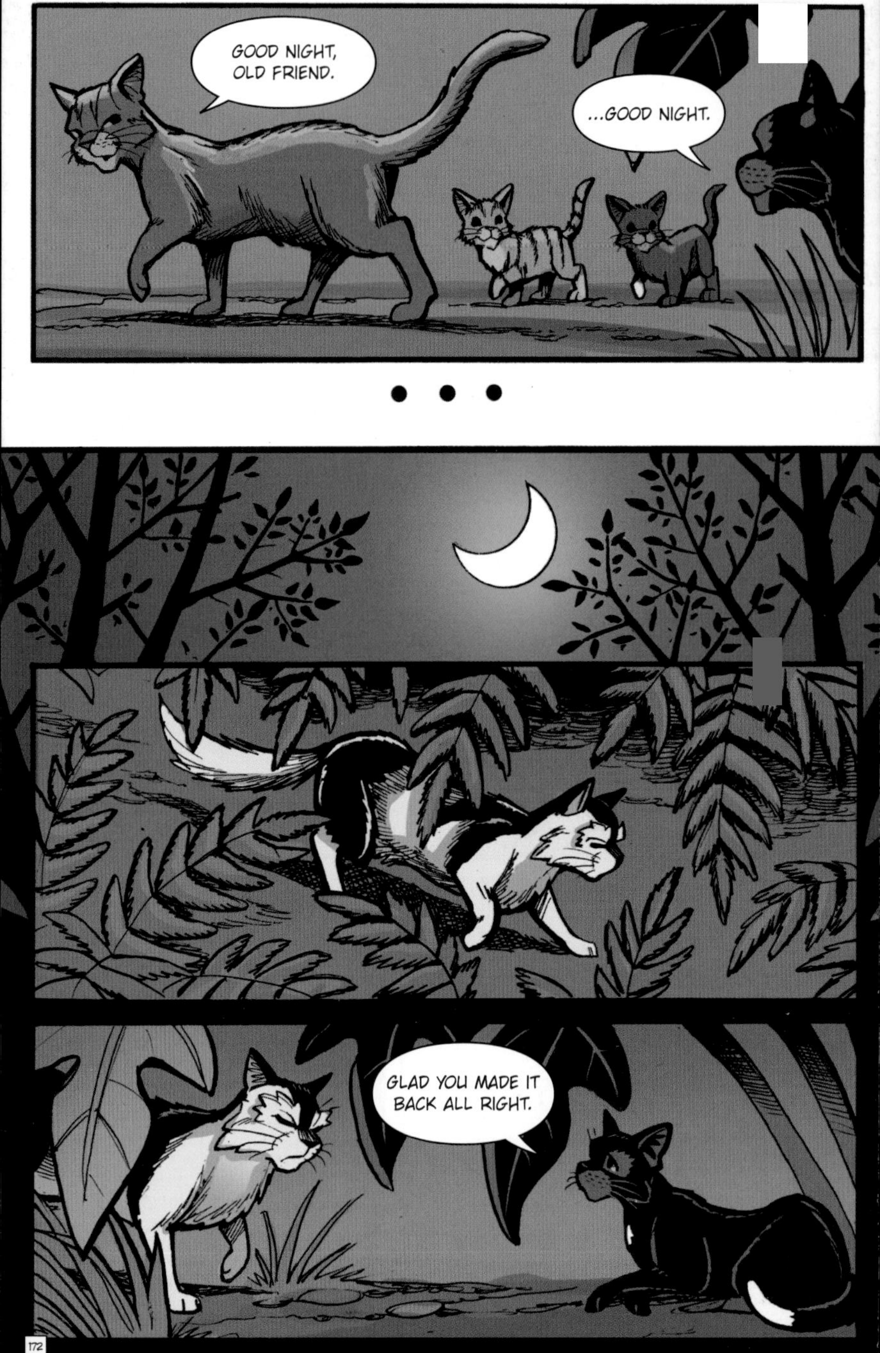
GOOD NIGHT, OLD FRIEND.
...GOOD NIGHT.
GLAD YOU MADE IT BACK ALL RIGHT.

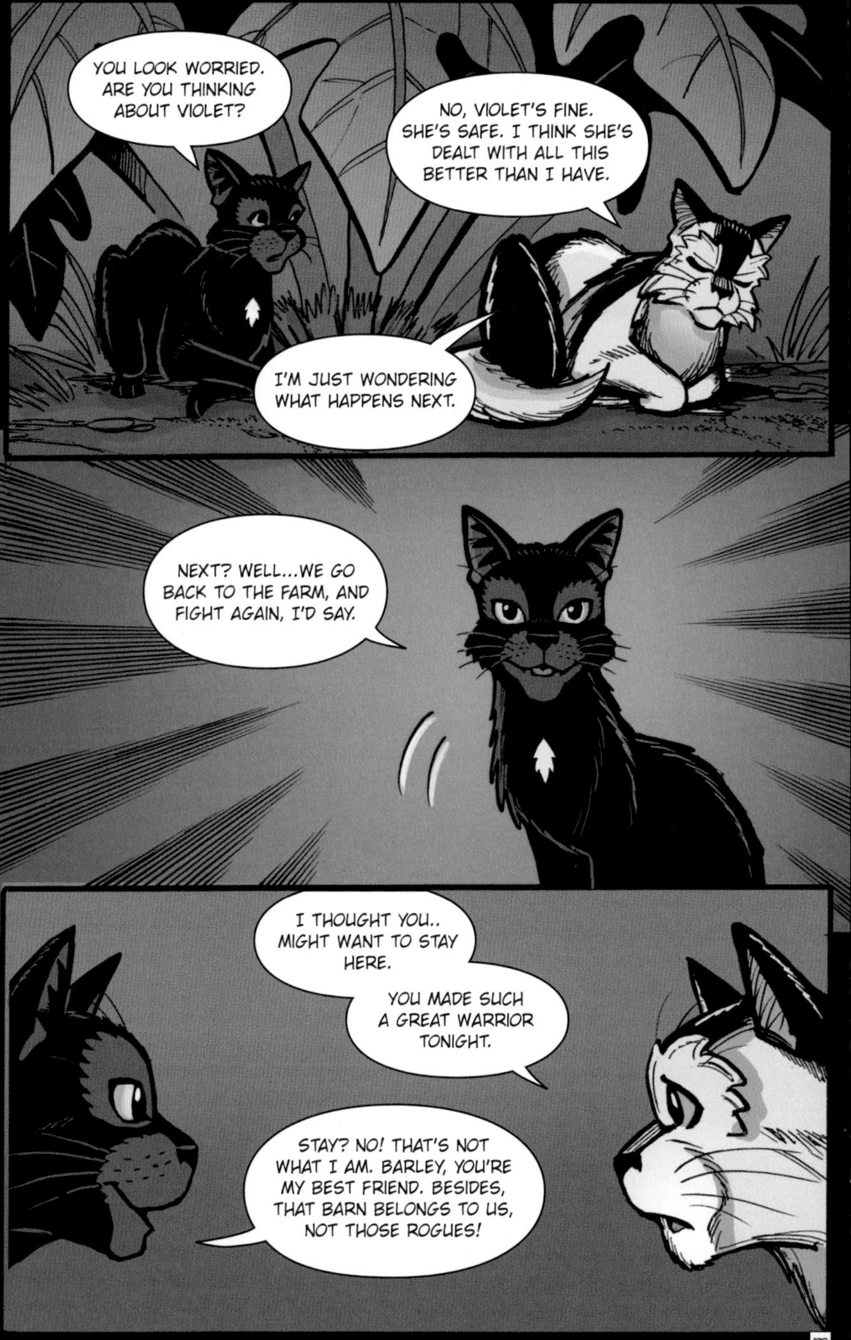
YOU LOOK WORRIED. ARE YOU THINKING ABOUT VIOLET?
NO, VIOLET'S FINE. SHE'S SAFE. I THINK SHE'S DEALT WITH ALL THIS BETTER THAN I HAVE.
I'M JUST WONDERING WHAT HAPPENS NEXT.
NEXT? WELL...WE GO BACK TO THE FARM, AND FIGHT AGAIN, I'D SAY.
I THOUGHT YOU.. MIGHT WANT TO STAY HERE.
YOU MADE SUCH A GREAT WARRIOR TONIGHT.
STAY? NO! THAT'S NOT WHAT I AM. BARLEY, YOU'RE MY BEST FRIEND. BESIDES, THAT BARN BELONGS TO US, NOT THOSE ROGUES!

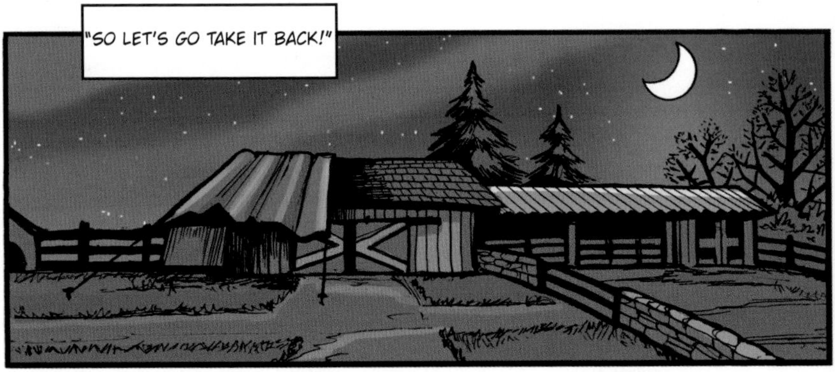
"SO LET'S GO TAKE IT BACK!"

WARRIORS
RAVENPAW'S PATH

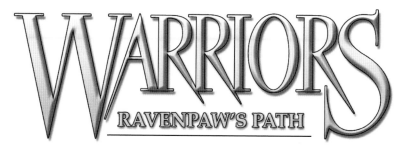

#3: THE HEART OF A WARRIOR

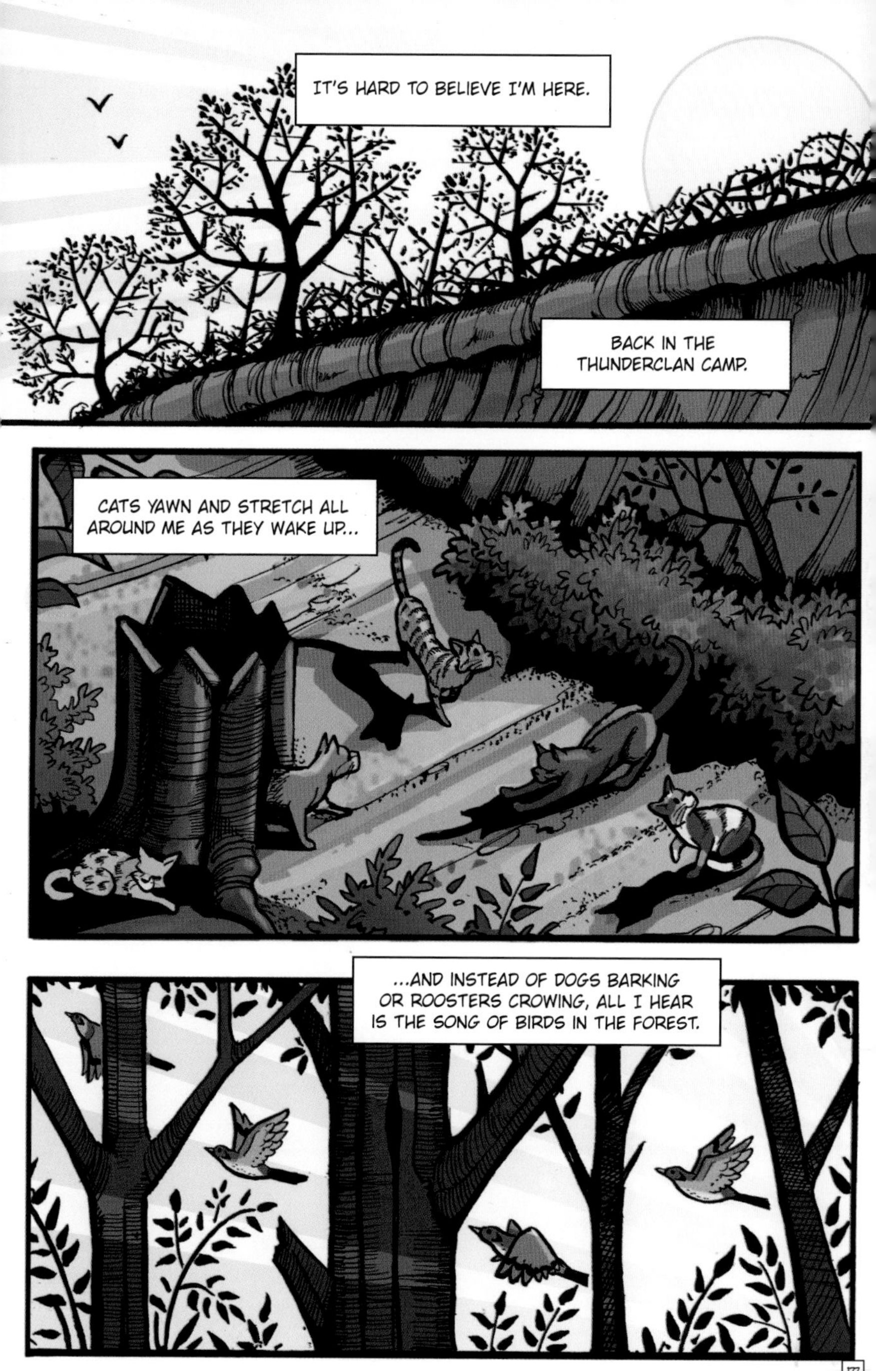
IT'S HARD TO BELIEVE I'M HERE.
BACK IN THE THUNDERCLAN CAMP.
CATS YAWN AND STRETCH ALL AROUND ME AS THEY WAKE UP...
...AND INSTEAD OF DOGS BARKING OR ROOSTERS CROWING, ALL I HEAR IS THE SONG OF BIRDS IN THE FOREST.

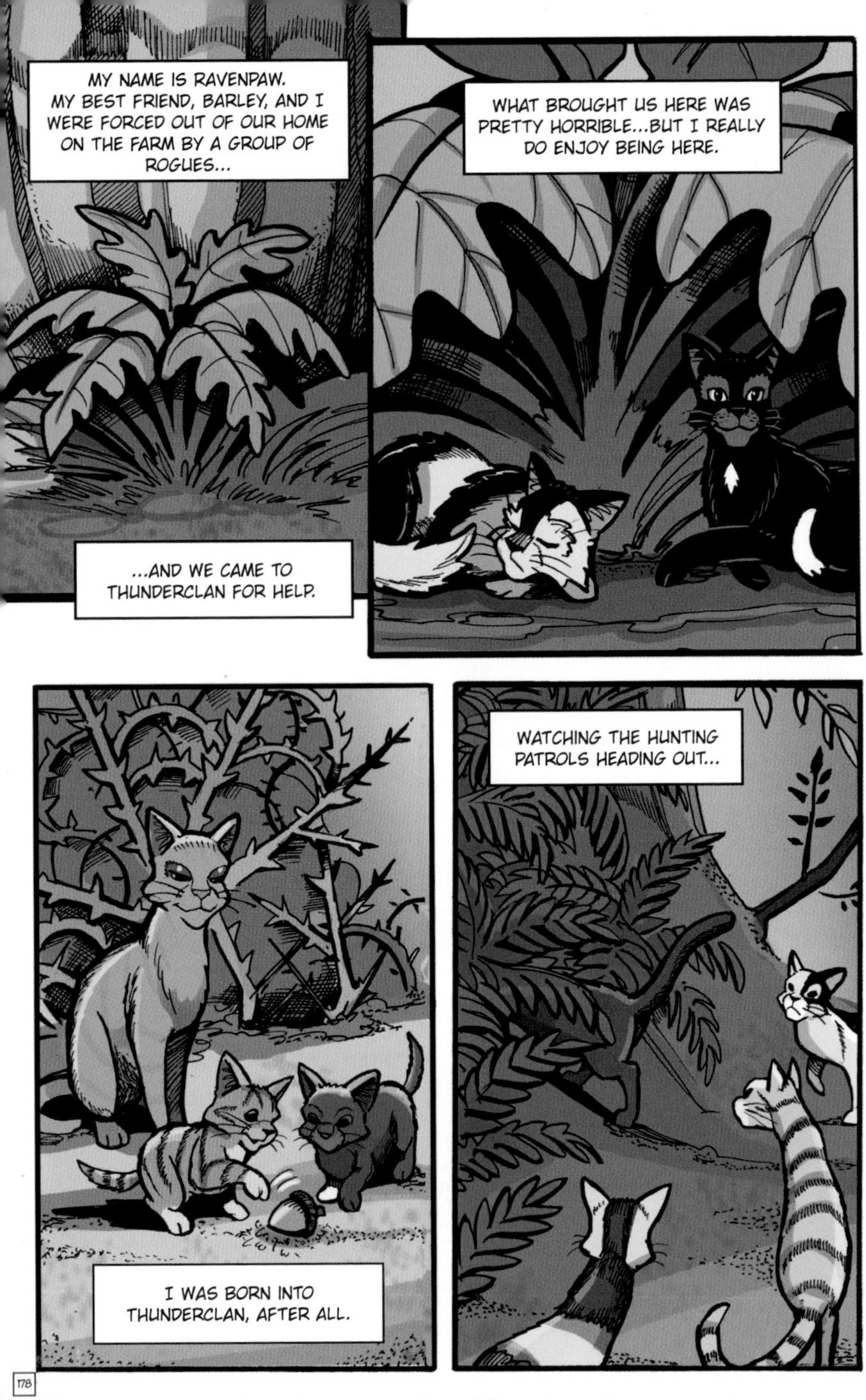
MY NAME IS RAVENPAW. MY BEST FRIEND, BARLEY, AND I WERE FORCED OUT OF OUR HOME ON THE FARM BY A GROUP OF ROGUES...
...AND WE CAME TO THUNDERCLAN FOR HELP.
WHAT BROUGHT US HERE WAS PRETTY HORRIBLE...BUT I REALLY DO ENJOY BEING HERE.
I WAS BORN INTO THUNDERCLAN, AFTER ALL.
WATCHING THE HUNTING PATROLS HEADING OUT...

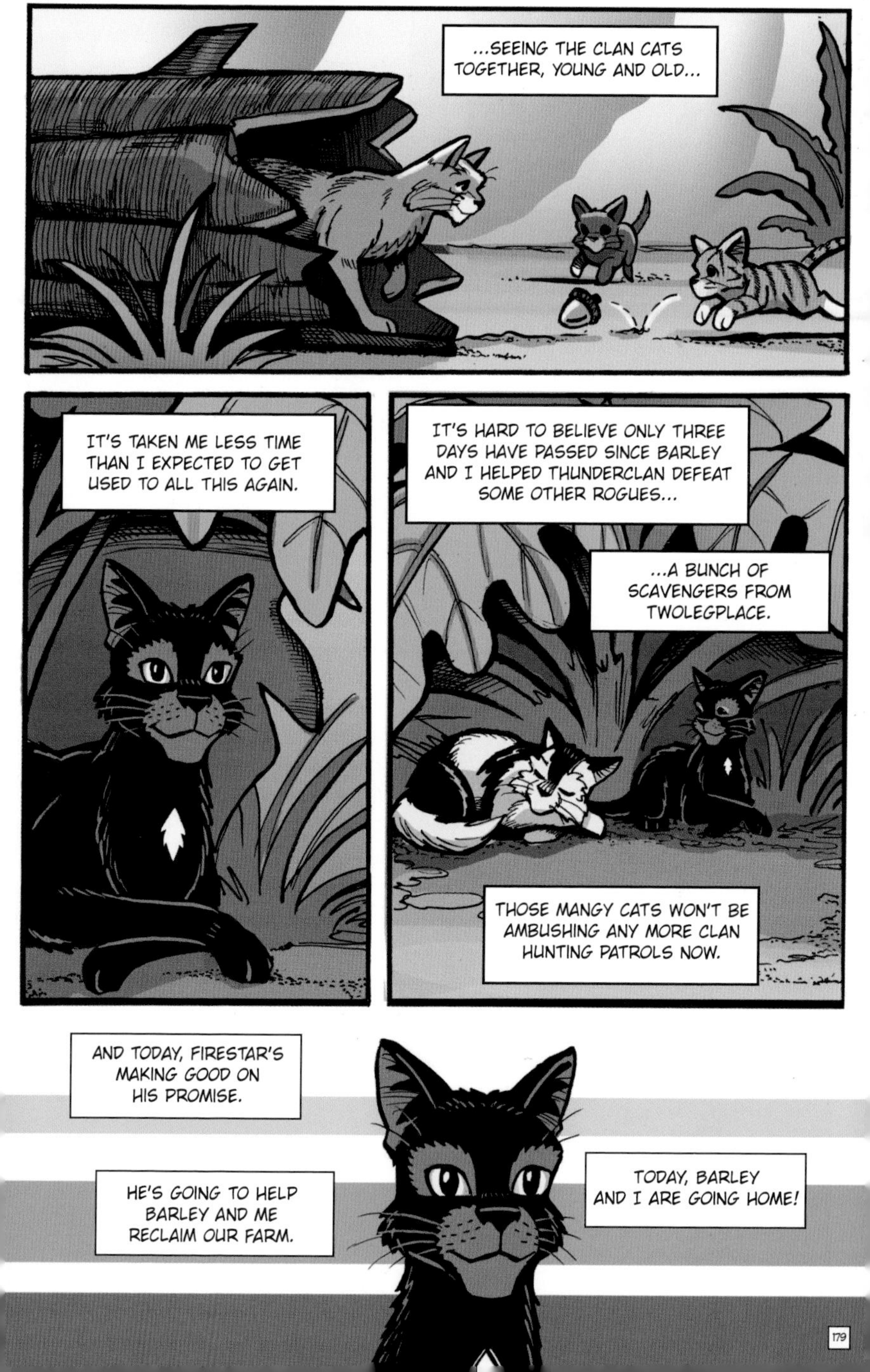
...SEEING THE CLAN CATS TOGETHER, YOUNG AND OLD...
IT'S TAKEN ME LESS TIME THAN I EXPECTED TO GET USED TO ALL THIS AGAIN.
IT'S HARD TO BELIEVE ONLY THREE DAYS HAVE PASSED SINCE BARLEY AND I HELPED THUNDERCLAN DEFEAT SOME OTHER ROGUES...
...A BUNCH OF SCAVENGERS FROM TWOLEGPLACE.
THOSE MANGY CATS WON'T BE AMBUSHING ANY MORE CLAN HUNTING PATROLS NOW.
AND TODAY, FIRESTAR'S MAKING GOOD ON HIS PROMISE.
HE'S GOING TO HELP BARLEY AND ME RECLAIM OUR FARM.
TODAY, BARLEY AND I ARE GOING HOME!

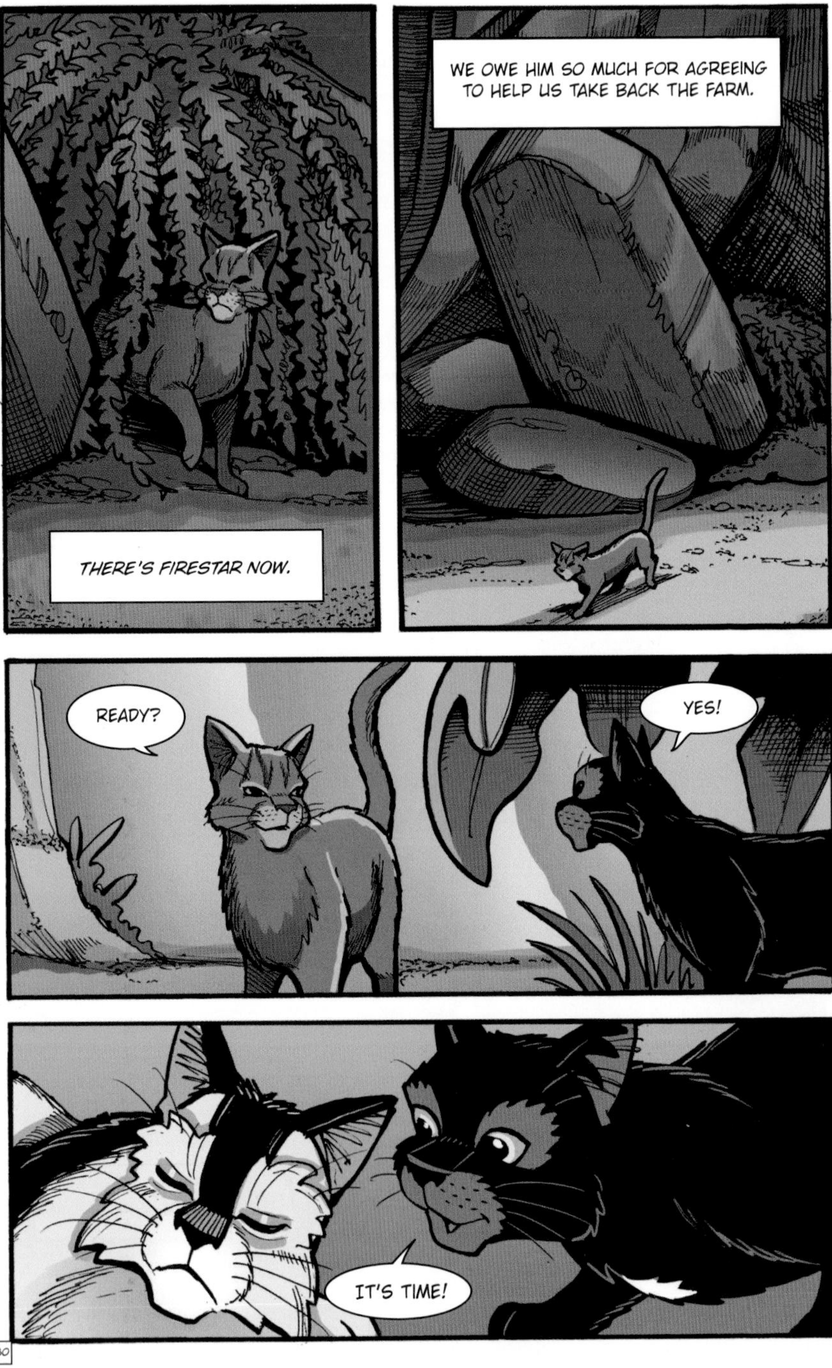
THERE'S FIRESTAR NOW.
WE OWE HIM SO MUCH FOR AGREEING TO HELP US TAKE BACK THE FARM.
READY?
YES!
IT'S TIME!

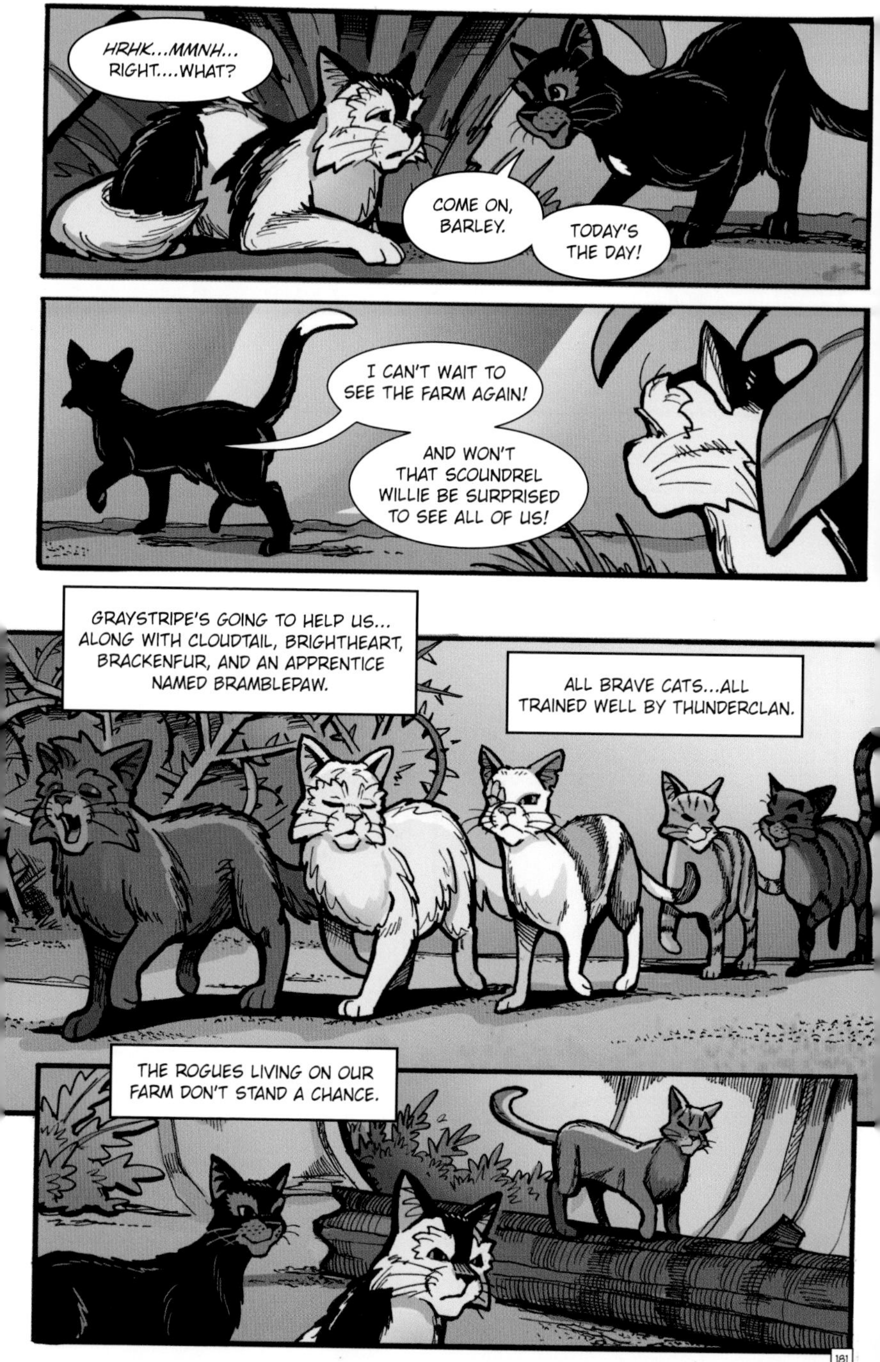
HRHK...MMNH... RIGHT....WHAT?
COME ON, BARLEY.
TODAY'S THE DAY!
I CAN'T WAIT TO SEE THE FARM AGAIN!
AND WON'T THAT SCOUNDREL WILLIE BE SURPRISED TO SEE ALL OF US!
GRAYSTRIPE'S GOING TO HELP US... ALONG WITH CLOUDTAIL, BRIGHTHEART, BRACKENFUR, AND AN APPRENTICE NAMED BRAMBLEPAW.
ALL BRAVE CATS...ALL TRAINED WELL BY THUNDERCLAN.
THE ROGUES LIVING ON OUR FARM DON'T STAND A CHANCE.

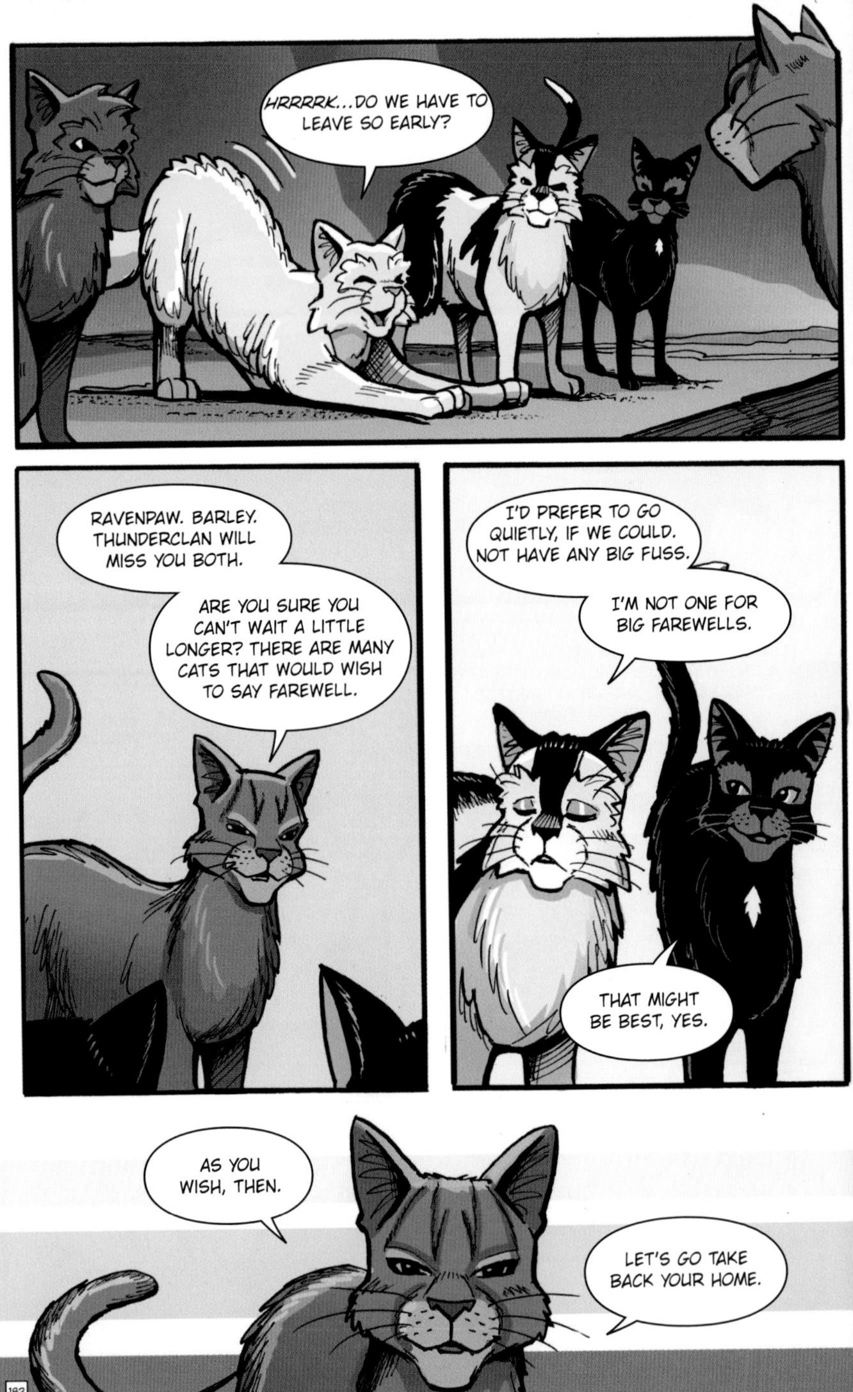
HRRRRK...DO WE HAVE TO LEAVE SO EARLY?
RAVENPAW. BARLEY. THUNDERCLAN WILL MISS YOU BOTH.
ARE YOU SURE YOU CAN'T WAIT A LITTLE LONGER? THERE ARE MANY CATS THAT WOULD WISH TO SAY FAREWELL.
I'D PREFER TO GO QUIETLY, IF WE COULD. NOT HAVE ANY BIG FUSS.
I'M NOT ONE FOR BIG FAREWELLS.
THAT MIGHT BE BEST, YES.
AS YOU WISH, THEN.
LET'S GO TAKE BACK YOUR HOME.

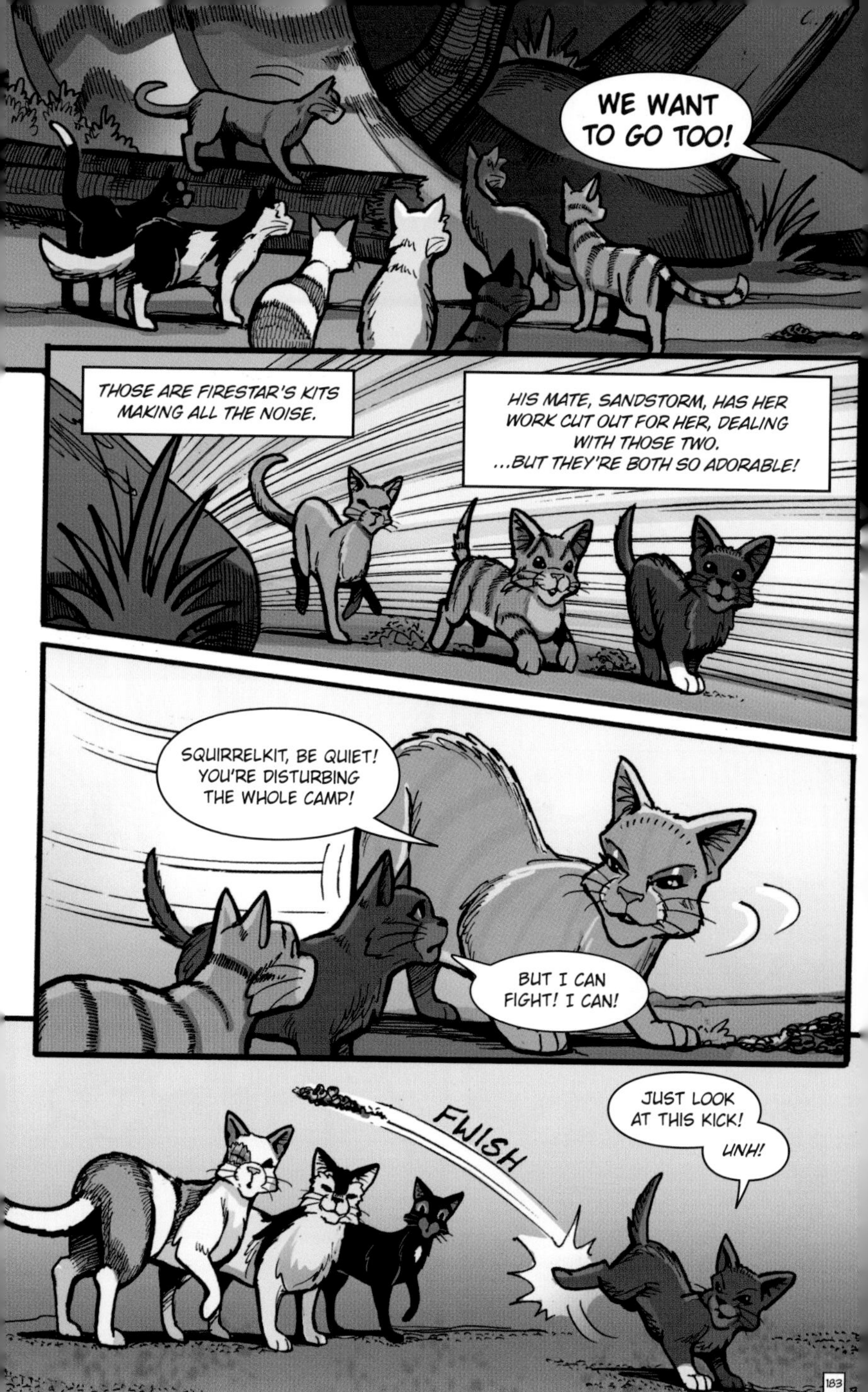
WE WANT TO GO TOO!
THOSE ARE FIRESTAR'S KITS MAKING ALL THE NOISE.
HIS MATE, SANDSTORM, HAS HER WORK CUT OUT FOR HER, DEALING WITH THOSE TWO. ...BUT THEY'RE BOTH SO ADORABLE!
SQUIRRELKIT, BE QUIET! YOU'RE DISTURBING THE WHOLE CAMP!
BUT I CAN FIGHT! I CAN!
FWISH
JUST LOOK AT THIS KICK!
UNH!

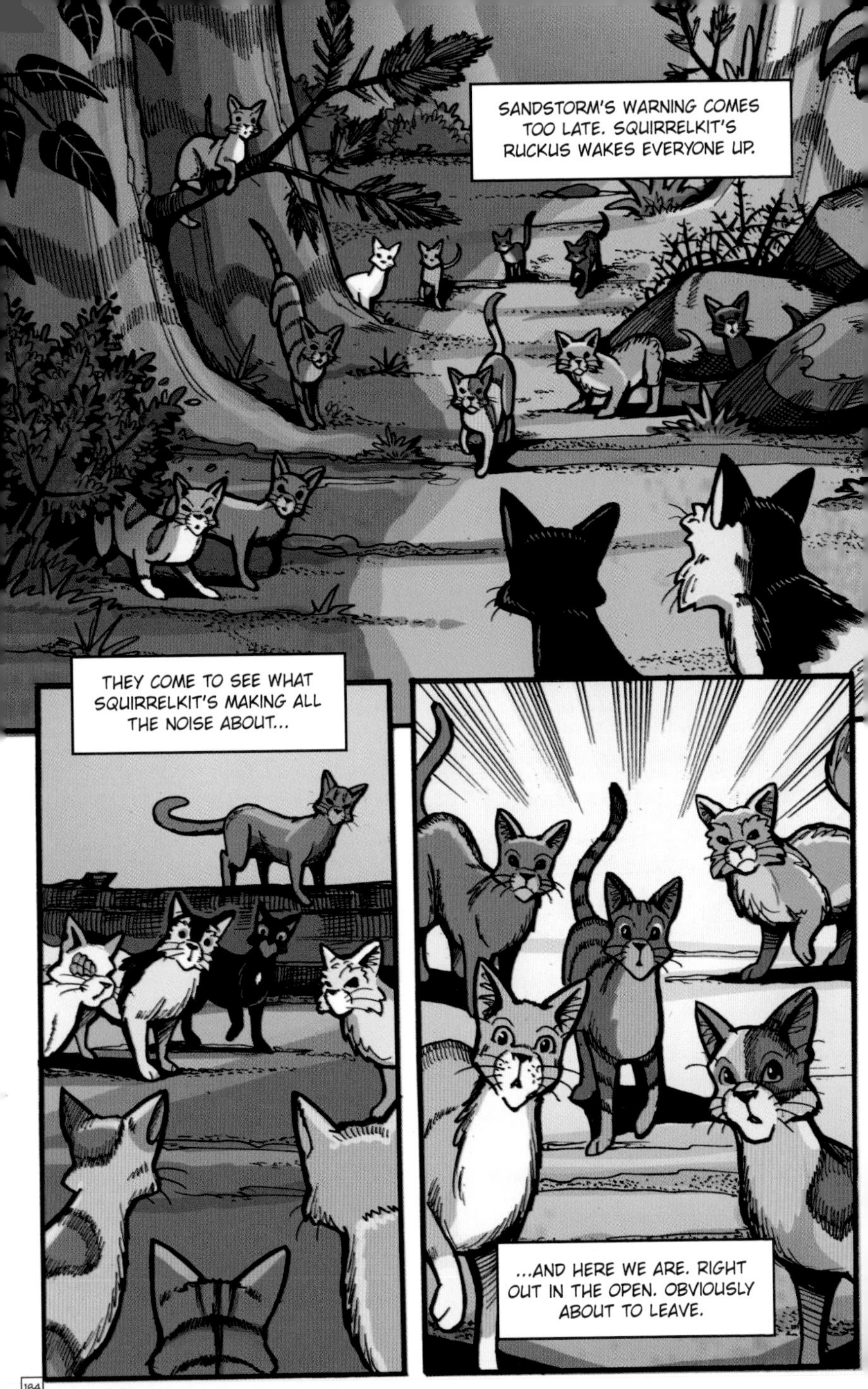
SANDSTORM'S WARNING COMES TOO LATE. SQUIRRELKIT'S RUCKUS WAKES EVERYONE UP.
THEY COME TO SEE WHAT SQUIRRELKIT'S MAKING ALL THE NOISE ABOUT...
...AND HERE WE ARE. RIGHT OUT IN THE OPEN. OBVIOUSLY ABOUT TO LEAVE.

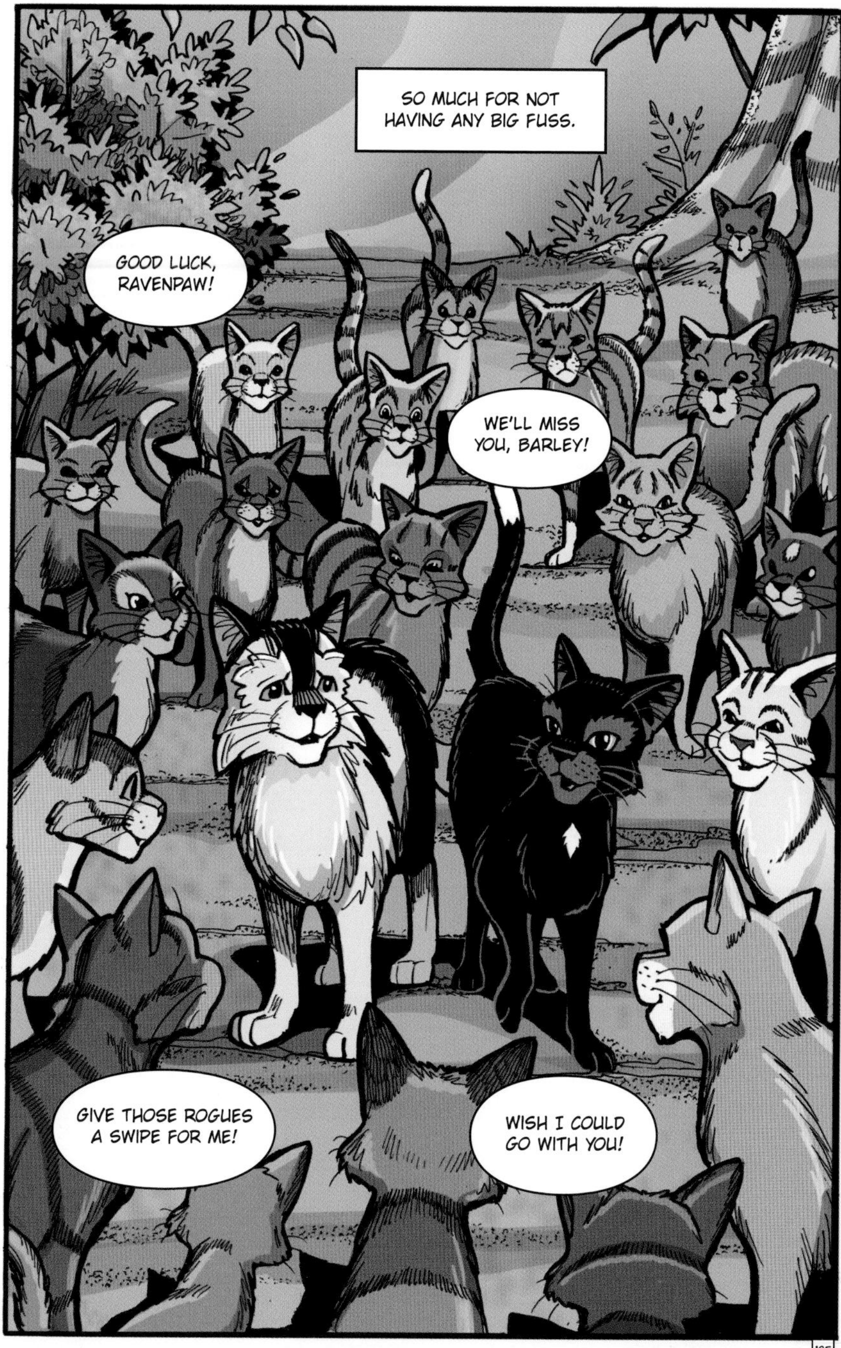
SO MUCH FOR NOT HAVING ANY BIG FUSS.
GOOD LUCK, RAVENPAW!
WE'LL MISS YOU, BARLEY!
GIVE THOSE ROGUES A SWIPE FOR ME!
WISH I COULD GO WITH YOU!

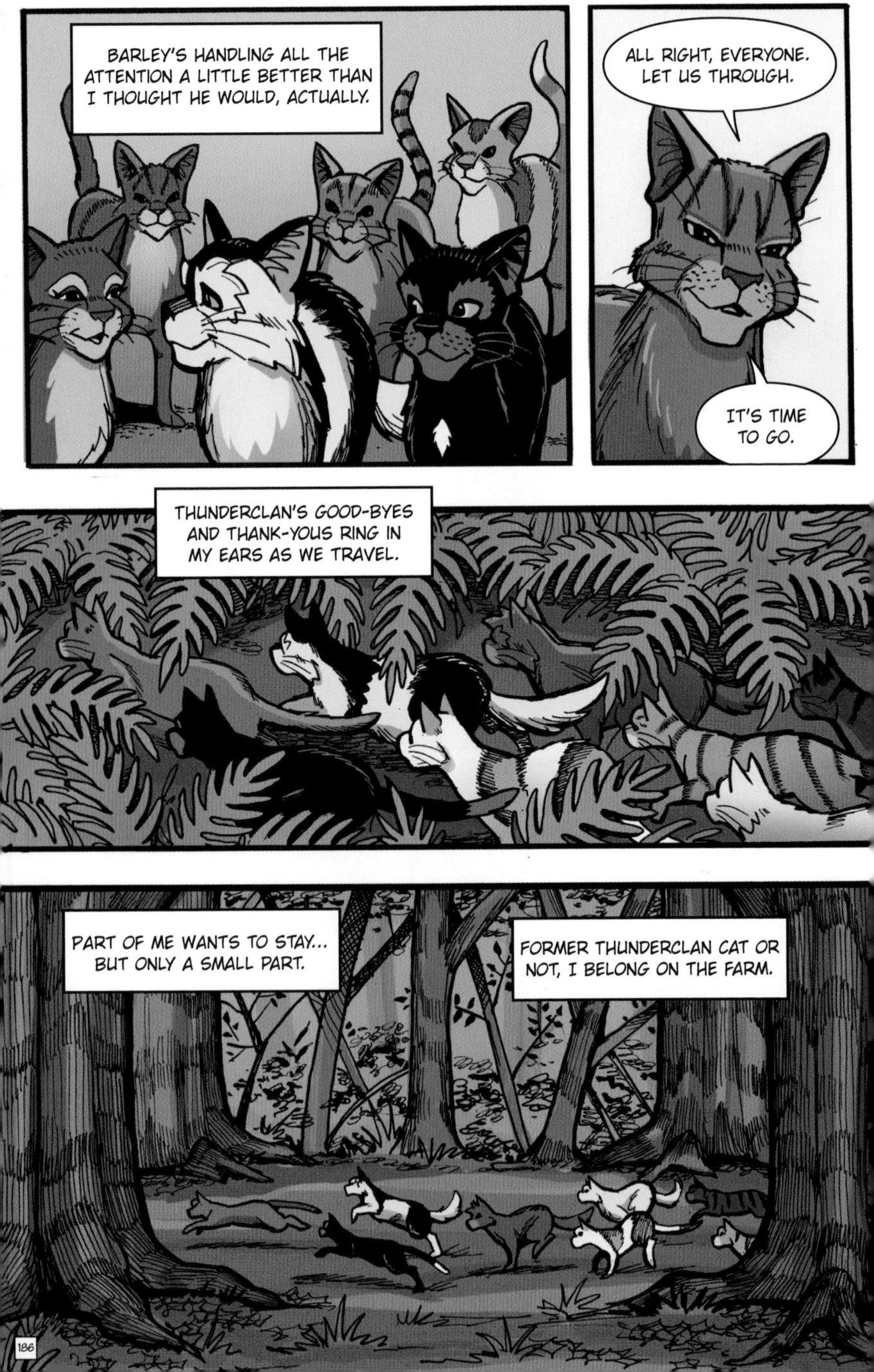
BARLEY'S HANDLING ALL THE ATTENTION A LITTLE BETTER THAN I THOUGHT HE WOULD, ACTUALLY.
ALL RIGHT, EVERYONE. LET US THROUGH.
IT'S TIME TO GO.
THUNDERCLAN'S GOOD-BYES AND THANK-YOUS RING IN MY EARS AS WE TRAVEL.
PART OF ME WANTS TO STAY... BUT ONLY A SMALL PART.
FORMER THUNDERCLAN CAT OR NOT, I BELONG ON THE FARM.

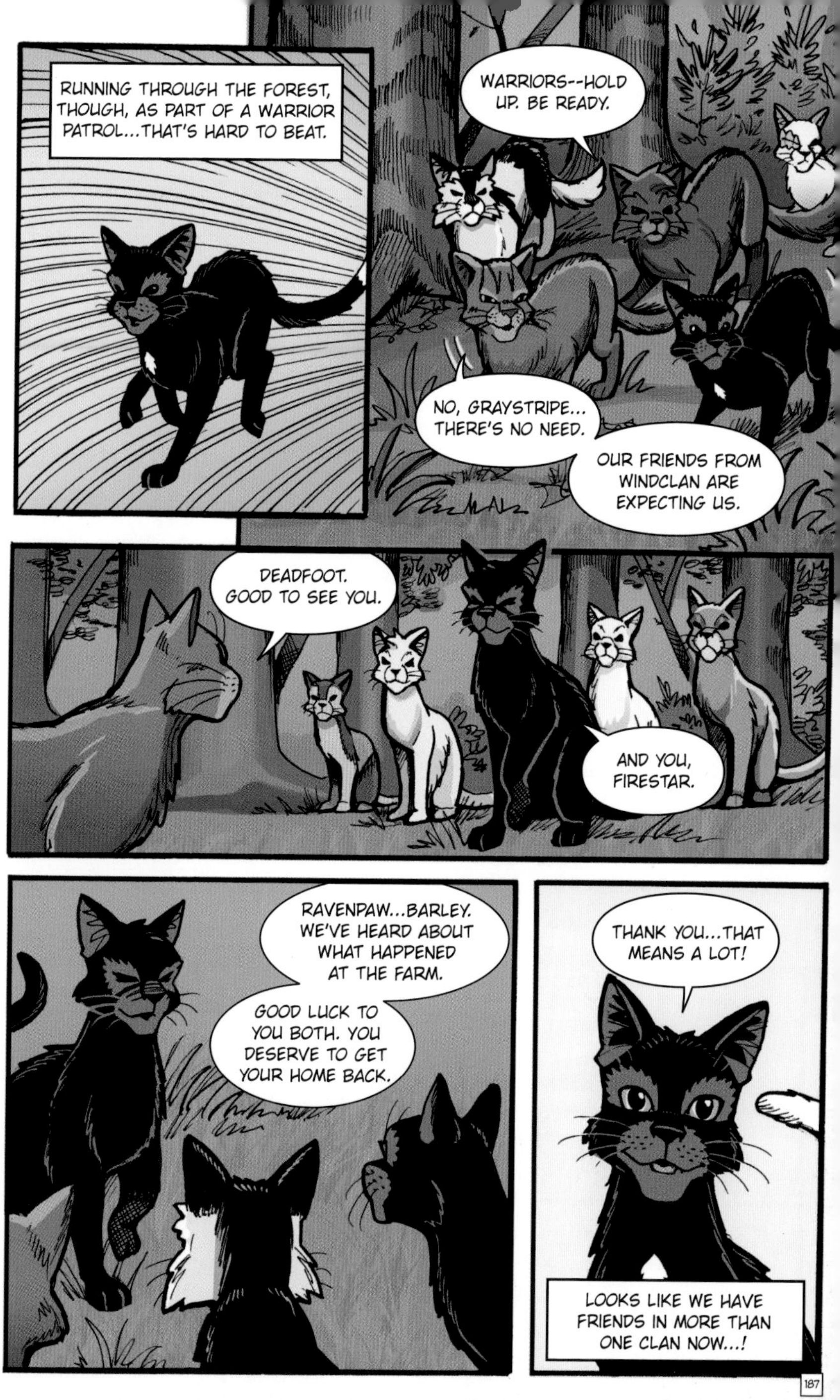
RUNNING THROUGH THE FOREST, THOUGH, AS PART OF A WARRIOR PATROL...THAT'S HARD TO BEAT.
WARRIORS--HOLD UP. BE READY.
NO, GRAYSTRIPE... THERE'S NO NEED.
OUR FRIENDS FROM WINDCLAN ARE EXPECTING US.
DEADFOOT. GOOD TO SEE YOU.
AND YOU, FIRESTAR.
RAVENPAW...BARLEY. WE'VE HEARD ABOUT WHAT HAPPENED AT THE FARM.
GOOD LUCK TO YOU BOTH. YOU DESERVE TO GET YOUR HOME BACK.
THANK YOU...THAT MEANS A LOT!
LOOKS LIKE WE HAVE FRIENDS IN MORE THAN ONE CLAN NOW...!

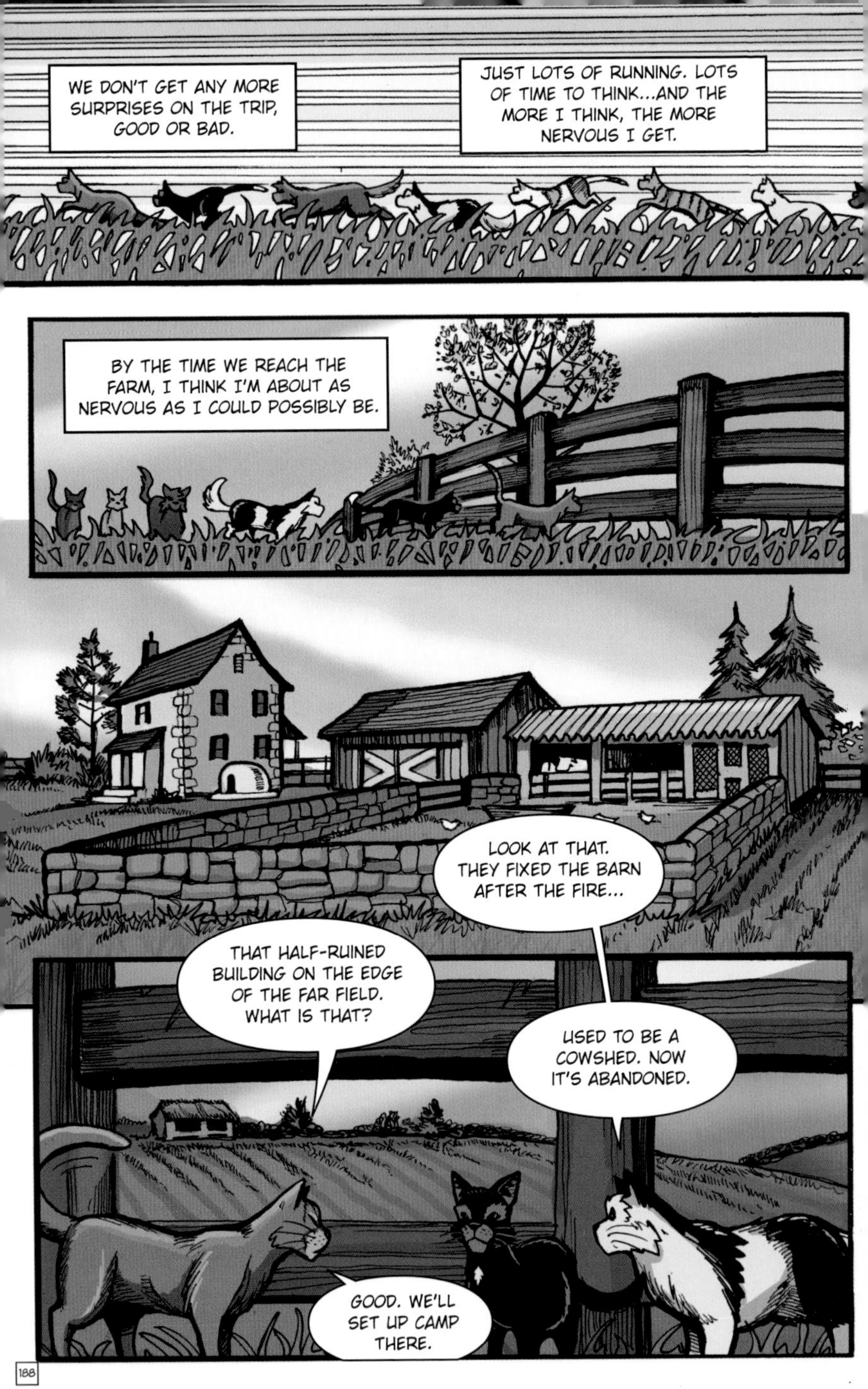
WE DON'T GET ANY MORE SURPRISES ON THE TRIP, GOOD OR BAD.
JUST LOTS OF RUNNING. LOTS OF TIME TO THINK...AND THE MORE I THINK, THE MORE NERVOUS I GET.
BY THE TIME WE REACH THE FARM, I THINK I'M ABOUT AS NERVOUS AS I COULD POSSIBLY BE.
LOOK AT THAT. THEY FIXED THE BARN AFTER THE FIRE...
THAT HALF-RUINED BUILDING ON THE EDGE OF THE FAR FIELD. WHAT IS THAT?
USED TO BE A COWSHED. NOW IT'S ABANDONED.
GOOD. WE'LL SET UP CAMP THERE.

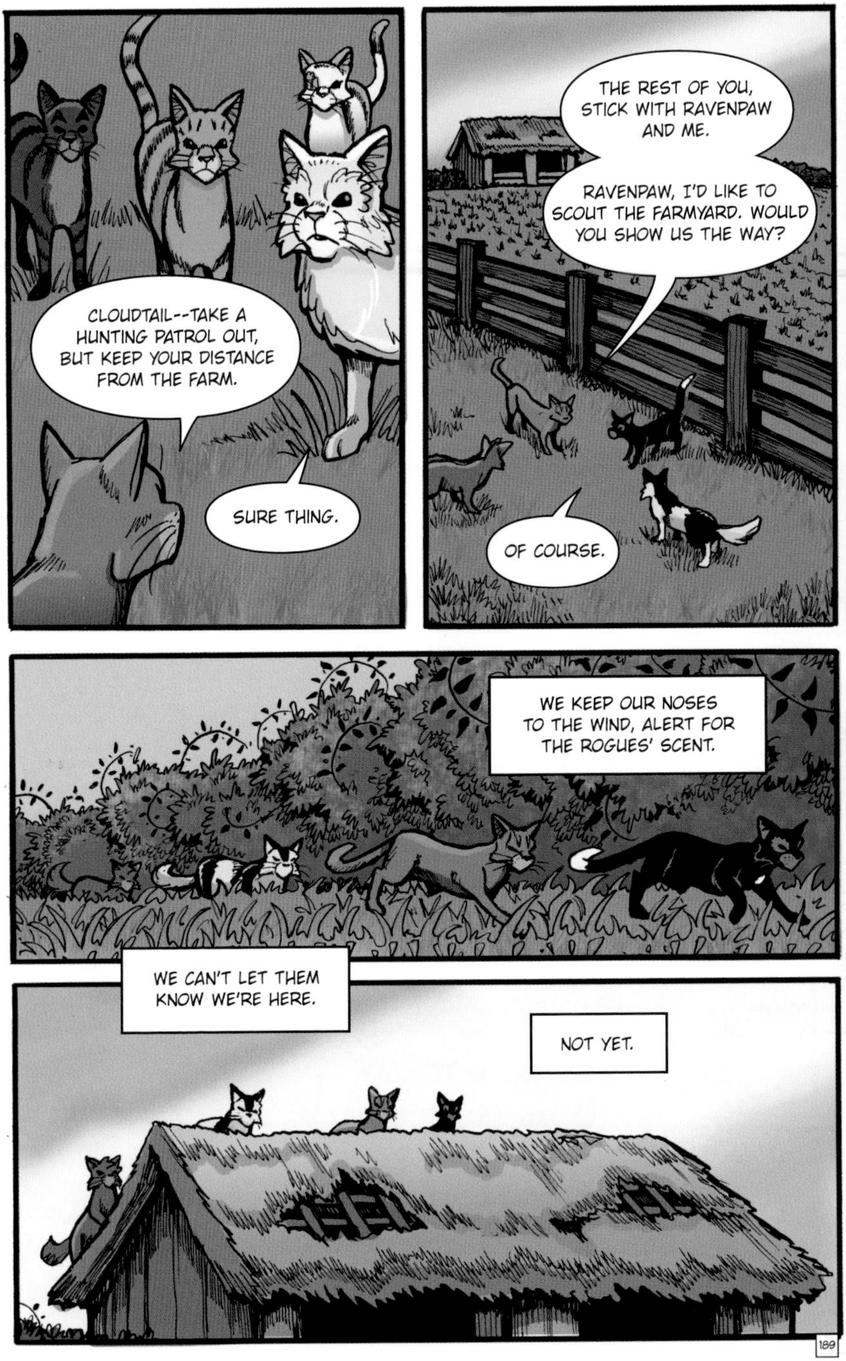

CLOUDTAIL--TAKE A HUNTING PATROL OUT, BUT KEEP YOUR DISTANCE FROM THE FARM.
SURE THING.
THE REST OF YOU, STICK WITH RAVENPAW AND ME.
RAVENPAW, I'D LIKE TO SCOUT THE FARMYARD. WOULD YOU SHOW US THE WAY?
OF COURSE.
WE KEEP OUR NOSES TO THE WIND, ALERT FOR THE ROGUES' SCENT.
WE CAN'T LET THEM KNOW WE'RE HERE.
NOT YET.

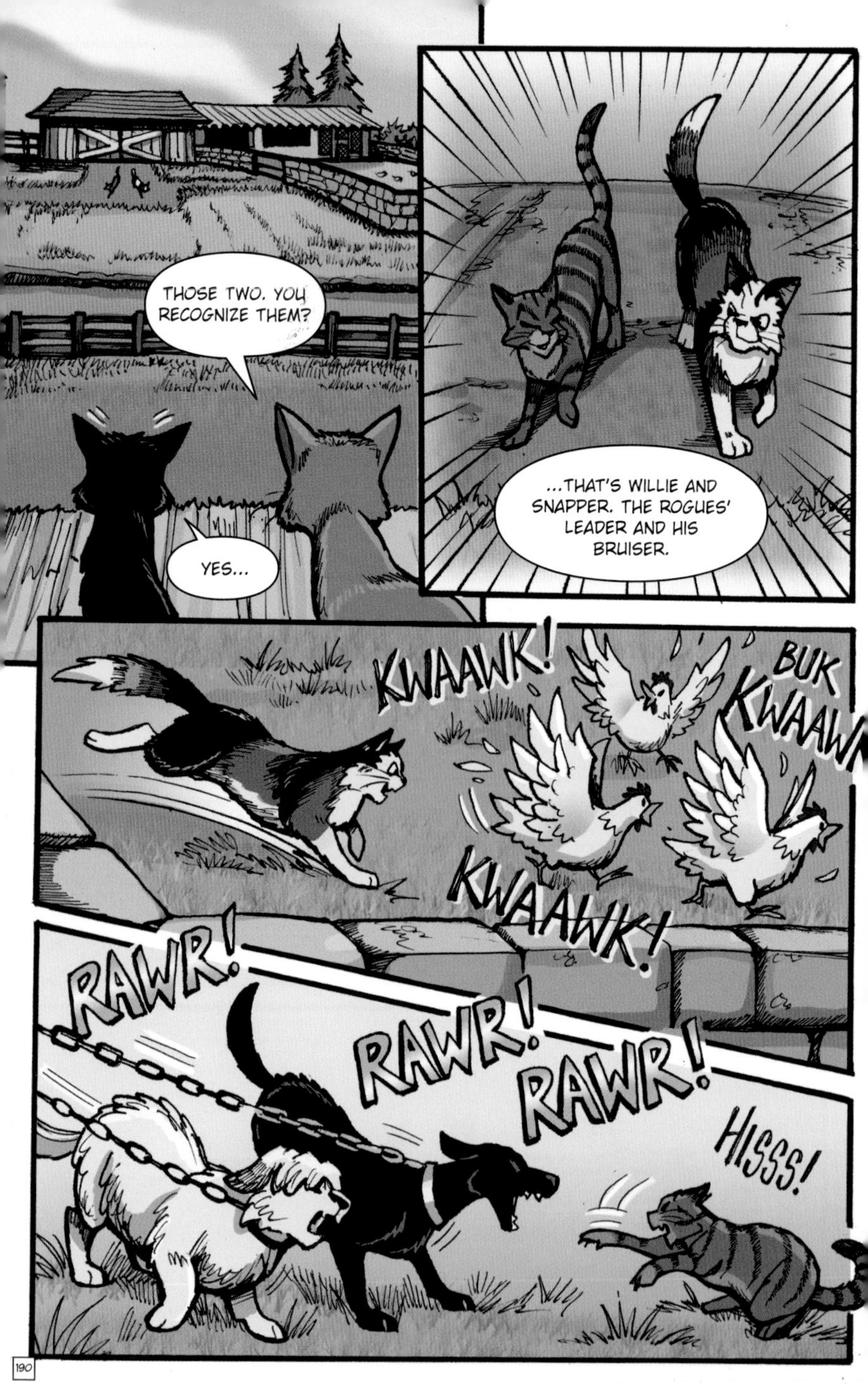
THOSE TWO. YOU RECOGNIZE THEM?
YES...
...THAT'S WILLIE AND SNAPPER. THE ROGUES' LEADER AND HIS BRUISER.
KWAAWK!
BUK
KWAAWK!
RAWR!
RAWR!
RAWR!
HISSS!

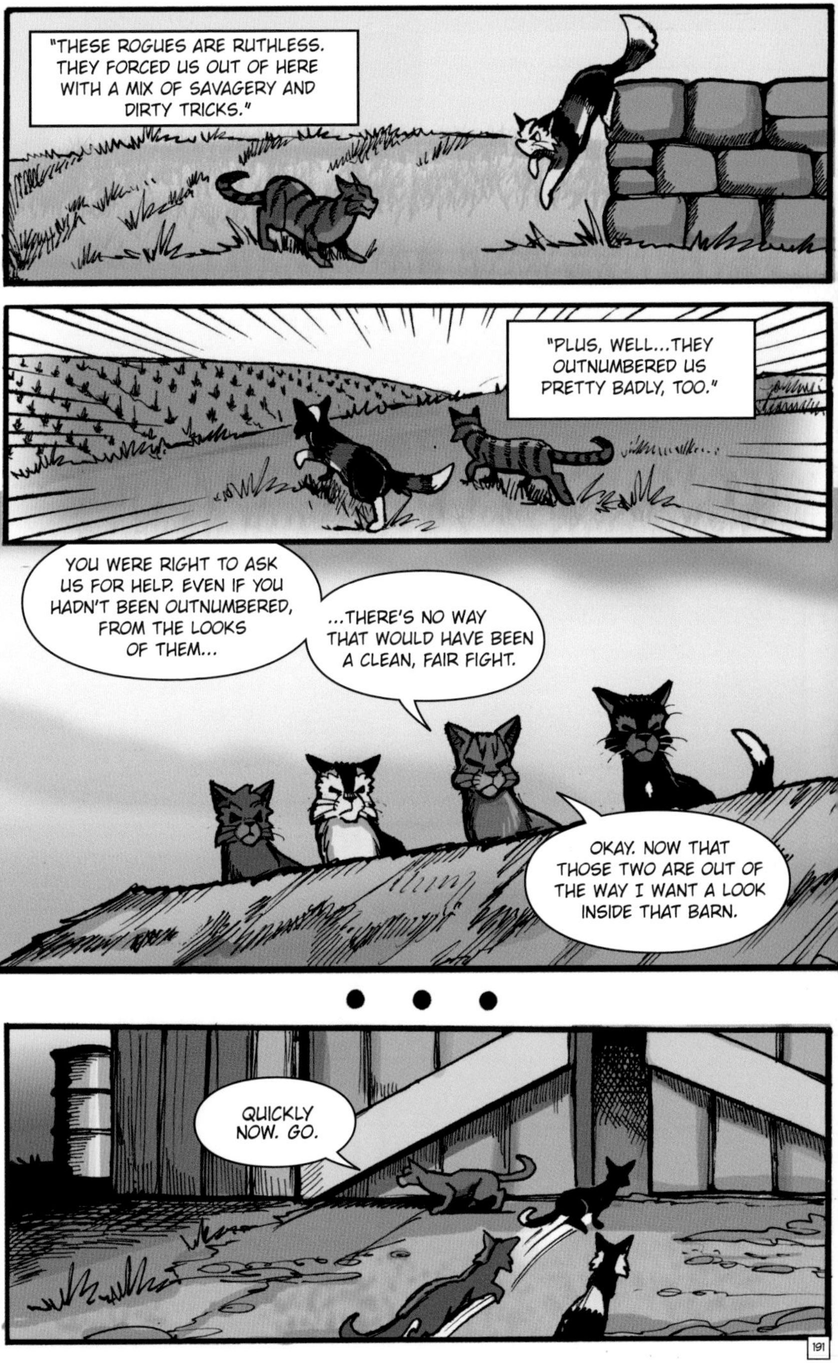
"THESE ROGUES ARE RUTHLESS. THEY FORCED US OUT OF HERE WITH A MIX OF SAVAGERY AND DIRTY TRICKS."
"PLUS, WELL...THEY OUTNUMBERED US PRETTY BADLY, TOO."
YOU WERE RIGHT TO ASK US FOR HELP. EVEN IF YOU HADN'T BEEN OUTNUMBERED, FROM THE LOOKS OF THEM...
...THERE'S NO WAY THAT WOULD HAVE BEEN A CLEAN, FAIR FIGHT.
OKAY. NOW THAT THOSE TWO ARE OUT OF THE WAY I WANT A LOOK INSIDE THAT BARN.
QUICKLY NOW. GO.

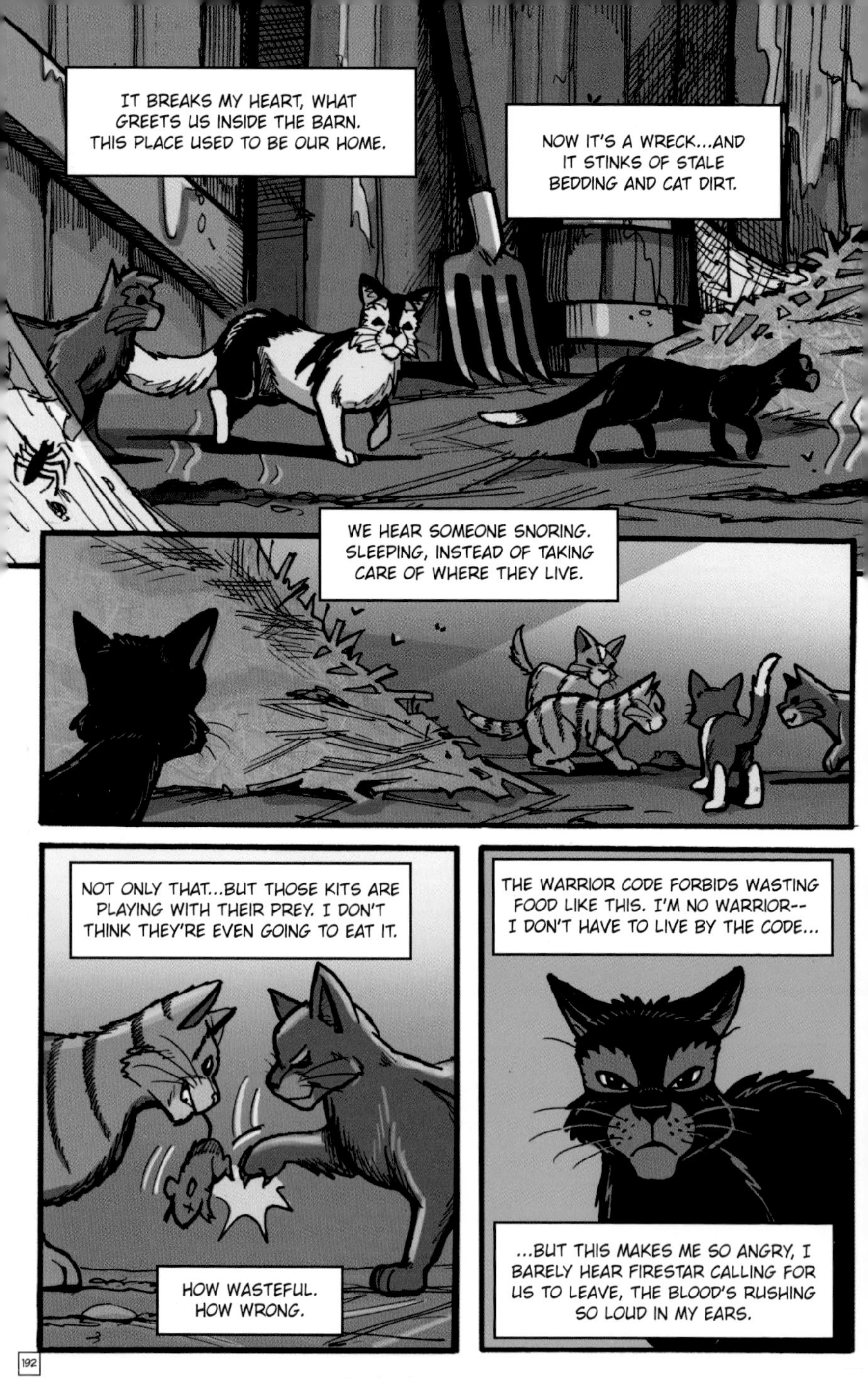
IT BREAKS MY HEART, WHAT GREETS US INSIDE THE BARN. THIS PLACE USED TO BE OUR HOME.
NOW IT'S A WRECK...AND IT STINKS OF STALE BEDDING AND CAT DIRT.
WE HEAR SOMEONE SNORING. SLEEPING, INSTEAD OF TAKING CARE OF WHERE THEY LIVE.
NOT ONLY THAT...BUT THOSE KITS ARE PLAYING WITH THEIR PREY. I DON'T THINK THEY'RE EVEN GOING TO EAT IT.
HOW WASTEFUL. HOW WRONG.
THE WARRIOR CODE FORBIDS WASTING FOOD LIKE THIS. I'M NO WARRIOR-- I DON'T HAVE TO LIVE BY THE CODE...
...BUT THIS MAKES ME SO ANGRY, I BARELY HEAR FIRESTAR CALLING FOR US TO LEAVE, THE BLOOD'S RUSHING SO LOUD IN MY EARS.

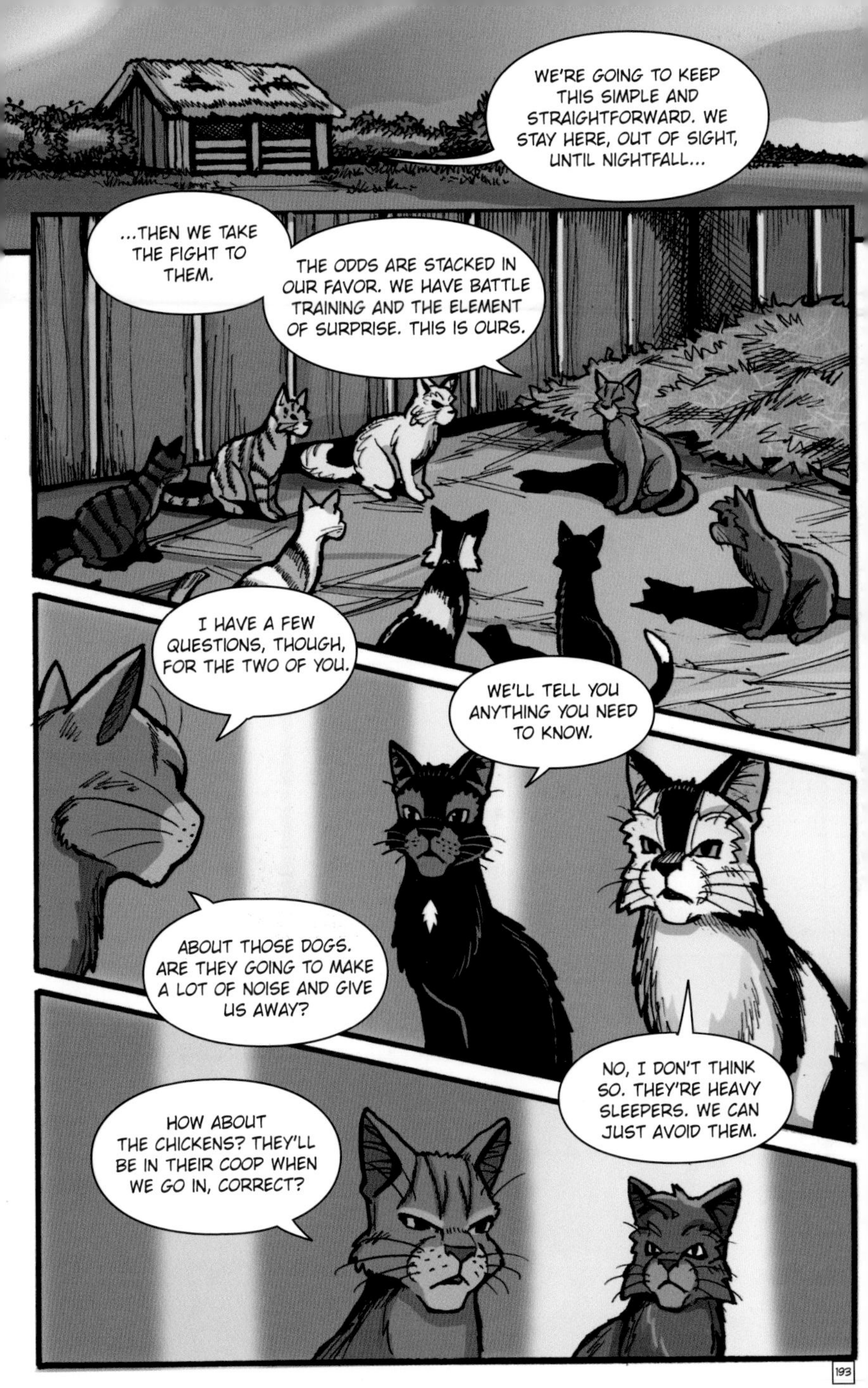

WE'RE GOING TO KEEP THIS SIMPLE AND STRAIGHTFORWARD. WE STAY HERE, OUT OF SIGHT, UNTIL NIGHTFALL...
...THEN WE TAKE THE FIGHT TO THEM.
THE ODDS ARE STACKED IN OUR FAVOR. WE HAVE BATTLE TRAINING AND THE ELEMENT OF SURPRISE. THIS IS OURS.
I HAVE A FEW QUESTIONS, THOUGH, FOR THE TWO OF YOU.
WE'LL TELL YOU ANYTHING YOU NEED TO KNOW.
ABOUT THOSE DOGS. ARE THEY GOING TO MAKE A LOT OF NOISE AND GIVE US AWAY?
NO, I DON'T THINK SO. THEY'RE HEAVY SLEEPERS. WE CAN JUST AVOID THEM.
HOW ABOUT THE CHICKENS? THEY'LL BE IN THEIR COOP WHEN WE GO IN, CORRECT?

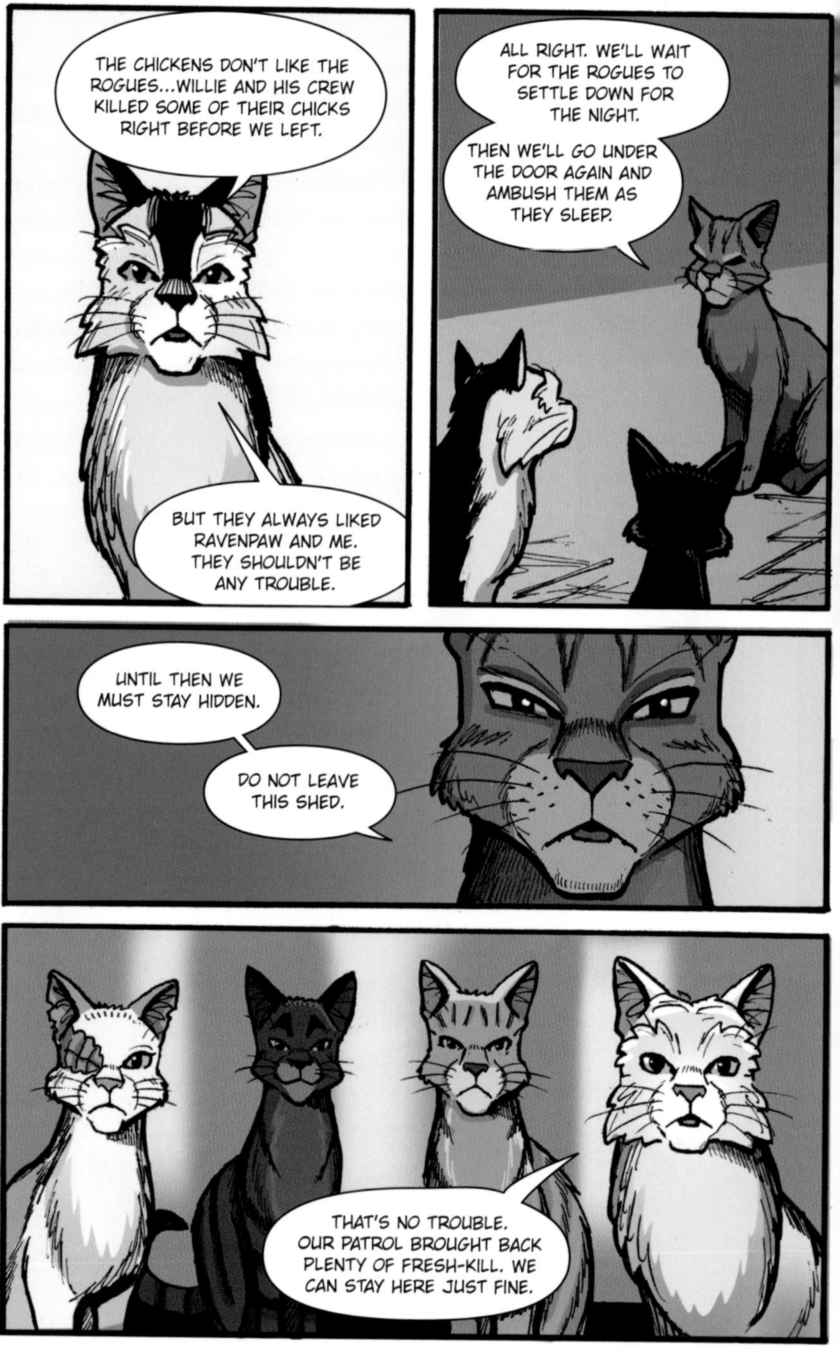
THE CHICKENS DON'T LIKE THE ROGUES...WILLIE AND HIS CREW KILLED SOME OF THEIR CHICKS RIGHT BEFORE WE LEFT.
BUT THEY ALWAYS LIKED RAVENPAW AND ME. THEY SHOULDN'T BE ANY TROUBLE.
ALL RIGHT. WE'LL WAIT FOR THE ROGUES TO SETTLE DOWN FOR THE NIGHT.
THEN WE'LL GO UNDER THE DOOR AGAIN AND AMBUSH THEM AS THEY SLEEP.
UNTIL THEN WE MUST STAY HIDDEN.
DO NOT LEAVE THIS SHED.
THAT'S NO TROUBLE. OUR PATROL BROUGHT BACK PLENTY OF FRESH-KILL. WE CAN STAY HERE JUST FINE.

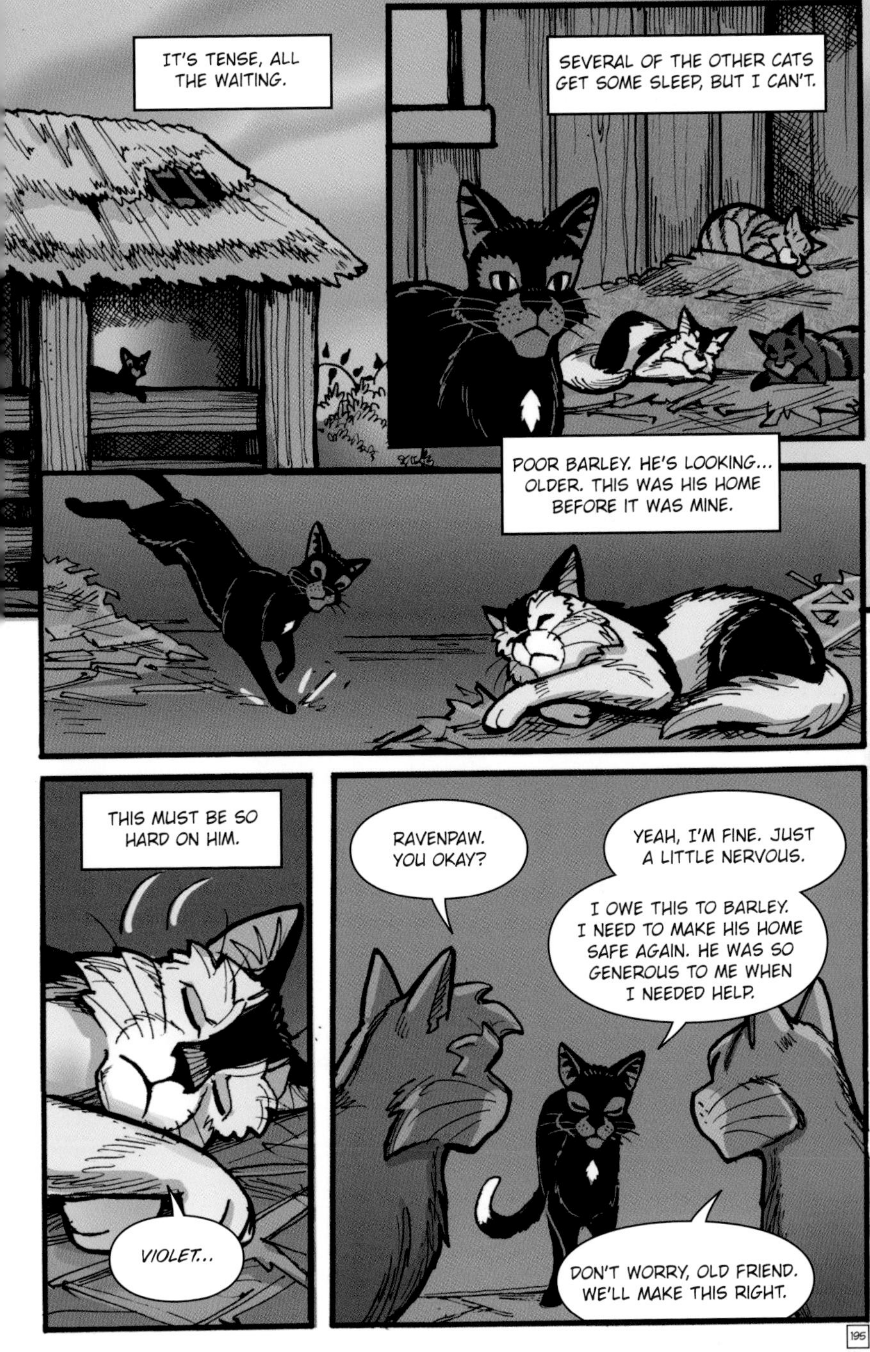
IT'S TENSE, ALL THE WAITING.
SEVERAL OF THE OTHER CATS GET SOME SLEEP, BUT I CAN'T.
POOR BARLEY. HE'S LOOKING... OLDER. THIS WAS HIS HOME BEFORE IT WAS MINE.
THIS MUST BE SO HARD ON HIM.
VIOLET...
RAVENPAW. YOU OKAY?
YEAH, I'M FINE. JUST A LITTLE NERVOUS.
I OWE THIS TO BARLEY. I NEED TO MAKE HIS HOME SAFE AGAIN. HE WAS SO GENEROUS TO ME WHEN I NEEDED HELP.
DON'T WORRY, OLD FRIEND. WE'LL MAKE THIS RIGHT.

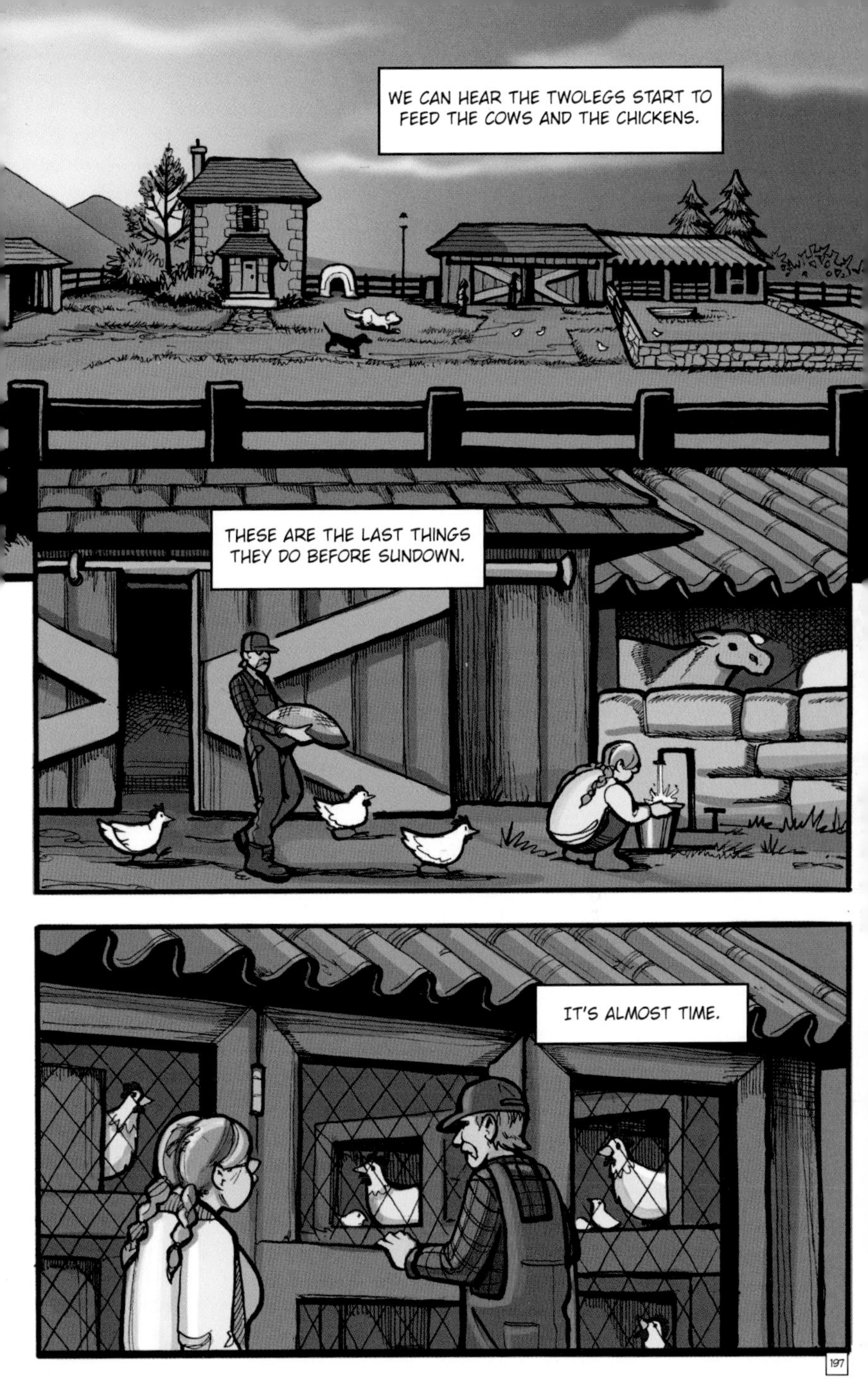
WE CAN HEAR THE TWOLEGS START TO FEED THE COWS AND THE CHICKENS.
THESE ARE THE LAST THINGS THEY DO BEFORE SUNDOWN.
IT'S ALMOST TIME.

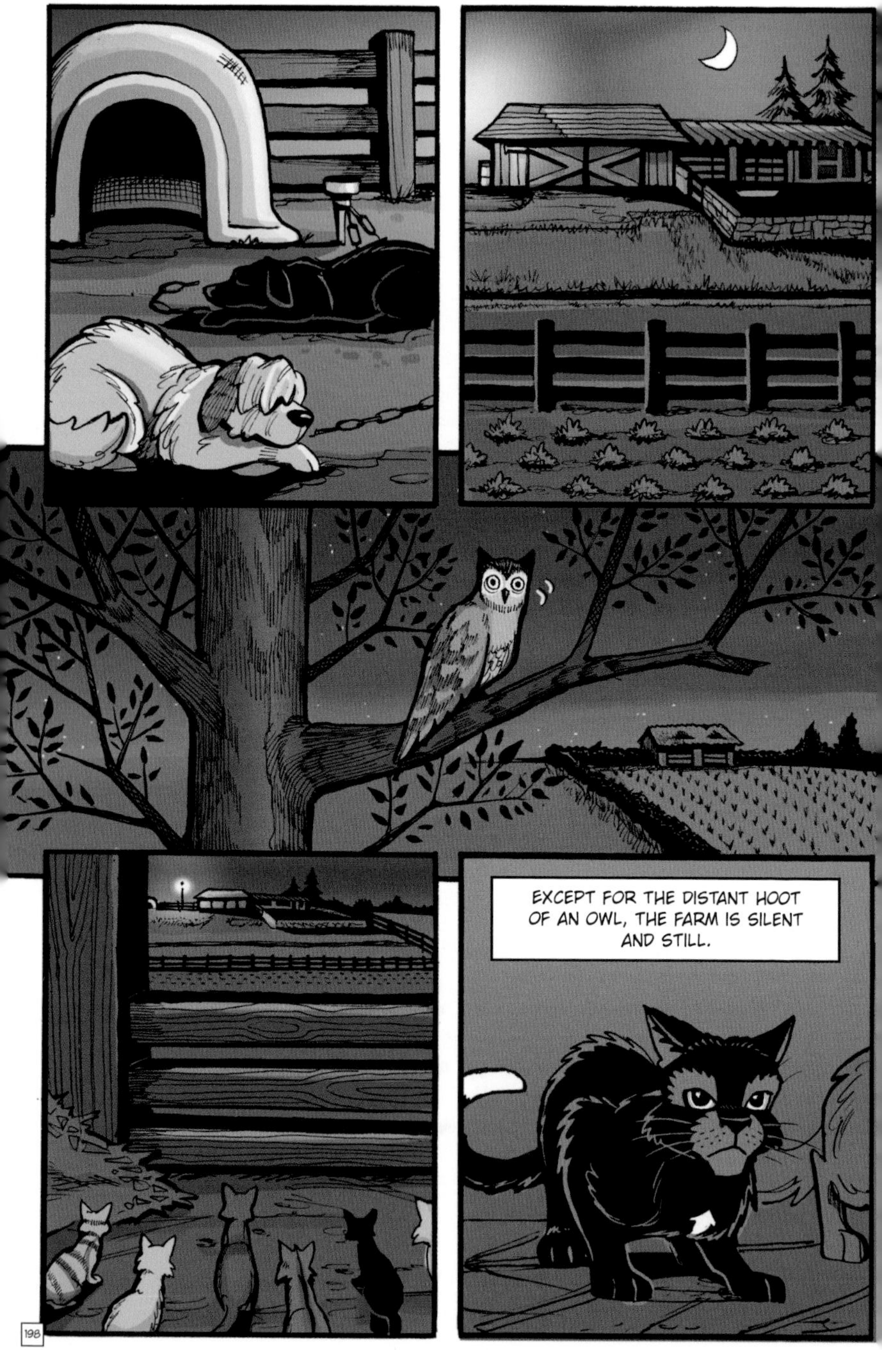
EXCEPT FOR THE DISTANT HOOT OF AN OWL, THE FARM IS SILENT AND STILL.

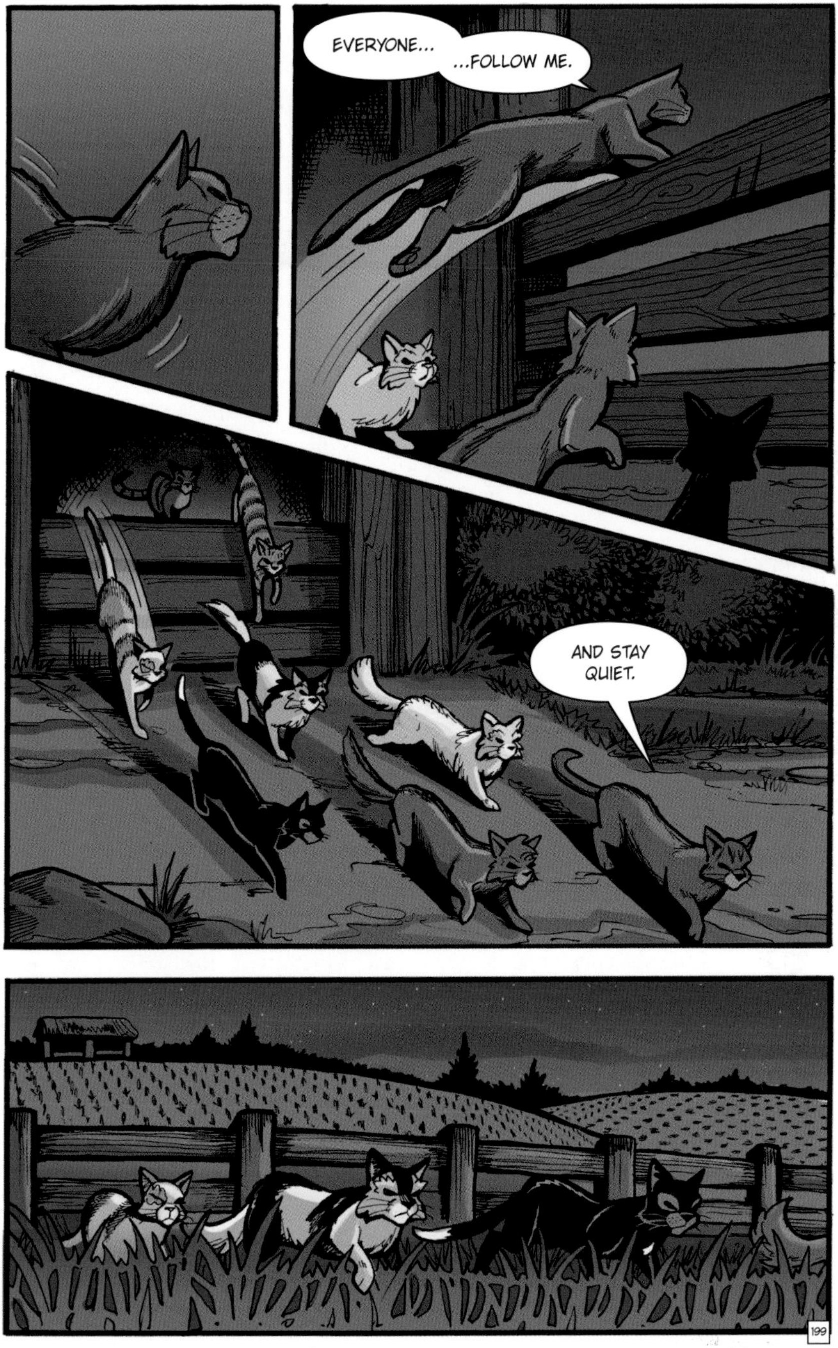
EVERYONE...
...FOLLOW ME.
AND STAY QUIET.

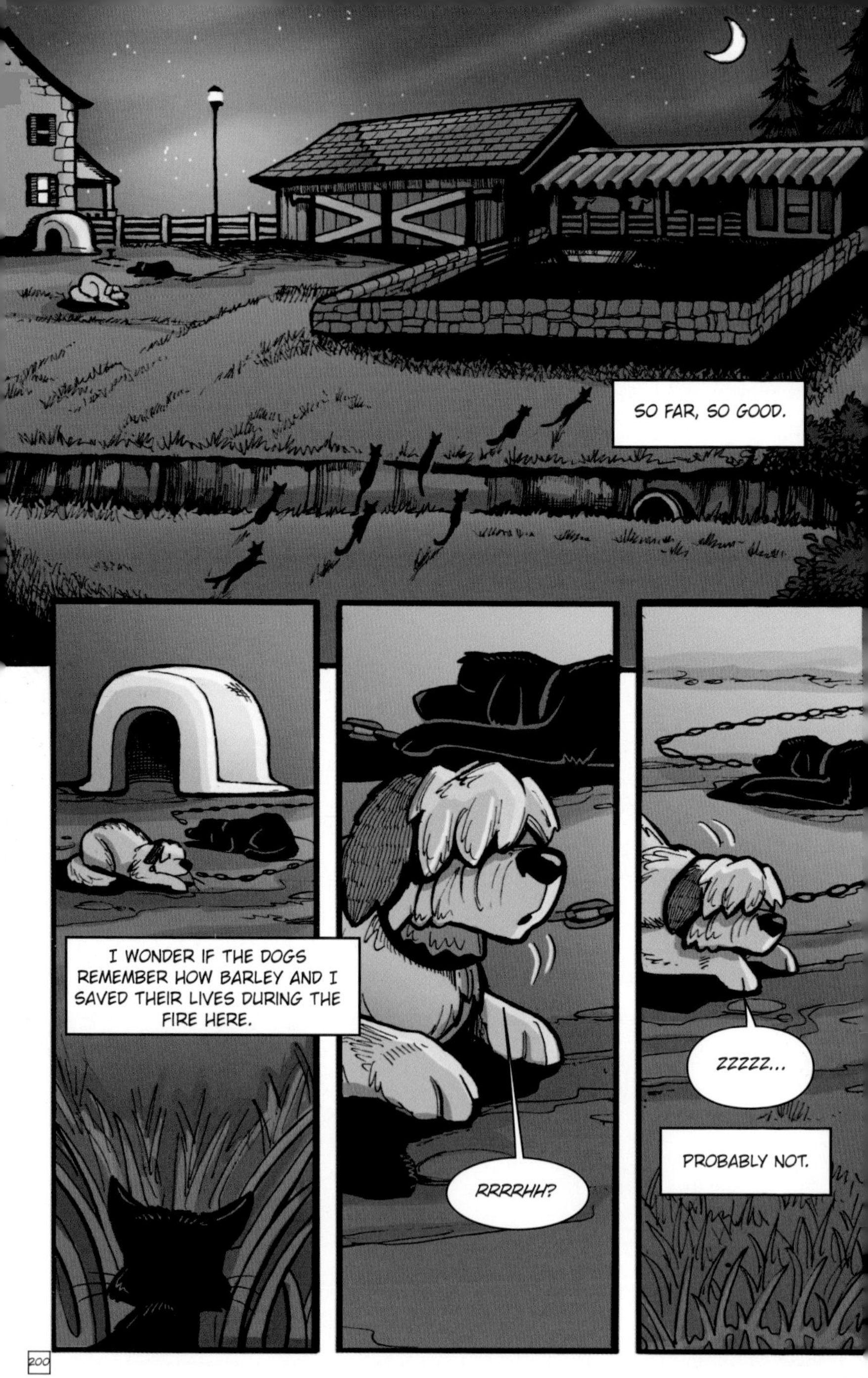
SO FAR, SO GOOD.
I WONDER IF THE DOGS REMEMBER HOW BARLEY AND I SAVED THEIR LIVES DURING THE FIRE HERE.
RRRRHH?
ZZZZZ...
PROBABLY NOT.

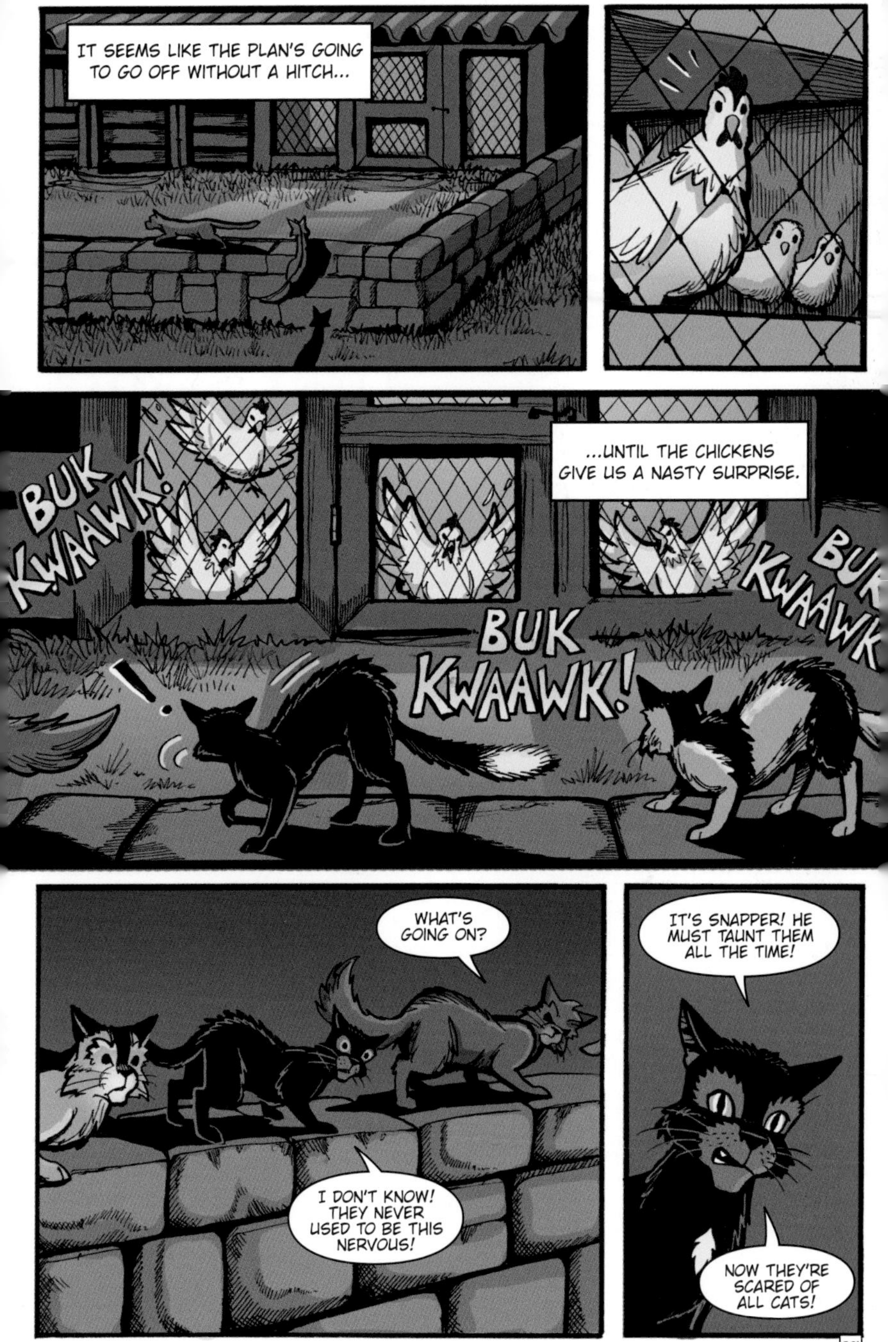
IT SEEMS LIKE THE PLAN'S GOING TO GO OFF WITHOUT A HITCH...
BUK KWAAWK!
...UNTIL THE CHICKENS GIVE US A NASTY SURPRISE.
BUK KWAAWK!
WHAT'S GOING ON?
I DON'T KNOW! THEY NEVER USED TO BE THIS NERVOUS!
IT'S SNAPPER! HE MUST TAUNT THEM ALL THE TIME!
NOW THEY'RE SCARED OF ALL CATS!

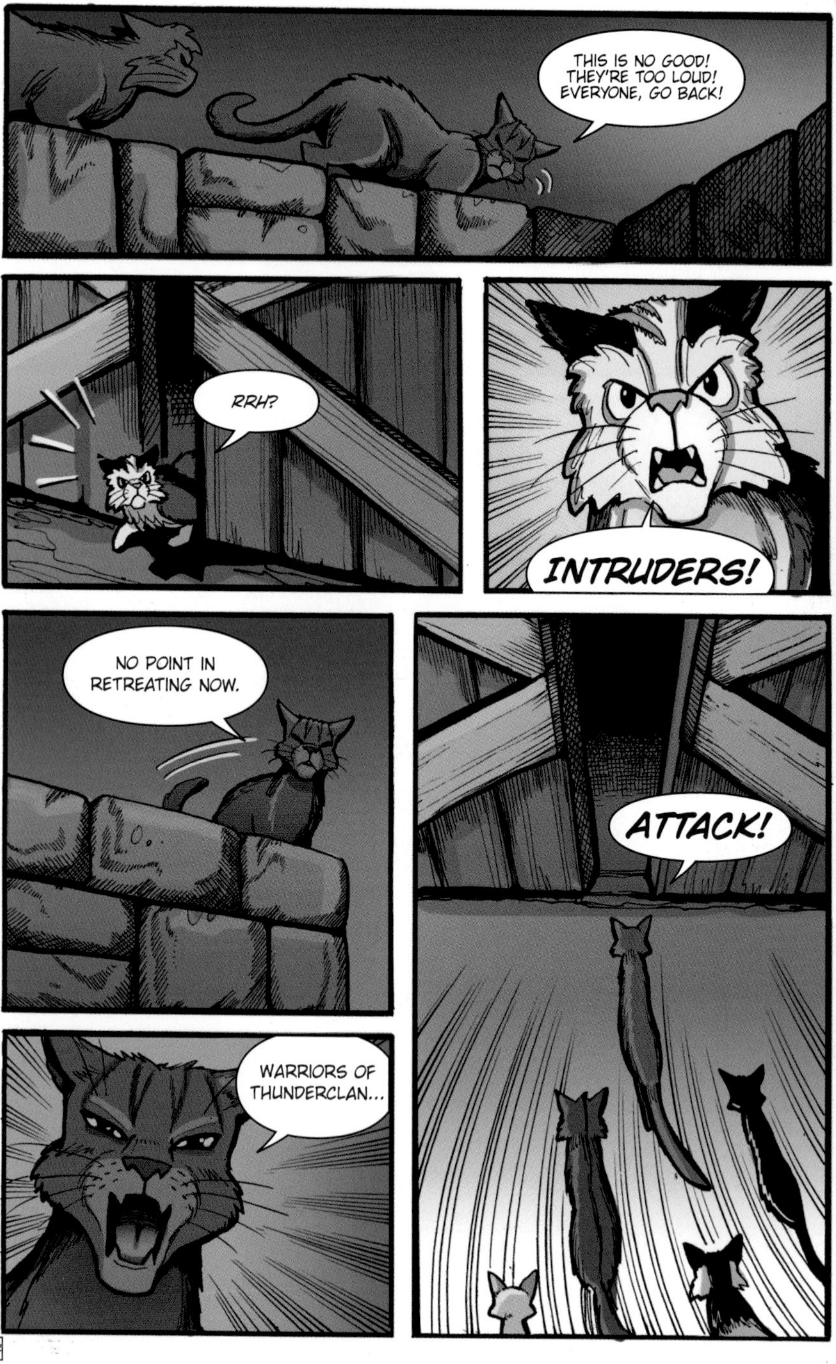
THIS IS NO GOOD! THEY'RE TOO LOUD! EVERYONE, GO BACK!
RRH?
INTRUDERS!
NO POINT IN RETREATING NOW.
WARRIORS OF THUNDERCLAN...
ATTACK!

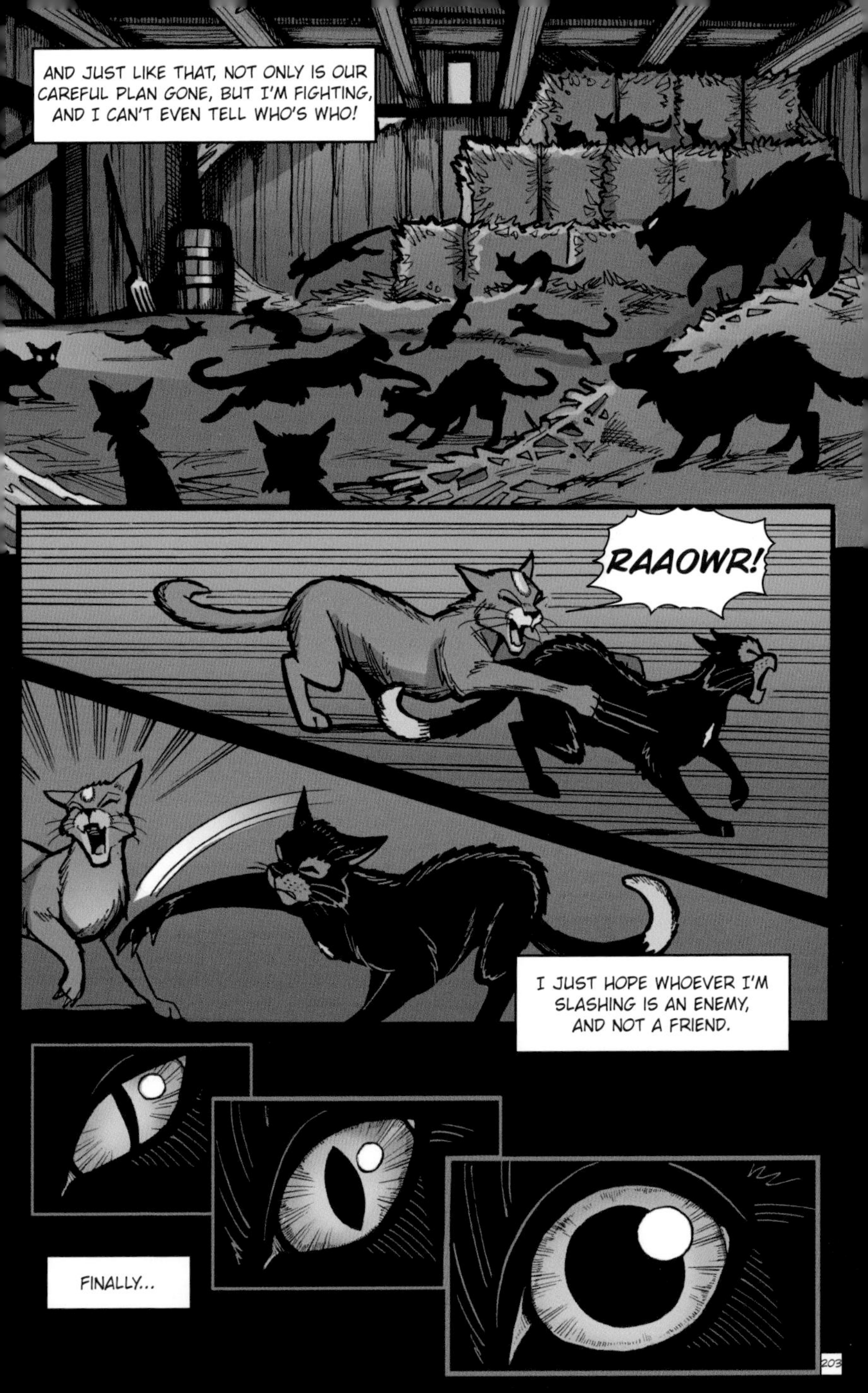
AND JUST LIKE THAT, NOT ONLY IS OUR CAREFUL PLAN GONE, BUT I'M FIGHTING, AND I CAN'T EVEN TELL WHO'S WHO!
RAAOWR!
I JUST HOPE WHOEVER I'M SLASHING IS AN ENEMY, AND NOT A FRIEND.
FINALLY...

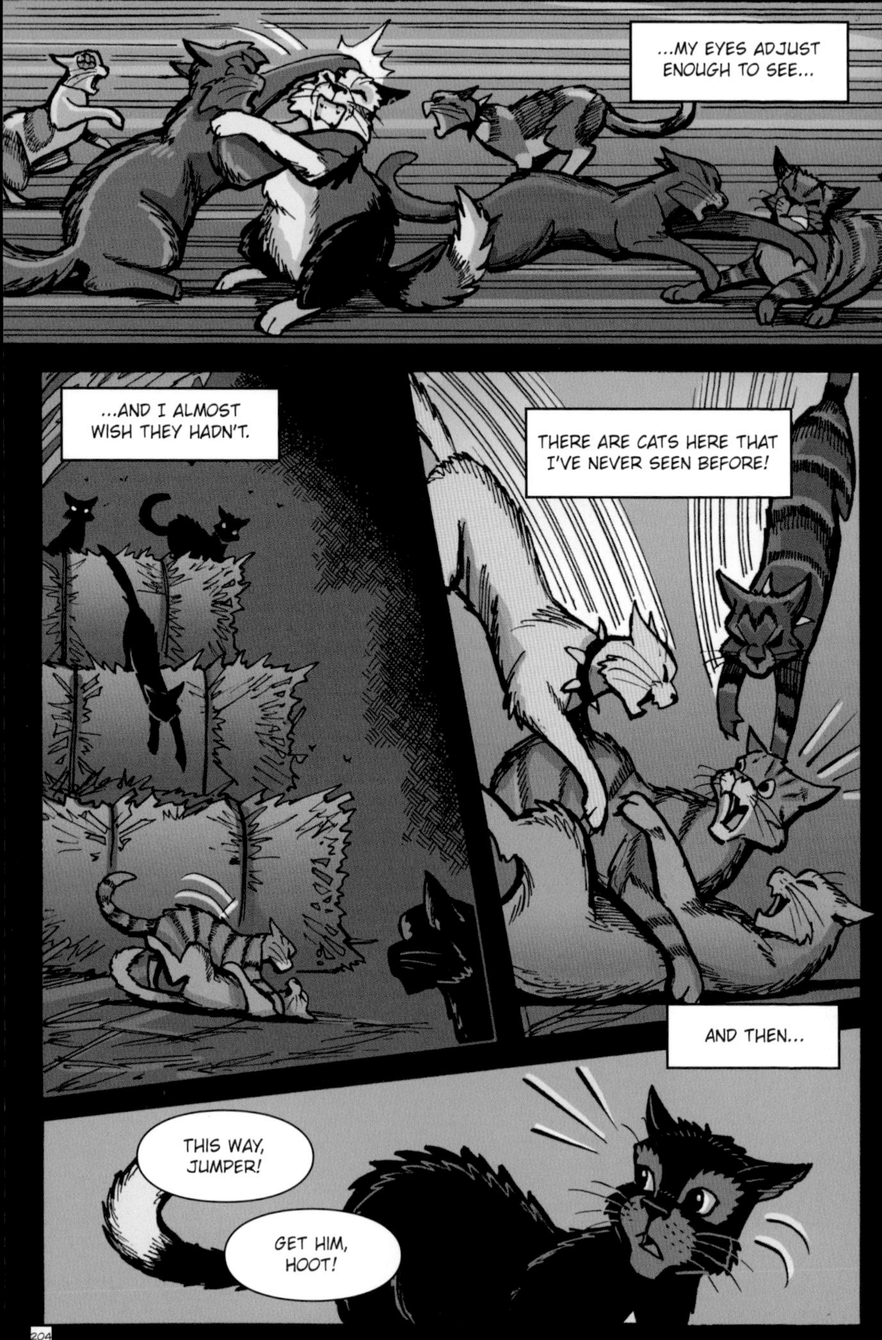
...MY EYES ADJUST ENOUGH TO SEE...
...AND I ALMOST WISH THEY HADN'T.
THERE ARE CATS HERE THAT I'VE NEVER SEEN BEFORE!
AND THEN...
THIS WAY, JUMPER!
GET HIM, HOOT!

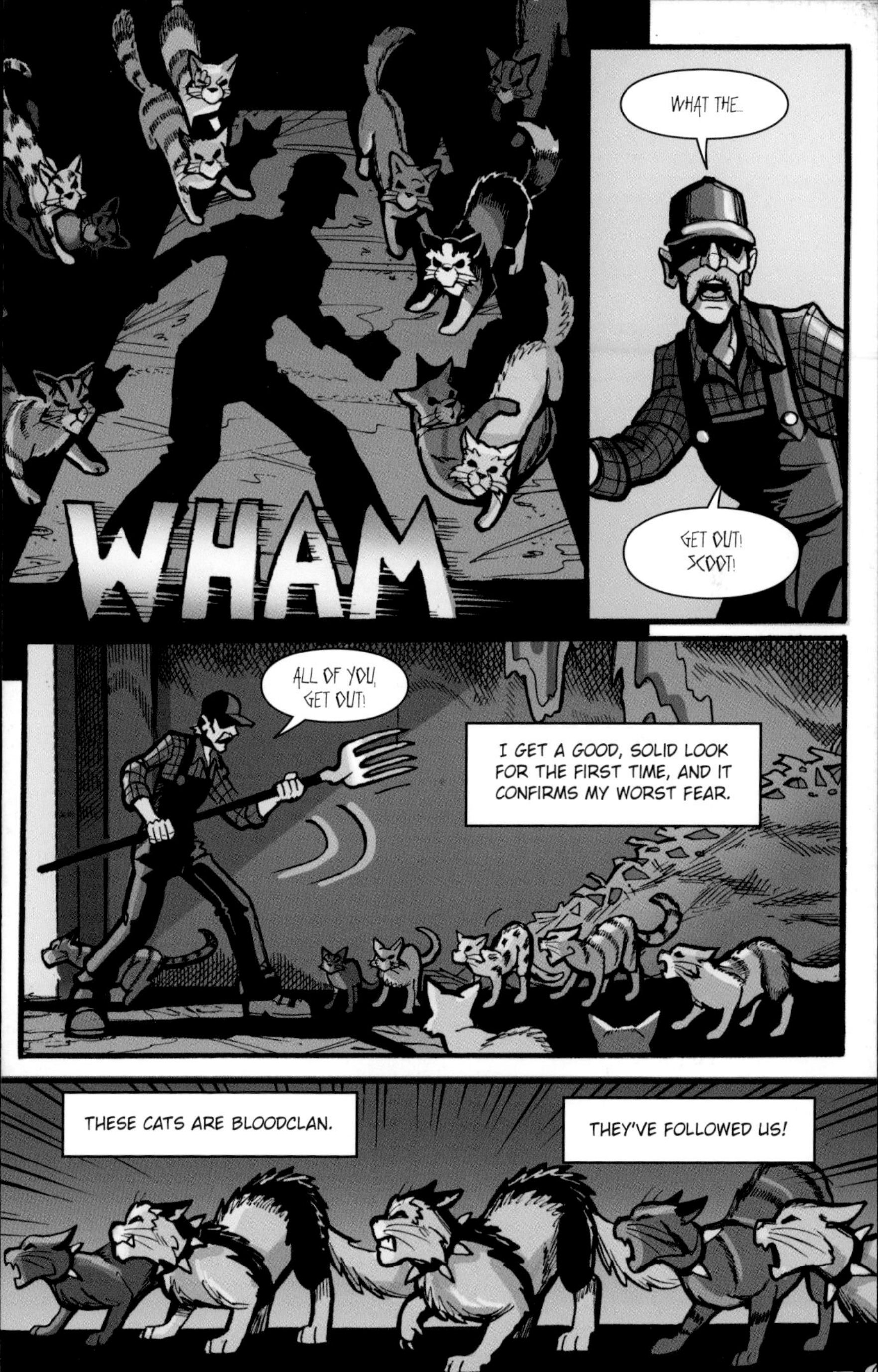
WHAM
WHAT THE...
GET OUT! SCOOT!
ALL OF YOU, GET OUT!
I GET A GOOD, SOLID LOOK FOR THE FIRST TIME, AND IT CONFIRMS MY WORST FEAR.
THESE CATS ARE BLOODCLAN.
THEY'VE FOLLOWED US!

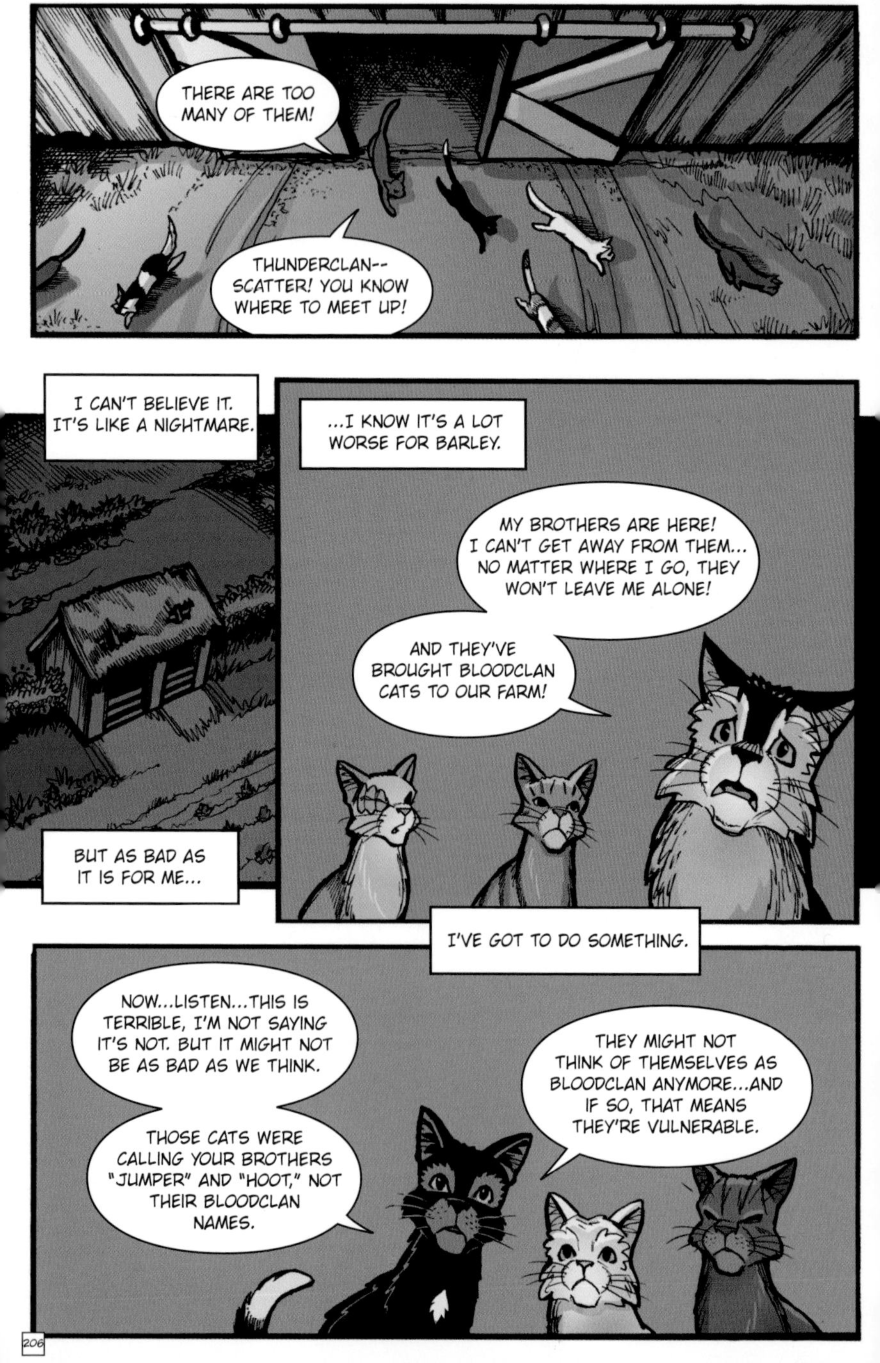
THERE ARE TOO MANY OF THEM!
THUNDERCLAN-- SCATTER! YOU KNOW WHERE TO MEET UP!
I CAN'T BELIEVE IT. IT'S LIKE A NIGHTMARE.
BUT AS BAD AS IT IS FOR ME...
...I KNOW IT'S A LOT WORSE FOR BARLEY.
MY BROTHERS ARE HERE! I CAN'T GET AWAY FROM THEM... NO MATTER WHERE I GO, THEY WON'T LEAVE ME ALONE!
AND THEY'VE BROUGHT BLOODCLAN CATS TO OUR FARM!
I'VE GOT TO DO SOMETHING.
NOW...LISTEN...THIS IS TERRIBLE, I'M NOT SAYING IT'S NOT. BUT IT MIGHT NOT BE AS BAD AS WE THINK.
THOSE CATS WERE CALLING YOUR BROTHERS "JUMPER" AND "HOOT," NOT THEIR BLOODCLAN NAMES.
THEY MIGHT NOT THINK OF THEMSELVES AS BLOODCLAN ANYMORE...AND IF SO, THAT MEANS THEY'RE VULNERABLE.

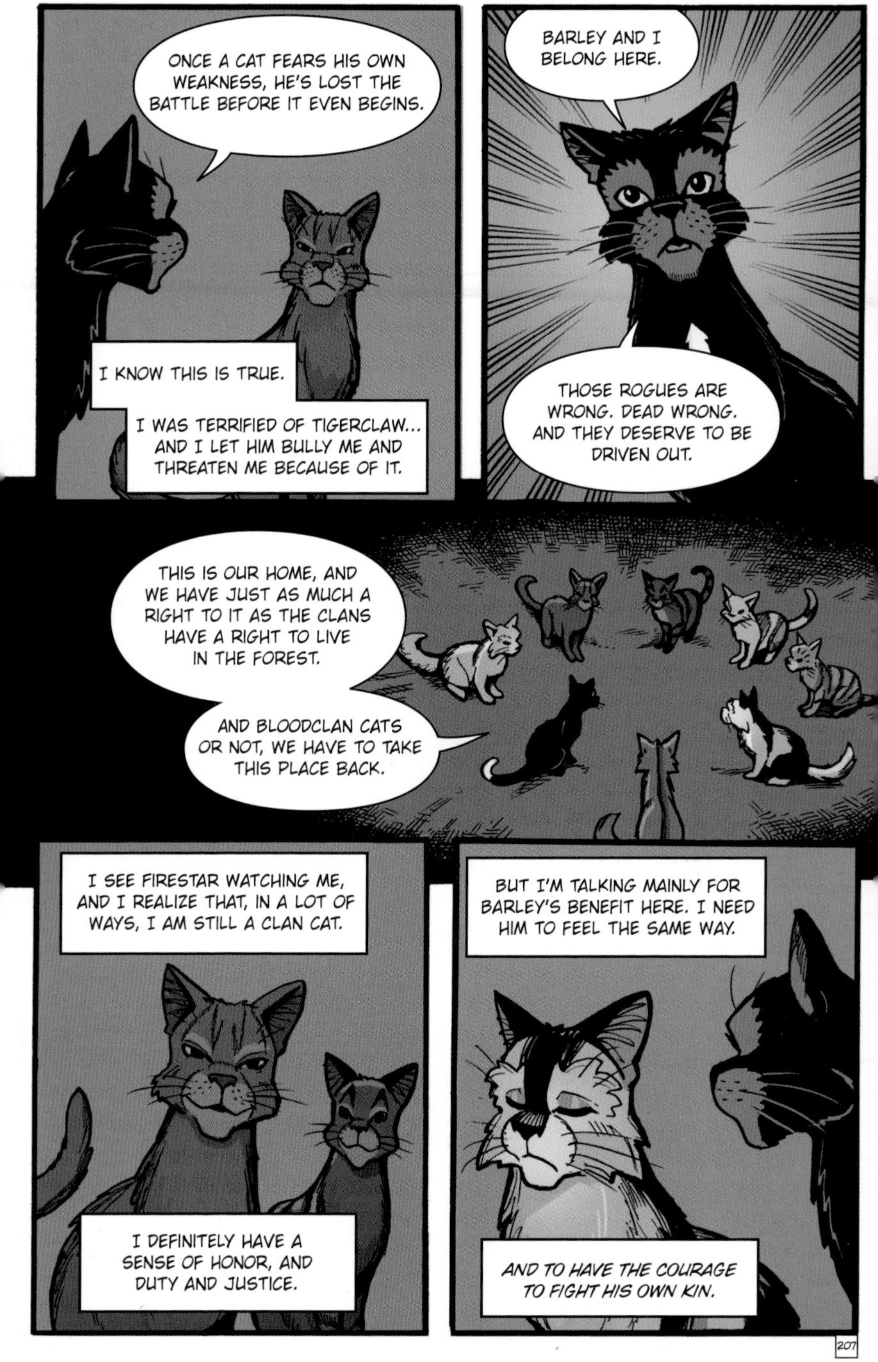
ONCE A CAT FEARS HIS OWN WEAKNESS, HE'S LOST THE BATTLE BEFORE IT EVEN BEGINS.
I KNOW THIS IS TRUE.
I WAS TERRIFIED OF TIGERCLAW... AND I LET HIM BULLY ME AND THREATEN ME BECAUSE OF IT.
BARLEY AND I BELONG HERE.
THOSE ROGUES ARE WRONG. DEAD WRONG. AND THEY DESERVE TO BE DRIVEN OUT.
THIS IS OUR HOME, AND WE HAVE JUST AS MUCH A RIGHT TO IT AS THE CLANS HAVE A RIGHT TO LIVE IN THE FOREST.
AND BLOODCLAN CATS OR NOT, WE HAVE TO TAKE THIS PLACE BACK.
I SEE FIRESTAR WATCHING ME, AND I REALIZE THAT, IN A LOT OF WAYS, I AM STILL A CLAN CAT.
I DEFINITELY HAVE A SENSE OF HONOR, AND DUTY AND JUSTICE.
BUT I'M TALKING MAINLY FOR BARLEY'S BENEFIT HERE. I NEED HIM TO FEEL THE SAME WAY.
AND TO HAVE THE COURAGE TO FIGHT HIS OWN KIN.

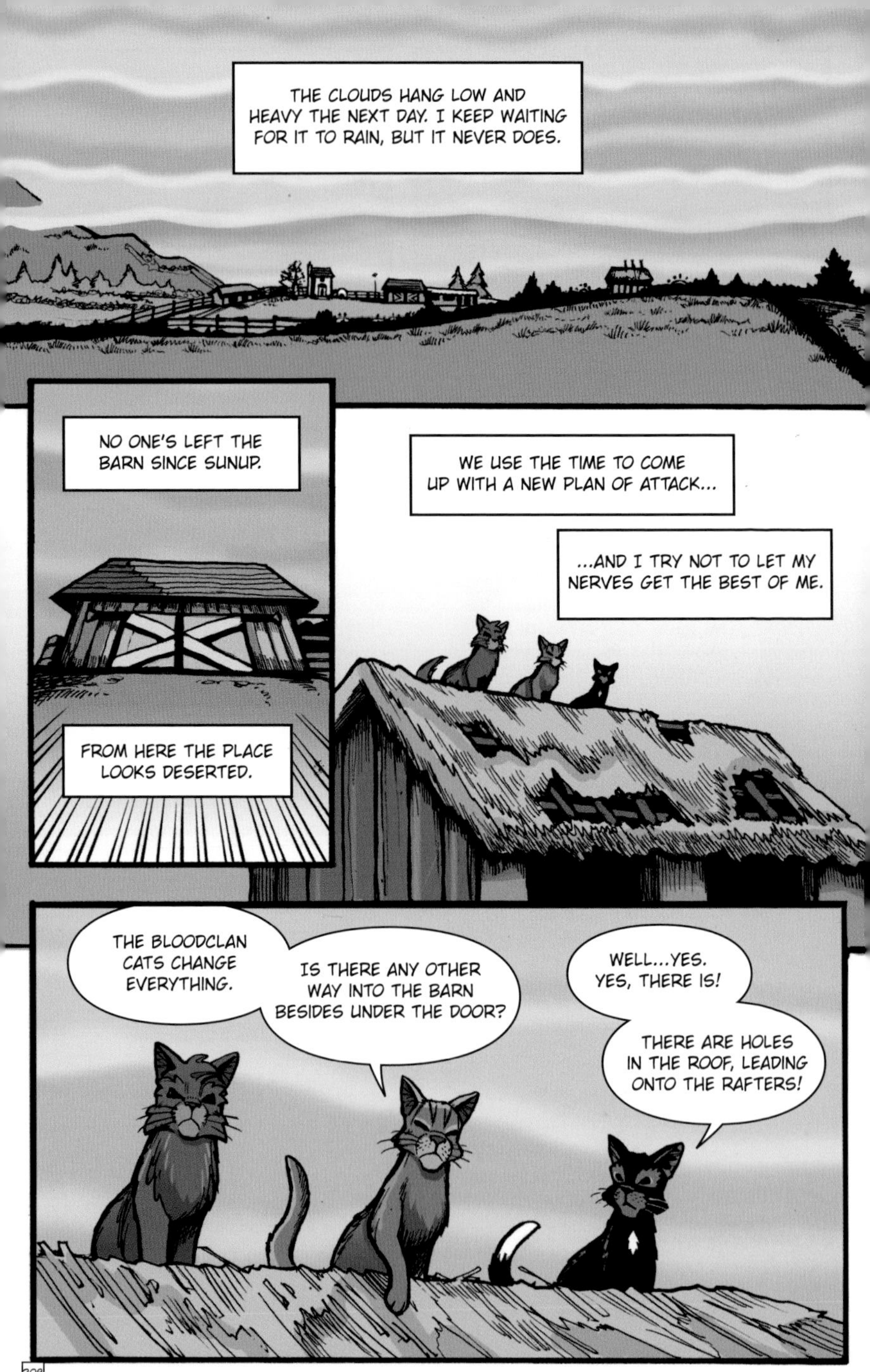
THE CLOUDS HANG LOW AND HEAVY THE NEXT DAY. I KEEP WAITING FOR IT TO RAIN, BUT IT NEVER DOES.
NO ONE'S LEFT THE BARN SINCE SUNUP.
FROM HERE THE PLACE LOOKS DESERTED.
WE USE THE TIME TO COME UP WITH A NEW PLAN OF ATTACK...
...AND I TRY NOT TO LET MY NERVES GET THE BEST OF ME.
THE BLOODCLAN CATS CHANGE EVERYTHING.
IS THERE ANY OTHER WAY INTO THE BARN BESIDES UNDER THE DOOR?
WELL...YES. YES, THERE IS!
THERE ARE HOLES IN THE ROOF, LEADING ONTO THE RAFTERS!

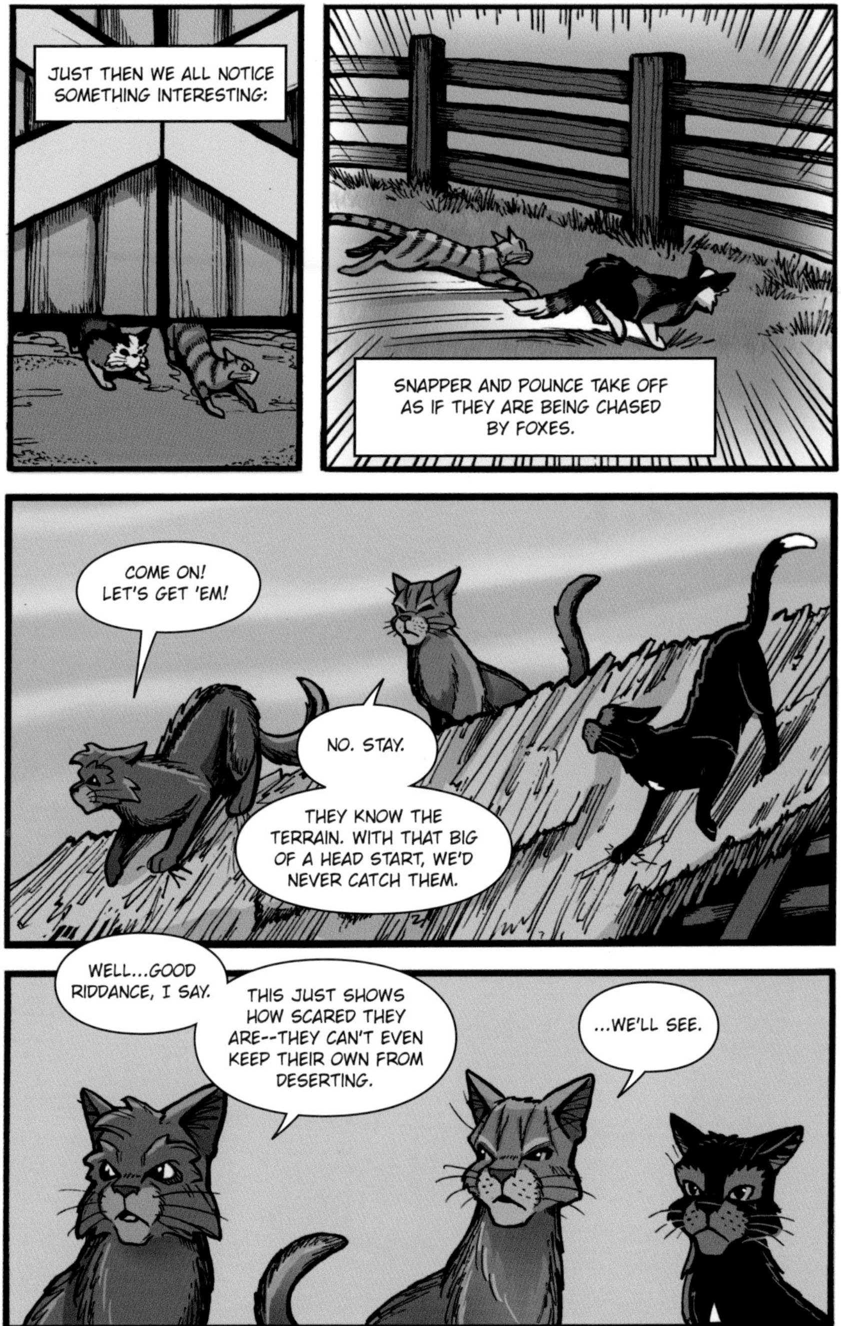
JUST THEN WE ALL NOTICE SOMETHING INTERESTING:
SNAPPER AND POUNCE TAKE OFF AS IF THEY ARE BEING CHASED BY FOXES.
COME ON! LET'S GET 'EM!
NO. STAY.
THEY KNOW THE TERRAIN. WITH THAT BIG OF A HEAD START, WE'D NEVER CATCH THEM.
WELL...GOOD RIDDANCE, I SAY.
THIS JUST SHOWS HOW SCARED THEY ARE--THEY CAN'T EVEN KEEP THEIR OWN FROM DESERTING.
...WE'LL SEE.

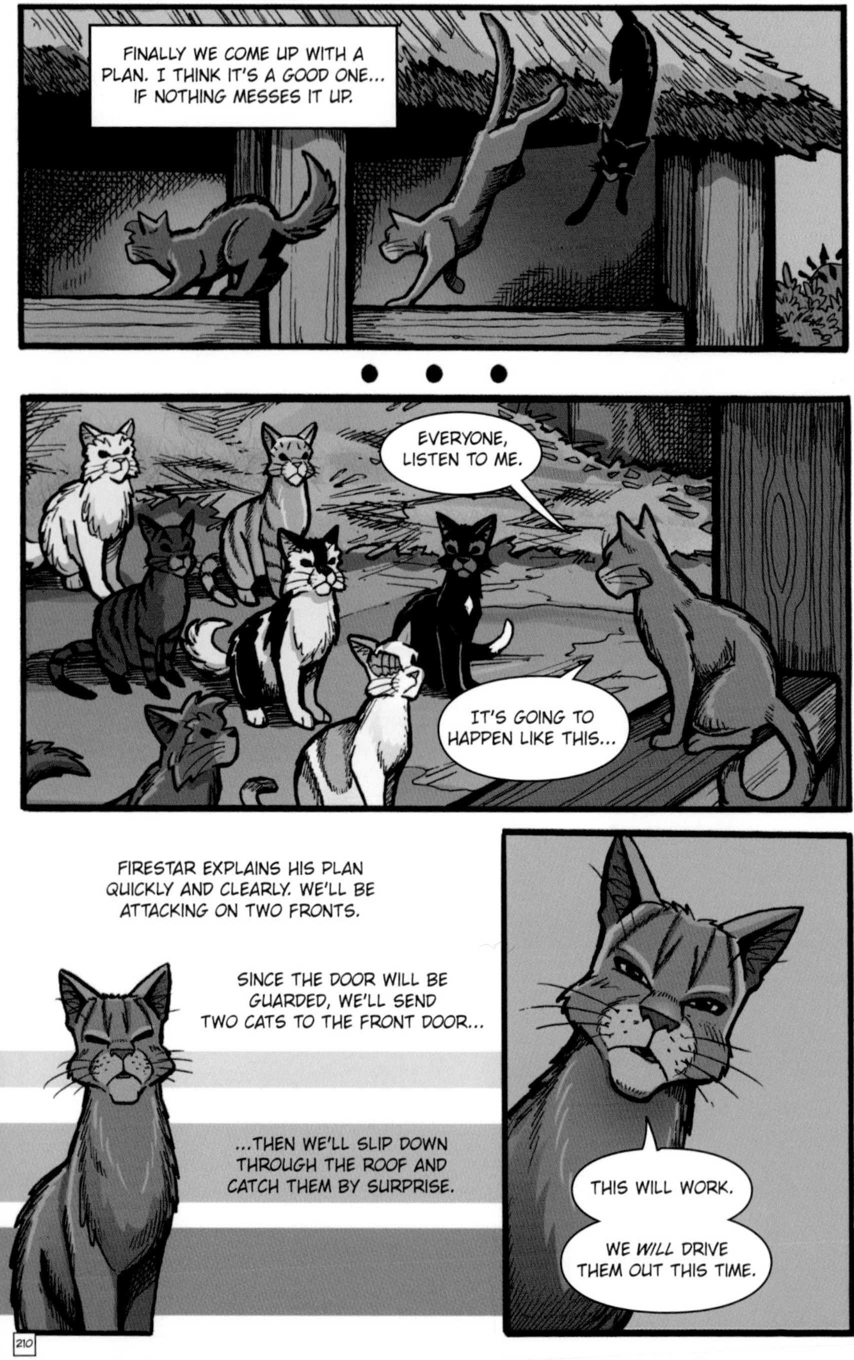

FINALLY WE COME UP WITH A PLAN. I THINK IT'S A GOOD ONE... IF NOTHING MESSES IT UP.
EVERYONE, LISTEN TO ME.
IT'S GOING TO HAPPEN LIKE THIS...
FIRESTAR EXPLAINS HIS PLAN QUICKLY AND CLEARLY. WE'LL BE ATTACKING ON TWO FRONTS.
SINCE THE DOOR WILL BE GUARDED, WE'LL SEND TWO CATS TO THE FRONT DOOR...
...THEN WE'LL SLIP DOWN THROUGH THE ROOF AND CATCH THEM BY SURPRISE.
THIS WILL WORK.
WE *WILL* DRIVE THEM OUT THIS TIME.

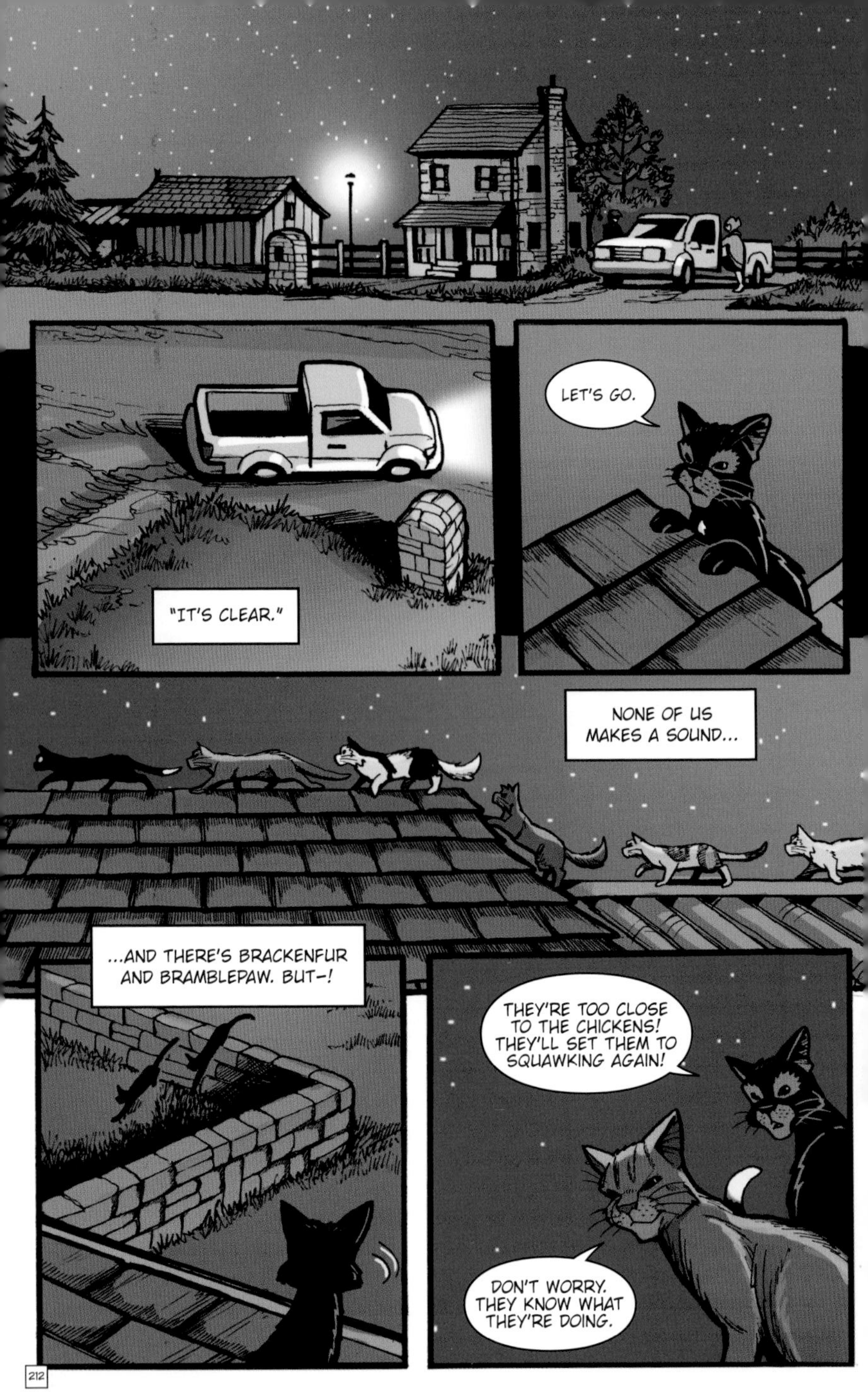

"IT'S CLEAR."
LET'S GO.
NONE OF US MAKES A SOUND...
...AND THERE'S BRACKENFUR AND BRAMBLEPAW. BUT-!
THEY'RE TOO CLOSE TO THE CHICKENS! THEY'LL SET THEM TO SQUAWKING AGAIN!
DON'T WORRY. THEY KNOW WHAT THEY'RE DOING.

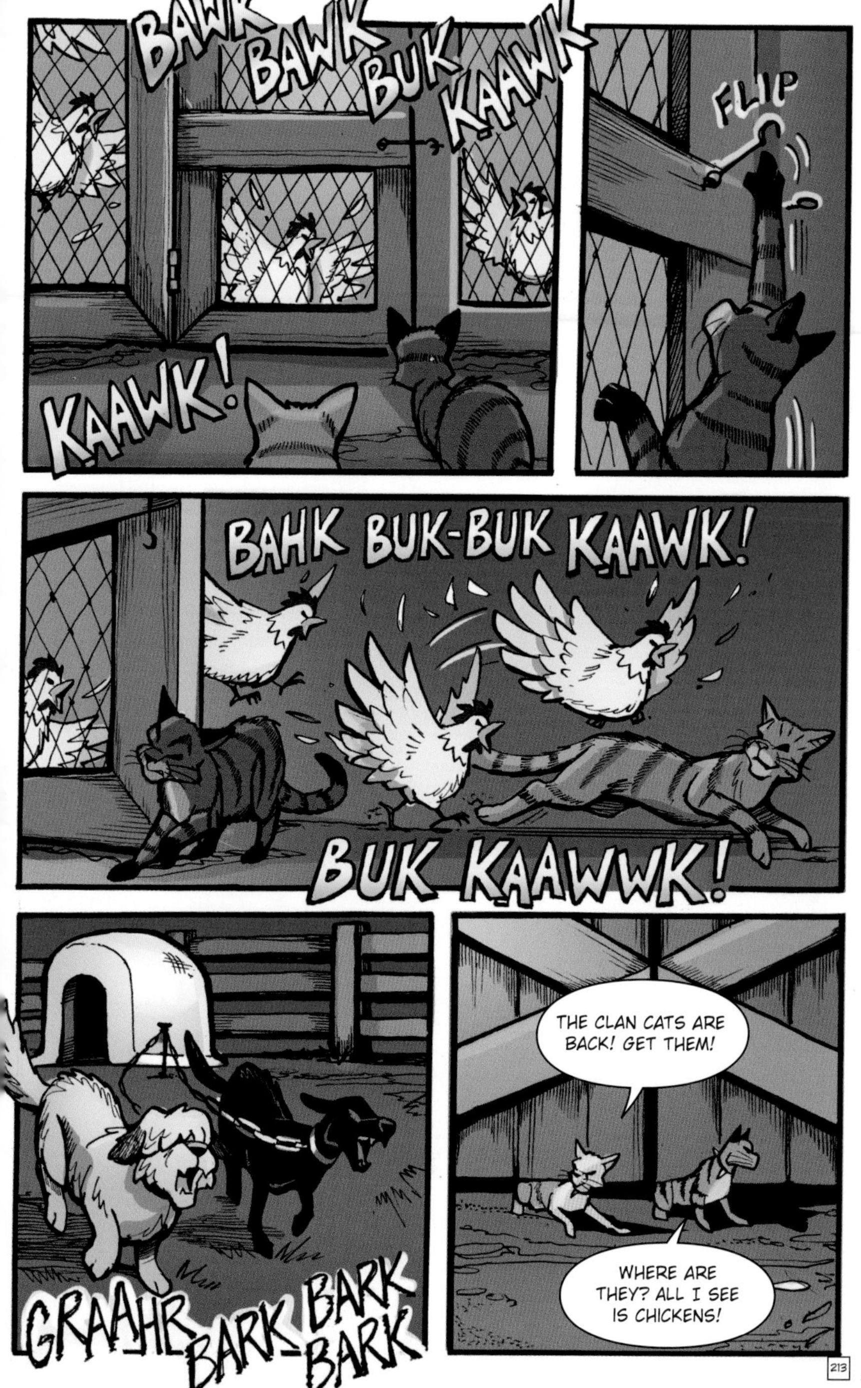
BAWK BAWK BUK KAAWK
KAAWK!
FLIP
BAHK BUK-BUK KAAWK!
BUK KAAWWK!
GRAAHR BARK BARK BARK-BARK
THE CLAN CATS ARE BACK! GET THEM!
WHERE ARE THEY? ALL I SEE IS CHICKENS!

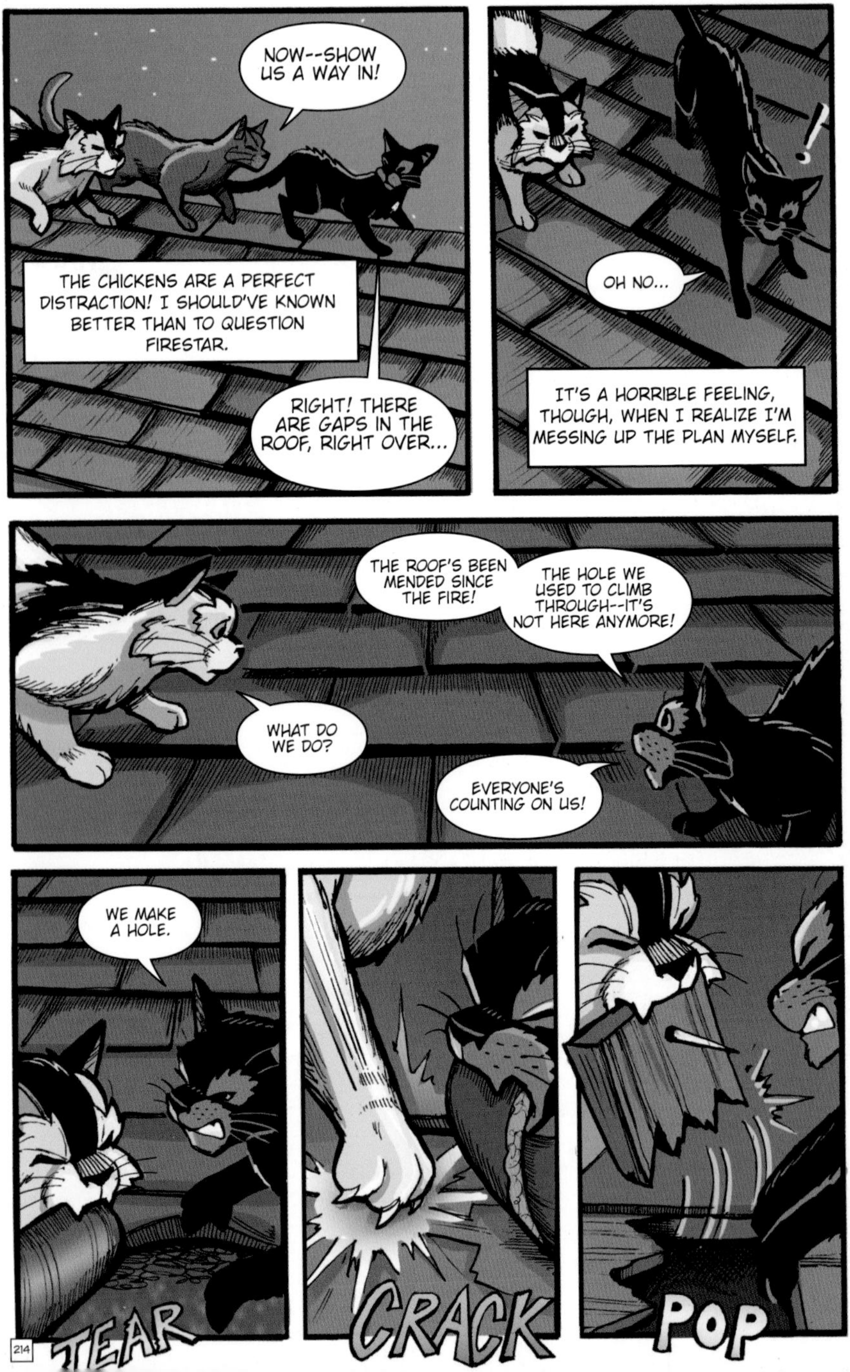
NOW--SHOW US A WAY IN!
THE CHICKENS ARE A PERFECT DISTRACTION! I SHOULD'VE KNOWN BETTER THAN TO QUESTION FIRESTAR.
RIGHT! THERE ARE GAPS IN THE ROOF, RIGHT OVER...
!
OH NO...
IT'S A HORRIBLE FEELING, THOUGH, WHEN I REALIZE I'M MESSING UP THE PLAN MYSELF.
THE ROOF'S BEEN MENDED SINCE THE FIRE!
THE HOLE WE USED TO CLIMB THROUGH--IT'S NOT HERE ANYMORE!
WHAT DO WE DO?
EVERYONE'S COUNTING ON US!
WE MAKE A HOLE.
TEAR
CRACK
POP

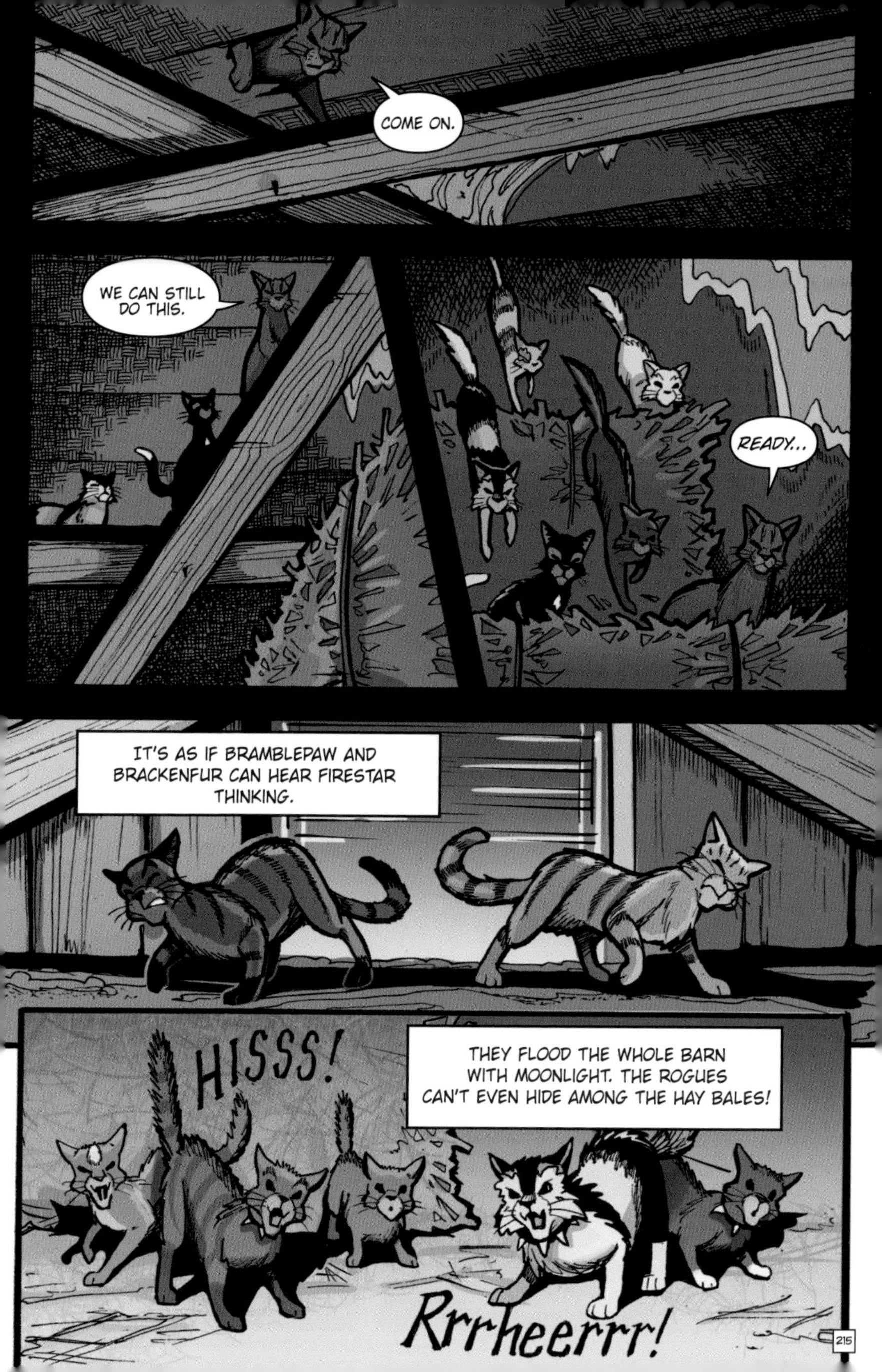

COME ON.
WE CAN STILL DO THIS.
READY...
IT'S AS IF BRAMBLEPAW AND BRACKENFUR CAN HEAR FIRESTAR THINKING.
HISSS!
THEY FLOOD THE WHOLE BARN WITH MOONLIGHT. THE ROGUES CAN'T EVEN HIDE AMONG THE HAY BALES!
Rrrheerrr!

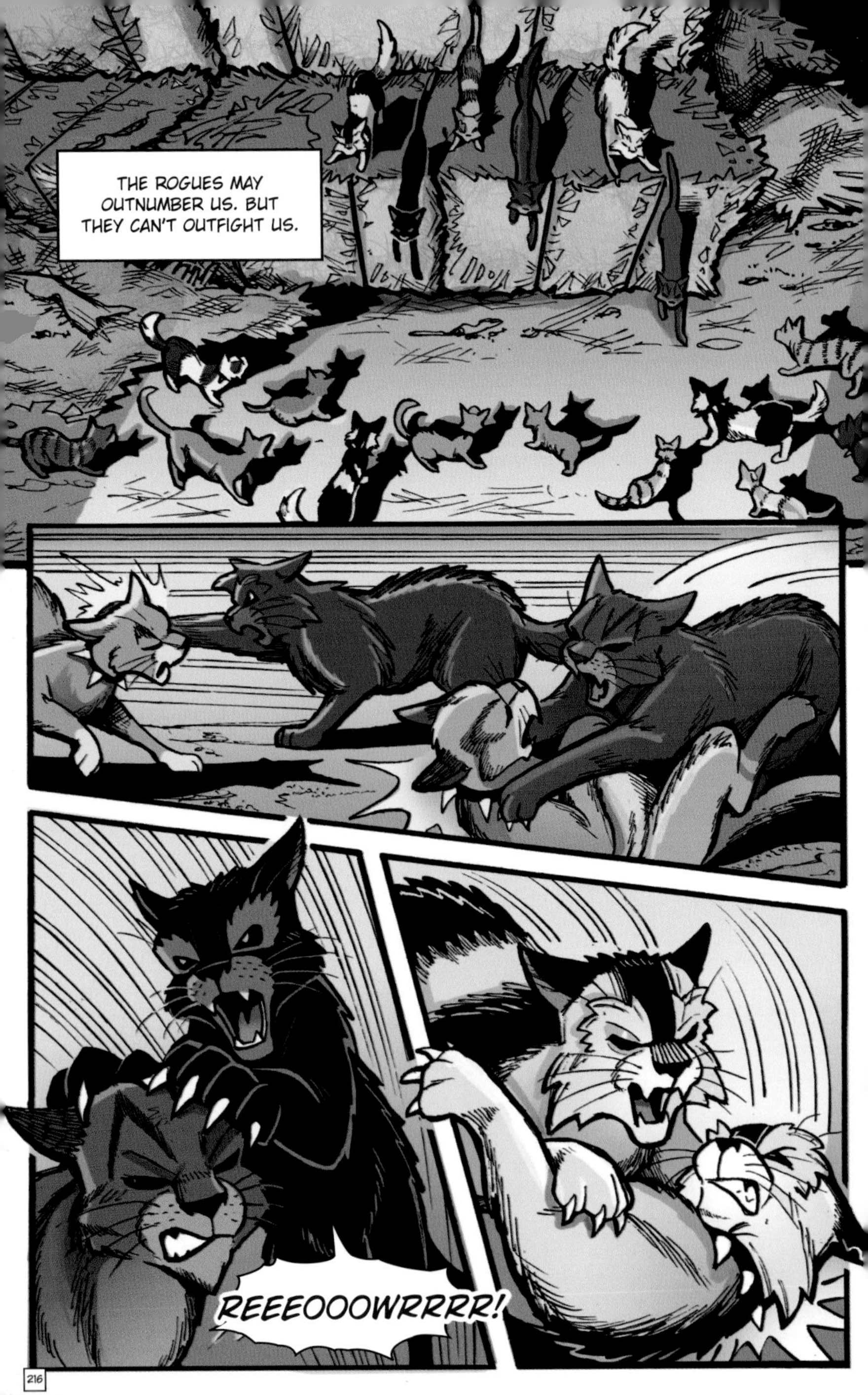
THE ROGUES MAY OUTNUMBER US. BUT THEY CAN'T OUTFIGHT US.
REEEOOOWRRRR!

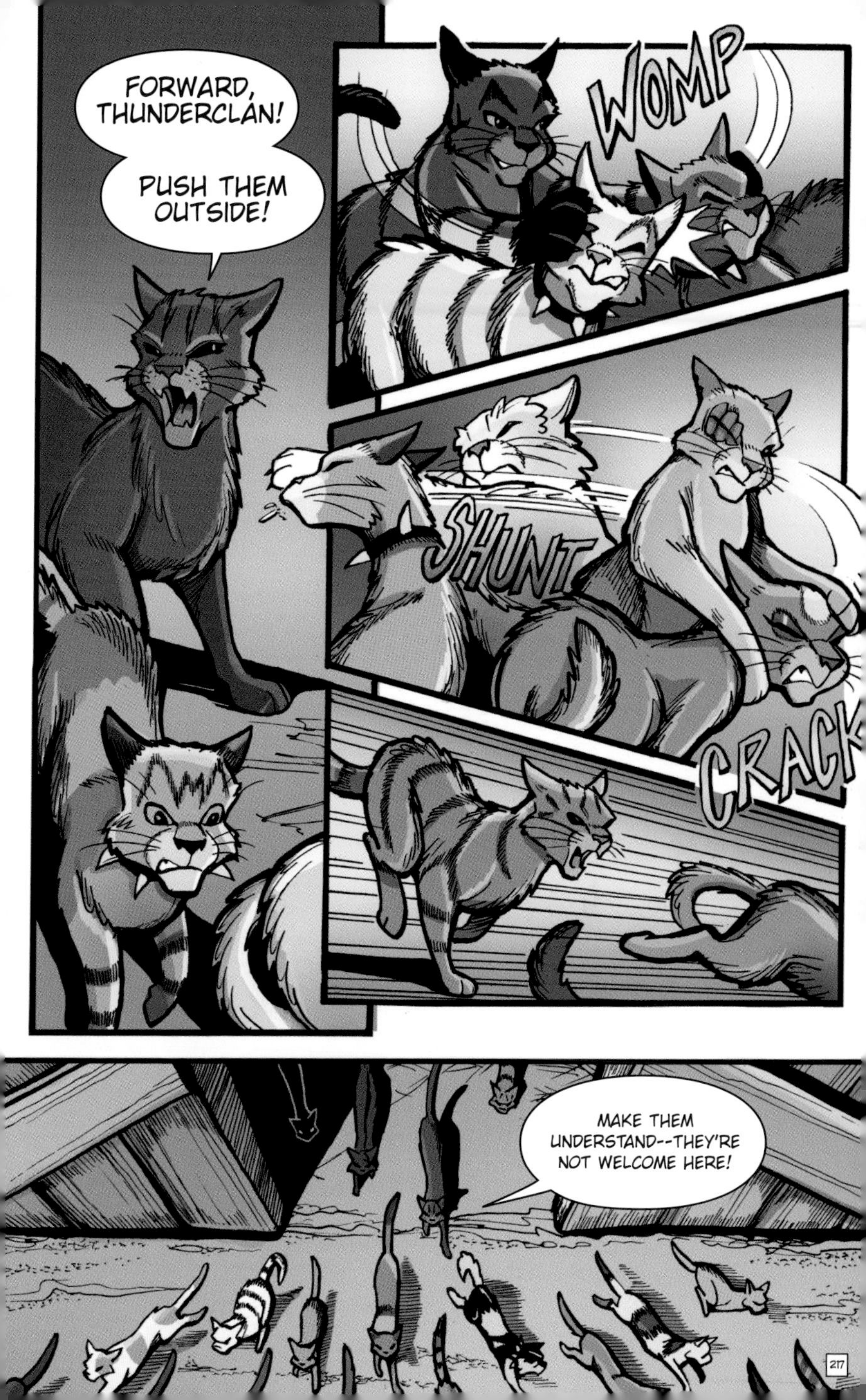
FORWARD, THUNDERCLAN!
PUSH THEM OUTSIDE!
WOMP
SHUNT
CRACK
MAKE THEM UNDERSTAND--THEY'RE NOT WELCOME HERE!

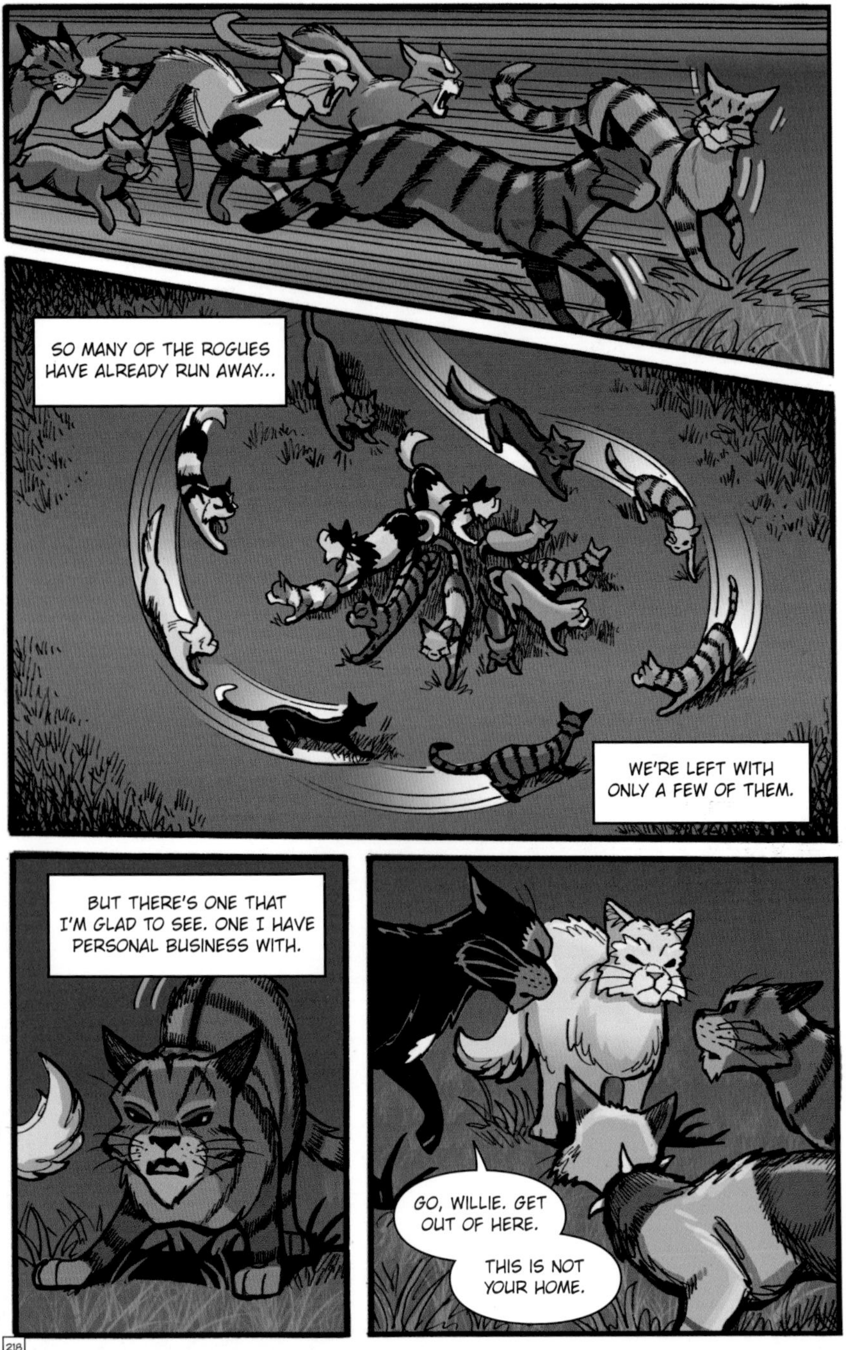
SO MANY OF THE ROGUES HAVE ALREADY RUN AWAY...
WE'RE LEFT WITH ONLY A FEW OF THEM.
BUT THERE'S ONE THAT I'M GLAD TO SEE. ONE I HAVE PERSONAL BUSINESS WITH.
GO, WILLIE. GET OUT OF HERE.
THIS IS NOT YOUR HOME.

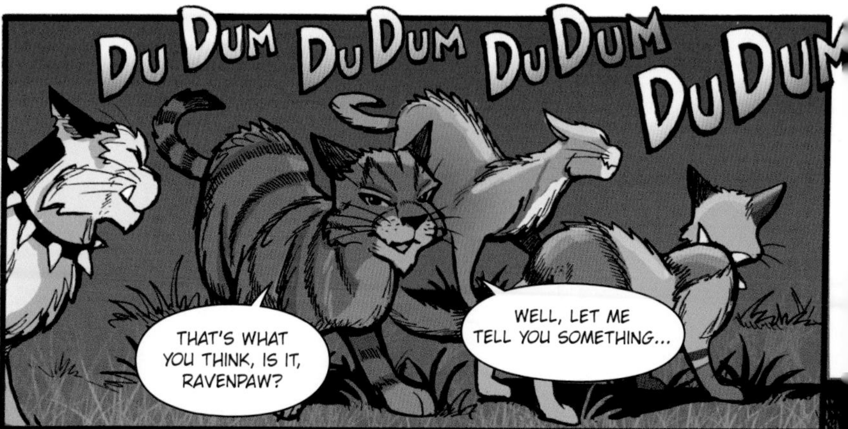
DU DUM DU DUM DU DUM DU DUM
THAT'S WHAT YOU THINK, IS IT, RAVENPAW?
WELL, LET ME TELL YOU SOMETHING...

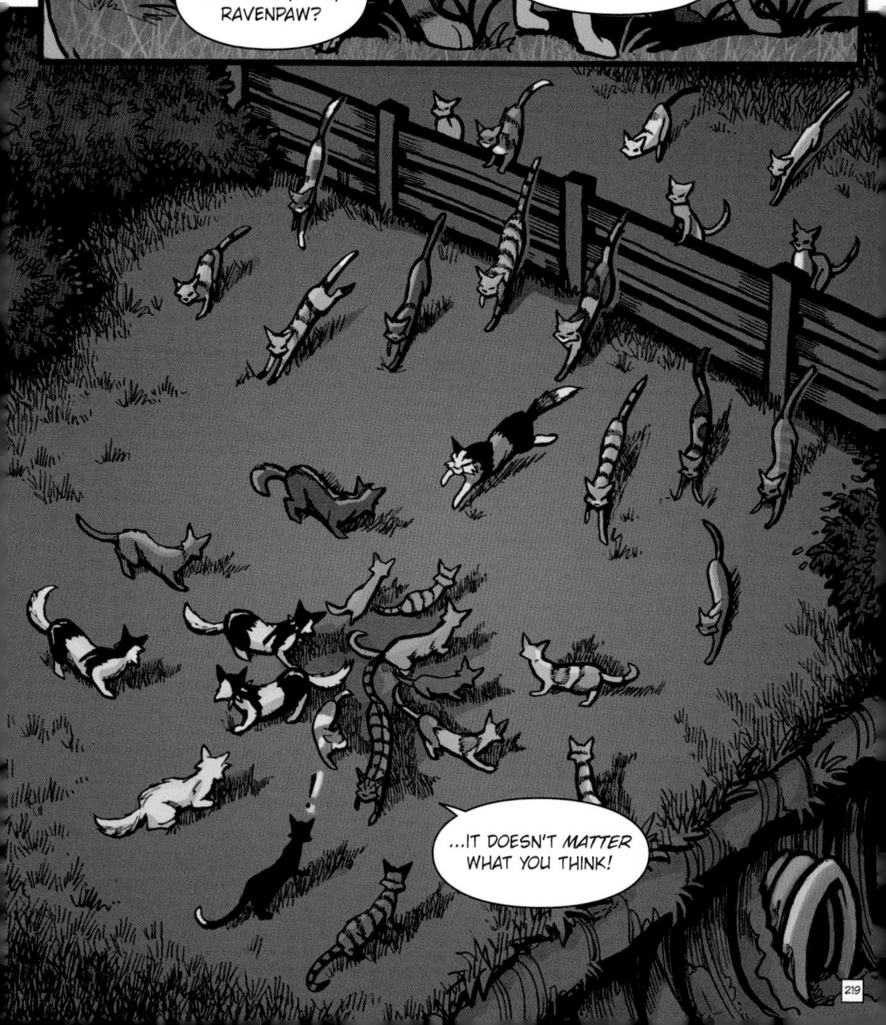
!
...IT DOESN'T *MATTER* WHAT YOU THINK!

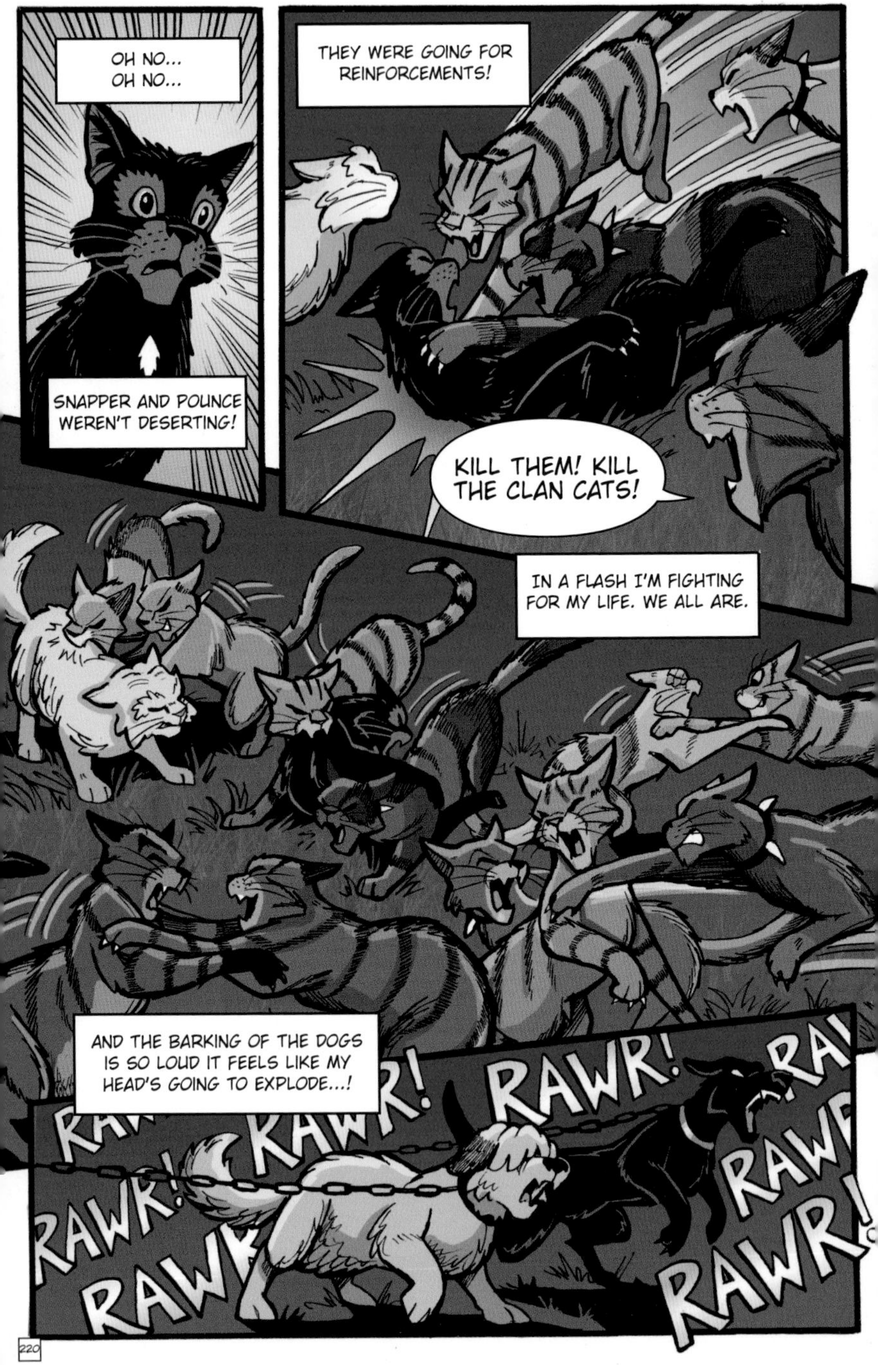
OH NO...
OH NO...
SNAPPER AND POUNCE WEREN'T DESERTING!
THEY WERE GOING FOR REINFORCEMENTS!
KILL THEM! KILL THE CLAN CATS!
IN A FLASH I'M FIGHTING FOR MY LIFE. WE ALL ARE.
AND THE BARKING OF THE DOGS IS SO LOUD IT FEELS LIKE MY HEAD'S GOING TO EXPLODE...!
RAWR!
RAWR!
RAWR!
RAWR!
RAWR!

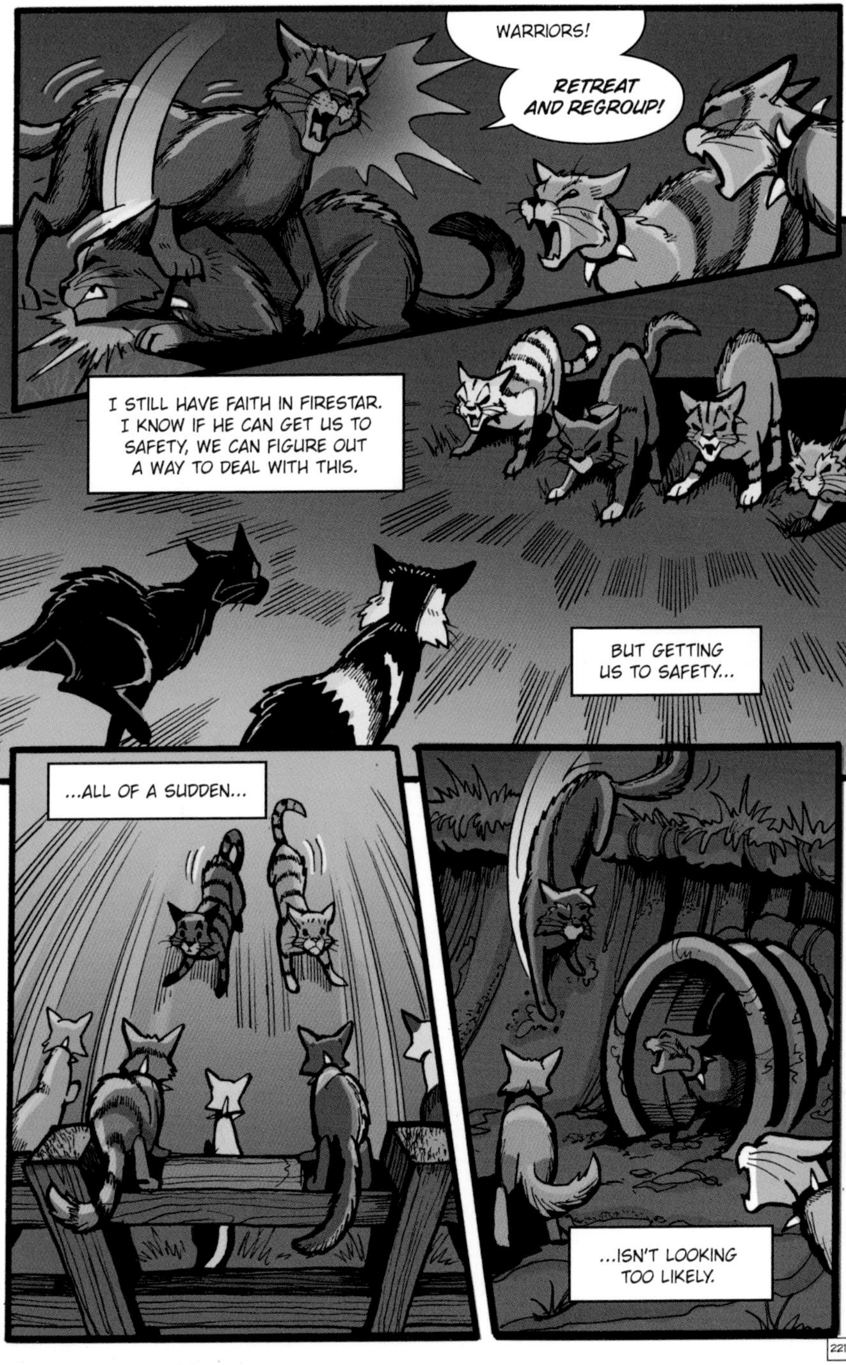
WARRIORS!
RETREAT AND REGROUP!
I STILL HAVE FAITH IN FIRESTAR. I KNOW IF HE CAN GET US TO SAFETY, WE CAN FIGURE OUT A WAY TO DEAL WITH THIS.
BUT GETTING US TO SAFETY...
...ALL OF A SUDDEN...
...ISN'T LOOKING TOO LIKELY.

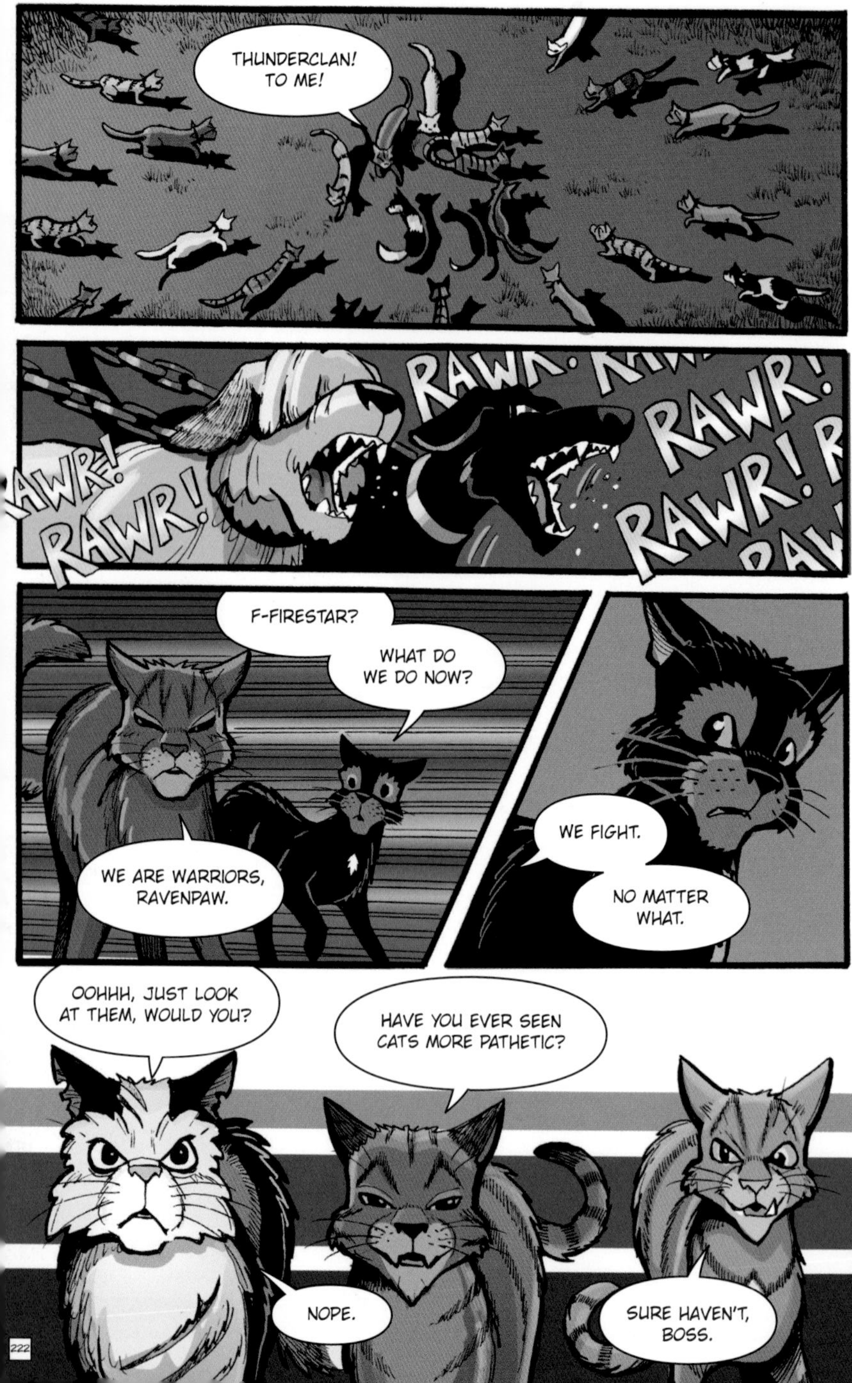
THUNDERCLAN! TO ME!
RAWR! RAWR!
RAWR! RAWR! RAWR!
F-FIRESTAR?
WHAT DO WE DO NOW?
WE ARE WARRIORS, RAVENPAW.
WE FIGHT.
NO MATTER WHAT.
OOHHH, JUST LOOK AT THEM, WOULD YOU?
HAVE YOU EVER SEEN CATS MORE PATHETIC?
NOPE.
SURE HAVEN'T, BOSS.

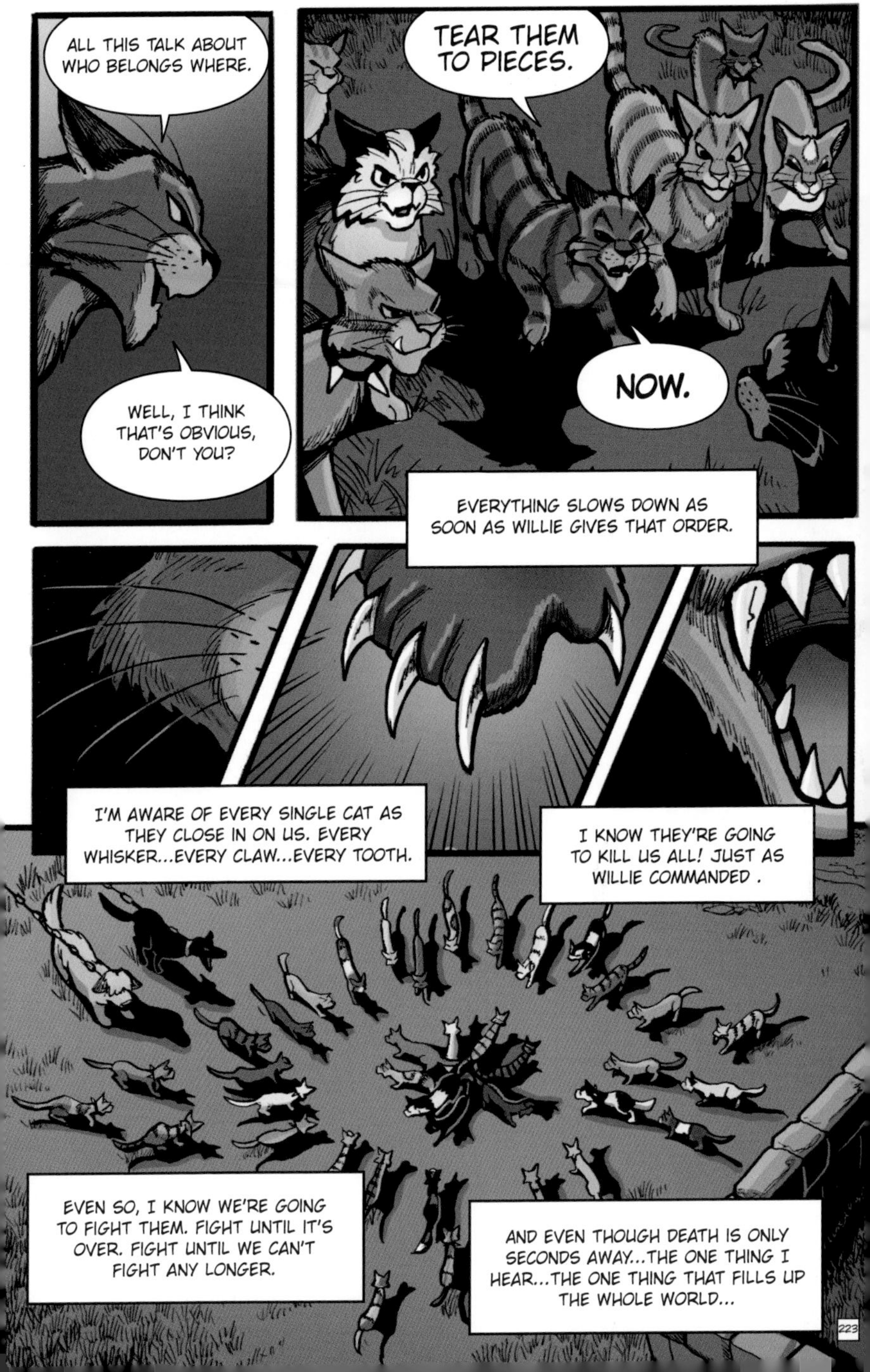
ALL THIS TALK ABOUT WHO BELONGS WHERE.
WELL, I THINK THAT'S OBVIOUS, DON'T YOU?
TEAR THEM TO PIECES.
NOW.
EVERYTHING SLOWS DOWN AS SOON AS WILLIE GIVES THAT ORDER.
I'M AWARE OF EVERY SINGLE CAT AS THEY CLOSE IN ON US. EVERY WHISKER...EVERY CLAW...EVERY TOOTH.
I KNOW THEY'RE GOING TO KILL US ALL! JUST AS WILLIE COMMANDED .
EVEN SO, I KNOW WE'RE GOING TO FIGHT THEM. FIGHT UNTIL IT'S OVER. FIGHT UNTIL WE CAN'T FIGHT ANY LONGER.
AND EVEN THOUGH DEATH IS ONLY SECONDS AWAY...THE ONE THING I HEAR...THE ONE THING THAT FILLS UP THE WHOLE WORLD...

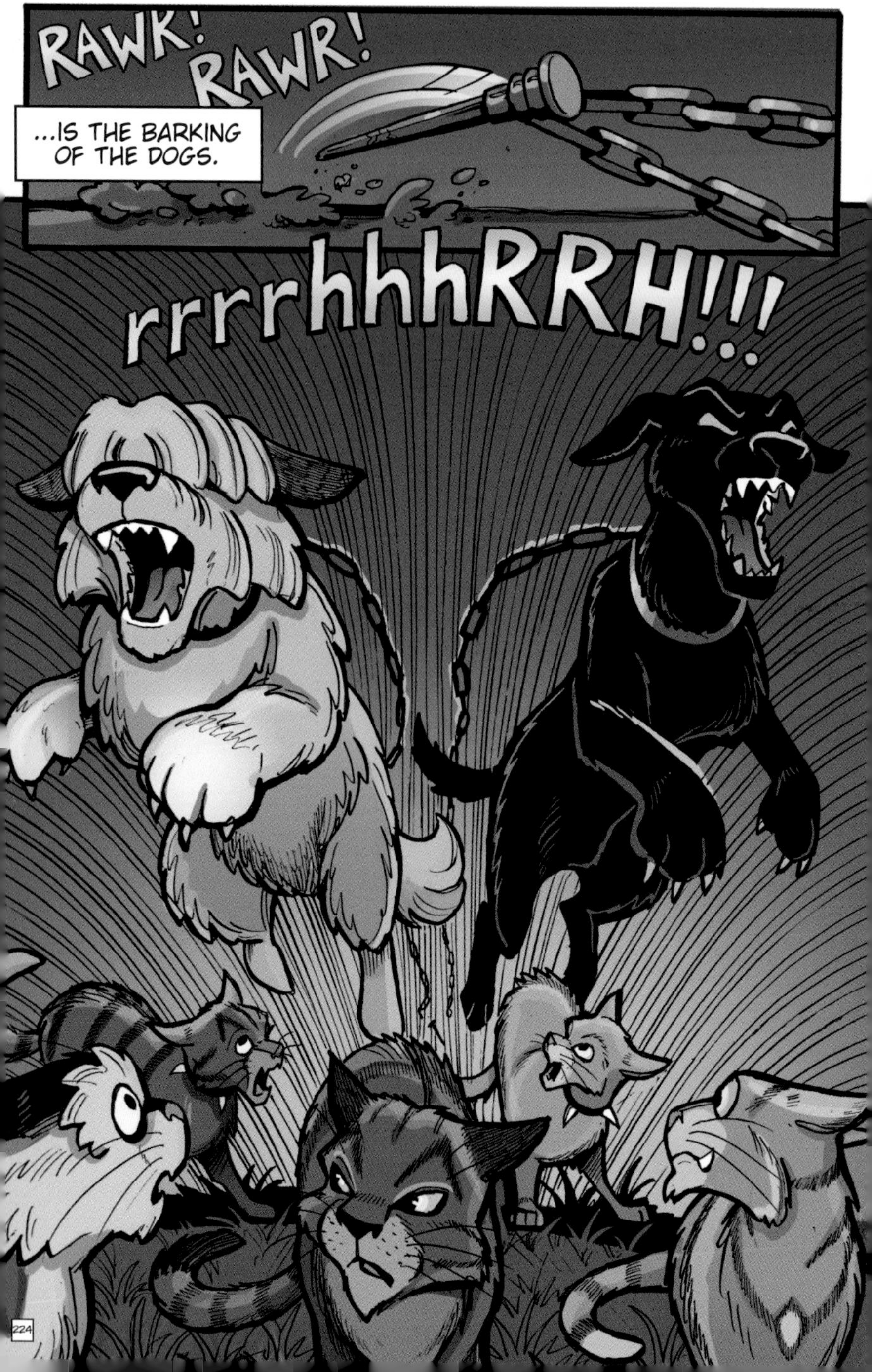
RAWR! RAWR!
...IS THE BARKING OF THE DOGS.
rrrrhhhRRRH!!!

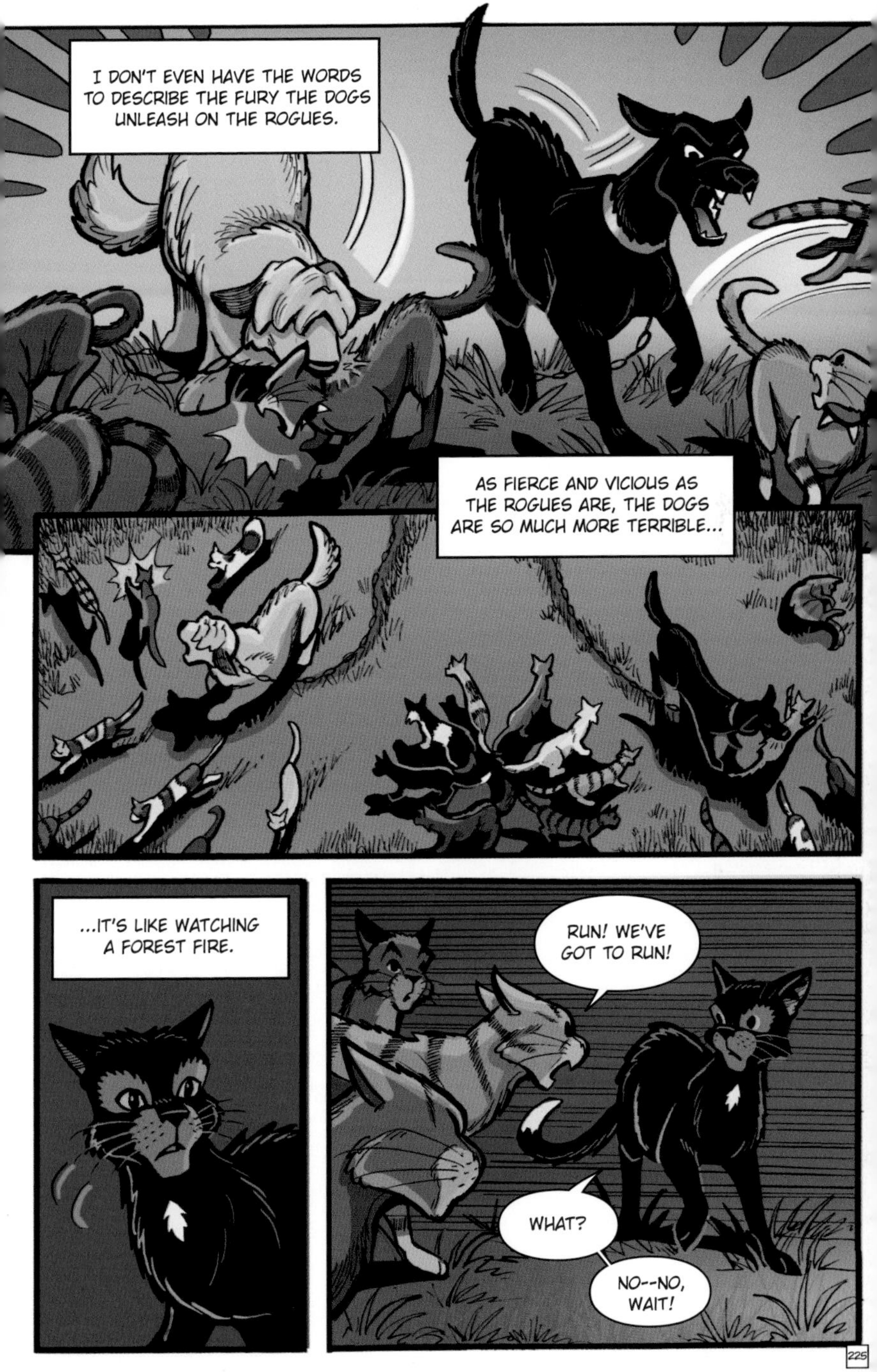
I DON'T EVEN HAVE THE WORDS TO DESCRIBE THE FURY THE DOGS UNLEASH ON THE ROGUES.
AS FIERCE AND VICIOUS AS THE ROGUES ARE, THE DOGS ARE SO MUCH MORE TERRIBLE...
...IT'S LIKE WATCHING A FOREST FIRE.
RUN! WE'VE GOT TO RUN!
WHAT?
NO--NO, WAIT!

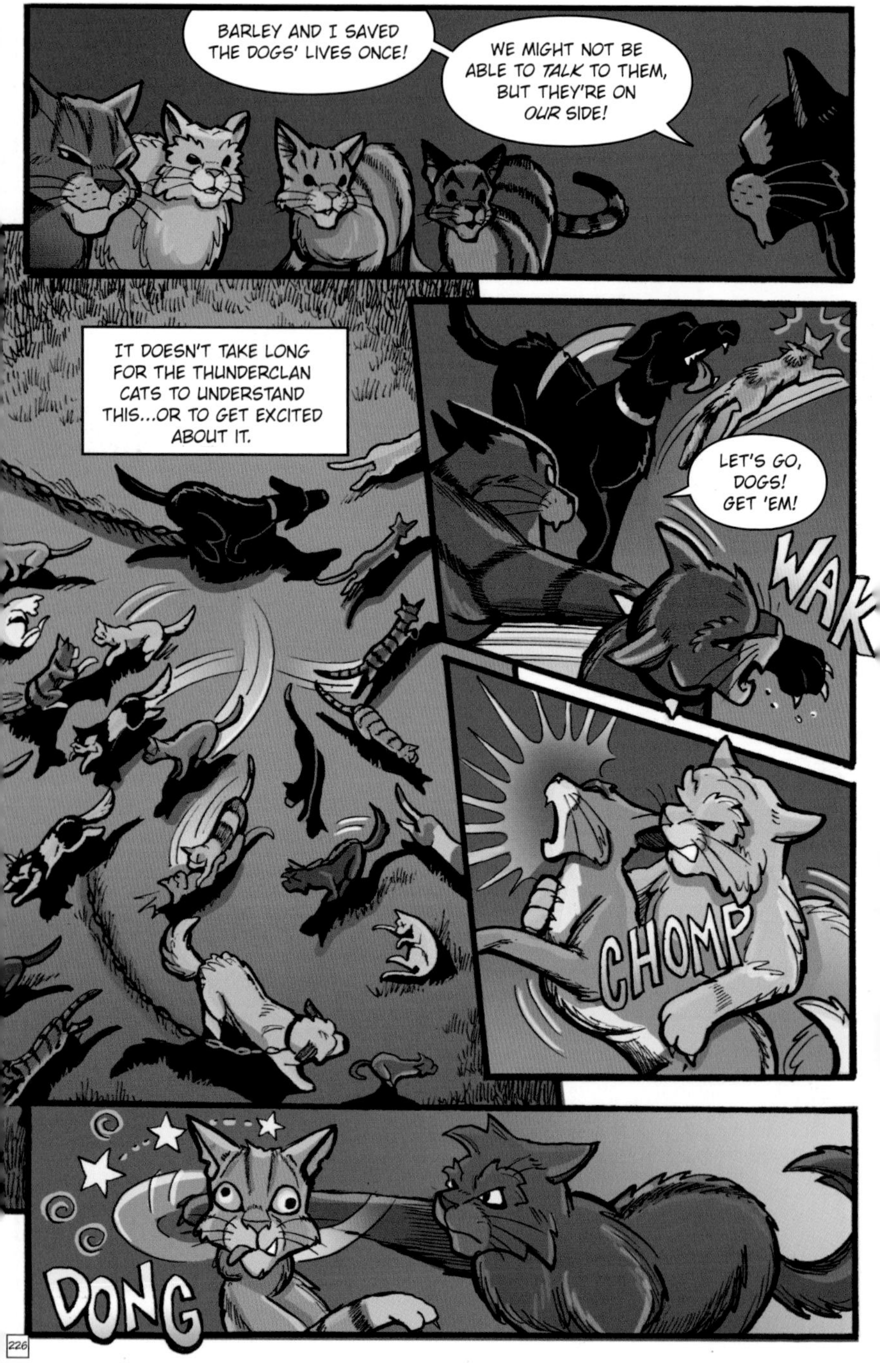
BARLEY AND I SAVED THE DOGS' LIVES ONCE!
WE MIGHT NOT BE ABLE TO *TALK* TO THEM, BUT THEY'RE ON *OUR* SIDE!
IT DOESN'T TAKE LONG FOR THE THUNDERCLAN CATS TO UNDERSTAND THIS...OR TO GET EXCITED ABOUT IT.
LET'S GO, DOGS! GET 'EM!
WAK
CHOMP
DONG

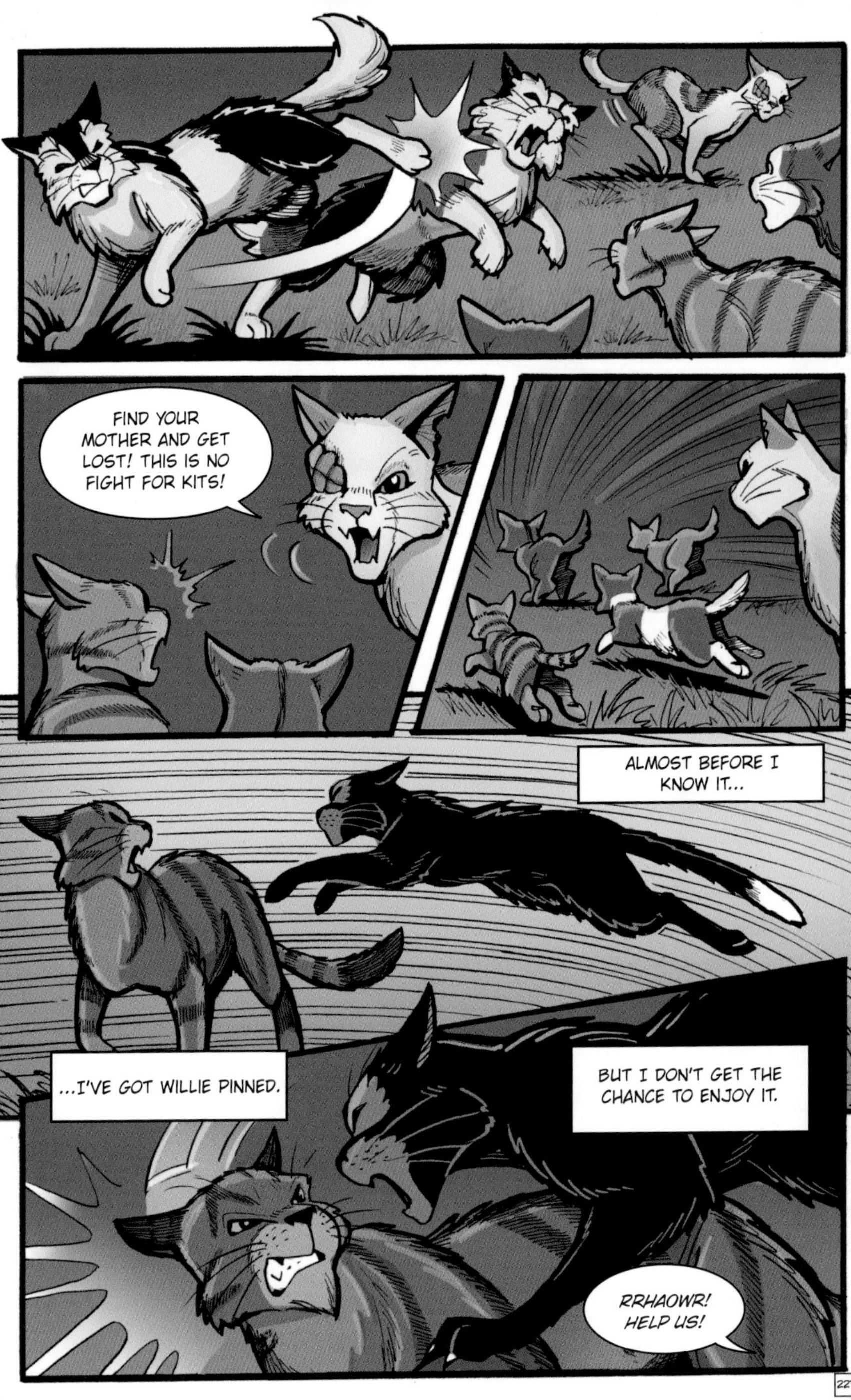
FIND YOUR MOTHER AND GET LOST! THIS IS NO FIGHT FOR KITS!
ALMOST BEFORE I KNOW IT...
...I'VE GOT WILLIE PINNED.
BUT I DON'T GET THE CHANCE TO ENJOY IT.
RRHAOWR! HELP US!

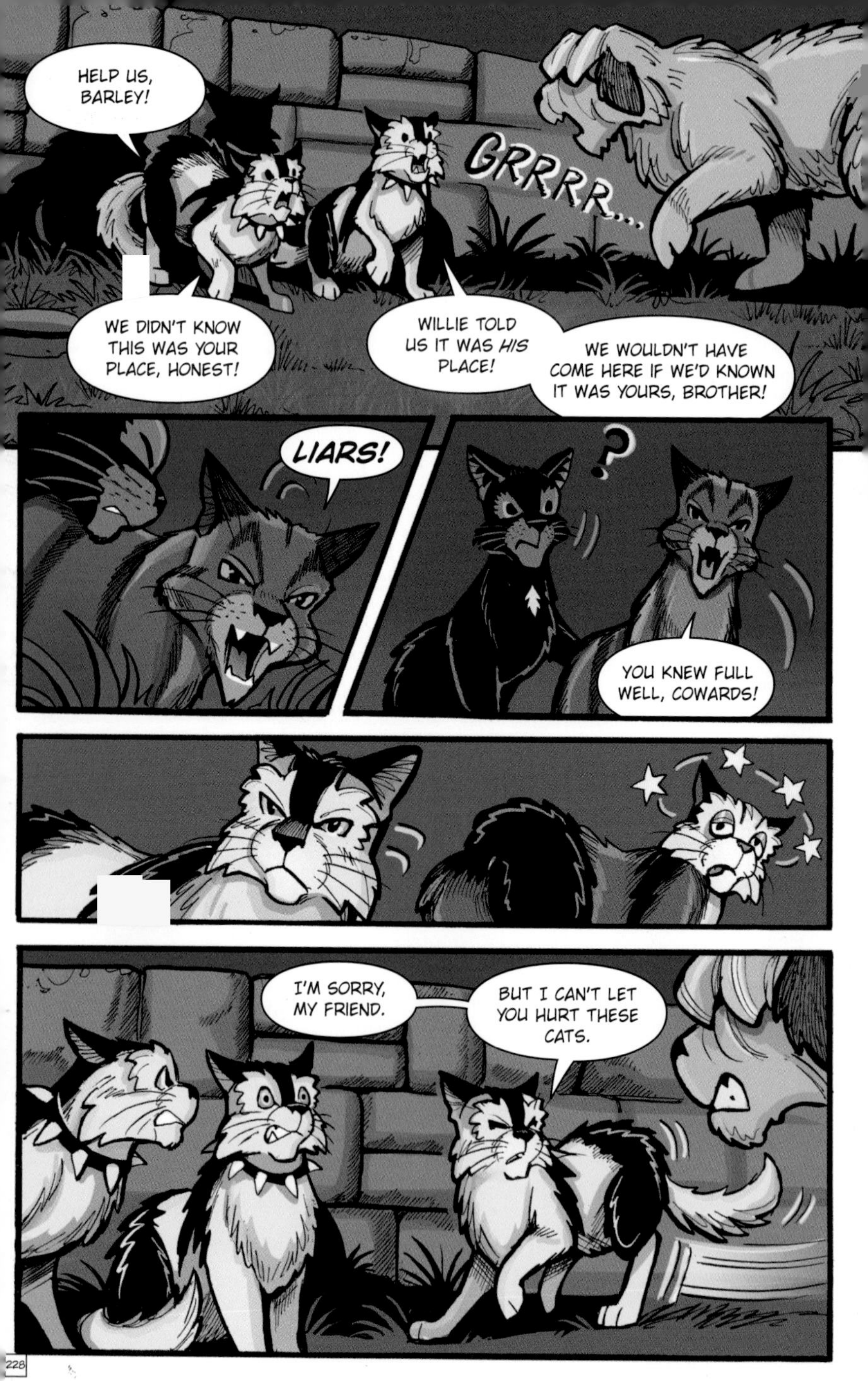
HELP US, BARLEY!
GRRRRR...
WE DIDN'T KNOW THIS WAS YOUR PLACE, HONEST!
WILLIE TOLD US IT WAS *HIS* PLACE!
WE WOULDN'T HAVE COME HERE IF WE'D KNOWN IT WAS YOURS, BROTHER!
LIARS!
?
YOU KNEW FULL WELL, COWARDS!
I'M SORRY, MY FRIEND.
BUT I CAN'T LET YOU HURT THESE CATS.

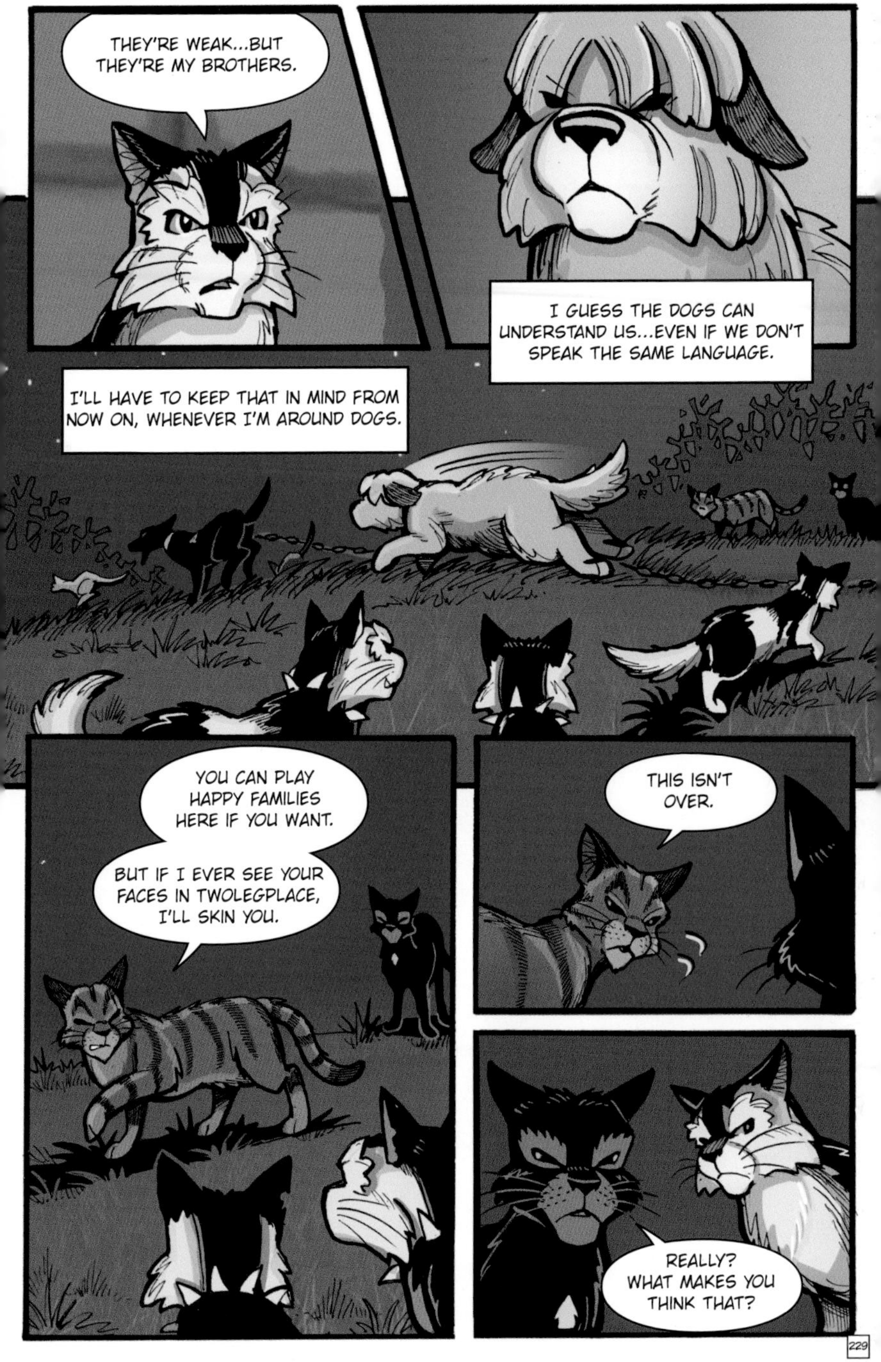

THEY'RE WEAK...BUT THEY'RE MY BROTHERS.
I GUESS THE DOGS CAN UNDERSTAND US...EVEN IF WE DON'T SPEAK THE SAME LANGUAGE.
I'LL HAVE TO KEEP THAT IN MIND FROM NOW ON, WHENEVER I'M AROUND DOGS.
YOU CAN PLAY HAPPY FAMILIES HERE IF YOU WANT.
BUT IF I EVER SEE YOUR FACES IN TWOLEGPLACE, I'LL SKIN YOU.
THIS ISN'T OVER.
REALLY? WHAT MAKES YOU THINK THAT?

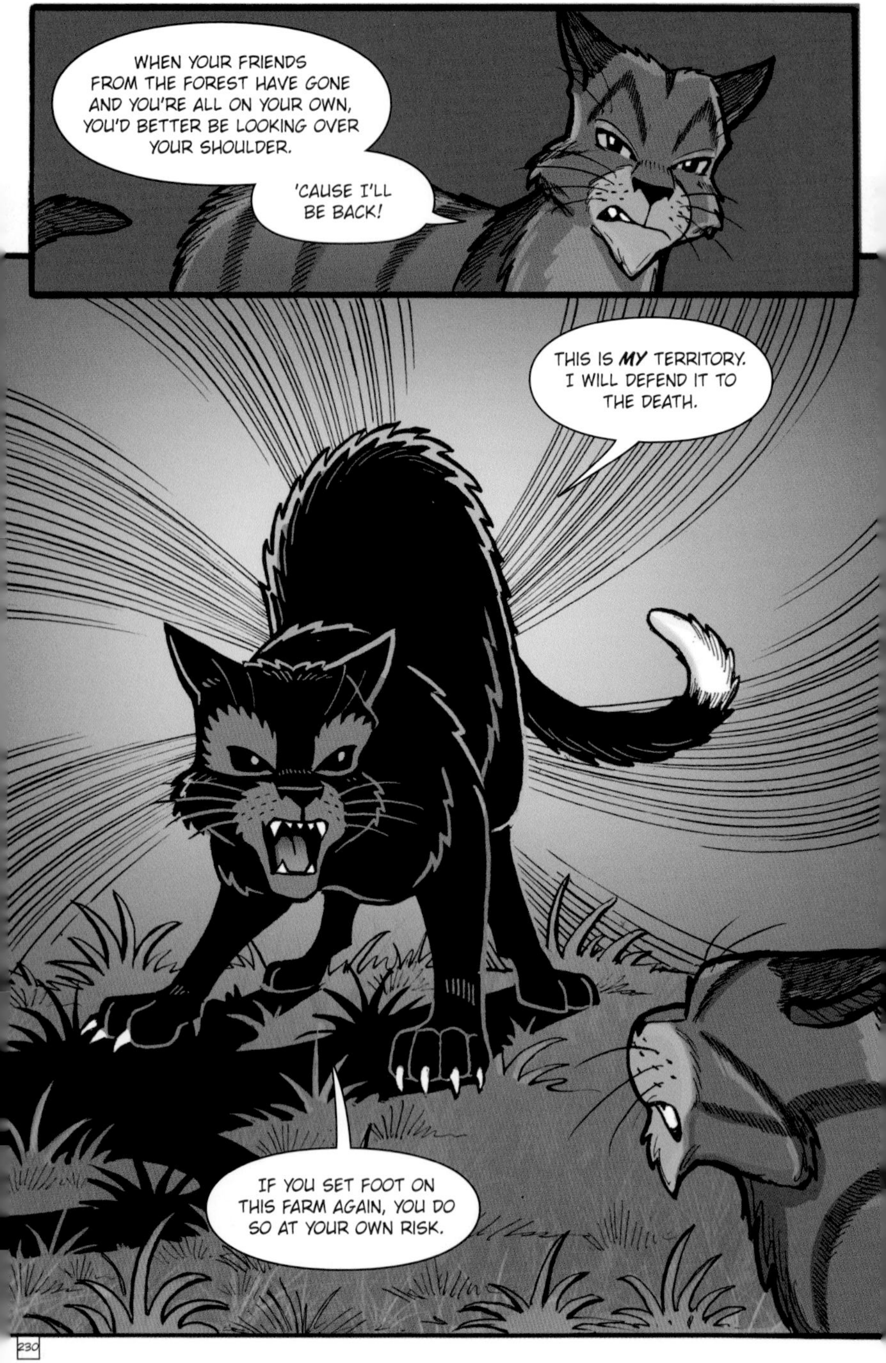
WHEN YOUR FRIENDS FROM THE FOREST HAVE GONE AND YOU'RE ALL ON YOUR OWN, YOU'D BETTER BE LOOKING OVER YOUR SHOULDER.
'CAUSE I'LL BE BACK!
THIS IS ***MY*** TERRITORY. I WILL DEFEND IT TO THE DEATH.
IF YOU SET FOOT ON THIS FARM AGAIN, YOU DO SO AT YOUR OWN RISK.

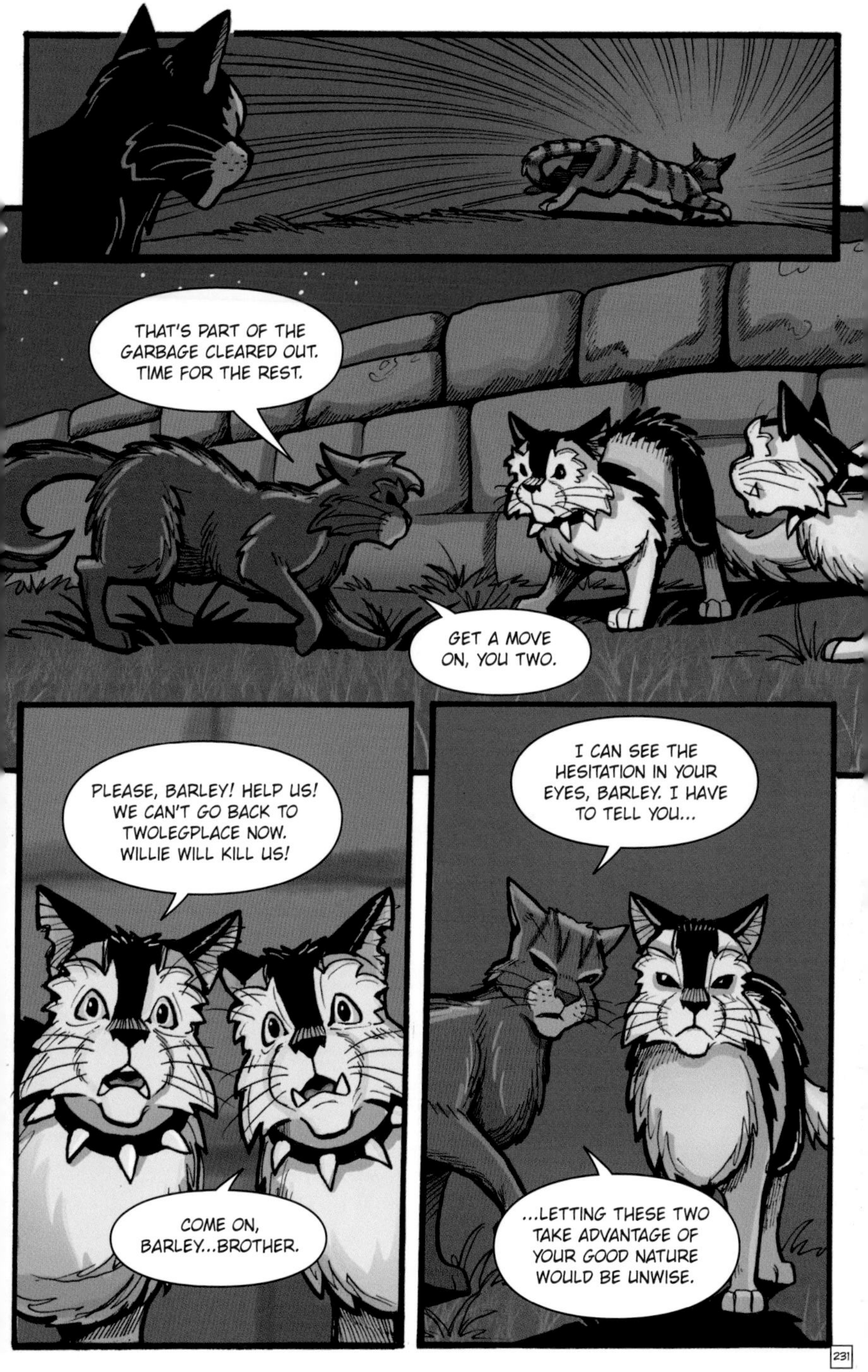
THAT'S PART OF THE GARBAGE CLEARED OUT. TIME FOR THE REST.
GET A MOVE ON, YOU TWO.
PLEASE, BARLEY! HELP US! WE CAN'T GO BACK TO TWOLEGPLACE NOW. WILLIE WILL KILL US!
COME ON, BARLEY...BROTHER.
I CAN SEE THE HESITATION IN YOUR EYES, BARLEY. I HAVE TO TELL YOU...
...LETTING THESE TWO TAKE ADVANTAGE OF YOUR GOOD NATURE WOULD BE UNWISE.

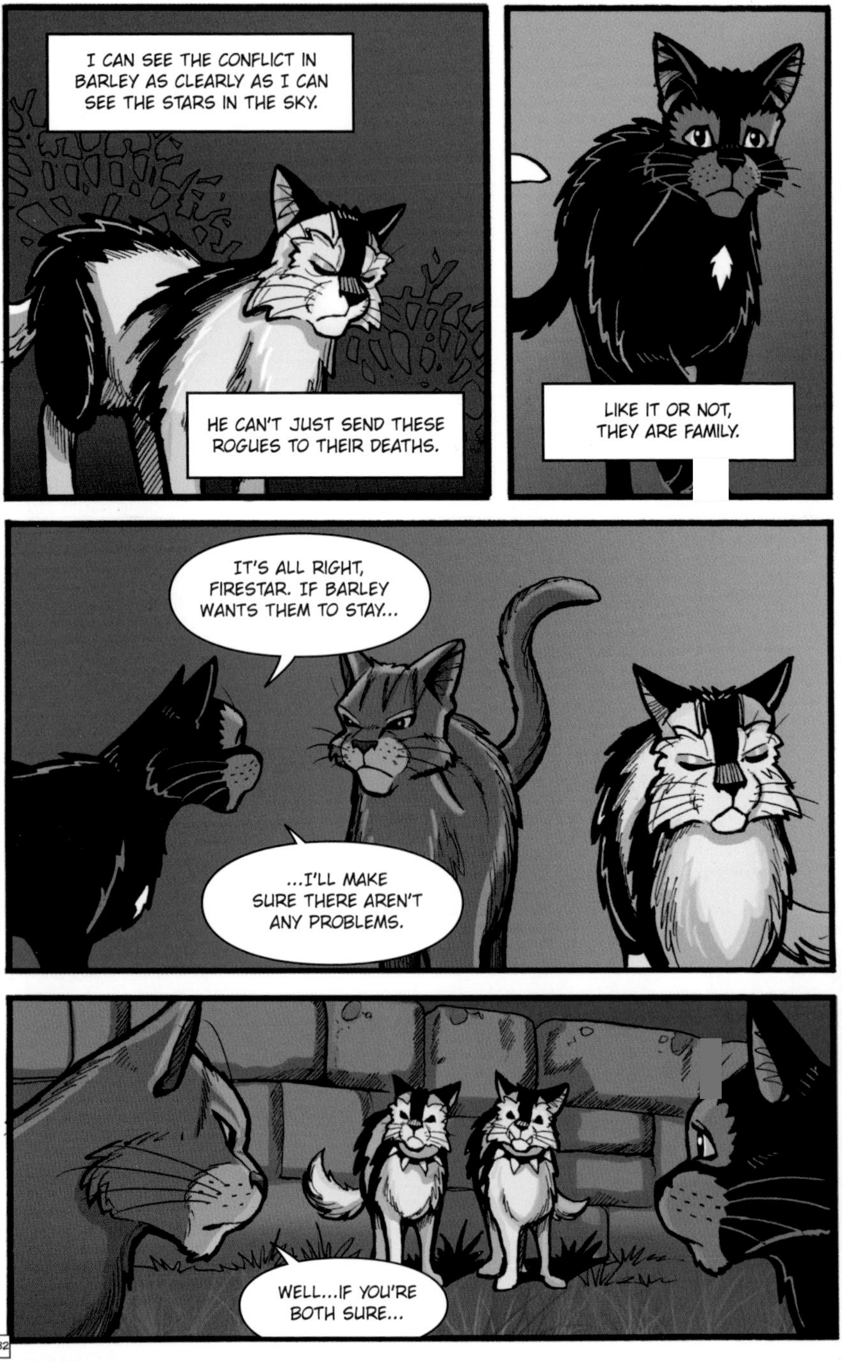
I CAN SEE THE CONFLICT IN BARLEY AS CLEARLY AS I CAN SEE THE STARS IN THE SKY.
HE CAN'T JUST SEND THESE ROGUES TO THEIR DEATHS.
LIKE IT OR NOT, THEY ARE FAMILY.
IT'S ALL RIGHT, FIRESTAR. IF BARLEY WANTS THEM TO STAY...
...I'LL MAKE SURE THERE AREN'T ANY PROBLEMS.
WELL...IF YOU'RE BOTH SURE...

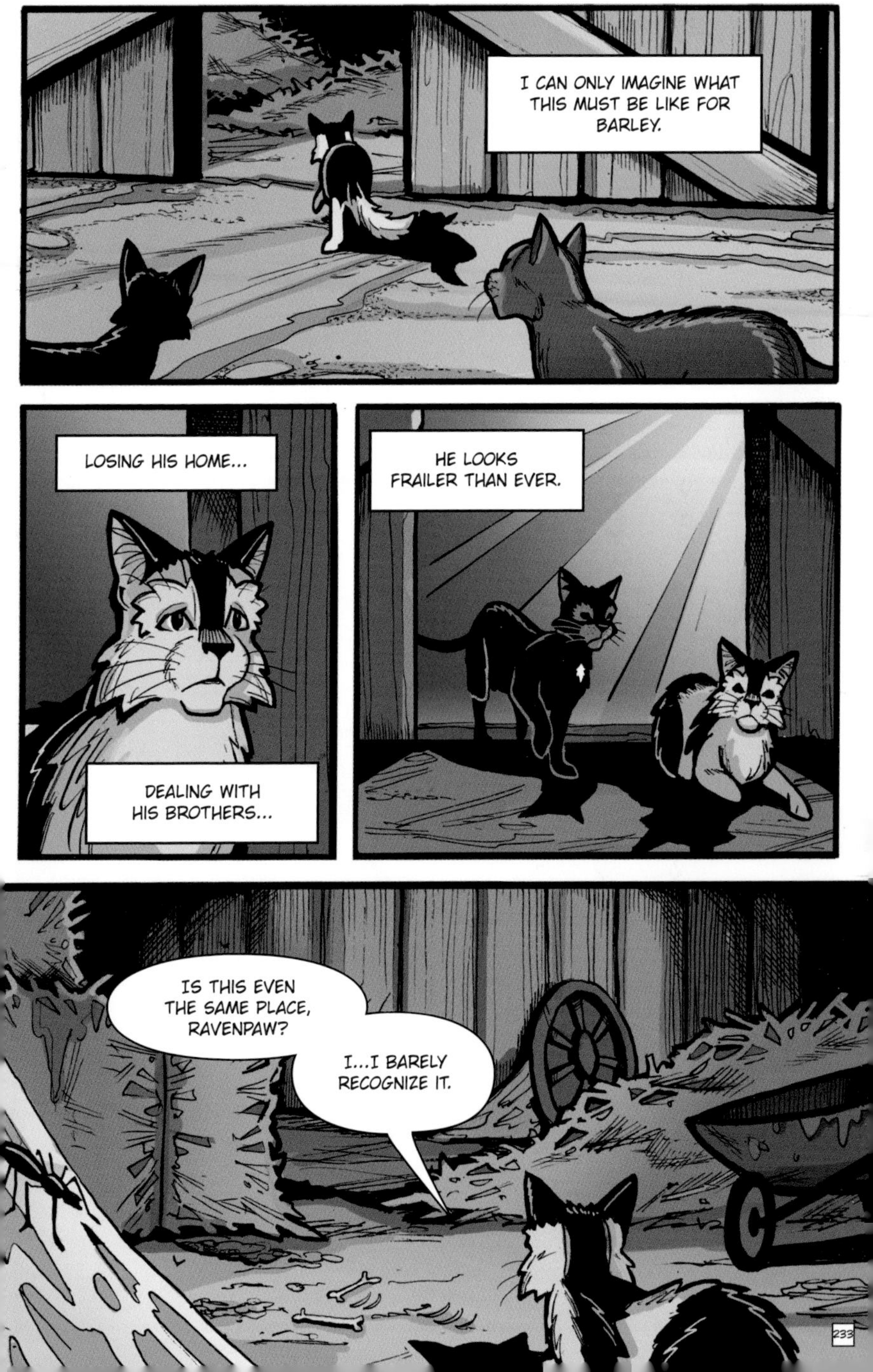
I CAN ONLY IMAGINE WHAT THIS MUST BE LIKE FOR BARLEY.
LOSING HIS HOME...
DEALING WITH HIS BROTHERS...
HE LOOKS FRAILER THAN EVER.
IS THIS EVEN THE SAME PLACE, RAVENPAW?
I...I BARELY RECOGNIZE IT.

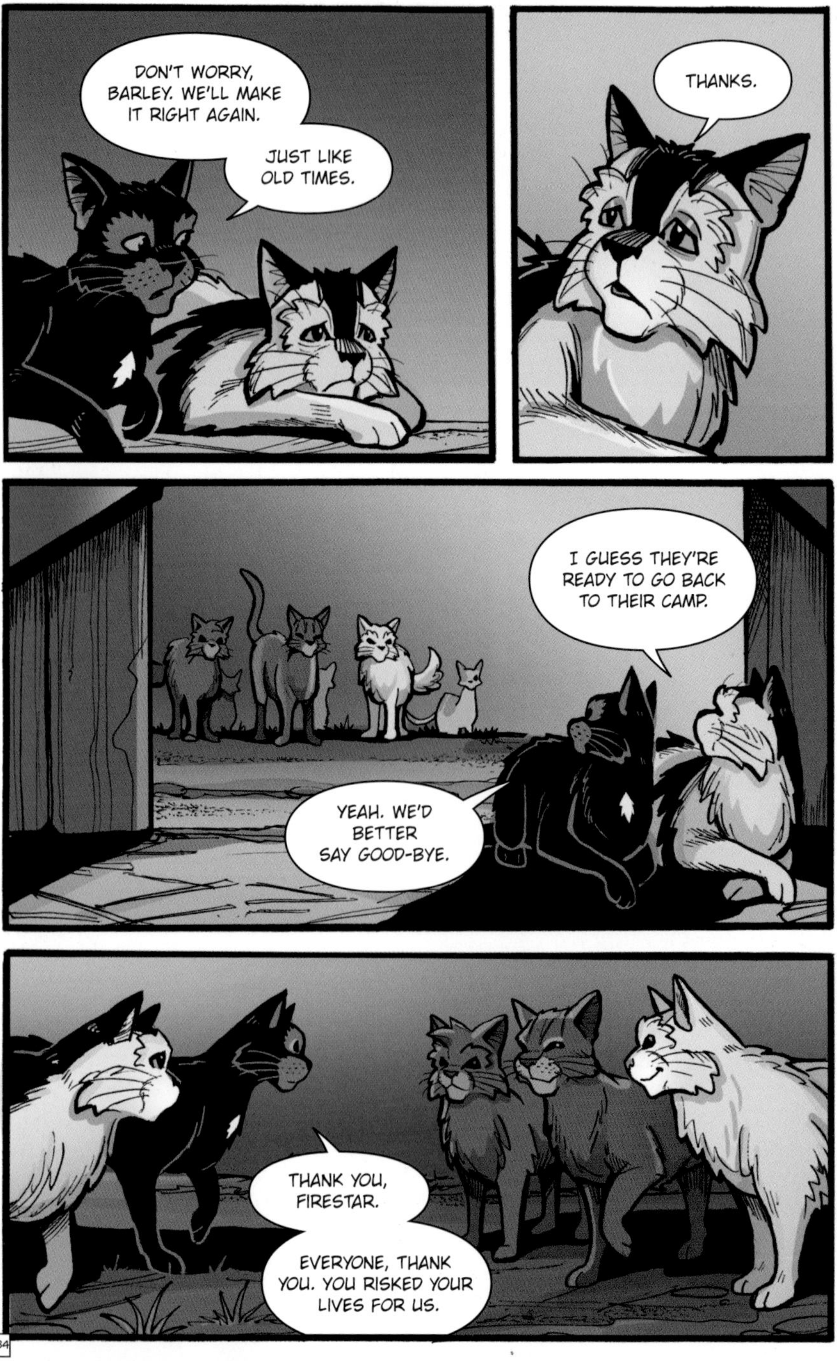
DON'T WORRY, BARLEY. WE'LL MAKE IT RIGHT AGAIN.
JUST LIKE OLD TIMES.
THANKS.
I GUESS THEY'RE READY TO GO BACK TO THEIR CAMP.
YEAH. WE'D BETTER SAY GOOD-BYE.
THANK YOU, FIRESTAR.
EVERYONE, THANK YOU. YOU RISKED YOUR LIVES FOR US.

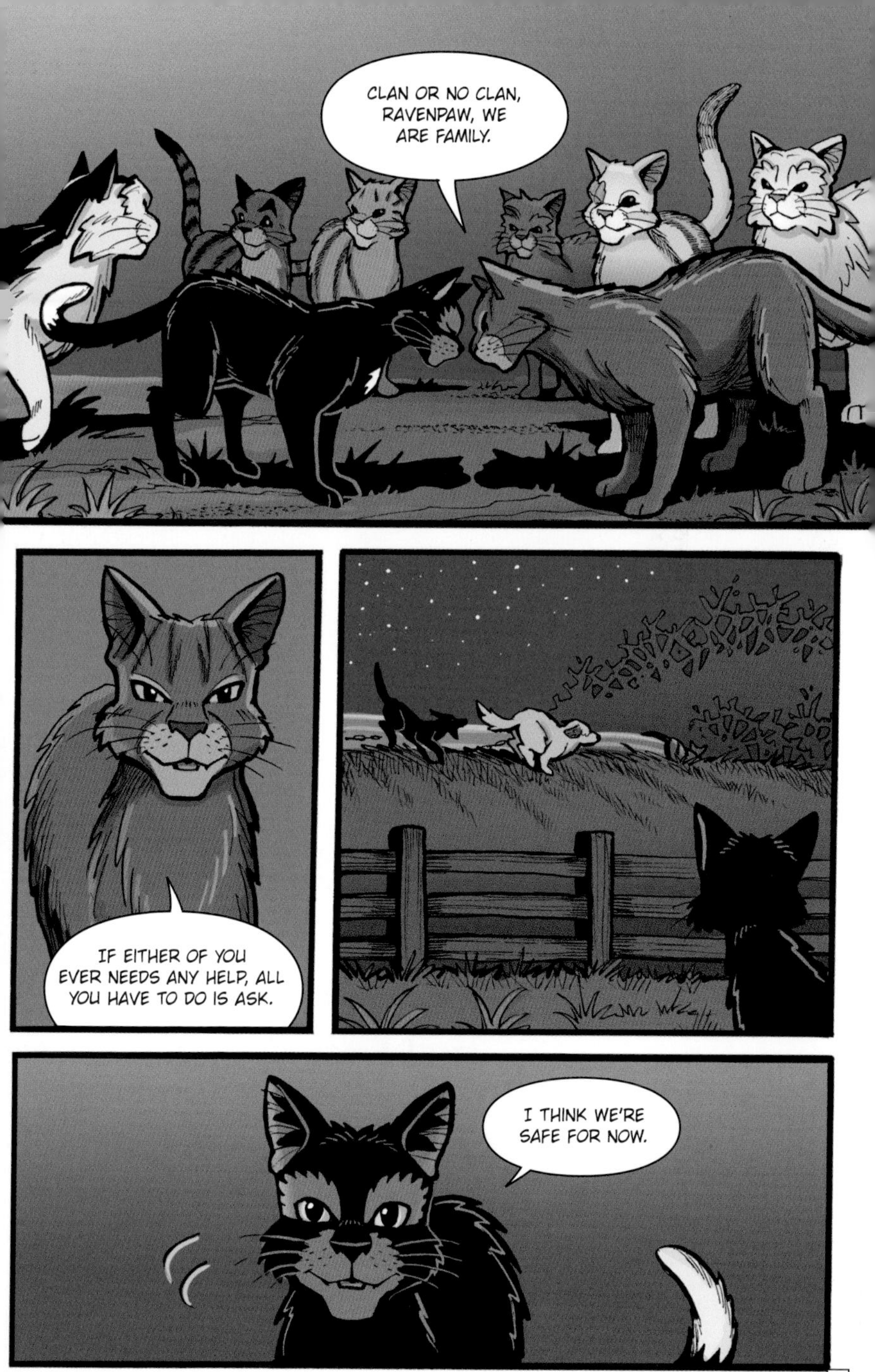
CLAN OR NO CLAN, RAVENPAW, WE ARE FAMILY.
IF EITHER OF YOU EVER NEEDS ANY HELP, ALL YOU HAVE TO DO IS ASK.
I THINK WE'RE SAFE FOR NOW.

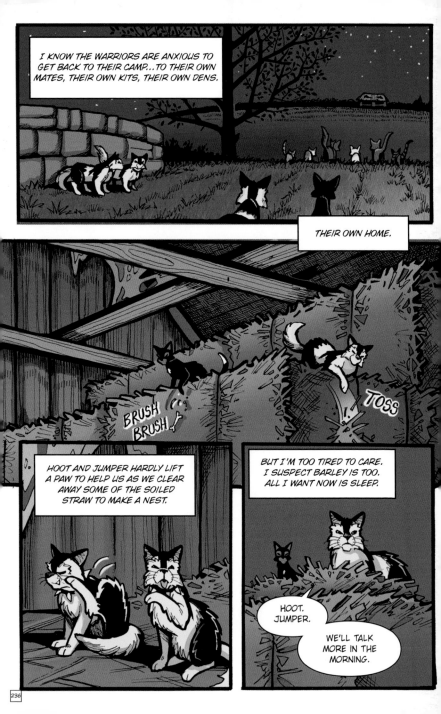

I KNOW THE WARRIORS ARE ANXIOUS TO GET BACK TO THEIR CAMP...TO THEIR OWN MATES, THEIR OWN KITS, THEIR OWN DENS.

THEIR OWN HOME.

BRUSH BRUSH

TOSS

HOOT AND JUMPER HARDLY LIFT A PAW TO HELP US AS WE CLEAR AWAY SOME OF THE SOILED STRAW TO MAKE A NEST.

BUT I'M TOO TIRED TO CARE. I SUSPECT BARLEY IS TOO. ALL I WANT NOW IS SLEEP.

HOOT. JUMPER.

WE'LL TALK MORE IN THE MORNING.

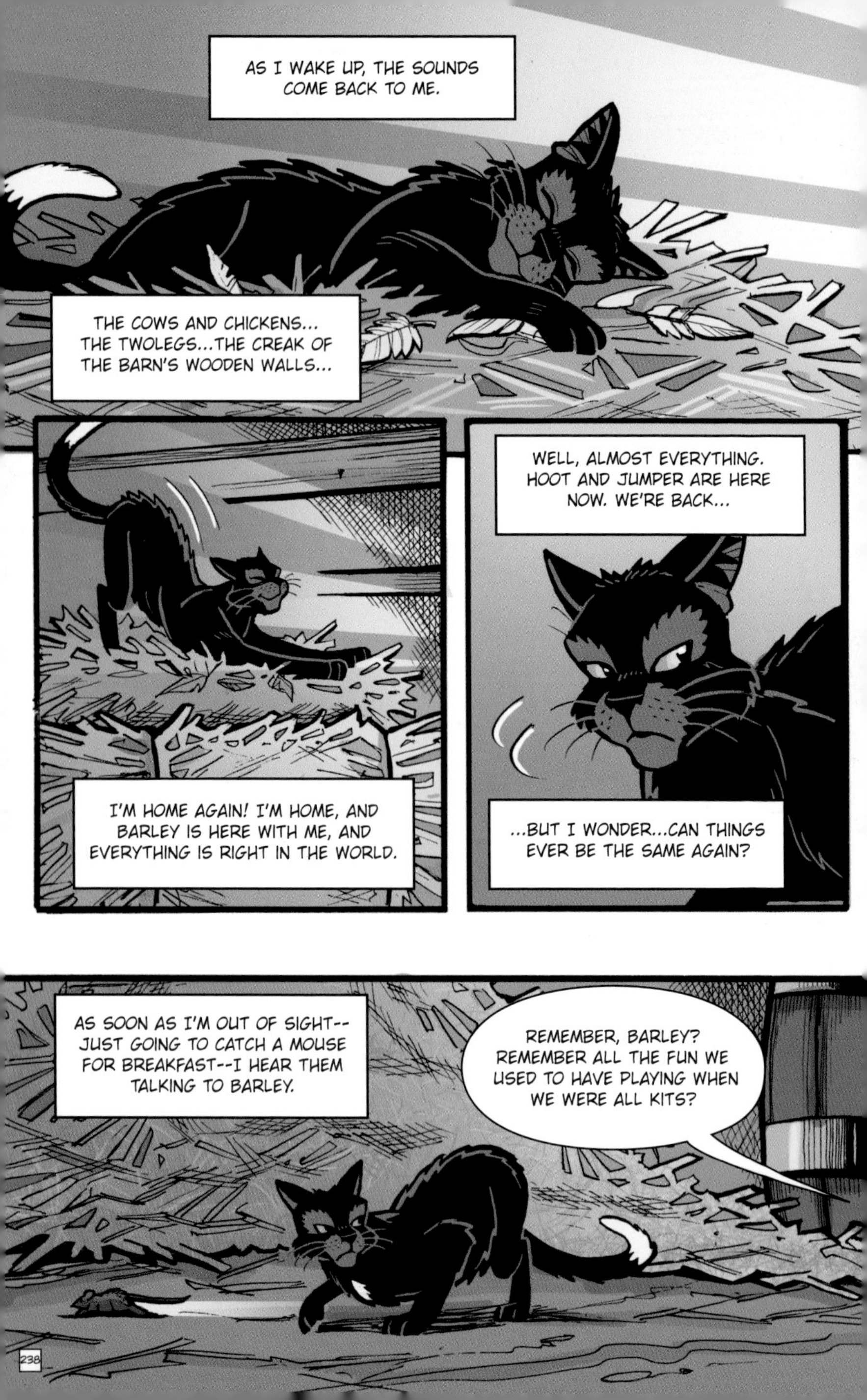
AS I WAKE UP, THE SOUNDS COME BACK TO ME.
THE COWS AND CHICKENS... THE TWOLEGS...THE CREAK OF THE BARN'S WOODEN WALLS...
I'M HOME AGAIN! I'M HOME, AND BARLEY IS HERE WITH ME, AND EVERYTHING IS RIGHT IN THE WORLD.
WELL, ALMOST EVERYTHING. HOOT AND JUMPER ARE HERE NOW. WE'RE BACK...
...BUT I WONDER...CAN THINGS EVER BE THE SAME AGAIN?
AS SOON AS I'M OUT OF SIGHT--JUST GOING TO CATCH A MOUSE FOR BREAKFAST--I HEAR THEM TALKING TO BARLEY.
REMEMBER, BARLEY? REMEMBER ALL THE FUN WE USED TO HAVE PLAYING WHEN WE WERE ALL KITS?

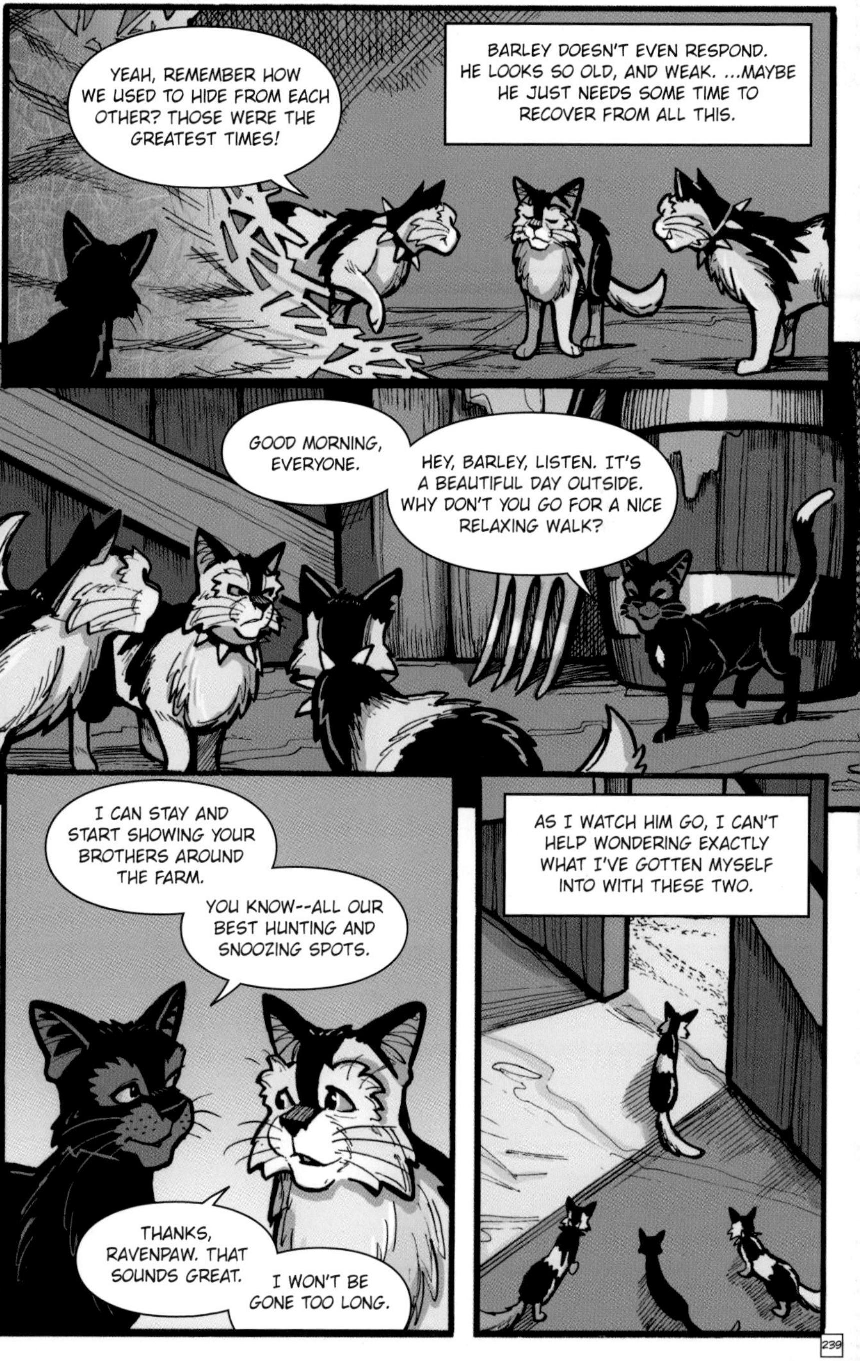
YEAH, REMEMBER HOW WE USED TO HIDE FROM EACH OTHER? THOSE WERE THE GREATEST TIMES!
BARLEY DOESN'T EVEN RESPOND. HE LOOKS SO OLD, AND WEAK. ...MAYBE HE JUST NEEDS SOME TIME TO RECOVER FROM ALL THIS.
GOOD MORNING, EVERYONE.
HEY, BARLEY, LISTEN. IT'S A BEAUTIFUL DAY OUTSIDE. WHY DON'T YOU GO FOR A NICE RELAXING WALK?
I CAN STAY AND START SHOWING YOUR BROTHERS AROUND THE FARM.
YOU KNOW--ALL OUR BEST HUNTING AND SNOOZING SPOTS.
THANKS, RAVENPAW. THAT SOUNDS GREAT.
I WON'T BE GONE TOO LONG.
AS I WATCH HIM GO, I CAN'T HELP WONDERING EXACTLY WHAT I'VE GOTTEN MYSELF INTO WITH THESE TWO.

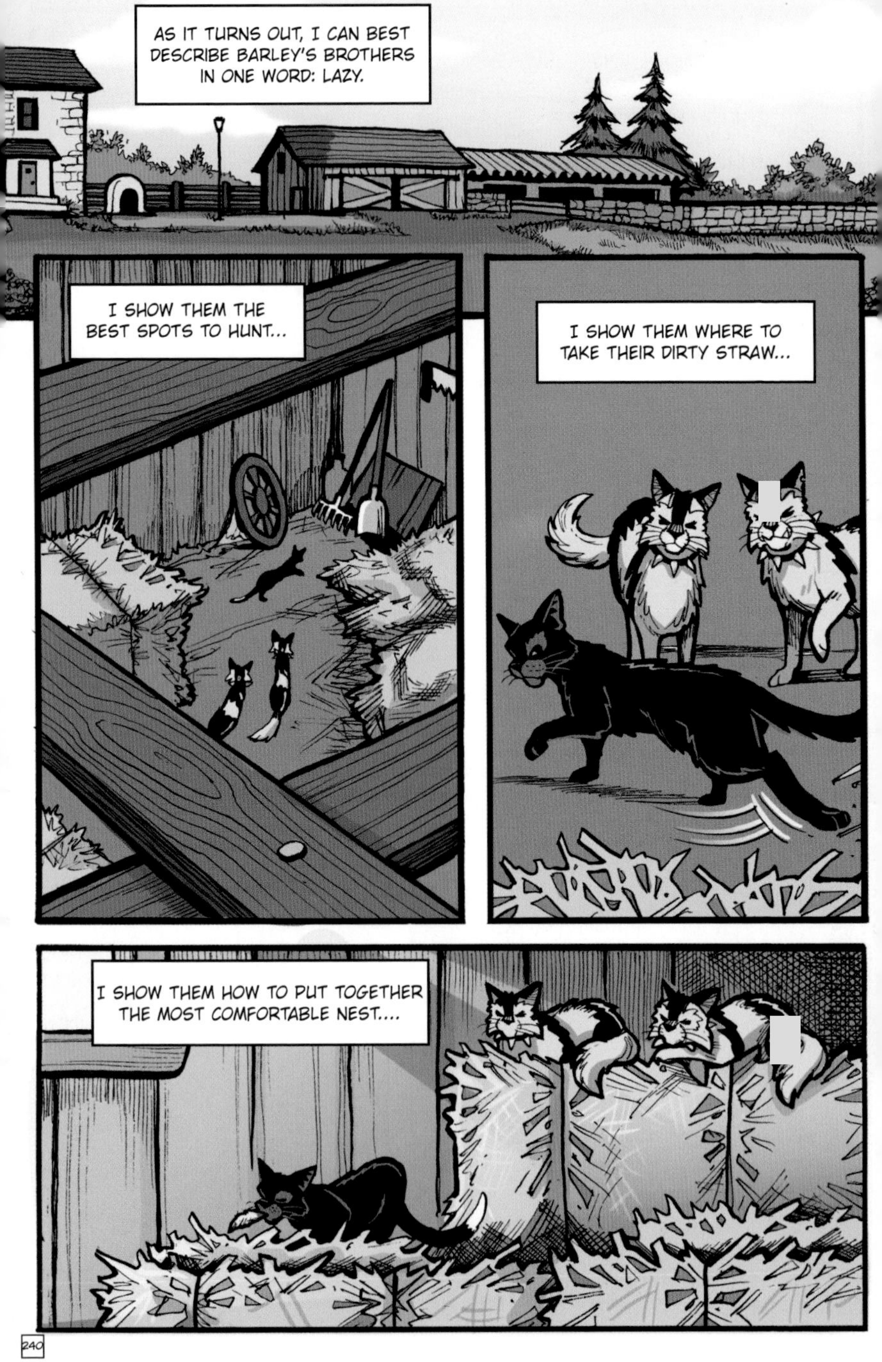
AS IT TURNS OUT, I CAN BEST DESCRIBE BARLEY'S BROTHERS IN ONE WORD: LAZY.
I SHOW THEM THE BEST SPOTS TO HUNT...
I SHOW THEM WHERE TO TAKE THEIR DIRTY STRAW...
I SHOW THEM HOW TO PUT TOGETHER THE MOST COMFORTABLE NEST....

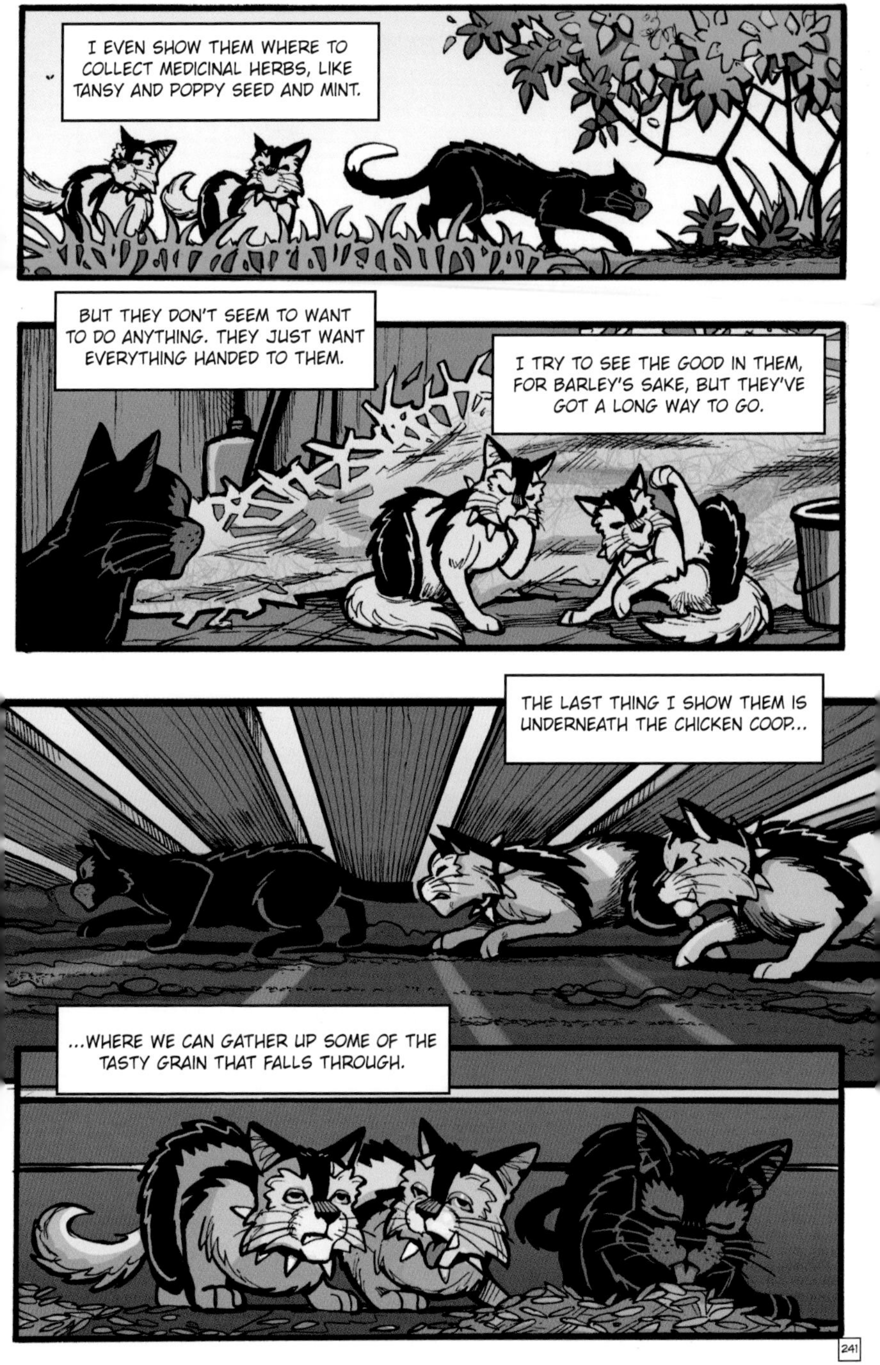
I EVEN SHOW THEM WHERE TO COLLECT MEDICINAL HERBS, LIKE TANSY AND POPPY SEED AND MINT.
BUT THEY DON'T SEEM TO WANT TO DO ANYTHING. THEY JUST WANT EVERYTHING HANDED TO THEM.
I TRY TO SEE THE GOOD IN THEM, FOR BARLEY'S SAKE, BUT THEY'VE GOT A LONG WAY TO GO.
THE LAST THING I SHOW THEM IS UNDERNEATH THE CHICKEN COOP...
...WHERE WE CAN GATHER UP SOME OF THE TASTY GRAIN THAT FALLS THROUGH.

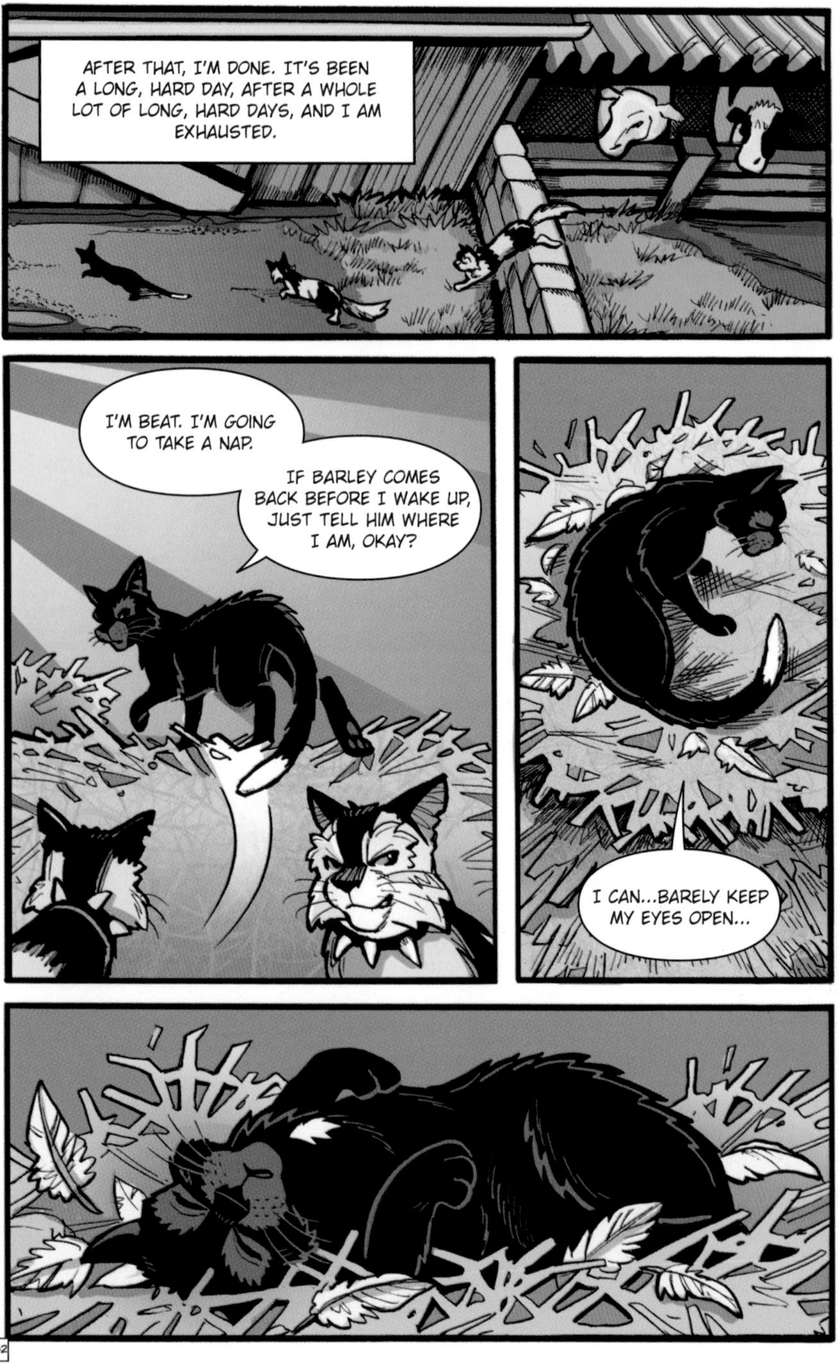
AFTER THAT, I'M DONE. IT'S BEEN A LONG, HARD DAY, AFTER A WHOLE LOT OF LONG, HARD DAYS, AND I AM EXHAUSTED.
I'M BEAT. I'M GOING TO TAKE A NAP.
IF BARLEY COMES BACK BEFORE I WAKE UP, JUST TELL HIM WHERE I AM, OKAY?
I CAN...BARELY KEEP MY EYES OPEN...

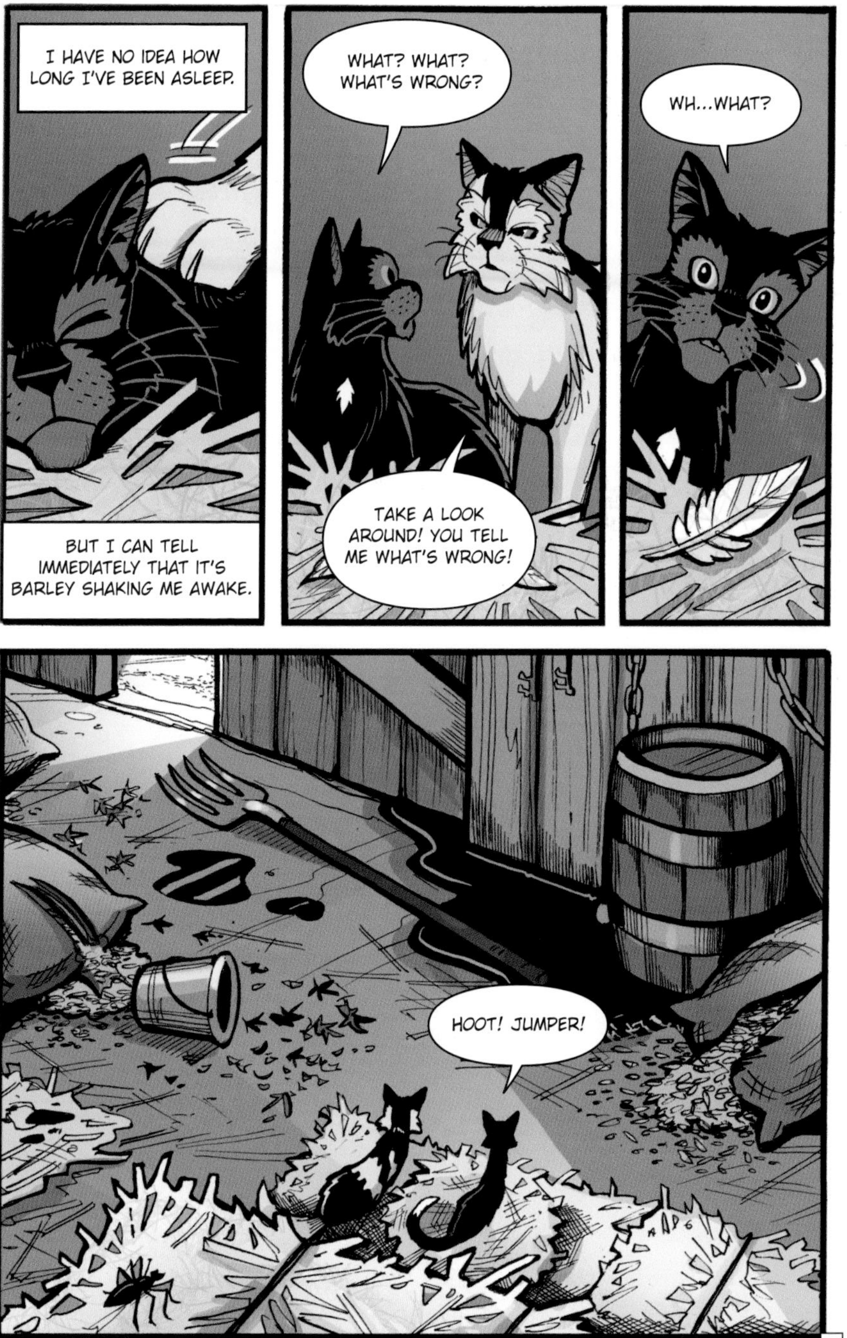
I HAVE NO IDEA HOW LONG I'VE BEEN ASLEEP.
BUT I CAN TELL IMMEDIATELY THAT IT'S BARLEY SHAKING ME AWAKE.
WHAT? WHAT? WHAT'S WRONG?
TAKE A LOOK AROUND! YOU TELL ME WHAT'S WRONG!
WH...WHAT?
HOOT! JUMPER!

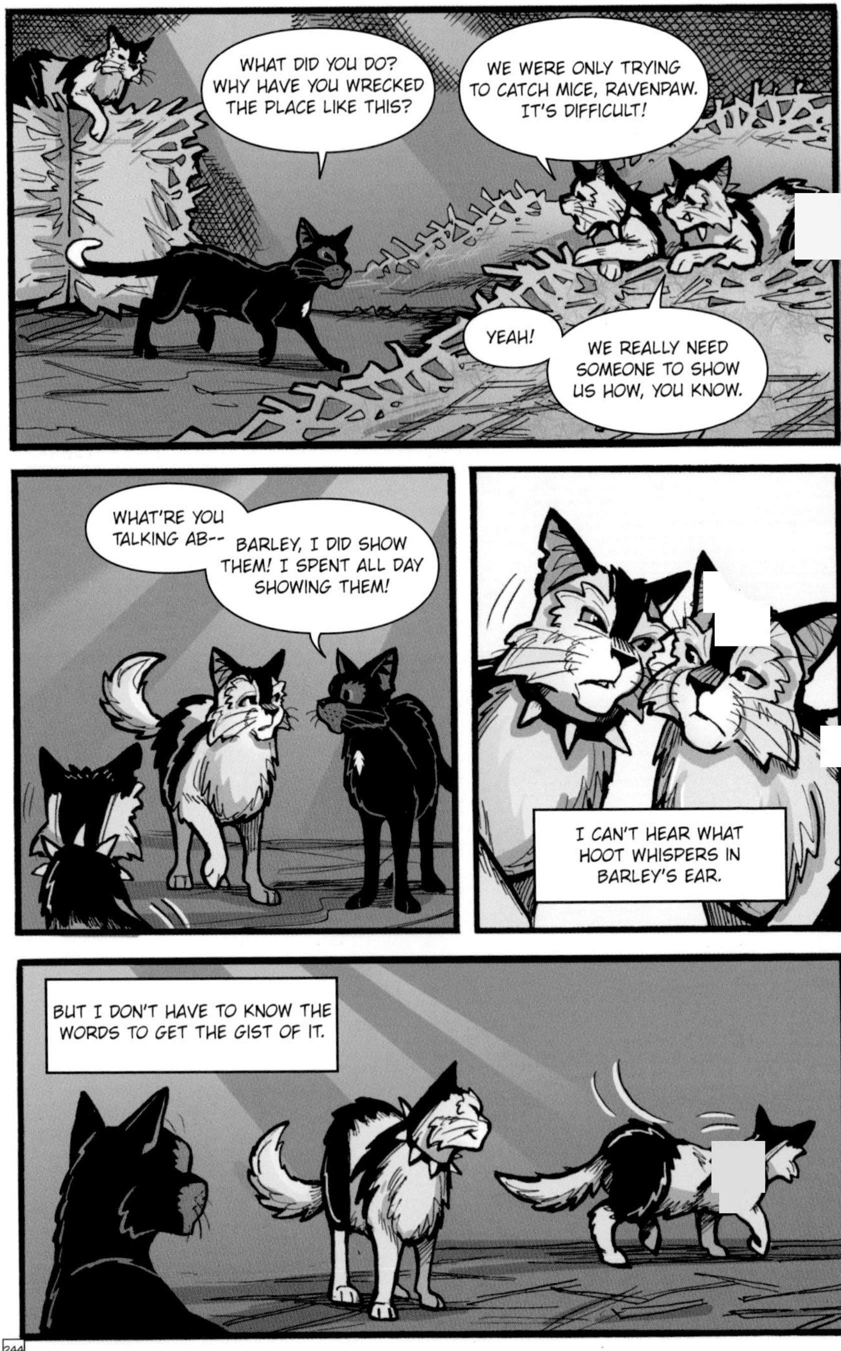
WHAT DID YOU DO? WHY HAVE YOU WRECKED THE PLACE LIKE THIS?
WE WERE ONLY TRYING TO CATCH MICE, RAVENPAW. IT'S DIFFICULT!
YEAH!
WE REALLY NEED SOMEONE TO SHOW US HOW, YOU KNOW.
WHAT'RE YOU TALKING AB--
BARLEY, I DID SHOW THEM! I SPENT ALL DAY SHOWING THEM!
I CAN'T HEAR WHAT HOOT WHISPERS IN BARLEY'S EAR.
BUT I DON'T HAVE TO KNOW THE WORDS TO GET THE GIST OF IT.

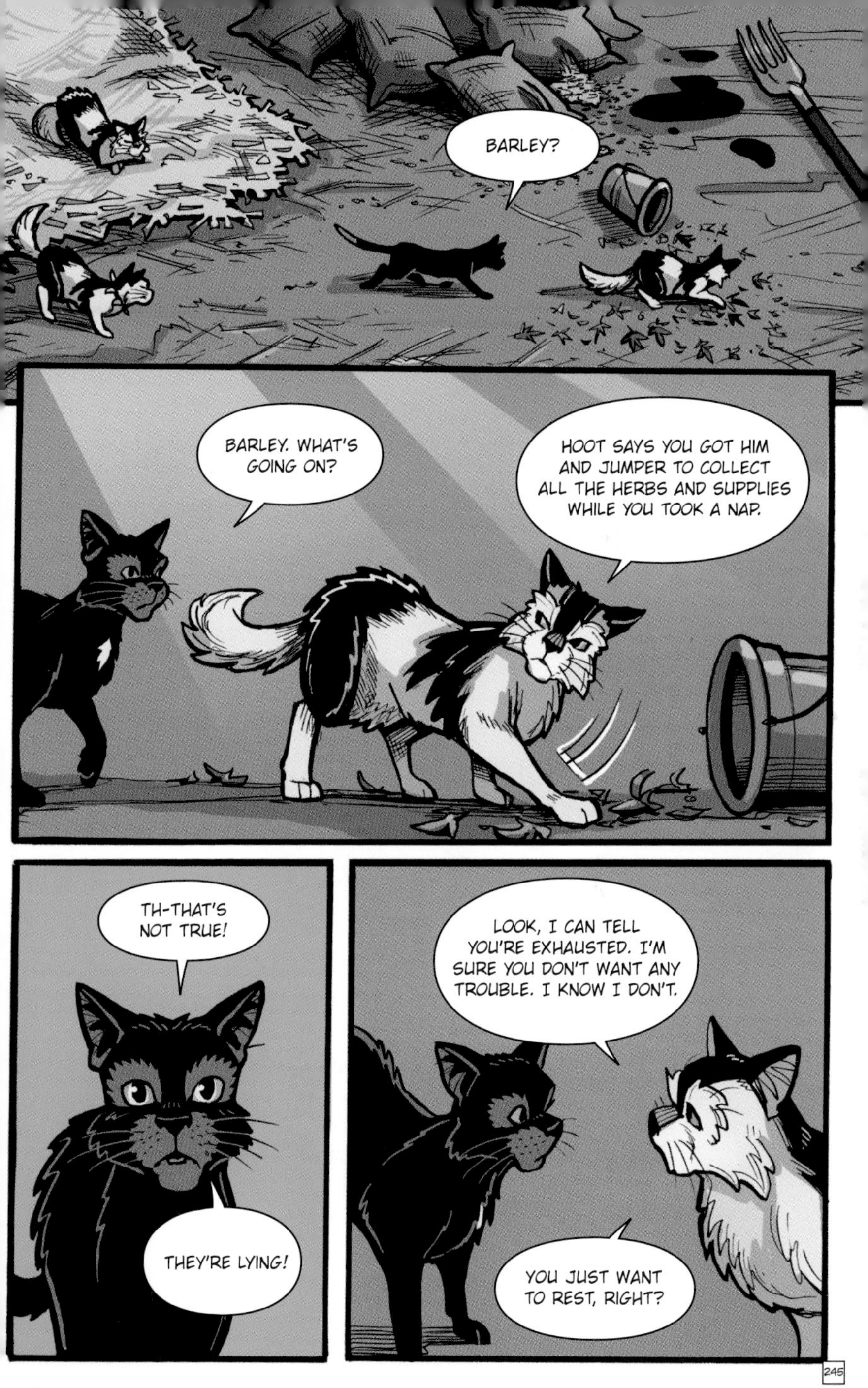

BARLEY?
BARLEY. WHAT'S GOING ON?
HOOT SAYS YOU GOT HIM AND JUMPER TO COLLECT ALL THE HERBS AND SUPPLIES WHILE YOU TOOK A NAP.
TH-THAT'S NOT TRUE!
THEY'RE LYING!
LOOK, I CAN TELL YOU'RE EXHAUSTED. I'M SURE YOU DON'T WANT ANY TROUBLE. I KNOW I DON'T.
YOU JUST WANT TO REST, RIGHT?

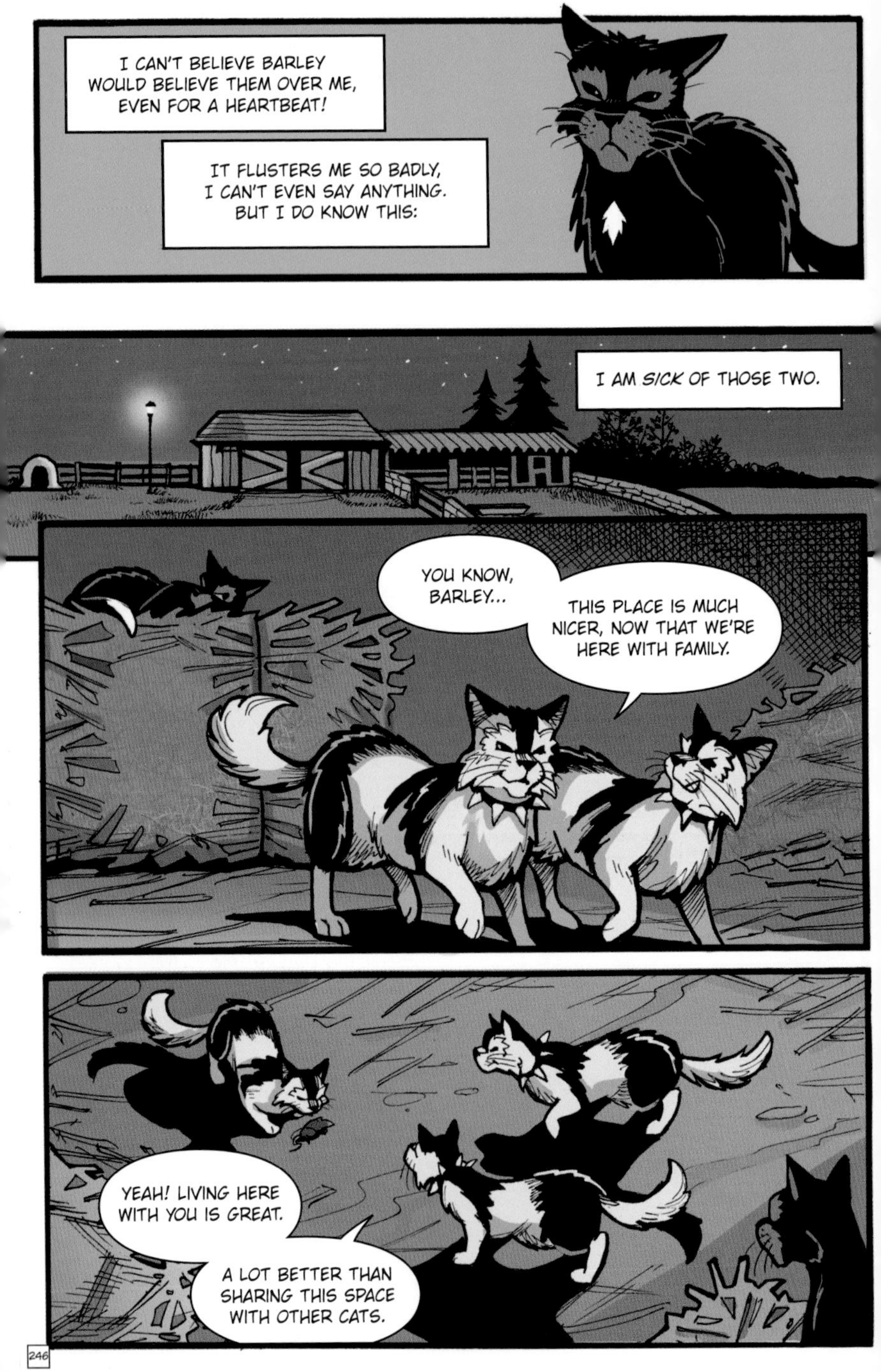
I CAN'T BELIEVE BARLEY WOULD BELIEVE THEM OVER ME, EVEN FOR A HEARTBEAT!
IT FLUSTERS ME SO BADLY, I CAN'T EVEN SAY ANYTHING. BUT I DO KNOW THIS:
I AM *SICK* OF THOSE TWO.
YOU KNOW, BARLEY...
THIS PLACE IS MUCH NICER, NOW THAT WE'RE HERE WITH FAMILY.
YEAH! LIVING HERE WITH YOU IS GREAT.
A LOT BETTER THAN SHARING THIS SPACE WITH OTHER CATS.

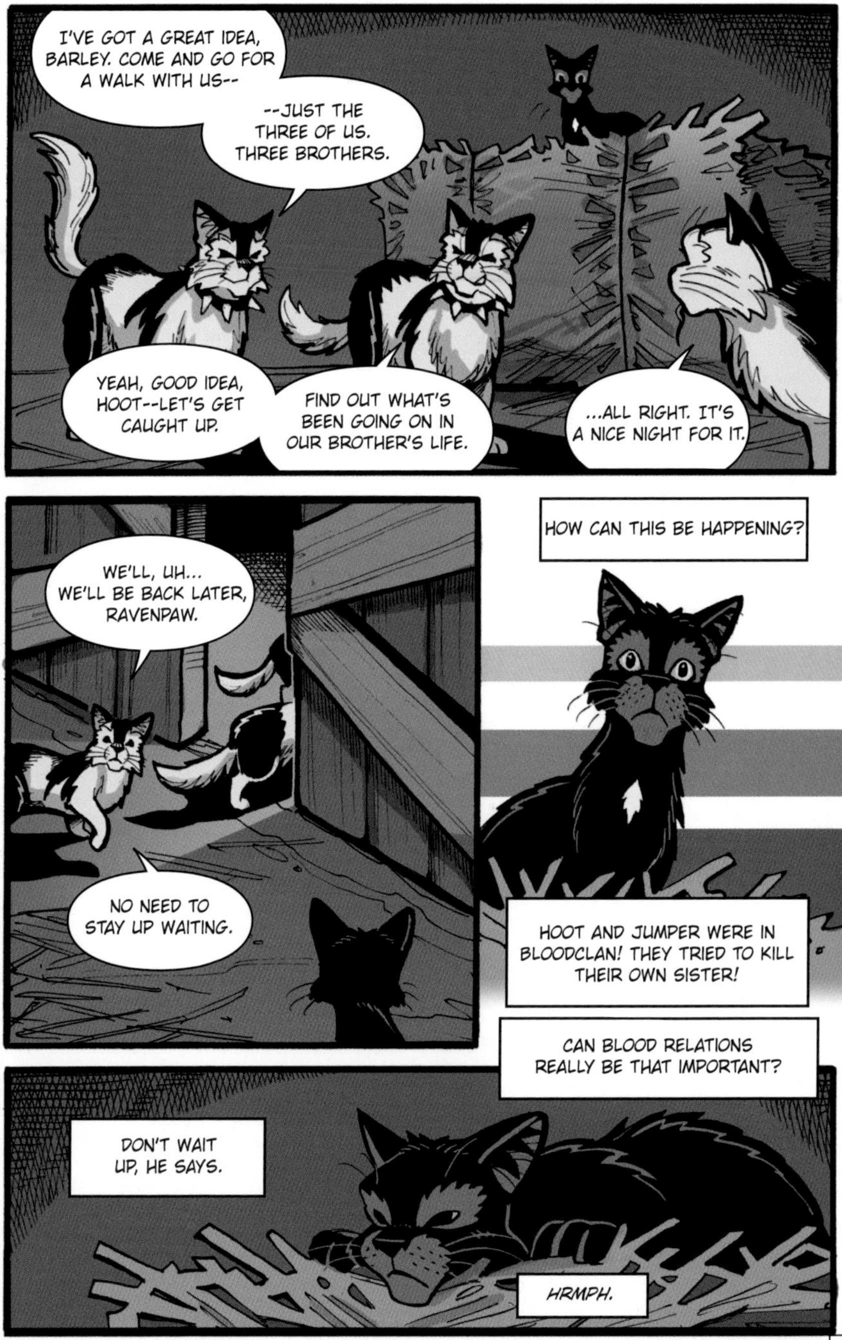

I'VE GOT A GREAT IDEA, BARLEY. COME AND GO FOR A WALK WITH US--
--JUST THE THREE OF US. THREE BROTHERS.
YEAH, GOOD IDEA, HOOT--LET'S GET CAUGHT UP.
FIND OUT WHAT'S BEEN GOING ON IN OUR BROTHER'S LIFE.
...ALL RIGHT. IT'S A NICE NIGHT FOR IT.
WE'LL, UH... WE'LL BE BACK LATER, RAVENPAW.
NO NEED TO STAY UP WAITING.
HOW CAN THIS BE HAPPENING?
HOOT AND JUMPER WERE IN BLOODCLAN! THEY TRIED TO KILL THEIR OWN SISTER!
CAN BLOOD RELATIONS REALLY BE THAT IMPORTANT?
DON'T WAIT UP, HE SAYS.
HRMPH.

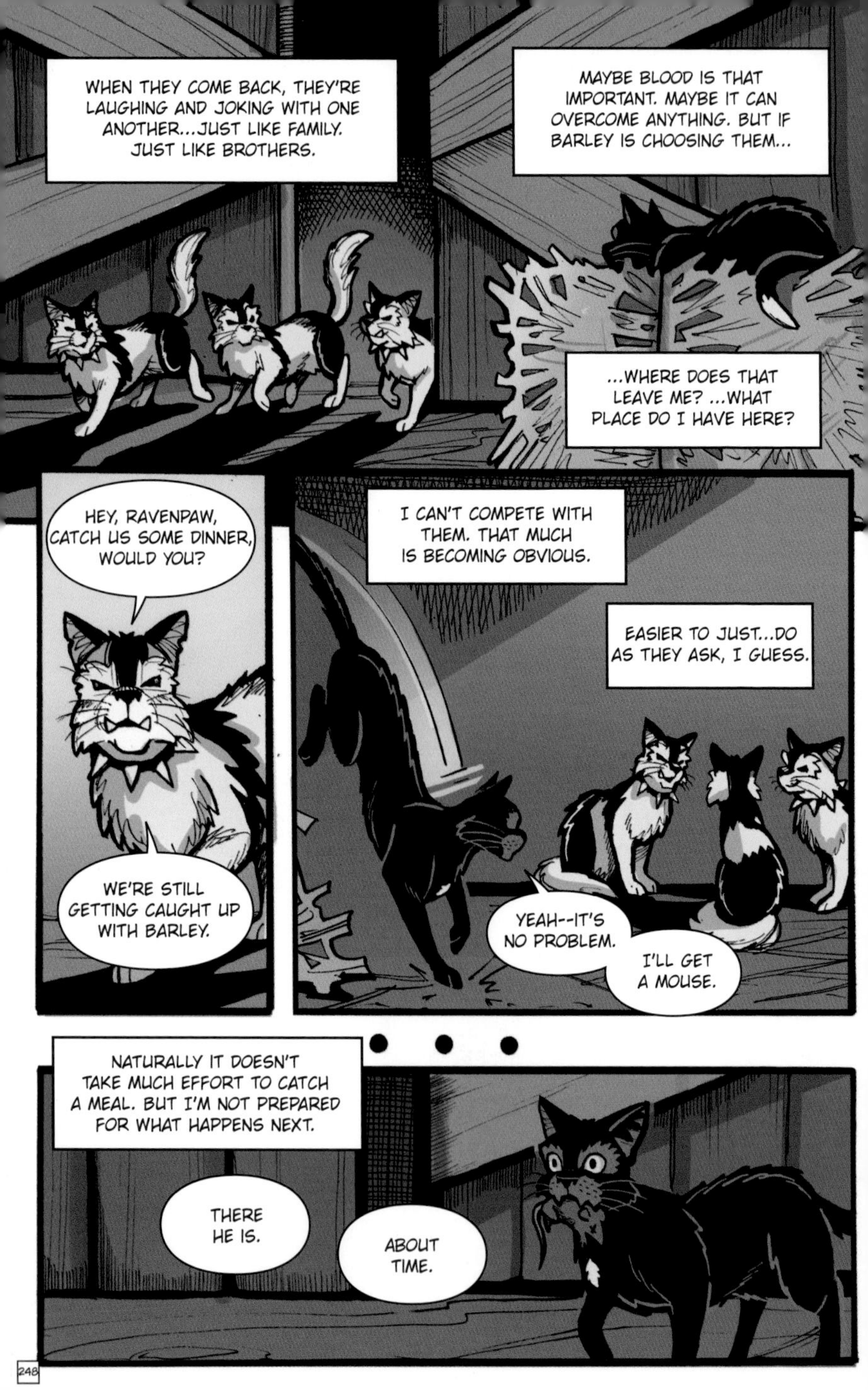
WHEN THEY COME BACK, THEY'RE LAUGHING AND JOKING WITH ONE ANOTHER...JUST LIKE FAMILY. JUST LIKE BROTHERS.
MAYBE BLOOD IS THAT IMPORTANT. MAYBE IT CAN OVERCOME ANYTHING. BUT IF BARLEY IS CHOOSING THEM...
...WHERE DOES THAT LEAVE ME? ...WHAT PLACE DO I HAVE HERE?
HEY, RAVENPAW, CATCH US SOME DINNER, WOULD YOU?
WE'RE STILL GETTING CAUGHT UP WITH BARLEY.
I CAN'T COMPETE WITH THEM. THAT MUCH IS BECOMING OBVIOUS.
EASIER TO JUST...DO AS THEY ASK, I GUESS.
YEAH--IT'S NO PROBLEM.
I'LL GET A MOUSE.
NATURALLY IT DOESN'T TAKE MUCH EFFORT TO CATCH A MEAL. BUT I'M NOT PREPARED FOR WHAT HAPPENS NEXT.
THERE HE IS.
ABOUT TIME.

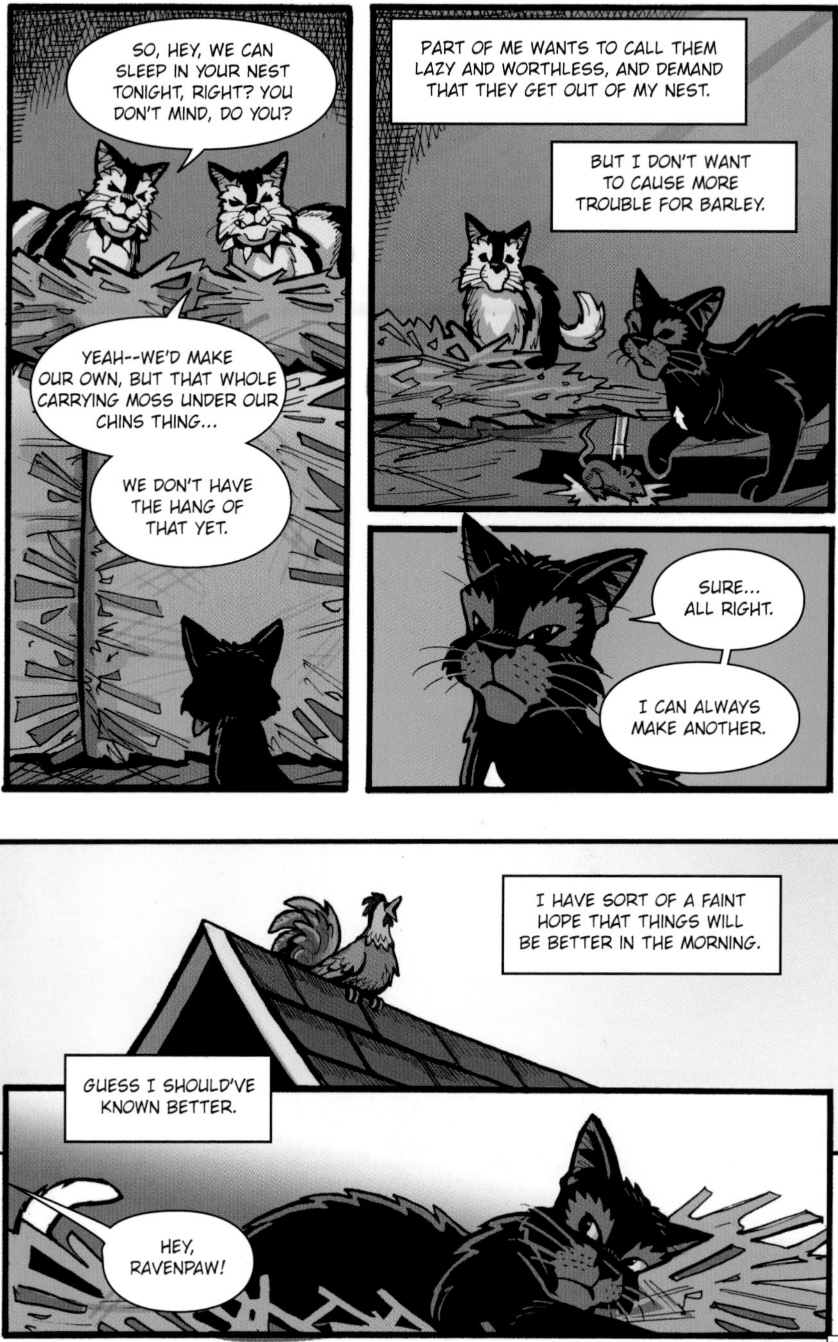
SO, HEY, WE CAN SLEEP IN YOUR NEST TONIGHT, RIGHT? YOU DON'T MIND, DO YOU?
YEAH--WE'D MAKE OUR OWN, BUT THAT WHOLE CARRYING MOSS UNDER OUR CHINS THING...
WE DON'T HAVE THE HANG OF THAT YET.
PART OF ME WANTS TO CALL THEM LAZY AND WORTHLESS, AND DEMAND THAT THEY GET OUT OF MY NEST.
BUT I DON'T WANT TO CAUSE MORE TROUBLE FOR BARLEY.
SURE... ALL RIGHT.
I CAN ALWAYS MAKE ANOTHER.
I HAVE SORT OF A FAINT HOPE THAT THINGS WILL BE BETTER IN THE MORNING.
GUESS I SHOULD'VE KNOWN BETTER.
HEY, RAVENPAW!

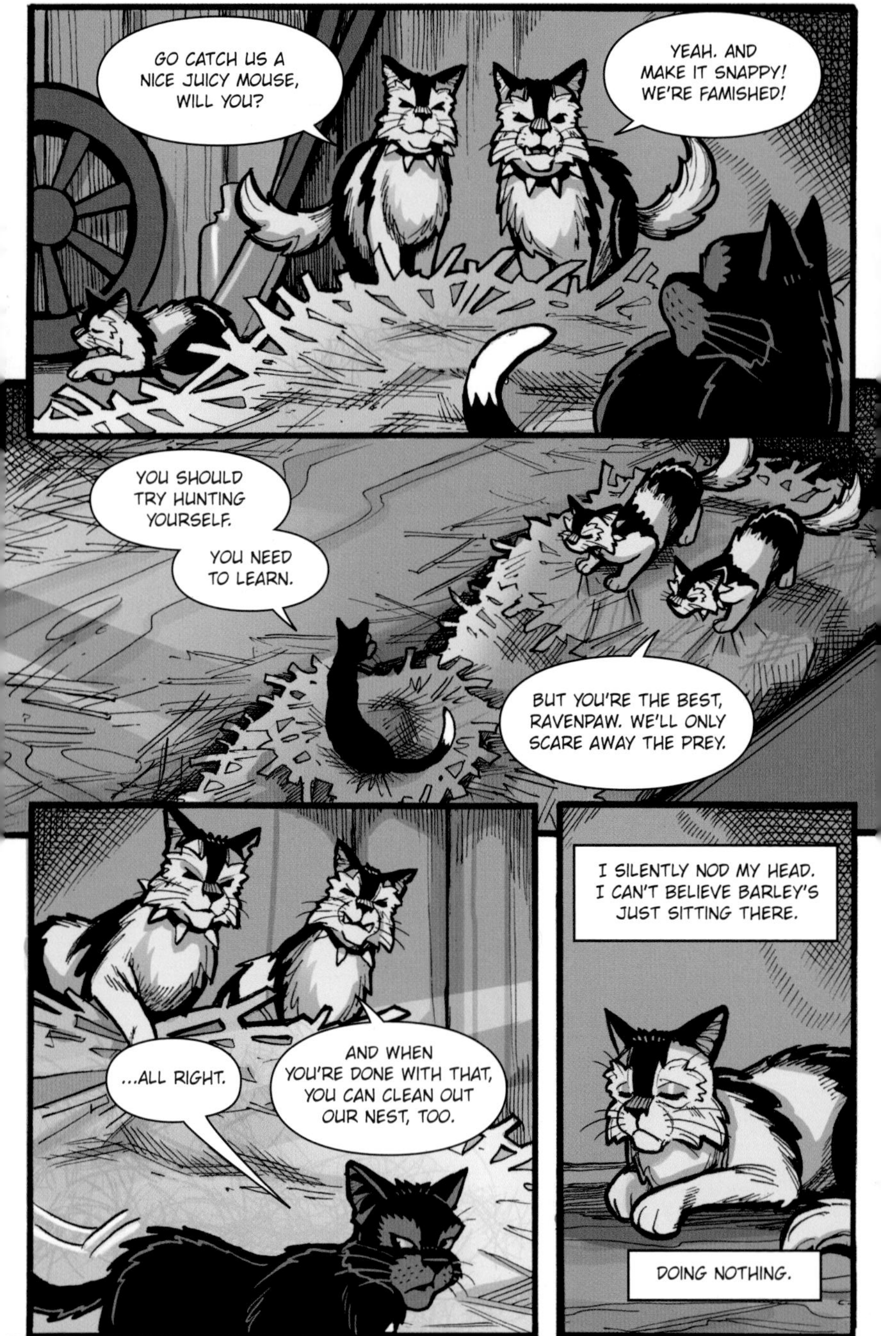
GO CATCH US A NICE JUICY MOUSE, WILL YOU?
YEAH. AND MAKE IT SNAPPY! WE'RE FAMISHED!
YOU SHOULD TRY HUNTING YOURSELF.
YOU NEED TO LEARN.
BUT YOU'RE THE BEST, RAVENPAW. WE'LL ONLY SCARE AWAY THE PREY.
...ALL RIGHT.
AND WHEN YOU'RE DONE WITH THAT, YOU CAN CLEAN OUT OUR NEST, TOO.
I SILENTLY NOD MY HEAD. I CAN'T BELIEVE BARLEY'S JUST SITTING THERE.
DOING NOTHING.

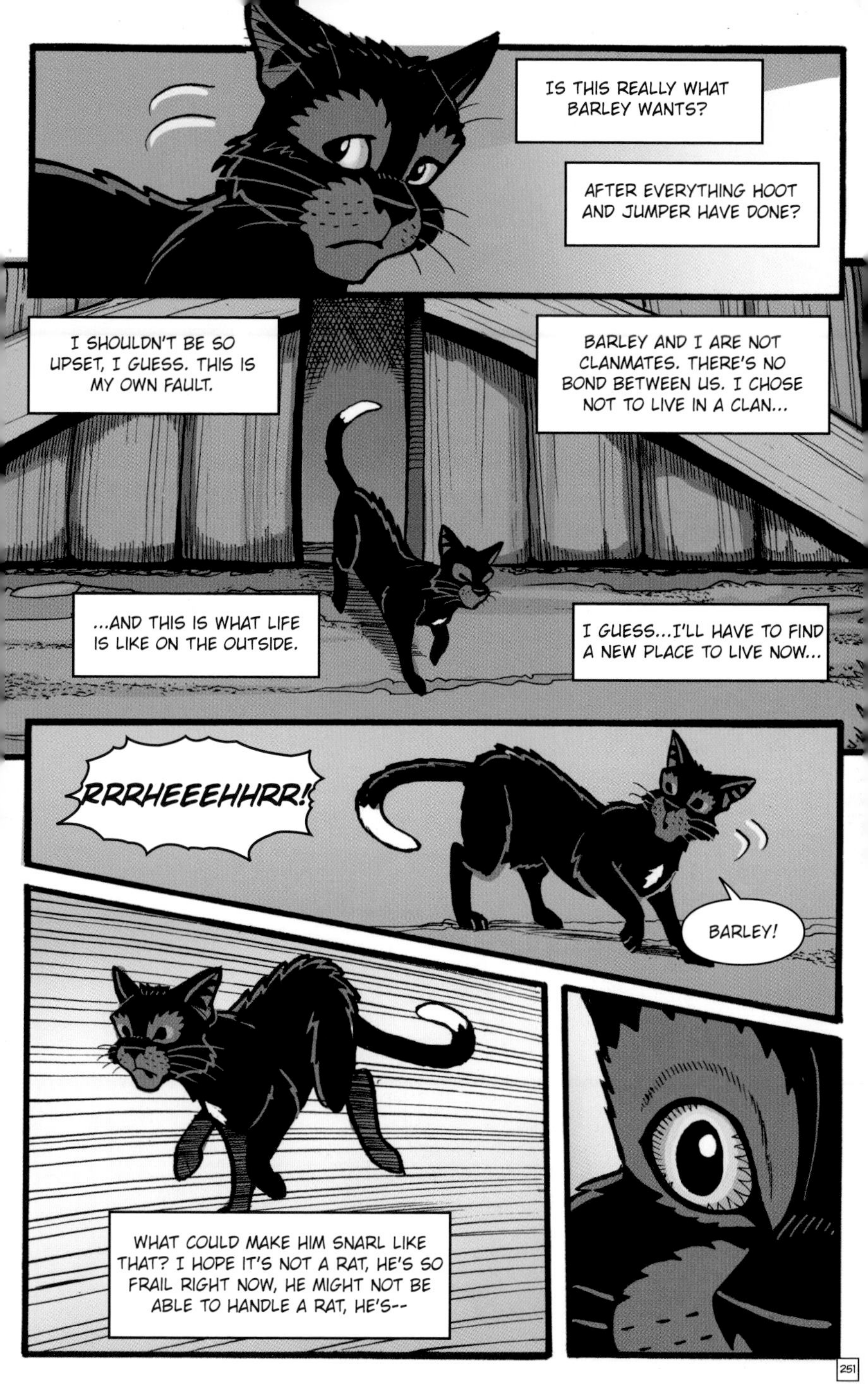
IS THIS REALLY WHAT BARLEY WANTS?
AFTER EVERYTHING HOOT AND JUMPER HAVE DONE?
I SHOULDN'T BE SO UPSET, I GUESS. THIS IS MY OWN FAULT.
BARLEY AND I ARE NOT CLANMATES. THERE'S NO BOND BETWEEN US. I CHOSE NOT TO LIVE IN A CLAN...
...AND THIS IS WHAT LIFE IS LIKE ON THE OUTSIDE.
I GUESS...I'LL HAVE TO FIND A NEW PLACE TO LIVE NOW...
RRRHEEEEHHRR!
BARLEY!
WHAT COULD MAKE HIM SNARL LIKE THAT? I HOPE IT'S NOT A RAT, HE'S SO FRAIL RIGHT NOW, HE MIGHT NOT BE ABLE TO HANDLE A RAT, HE'S--

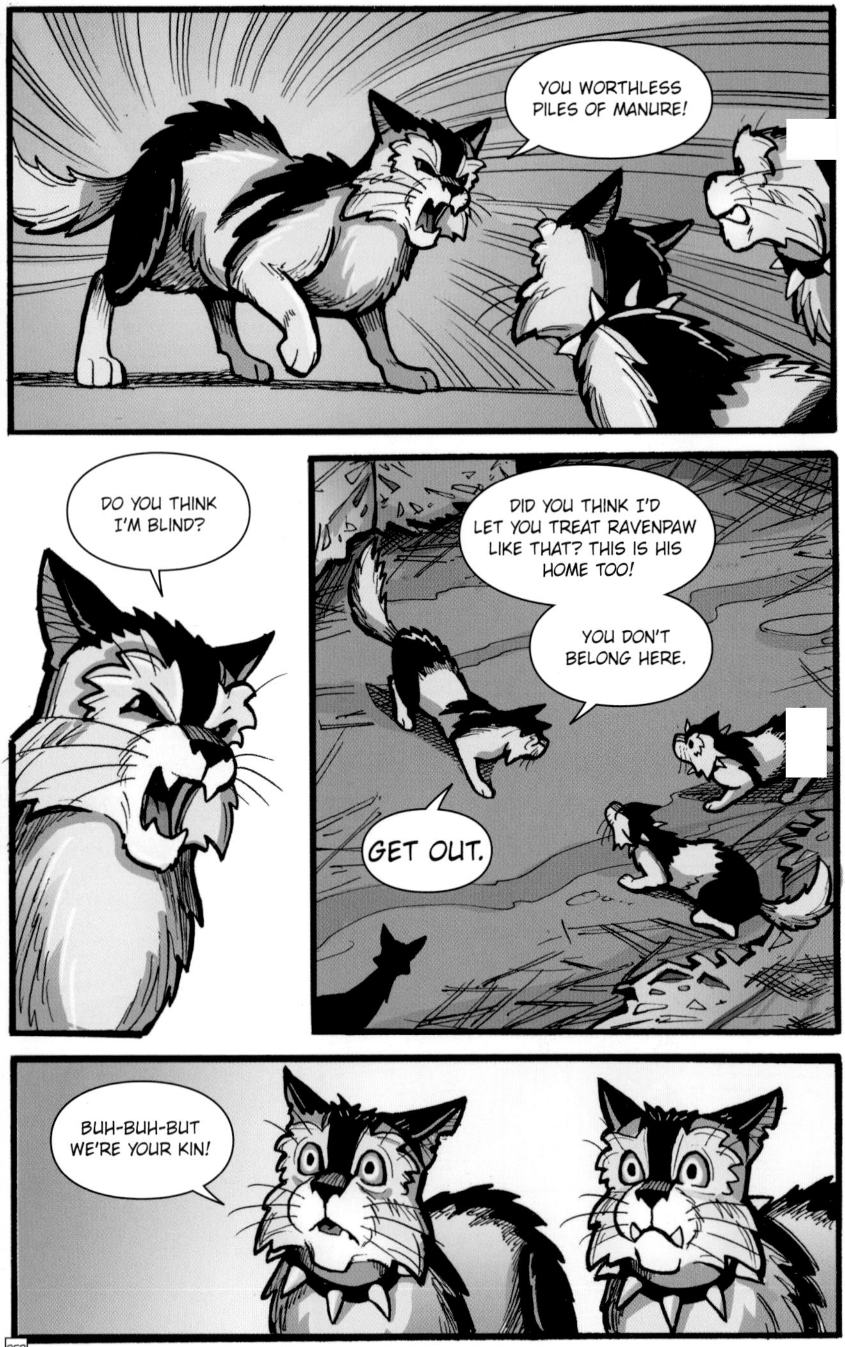

YOU WORTHLESS PILES OF MANURE!
DO YOU THINK I'M BLIND?
DID YOU THINK I'D LET YOU TREAT RAVENPAW LIKE THAT? THIS IS HIS HOME TOO!
YOU DON'T BELONG HERE.
GET OUT.
BUH-BUH-BUT WE'RE YOUR KIN!

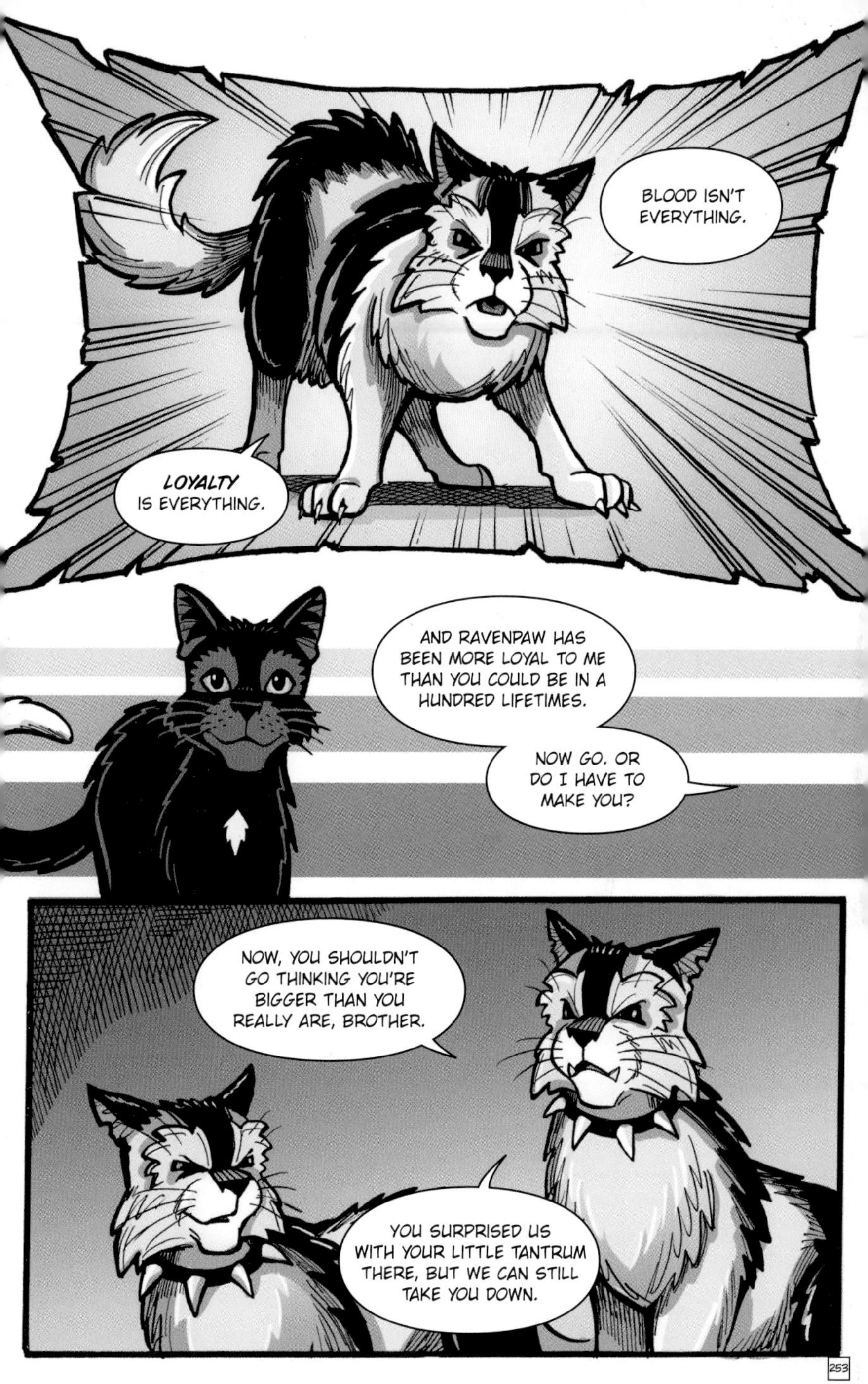
BLOOD ISN'T EVERYTHING.
LOYALTY IS EVERYTHING.
AND RAVENPAW HAS BEEN MORE LOYAL TO ME THAN YOU COULD BE IN A HUNDRED LIFETIMES.
NOW GO. OR DO I HAVE TO MAKE YOU?
NOW, YOU SHOULDN'T GO THINKING YOU'RE BIGGER THAN YOU REALLY ARE, BROTHER.
YOU SURPRISED US WITH YOUR LITTLE TANTRUM THERE, BUT WE CAN STILL TAKE YOU DOWN.

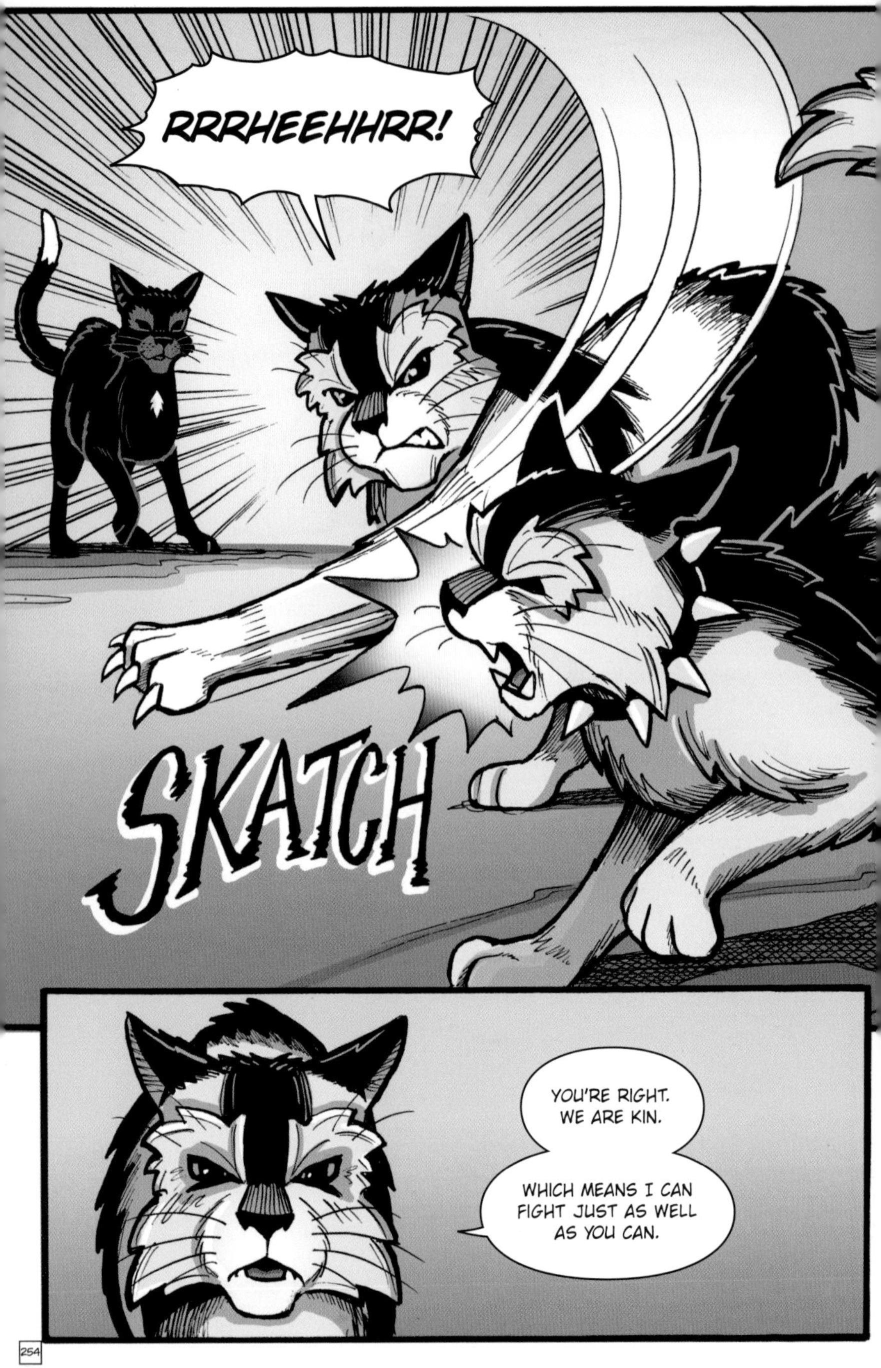
RRRHEEHHRR!
SKATCH
YOU'RE RIGHT. WE ARE KIN.
WHICH MEANS I CAN FIGHT JUST AS WELL AS YOU CAN.

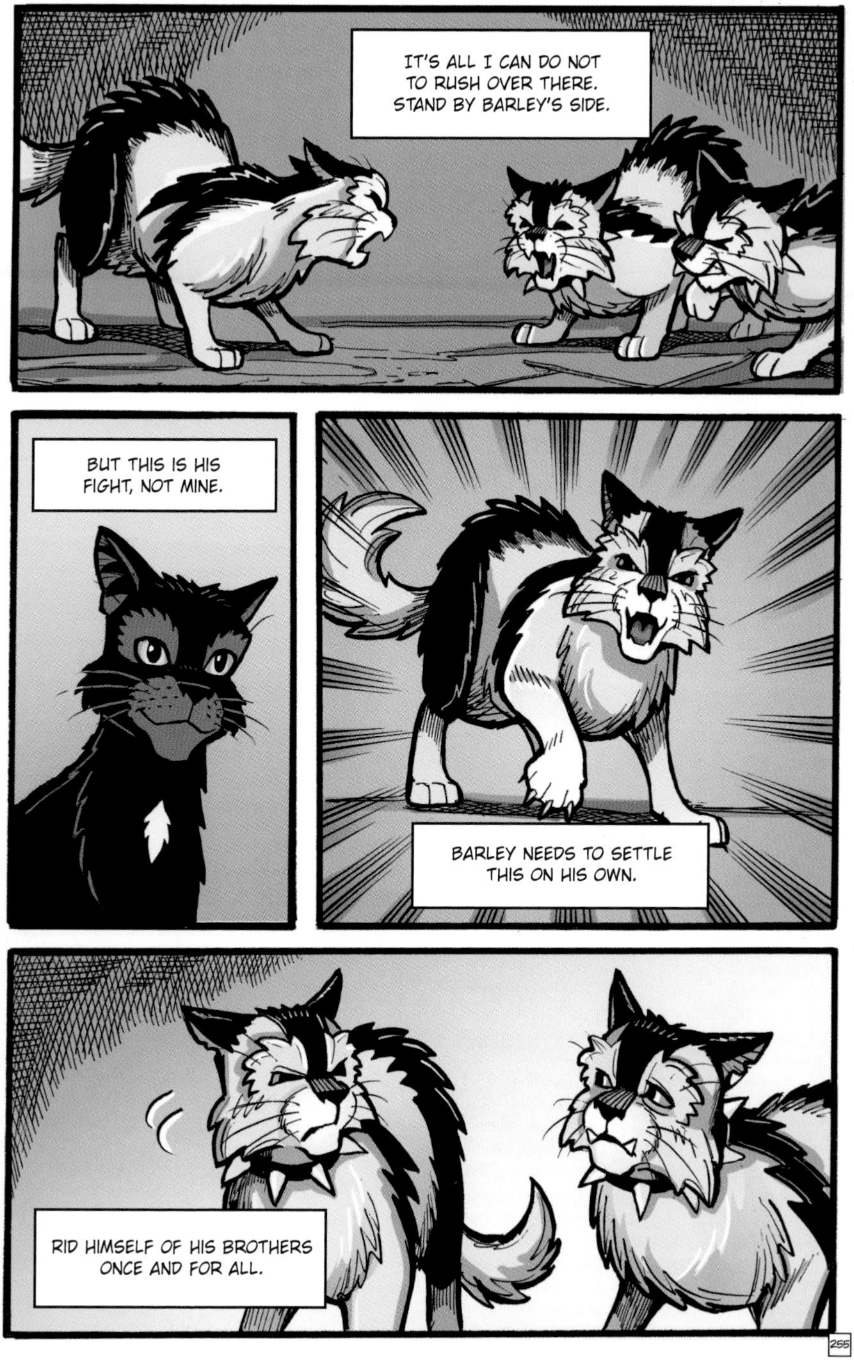
IT'S ALL I CAN DO NOT TO RUSH OVER THERE. STAND BY BARLEY'S SIDE.
BUT THIS IS HIS FIGHT, NOT MINE.
BARLEY NEEDS TO SETTLE THIS ON HIS OWN.
RID HIMSELF OF HIS BROTHERS ONCE AND FOR ALL.

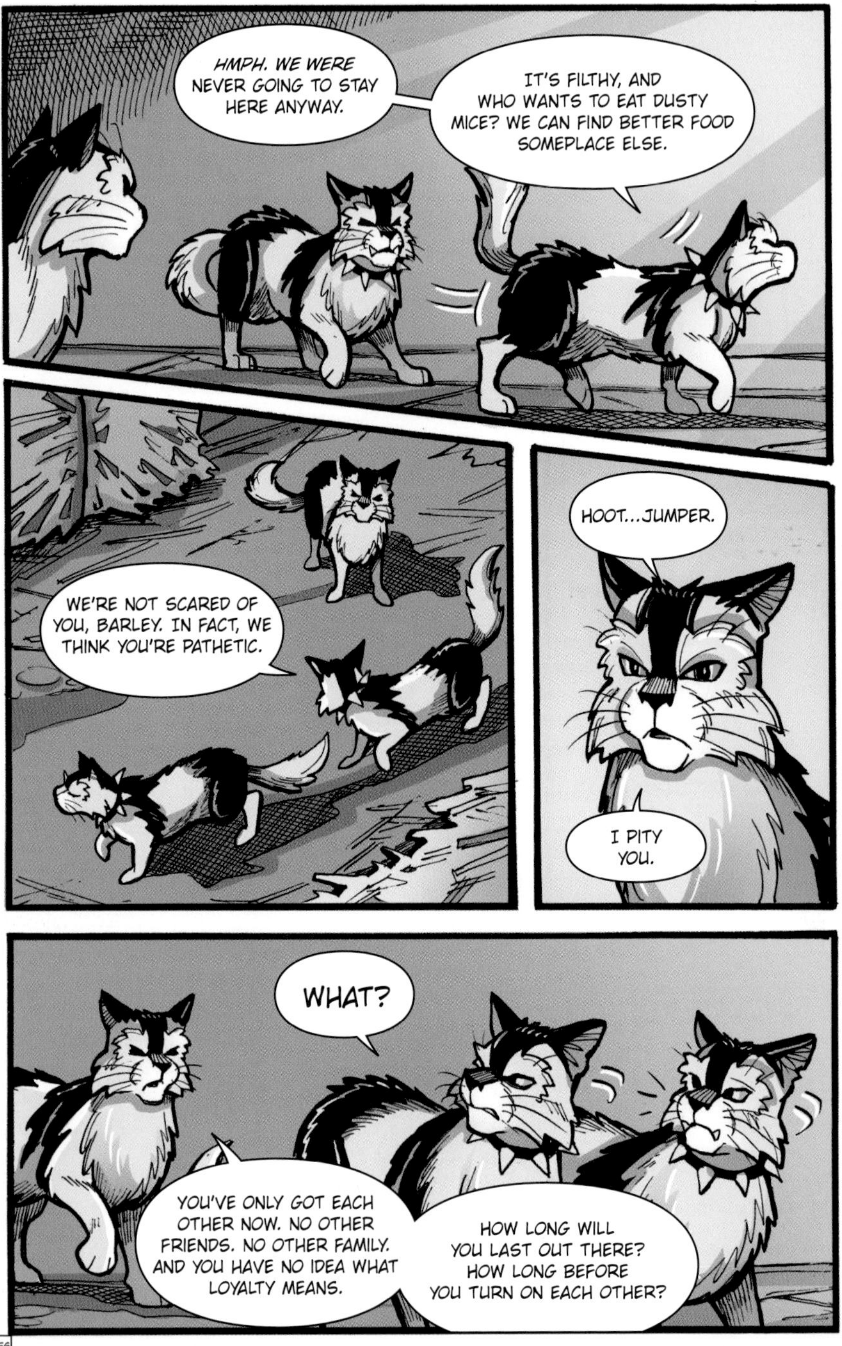
HMPH. WE WERE NEVER GOING TO STAY HERE ANYWAY.
IT'S FILTHY, AND WHO WANTS TO EAT DUSTY MICE? WE CAN FIND BETTER FOOD SOMEPLACE ELSE.
WE'RE NOT SCARED OF YOU, BARLEY. IN FACT, WE THINK YOU'RE PATHETIC.
HOOT...JUMPER.
I PITY YOU.
WHAT?
YOU'VE ONLY GOT EACH OTHER NOW. NO OTHER FRIENDS. NO OTHER FAMILY. AND YOU HAVE NO IDEA WHAT LOYALTY MEANS.
HOW LONG WILL YOU LAST OUT THERE? HOW LONG BEFORE YOU TURN ON EACH OTHER?

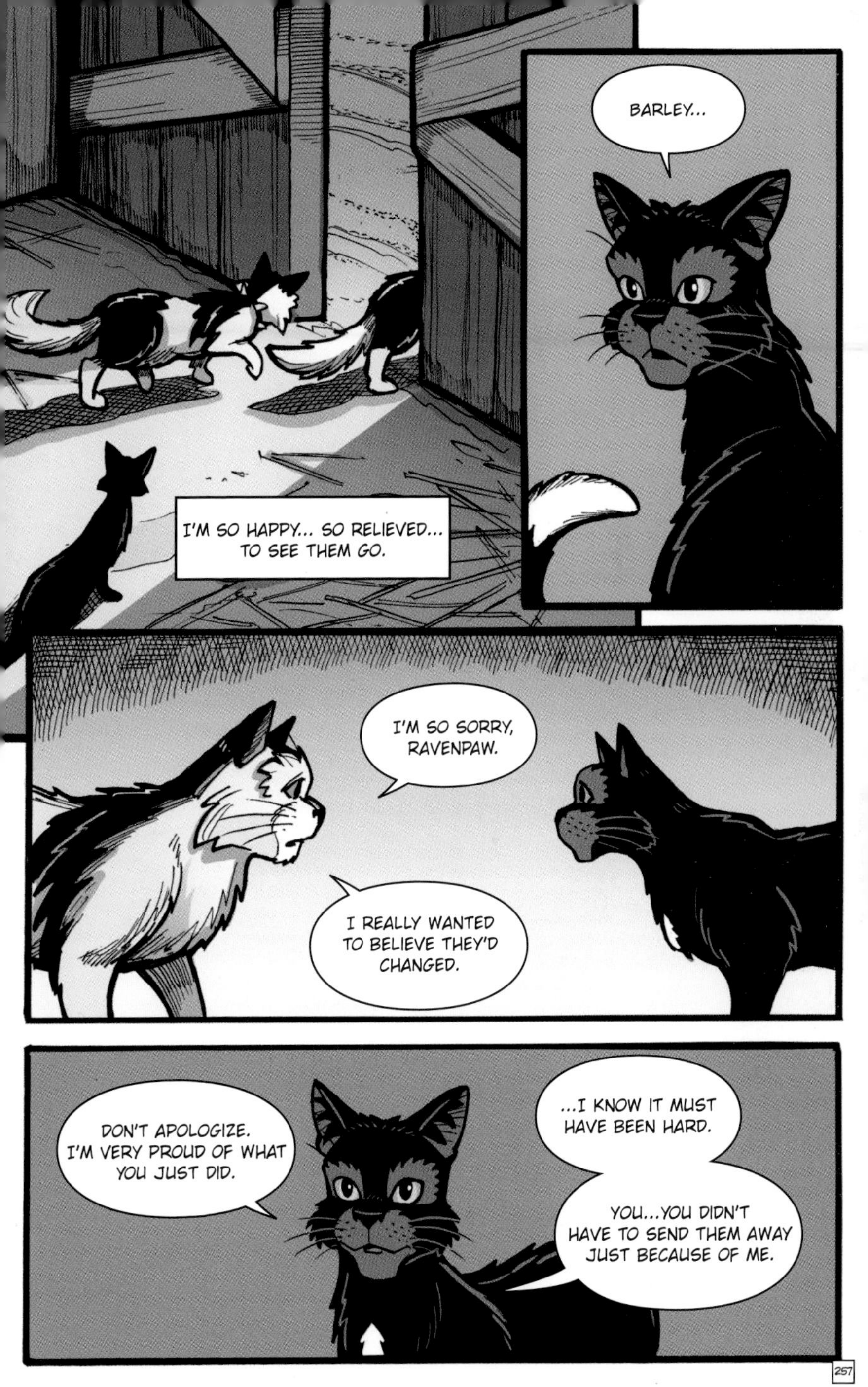

BARLEY...
I'M SO HAPPY... SO RELIEVED... TO SEE THEM GO.
I'M SO SORRY, RAVENPAW.
I REALLY WANTED TO BELIEVE THEY'D CHANGED.
DON'T APOLOGIZE. I'M VERY PROUD OF WHAT YOU JUST DID.
...I KNOW IT MUST HAVE BEEN HARD.
YOU...YOU DIDN'T HAVE TO SEND THEM AWAY JUST BECAUSE OF ME.

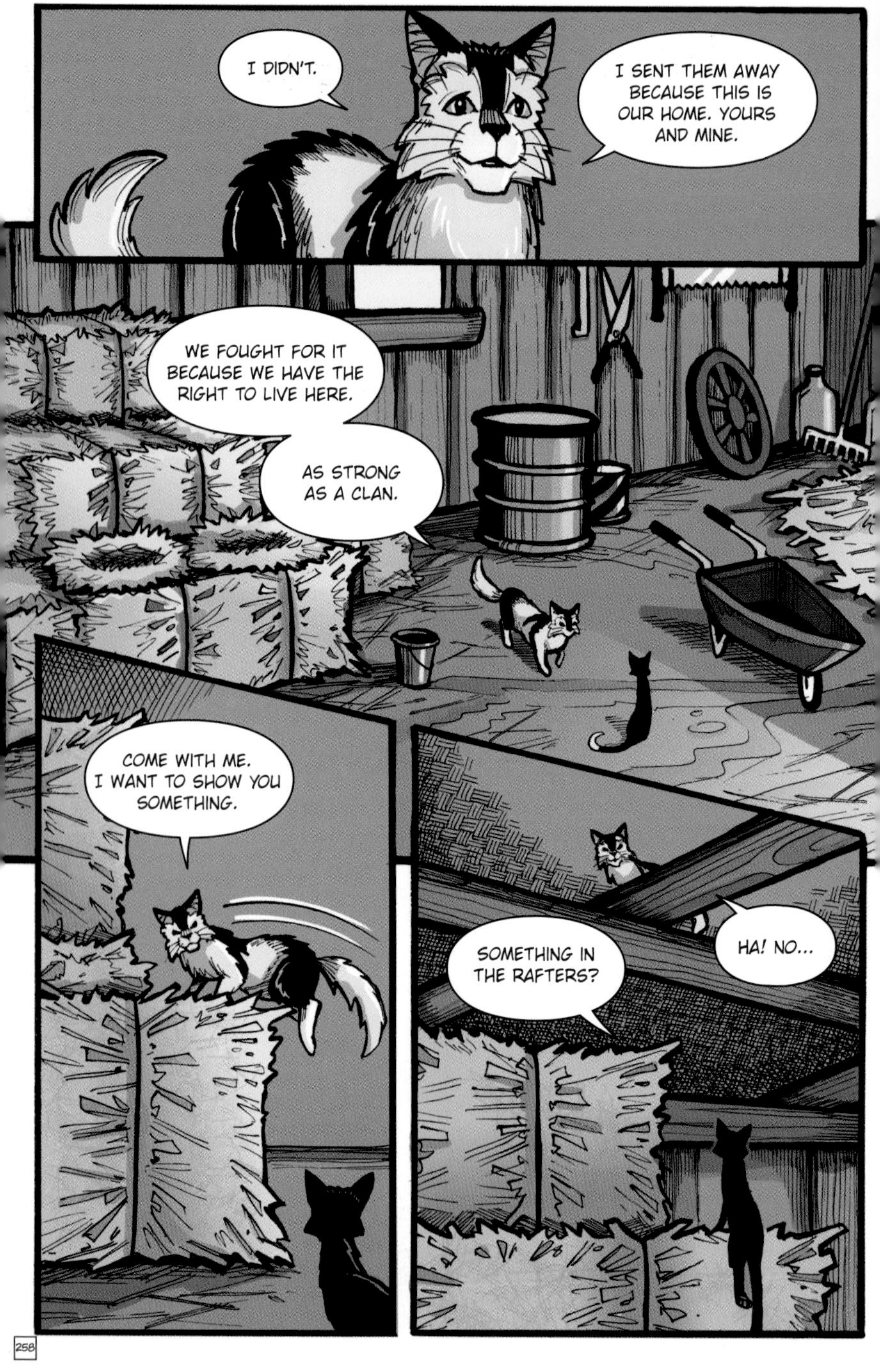
I DIDN'T.
I SENT THEM AWAY BECAUSE THIS IS OUR HOME. YOURS AND MINE.
WE FOUGHT FOR IT BECAUSE WE HAVE THE RIGHT TO LIVE HERE.
AS STRONG AS A CLAN.
COME WITH ME. I WANT TO SHOW YOU SOMETHING.
SOMETHING IN THE RAFTERS?
HA! NO...

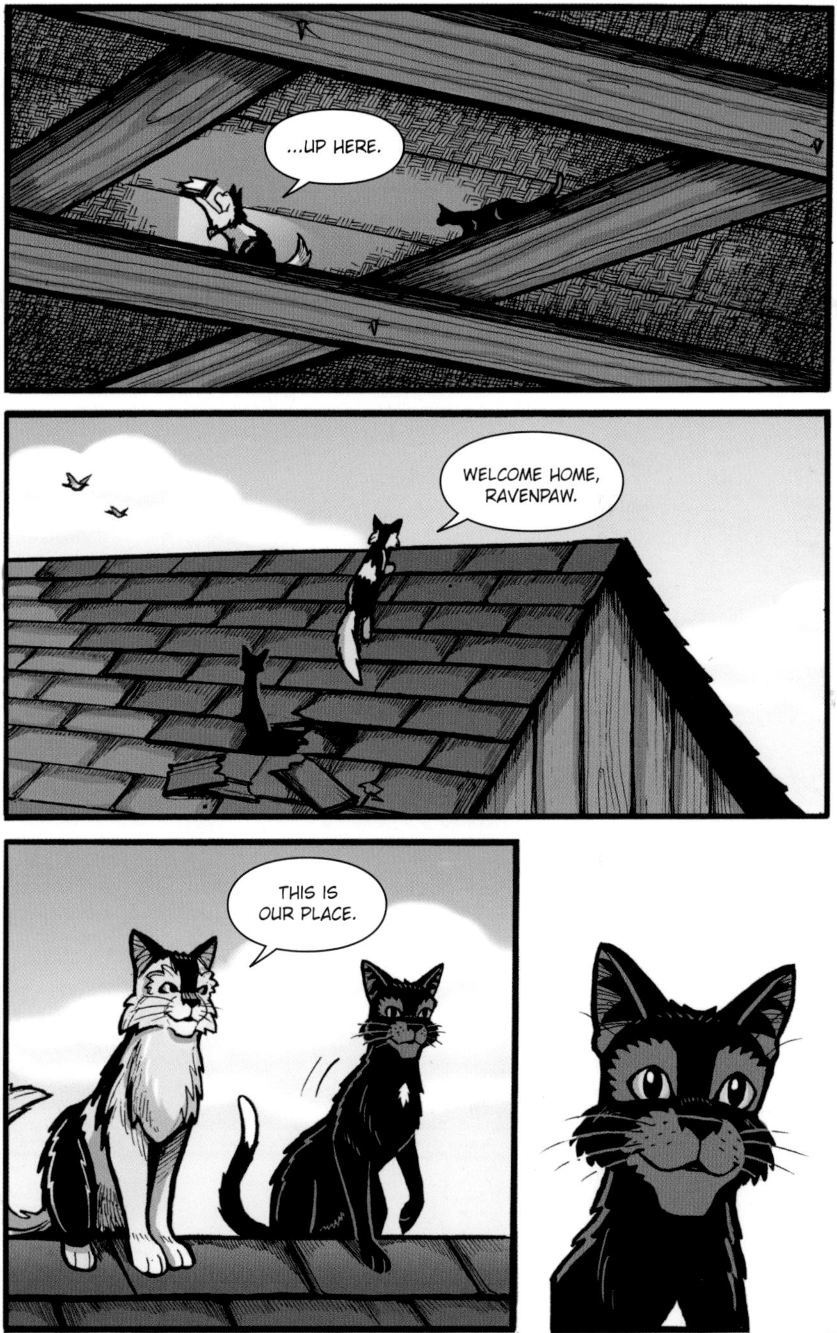
...UP HERE.
WELCOME HOME, RAVENPAW.
THIS IS OUR PLACE.

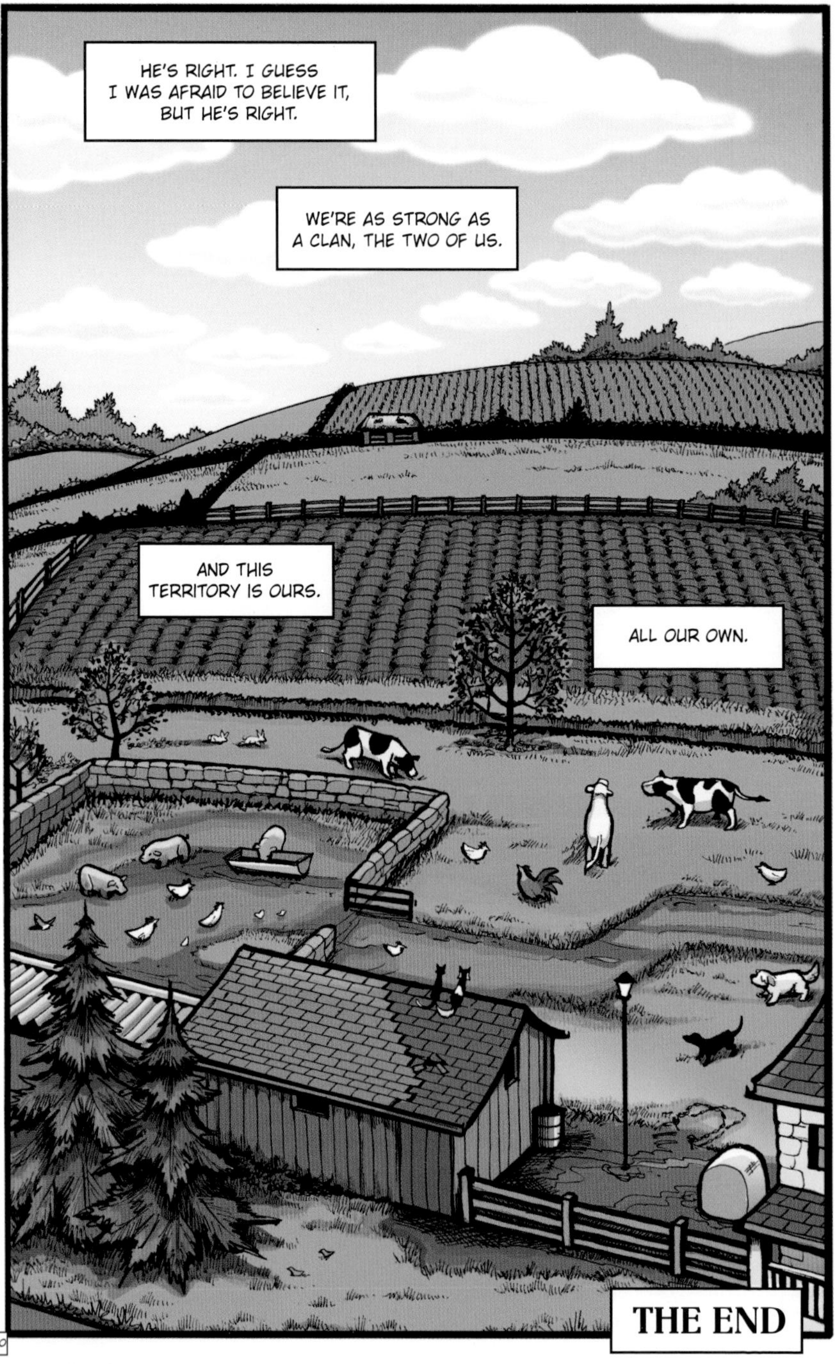
HE'S RIGHT. I GUESS
I WAS AFRAID TO BELIEVE IT,
BUT HE'S RIGHT.
WE'RE AS STRONG AS
A CLAN, THE TWO OF US.
AND THIS
TERRITORY IS OURS.
ALL OUR OWN.
THE END

ERIN HUNTER

is inspired by a love of cats and a fascination with the ferocity of the natural world. As well as having great respect for nature in all its forms, Erin enjoys creating rich mythical explanations for animal behavior. She is also the author of the Seekers, Survivors, and Bravelands series.

Download the free Warriors app at www.warriorcats.com.

ENTER THE
BRAVELANDS

1

2

Heed the call of the wild in this
action-packed series from **Erin Hunter**.

WARRIORS: A VISION OF SHADOWS

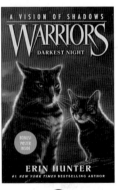

Alderpaw, son of Bramblestar and Squirrelflight,
must embark on a treacherous journey
to save the Clans from a mysterious threat.

WARRIORS: THE PROPHECIES BEGIN

In the first series, sinister perils threaten the four warrior Clans. Into the midst of this turmoil comes Rusty, an ordinary housecat, who may just be the bravest of them all.

Also available as audiobooks!

WARRIORS: THE NEW PROPHECY

In the second series, follow the next generation of heroic cats as they set off on a quest to save the Clans from destruction.

WARRIORS: POWER OF THREE

In the third series, Firestar's grandchildren begin their training as warrior cats. Prophecy foretells that they will hold more power than any cats before them.

HARPER
An Imprint of HarperCollinsPublishers

WARRIORS: OMEN OF THE STARS

In the fourth series, find out which ThunderClan apprentice will complete the prophecy.

WARRIORS: DAWN OF THE CLANS

In this prequel series, discover how the warrior Clans came to be.

HARPER
An Imprint of HarperCollinsPublishers

www.warriorcats.com

WARRIORS: MANGA

WARRIORS
ERIN HUNTER
NOW IN FULL COLOR!

Don't miss the original manga adventures!

WARRIORS: BONUS STORIES

WARRIORS
The Untold Stories
ERIN HUNTER
WARRIORS
Tales from the Clans
ERIN HUNTER
WARRIORS
SHADOWS OF THE CLANS
ERIN HUNTER
WARRIORS
LEGENDS OF THE CLANS
ERIN HUNTER

Discover the untold stories of the warrior cats and Clans when you read these paperback bind-ups—or download the ebook novellas!

WARRIORS: FIELD GUIDES

WARRIORS
Secrets of the Clans
ERIN HUNTER
WARRIORS
Cats of the Clans
ERIN HUNTER
WARRIORS
Code of the Clans
ERIN HUNTER
WARRIORS
Battles of the Clans
ERIN HUNTER
WARRIORS
Enter the Clans
ERIN HUNTER
WARRIORS
THE ULTIMATE GUIDE
ERIN HUNTER
FOR THE ULTIMATE FAN!

Delve deeper into the Clans with these Warriors field guides.

HARPER
An Imprint of HarperCollinsPublishers

www.warriorcats.com

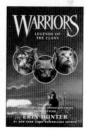

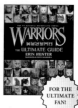

ALSO BY ERIN HUNTER:

SURVIVORS: THE ORIGINAL SERIES

SURVIVORS
ERIN HUNTER
SURVIVORS
ERIN HUNTER
SURVIVORS
ERIN HUNTER
SURVIVORS
ERIN HUNTER
SURVIVORS
ERIN HUNTER
SURVIVORS
ERIN HUNTER

The time has come for dogs to rule the wild.

SURVIVORS: THE GATHERING DARKNESS

THE GATHERING DARKNESS
SURVIVORS
A PACK DIVIDED
ERIN HUNTER
THE GATHERING DARKNESS
SURVIVORS
ERIN HUNTER
SURVIVORS
ERIN HUNTER
THE GATHERING DARKNESS
SURVIVORS
ERIN HUNTER

In the second series, tensions are rising within the pack.

SURVIVORS: BONUS STORIES

SURVIVORS
ERIN HUNTER
SURVIVORS
ERIN HUNTER
SURVIVORS
ERIN HUNTER
SURVIVORS
TALES FROM THE PACKS
ERIN HUNTER
Paperback

Download the three separate ebook novellas or read them in one paperback bind-up!

HARPER
An Imprint of HarperCollinsPublishers

www.warriorcats.com/survivors/